The Queen's Starfire Throne

INFERNAL WAR SAGA III

HAILEY TURNER

To Bear.
For all your support over the years.

There is no future without a road
No lasting sunset without the breaking dawn
A life is all that should ever be owed
To the ashes of memory there and gone

~ Remembrance hymn from a Star Order prayer book

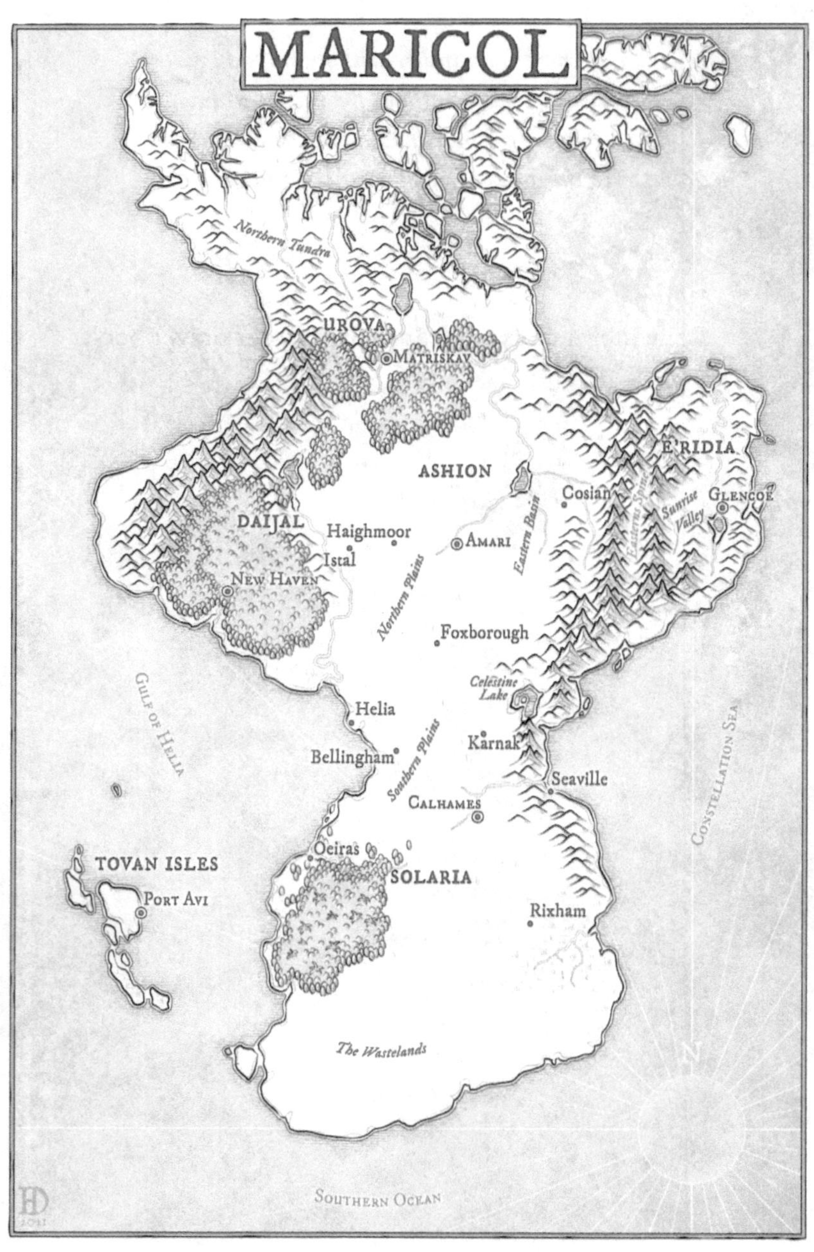

MARICOL
Northern Tundra
UROVA
MATRISKAV
ASHION
E'RIDIA
Cosian
Eastern Spine
Sunrise Valley
GLENCOE
DAIJAL
Haighmoor
AMARI
Istal
Eastern Basin
NEW HAVEN
Northern Plains
Foxborough
GULF OF HELIA
Celestine Lake
Helia
Southern Plains
Karnak
Bellingham
Seaville
CONSTELLATION SEA
CALHAMES
Oeiras
TOVAN ISLES
SOLARIA
PORT AVI
Rixham
The Wastelands
SOUTHERN OCEAN

Hostilities

937 A.O.P.

EIMARILLE

Haighmoor was a city in a western province of Ashion that lacked the cheerful color of New Haven in its buildings. Its layout was filled with dreary streets surrounded by multiple city walls. Once known for its military school and the location of the commanding officers of Ashion's army, it had slowly been picked apart by policy, the troop numbers wound down to a weak force the Ashion parliament had been pleased with.

Except the army hadn't really lost its ranks, even if they'd lost the city. The battalions once thought broken up had merely been transported to the eastern provinces of Ashion in secret under the auspices of the military leaders whose loyalty was still to the old queen. They'd willingly let the politicians in two countries believe the army had been practically disbanded when, in fact, its force had remained intact, waiting to be called to the battlefield again.

Queen Eimarille Rourke thought the Ashion army was digging its own grave in a misguided attempt to rally behind an imposter. The bodies that fell in the poison fields were useful, though, even if they had to be transported to the field locations where the death-defying machines were positioned. Still, even with thousands of revenants to help aid their advance, the Daijal army had yet to break through the front line stretching from Urova down to Solaria east of Amari.

"The winter weather made advancing difficult, but our forces are in a better position now for a frontal assault. We can deploy our war airships with better accuracy and less risk to the crews," High General Kote Akina said.

He stood at strict attention in the receiving room of the Beltre bloodline's ancestral estate. The family's name had been written into the nobility genealogies generations ago, a well-regarded and old bloodline whose political power had never quite been able to rival the Auclair bloodline's over the years. Since the Inferno, they'd been partial to Daijal propaganda, putting them at odds with half the citizens of Haighmoor. Many of the citizens who favored Daijal over Ashion had filled the streets to greet her arrival yesterday with screaming fanfare.

Eimarille looked up from the map spread across the low table, its markings showing their troops' positions and the always shifting front lines that didn't match up with the dash marks delineating the interior province borders of Ashion. It had fluctuated over winter, the Ashion army providing a rather spirited defense of their provinces with the aid of wardens and bad weather.

The lack of wardens in Daijal and western Ashion was another detail hampering their push forward. While her army could create revenants, controlling them was impossible. The high numbers were becoming an issue in Daijal, with complaints being sent to New Haven about trade being disrupted because of unsafe roads, and the cost of transportation by airship was rising. Eimarille's representatives were quick to say the risk and associated costs would ease once the war was over and won, but that excuse wouldn't be acceptable forever.

"Targeting Cosian should be a priority," Eimarille said.

"We sent a squadron after unloading another revenant horde for a bomb drop. Reports coming back from behind the enemy line indicated some of the airships were forced back on the flight over by

Ashion airships and aeroplanes. Those of ours that did make it to Cosian were faced with upgraded ground-to-air defenses."

"Were they successful in their attempted bombardment?"

"Some, not all."

Eimarille curled her hands together over her knees, the heavy skirt of her deep blue ball gown falling in layers around her legs. She was here with Kote for an in-person update on the war, though it was running longer than she'd anticipated. She risked the evening's schedule being delayed since the welcoming ball to tout the province's support for Daijal and their queen wouldn't truly start until Eimarille joined the revelry in the estate's ballroom.

"And the revenants?"

"Poison grenades eventually eradicated them."

"Warden-make?"

"Yes, Your Royal Majesty."

Eimarille frowned at the map before looking at Kote. The high general wore his formal uniform with all its gold medals, braid, and ranking pins on display. The white peaked cap was tucked under one arm, his gloved fist pressed against his torso as he stood before her, delivering news she didn't like and for which his orders were responsible.

The former king—long since burned by starfire—would have taken Kote to task for what Bernard would have seen as a failure. Bernard had never been one to see the big picture—truly, he had never even known about the ways Eimarille had worked to undermine his rule as his ward. That had been to her advantage. He'd thought her weak, despite the favor granted to her by the Twilight Star and the protection that came with it.

Innes had guided Eimarille down her road since she was a child taken from Amari as the Inferno burned away everything she once knew. Every step forward had brought her closer to the starfire throne and the decree still burning on that symbol of power. As much as she wanted to fly to Amari and claim what was rightfully hers, she could not do so until her younger brother and sister were dead.

If the only Rourke left alive was herself, then the North Star would have no choice but to let Eimarille take the throne, crown, and country that were, by right, always meant to be hers.

"Send another bombing run," Eimarille said.

Kote inclined his head. "That can be done."

"Good. I trust your skill in the battlefield and know this setback will not remain for long."

Kote nodded sharply, all stiff shoulders and resolute expression. He'd ever been her staunchest supporter in the Daijal military, never hesitating in executing her orders over the years, both in secret and publicly after she was crowned queen of Daijal.

"The rebellion doesn't have the production capacity to keep up with ours. We believe they won't last through the end of the year, not with our war machines in the field. My understanding is that Solaria and E'ridia still have not agreed to an alliance with them. Solaria's Legion has not crossed our southern border, and E'ridia's air force remains behind the Eastern Spine."

"What of the contested land in the south?"

"We are holding that line. Our war machines are a match when it comes to the Legion's. The *vasilyet* around Bellingham remains in our control."

Emperor Vanya Sa'Liandel, of the House of Sa'Liandel, still ruled Solaria, but his claim to the Imperial throne was tenuous at best despite the Dawn Star's blessing. The Conclave of the Houses had ended with the Imperial palace burned to the ground and a *vasilyet* seceding from Solaria. The emperor refused to accept the secession, and the fighting along that border was particularly intense, even now. Still, holding that *vasilyet* was necessary to divide and conquer. Whatever support Kote deemed the southern fighting required, Eimarille would approve it.

The sound of the knob turning had Eimarille looking over at the gilded door as it opened. A familiar and well-loved figure stepped into the room, carrying Eimarille's whole world in her arms. Terilyn smiled at Eimarille as she crossed the room, Lisandro propped on one hip despite Eimarille's five-year-old son being more than capable of walking. Her Blade spoiled him so, and Eimarille could not fault her lover's habits in that regard. If she had her way, she'd give her son the world.

"Mama!" Lisandro said excitedly, wriggling in Terilyn's arms. She bent to set him down on the floor, and the boy immediately ran to her. "Terishka said you are going to a ball. I want to come."

Eimarille reached for her son, scooping him up into her lap with practiced ease. He was dressed in the soft sleeping gown and slippers that he wore when playing in the nursery before bed. She smoothed back his blond hair before kissing his forehead. "My darling, I would love to have you escort me, but you know your bedtime is soon."

He pouted at her but giggled when she tickled his stomach. His bright laughter was a sound she always wanted to hear, and Eimarille wrapped her arms around him, hugging him tightly. Lisandro had always been hers more than he'd ever been Wesley's. She'd raised him as a Rourke rather than an Iverson, whispering about the world she was going to give him. Despite Wesley being dead, Lisandro never asked for his father, not how he asked for Terilyn when the Blade was absent from his life.

Eimarille hadn't been willing to risk leaving him behind in New Haven, not with the ongoing war. Daijal's capital might be far from the front lines, but it had an ocean to think of. The Daijal navy had patrols in the Gulf of Helia, aided by Urovan submersibles. For now, their presence was for defensive purposes only.

Eimarille rested her chin on Lisandro's head, smiling at Terilyn as the other woman sat beside her on the sofa. Terilyn wore a ball gown similar to Eimarille's, but the skirt had been tailored with the ability to be discarded with a firm tug at several lace points. Eimarille knew that other design changes had been incorporated to make it easier for Terilyn to reach the wealth of weapons hidden beneath her clothes that she never went without.

Her long black hair was pinned back and twisted into a bun, the metal hair sticks piercing it decorated with diamonds and the hidden blades sharp enough to slit a throat. Eimarille had gifted them to her during the new year festivities, and Terilyn had bloodied them a dozen times over since then.

"Lady Beltre is asking after you. I informed her you were delayed but would be out shortly," Terilyn said.

"We're finished here for the moment," Eimarille said.

Kote put his cap back on. "I can escort you both to the ballroom."

"The nursemaid is waiting outside to take Lisandro back to the nursery," Terilyn said.

Of course, her son protested that, begging to join her. Eimarille hushed his pleading with a touch of her fingers to his cheek and a gentle tsking of her tongue. "None of that now, my darling boy. A prince doesn't beg."

Lisandro pouted but allowed her to hold him close as she stood. "Yes, Mama."

She carried him to the door, which Terilyn opened for her. The nursemaid out in the hall dipped into a deep curtsy, head bowed. "I'll take the prince, Your Royal Majesty."

Eimarille handed her son over to the nursemaid, glancing at the pair of guards who must have escorted Terilyn to the receiving room. From a distance, she could hear the muffled music from the live orchestra quartet and the faint murmur that signified many voices. The ball tonight was one of the first of the season and not to be missed with Eimarille in attendance. That meant many people she would never trust being within reach of her son, but the guards watching over Lisandro had come with her from Daijal. Their loyalty wasn't in doubt—it was everyone else's she would always worry about.

"We'll keep watch, Your Royal Majesty," the lieutenant assured her after snapping off a salute.

"See that you do," Eimarille said.

She watched them leave with her son, never turning away until they were out of sight. Terilyn brushed her hand against Eimarille's, her fingers cool. "He'll have a Blade with him tonight."

Eimarille grasped Terilyn's fingers and lifted her hand, brushing a kiss over scarred knuckles before letting go. "Thank you, my darling."

She turned toward Kote, who bowed and gestured for her to go ahead of him. "After you, Your Royal Majesty."

Eimarille reached up to adjust the weight of her crown one last time before walking past him toward the revelry happening elsewhere in the estate. Terilyn settled to her right and one step behind while Kote took up position on her left. The royal guards on duty in this wing all snapped to attention as she passed, making her way to the staircase that led to the main foyer and hallway.

Guests mingled in that space, their jewelry glittering beneath the gas lamp light from the grand chandelier. The Lord and Lady Beltre waited in the foyer, chatting with a handful of guests. Their chamberlain saw her first, attention riveted on the stairs. He immediately came to attention, voice rising over the chatter with a clear and deep projection. "Announcing the arrival of Her Royal Majesty Queen Eimarille Rourke."

The crowd shifted, pulling back. Heads turned to catch a glimpse of Eimarille as she descended. Men bowed, women curtsied, as was expected of them. She extended her hand to Lady Ximena Beltre, who took it and curtsied deeply. "It is our greatest honor to have you as our guest, Your Royal Majesty."

"A pleasure as always to be back in Ashion," Eimarille said with a winning smile.

Ximena straightened, the corners of her brown eyes creasing slightly when she smiled. She was a little older than Eimarille, dressed in a gown that was at least two seasons behind in fashion, though the rest of the guests seemed to have followed their lady's lead rather than Eimarille's. The gold, diamond, and pearl tiara she wore shone against the dark chestnut of her curled updo. She looked radiant but couldn't hope to outshine Eimarille.

Her husband, Felipe, was five years her senior and had married into her bloodline. Tonight, he wore a fashionable evening suit, shined black shoes, and white gloves. His cravat was neatly done, the pale peach color a match to his wife's ball gown. Felipe had been gone from the city and only just arrived in time for the ball. Ximena had offered her sincere apologies yesterday for his absence, but he was here now and playing a game Eimarille was a master at.

"You grace us with your presence, my queen," Felipe said.

Eimarille smiled at the praise before gesturing at the two with her. "My companions for the evening, the Lady Terilyn and our guest of honor, High General Kote Akina."

Ximena greeted the pair smoothly. If Felipe hesitated a split second before turning his smile on Terilyn, one could forgive the man. Eimarille well knew the rumors that followed in Terilyn's wake and had since they were children. Blades were trained and deployed out of Daijal, adhering to a secretive branch of the Star Order that existed in that country. Some people called them zealots; others labeled them assassins. Both would be right.

"Lady Terilyn," Felipe said while his wife greeted Kote.

Terilyn's smile was cool and polite, though she said nothing, ever Eimarille's silent shadow. She'd never quite lost her Urovan accent and been horribly teased for it in the Daijal court before Eimarille had consolidated enough social and political clout to make people think twice about letting insults leave their lips. These days, Terilyn's silence heard much around her, and she always had such interesting things to say after evenings like this.

Eimarille glided down the receiving line that extended into the hallway leading to the ballroom, Ximena facilitating every introduction. Eimarille committed faces and names to memory, noted those whose smiles never reached their eyes and those who looked at her as if she were their savior. When she finally swept into the ballroom, it was to a flare of music from the quartet orchestra and a round of applause that lasted over a minute.

When the applause died down and the last musical notes faded away, Eimarille greeted those gathered before her with a dazzling smile. "I am here tonight to celebrate the efforts of the Daijal army fighting against the rebellion entrenched in the eastern provinces and, most importantly for all of you, keeping the revenants at bay from Haighmoor's city walls. High General Kote Akina continues to lead with exceptional skill, and I am pleased with his efforts of leading us toward the reunification of our countries."

Eimarille turned toward Kote with a smile, leading the applause for his war efforts. He came to attention and saluted her, looking nowhere else. "I live to serve you, my queen."

"You do it so well, High General. With your steady hand, we'll take the eastern provinces before the year is up." More applause followed her words, and she turned her attention to Ximena. "And to our gracious host, for opening up your home on this grand night, I thank you."

Ximena curtsied smoothly, the skirt of her gown fluttering around her. "No thanks is ever needed for you to grace our home, Your Royal Majesty."

Eimarille smiled at that and took Felipe's hand for a waltz when he approached. The music picked up, and she let herself be spun around the quaint ballroom, the pair of them the center of everyone's attention. That focus never wavered from her as the night went on. Eimarille danced with no other, despite the men and one blushing young woman who asked.

She drifted through the conversation circles instead, sipping from the wineglass Terilyn had fetched for her. The servants discreetly sliding through the crowds with their silver platters of finger food always attended her. Eimarille enjoyed several bites to help soak up the wine, letting herself and Kote be drawn into conversations about the war efforts with various people inside the ballroom.

The clock on the wall ticked later and later, until it chimed an hour tone, calling for everyone to end the festivities in the garden. Ximena found her again, holding on to Felipe's arm, and the pair escorted Eimarille outside.

"We thought to celebrate our queen with a fireworks show," Ximena said.

Around them, guests received glasses of sweet wine or brandy from the servants, chattering about what was to come. Eimarille kept her eyes on the night sky with its blanket of stars scattered across that inky black. "I'm flattered you think of me with such kindness when your husband does not."

Ximena froze, thin brows furrowed in confusion. "I'm not sure what you mean. The Beltre bloodline favors Daijal and believes in the road you are building."

"Yes, but your husband is not of your bloodline, and I've decided his betrayal is his own." Eimarille dropped her gaze from the sky and turned her head to look at where Felipe stood rigidly beside his wife. In the gas lamp light that brightened the courtyard, backlit by the glow spilling out of the ballroom doors, Felipe appeared washed out to a sickly white. "Is that not correct, my dear little cog?"

Ximena stared at her husband with a sort of disbelieving horror in her eyes. In the low light, Eimarille couldn't tell if it stemmed from Felipe's betrayal or the impending loss—whether she knew it or not—that she was about to endure.

"I don't know what you speak of," Felipe said, his voice quiet and tight.

Eimarille arched an eyebrow. "Don't you? All these trips you take under the guise of business have you assisting the Clockwork Brigade in secret meetings. Come now, did you think your chain would remain intact forever?"

"I am no cog."

It was the worst thing to be with Daijal's occupation and propaganda spreading through Ashion. The Clockwork Brigade had spent decades working to undermine Daijal's permissive use of debt bondage and debt slaves. People who tried for a better life mortgaged their own with banks, and if they couldn't pay, their indentured servitude became the price owed.

Eimarille had allowed many debt slaves to be fed to the death-defying machines in the lead-up to crossing the central border between Daijal and Ashion. Debt collectors had worked overtime to fill that need, but many more debt slaves still existed in Daijal in their original capacity, toiling away under banking contracts that would never be fulfilled. The bank numbers tattooed on their necks marked them forever.

Despite his betrayal, Felipe would never receive one.

"I've been breaking chains for quite some time," Eimarille said, her words heard by only their small circle as the fireworks erupted overhead. "I'm not cruel, you must understand that. I do what I do for the sake of two countries that should have never split. The Clockwork Brigade has always stood in the way of that."

"Felipe," Ximena begged, reaching for him. "My dear, tell me you didn't. You risked our *children*—"

"Your children will be fine," Eimarille interrupted. "I could no more harm them than harm my own son."

Which was true, to an extent. The Beltre children were young, barely older than Lisandro, incapable of being indoctrinated by their father and assisting the Clockwork Brigade. If they'd been older, if Eimarille had records of them traveling with Felipe, then things would be different. Ximena could forgive Eimarille the execution of her husband but not her children, and Eimarille still had use for the highest-ranking noble lady in Haighmoor.

Which was why Terilyn silently appeared behind Felipe and not Ximena, one slim hand gripping his hair and forcing his head back. The slender stiletto in Terilyn's other hand flashed in the gas lamp light as the Blade carved a red line through the man's cravat and throat from ear to ear. Blood poured out of the wound, and Felipe jerked his hands to his throat, eyes wide in agonized disbelief as blood bubbled at his lips.

His dark suit hid the sickly crimson of his lifeblood as it flowed from his neck. Felipe staggered toward his wife, white-gloved hands drenched in blood, reaching for her, but Ximena stepped back, her expression twisting with grief and regret, voice aching from it. "Oh, Felipe. My love, you chose the wrong road."

The guests nearest them finally realized something was wrong when Felipe's knees hit the cobblestone courtyard, hands scrabbling at his ruined throat. Eimarille took a half step back, twitching the skirt of her gown away from the pool of blood growing on the ground. Loud gasps echoed in the air, drowning out the booms from the fireworks. More attention was turned toward the death of a lord than the celebration of war.

Terilyn glided around Felipe's body, her stiletto nowhere in sight, and came to stand next to Eimarille. Ximena's eyes shone with a wetness she couldn't hide as she lifted her gaze to Eimarille. "I swear, I had no knowledge of his betrayal, my queen."

"I know you didn't," Eimarille said soothingly. "If you had, I would know, and you would have shared your husband's funeral shroud."

Ximena flinched at that, hands fisted at her side, but her eyes held no hatred as they stared at Eimarille. "I don't want the children to see."

"Kote will coordinate the body being taken to the crematorium. You'd do well to summon a star priest in the morning and strike your former husband's name from the nobility genealogies."

Ximena nodded, still in shock but willing to do whatever Eimarille wanted in order to keep what remained of her family alive and her bloodline intact.

Eimarille stepped around the body bleeding out on the cobblestones and extended her hand to Ximena. She jerked her gaze away from her husband's lifeless form and automatically reached for Eimarille's hand, ever the lady and gracious hostess. "My queen."

"Come, Lady Ximena Beltre. We'll adjourn to your private study so I may explain why I favored your loyalty over a traitor's. You must understand that cogs have no place in this world, no matter their bloodline."

Ximena swallowed, the peach silk of her gown no longer a match for a bloodstained cravat. But she was alive, and like anyone who knew how close they'd come to death, Ximena was willing to never look back at the body of the man she'd loved and married and raised children with because his road had ended and hers still yet needed to be walked.

Two

EIMARILLE

Istal was a frontier military city Eimarille had first seen as a child, when Innes had helped steal her out of Amari on a train heading west. Growing up, Eimarille had focused her attention on the Daijal court and all the many bloodlines that paraded through the palace in New Haven. Some had longstanding ties to Istal, many of them military men and women, all of whom had been quietly grateful for the respect she had shown their duty to country.

The Daijalan officers who joined herself, Terilyn, and Kote for a command meeting in Istal that day all wore their ranking pins with pride and saluted her when she swept into the large room. The space was grand, all dark wood and rich carpeting, with a window that overlooked the parade grounds outside where soldiers performed drills. Oil paintings depicting victorious battles hung from the wall while the flags of Daijal and Ashion were positioned on poles at the end of the table, joined by the Urovan flag.

Half the table was filled with Urovans, most from the diplomatic corps, but several officers from that northern country had also joined them. The contingent was led by their ambassador, Maksim, a man who belonged to Eimarille more than he ever would anyone else these days. Hidden beneath the fur-lined brocade jacket Maksim wore were the scars of a *rionetka*. He'd been the first one Eimarille had ever seen made, a living embodiment of control, and she held the strings.

Maksim stood at her arrival, smiling warmly across the table at her. "Your Royal Majesty."

"Ambassador Maksim." She smiled at everyone after that greeting, giving a graceful little nod as she took a seat. "My thanks to you all for making yourselves available on such short notice."

She and her entourage had been in Haighmoor a few days ago, having flown to Istal on the royal airship that morning. Lisandro was ecstatic to be around so many soldiers, having a fascination for them that she gently encouraged. When he was older, after he completed his general schooling, she'd let him join Evergreen if he liked. The military school back in New Haven was the premier education spot for officers, and Eimarille knew it would only instill a sense of duty in Lisandro his father had never found.

For now, her son was safely tucked away in the visiting quarters of the garrison, watched over by his attendants, the royal guards, and a Blade who had met them at the end of the gangplank when they'd docked in the airfield. He was safe, but Eimarille always worried about her son when he wasn't by her side.

"High General Kote updated me when we were in Haighmoor on the status of the front lines in the east. To that end, I am here to talk about our southern efforts and our foray into the Gulf of Helia." Eimarille looked across the table at Maksim, meeting his gaze. "I understand we are to expect another flotilla of submersibles to take up position in the Gulf of Helia. What of the rest of your fleet?"

"Our icebreaking ships are carving a path through the ice floes of the Northern Tundra in the east. When it is open, the fleet of submersibles will make their way to our agreed-upon eastern targets," a Urovan officer said. Judging by the gold ranking pins on the lapels of his coat, he was a captain who most likely commanded a submersible.

"How long until the path to open water is completed? We are already at Fifth Month."

"At least another month. We had a harsh winter, and the ice is slow to melt this year, but we are still within the approved timeframe. Once the way is cleared, the submersibles will be prepared to launch from Matriskav at your command. It will take several weeks to reach their assigned targets as they must move carefully so as to not be discovered once they make it up the rivers."

Eimarille nodded before glancing to her left at where Kote sat. "Your thoughts on this course of action?"

"The Urovans have proven to be worthy allies, my queen. The targets were well thought out on their end and will only aid our efforts on land. I and my fellow officers have no concerns about their command decisions," Kote said.

"Excellent. And what of our southern border?"

"*Vezir* Joelle has requested additional troops, but to deliver those numbers requires reassigning some companies," another officer said. She was looking at her notes, the paper marked up with the Secured stamp that limited who had the authority to view it. "We wanted your approval to do so, as we're unsure if you have any ongoing communications with the *vezir* we should be aware of, my queen."

Eimarille was careful to keep the distaste off her face at the mention of *vezir* Joelle Kimathi, of the House of Kimathi. Joelle was a needed ally, but she'd overstepped herself more than was helpful last summer. She'd never managed to claim the Imperial throne during the Conclave of Houses, which had forced Eimarille to settle on her fallback plan, one that didn't have Solaria as her country's ally through Joelle as the Imperial empress.

A problem, to be sure, but Eimarille excelled at overcoming those. Presently, the Legion guarded the border that ran through the Southern Plains between Solaria and Daijal and Ashion. The southern part of the continent belonged to Solaria, though not all the land was safe to travel through. The Wastelands were a breeding ground of spores and revenants, and she knew wardens hadn't left those borders the way they'd left Daijal.

"My communications with *vezir* Joelle have no bearing on this decision. Spare who you can to head south and shore up that border.

We need to maintain our defense there. I'll leave the details to High General Kote," Eimarille said.

Kote nodded. "I'll see it handled after the meeting. We have war machines coming off the production line we can send south to hold the line."

Companies owned by Daijalan bloodlines and merchants had thrown their support into the war effort back home. Steel and clarion crystal remained in abundance and were being transported weekly to the factories in the middle of Daijal churning out weapons, ordnance, automatons, and transport vehicles. War was expensive, but the Daijalan parliament had put forth a new tax break bill that was being lauded in the business circles.

It didn't matter that E'ridia and Solaria had embargoed trade with her country. Daijal had stored up what it needed for the war effort over the years, and Urova's clarion crystal mines were open to Daijal's needs. The war might not be won yet, but they were in the best position to see it finished before the end of the year.

"What of the Tovan Isles?" an officer farther down the table asked.

Maksim waved off the question with an imperious hand. "The Tovan Isles are more neutral than even E'ridia claims to be. They will not give aid to those of us on land."

"But if they do?"

"Then we will sink their ship-cities."

A few Urovan officers banged their fists on the table in agreement, prideful in their people's underwater sea prowess. While their expertise in navigating freezing waters beneath the ice floes that lined the Northern Tundra was great, Eimarille knew it wouldn't exactly translate to open-sea warfare. The Tovanians and their ship-cities were the undisputed rulers of Maricol's oceans and seas. Conquering that country wouldn't happen until after she'd claimed the continent, and it would take a different plan of attack than what was currently on the table.

The meeting lasted for quite some time. An aide came in halfway through with tea for everyone, the conversation momentarily paused as they took a brief break. Eimarille never left her seat, and neither did Terilyn. Eimarille was aware of the glances thrown her Blade's way. It was atypical that a lady-in-waiting would attend such a high-status meeting, but no one commented on her presence. Some eyed her with enough wariness that Eimarille knew they must be aware of Terilyn's true calling.

When the meeting commenced again, Eimarille was content to let Kote take the lead, solidifying the working relationship between the officers of both countries. Typically, a monarch wouldn't be so involved. Certainly, Bernard had never cared for the details when he'd been king. He'd issued the orders he liked, expecting to be obeyed, and it had been the duty of the military commanders to execute them.

But he'd never had respect for those in the military, and neither had Wesley. Eimarille knew their worth, though, and that meant she never contradicted Kote's decisions. The high general knew war, and the rest of the high-ranking officers trusted his command. His social status had certainly increased, and the gushing news stories of his command had many women and some men asking for him to dance at the balls he could find the time to attend, usually at her urging.

Eimarille knew he'd have plenty of admirers at the one occurring tonight. The fight in the east would give them victories, but the ones at home were just as important. Which was why, when the meeting ended, Eimarille opted to return to their quarters to check on Lisandro before getting ready for the ball and perhaps, if time allowed, a moment of respite with Terilyn.

The ball was set to occur at the home of the Khaur bloodline. They'd only had half a week's notice to prepare for such a grand occasion, as Eimarille's travel schedule was closely guarded information. Terilyn had dispatched royal guards and a Blade to oversee the estate's security that morning, ever diligent about Eimarille's safety. The Khaur bloodline had offered her a wing to use in their estate, but this close to the central border and Ashion meant Kote had requested she stay in the garrison, surrounded by soldiers to keep her safe.

Eimarille's private rooms were guarded by soldiers and a magician who had orders from Terilyn herself to let no one pass. Innes seemed quite content to continue sipping his brandy in the room that acted as a parlor, cravat undone and shirt unbuttoned at the top, revealing a hint of the Viper constellation tattoo on his pectorals. The brilliant golden lines never ceased to catch Eimarille's attention, the aether that burned in them similar to the starfire she herself could summon.

She immediately dipped into a deep curtsy, subjugating herself to the only person she had ever lowered her gaze to. "My lord."

Innes raised his hand and curled his fingers at her. "Come here, my child."

Eimarille rose from her curtsy and approached the sofa, settling herself beside Innes. The Twilight Star set his brandy aside on the low table and shifted on the cushion to face her. His face remained exactly as it looked when she'd first met him as a ten-year-old child, all sharp features, blond hair, and blue eyes, with the burn of starfire in his veins.

Innes was forever born of the aether, as all Star Order scripture espoused. But he felt real to her when he took her hand, giving it a squeeze, and offered up a smile that made him oh so human there in that room. "Your prayers have been only for your people lately."

"We are at war. Of course I pray for them," Eimarille said.

"The mark of a good queen." Innes let her hand go to curl his fingers over the point of her chin, holding her still as he studied her face. "But the war is not all that you are worried about."

"The starfire throne is not under our control, even if Amari is."

"Aaralyn is not yours to worry about."

The North Star guided Ashion, her claimed country, and Maricol as a whole. Eimarille used to pray to the world's guiding star when she was young and still called her birth country home. Innes was who she prayed to now, but for all his power and influence, his wife was the apex of Maricol's religion, and Eimarille knew they had to tread carefully. "I would go to Amari and claim my birthright."

Innes' hand moved to frame her face, and he leaned forward to kiss her other cheek. His lips were dry and warm against her skin, the touch of an indulgent father over anything else. Innes might not have raised her, but he'd dipped in and out of her life over the years, a reminder to those who'd controlled her before she controlled herself that she wasn't to be harmed.

"Your birthright needs no claiming. You've had it all your life. It is reunification of all of Maricol we must prove. Your bloodline will sit on the starfire throne in due time. Until then, let your high general here wage your war."

Out of the corners of her eyes, Eimarille saw Kote bow deeply. "You honor me, my lord."

Innes nodded before drawing away from Eimarille. "I understand you have a ball tonight."

"There are chains to break. My love does so enjoy such activities," Eimarille said lightly. She reached for Terilyn without looking, smiling when the other woman took her hand. Eimarille got to her feet so she could more easily kiss Terilyn on the cheek.

Nathaniel Clementine's stolen memories had been more than useful to their side. The cogs he'd been responsible for had led them to others in the Clockwork Brigade. Eimarille's spies and Blades had been breaking chains since last summer. Meleri might have sent her cogs a warning. Many may have gone on the run if they hadn't outright joined Ashion's war efforts, but many others had paid the ultimate price for siding against Eimarille.

She doled out punishment in increments, knowing that to raze the Clockwork Brigade to the ground immediately would risk losing potential information. So she'd taken her time, allowed Terilyn to uncover those still in positions of power and send Blades to monitor the traitors. Eimarille had been grudgingly impressed with the reach Duchess Meleri Auclair had obtained over the years. Some cogs had worked their way deep into Daijalan society, and tonight, she was set to rectify that betrayal.

An important fact about war Eimarille had learned was one had to get the strategy and overall decisions right. War for war's sake would earn her no goodwill with the people she ruled. There needed to be a goal, one worthwhile enough for people to die for, and sometimes society needed to be reminded about the enemy up close and personal.

"I'm sure you will all enjoy tonight," Innes said as he stood.

"Will you be joining us, my lord?" Eimarille asked.

Innes did up his shirt and cravat, a smile tugging at his mouth. "I am expected elsewhere, but I am certain I'll hear your guests' prayers tonight."

Eimarille and Terilyn curtsied as Innes left, while Kote held a salute with straight-shouldered precision. The door clicked shut behind the Twilight Star, and Eimarille let out a slow breath, the heavy presence of a star god fading from the room. Terilyn touched a hand to her elbow, and Eimarille glanced at her lover.

"Come, let us prepare for tonight," Terilyn said.

Kote left with a quiet goodbye, leaving them in the care of the servants who had traveled with them over the last week. Eimarille didn't mind, for Terilyn stayed by her side, and she would never tire of such company.

Three

MELVIN

Melvin Khaur, a member of the Khaur bloodline, albeit a cadet branch, strode down the ground-floor hallway in the eastern wing of his family's Istal estate. Servants darted about, tending to the last-minute decorating and setup that always occurred when a ball was held in his bloodline's estate. Occasionally, he was stopped on his way to the stairs at the end of the hallway, and Melvin made himself available to whatever servant needed guidance. Guests were set to arrive shortly, and Melvin well knew how frantic his chamberlain and servants got at a time like this.

The Istal estate was his and his husband's home, given to them by his uncle. They oversaw those in the bloodline who worked out of the frontier city, which weren't all that many. Most of his prominent cousins resided in New Haven or Helia, working in politics or for the bloodline's many casinos. The rest were scattered across Daijal, calling the major cities and larger towns home, creating a web of information that was easily explained away by familial presence and visits.

Their bloodline's wealth came from gambling, which made keeping up so many properties possible. They paid their taxes on time and in full, and despite their own personal misgivings, those with a

25

seat in the Daijal parliament voted with the majority most of the time unless it directly affected their bottom line. They tried to never use debt slaves if they could help it, but sometimes such horror was required to keep up the façade of a loyal bloodline.

In all, the Khaur bloodline was a bloodline in good standing through exceptional effort.

Istal allowed no casinos within its walls, but his husband's wind-up toy company was a perfect excuse for them to stay in the city. That it also doubled as a means to aid debt slaves through the Clockwork Brigade was a secondary perk. While his uncle might be Lord Khaur and head of the bloodline, Melvin had held the title of Marshal within the Clockwork Brigade for almost two decades, overseeing chains of cogs for Fulcrum.

The Khaur bloodline had distant ties to the Auclair bloodline, a connection he prayed to the North Star that Queen Eimarille Rourke would never uncover. When Daijal had split from Ashion after the civil war, the Star Order's genealogies had also been cleaved. Daijal records might no longer indicate his bloodline's distant past, but there was no guarantee the Ashion records had done the same.

Still, the Khaur bloodline had made a point of aligning itself with the Daijal court, even as it undermined the old Iverson bloodline's power over the years. These days, with Eimarille wearing the crown, Melvin couldn't find it in himself to be pleased that a Rourke ruled once again, not when the result was a grinding war out east that threatened everyone across the continent, whether they wanted to believe so or not.

Melvin let such thoughts slide away as he took the stairs up to the second floor of the estate and then the third. The rooms on that floor were private, meant for the family's use alone, and none of the decorations from below had made their way above. The walls only held portraits of his ancestors and artwork of distant cities, and the private office Melvin favored only held his husband.

Ezra looked up at his arrival, the gas lamps burning brightly on the desk and wall sconces casting a shine to his blond hair. He smiled at Melvin's arrival, blue eyes crinkling at the corners. Even after all these years, Melvin never got tired of being greeted with a kiss from his husband.

"You look harried," Ezra murmured against his lips.

"I am glad no one else in the family could make it in time for the ball," Melvin admitted.

A strong arm wrapped around his waist, pulling him close against his husband's side. Ezra set the telegram he'd been reading down on the desk to hold him more tightly. Melvin glanced at it, noting that the missive was from his uncle and completely innocuous. It wasn't even in code, merely plain language, giving them authority to act in his place when the queen was present.

Ezra pressed his lips against the shell of Melvin's ear, voice barely louder than a whisper. "Have faith, my love. We will see the dawn."

Melvin closed his eyes, taking in a steadying breath. It was a risk to speak of such things in a home where Blades walked. The Star Order's never-acknowledged assassins had shown up midweek with soldiers wearing uniforms of the guards typically on duty at the palace in New Haven. Melvin had no recourse but to allow them entry and give them the run of the estate.

He and Ezra kept no security—magical or otherwise—in the office they shared save for a regular lock. To have anything more than that within the estate was to invite questions they could ill afford. Most of their communications with the cogs in the chains they were responsible for came through dead drops and veiled conversation out in public. If Melvin had learned anything from his uncle since taking up the mantle of Marshal, it was how to keep secrets.

They had a reputation as indulgent nobility, with a philanthropic focus on mechanical engineers and a business that focused on children. He and Ezra made it a point to be as careful as possible with how they acted in public to shield themselves and the rest of the bloodline from the actions they took on behalf of the Clockwork Brigade. But for all their carefulness, everyone's secrets were being found out.

The death of Lord Felipe Beltre in Haighmoor had spread like wildfire in the nobility's private parlors and public broadsheets across two countries within the span of a day. The accusations levied against him—of being a cog, of colluding with the Clockwork Brigade and the Ashion rebellion—had been a guilty verdict issued by Eimarille and not a court, the execution rumored to have been carried out by the only lady-in-waiting to never leave her side.

However Eimarille had come into possession of the identities of cogs, a full cascade failure of the entire Clockwork Brigade had yet to occur. Melvin and Fulcrum had worked fanatically to pick apart the chains at issue, trying to salvage who they could amidst the growing war. But Eimarille's actions of late proved they couldn't shield everyone.

Perhaps not even themselves.

It was why, as soon as the courier had arrived with their military escort and the queen's expectations and a list of invitees, Melvin had only ever been agreeable to everything requested. He'd put on a show of calm pride despite the logistical nightmare of throwing a ball worthy of the Daijalan queen with only a few days' notice.

That had been enough of a reason to call his uncle, and if, in the course of the conversation, he slipped in a code for the rest of the family to *stay away*, well, no one would know. He hoped, if asked, that Eimarille would accept the excuse of being greeted not by Lord Khaur himself but by a favored nephew and not consider it a slight.

Ezra pulled back a little, letting his hands move to grip Melvin's waist. The expensive blue fabric of his evening coattails brought out the color of his eyes, the fondness in his gaze as familiar as breathing. "Let's get downstairs before the guests arrive. If we aren't in the receiving line before the first knock, we'll never live it down."

Melvin snorted. "Of course not."

Tonight's ball had most certainly not been on their schedule, neither their public nor private ones. It had necessitated pushing back several business meetings and one very important clandestine one dealing with the abhorrent prisoners of war camp that had cropped up a mile away beyond Istal's outer wall.

The sprawling camp of tents and temporary barracks—overseen by better-built watchtowers and guarded by soldiers and automatons alike—was surrounded by temporary fencing meant to keep prisoners in and revenants out. It didn't always hold up.

Several breaches had occurred, necessitating the murder of POWs under the guise of ensuring spores couldn't spread. The bodies were always shipped away, most likely to wherever the death-defying machines were being kept in the field. That they weren't even given proper funeral rites in a crematorium, or their names listed on a memory wall, was sickening.

The location of the death-defying machines was information Melvin had yet to uncover, but the most critical information he had come into possession of was the identity of two high-profile prisoners who were relegated to the barracks in the camp, ever under guard. Baron Emmitt Dhemlan and Baroness Portia Dhemlan, late of Ashion, had been smuggled into the camp after winter receded and were under the heaviest guard.

Since Caris had claimed Rourke as her bloodline, everyone had wondered what had befallen the Dhemlans. Melvin knew they'd been under house arrest in Amari before that shocking announcement. Since then, no one could or would confirm their whereabouts, not until a cog who worked as a prostitute plied a Daijalan officer with enough whiskey to loosen a tongue.

The officer in question helped oversee the POW camp and knew the records of those brought inside its fences that did nothing to keep out the wind that screamed across the Northern Plains. The POW camp outside Istal's walls was a place of death. Melvin couldn't leave Caris' parents out there to die, but any attempt to access the camp without the proper clearance meant one would join the prisoners.

Melvin was skilled at facilitating the movement of debt slaves, at hiding them and passing them off to other chains for escape out of Daijal. When it came to emergency extractions, the best cog for such tasks came out of Helia.

Lady Sabine Garnier was married to a naval captain, doted on by her husband whenever he was ashore, the man ignorant of her position in the Clockwork Brigade. She wasn't directly connected to Melvin through a chain, but as the Marshal, he was aware of her position, and they ran in the same social circles. They'd become friendly acquaintances ever since their first introduction some years back. They were careful to keep their interactions few and far between while adhering to the social manners required of them for their individual stations.

Tonight, in the receiving line, Lady Sabine smiled winsomely at them both as she held on to her husband's arm. She looked splendid in a gauzy sheath gown with a high waist, the deep green fabric picked through at the hem and high collar with bright gold thread. The floral design was meant to invoke the new spring season, a familiar trend everyone indulged in wearing after the snows melted and the barrenness of winter passed.

"A most envious evening, if I do say," Sabine said with a smile that showed off her dimples as she offered her free hand to Ezra, who bowed over it. "I would be ecstatic at the chance to welcome the queen to our estate in Helia."

"It is certainly an honor for us," Ezra replied. "Lord and Lady Garnier, the Khaur bloodline welcomes you. So nice to see you away from the sea."

Lord Payton Garnier was a tall man five years Sabine's senior, with a rugged face carved from the sea winds that blew across the Gulf of Helia. His smile was genuine, and he'd always been friendly at previous social gatherings in Helia where they'd interacted. Tonight, he looked quite dashing in his naval uniform, the ranking pins and medals showcasing valor glinting against the crimson of his jacket. When he offered his gloved hand in greeting, his grip was firm but not overwhelming how some officers' were.

"Well met, Mr. Khaur. You do your bloodline a great service for putting on such a grand occasion in such a short amount of time," Payton said.

"A pity my uncle could not be here to see it. I would like to think we did him proud," Melvin said.

"You most certainly have."

"I'd ask if you were here on holiday, but the war gives no time for breaks. How fares Daijal's navy?"

Payton smiled, the pride in his gaze that of a military man who knew his place. "I was granted leave for a few weeks and ended up being summoned to Istal for some strategy meetings. Sabine decided to join me. As to the navy, we are holding the waters that belong to us."

Sabine smiled up at her husband, the adoration in her gaze not a lie, for Melvin knew how much she cared for Payton. "I couldn't bear the thought of not seeing you while you were on land."

Payton lifted her gloved hand to his lips to kiss her knuckles. "I am glad you wanted to accompany me. I'm even more thrilled we were invited tonight."

Melvin knew it was as much to be with her husband as it was to do the work of cog, though she would never admit it. Sabine and Payton smiled their goodbyes and moved away. Melvin and Ezra didn't pay the pair any more attention than they did with their other arriving guests. Melvin's throat was dry by the halfway mark of the arrival hour, but his chamberlain had positioned a servant nearby, who quickly offered up a tray of water and wineglasses. He chose water for the moment, passing the glass to Ezra to drink out of when he finished.

They were in the midst of welcoming one of the city's court justices when the sound of trumpets echoed through the open doors, signaling Queen Eimarille Rourke's arrival. Melvin smoothed his hands down the front of the waistcoat that matched the color of Ezra's suit, hiding his nerves behind a quick smile directed at his husband. "Let's hope we did our bloodline proud."

The receiving line broke up, their chamberlain quickly ushering the latecomers to the side as Melvin and Ezra left their spot beside the grand stairway to position themselves closer to the double doors. Melvin resisted the urge to crane his head about to peer through the doorway for a better view of the drive and the people present there. He didn't fidget, having learned not to when he was a boy, but he couldn't help but brush his hand over the front of his jacket again, palm skimming over the faint shape of his wand secured in an inside pocket.

Melvin had long made a name for himself as a magician skilled in parlor tricks. He would never be a match for someone who could cast starfire, but having his wand close at hand brought him a false sort of comfort. These days, with the war in full fight, he never went anywhere without it.

A flurry of motion on the porch made him straighten up, smile perfectly in place and attention on Daijal's queen as she stepped through the doors amidst the chamberlain loudly announcing her arrival. "Her Royal Majesty Queen Eimarille Rourke."

The applause that rang through the large foyer echoed against the walls. Eimarille paused just past the threshold, gracing everyone with a lovely smile, head held high beneath the weight of the crown she wore. She was beautiful, Melvin could admit, but her beauty hid a cruelty she couched as service to her country.

He let those thoughts slide away, allowing no hint of his true feelings to show on his face or in his voice as he bowed deeply to the degree appropriate for the monarch, no more and no less. "Your Royal Majesty, on behalf of my uncle, Lord Khaur, my husband and I are honored and delighted to welcome you to the Khaur bloodline's Istal estate."

Eimarille's gown was a shimmering green with gold details around the full skirt. Melvin could just make out the repeating constellation of the Viper, the representation of Daijal's guiding star god. Her gold-and-diamond crown had lone spines protruding from the flower fili-gree base, a representation of sunbeams. It sparkled with every move-ment of her head, her thick blonde hair styled into an updo that put the long line of her neck and back on display.

She smiled at him, her expression open and pleased, as if she truly did care. "I know Lord Khaur is diligently working on several war bills back in New Haven with his heir. It was kind of you to fill in for him on such short notice."

"No notice is ever too short when it comes to making you feel welcome, my queen. We are proud that you chose our bloodline for your ball." Melvin gestured subtly at Ezra, smiling fondly at the other man. "May I introduce my husband, Mr. Ezra Khaur?"

Ezra bowed again. "Queen Eimarille, it is an honor."

Eimarille kept smiling, gloved hands clasped together in front of her. Terilyn stood to her right and a little behind, the Urovan wearing a sheath gown much in the style of Sabine's from earlier. Her jewelry was more delicate and refined than Eimarille's, but Melvin didn't trust she wasn't armed. She wouldn't be a Blade if that were the case.

"Ezra, so nice to meet you. I understand you are a toymaker?"

"Yes, my queen. I own a business that makes wind-up toys."

Eimarille brightened at that. "Oh, lovely! I'm sure Lisandro would love a toy from your workshop."

"I would be happy to gift the young prince a set."

They chatted a little longer before Melvin smoothly segued their conversation into escorting Eimarille through the guests toward the ballroom. Ezra offered Terilyn his arm as well, and the other woman took it with a polite smile. Eimarille was adept at social niceties, remembering everyone's name and social status as they orbited around her through the next hour of greetings.

Melvin kept close, facilitating introductions and giving Eimarille the spotlight she didn't need to fight for, not as queen. If she wasn't the architect of the war—wasn't the one signing off on the murders of cogs and debt slaves—he could possibly appreciate her political deftness. But that would happen only if she walked a different road, and as everyone knew, the Twilight Star had set her down this one.

"Have you and your husband always lived in Istal?" Eimarille asked him in a rare break between guests.

"Yes. It is where I went to school and where his family's business is located. We met here, and we feel safe here," Melvin said, lying just a little bit.

"Even with the war?"

The question was innocuous if it had come from anyone but Eimarille. "The war is needed, my queen. How else are we to bring Ashion back into the fold? You are doing what the previous king could not, and my bloodline supports your efforts wholeheartedly."

"Yes, your uncle is quite vocal in cajoling others to vote his way in parliament back in New Haven. I do appreciate his support. Are you happy out here in Istal?"

"I must admit, the bustle of New Haven is a bit much some days. Even with the war, Istal has always been slower-paced."

Eimarille smiled gently at him, her gaze warm. "You stay for your husband, do you not? He married into nobility, as I recall."

Melvin was glad for the gloves he wore, that the sudden clammy sweat on his palms would be absorbed by the white cotton. "Yes. Politics has never been his favorite thing. He has always much preferred making toys for children."

"A worthy job if ever there was one. Your bloodline has been nothing but supportive, unlike some over the years."

He inclined his head, keeping his voice steady. "You are our queen."

"Some don't believe so."

"Then they are wrong."

Eimarille nodded, her gaze cutting away, and Melvin felt as if he could breathe again. "Of course they are."

Melvin escorted her onward, trying not to hold himself so stiffly that she noticed, but her words were like the klaxon of a warning siren. They rang in the back of his head for the next few hours, through dances and conversation, through the well-wishes of Istal's high society as he did right by his bloodline.

The estate wasn't as large as others in Istal, but it was well maintained, and the rear garden, with its topiary maze and bubbling creek, was a favorite for quiet assignations. It was in one of the groves, as they waited for the fireworks to burst in the sky at the end of the ball, that Melvin came to understand his road would continue.

Another guest's would not.

"You and your husband have been excellent hosts, Mr. Khaur," Eimarille murmured as she stared at the sky. "It is a pity not everyone's loyalty is as unquestioned as yours."

Melvin couldn't help but stiffen at her words, gaze flickering to Ezra, finding his husband looking back at him with a blank gaze, expression still that of someone enjoying the ball.

The night air was warm enough, but Melvin felt chilled to his bones. He abruptly realized Terilyn had disappeared from Ezra's side, but Melvin couldn't afford to look for her. Eimarille required all of his attention. "Pardon?"

"I know what occurred in Haighmoor is being whispered about amongst high society. I take no pleasure in removing traitors in such a way, you must understand."

Eimarille gestured almost lazily with one hand, and a moment later, Sabine was shoved out of Payton's arms and into the center of the small garden grove. She fell to her knees on the flagstones with a cry, catching herself with her hands. Payton lurched toward her with a protesting sound that he immediately strangled when Terilyn pressed the blade of her stiletto against his throat.

"None of that, please," Terilyn said in a low voice. "You are not being judged here, but if you persist, you will be."

Payton's eyes were wide, face gone bone white beneath the distant illumination of gas lamp lights. His arm remained outstretched, but he didn't move, Terilyn's warning keeping him rooted where he stood. The distant boom of fireworks filled the eerie quiet that had settled over this small corner of the gardens.

Sabine raised her head, gaze focusing not on her husband but on Eimarille. She leaned back, resting her weight on her heels, hands clenched in the gauzy fabric of her gown. "My queen, there must be some mistake."

"I am no queen to cogs," Eimarille said, staring Sabine down.

Her words drew sharp gasps from those nearby and privy to the execution about to take place. Melvin reached without looking, his hand finding Ezra's and gripping tight. He didn't look away from Sabine, didn't want to know if some other Blade was coming up behind them in the shadows. If they died tonight, they'd die together.

Eimarille stepped forward, her heels clicking against the flagstone in between the sound of exploding fireworks. "You have operated out of Helia on behalf of the Clockwork Brigade for quite some time. While your husband has served his country well at sea, you have betrayed it."

"I know not what you speak of. I am loyal to Daijal."

"You are loyal to a false queen in the east."

Sabine pushed herself to her feet, the motion somehow hiding her retrieval of her wand until it didn't. She raised it not at Eimarille but at herself, resting the tip against her right temple. The clarion crystal there brightened as she called forth the aether, her magic curling against the skin of her face and loose strands of hair. Payton's shocked gasp told Melvin the naval captain had never been privy to Sabine's most closely guarded secret. "Caris Rourke is the rightful queen of Ashion."

Gone was her subservience, and in its place was a righteous fury that Melvin felt in his bones, though he dared not ever show it. Sabine stood beneath the glow of gas lamps and magic, facing off against a woman who had signed her death sentence before she'd ever set foot on the Khaur bloodline's estate.

The sound of safeties being clicked off pistols made Melvin jerk, and he gazed wildly about at the guards whose weapons were now drawn and pointed at Sabine. Terilyn hadn't moved from Payton's side, her stiletto still resting against his throat. The Blade's attention wasn't on anyone but Eimarille, who stopped arm's distance from Sabine, one slender hand turning palm up, starfire flickering into existence in the cradle of her fingers.

The molten light of starfire brightened the area considerably, as if an impossible miniature sun rested in her hand. Melvin couldn't see Eimarille's face, only the back of her, but her voice was thick with regret he almost believed she truly felt. But it was all a lie, he knew. Eimarille was the puppet master holding Maricol's strings, granted that right by a star god at odds with the rest of his brethren.

"You dishonor your husband's bloodline," Eimarille said.

"I loved my husband, unlike the way you pretended to love yours," Sabine said. The magic at her temple grew brighter, gaze becoming distant. "And I loved my queen. For her, I will forget."

Sabine was a magician skilled in mind magic, and to turn it on herself to protect the memories and names of the cogs she worked with was a sacrifice Melvin didn't feel worthy of. Not when he stood silently by as Eimarille cast her starfire at Sabine, the magic-driven flames licking at the gown she wore and the flesh beneath it.

Payton's cry couldn't be drowned out by the fireworks as Sabine went up in starfire, never uttering a sound, forgetting how to at the behest of her own magic if she was lucky. Ezra's grip on Melvin's hand was bone-bruising, and he could hear the shallow way his husband breathed beside him. The smell of burning human flesh had Melvin turning his face aside, trying not to gag, trying not to cry, feeling desperately, achingly guilty that it was neither himself nor Ezra who'd been the focus of Eimarille's ire and glad for it.

The ball in Haighmoor and the one tonight and all the rest on Eimarille's social calendar were nothing but staged executions. In every home that held them, a cog would die, and there was precious little Melvin could do from here on out other than order the chains to flee east. Doing so would cripple the Clockwork Brigade in Daijal, and perhaps that was Eimarille's desire all along.

"I am sorry you had to find out this way, Captain," Eimarille said in a soothing voice that did little to slow the trip-hammer of Melvin's heart.

Melvin watched Eimarille comfort Payton, breathing shallowly so as not to take in the smell of Sabine's death. The captain's grief and shock was like an opera mask painted on his face, the man having aged a decade in moments. Payton's gaze remained riveted on the smoldering remains of his wife, who was nothing but ash and whose name would never be written on a memory wall.

Despite the roiling in his gut, Melvin rallied himself to do his duty to his family, hoping that Eimarille's edicts were for Sabine alone tonight. He let go of Ezra despite it being the last thing he wanted to do. Melvin didn't need to fake the solemn expression on his face at all as he approached Eimarille and Payton. He dutifully rocked to a halt when a soldier got in his way, pistol holstered now but hand resting on the sturdy brass grip. Melvin sketched a shallow bow in Eimarille's direction when she looked over at him, no hint of remorse in her eyes.

"I'll have my servants handle the...mess, my queen. Perhaps it would be best if we finished up inside?" Melvin asked.

"An excellent idea. If you've a private room we may use? I fear the good captain is in need of a respite," Eimarille said.

"Of course. Let me escort you both there."

The guard let him pass after that, and Melvin wasn't at all surprised to find that Terilyn remained by Eimarille's side. Ezra stayed behind long enough to usher everyone who had borne witness to Sabine's execution back into the estate, the whispers about what had occurred already spreading amongst the guests. Melvin desperately wanted to keep Ezra with him, but Eimarille required all of his focus.

He escorted the queen and the shell-shocked captain into the library at the other end of the wing, allowing Terilyn to enter first. Only when she gave a nod did Eimarille guide Payton inside, speaking low and soft to a man whose world she'd burned to ash. Melvin was careful to keep the horror, anger, and grief off his own face, knowing that to mourn now would leave his bloodline suspect.

Payton sank onto the chaise, cradling his head in his hands, not quite able to muffle his sobs. Eimarille didn't try to console him for his loss, only his ignorance. "You didn't know. She hid her lies well."

"She was my *wife*," Payton gasped out.

"She was a cog, but that has no bearing on you or your bloodline. You are not at fault."

Payton finally lifted his head, eyes wet and reddened, and looked up at her beseechingly. "My queen, I am no traitor."

Eimarille touched her fingers to his cheek. "I know. You would have met her same fate if I had information otherwise. Be at ease, Lord Garnier. Your bloodline remains untarnished. I only execute those that are disloyal."

"I am loyal, my queen."

"I know you are."

Melvin stayed put, watching as Eimarille promised lies to a man too grief-stricken to appreciate them. He knew, even if Payton didn't, that if Eimarille wanted the Garnier bloodline excised from the nobility genealogies, it would be.

Eventually, Payton was given a glass of whiskey from Terilyn, handed off to a guard, and hopefully escorted home and not some-place where his body might turn up in a gutter.

Then it was just Melvin and Eimarille and the lies he lived that he hoped were enough to save him. Sabine had, in the end, saved the chains around her, as well as keeping secret Melvin's position as the Marshal. Her own magic had carved out her memories, so even if Eimarille had imprisoned her, there would be nothing left to take. Merely a husk of flesh that was little more than a revenant, and Eimarille had seen her be not even that in the end.

There in that room, he silently prayed that Sabine danced amongst the stars.

Eimarille studied Melvin with keen eyes. "This war makes strange bedfellows of those who should know better."

Somehow, he unstuck his tongue from the roof of his mouth. "So it seems."

"Your bloodline will hold only good favor for allowing my Blade to flush out traitors to the crown."

At that, he sketched another bow, all the years of his boyhood learning the dance of manners guiding him when he only wanted to hide. "The Khaur bloodline only ever wishes to aid the war effort and support your rule. We are at your command."

"Indeed."

Melvin straightened, forcing himself to meet Eimarille's gaze, wondering if he'd soon feel the sharp edge of a knife slide into his back. She studied him with gray-blue eyes that gave nothing away, but in the end, she let him keep his life.

Eimarille headed for the door. "I believe it is time we said our farewell to the guests. You have been an excellent host, Mr. Khaur."

Melvin turned to follow her out, doing his best to pretend he wasn't lightheaded at escaping death in that room. Still, her actions were a reminder of the damage done to the Clockwork Brigade, and he knew his family's future faced a ticking clock.

After Eimarille and the guests departed, after the remnants of Sabine's life had been swept up into a vase as a makeshift urn to be dealt with in the morning, after silence settled like mourners at a memory wall, Melvin and Ezra found themselves alone in their bedroom. They undressed in silence, sliding beneath the covers and holding each other close. Melvin never once let go of his clarion crystal-tipped wand, for all the good it would do if a Blade slipped through the shadows.

In the dark, with the memory of Sabine's death playing through his mind, Melvin was never more cognizant of what was at stake than in that moment when war came knocking at his door. For war was never famine; it was always feast. It ate the lives of people in its path, swallowed their hope, and burned their freedom to ash. War was a glutton never satisfied, bones of the conquered churning beneath the boots of an army that kept driving forward.

War had teeth, and it would always bite.

Four

PORTIA

When the door to her locked cell pushed open, Baroness Portia Dhemlan couldn't bring herself to rise to her feet from the narrow bed she lay in. The barracks housing herself and other high-profile prisoners were located in the center of the POW camp. Weapons from the soldiers and automatons that guarded the camp against revenants had gone off all night, keeping her awake.

"Get up. You're wanted in the city."

She tried not to flinch at that order. Being summoned like this had never gone well in the past—the last time had seen her put on a steam train at the rail station in Amari. It had taken her and Emmitt west, out of reach of anyone who might think to try to save them from an occupied city.

Portia carefully sat up, swinging her legs over the side of the bed. The thin mattress and patched blanket weren't enough to ward off the morning chill, but it was spring, she thought, and the floor wasn't as icy as it had been even a few weeks ago.

Portia slipped her feet into the thin-soled shoes allotted to each prisoner in the camp once they were processed through the gates. The drab gray pants and loose long-sleeved shirt matched the clothes worn by other prisoners. Being nobility didn't mean anything there in that hellish place. Her rank as a baroness only afforded herself and her husband separate tiny rooms in the barracks with other high-profile prisoners when everyone else in their same predicament lived in rows of tents, at the mercy of the elements.

The soldier snapped a pair of shackles around her wrists once she stood. The metal dug against her wristbones, but she knew better than to protest. Portia followed her jailer out of the cell, the heavy metal door clanging shut behind her. She looked past the soldier, heart skipping a beat at the sight of her husband as Emmitt came out of a cell at the other end of the hallway.

They locked eyes, and Portia bit her lip, swallowing the urge to call out to him. It had been weeks since she last saw him, and she ached to hold him and be held in return. Portia blinked back tears and drew in a shaky breath, refusing to cry before their jailers.

Emmitt and his guard joined them at the landing. His shackled hands twitched toward her before he fisted them and pressed them close to his stomach. The hollows in his cheeks seemed worse, though the cough he'd had the last time they saw each other seemed to have gone away. Portia had begged for a healer for him, and she hadn't known if one had been granted to see him. Looking at Emmitt now, one must have, for all the good it had done.

"Portia," Emmitt murmured right before he was prodded down the stairs.

She squared her shoulders, following him down, aware of the soldiers at their back, waiting for a shove that never came. She and Emmitt were spared the violence most other prisoners had to live through in the rest of the camp, though Portia wasn't grateful for that reprieve at all. It singled them out, and the reason for that had escaped Amari and was rallying the Ashion army if the rumors from other prisoners were true.

But oh, how she missed her daughter. Knowing that Caris was hopefully still alive did nothing to ease Portia's worry. Caris was her daughter and always would be, no matter the name she now used. She might have been born a Rourke, but she would always be a Dhemlan in Portia's heart.

Their transportation from the POW camp to Istal was in a motor carriage whose engine needed an oil change if the grinding sound of the pistons was anything to go by. Portia ignored the sound on the fast drive toward the city, leaning hard against Emmitt on the back seat, taking what comfort she could from his presence. He didn't smell like the cologne he used to wear, but the press of his lips to her temple was achingly familiar.

The driver bypassed the main entry line through the city gates for the one used by the military. Whatever papers he brandished got them waved through to a bustling street. Portia stared at the passing buildings and the people who went about their business as if a war wasn't being fought and they didn't have the dead clawing at their walls every day.

Revenants were a scourge Daijal was no longer safe from. Portia had read the broadsheets when they'd been imprisoned in Amari. She knew the atrocity Queen Eimarille Rourke had perpetuated against the wardens, damning her country to the walking dead and poison fields that would never be cleansed. Eimarille had done it in the name of progress, a fitting reason for the Age they were in. But all progress came with a price, and Portia wondered if Eimarille would damn all of Maricol for a future not everyone believed in.

Portia would never ask that question out loud, but it lingered in her thoughts when the motor carriage finally drove into the military garrison within Istal's walls and saw who waited for them in the fore-court. She remembered the Urovan from the debutante ball back in Amari last year and, later, when Terilyn had overseen their transfer from Ashion to Daijal. Wearing a long brown skirt and a white short-sleeved blouse, with her black hair pulled back in a queue, her outfit was quite plain, not indicative of a noble at all.

Terilyn's quiet demeanor hid sharp eyes and an even sharper mind. Ever Eimarille's companion and trusted lady-in-waiting, she was not above murdering for her queen, as Portia well knew. She couldn't quite hide the flinch when Terilyn's steady, brown-eyed gaze landed on her as she exited the motor carriage.

"This won't do," Terilyn said, taking their measure. "Remove their shackles."

The guards who had come with them obeyed the order without argument. It wasn't as if Portia or Emmitt had any weapons or magic at their disposal. With her hands free, Portia reached for Emmitt and found him reaching back. Their fingers tangled together tightly, his palm rough against hers, but it felt so good to hold on.

Terilyn circled them once before gesturing sharply. "You will follow me."

The soldiers didn't join them, and no one tried to separate them. Portia took advantage of that tiny bit of freedom to press close to her husband. Emmitt wrapped his arm tight around her waist, his fingers digging into her hip with bruising desperation.

Terilyn led them to a washroom with attendants who looked more suited to being at court than a garrison. She and Emmitt were stripped of their prison clothes and scrubbed down while they stood in the center of the tiled space. Portia's cheeks burned with shame at being on display in such a manner, but she didn't complain. At least the water was warm enough, but Portia was still chilled by the time she was handed a towel and told to dry off. She didn't dally, thankful that she'd been able to wash off the accumulated grime. Her daily ablutions in the POW camp were little more than sluicing a tiny amount of water over her hands and face.

Once they were dry, the attendants dressed them in clothes Portia knew they wouldn't get to keep. The fabric was too fine, the style too new, to be anything but a façade for political purposes.

That's all they were now—no longer cogs but political pawns.

Terilyn nodded her approval at their cleaned-up state before stepping out of the room. "This way."

Portia and Emmitt followed after her, escape a distant dream. Terilyn led them deeper into the garrison to a room that had been rearranged to allow a military photographer to set up his camera stand. The painting that once hung from a white-painted wall now leaned against the back of a pushed-aside sofa. In its place hung the Daijal flag. Portia and Emmitt were made to sit and stand, always facing the camera with grim expressions on their faces as the bulbs popped and flashed throughout the process. Whatever propaganda the photographs would be used for, Portia hoped Caris knew they were unwilling participants in the designs.

"I'll have them ready for the queen by tomorrow morning," the man said with a stiff nod in Terilyn's direction.

"See that you do. We depart Istal at noon tomorrow," Terilyn said.

With the appointment finished, Terilyn led them once more through the garrison on a route Portia didn't bother to keep track of. Eventually, Terilyn escorted them into a library where Queen Eimarille Rourke waited. Portia tried to still her pounding heart as Eimarille looked at them over the tea tray situated on the low table.

Eimarille was dressed in a rich maroon gown with sheer gold voile layered over the skirt. Her bodice had delicate gold thread embroidered in a repeating Viper constellation pattern along the collar, drawing attention to the layered strands of gold and pearl necklaces. She wore no crown, only a tiara with intricate floral filigree done in gold, pearl, and diamonds.

As beautiful as she looked, Portia found no warmth in Eimarille's gaze. But even as she stared, she could see bits of Caris in Eimarille's face, the resemblance there only in the physical, for her daughter would never be so cruel.

"Have you forgotten your manners?" Terilyn asked with an amused lilt to her voice.

Belatedly, Portia sketched a curtsy while Emmitt bowed. Neither one of them spoke, choosing silence over the political pitfalls that came with words these days. Eimarille's lips quirked into a smile as she gestured at the sofa across from hers. "Baron and Baroness Dhemlan, do take a seat. I thought it time the three of us finally had a conversation."

When they'd been imprisoned under house arrest in Amari after the riot last summer, Eimarille had not summoned them before her. They'd been held under false pretenses, Portia had argued, but it made no difference at the time. Portia and Emmitt might have been Ashionen citizens, not subject to Daijalan law, but the courts saw differently. Their detainment had been orchestrated by the very woman who now offered them a spread of tea and food too rich for their stomachs after months of poor rations.

Emmitt squeezed Portia's hand before letting go and ushering her to a seat. They sat, so close their thighs touched, and Portia clasped her hands together over her lap. Terilyn gracefully sat next to Eimarille and set about pouring tea for everyone. Two pots were available, one with the pale gold flowering tea favored by Daijal and another of the bitter black favored by some provinces in Ashion. There was cream and sweetener in the form of sugar, honey, and jam, along with elegantly made cakes and tea sandwiches.

Terilyn passed out teacups to everyone, and Portia had to force herself to reach for hers, opting not to add anything to it. She wondered, idly, if it was poisoned in some way. Eimarille had stolen war machine designs from Solaria; she wouldn't put it past the other woman to borrow the Houses of Solaria's habits of murdering each other by way of poison in order to claim power.

"Not to your liking?" Eimarille asked, the kindness in her tone a lie.

"It's been quite some time since I've had tea," Portia demurred. She braced herself for a careful sip, the hot beverage tasting how she remembered.

"I am aware."

Portia said nothing to that, knowing better than to lay the blame for their current predicament at the feet of the woman who quite literally controlled their lives. Her sip taken, Portia set the teacup on the table, steeling herself to meet Eimarille's gaze. The younger woman's attention was a heavy thing, leaving Portia's chest tight as she wondered how to dance like a puppet to ensure their road continued.

"You must understand I did not wish for things to turn out this way, but your daughter gave me no recourse," Eimarille said after a moment. Portia bit her lip, swallowing her words. Emmitt stayed silent as well. Their reticence to speak seemed to amuse Eimarille. "No defense for your daughter?"

"Would it do us any good, Your Majesty?" Emmitt asked carefully.

Eimarille's mouth quirked up at the corners, but there was no humor to be found in her eyes. "No, it wouldn't. It is good that you understand that."

The taste of the tea soured on Portia's tongue. "We understand that we are at your mercy."

"My mercy can be kind." Eimarille set her teacup down on the table, sharing an unreadable glance with Terilyn. "Your memories show no recollection of how Caris came to you."

Portia couldn't hide the flinch those words caused, mind spinning back to one horrible afternoon last year shortly after they'd been put under house arrest. A man dressed like a warden had arrived at their Amari home, wand in hand, commanding insidious magic that carved its way through her thoughts. He'd dredged up every moment of Caris' life from the recess of Portia's mind, from infancy to the last sight of her at the start of the riot.

Portia hadn't been able to feel clean for weeks after that visit. Whatever he'd been searching for, he hadn't found it, his magic incapable of breaking through the hidden, fuzzy memory of the night Caris had come to them. Even now, it was like a distant dream, and the words to describe that moment were impossible to speak, held back by the power of a star god, so she didn't even try.

"She has always been with us."

"You did not give birth to her. Someone brought her to you. I want to know who."

"We have only ever known our daughter. Her name was written in the nobility genealogies."

"I am aware of that record. What is strange is that you have no memory of how she came to you. Few magicians are that skilled, and I know all of those weren't in your province during the Inferno. Outside of magicians, only star gods have that skill."

Portia didn't flinch this time. Perhaps some leftover bit of manipulation in her mind from so long ago allowed her body to remain truthful. "We are not favored by the star gods."

"I think you are, as is your daughter." Eimarille sipped her tea and was quiet for a moment before she resumed speaking. "Caris claims the Rourke bloodline, but her name was never written down in the royal genealogies. The ability to cast starfire doesn't give her the right to claim the starfire throne. Ashion is not like Solaria. We are not the Houses. My understanding from all the cogs we've uncovered is that she has been a figurehead for years, whether she knew it or not."

Portia dropped her gaze to the table and the food she had yet to touch. The magician who'd scoured their minds for memories of Caris had also pulled forth their status as cogs in the Clockwork Brigade. That alone should have been a death sentence in Daijal, but their association to Caris had spared them.

Their chain hadn't been high up, and they'd lived too far east to be of any political use—or so she'd thought. Portia hadn't known the leaders of the Clockwork Brigade until one afternoon years ago when the Duchess Auclair had voiced that critical secret. Now, those memories and their ties to Caris had turned them into pawns.

"What will you do with us?" Emmitt asked.

"Use you, of course," Eimarille said with a lightness that wasn't promising. "Caris won't be able to save you, but I want her to think that is still an option as the war claims Ashion's eastern provinces. You will be the reason she dies."

Portia opened her mouth to protest, but the words died on her lips in favor of begging. "Please don't kill her."

Eimarille leaned forward slightly, the layers of necklaces hanging from her throat swaying a little. "I despise martyrs, and the only way to eradicate one is to burn the foundation that upholds them."

Portia's lips trembled when she pressed them together, blinking back tears. She knew nothing would change Eimarille's mind, that the Daijal queen who wanted Ashion and the rest of Maricol beyond those borders had engineered this war with the deft touch of a master manipulator. Begging wouldn't change her intentions.

Eimarille's mercy was cruelty. It wasn't an accident or a secret; it was the point.

"You will be your daughter's downfall," Eimarille promised before nodding at Terilyn. "See that their transport back to Amari happens this week. We'll have the stories printed as we discussed."

"Of course," Terilyn murmured.

Terilyn stood with a smooth grace, gesturing at Portia and Emmitt to stand as well. She led them out of the room and back into the hands of their jailers. They changed out of the clothes that had been given to them to shape the propaganda Eimarille needed in favor of the ones they'd worn to Istal.

On the drive back to the POW camp, Portia couldn't stop crying, salty teardrops stinging her dry lips. The chain connecting the shackles around her wrists clanked against Emmitt's when he took her hands in his and held on, neither of them giving voice to the prayers in their thoughts.

Portia only hoped the North Star heard them.

Five

CARIS

Fifth Month in the Eastern Basin of Ashion came with cool winds blowing off the Eastern Spine, rolling down over frontier cities and towns scattered at the base of the mountains. The spring winds brought with them the insidious risk of poison and threat of spores all citizens of Maricol had learned to live with over time.

Growing up, the former Honorable Caris Dhemlan never went anywhere in the frontier city of Cosian without a gas mask hooked to her belt or strapped over her face. Now, carrying the name Rourke and the shadow of a crown she had never wanted, her old habits refused to break.

Some of the people who now called Cosian home weren't used to such habits, but they learned, as did the soldiers trying to hold their defenses on the front line stretched through the eastern provinces. Fighting past the safety of a city's thick outer walls was a frightening prospect that had become all too real. Nine months since the first illegal border crossing by Daijal, and many citizens in Ashion's eastern provinces were learning how to survive in places where only wardens once walked.

All because of Caris.

She might be considered queen to the half of Ashion who backed her, but the employees of the Six Point Mechanics Company she'd retaken control of last year knew her as an exacting supervisor these days. In the quiet hours of the night, when no one could see her uncertainty, Caris wished her family's company was all she had to worry about. War wasn't anything she'd been raised for, but then, neither had she been raised to be queen.

A familiar figure took up the empty space next to her at the long table in the meeting room typically used to present new engineering designs for them to be picked apart and reworked. Lately, it was used to discuss weapons. Lady Lore Auclair graced Caris with a tired smile. "It won't be much longer. We're waiting on one more officer."

She spoke with a cut-glass accent favored by the nobility in Amari, but Caris had heard her affect various others over the years. Lore could become anyone when wearing a veil, as Caris well knew. No matter the identity, Lore carried herself differently when undercover, using her entire body to become someone else.

She'd had practice for most of her adult life as Mainspring, one of the key cogs that oversaw the Clockwork Brigade. Caris had always admired the way Lore could read people and situations and tailor herself to each in order to gain information. It was a skill Caris lacked. She always felt she was better at engineering than she was with people.

True to Lore's prediction, the door was pushed open, letting inside the last officer needed for this meeting of military minds. Caris didn't know his name, but he crisply saluted General Clarence Votil before snapping another one off in Caris' direction. She nodded an acknowledgment, even as Clarence started speaking.

"With the season change, we'll be faced with an escalation of attacks now that the snow has melted. The army is implementing strategy for the front lines, but we must also focus on the logistics of our supply lines," Clarence said.

"Defending our critical cities should also be a priority as well, should it not?" Caris asked, hoping she didn't sound ignorant of the situation.

"Any city where you are will be defended."

Caris tried not to flinch at that statement. "A single city does not a country make. The rivers need to be defended as well. Myself and other engineers didn't spend all winter working on devices only to see them collect dust."

Clarence nodded. "I know our engineers built new devices to defend the rivers in this province. I commend everyone's efforts on that front. The transportation and implementation of these new devices is critical, but the Ashion army has very little manpower to spare an escort. Neither do we have the ships necessary to blockade the river farther downstream while the engineering corps works to deploy the devices. Even if we did, we'd have to contend with Urova's submersibles once word got out, and they've proven damnably difficult to target. It's a risky endeavor right now with Daijal forces entrenching themselves in the province west of the Serpentine Lake for another attack."

Clarence tapped at the image of the lake on one of the large maps spread out over the table with a pointer stick. This particular map showed the eastern provinces that surrounded the Serpentine Lake and the waterways that branched off it. The maps were gridded in a way favored by wardens as opposed to general cartographers. Different shaded areas showcased the poison fields and the degree of poison embedded in the land. Caris knew these days it had probably spread more than the wardens would have ever allowed in the past.

The date on the map's corner showed it had been drawn up in the summer of 936, most likely finished before the unconscionable attack on the Warden's Island in the southeast by the Daijal army. Since then, wardens had pulled out of Daijal and Urova completely, leaving those countries to deal with revenants on their own. If wardens weren't guarding their assigned borders or working to rebuild the half-destroyed fort on the Warden's Island, then they were giving aid to the Ashion army where revenants were concerned.

The Poison Accords demanded wardens be neutral for the sake of Maricol's survival. Queen Eimarille Rourke had broken the agreement in such a way the wardens had been forced to choose a side for the first time in their long-established history.

Their ranks had been thinned in the attack—too many tithes and wardens on the island killed—and the destruction of infrastructure and the loss of historical border reports had dealt a heavy blow. While the underground laboratories had survived, much of the wardens' alchemy tools and devices used to help cleanse the land and fight revenants not already in use in the poison fields had been destroyed.

These days, the wardens were putting their alchemy skills to use for war.

Many had followed Caris from Veran to Cosian, where the Ashion army command was running the war out of. Caris' childhood city had become the de facto capital of Ashion, with Amari still occupied by Daijal, the citizens there unable to leave. The Ashion parliament was all but controlled by Eimarille these days, and those who had voted against her favored bills hadn't been heard from since the gates closed.

The walls still stood around Amari, just as they did around Cosian, and the wardens had worked to keep it that way in the east. Ksenia, a master alchemist, had overseen the wall defense upgrades for most of autumn before leaving for the Warden's Island. The warden who had taken her place as advisor to Caris and Meleri Auclair, Duchess of Auclair and Lore's mother, was a tall man with a grizzled look to his weather-worn face at odds with the smoothness of his voice.

Enmei understood alchemy as well as any warden, but he excelled more as an engineer. He'd been in E'ridia when the Warden's Island had almost fallen, and his knowledge had thankfully not been taken from them. Caris had given Enmei free rein of her company's laboratories in Cosian. They'd worked together throughout winter, along with other civilian and military engineers, to create new devices to aid in the war effort. Many of those had gone into production in nearby factory towns more used to sending heavy farming equipment and mining tools off the line rather than war machines.

Some of those devices were why Caris had tried to convince Clarence she should be allowed beyond the walls, a request that had been immediately denied. Meleri had also been adamantly against her leaving, despite knowing that securing the river that provided Cosian water was critical.

Aside from being able to hear clarion crystals sing better than anyone, Caris' command of starfire was more than enough to keep herself safe against revenants and Daijalan soldiers. No one else was in agreement with her. Meleri insisted using starfire would put a target on Caris' back. She'd been warned to cast it only as a last resort whenever she was allowed to travel, for if the enemy knew she was beyond Cosian's walls, they'd muster a team of Blades or worse to neutralize her.

Caris had lived with a warrant hanging over her head since the protest in Amari last year and refused to be cowed by such a threat, not when she had other problems to worry about. Urova, with their icebreaker ships and submersibles capable of traveling through frozen-over rivers, had launched a dozen attacks against Cosian during winter. Nine months on since the start of the war, with winter fading away in Ashion everywhere but on the mountaintops, the Ashion army was struggling to stop Daijal's advance.

Enmei uncrossed his arms and picked up another pointer stick. He used it to tap at the mouth of the river that branched off in an easterly direction from the Serpentine Lake. "Blockading the river isn't advisable. You risk your barges and ships if you do and putting the other side on notice that something is going on. Your submersibles on watch duty near the fork haven't signaled to the soldiers on land of any approach by Urovan forces in the last few days. If we're going to implement the crystal-breaking devices, now is the time to do so."

"We're ready to load the airships," Caris said.

Clarence's gaze flicked to where she stood shoulder to shoulder between Enmei and Lore, watched over by a trio of Royal Guards in their distinctive uniforms. "I'd ask that you remain inside the walls, Your Royal Majesty."

"If you won't let me see the devices to the river, I'll see them onto the airships."

"She'd be safe enough at the river if you let her go, especially if she wore a veil. No one would know who she was," Enmei said.

Clarence frowned deeply. "No."

Enmei shrugged in the face of that flat denial, catching Caris' eye. "We'll hope the readouts match the results we obtained here in the laboratories. I'll know what to look for."

"If they don't, then I'll make my way to the river," Caris promised.

Clarence seemed appalled by that statement. "Your Royal Majesty—"

"I understand everyone's concern about my safety, but my concern revolves around the safety of everyone in this city and those towns residing by the rivers. If the clarion crystals need to be recut for any reason, I'm the only one who can do that quickly on the spot. I hear the way clarion crystals sing better than anyone."

Every nation cut clarion crystals differently. Steam power had long been the predominant form of providing heat and energy throughout every Age. While magicians could cast magic with energy drawn from the aether through clarion crystal–tipped wands, engineers had been studying the use of clarion crystals as a power source for some time now.

Televoxes were one such device come into recent play, used by every nation's military as well as by government officials, to say nothing of those who claimed bloodlines written down in the nobility and royal genealogies. Powered by clarion crystals, the communication devices had no need of the wires that connected telephones and telegraph machines.

The crystal-breaking devices Caris and several other engineers had created over winter operated under the same design, powered by the aether as opposed to steam. Divers had taken clarion crystal off sunken Urovan submersibles and brought the pieces to Cosian for engineers to study how the Urovans cut them. The notes of those songs had been different than the clarion crystals used on land, meant for the water rather than the air.

It had taken Caris weeks to find the difference in pitch and tone in the Urovan clarion crystals. She'd broken more clarion crystal than she'd have liked, considering they only had access to E'ridia for limited trade of the commodity these days. But the end result was worth her efforts during long winter nights.

The crystal-breaking devices engineering teams were readying to deploy into the river were set up like a filtration machine, the design meant to disguise their true purpose. Each crystal had been painstakingly cut in order to amplify their song in the water and channel the splintering spell a warden who was also a magician had come up with for use in the poison fields. She'd created the spell through trial and error over the years and these days could shatter bone from half a mile away with a flick of her brass-plated wand. It made eradicating revenants on her border route easier, to be sure.

The engineers and fellow magicians had taken the framework of that spell and applied it against the Urovan-cut clarion crystal. Caris had found the shape that worked best in creating a song that shattered the clarion crystal used in Urovan submersibles, sinking them. The devices were less dangerous to soldiers, trade boats, and barges than using water mines.

While they'd been tested as extensively as they could in a scant few months, no one knew how well they would work when pressed into the war effort. But they had to try because if the devices worked, they'd keep Cosian and its citizens safe just a little longer.

It was the small victories Caris hoped for, because they'd had so few of those lately.

"We'll work with our engineers to get the airships loaded quickly. Caris can help coordinate that effort. You needn't worry that Caris will be on board when they launch," Lore said to the general.

"If that's settled, let's get the cargo onto the trucks and out to the airfield. You can let the soldiers at Lockwood know we'll be coming," Enmei said.

Clarence looked as if he'd bit into the black coriche candies favored by miners and found it too bitter for his taste. Caris knew he'd rather she stay behind Cosian's walls and never leave the city, but she'd sworn when she took up the mantle Meleri had guarded for her that she'd never be anyone's puppet.

"Let me know the number of people going so we can figure out the housing situation," Clarence said.

"We can bunk in the airships if need be."

The Ashion army had slowly drawn out of Haighmoor after the Inferno. When parliament, at the behest of the Daijal court, cut funding for the military, it had been easy to close some of the army's production factories while secretly appropriating others in eastern provinces with the help of the Clockwork Brigade. The sleight of hand had taken years to accomplish. The foresight of Meleri and the Ashion officers who still believed in the old monarchy was the only reason they'd been able to stand against the Daijal army for so long.

Lockwood used to be a frontier factory town that handled trade by river, filled with people who knew what hard work meant. They should have been far removed from the front lines, but war had found them anyway over winter. The Urovans had attacked from the river, damaging the town's outer wall and forcing its citizens in that residential section to retreat behind the town's inner wall for the duration of winter.

The damage to the outer wall hadn't been fixed quickly enough to stop revenants getting through. It had taken wardens an entire week to flush out every last revenant hiding in the residential section before they could comfortably say it was safe. With most of the citizens already pulled back, the Ashion army had chosen to take over that part of the town, with soldiers bunking up in homes behind remade walls.

The people of Lockwood had traded in their old livelihoods for the war effort, and most everyone in that town worked to support the army now. Its production factory, once used to build farming tractors, armored crawlers, and other heavy vehicles, now churned out motor carriages meant to traverse rough terrain, trucks for troop transport, tanks, and digging machines for the trenches.

Enmei headed for the door, ending the meeting with his departure. Caris turned to follow him out, with Lore staying by her side. The Royal Guards fell in around them, a constant presence Caris had taken months to get used to.

Caris pulled her brass goggles down over her eyes once they stepped outside into the laboratory's shipping yard. She slipped her fingers beneath the collar of her blouse to touch the gold necklace that held Nathaniel Clementine's signet ring and a pair of clarion crystal shards.

The man she loved wasn't nobility but came from a merchant family who had lost everything due to his and his parents' ties to the Clockwork Brigade. Daijal had seized their Clementine Trading Company, his family shipped west after being snatched up by debt collectors, and Nathaniel had been turned into a *rionetka*. He lived only because of a clockwork metal heart, thought a traitor by many because of it, despite the alchemist manipulation wardens had provided to give him back his mind and a fragile sense of free will.

People still saw Nathaniel as a risk—to the war effort and to Caris. Meleri no longer considered him a cog, and Nathaniel was kept away from all details on the war effort. Caris had fought to keep him involved because he'd suffered more than any of them, but Meleri— and later, the military command—had been against it. Caris had abided by their wishes, and even Nathaniel agreed with them, but it still felt like a betrayal on her part.

She wished desperately that he were there with her, despite the risks. She loved him when she hadn't thought she'd ever learn how to want someone the way her peers had back when all she had to worry about was school and her company and being a cog.

Lore glanced at her, her expression softening. "You'll see Nathaniel tonight. He's always waiting for you at your home, no matter the hour."

Caris dropped her arm to her side. "I know."

Lore hooked her elbow around Caris', veering in the direction Enmei was headed. The warden walked with a sure stride, his field leathers distinctive amidst everyone else's uniform or everyday clothes. He was kitted out in the typical gear of a warden, though his bladed weapon of choice was a heavy battle-axe that he carried across his back at an angle with ease. The clockwork gears hidden in the handle distributed poison across the blade for fighting revenants but were just as deadly against the living.

Caris knew the devices they were putting into use in the battlefield were needed, but they were a stopgap measure at most. What Ashion desperately needed was allies, and so far, none had answered her envoys' calls. Solaria had closed its border in the south, E'ridia was reluctant to give aid of any sort, and they'd not had any direct outreach to the Tovan Isles since the Inferno.

Honovi, *jarl* to Clan Storm and a fine aeronaut captain, was doing his best to convince his country's ruling body to break out of its insular habit. So far, the *Comhairle nan Cinnidhean* had yet to pay heed to his arguments despite the atrocity E'ridia had sustained to their own government from *rionetkas*. Honovi knew, like Caris did, that neutrality would save no country in the face of Eimarille's desire to rule all of Maricol.

"This way," Lore said, tugging at Caris' arm.

The yard was lined with trucks that were already being loaded with their precious cargo while the motor carriages were parked in a designated section. Lore led her to one of those, neither of them surprised at being flagged down by a clerk who gladly gave them an update on the loading process so far.

After Caris finished speaking to the clerk, she and Lore climbed into the back seat of a motor carriage. Maurus Nash, captain of her Royal Guard, got behind the steering wheel. He closed the door to the motor carriage with a sigh. "It's dangerous beyond the walls even if no sighting of the enemy has occurred, my queen."

"My parents took me beyond the walls as a young girl because our business depended on tracking the poison data from field markers for testing purposes. I'm well aware of the dangers, captain. It won't stop me from doing my duty," Caris replied.

Maurus said no more to that and drove off the lot, keeping his attention on the street around them, pistol ever close at hand. The remaining Royal Guards were in the motor carriages directly before and after theirs, and the vehicles drove down the cobblestone street for the main city gate, following after several trucks.

They drove through two sections of the city, passing through one of the inner walls as they made their way to the main city gate in the outer wall that led to the airfield. When they approached it, Caris' gaze lingered on the automatons standing guard on the wall over the gate, Zip gun arms bent and at the ready to fire on any threat. Other soldiers were up on the wall as well or posted at the gate proper, checking the arrival of everyone wanting to enter the city.

Physical checks for *rionetkas* were still a requirement for everyone, no matter their status. It made the customs officers' jobs harder and the lines to gain entry longer, but everyone grimly adhered to the requirements. Spell-detecting devices couldn't be mass-produced and sometimes didn't work well in crowds. False positives had resulted in incorrect detentions of people in the past in Cosian, but the devices were still in use at the city's gates. Meleri had kept the ones installed in her temporary home, and the military command had kept theirs.

Caris had declined to have them put up in her home, for that was where Nathaniel stayed, and the spell-detecting devices would go off constantly if he were around. Besides, she could hear the distinctive song of the clarion crystals that powered a clockwork heart. Caris didn't need a machine to tell her when a *rionetka* was nearby.

Their motor carriage drove through the gate and into the airfield. It was located south of the city, spread out with dozens of long piers and hangars to anchor airships. Mixed in with the airfield workers were wardens keeping watch.

The trucks and the motor carriages were directed to a set of berths in the middle of the airfield. The airships waiting there were owned by her bloodline's company but hadn't been used for merchant purposes since last summer. Maurus pulled off to the side, giving more room for the trucks to get unloaded, and set the brakes.

Maurus got out first, hand on the grip of his pistol and gaze sweeping the nearby area. Caris got out as well, ignoring the frown he sent her way. She rather thought he wanted to lecture her about making herself a target again, but this time, at least, he held his tongue.

Enmei jumped out of one of the trucks and strode over to them, giving Caris a quick nod. "The airfield workers on the drive over said they're ready to start loading what we've brought."

Caris squared her shoulders, looking up at where the sun burned bright in the sky, having cleared the distant peaks of the Eastern Spine some time ago. "Let's get the machines onto the airships and pray they work."

"I leave my faith to science, not the star gods."

Caris cracked a smile. "Then I'll pray for the both of us."

Six

CARIS

The sky was streaked with rich oranges and reds, the east dark over the mountaintops and the sun touching the horizon in the west when they finally left the airfield. A cool breeze blew across the pier, making Caris glad for the fitted coat she wore over her long-sleeved blouse and corset belt.

"Mother promised to hold the evening meal until we arrived. It will only be family tonight," Lore said.

Caris was looking forward to a meal where war wasn't the topic of conversation. "Sounds lovely."

They walked down the pier away from the last airship they'd overseen the loading of, flanked by Royal Guards. That airship was going to launch tomorrow morning rather than risk a night flight and landing. Cities and towns were much more strict about gate closures these days. Revenants were more numerous now than they had ever been before, their numbers helped along by the death-defying machines Daijal employed, fed by debt slaves and the dead left on the battlefields.

But no sirens wailed a warning, and no sense of urgency filled the air of everyone trekking back into Cosian. Most of the airfield workers had finished their shift, and the stragglers were making their way toward the safety of the gates and the soldiers manning it. The young woman with lieutenant pins on her uniform's collars drew up smartly when Caris and Lore stepped into her queue. Her eyes widened a bit in the gas lamp light, and she snapped off a quick salute. "Your Royal Majesty."

"Just Caris, if you please," she said lightly, already shrugging one arm free of her coat to better tug aside the collar of her blouse. "How's your shift been?"

"Well enough."

The skin over Caris' collarbone was unmarked, no vivisection scars to be seen and no hidden, sewn-on veil snagging on her nails when she dragged her fingers over her skin. The spell-detecting devices installed over the arched gates remained quiescent, the clarion crystals there a faint hum in her ears. The lieutenant nodded her approval for Caris to pass and put Lore through the same inspection.

Their motor carriages waited for them on the street beyond the gate. Maurus opened the door of one for her, and Caris climbed in with the aid of his hand. Lore followed after her, and Maurus shut the door before settling himself behind the steering wheel.

"The Auclair estate for us both," Lore said.

Maurus nodded before undoing the brake and driving forward, gas lamp headlights shining the way over cobblestone streets. The ride was a little bumpy, as it always was, and Caris was tired from a long day of work. She didn't mind the lack of conversation for the moment, knowing more would be had at the coming dinner table.

The Auclair bloodline's ancestral home was to the southwest of Cosian, Veran currently a major launching point for the Ashion war effort despite the town's small size. When Caris had decamped to Cosian last year, the Auclairs had followed. The duchess had spent her life being in the thick of politics, and her expertise was greatly needed when it came to diplomatic efforts. Once the old queen's spymaster, Meleri had taken up the leadership role of Fulcrum in the Clockwork Brigade, working against Daijal's permissive attitude toward debt bondage. Her seat in parliament had been filled by her oldest daughter, Lady Brielle Auclair, whom no one had heard from since last summer.

Politics was deeply entrenched in the Auclair bloodline, and people tended to listen to Meleri. Caris had learned much about politics and what it meant to be a lady as well as a cog when she'd been the duchess' ward while attending Amari's Aether School of Engineering. Despite the secrets Meleri had kept from her, Caris still respected the duchess. With her own parents prisoners of war, she had no family save that which she built, and she was reluctant to give up any of them.

Still, Cosian was a long way from the fashionable capital. The Auclairs had chosen to borrow an estate from another absent bloodline, the manor home nowhere close to the grand one in Amari or the one in Veran. Meleri's servants hadn't bothered changing up the décor, though they had flown their own heraldic flag displaying their bloodline's coats of arms from the post on the roof.

Meleri had gifted Caris a heraldic flag when she'd settled in Cosian last year, the colors that of the Rourke bloodline rather than the Dhemlan bloodline. Caris had yet to fly any above the home she'd shared with her parents when she was younger and which now felt haunted with memories.

Soldiers guarded the Auclair home in Cosian the same way they guarded Caris'. A few of the soldiers on duty wore the uniform of the Royal Guard. All of them came to attention as the motor carriage rolled up the drive and stopped in front of the home's entrance. The gas lamp on the porch flickered, casting a soft glow over the man who waited there.

Caris' heart lightened at the sight of Nathaniel, a smile coming unbidden to her lips. She unbuckled her lap belt and exited the motor carriage without aid, hurrying to the porch. When she reached Nathaniel, he caught her up in his arms in an embrace that made all her tiredness and stress wash away.

"I missed you," she said, holding him close and breathing in the scent of him.

It was improper for him to kiss her in public, despite the fact that

Lore could conceivably be considered their chaperone. Caris was an adult—her birthing day had been celebrated by everyone in this very home last month—and had been for quite some time now. But propriety and the unspoken rules of manners her mother had desperately tried to teach her over the years meant Caris was considered by high society as someone who still needed social guidance.

With her newfound ancestry, that social guidance had become something of a prison, in her opinion. Being queen came with many requirements she didn't have time for during the war efforts. What use did she have for a court when there was no palace to see them in? What use did she have for ladies-in-waiting when the social interactions had been replaced with meetings with military officers and high-ranking nobility more worried about the enemy at their borders than a ball?

But Meleri had been insistent she create a court because every Ashion ruler listed out in the royal genealogies had overseen one. It made her seem the queen, even when she didn't quite act like one. Lore had taken up duties as Caris' lone lady-in-waiting, which consisted of mostly continuing on as she had been. She lived in Caris' home these days, a permanent chaperone if anyone asked, but more a friend than anything else.

Nathaniel stood outside everything these days, even as he'd made a home in her heart. Caris knew it was for everyone's safety, including her own, but she still wished she could confide in him about the things that weighed on her. She squeezed her eyes shut for a moment, listening to the quiet workings of his clockwork metal heart and the clarion crystal song, finding comfort in the way it still beat.

Nathaniel's lips brushed over the top of her head, the ghost of a kiss she wished she could feel on her lips. "How was work, my darling?"

"Worth the effort," Caris said as she reluctantly pulled back.

He reached up and tucked one of her curls behind her ear before touching his fingertips to the side of her face. "The duchess has the meal ready on the table if you are hungry."

"Famished."

She slid her hand over the bend of his elbow and let him lead her inside the home. It was warmer inside, brighter, too, with the gas lamps all turned up to their highest setting behind their clear glass coverings. A servant took her coat, and Lore's as well, with Maurus slipping off to confer with the officer left in charge of the home's security while he'd been gone.

Lore had been right when she said it was only a family meal, the long table set for five and no more. Meleri and Dureau were both already sitting at the table, though they stood at her entrance, a courtesy afforded her rank, when before, she would have been the one to curtsy to Meleri. Caris nodded at the show of respect, having long since given up on arguing they needn't stand on ceremony with her.

The duchess looked well, if tired. Her hair was trending more gray than her natural pale red and had been recently cut, the shortness a style she'd worn for years. Her dress was practical but still well made, the style something Caris had seen quite a few of the nobility still in Cosian requesting their tailors and seamstresses emulate. Caris favored trousers and utilitarian blouses with corset belts over dresses, finding them less constricting for the work she had to perform. She, too, had seen others her age wearing that style more and more.

Dureau smiled at her, the young man more like a brother to her than anything else these days. He went by the moniker of Locke in the Clockwork Brigade, in charge of code work once relegated to just the cogs but now shared with the military. He, like the rest of his family, knew how to keep secrets. He'd been in Veran all last week and only recently returned, and Caris was glad to see him.

"A telegram came for you today on the private wire," Dureau said, nodding at the folded missive near her place setting.

If it had pertained to the war effort, he would have given it to her after dinner, alone in the library where they had such conversations, while Nathaniel waited elsewhere in the estate. Which meant it was personal to her, and Caris had to refrain from immediately snatching it up. She managed to wait until Nathaniel pulled her seat out for her, and she sat before reaching for the paper. The block lettering was short, the words innocuous, but they left her feeling giddy none-theless. "Blaine and Honovi will arrive tomorrow."

She missed Blaine, having long since forgiven him for the secrets he'd kept where her birthright was concerned. She hadn't seen him or his husband in months, the pair working to convince the *Comhairle nan Cinnidhean* to give aid to Ashion. So far, even with her envoys pleading their case, the ruling body of E'ridia hadn't budged. Caris didn't expect the two would be arriving with good news, but it would be lovely to see them again, and she wanted another look at Blaine's mechanical prosthetic.

Caris still felt guilty over the torture Blaine had endured when he'd been taken by Daijal during the attack on the Warden's Island. Honovi had led the rescue of him at Foxborough last summer, and Blaine had been immediately transported back to Glencoe once he was snatched from the enemy's hands. By the time he'd been well enough—both physically and emotionally—to travel, the winter storms had made passage over the Eastern Spine difficult and E'ridia had partially closed its borders.

They'd kept in touch by telephone and diplomatic letters and couriered the design for his mechanical prosthetic back and forth before autumn ended. No news that would endanger the war effort was ever shared, but she always cherished hearing his voice on the other end of a wire. She'd cut the first set of clarion crystals for him and only wished she could have done more, could have saved him from the horror of his brief captivity before he'd lost half his left arm.

"I'll have the servants make up a room for them here," Meleri said.

Caris set the telegram aside. "They can stay with me."

Meleri pursed her lips but didn't argue. "Very well. I'll have my secretary retrieve their flight itinerary from the airfield in the morn-ing. I'll pencil in a meeting with General Votil in our schedules for two days hence."

"They may have no news."

"They'll have something to report either way." Meleri's gaze cut to Nathaniel, her lips firming ever so slightly before she pasted on a cheerful smile. "Come now, let's start the meal."

The roast chicken and vegetables, fresh bread, and crisp greens were plated family-style, as was typical in Cosian households. Dureau served his mother and himself while Caris and the others filled their own plates. It was how every meal had been spent when she lived with her parents, and the ache when she thought of them remained sharp.

Conversation was light and easy. Nothing about the war was touched upon, and Meleri was too deft of a conversationalist to fall into the trap of pauses and redirects. She kept the dinner conversation going in ways Caris would have failed at. Still, the meal was delicious, and the company was good. Having Nathaniel by her side was better than any dessert, which Meleri apologized for not having.

"There's still a sugar shortage going on for our province," Meleri said.

Farms were fenced off and guarded areas that tended to be less than half a day's travel from a city or town. Some of the ones that grew sugar grasses were outside Foxborough, and Daijal had burned most of those fields last autumn.

The tea that was served in place of a dessert carried its own kind of sweetness from the flowers it was made from. Caris enjoyed her cup and enjoyed the press of Nathaniel's knee to hers beneath the table even more.

By the time the meal was over and they were ready to depart, the clock on the wall chimed a late hour indeed. Caris gave Meleri a quick hug before Nathaniel helped her into her coat. "We'll be back tomorrow with Blaine and Honovi."

"Of course," Meleri said.

Maurus waited for them outside, the captain giving her a quick nod before opening up the door to the motor carriage that would take them home. Caris and Nathaniel took the back seat while Lore rode up front with Maurus.

Her family's estate wasn't very far from the one Meleri lived in. At this late an hour, only those out at local restaurants and pubs were on the street, the shops all closed up and most other people taking their meals at home. The motor carriage drove down the cobblestone street toward home, Caris' hand held in Nathaniel's for the entire way. They didn't speak, not until they exited the motor carriage and made their way inside. A maid greeted them in the small foyer with a quick curtsy and took their coats with deft hands.

"I'll be in my office if you need me," Lore said.

She walked off, boot heels clicking against the floor. Maurus took his leave as well, heading toward the set of rooms the Royal Guard worked out of when coordinating her protection. Nathaniel offered Caris his hand again, mouth tugging upward at one corner. "Just us, it seems."

Caris laughed, gladly taking his hand and letting him kiss the back of it with warm lips. "I quite like that."

They went to her favorite spot in the home, what had once been her nursery and long since turned into a study room with a balcony that overlooked the back garden. The glass doors were closed and the curtains drawn, but the gas lamps burned bright when she turned them on, illuminating a room filled with books, folios, and a comfortable sofa that fit two easily enough.

Perhaps it wasn't proper to sit beside Nathaniel and curl in close, to let him wrap his arms around her and have his mouth press to hers. But it felt strangely good, made her stomach clench in a delicious way, though she never wanted more than that.

Nathaniel had always been respectful of her desires and boundaries, even when they were alone. He was ever the gentleman outside of the kiss. When they broke apart, Caris rested her head on his chest, over his clockwork metal heart, the sound of it beating an odd but welcome cadence in her ear. She could hear the hum of the clarion crystals that powered it, the song one she hoped would always be present.

He was self-conscious these days about the vivisection scars on his chest, always keeping his shirt buttoned up to his throat and his cravat securely knotted. The clarion crystal shards hanging from the necklace around Caris' throat were matched by the one Blaine wore on a necklace and the one embedded in Nathaniel's chest that he didn't know about. The pieces could track each other on a spelled map the way Meleri's metal map had done so for the cogs who traversed the catacombs back in Amari. Honovi had used his shard to find Blaine in Foxborough last year, and Caris intended to find Nathaniel if he was ever lost to her again.

His hand stroked up and down her arm, the light touch comforting as she listened to him breathe. "You yawned quite a bit during dinner. I don't want to keep you up too late."

Caris reached up to frame the side of his face, stroking her thumb over his cheek. "I like spending time with you."

Nathaniel turned his head so that he could kiss the palm of her hand. Everyone kept insisting she shouldn't be with him, that Nathaniel was a danger to herself and so many others. Caris knew otherwise. The one and only time he'd ever put his hands on her to harm, it hadn't been him. When one was bound by the compulsion of a *rionetka*, they weren't themselves. In his right mind, Nathaniel could *never* hurt her.

His hand settled over her shoulder, anchoring her against him. "The broadsheets aren't as optimistic as they used to be. I know you can't speak of what's going on with the war effort with me, but the public could do with some good news."

Caris closed her eyes. "We all could."

The Ashion army was doing its best, but Eimarille had played a very long game indeed with her death-defying machines, stolen automaton war designs, and the favor of a star god. Some days, Caris wasn't sure how she could ever hope to compete with the woman who was her sister in name and bloodline only. They were nothing alike, she and Eimarille, the same way Caris knew she wasn't like the brother that Blaine swore was alive.

For all the wardens she had met over the past many months, Caris had yet to meet the one who'd once been a prince.

"You're giving people hope with what you're doing. I don't mean to dismiss that," Nathaniel said softly.

Caris reached for his other hand and tangled their fingers together. "Hope isn't enough."

Winning would be, but all her prayers toward that had so far gone unanswered by the North Star.

Seven

BLAINE

The *Celestial Sprite* juddered as it settled into the anchor berth inside the hangar the colored smoke marker had guided them to. Blaine looked away from the engine readouts in the flight cabin, watching Honovi converse with air force Captain Caoimhe of Clan Sky. Honovi had flown them west over the Eastern Spine to Cosian, but since this was a military airship, Caoimhe was technically in charge.

Blaine flexed the fingers of his left hand, the sound of gears clicking softly as the mechanical prosthetic, powered by tiny clarion crystals and magic, moved with the intent buried in the remaining muscles of his left arm. He glanced down at the rods, plates, gears, and screws made from various kinds of metal that fit snugly around the stump of his forearm and the bend of his elbow, gripping his upper arm. It was a familiar sight these days.

He folded his fingers down one at a time against the metal cage of his palm, making a fist. Last autumn and winter had been a frustrating time for him as he came to terms with the torture he'd endured at the hands of Daijal soldiers and the recovery process once he'd been rescued. Losing part of his arm had shifted his worldview in terms of accessibility, but it hadn't deterred him from living his life how he had been.

Honovi had been there every step of the way as Blaine struggled through the learning curve of using the mechanical prosthetic and how it affected his role as an engineer. Honovi loved him just as he was, and for that, Blaine was grateful. Being here, back on an airship, was an important milestone for them both.

"We have clearance to disembark," Honovi said as he put down the radio.

Blaine nodded. "Let me log the numbers, and we can leave."

He did so quickly and then followed Honovi out of the flight deck. The flight leathers they wore had the plaid of their clan curving over their shoulders, with more embroidery than would be found in the uniforms the rest of the crew wore. In Cosian, he and Honovi would be treated not as aeronauts but as visiting foreign dignitaries.

Honovi, as *jarl* to Clan Storm, would one day take over his father's seat on the *Comhairle nan Cinnidhean* and aid in ruling E'ridia. He'd held many roles over the years, all of which served to make him a politician with a keen eye toward the future, not just for E'ridia but Maricol as a whole.

Blaine reached up to touch the gold marriage torc hanging around his throat. He'd missed it greatly during his time spent as a spy and a cog in Ashion. He'd meant to stay by Caris' side until he saw her claim the starfire throne, but the ties to the country that had become his home after escaping the Inferno had vied with his promise to stand witness to her. His recovery had been spent in Glencoe, and he'd only conversed with Caris through telegrams or telephone calls.

It felt as if he were letting her down, but she seemed safe enough tucked away in the eastern province of Ashion, where Cosian was located. The city was far from the front lines, but those lines were changing with every month that passed.

If Ashion fell to Daijal, only Solaria and E'ridia would remain on the continent to hold back Eimarille's desire to rule. E'ridia had no presence in Daijal, not after Blaine's kidnapping and the attack Honovi had led on Foxborough to rescue him. Trade had been embargoed with that country ever since Eimarille ordered the attack on the

Warden's Island. The Tovan Isles claimed Maricol's seas, and despite Urova's submersibles, the Tovanian navy was the strongest in the world. But Blaine had a feeling that even Maricol's oceans wouldn't be enough to stop Eimarille. Only Caris could, and Blaine still had a duty to her despite his ties to E'ridia.

Honovi went down the gangplank first, with Blaine right behind him. The person who greeted them on the pier was a surprise, though Blaine should have known Caris would send the one closest to her these days if she herself could not come.

"Welcome to Cosian," Nathaniel said in Ashionen with a smile.

The last time Blaine had been in this part of the country, he'd been an orphaned boy, hidden away on an E'ridian airship while the Dusk Star carried Caris down her road. It would be nice to see the city she'd grown up in. "I wish it were under better circumstances. How have you been?"

Blaine's gaze lingered for a few seconds on the pair of Royal Guards standing behind Nathaniel who were clearly acting as his escort rather than peacekeepers, most likely at the behest of Caris. He wondered, though, if they had underlying orders to take out the threat Nathaniel represented and if Caris knew or not. Meleri had been in charge of resurrecting that vaunted military unit, so he rather thought she would have and kept Caris in the dark for her own safety.

Nathaniel shrugged, his smile becoming thin. "Well enough, these days."

Blaine nodded, willing his gaze not to drop lower than Nathaniel's face. For all that he'd suffered at the hands of Daijal, Nathaniel had endured worse. The merchant would always be a risk—to the war effort, to the secrets cogs needed to keep, and to Caris—but Caris wanted Nathaniel by her side. Blaine could understand that want, and while he'd counseled against it, there was no arguing with the stubbornness of someone in love.

Honovi wrapped his arm around Blaine's waist, giving Nathaniel a polite nod. "Shall we head into the city?"

Nathaniel gestured for them to follow him out of the hangar. "The ground crew know where to bring your travel trunks. We have motor carriages waiting past the gates. I'll take you there."

Blaine had traversed many airfields over the years, but he couldn't recall one in recent memory where the majority of the anchored airships were built for the military as opposed to trade and travel. The closer they got to the city walls, the more Blaine became aware of weaponry and automatons that cities rarely deployed in the form of defense.

City walls were meant to keep revenants out, and wardens had always been enough for that threat. Now, the threat of fighting against the living meant the city gates were guarded by automatons and heavy artillery, and some number of airships were always ready to launch. He even saw a few ornithopters at some piers, and they'd seen more than a dozen aeroplanes lined up at the far runway during their approach.

They went through the security protocol at the gates and made it inside the city. Nathaniel led them to a pair of motor carriages parked in the lot by the wall, drivers already behind the steering wheels.

"You'll be staying with us while you're here, but the duchess insisted on a dinner at her estate tonight. We'll head over later, but Caris wants to see you first," Nathaniel said.

"I didn't think the Auclair bloodline had property out this way," Blaine said.

"They followed Caris. Many people have."

Which was what they'd all hoped for over the months. But Ashion was a fractured country and had been ever since its civil war, whether historians liked to believe it or not. A country needed a government, and Meleri was struggling to build one around Caris. Blaine knew of their inability to gain allies and aid, and it was only a matter of time before the rebellion that had started with the Clockwork Brigade grew into something more burned out.

It wasn't a future Blaine wanted, wasn't a road he wanted to walk down.

The news he and Honovi were bringing out of Glencoe wasn't

going to change things, though he wished it would. Ashion had been his country once before. He didn't want to see it wiped off the maps.

It wasn't as long of a drive to their destination as it would have been in Glencoe. Cosian was a frontier city housing the military command for the war. The people they passed on the street weren't dressed in the highest fashion, and he saw more people in uniform than anything else in the outer sections.

"Have there been any protests?" Honovi asked.

Nathaniel craned his head around to look at them from the front passenger seat. "No. If anything, Cosian is bursting at the walls with volunteers wishing to join the army."

"Where are you training them?"

"Here and elsewhere. The army had to recruit and train in secret since parliament ordered it to wind down years ago. It's why losing Haighmoor wasn't as terrible as it could have been."

That information had been gleaned last summer, so Blaine doubted it was something Nathaniel had learned recently. He knew from Meleri that Nathaniel was being kept out of all the high-level talks when it came to the war efforts. Caris might love the man, but no one trusted the clockwork metal heart beating in his chest. It wasn't through any fault of his own, but some part of Blaine would always distrust the magic, alchemy, and mechanics that kept Nathaniel alive.

Eventually, they turned down a street that had a security checkpoint at either end of the block and automatons guarding metal gates that barricaded the way through. The Royal Guards on duty nodded at Nathaniel but didn't let the motor carriage drive through until one of the Royal Guards in the other motor carriage handed over papers to the officer in charge.

"We've added you to the list of approved visitors to Caris' home. They're just confirming you have permission," Nathaniel said.

Honovi nodded approval. "That's good."

"We don't have a proper palace, so security has been an issue, but the Royal Guards have done exceptionally well in keeping her safe."

Blaine was glad to hear that. He watched as the Royal Guards handed back the paperwork and signaled to open the metal gates. Nathaniel drove forward, and it wasn't long before they pulled up in front of an estate Blaine knew the nobility back in Amari would describe as *charming*. Caris waited on the porch, flanked by yet more Royal Guards, offering a smile that Blaine found himself returning before he'd even left the motor carriage. He barely had both feet on the cobblestones before Caris clattered down the steps and threw herself at him.

"You're here," she got out in a muffled, hitching voice as Blaine swept her up in a hug. "You're okay."

Blaine held her close, carefully making a fist with his mechanical prosthetic hand against the curve of her lower back. "I'm here."

He hadn't realized he'd miss her so much; a voice on a telephone wasn't the same as seeing her in person. She'd been his focus for nearly half a decade at this point, ever since he'd learned she was the infant he'd carried out of Amari after the Inferno. Finding her again at the university had sparked so much of this. He was ten years her senior, and some days, that felt like a lifetime.

They held each other for a long moment before Caris finally pulled back, wiping discreetly at her eyes with the back of her hand rather than using a kerchief. Blaine thought about offering her one, but she'd moved on to hug Honovi hello, his husband nearly picking her up off her feet with his embrace. When they finally parted, Caris appeared more settled, and a brightness came to her gray eyes when her attention finally landed on his mechanical prosthetic.

"I hope you'll let me take a look at that today. I brought clarion crystals home from the laboratory in preparation for your arrival," she said.

Blaine glanced over at Honovi, raising an eyebrow. "Do you mind if we do some lab work first?"

Honovi snorted. "Nathaniel here can help me find a glass of whiskey."

Caris laughed, grabbing Blaine by his right hand and leading him into the home. "We'll be in the back garden."

The Royal Guards snapped to attention as she passed, but she paid them no mind. Blaine didn't bother digging in his heels at Caris' headlong rush, but he did say to those on duty, "Send your captain to me."

The soldier on his left nodded sharply, and Blaine knew his message would be passed along. While Meleri had handled the reactivation of the Royal Guard, the Westergard bloodline had led that military unit for centuries, ever guarding the Rourke bloodline. Blaine might have left the Westergard bloodline behind at the urging of the star gods, but he still knew his duty. His father had died for it long ago, and Blaine wouldn't dishonor that sacrifice by walking away from it. His road would always be intertwined with Caris'.

The hallways and rooms they passed were warmly decorated, lived-in, and cozy in a way that instantly made Blaine feel at ease. It reminded him of the shared clan home he and Honovi resided in back in Glencoe, a place filled with memories and people and meant to raise a family in. If this was where Caris had grown up, well loved and well guided, he couldn't be regretful that he hadn't tried to fight the Dusk Star to keep her.

Caris' personal laboratory was thankfully not in a basement but outside in the back garden, the little detached building cluttered and well used. It was a bit warm inside, and Blaine shrugged out of his leather flight jacket, hanging it over the back of a wooden chair. He watched as Caris flitted about, turning on the mechanical fans in the corner and switching on the gas lamps. The little lab had windows, but extra light was always welcomed when working.

When she finally came to a stop on the other side of the worktable, she rested her hands on top of the work mat, meeting Blaine's gaze. There was a gravitas to her gaze that hadn't been there even last summer, war and her new position weighing on her. "You look better. Your hair has gotten longer."

Blaine reached up to tug on the short braid that lacked the metal hair adornments he'd worn in E'ridia. They got in the way during a flight, but they were packed away in the truck for later, along with his formal kilt and plaid. It wouldn't do to present themselves before the

Ashion dignitaries without being properly attired. "I promised Honovi I wouldn't cut it again."

E'ridians kept their hair long, braided in various ways to denote age and social status, the hair adornments hinting at clan affiliation and more. One could tell someone's rank and clan just as much from their hair as the plaid they wore. Cutting his hair several years ago had been excruciatingly difficult, but he'd done it.

Caris smiled, her gray eyes crinkling at the corners. The shadows underneath them were like tiny bruises, and he wondered about the stress she must be under right now. She gathered up her shoulder-length dark curls and tied them back in a queue as best she could. "Let's have a look at your arm, shall we? I want to check the settings of your clarion crystals."

"I did incorporate some of your design suggestions into it."

"Yes, but I didn't build it with you."

"Some of the best E'ridian engineers did."

"Good."

Caris came around the table to stand beside him and waited until Blaine placed his mechanical prosthetic hand in hers. She explored it with sure fingers, and Blaine tracked the shape of where she touched.

When he'd first woken up in Glencoe after being held prisoner and could think without the potions or drugs keeping the pain at bay, he'd been terrified at not being able to live his life how he once had. No more engineering work, no more flying, not with the loss of his hand and forearm—grounded in a way he never thought he would be. But the absence of part of his limb didn't define him, and Honovi had reinforced that belief until Blaine actually *believed* it.

He'd learned he wasn't the only aeronaut crewing an airship who had a missing limb. Granted, there were certain aspects of his job as a flight engineer that required additional help—fine motor control was still something he was working on—but the loss hadn't affected his dominant arm, and he didn't need the mechanical prosthetic to feel whole. As Honovi was always reminding him, Blaine was still himself, with or without two flesh-and-bone hands.

As for the mechanical prosthetic itself, he was proud of the design he'd created with Caris' input. The engineers who'd helped him build it to his exact specifications had done a fine job, but it wasn't going to be the final version he wore. Even with magic to ease along the healing, it would be months more until the shape of the stump of his arm settled into its final form. Once the healing was complete, then he could work on the permanent fitting.

"Have you thought about adding a mini Zip gun to it?" Caris asked, tapping at a brass plate on the outside of the metal forearm.

Blaine laughed. "I heard about the weaponry addition you gave that racing carriage when you rescued me from Foxborough. I don't think Honovi would approve, and it would be a danger on an airship. What if it accidentally discharged?"

Caris wrinkled her nose and let his arm go, nodding at the worktable. "I'm sure a magician could work a spell on the switch so it wouldn't fire unless you intended it to. Sit, please. The crystals are good, but their song is off. You have a gear that catches sometimes in the elbow joint, don't you?"

He eyed the metal prosthetic, the shape of it larger around his elbow for stability purposes. "It does sometimes. How did you know?"

"Discordant notes. I can fix it today, if you like."

Which was how Blaine found himself sitting at the worktable, mechanical prosthetic removed and in Caris' capable hands. She had a pair of magnifying goggles on as she worked within the casing of the forearm, the gears, springs and clarion crystals on full display beneath her tools.

"The spells in the gears are still learning how I move," Blaine said.

"Replacing the crystals will help with that. The shapes are correct. Whoever cut them just cut wrong across the crystal rod they used. The crystal didn't quite like that."

"Are the ones you have from E'ridia?"

Caris nodded, never taking her eyes off her work. "We received them in a shipment during winter. Urova has blocked all clarion crystal trade with Ashion since the start of the war."

"How is the war effort going?"

They could speak freely there in her small laboratory, without

Nathaniel to overhear what he shouldn't. Caris didn't immediately pick up the conversation, and Blaine patiently waited for her to find her voice.

"Badly now, I think," she admitted softly. "We're doing the best we can, but I don't think it will be enough, despite the wardens helping. Daijal has war automatons they stole from Solaria, but that's not enough for the Imperial emperor to give us aid. Even with the new alchemy bombs the wardens have cooked up, it's not enough to keep the amount of revenants at bay. Daijal is taking the fallen in skirmishes off the battlefield and sending them through their death-defying machines. And E'ridia—"

She broke off with a sigh. When she didn't immediately continue, Blaine picked up where she'd left off. "E'ridia is reluctant to get involved."

Caris' mouth twisted, eyes on the clarion crystal she was extracting from his mechanical prosthetic with thin tweezers. "I gave E'ridia permission to use our airspace to rescue you. I wanted you back, that was never in question, but I thought the situation would be enough to get the *Comhairle nan Cinnidhean* to see the threat Eimarille represents. My ambassadors tell me nothing comes of their requests to your ruling body."

Blaine knew the *cinn-chinnidh* who made up the *Comhairle nan Cinnidhean* were focused on quietly rooting out *rionetkas* from the government. Even with the wardens having found a way to push aside the compulsion to give *rionetkas* back their own minds, they couldn't remove the intricate spell completely without risking the destruction of the clockwork metal hearts. It meant his country's Seneschal could no longer hold that office, and an election for the clans to choose a new one had been handled carefully over winter.

While everyone believed *rionetkas* were created by Daijal to infiltrate the political spheres of foreign countries, they didn't have any proof. Without proof, Eimarille would deny to her last breath that she had anything to do with the destruction of so many lives and the interference of a sovereign nation's right to rule.

"Taking the starfire throne would go a long way toward breaking Eimarille's propaganda," Blaine said.

"It wouldn't stop the war."

"Wouldn't it?"

Caris set her tools down with a sigh, lifting her gaze from Blaine's mechanical prosthetic. "Amari is occupied by Daijal. Eimarille hasn't been to that city since last year, and we don't know why. But trying to take the capital would decimate the army that we have, and we don't have allies to fall back on. Sitting on the starfire throne to put out the North Star's decree won't end what she started."

"Then perhaps it is the North Star keeping it safe."

He'd never seen Ashion's guiding star; the Dusk Star had been the one to help him flee the Inferno and the ravages that coup had produced. But Aaralyn was the star god that Ashion prayed to, and if anyone would have a say in who claimed the starfire throne, he rather thought it would be the North Star. Though it wasn't only Caris and Eimarille who had the right to it these days.

"Have you spoken to Alasandair yet?" Blaine asked.

Caris picked up the rod of clarion crystal and the cutting tool resting near her elbow, not meeting his gaze. "Meleri doesn't think it would be a good idea to reach out to him."

"But do you want to?"

"I don't know him, the same way I don't know Eimarille. I was a Dhemlan before I was a Rourke and had no siblings until recently, and then in name only. Claiming a bloodline doesn't make a family."

She sounded frustrated, as if she'd had this argument before, though Blaine's intention wasn't to argue. He rested the stump of his left arm on the worktable and leaned forward. "Meleri believes him to be a risk to your right to rule."

"She believes much is a risk to my right to rule, including the decisions I make."

The bitterness he could hear was a keen identifier of her state of mind, something anyone could pick up on. For all that Meleri had taught her spywork over the years in the Clockwork Brigade, Caris' political savviness when it came to court and keeping one's opinion veiled was not the best.

He could understand, too, Meleri's desire to keep the siblings apart. If Blaine hadn't seen for his own eyes the shocking similarities in looks between the warden who went by Soren and Caris, he never would have known. But he'd seen the same gray eyes Caris had in the warden's face, the same dark hair, and the same missing road beneath their feet.

Soren had denied being a Rourke when he'd met with Blaine, Honovi, and the wardens' governor that day in Glencoe. But Delani had seen what he had, and she'd moved to keep Soren's identity a secret going forward for as long as possible. Because if Soren *was* a Rourke, then the possibility he could cast starfire was high, no matter his denials, and that meant the wardens had broken the Poison Accords of their own volition in the past. They were meant to be neutral, and the only way to truly be was to never take those whose names were written in the royal genealogies as tithes.

The wardens didn't know which of their governors had made that decision, as Soren's records had been destroyed—along with so many others—during the attack on the Warden's Island. Unlike with Caris, Blaine couldn't stand witness for the prince, if he ever even reclaimed that title. Soren, Blaine had come to learn, was very much a warden, and he didn't know how the nobility would react to Ophelia's only son having been remade through alchemy into someone who spent more time outside city walls in the poison fields than anywhere else.

"Perhaps he is, or perhaps he can be an ally," Blaine said.

Caris didn't look away from the clarion crystal as she started cutting the rod. The deep violet color was different from the aquamarine ones currently powering his mechanical prosthetic. "And if he wanted the throne? He could claim it, you know. He is older than I am."

By five years, if Blaine recalled correctly. He wondered if Soren remembered how he had escaped the Inferno, if there had been someone to carry him out of that city the way Blaine had with Caris. "He hasn't claimed anything."

Caris' mouth twisted as she delicately changed the cutting angle on the clarion crystal, hands moving with a deftness Blaine missed. "He could, and what then?"

"He can't," Blaine said reluctantly. Caris arched one eyebrow in a silent question, to which Blaine answered with a faint sigh. "Alasandair Rourke was struck from the royal genealogies after the Inferno. Soren's records were destroyed during the attack on the Warden's Island. We can't trace his lineage, not how we can with you if I stand witness."

"Would you need to if he could cast starfire?"

Blaine picked at a tear in the soft work mat laid across the table, dodging the question. "If he could cast starfire, he'd be an asset on the front lines."

Caris paused, drawing her hands apart so she didn't accidentally nick the crystal. "You'd truly send him out to fight?"

"We can't send you, though I know you wish you could be out there."

Blaine had taken enough calls from Meleri over the winter about Caris' wish to give aid to the soldiers dying in her name. As admirable as it was, they'd lose her if she tried. Already, the wardens and Royal Guards had quietly dispatched several attempts on Caris' life from Blades sneaking past the city's defenses. He didn't know if she knew how close she'd come to an assassin's blade, but the attempts were further proof that Eimarille considered Caris a threat like nothing else on the continent.

"Would he go?" Caris asked.

"Other wardens have."

"None of them are supposedly a prince."

"He is a warden. I don't think a crown could ever change that."

Caris repositioned her hands and elbows and started cutting again, head bent over her work. "If he helps, that's more aid than others have given us."

Blaine didn't wince, but it was a near thing. "We're trying to press your case, but the *Comhairle nan Cinnidhean* is reluctant to commit our country's air force to your cause."

"You must realize it's all our cause. Eimarille won't stop at the Eastern Spine."

She said it with a sureness that made Blaine want to duck his head in shame. "I know that. Honovi does, too. We're working on convincing our people that we can't stay isolated and neutral while the rest of the world goes to war."

"Would a request directly from me move them to reconsider their position?"

"You can't leave Cosian."

"Then I'll send a personal letter of entreaty when you fly home."

She spoke as if she knew he wouldn't stay, despite his promise to her and the Dusk Star. It shamed him to know that his country could give Ashion support and aid, but they weren't. Swallowing, Blaine curled his hand over the stump of his arm, running his fingers over the scars there, barely feeling the touch in places. "How's Nathaniel been?"

"Keeping busy. Meleri won't let him be a cog again."

"You know he—"

"I know," she said, cutting him off. "But he's lost more than so many others, and I hate that his sacrifice isn't worth the trust he deserves."

"How's his heart been?"

"It beats the same as always. The clarion crystal doesn't sing like it did when he was a *rionetka*."

Blaine bit his tongue so he didn't protest that Nathaniel still *was* a *rionetka*. He knew that was an argument that would do nothing but give hurt. "I'm glad you have him."

Caris glanced up from the work she was doing, a tentative, happy smile curving her lips. "Me, too. He's a kind man, and I care for him dearly."

And a danger, but Caris was stubborn in a way Blaine had only the vaguest recollections of how her birth mother, Queen Ophelia, had been. There would be no telling Caris to take the fork in her road if she wanted to walk it straight toward the unknown with Nathaniel by her side. He hoped Meleri was prepared for that.

Blaine returned the smile. "Catch me up on what's going on?"

Caris kept cutting clarion crystal, but she pitched her voice louder than the noise from the cutting machine, talking about the war effort and the diplomats she kept sending to the east and south, never blaming him for his people's failing. Ashion had been his people, once, years ago. Despite everything, Blaine wasn't prepared to turn his back on the country he'd lost in order to survive.

Eight

HONOVI

The borrowed estate that passed as the Auclair bloodline's home in Cosian was a far cry from the one in Amari where Honovi had once been received. Still, the servants who greeted him were just as professional, and the duchess was her same regal self when he was escorted into the parlor with its violet-colored wallpaper, glass display shelves of porcelain figurines, and enough flowers in vases to make him want to sneeze.

Meleri rose to her feet at his arrival, giving Honovi a quick and shallow curtsy as due his social station of a *jarl* to Clan Storm. In the grand hierarchy of manners, he outranked her, but her own political reach was nothing to discount.

"It is good to see you again, *jarl* Honovi," Meleri said.

"Duchess Auclair," Honovi replied. "Thank you for having me."

Meleri gestured at the only other seat at the small round table. The wooden chair was nicely cushioned, the fabric a pale blue that went well with the violet saturating the room. The spread on the table looked delicious, and the tea the servant poured for him after he sat was the green he preferred over the floral one Meleri favored.

The servant set the teapot down on its silver tray before sketching a bow and leaving the parlor, closing the door behind them for privacy. Meleri's gaze never wavered from Honovi's. "Is Blaine with Caris today?"

They'd all met for a many-course dinner last night at the dining room here in the estate, where nothing of the war was discussed. Nathaniel had sat by Caris for the entire meal, and his presence alone had required careful conversation.

"They're still working on his mechanical prosthetic, and she wanted to introduce him to a warden she's been partnering with in her company's laboratory."

"Ah, Enmei. A pragmatic fellow."

"How many wardens do you have in the city?"

"They come and go, but there are at least two dozen who have resided here on a continuous basis since last year. A few of those have been in the thick of command meetings. My understanding is the fort on the Warden's Island is still undergoing cleanup and construction. Creating alchemy-based weapons here takes the heat off the island."

The wardens had lost many tithes and those wardens with specialized knowledge during the attack on the island, to say nothing of the vast historical records they'd meticulously kept since the Poison Accords were signed. The attack by Daijal had seen every warden retreat out of that country as well as Urova, leaving the revenants for the living to handle on their own.

E'ridia's diplomats still had a presence in Urova out of political necessity, even if they'd been recalled from Daijal. Honovi knew smaller towns and even some cities in Urova were concerned about the uptick in revenants clawing at their walls. But when one allied themselves with an aggressor, they couldn't be surprised at the fallout.

Revenants were impossible to control. Daijal could send bodies through their death-defying machines to create revenants, but unlike with *rionetkas*, the walking dead took orders from no one.

"The wardens are still assisting the war effort?" Honovi asked.

Meleri reached for one of the tiny squares of sweet cake on the tray with a pair of silver tongs, placing it on her ceramic plate. The savory dishes outnumbered the sweet ones due to a sugar shortage. "They have pledged their support against Daijal."

It was telling that she didn't say it was for the Ashion cause. "For how long?"

"The wardens' governor promised until the war was over."

"And if Daijal wins?"

Meleri took a dainty sip of her tea, gaze never leaving Honovi's face. "You and your people could be the deciding factor in that never happening."

"I know Daijal won't stop at Ashion's borders. My father believes the same as well, especially after the *rionetka* infiltration of our government. But the *Comhairle nan Cinnidhean* believes closing the border will keep us safe."

"That's a death sentence with the way Eimarille is fighting. Even the Eastern Spine won't protect you."

"Getting troops across it isn't feasible. There's only a handful of railroads that traverse it."

"One can go above or around."

He tipped his head in acknowledgment of that before reaching for one of the small, neatly cut sandwiches on the tiered tray between them. "E'ridia survived your civil war in the past."

Meleri set her teacup down. "This isn't a civil war."

Which was true. In no other war in Maricol's history had someone attacked the Warden's Island. That alone had changed the fundamental details of the fight happening within Ashion's borders. But it wasn't enough for E'ridia or Solaria to lend their military might to the fight. "I've said as much to my father."

"And has that swayed him?"

"If it had, I would have arrived with more airships than just the one."

Meleri sighed tiredly, looking every year her age in that moment. "Our capital is under occupation, and the starfire throne is inaccessible. If Caris put out the North Star's decree, if she was seen as the rightful queen, would your people find sympathy with our plight and give us aid?"

"You'd have to get her into Amari. My understanding is that's a losing battle for you right now."

Honovi was aware of the restrictions placed on that capital city and the broken chains of cogs that stretched away from it. Nathaniel, in his role as a *rionetka*, had done his damnedest to destroy the cogs he'd been in charge of, creating a cascade failure of death the Clockwork Brigade hadn't yet recovered from. More than that was the fierceness with which the Daijal army had moved to control that central province. The front lines of the war had started in the western provinces last year but were farther east now, a testament to Daijal's strength.

"I haven't heard from my oldest daughter since we left for Veran last year," Meleri said quietly. "We've stopped the rescue of debt slaves because we haven't the people to spare. The Marshal managed to send news that Eimarille is feeding not just the fallen but prisoners of war and debt slaves to her death-defying machines. She doesn't care about the living, and the dead are just cannon fodder to her."

"Does Caris know?"

Meleri curled her finger through the delicate handle of her teacup but didn't raise it to her mouth. "She's aware of the use Eimarille has for the battlefield fallen. I haven't spoken to her about the possibility her parents might already be dead."

Honovi remembered well how badly Caris took being lied to. "You should tell her."

"I only mean to spare her that grief."

"She won't think kindly of your efforts. You can't coddle her if you want an independent queen."

Meleri smiled, though there wasn't any humor in her expression. "Your husband said something similar to me once."

"You should probably listen to him."

Meleri finally picked up her teacup and sipped the sweet-smelling liquid. "Is it your opinion that your country will not give military aid? Are the ambassadors we sent a wasted effort?"

"Keep your people in Glencoe. Having an Ashionen presence to remind our contemporaries of the ongoing threat is important."

They made small talk for the rest of the meeting, Meleri's disappointment at Honovi's inability to promise military aid from E'ridia swept away with political deftness. When Honovi had only crumbs on his plate and the teapots were empty, Meleri stood. "I want to thank you for meeting with me, *jarl* Honovi."

"I'm sorry I couldn't bring better news," Honovi said as he pushed his chair back and stood. "I—"

The piercing sound of a warning siren ripped through the air, freezing them both. The color left Meleri's face as she reached for the back of her chair to hold herself steady. Honovi's hand went immediately to the gas mask hanging from his belt. He didn't see one on Meleri's person, but a quick glance around showed one resting on a nearby side table. He hurried to retrieve it, bringing it over to her.

"It's not the tone pattern for spores, but thank you," Meleri said.

"Revenants, then?"

Meleri nodded. "Yes. They come in a horde not typically seen in the wild. We believe Daijal is transporting them somehow but not using the regular roads."

"The back roads are dangerous." The only people known to frequent those areas were wardens, and no warden would give aid to Daijal.

"It hasn't stopped their attacks."

Meleri clutched the gas mask to her chest and headed for the door. Honovi followed after her, unsurprised when, moments later, Dureau came racing around the corner right when the warning sirens changed pitch. "Mother! There are airships in the sky and revenants making their way to the walls."

Meleri rocked to a halt so abruptly Honovi had to put a hand beneath her elbow to make sure she stayed upright. "They'll try to bomb us again."

"Again?" Honovi asked sharply.

Meleri reached for her son, urging him back down the hallway. "Eimarille knows Caris calls Cosian home. She'll keep dropping bombs until her air force finds its target. Didn't you see the damage to the city on your flight in?"

Honovi remembered the pockets of rubble between the city's inner walls, knowing the damage must have been from an attack, but hadn't thought much of it until now. "What is your protocol for an aerial bombardment?"

Dureau grimaced as he slipped his arm around his mother's waist to guide her forward. "We head to the basement and leave the defense of the city to the military."

As much as Honovi wanted to leave to go to his husband, he knew the streets wouldn't be safe in a time like this. Caoimhe would have left a skeleton crew on the *Celestial Sprite*. He didn't know if she'd give an order for them to lend support to the Ashionen military airships anchored in the airfield or not. Despite captaining the airship into Ashionen space, he wasn't the officer in charge of the crew, and Caoimhe knew the restrictions placed on E'ridia's air force just as surely as he did.

That didn't stop Honovi from pausing at the basement door near the servants' quarter and pulling his televox from a belt pouch. The clarion crystal–powered device wasn't widely available to the general public in any country, but his position as *jarl* meant he couldn't do without. As his husband, Blaine carried his own as well.

"We're safe," Blaine assured him when he answered. "We're heading to a bunker beneath the Six Point Mechanics laboratory. I'll lose connection soon."

The cage around Honovi's heart loosened a bit. "We're heading to our own. I just wanted to hear your voice."

"I'm here, and I will come to you after this is over. I love you. Be safe."

"I love you, too."

The call ended, and Honovi ignored the soldier frantically gesturing at him to head down into the basement in favor of ringing Caoimhe. As the ranking military officer on their flight, she had her own televox, and she picked up after the first chiming ring.

"*Jarl*," she said, sounding a bit breathless, as if she were running.

"I'm with the Duchess Auclair. Blaine is safe with Caris," he said.

"They've closed the city gates, but I'm hoping to get through to the airfield with the other military assets."

"Are you going to launch?"

"Being anchored makes us a target."

"Will you go for altitude, or will you fight?"

"I'd be a poor aeronaut if I ran from a Daijalan airship. We didn't go searching for the fight; it came to us."

It might not be enough of an excuse for the commanding officers back in E'ridia to accept, but Honovi would back her if she faced a disciplinary board. "May the Dusk Star guide you true."

Caoimhe didn't respond, the repetitive sound of an ended call echoing in his ear. She'd do her duty while Honovi hid, and it galled him that he couldn't be on the flight deck with her. Tucking the televox away, he descended the stairs to the basement, where Meleri and Dureau huddled with their people and a handful of soldiers as well for security reasons.

Someone had brought Meleri a coat, and the duchess was wrapped up in warm wool to ward off the chill in the underground space that acted both as storage and safety. Honovi could see areas of the cement floor that were less stained than others, whatever crates that had once been there now removed, most likely to make room for moments like this. While some people appeared frightened, most were quietly resigned, with a weariness in their faces that spoke of having been in this exact situation before.

Honovi went to sit beside Meleri on an old wooden bench, Dureau scooting over to make room for him. She nodded at his approach, lips pressed into a trembling line, the gas lamps burning in the ceiling casting a sickly sort of color across her face. Still, she kept the fear she must be feeling off her face, and her voice, when she spoke, was steady enough.

"Winter storms kept Daijal's airships grounded more often than not. With the weather clearing, I fear they'll try to wipe this city off the map and Caris with it," Meleri said softly, her words meant for Honovi alone. "You see now why we need E'ridia's air force?"

Honovi had nothing to say in the face of her plaintive statement, knowing that the promises he wanted to give her were meaningless when bombs would soon be falling on the city above while revenants clawed at Cosian's walls.

Nine

AARALYN

Memories of the time before the first city they'd ever built on Maricol were like fragmented pieces of clarion crystal—shattered moments that never quite fit after all these many years.

The sound of Aaralyn's footsteps echoed against the walls of the catacombs beneath Amari as the North Star walked the length of a tunnel. She trailed her fingers across the cold metal walls that had survived the Ages on this planet and the one that came before, between the stars. Starfire dripped from the Wolf constellation tattoo wrapped around her right arm, providing never-dying illumination there in the dark.

She wandered below, aware of the weight of prayers above in Ashion's capital city from all the people hoping to escape the noose of Daijal's rule and those who didn't mind it. The catacombs were quiet, though, the prayers once whispered within those expansive walls long since lost to history. But Aaralyn knew what they had prayed for, once, when desperate people had dug into the poisoned earth to survive.

Much of the catacombs had fallen into disrepair, hallways and rooms blocked off by past efforts, the full map of the underground city lost to those above, even the ones who purported to know it. They didn't, not truly, not how Aaralyn once had.

This had been home, their beginning before the aether ate through their veins.

Before they were changed.

What the Duchess Auclair and those in the Clockwork Brigade didn't know was how deep the catacombs truly went. The underground tunnels they walked merely scratched the surface of places hidden away in the dark for Ages. But the barricaded entrances, hidden behind packed earth and other efforts, weren't a problem for a star god. Aaralyn passed through them all like a ghost, breathing in cold air and dust that reminded her, there beneath the ground, of the coldness found in a sleep with no memories that lasted years and years as they streaked through an impossible darkness like a comet.

Some vast, distant part of Aaralyn remembered the relief she felt when the stars fell on Maricol so long ago, like finally reaching the shore after so long at sea. She remembered, too, the husband she'd first breathed the fresh air with, before they knew about the spores and the poison and the revenants and the aether that would not let them go.

Down, down, she walked between cold metal walls, through closed doors and barriers of earth, the dark easy enough to see through when lit by starfire. Aaralyn made her way with unerring steps to a room where the metal walls were painted black, with flecks of gold that would have gleamed in the light of starfire if not for the thick layer of dust blanketing everything.

They'd called it a reflecting room, a place to pray and remember the dead burned above. The stars they would become were painted across the walls and ceilings, so different from the ones they'd left behind in some other life, some other Age, some other world.

But they could not leave each other, and Aaralyn would not break the vows she'd sworn at the start of their journey. Innes looked the same now as he did then, ever her husband, ever her regret in moments like this.

"Husband," Aaralyn said into the deep, deep quiet there below the living, her voice echoing in a room that hadn't heard sound in Ages.

Innes smiled at her in the glow of starfire that dripped off his shoulders like a cape, bleeding aether from his Viper constellation tattoo. "Wife."

She looked away from him, looked up at a ceiling that could have doubled as the night sky behind the dust and dirt and grime of their past. "This world isn't meant to be owned how you wish."

"You would deny our children progress."

"I would deny them nothing, but your dream will be their nightmare." Aaralyn met his gaze once more, the love in his eyes as steadfast as his hate. "Our hope of leaving has long been dead. Do not try to resurrect it like a revenant. That way only lies madness."

Innes stepped forward, hands reaching for hers, and she let him take them. His grip was firm and familiar, as was the tired smile on his face. When he pressed his forehead to hers, she couldn't help but close her eyes.

"We are the stars that guide, and you guided us here, forever the captain of my heart, but this world was never meant to be our home."

His power tugged at hers, drawing her upward through the long-ago safety of that underground home and back to the surface of dangers that would never die. The cold changed, that ancient quiet replaced by the sound of the wind and a city waking up. A burning heat to her left that chased away the chill of below had Aaralyn opening her eyes and pulling back.

The starfire throne burned at the center of the park that had grown up around it in the last two decades. The new palace was close by and walled off for privacy, but the old broken throne room remained accessible as a reminder of what a country had lost and could regain.

The throne that every king and queen of the Rourke bloodline had sat on burned with starfire that never went out. The glass cupola above it was supported by iron pillars, the space between them open so people could see the remnants of all that was left of the old palace. The old marble floor was streaked with ashes from the people who still sought to claim the power of rulership denied to them by her decree.

"Maricol was our lighthouse in a storm," Aaralyn said, letting her husband go. She took a step back, looking away from the starfire throne to meet Innes' gaze once more beneath the dawn's encroaching light. "Our miracle."

Innes skimmed the knuckles of one hand down her cheek. "Our grave."

He wasn't wrong, but they'd long since accepted their roads. "And for your anguish, you would damn the world."

"My only goal is to rebuild it through our children, to give them a chance to see the stars one day, to know what we once knew."

She gave him a pitying look, and that deep well of love in his eyes faded into something bitter and angry and mournful. Aaralyn caught his wrist in her hand, pulling his away from her face. "Husband, don't you remember? We ran from that future once before and promised each other never to strive for it again."

"You cannot kill progress."

"Progress has many roads, and I will not let our children walk yours."

Innes wrenched his hand free, walking away from her as was his habit these last few centuries. Ever since Daijal had cleaved itself of Ashion, he had cleaved himself from her. She missed him—she always would—but she would not give up Maricol without a fight.

It was, after all, the only home they had left.

Conflagration

937 A.O.P.

One

SOREN

Soren was certain he'd hear the sounds of telegraph machines in his sleep for years to come.

The building he'd worked out of ever since returning to the Warden's Island from Glencoe in Thirteenth Month of last year had once been a warehouse used for storage. After the attack on the Warden's Island last summer, they'd repurposed it for what salvaged telegraph machines were found in other buildings and those that were shipped to them from Solaria or E'ridia.

It didn't have the best insulation, and the high roof meant the sound from the ranks of telegraph machines stretching from wall to wall echoed loudly. At the far end of the building was a large analytical machine that helped coordinate which telegraph got which incoming message.

The setup wasn't as elaborate or as entrenched as it once had been before the original administrative building was destroyed by Daijal forces. But it worked, and wardens made do with what they had. So far, it was holding up to the heavy influx of messages coming from the borders and the battlefields where wardens were assigned.

Shifts were nine hours each, with the telegraph machines needing to be manned for three shifts a day. Soren had been assigned the mid-shift, which meant he didn't have to disrupt his sleeping hours, but the bulk of messages came in during that time. He'd gotten good at transcribing the coded clicks and beeps into the trade tongue wardens used, his recordings clean and precise. When a message was received and documented, he returned his own confirmation and then waited for the next one to come through.

It was tedious work that required focus, for which he was grateful. Given half a chance, Soren would spend every day since leaving Solaria thinking about the man whose heart he'd inadvertently broken.

Vanya Sa'Liandel, of the House of Sa'Liandel, was the Imperial emperor of Solaria and had once been Soren's longtime lover ever since he'd saved Vanya's life from a train wreck. These days, Vanya was an ache in Soren's chest and painful memories he couldn't let go of the same way he couldn't let go of the vow that still hung around his throat.

He was pulled from his thoughts by someone clearing their throat beside his desk. Soren looked up from the pages he'd been sorting to see a tithe standing next to his desk, wearing a brass pin that marked her as on messenger duty. The girl couldn't have been more than ten years old, but Soren knew she was probably one of only a dozen or so in her year group who had survived the attack last year. The Daijal forces had known where to target to do the most damage due to a warden turning traitor and feeding them information as well as prisoners.

The school and training buildings had been targeted first, along with the civic buildings. Both were critical infrastructure, and while buildings could be easily rebuilt, the ranks of tithes and wardens with specialized knowledge could not. Daijal had eradicated the next few generations of wardens, to say nothing of the archives that had once held records of alchemic information of the poison fields dating back to the Age of Starfall, before the current countries even existed. So much had been lost, and they were losing even more wardens to the war between Daijal and Ashion.

"The governor wants to see you," the tithe said.

Soren nodded and hit the button on the telegraph machine that would turn it off. He gathered his reports and placed them in the outgoing tray for pickup. They would be taken to a different building and entered into proper record-keeping ledgers, organized between border updates or pertaining to the war, and passed on to those who needed to know. Soren left his desk behind, the tithe enough of a reason for him to end his shift early. He followed her out of the building into a steady rain that was typical of weather during Fifth Month.

The wind accompanying the rain wasn't poisonous enough to merit a gas mask for wardens. Soren ducked his head against the rain as he jogged after the tithe across the grassy open space situated between the telegraph building and the one that now held the administrative offices after the original one was destroyed. The interior of the fort was still recovering from the attack last summer, and rebuilding all the damaged areas was slow going, even with aid provided by Solaria and E'ridia.

They reached the administrative building—previously used as barracks but no longer needed, not with the drastic decline in tithes—and he knocked his boots against the porch step to get some of the mud off his soles. The tithe left him to it and disappeared inside. Once his boots were clean enough, Soren stepped inside and nodded at the wardens manning the desks there. Only one nodded back, the other two wardens bent over their work as they sorted through paper and ledgers.

"Head on down. She's expecting you," the warden said.

The walk to the governor's office was a route Soren could do with his eyes closed. The building had been gutted in places to open up space for wardens to work in, and he passed quite a few going about their duties. The layout was temporary, at least until the new administrative building was finished. Most of the wardens who could have helped with the construction were on border patrol in other countries or fighting in the poison fields alongside the Ashion army—two places where Soren wished he could be but was denied.

Ever since Soren's arrival in Glencoe after the attack on the Warden's Island and the destruction of the Imperial palace in Calhames last year, Delani had refused to assign him a border. It had as much to do with the miscalculation of his efforts in Solaria and the Imperial court as it did with the realization that Soren may very well be someone who should have never become a warden at all. As much as he wanted to be off the island and fighting with his brethren, to be a warden meant abiding by the governor's orders. Delani had refused to let him leave the Warden's Island once they returned, and so here Soren remained.

What Soren wanted—desperately, perhaps selfishly—was his border in Solaria back. But that was lost to him, as much as Vanya was as well. Even these many months after that ugly, wretched night trapped by revenants in the Imperial palace and the one after when he'd last felt Vanya's touch, Soren still ached for the other man. The vow hanging from his throat was a reminder of what he'd lost, but Soren still couldn't find it in himself to give it up, to send it back, not when it was the last feasible connection he had to Vanya.

Even if he could return to Solaria, he knew Vanya wouldn't want to see him, much less forgive Soren for lying about being able to cast starfire. No matter that his secret had saved Raiah's life—it had irrevocably damaged the trust between Vanya and Soren. After all the betrayal Vanya had suffered, Soren had made it so much worse by hiding a past he had never claimed but which others had bestowed upon him.

As for starfire, even now, Soren was loath to ever cast it again. That power was anathema to being a warden, and this life was the only one he knew. He wasn't ready to give it up for a different road.

Soren let those melancholy thoughts slide away once he made it to Delani's office. He could see her door was propped open, and he had to edge his way past pushed-together desks filled with wardens and tithes working on filing reports and filtering vital information for the governor to review. Soren had spent his own fair share of duty at those desks before getting assigned to the telegraph building.

He reached the doorway and knocked on the frame, waiting until Delani looked up from the half dozen reports scattered across her desk before stepping inside. "You wanted to see me?"

The governor leaned back in her chair, a creaking sound coming from the motion. "Close the door and take a seat."

Soren did as ordered before sitting in one of the wooden chairs in front of her desk. He leaned back, rolling his shoulders a little as the sheath holding his poison short sword pulled at them. No warden went weaponless in the fort these days, when before, those wardens who returned for a respite from their border patrol didn't mind leaving their weapons in the barracks.

Delani studied him with her one good eye, the other a pitch-black prosthetic painted with gold flecks to look like the night sky. The monocle goggle that helped with her depth perception was strapped securely around her head. Her short, dark hair sported more white these days. Signs of stress were in everyone, but they didn't have the luxury to succumb to it.

"You're aware of the doubling of revenant numbers in Daijal and Ashion since winter, correct?" Delani said.

"Every warden is," Soren said.

"Even pulling our ranks out of Daijal and Urova, wardens are barely able to clear the poison fields before more revenants come through. Winter brought heavier rains and snowfall than the previous years, and there are more bogs to deal with. We're losing too many wardens to the dead and the war, and we don't have enough tithes ready to graduate, to say nothing of those tithes we lost in the attack. We need to replenish our ranks for the future."

Soren went still beneath her piercing, knowing gaze. "Have you decided if you will lift the stay on Solaria's sanctions?"

Since the founding of their country, the Houses of Solaria that claimed the Imperial throne had buried their royal dead rather than burned them. That adherence to a form of worship for the Dawn Star had resulted in a secret crypt underneath the royal grounds, accessed through the private star temple used by the Imperial family.

Soren had become aware of the crypt during the funeral for Vanya's parents when Vanya had invited him to participate in the funeral rites. The iron coffins with their welded-shut lids in the crypt below the Imperial palace had held an unknown number of revenants —revenants the House of Kimathi, in an unconscionable attack backed by the Daijal queen, had let loose during the Conclave of Houses.

He still woke sometimes from the nightmare of being trapped in a metal coffin, listening to the sounds of a revenant trying to claw its way inside. He might be a warden, used to fighting against the walking dead, but being at their mercy like that was something he never wanted to experience again.

The crypt with its buried dead had been something Soren couldn't hold back from Delani, no matter how much he cared about Vanya and the other man's precarious hold on the Imperial throne. It was law in every country on Maricol for citizens to burn their dead and leave names on a memory wall. Burning the dead was the only way to ensure a body didn't rise as a revenant, an action written into the Poison Accords that governed the relationship between wardens and Maricol's countries.

Because Solaria had broken the Poison Accords—at the risk to their own citizens and others—that country owed the wardens enough tithes they could replenish their ranks within the next few decades. Neither was Solaria the only country to be hit with sanctions. Daijal, too, had been slapped with them, albeit for vastly different reasons. The wardens couldn't enforce the sanctions on Daijal so long as the war was ongoing, but already Daijal was feeling the bite of having no wardens to lend aid against revenants or cleanse the poison fields.

Right now, the war was giving ground to the dead. Soren knew they needed more tithes, but he also knew handing down the sanctions now would weaken Vanya's grip on power and leave Solaria vulnerable.

"I'd send you to deliver the news if I thought it would get us anywhere," Delani said.

Soren had spent many years in the Imperial court learning how not to show his feelings. He doubted he was fooling Delani. "If you hand down sanctions now, it might destabilize the war effort."

"Solaria's Legion is deployed to their northern border and no further. Neither Daijal nor Ashion has risked a skirmish with that country's army. They are not involved in any war effort, despite Ashion's numerous requests for support and aid."

"They fight over the *vasilyet*."

Delani made a throwaway gesture with her hand. "That is a proxy fight. If the emperor had proof of Eimarille being responsible for the destabilization of his country's government, the Legion would have marched on Daijal last year. We need tithes if we're to handle the dead once the war is over. Our records might have been destroyed, but I know from previous research us wardens needed to double our ranks in the aftermath of Ashion's initial civil war. We number less now than we did then. We can't do our duty unless we fill our ranks."

"And if doing so causes the House that holds the Imperial throne to lose power to one who won't care to pay sanctions, what then?"

"We will pull our people out of Solaria the same way we did with Daijal and Urova."

Soren swallowed tightly. "What about the Wastelands and Rixham?"

Delani leveled him a flat stare. "We would guard Solaria's northern border. Your concern is noted, but I know your feelings toward the House of Sa'Liandel. As I recall, I sent you to observe the Imperial court, not bed the emperor."

Soren refused to feel shame about that, even if his cheeks did heat a little. He knew he'd overstepped when it came to Vanya, but he couldn't regret the days he'd woken up in Vanya's bed. He ached for those moments, even now, missing the other man in a way he'd missed no other. His relationship with Vanya was complicated. Soren had tried his best to keep it out of the public eye, but the Imperial court ran on whispers, and there'd been no hope of hiding where Vanya's favor lay.

Other wardens had expressed their displeasure with his choices since his return to the island, but at least none had tried to kill him like the *rionetka* in that Ashion border town. Amidst everything else that had happened, Soren's past indiscretion with a head of state wasn't the worst problem they were dealing with.

"Solaria is the only country with a military that can stand against Daijal's and win, but only if they're not rocked by internal divisions, which will surely happen if you insist on the delivery of tithes," Soren said carefully.

"They haven't chosen to engage."

Soren wondered what Vanya would think of his defense of Solaria, if Vanya even thought of him at all these days. "If Eimarille's war continues how we believe it will, Solaria will have no choice but to be drawn into the conflict. Would you rather have them solidly capable or the Houses at each other's throats again because you demanded sanctions from all their people?"

The Conclave of Houses hadn't fixed the animosity between some of the bloodlines, merely patched over the cracks at the behest of the Dawn Star. Still, all the news coming out of Solaria spoke of the palace being rebuilt and Vanya conducting government out of Oeiras.

"You act like they have a choice about their payment. You don't have the authority to argue for them. You are a warden, not Solarian." Delani paused, raising the brow over her good eye. "Though I wonder if you were supposed to be even that."

Soren shoved down his anger, knowing it wouldn't help him here. "I *am* a warden. This is the only road I have ever known."

"You have a sister. Two of them, if the broadsheets out of Ashion are correct. Your records as a tithe were destroyed along with everything else, and there is the question of starfire that runs in the Rourke bloodline."

"We give up our countries and we give up our names when we become tithes. My loyalty is to the wardens, and it always has been. Whatever people think I am, they are wrong."

The Dawn Star had set him on this road, and Soren would walk it as a warden until he died and his ashes danced amongst the stars.

Whatever crown he may have once worn in some other life, whatever name he may have once had, he didn't want it.

All he truly wanted was the love of a man who wanted nothing to do with him anymore.

Delani sighed, leaning forward to rest her elbows on the desk. "We both know you are not just a warden, and I can't ignore that fact forever, the same way I can't ignore the sanctions owed to us. Daijal is readying for a heavy push east now that the snows have melted. You are right that we can't afford for Solaria to be splintered when Eimarille eventually turns her attention to that country. War will only delay the inevitable, but the sanctions will be paid."

"Will you tell the emperor that?"

"It will be relayed, but not by you. Your duty remains here on the island."

Soren knew it was too much to hope that he'd be assigned his old border again, but with the crypt emptied, there was nothing left for a warden to guard. Still, he tried not to be disappointed. "I would be of better use in Ashion with the war effort."

Delani snorted. "I have it on good authority Eimarille hunts for her brother, and I'm not inclined to give her what she wants."

"I'm not—"

"I'll believe what I want," Delani said, cutting him off. "Because to ignore the fact staring at me with the same gray eyes in a face with similar features as a purported Ashion queen would risk what the wardens stand for, and I won't break the Poison Accords like those before me apparently did."

Soren snapped his mouth shut, teeth clacking together. "I'll do my duty."

"Of that, I have no doubt."

It was as much a dismissal as any, and Soren left the governor's office wishing for a world that didn't end at the shores of an island in the middle of the Celestine Lake. He wanted—more than anything—a road that would lead him back to Vanya. That was a prayer he had no right to speak, because wardens were Maricol's starless, nameless children, and there would be no star god to hear his words.

It didn't stop Soren from dreaming of Vanya that night and waking the next morning aching for the touches that had seemed so real in the middle of the night.

Two

VANYA

The Tirsha River fed the sprawling tropical rainforests that Oeiras overlooked, that vast green canopy hiding dangerous revenant wild beasts. The port city sat at the mouth of the river and was known for its trade with the Tovan Isles, the same way Seaville was known for trade with E'ridia in the east. Unlike that city, Oeiras now held the honor of the Imperial family calling it home while the palace was rebuilt in Calhames.

The House of Dayal oversaw the surrounding *vasilyet*, a House that had thrown its support behind the House of Sa'Liandel during the Conclave before the Dawn Star had given her blessing. That was more than some other Houses had done, and it was one reason why Vanya Sa'Liandel, of the House of Sa'Liandel, had chosen the Imperial estate in Oeiras over all others to temporarily rule out of.

While Vanya could have stayed in his House's ancestral estate in Calhames, he'd needed to escape Solaria's capital and all the terrible memories that city held for him these days. More than even escaping heartache, he'd wanted to protect his daughter. Oeiras wouldn't have been his first choice to return to, but of the major cities he could temporarily rule out of, Seaville was held by a House whose loyalty was still in question, Karnack was too close to the northern border and the war happening in neighboring countries, and Bellingham would never be an option.

So to Oeiras they had gone, and Vanya had been tasked with turning a temporary residence into a home. Unlike the last time he and Raiah had resided in Oeiras, Vanya and the *praetoria* legionnaires were well aware of the threat from *rionetkas* and had planned security accordingly. He did his best to shield his daughter from the threats aimed at their House. Raiah was the brightest start of his day, and that never changed.

"Papa!" Raiah cried out as she raced across the inner courtyard, her long hair flowing behind her in thick waves. The white robes she wore were perhaps an inch too short, courtesy of the growth spurt she was going through. She was all legs even at five years old, and Vanya had a feeling she'd take after him in height rather than her mother.

Vanya scooped Raiah up into his arms and tossed her into the air, causing her to shriek happily. He caught her easily and held her close. "How is my favorite girl this morning?"

Raiah wrapped her skinny arms around his neck and pecked a kiss to his cheek. "I'm your only girl."

"Ah, your *valide* would argue otherwise."

Vanya tucked Raiah against his side and carried her over to the table set with a family-style breakfast spread. Taisiya Sa'Liandel, of the House of Sa'Liandel, sat on the low bench built beneath a curtain of flowering vines, watching them approach with a smile on her subtly scarred face, mouth dragged down at the left corner. She'd survived a poisoning on her wedding day while her husband had not and spent much of her days since then at a coastal estate.

She'd returned to Calhames before the start of the Conclave last year, becoming Vanya's advisor as was her right as *valide*, the matriarch of the ruling House that held the Imperial throne of Solaria. She'd stayed with them when Vanya decided to move the Imperial court to Oeiras, making her the only person he trusted with Raiah these days after the betrayals that had come to light last year.

He no longer had a majordomo for his household, reluctant to bring a stranger so close to his family again after Alida's treachery. Taisiya handled the running of the household for now, capable of doing so only because the Imperial estate here was smaller than the Imperial palace had been, meant to hold a family and not a government. Still, he knew it could not be her duty indefinitely, not with her age and other duties bearing down on her.

"She wants to join you when you meet with the Tovan Isles ambassador today," Taisiya said, the rasp of her voice familiar. In her youth, she'd been one of the most revered theater singers in the country before fervere stole her voice and her husband. But she'd survived, voice ever altered, speaking as if she'd smoked tabac all her life when she'd never touched it.

The loose curls of her graying auburn hair were similar in shape to Raiah's, styled today in a coiled updo held in place by hair combs made of pearlescent shell and inlaid with jewels. Her gown was a teal color, the light robe layered over it a pale gray that was almost white. It reminded Vanya of the waves in the port, and he knew the homage was done on purpose. Taisiya would be joining him when he and his other advisors met with the Tovanian ambassador after breakfast. Raiah would be otherwise occupied.

"I believe her tutors would protest Raiah missing her lessons," Vanya said as he sat on the bench opposite Taisiya, letting Raiah go so she could sit beside him.

"But Papa!" she protested. "I want to see what you do."

Taisiya reached for the teapot that held the strong red she favored, pouring herself a cup and then one for Vanya. He handled pouring Raiah her favorite chai, setting the cup beside her empty plate. "You will, but for now, you have lessons."

She pouted at him, brows furrowed in a way he knew she was trying to come up with an argument that would get her way. Raiah was as strong-willed as they came, despite the horrors she'd lived through in her short life. "Lessons are boring."

"Lessons until you are seven. Then you will be old enough to sit with me in court some mornings," Vanya said. It was never too early to learn how to rule, but he wanted her to have a childhood a little longer.

Raiah sighed loudly, clearly believing he was in the wrong but allowing his decision. "Yes, Papa."

Taisiya hid her smile behind her teacup. "Let us eat before the hour gets away from us."

Oeiras was known for their spicy dishes, and the rice mixed with eggs and chunks of pork was the main part of the morning meal. Vanya served Taisiya first, then Raiah, and finally himself. The flatbread was passed around, chunks torn off to dip in the bowls of sauces that added more flavor to the rice they scooped up.

"Have you heard any update from General Chu Hua?" Taisiya asked after several bites.

"Only what you know from the last report. The House of Kimathi's stolen *vasilyet* still remains under their control, and Daijal continues to claim their designs for the war machines they deploy against Ashion are their own. I fly to Calhames tomorrow," Vanya said, trying not to let the bitterness seep into his voice.

He would never forgive Joelle her machinations that had nearly gotten his daughter killed and risked Solaria's sovereignty. When his spies had come back from the north with information that Daijal had built war machines far too similar to those used by Solaria's Legion to be anything but stolen, Vanya discovered Joelle's treachery ran deeper than anyone had thought. Aligning herself with a country determined to interfere with other sovereign nations had cleaved the *vasilyet* her House had presided over for Ages from Solaria, and Vanya was spending resources and political capital to claw it back.

Despite their military prowess, the Legion had yet to take back the *vasilyet*. Joelle had provided quite a spirited defense of the land there in the northwest with Daijal's unofficial help. The worst problem the Legion faced wasn't war machines but the astronomical number of revenants roaming the *vasilyet* and the self-inflicted poison Joelle's side had ruined the cleansed land with on a wide scale.

Passage through the poison fields was a risk the Legion had no choice but to take. The officers in command were trying to mitigate losses as best they could. Add in the fact that Vanya couldn't commit the entirety of the Legion to that fight in the corner of Solaria when the bulk of the Legion's ranks were needed to guard the long stretch of the northern border meant it was a slow grind to gain ground.

The revenants would be more of a problem if not for the efforts of the wardens. Vanya knew his country was lucky to still have their support after the announcement of sanctions as payment for the actions of the Houses who'd held the Imperial throne. But the wardens numbered fewer now after Daijal's attack on the Warden's Island, and most of their numbers were in Ashion, aiding the war effort. Their alchemists could only do so much to help cleanse the poison fields in the northwest, and it wasn't enough yet to tilt the fight in Solaria's favor.

Solaria's borders still had wardens guarding them, and Vanya tried every day not to think about the only warden who had ever mattered to him. It was a losing battle, one Raiah was ignorant of.

"When is Soren coming back?" Raiah asked halfway through the meal.

Vanya had learned young not to let his pain show in the wake of questions that hurt, but hiding his reaction didn't diminish the way his chest went tight. Even these many months on, the heavy knot of hurt and betrayal that sat behind his ribs had yet to ease.

It was just as hard—if not harder—for Raiah. His daughter had grown up with Soren coming and going in her life, a familiar presence Vanya had never thought twice about, not until that fateful night of the Conclave ending. His absences were always paired with a return, but it was far past the time when Soren should have come back to them if all was right in the world. Only it wasn't.

For all of Vanya's simmering anger and hurt when he thought of the warden, he couldn't quite excise the curl of worry Soren's absence brought him. Nor could he be angry at his daughter for asking about the warden who had once kept her safe. He could only try to mitigate the hurt she felt at an absence she had a difficult time comprehending. Eventually, one day, she might forget Soren, even if Vanya knew he never could.

"Someday," Vanya said, hoping she would accept the vague answer that was no longer a promise.

Taisiya arched an eyebrow at him but held her tongue. Raiah frowned at her plate before raising her chin and giving Vanya a mulish look. "I want Soren. You should tell him to come back."

Vanya reached for a teapot and refilled his daughter's cup. "Drink your chai."

Raiah was so like himself at that age, stubborn and demanding. "He always comes back. Why hasn't he visited yet?"

"Raiah," Vanya said sharply. "The warden has his duty."

She scowled at him, crossing her arms over her chest. "He's not a warden. He's *Soren*, and I miss him."

"That's enough. Finish your meal."

She didn't wait to be excused, sliding off the bench with a huff and stomping away from the table. Vanya turned his head, frowning at her back. "Raiah. This tantrum isn't becoming of a princess."

Raiah whirled around, the hem of her robe fluttering around her skinny legs. "You could tell Soren to come back, but you *haven't*. I want to see him, and you won't let me."

Then she burst into tears and ran out of the courtyard, one of the *praetoria* legionnaires standing guard at the entrance swift to follow her. Vanya got to his feet, torn between going after her and knowing that he didn't have time in his schedule to try to soothe such a tantrum when they were due for their meeting with the ambassador soon.

"You let Soren into her life the same way you let him into yours. You should not be surprised at the hole he left," Taisiya said quietly.

Vanya clenched his hands into fists and let out a slow breath before turning to face his *valide*. "The warden is not open for discussion."

Unlike every other person in Solaria, Taisiya did not bow her head to him when faced with his anger. "Soren is the reason Raiah is not with Joelle, I am alive, and you still hold the Imperial throne."

"The wardens called him back."

"You never asked him to stay."

Her words were like salt in a wound that refused to heal. Vanya still dreamed of that last night he'd spent with Soren, wanting answers, wanting more than what the warden could give him, wishing the betrayal hadn't hurt so much. Knowing Soren could cast starfire, a skill that should have made him ineligible to be a warden if it weren't for the interference of the Dawn Star, was a secret he still hadn't spoken of, not even to Taisiya.

"He is a warden. His duty was never to me."

Taisiya snorted at that. "His duty perhaps, but not his heart."

She slid across the bench, and Vanya automatically stepped forward to offer his hand. She took it, and he helped her to her feet. Taisiya was shorter than him, thin and fragile-looking if one didn't know her internal strength. Her hazel eyes were more green than brown, filled with a compassion he hadn't seen directed his way since his mother was alive.

"Pretending Soren never existed in your life or Raiah's does a disservice to the memories he built with you," she said.

She didn't know Soren had lied, that it had been one lie too many after the Imperial palace had burned. All Taisiya knew, like Raiah, was that Soren had returned to the wardens. For all of Soren's betrayals, his secrets weren't Vanya's to tell.

"The Tovan Isle ambassador awaits us," Vanya said.

Taisiya sighed. "Stubborn child. Very well, let us depart."

He offered her his arm, and she curled her hand around the bend of his elbow. They left the courtyard and the unfinished meal behind them in favor of crossing the estate for the dignitary room used for trade talks with the Tovan Isles. Unlike other rooms in the estate, this one had a deep pool filled with salt water. Vanya could smell the sea before they reached the archway of open doors.

A servant announced his arrival with a voice that rang through the spacious room as he and Taisiya entered it. "May I present His Imperial Majesty, Emperor Vanya Sa'Liandel, of the House of Sa'Liandel, and *valide* Taisiya."

The Tovan Isles delegation stood on the elaborate floating cabana anchored to the edge of the pool. The thrum of the engines that kept it afloat was a soft hum at the edge of his hearing, and Vanya could feel the faint vibration of the mechanics filtering up through the floor. Ambassador Akeheni, of the ship-city *Matariki*, bowed at his arrival, as did the others with her. Vanya's advisors, political aides, and several high-ranking Legion officers who waited at the low table near the pool all bowed as well. A photographer waited nearby with their camera gear and an assistant, ready to document the meeting for the broadsheets.

Vanya escorted Taisiya to the pair of empty center seats meant for them and saw her settled in one before turning his attention to Akeheni. The ambassador stepped to the edge of the floating cabana and bowed to the Imperial degree. "Emperor."

"Ambassador," Vanya said. "Welcome. It is good to have you back with us."

Akeheni smiled, the thin tattooed lines that arced away from the outer corners of her hazel eyes and which framed her chin and mouth elongating a bit with the motion. Those tattoos marked her as a ship's captain, while the six-pointed star tattooed between her eyes marked her as a government official. She'd lived quite an illustrious life, something Vanya knew from their previous conversations. He found her stories of a life at sea interesting, her personality calming, even when they disagreed on particular points of diplomacy.

Typically, Vanya's people handled the minute details of trade, and he was brought in at the end of negotiations. Today's meeting was different—less about trade and more about the war creeping close to both their borders.

The photographer approached and bowed deeply. "If I might make a record of this meeting, Your Imperial Majesty?"

Vanya angled his body toward the camera, as did Akeheni. They composed themselves for the picture, the flash of the light almost blinding. He blinked spots out of his eyes and waited for an aide to escort the photographer out of the room before turning his attention back to Akeheni.

"Please, make yourself comfortable," Vanya said as he made his way to his seat.

Akeheni settled on the low chair screwed into the cabana's floor, comfortable with the slow rocking motion from the machine-generated waves. Tovanians suffered from land sickness when they spent too long away from their ship-cities, a debilitating affliction that could be counteracted with potions, but it wasn't a long-term solution. Hence, a room built to make them comfortable, which Vanya knew made negotiations easier.

"Your people are aware of the war happening between Daijal and Ashion, are they not?" Vanya asked.

"We know the Daijalan queen has much to answer for when it comes to the wardens. We know, too, she has an alliance with Urova. Their submersibles have traveled far from the icy north into the Gulf of Helia," Akeheni said.

"Have they attacked your ship-cities?"

"No, but the sailing routes to Daijal have become tighter, which we don't appreciate. We have no fear of Urova's submersibles. We have our own, and our depth charges sink deep. Urovans are used to the icy deep, not the stormy open sea."

The military officer on the other side of Taisiya leaned forward, gesturing with one hand. "Do you think Urova could become a problem for your people?"

"As much as any country. We have no quarrel with them—for now."

"Neither do we, but the war in the north is a concern of ours," Vanya said.

Akeheni nodded slowly. "I understand you fight against a House who seeks to break away."

Vanya bit back the bitter sting of those words. She meant it as a statement, not an insult. "Daijal's interference doesn't stop at just the wardens."

"We believe it won't stop at Ashion's borders either. We've our Legion in the north, but Solaria has more coastline than any other country," Taisiya added.

Which was true, even if a third of it was buttressed by the Wastelands, a desert that had spawned spores and revenants for Ages and which wardens meticulously guarded, even now with their numbers depleted. The Legion had come into being as a defense against the threat of the walking dead in the south. But the Wastelands weren't the only place in Solaria where revenants congregated.

Rixham was a dead city, one with its walls sealed off and citizens long since succumbed to spores, made that way by the decisions of his mother to keep Solaria whole when a House sought secession. Vanya knew he would have to make the same sort of decision with the House of Kimathi in Bellingham once the Legion fought its way through the numerous revenants in that *vasilyet*'s poison fields.

For now, he was trying to give the people caught in the crossfire a choice to leave, but finding safety outside a city's walls was never easy. The war machines Joelle deployed into the poison fields weren't commanded by humans but by magic. Paired with the frightening numbers of revenants in the battlefield, and the Legion was fighting for every mile while trying to keep legionnaires alive and uninfected by spores. It made Joelle's losses less than Vanya's, and that was an imbalance his military advisors worried about.

"Our countries have a long relationship when it comes to trade. I am here to see if your people would be amenable to expanding that into an alliance. Your ship-cities would be of great help monitoring our coasts," Vanya said.

Akeheni shifted on her seat, frowning slightly. "You ask for something I can't commit to without further discussion with the *Uri*. An alliance of any kind always makes rough seas that take time to settle."

Vanya had expected nothing less, for he knew the governing body of the Tovan Isles never made any decision without long deliberation. Somehow, he doubted Eimarille would wait for them to do so. "Daijal already allies itself with Urova. If you think Eimarille will stop her war at the shores, then you are wrong. I would not see either of our nations have their sovereignty weakened."

"I will carry your request to Port Avi, but I make no promises to what you ask," Akeheni warned.

For now, it would have to be enough.

"I will send a delegation west with you. They will speak for me about what transpires here so the *Uri* knows time is of the essence."

Akeheni nodded at that, gaze flicking to the military officers ranged down the table. "I hope your people have strong stomachs. The spring waters are never as calm as the stories say."

"We are Solarian. We will persist."

Vanya settled back into his seat, ready to talk about more than just war.

 Three

VANYA

The airship flight east from Oeiras to Calhames was choppier than usual due to a spring storm the captain had to navigate through. Vanya landed midmorning with a headache that only grew in size by the time he disembarked, went through the physical checks for *rionetkas,* and was driven through the city walls all the way to the Imperial Senate. The route took his motor carriage and its escort vehicles past the walled-off construction site that was the Imperial palace grounds.

Vanya stared through the golden gates that once led to the Imperial palace as he was driven down the street. Architects, engineers, and construction crews had been hard at work since autumn of last year to design and build the next Imperial palace that would see the Houses through future Ages. But it had fallen under his rulership, and that was an ignominy he could not escape.

He got a glimpse of the ongoing work as the motor carriage sped past: construction vehicles, workers, and automatons scattered around what once used to be the massive forecourt. He'd presided over a ceremony last year when the first foundation piece had been laid. That moment had been different from the one where he'd used starfire to melt metal and stone and seal off the entrance to the royal crypt.

Despite all the ongoing work, the palace wouldn't be fully ready for years, and some small part of him wondered if he would ever even set foot in the new Imperial residence in the future. But that was something he couldn't dwell on, as the present needed all his attention these days. So Vanya faced forward and let the palace disappear behind them.

When he arrived at the Senate building, Vanya was greeted by a woman who had become an unlikely ally during the Conclave of the Houses and someone who wasn't afraid to be blunt with him. Her presence was most likely why Taisiya had opted to remain in Oeiras to watch over Raiah. *Vezir* Cybele Balaskas, head of the House of Balaskas, was never one to mince words these days and had made a friend of his *valide* after the attack on the palace.

"Your Imperial Majesty," Cybele said with a bow where she waited just past the grand Senate doors. "The House of Balaskas welcomes your return to Calhames. How was the western coast?"

Vanya managed a smile for her, tight though it was. "Invigorating."

Cybele folded her hands in front of her midsection. The gown she wore today was a deep crimson trimmed in white, the rubies on the bone hair combs a perfect match. She was a decade older than him, head of a minor House that had never held the Imperial throne for all that they'd schemed after it. But she'd learned of the secret the major Houses had kept for generations—that of the buried royal dead—and had still thrown her support behind him during the Conclave anyway. For that, her loyalty was integral to shoring up his position, and he repaid it with royal favor.

The Houses would always vie for the Imperial throne. He knew Cybele would claim it for her own if ever presented with the opportunity, but unlike some other Houses, her concern was for Solaria right now.

"The vote stands in your favor, if you care for such news," Cybele said.

Vanya gestured for her to attend him as the *praetoria* legionnaires fanned out around them, ever keeping watch. "I knew it would fall that way."

Any senator who voted against the bill calling up reservists to the Legion would be soundly mocked and shouted down until they changed their vote. Solaria's borders had to be guarded, and Vanya wanted the reservists to get through training before summer. What information his spies had delivered from the war in Ashion had left Vanya and the high-ranking officers of the Legion worried and wanting to be prepared.

"There are whispers of those who doubt your fortitude to rule," Cybele said, keeping her voice even as she stared straight ahead.

"The same Houses as before, I assume?" At her nod, Vanya waved off her concern. "They know if they try to stand against me, they stand against Solaria and will be considered traitors in the way of the House of Kimathi. If that is the road they wish to walk, then let them."

"I'm doubtful that is what they want."

"What they want is my crown and the Imperial throne. So long as I have the Dawn Star's blessing, they shall have neither."

He knew he wouldn't rule forever. The Dawn Star was a finicky god who ignored her children as often as she listened to their prayers. Vanya knew, too, that he'd let Soren go when the Dawn Star had warned him to keep the warden close. He hoped Callisto wouldn't hold his heartache against him while he threw himself into the fight to keep Solaria whole.

Cybele left him at the stairs that branched off and led from the hallway to the mezzanine where the Houses could watch the proceedings. Vanya continued on toward the open double doors, *praetoria* legionnaires lining the hallway. Maurizio, the Senate's sergeant at arms, announced his arrival in a clear, ringing voice that drew everyone's attention. "His Imperial Majesty Emperor Vanya Sa'Liandel, of the House of Sa'Liandel."

The murmur of conversation in the room was drowned out by the sound of everyone rising to their feet and bowing at his entrance. Vanya made his way down the center aisle to the throne, the only one left in Calhames. Vanya had chosen to replace it with one similar in design to the throne that had resided in the Imperial palace. An artisan had delivered the new one at the beginning of First Month. The carved wooden body and gold-gilt design was different enough that it shouldn't always dredge up the memory of Soren sitting in his lap in a throne room that no longer existed, but it always did.

For all that he'd tried to ignore the holes that Soren had left behind, time didn't ease the ache any. But Vanya had gotten good at shoving aside the memories Calhames threw at him, glad, in a way, that he didn't have to walk the hallways of the Imperial palace's private royal wings and see the warden everywhere there.

Vanya made it to the low dais where the throne was positioned and sat down on it. He nodded at the *magister* of the Senate, who nodded back. "Let's begin."

Time ticked away slowly on the Senate chamber clock bolted to the wall over the main entrance. Vanya focused on the procedure that ultimately brought the reservist bill before him after a final vote. Only then did Vanya leave the throne for the table positioned to the side of the dais. He bent over the table and signed his name to multiple copies of the bill.

"The reserves will be activated," Vanya said once he stamped the Imperial seal over his name.

Despite the mistakes he'd made during his rulership last year, ensuring the Legion had enough soldiers to defend Solaria's borders would not be one of them.

Senators dutifully applauded as the bill became law, with some of the spectators in the mezzanine joining in. The noise didn't help Vanya's headache any, but he smiled through it anyway, taking time afterward to mingle with a few of the senators and get a feel for the current temperament of the Imperial Senate.

"My *vasilyet* is wondering why we haven't brought Bellingham to heel yet. Surely our Legion is capable of putting down a traitor," the senator from Seaville said.

Vanya studied the man, wondering if he'd been fed that line from the House of Aetos. That House had only reluctantly backed his at the end of the Conclave and only because he'd proven Joelle's betrayal to

Solaria. "When one has to fight through thousands of revenants to reach a city's walls, then you'll find the precautions taken worthwhile. I will not question the generals and their battlefield decisions, for they keep our people safe."

The senator smiled thinly, bowing his head before stepping back. "Of course."

Cybele's warning from earlier kept Vanya in the Senate chambers longer than he intended. Working out of Oeiras half the time meant the personal connections he'd taken for granted when he was mere streets and not *vasilyets* away took a little more effort. When he was finally escorted out of the Senate chamber by *praetoria* legionnaires, he found Caelum waiting for him in the hallway.

His Chief Minister elicited a true smile from Vanya. The formal robes of Caelum's office were matched by the elaborately patterned and brimless, round cap that marked his rank. His short, graying brown hair appeared to have recently been trimmed. Caelum always presented himself impeccably when in public. "Ah, Caelum. I was about to send an aide to find you."

Caelum bowed deeply, cradling the folios he carried to his chest through the motion, blue eyes creasing at the corners when he smiled. "Your Imperial Majesty, it is always good to see you. The Ashionen representatives are present and available whenever you are ready."

"The bill is signed, so let's see to the foreigners."

"They're in the Mosaic Room." Caelum situated himself one step behind Vanya as they walked. "How was your flight over?"

"A bit turbulent, but nothing the captain couldn't handle. How has Calhames fared in my absence?"

Caelum took the brief opening to bring Vanya up to date on the political pulse of the Senate and the Houses. While a small subset of political officials and aides had decamped to Oeiras to assist Vanya in ruling out of that city, the Senate couldn't be moved, and so Caelum was Vanya's eyes and ears in the capital when he was out west.

Not for the first time was Vanya glad that the older man had survived the attack on the Imperial palace. Too many had not, but the government persisted, as did the Houses, and Caelum was as loyal as they came these days.

The Mosaic Room was on the other side of the Senate building, where offices for the senators were located. Since they no longer had a functioning palace, rooms in the building had been repurposed for Imperial use. Vanya had refused to have his House's ancestral estate be used for governing. At some point, when he brought Raiah back, she would stay there, and he wasn't about to let unknown people near her in a place that should be her home.

Caelum had an office on the premises, close to the one given Vanya. Both were located near the Mosaic Room, which had once been a social space for senators and subsequently been turned into a formal receiving room. The wide windows allowed in the sunlight, hitting the hundreds of thousands of tiny colored pieces of broken tile and glass fit together on the walls, floor, and ceiling. When Vanya's arrival was announced, he saw the Ashionens turn toward the door, heads craning back down from where they'd been studying the sky of the grand mosaic. He couldn't fault them their admiration.

The artwork was grand, depicting the Dawn Star in all her glory as she led the sun across Solaria, with the eastern wall picked out in soft dawn colors, the middle bright like day, and the west shaded for sunset. The mosaic across three walls showcased the various major cities of Solaria from east to west on the continent. It was hundreds of years old, which meant it also depicted Rixham when it had once been a thriving city and not a prison for the dead.

The Ashionens all bowed or curtsied at his arrival, their formal attire not nearly as extravagant as their Daijalan counterparts. He could see the similarities in the tailoring of the clothes, though. Vanya wondered if that war up north had anything to do with it or if this particular group merely preferred a more subtle style. He knew the banking system in Ashion had split, resulting in disrupted capital and food shortages, and yet they persisted in their fight against Daijal.

"Your Imperial Majesty, may I introduce to you the Ashionen ambassador, Lord Dariush Zayed," Caelum said.

Vanya nodded at the ambassador as the *praetoria* legionnaires who'd followed them into the Mosaic Room settled themselves against the wall. Dariush was a tall man, perhaps a few years older than Vanya, with blue eyes that stood out against his tanned skin and brown hair. He held himself with a gravitas that Vanya could respect, considering the situation up north.

"Your Imperial Majesty," Dariush said in accented Solarian. "We thank you for agreeing to meet with myself and my diplomatic aides on behalf of Queen Caris Rourke and Ashion."

He spoke with an accent found in Karnak and had a fluency Vanya could appreciate. Whoever his teacher had been, they'd hailed from that city and been very good. Vanya had been prepared to conduct the meeting in Ashionen if need be, but any ambassador worth an auron would be fluent in the language of the country they'd come to do diplomatic business in. If he weren't, then their supposed queen was politically inept. "The Daijalan envoy has pressed upon the throne that you and your people do not speak for Ashion, Ambassador Zayed."

"You have been misinformed, Your Imperial Majesty. Daijal does not speak for Ashion. We speak for ourselves and always have."

"At least until the Inferno, perhaps." At the faint tightening of the other man's mouth, Vanya waved them in the direction of the formal seating arrangement that consisted of two leather sofas facing each other over a low, colorful glass table. "I speak nothing but the truth and mean no ill will by it. Your politics may not be ours, but I am aware of them for Solaria's sake."

"Then you must be aware of the threat Daijal poses to your country and others, especially after their attack on the Warden's Island."

More than they knew, though he'd never speak of such to foreigners. Vanya sat on one of the sofas, taking the folio that Caelum handed him, but didn't immediately open it. Caelum chose to stand behind the sofa and a little to Vanya's right, a clear indication that his Chief Minister didn't anticipate the meeting lasting long.

This was not the first time Vanya had been petitioned by the Ashionen envoy in Calhames to hear their entreaties, but it was the first time he'd agreed to speak with them. He knew such acceptance would give them false hope, but Vanya only meant to reiterate his country's stance.

"Solaria knows of the attack, and we sent aid once news reached us. Our engineers have been helping the wardens rebuild. Daijal has not officially targeted Solaria, and I will not send the Legion into a war that is not ours," Vanya said.

"Not officially means they haven't tried." Dariush wisely didn't reference the fighting in the northwest of Solaria, but that fact lingered between them. "What would it take for Solaria to give aid to Ashion? We could use ammunition and weapons, even if you won't order the Legion past the border."

A proxy war wasn't one Vanya thought he could push through the Senate without the Houses protesting. Too many of the Houses were against any effort to go to war or support Vanya's desires in that area. Guarding their northern border and going after Joelle had happened only in the aftermath of the Conclave when her betrayal had come to light. Eimarille's interference wasn't so easily proven, even with the *rionetkas* found inside their borders.

"Supporting a war outside our borders isn't something my government is willing to do. I know you have impressed your need upon senators and some minor Houses, but your situation is unfortunately not one we can commit an alliance to."

Dariush was a skilled enough ambassador to not show his disappointment, but Vanya knew the Ashionen did not like his answer. "My queen only thinks of her people, the same way you do. I cannot, in good conscience, return to her empty-handed. We ask for aid and supplies. Would you deny us a way to fight?"

"The Legion is already committed to the defense of Solaria. You are welcome to stay in Calhames and press your case to those senators who may have a sympathetic ear when it comes to supplies."

Ultimately, the final decision would be Vanya's, but he couldn't ignore the position of the Senate or the Houses, not if he wanted to keep hold of power. Even with the Dawn Star's blessing, he needed to take into consideration those opinions and positions of others who saw him as a rival. It was a balancing act that would have been far easier if he held support that was more freely given.

Dariush inclined his head, no hint of disappointment or frustration in his eyes or voice, ever the diplomat. "Thank you for your time, Your Imperial Majesty."

It wasn't the result the ambassador had hoped for, Vanya knew, but it was what was best for Solaria right now. Standing, he nodded farewell at the other man before leaving, a pair of *praetoria* legionnaires preceding him into the hallway.

"Has anyone answered their queen's request for aid?" Vanya asked once they were out of earshot.

"No. Urova has sided with Daijal in their war, and E'ridia has pulled back behind the Eastern Spine. They have no contact with the Tovan Isles as far as I am aware," Caelum replied.

Which placed Solaria as their one desperate hope for survival against an army of the living and the walking dead that was slowly grinding Ashion down. "If Ashion falls, Eimarille will not stop at any border."

Caelum glanced at him. "Your Imperial Majesty?"

"Summon a driver. I have a meeting with the commanding officers of the Legion."

Even if Solaria couldn't give aid, Vanya could ensure his country's borders were well guarded and the supply lines remained intact.

Four

SOREN

The start of Sixth Month brought clearer skies at the tail end of spring and a warmth that spoke of the oncoming summer. Soren was returning from the refractory for the second half of his shift at the telegraph machine when a warning siren cut through the air. The tone was pitched for revenants, but his head snapped up anyway, gaze skimming the partly cloudy blue sky for any oncoming airships. Soren didn't immediately see anything out of the ordinary, but he knew how quickly that could change.

Other wardens and tithes exited the surrounding buildings at a fast clip. Since the attack last summer, Delani had ordered all younger tithes to retreat to the laboratory entrance if they were within a certain range of it. Otherwise, they were supposed to find safety in several of the new bunkers that had been built at strategic points throughout the fort. The older tithes were assigned defense duties with wardens, and everyone knew the positions they needed to be at.

Soren sprinted across the grass for a narrow alley between two administrative buildings. That route took him to a street that had direct access to the wall. It was also where general-use velocycles were parked, and he wasn't the only warden flinging himself onto one of the two-wheeled vehicles. The length of the seat allowed for a passenger, and Soren only had to wait a handful of seconds before another warden vaulted up behind him.

"I'm heading to the western wall," Soren said as he kicked up the stand with his boot and revved the engine.

"I'm assigned to the north. I'll take the velocycle after you," she said.

Soren drove into the street, dirt churning beneath the velocycle's wheels. Other wardens fell in beside him as he drove toward the wall where automatons were already aiming Zip guns at the shoreline of the island. The deep sound of heavy-caliber bullets going off echoed in the air. The sirens kept sounding, but they never changed tone, which gave Soren hope the threat was only revenants and not Daijalan war machines.

Once they reached the wall, Soren braked to a halt by the stairs leading up to ramparts and one of the rebuilt defensive sentry towers. He pitched himself off the velocycle and let the other warden take over. She sped off before he even got his foot on the first step.

Soren took the stone steps up two at a time, coming up onto the ramparts just outside the tower with its grenade launcher. Spiderlike automatons clung to the ledge of the outer wall, their boxy bodies angled over the side to better aim the miniature Zip guns attached to their framework. When Soren looked down the length of the wall, he saw a sentinel-class automaton bracing itself, the warden inside the center space of its body manipulating the controls to raise its arms and aim two Zip guns at the shoreline.

Beyond the wall, revenants staggered out from the waters of the Celestial Lake and onto the blackened shore. The numbers were more than they'd normally see during the spring melt, and Soren wondered if any submersibles were in the water, waiting to attack. Turning away from the wall, he ducked into the sentry tower where the ranged defensive weaponry was kept. The tripod-mounted grenade launcher was manned by a warden who looked as if she might have been a tithe last season.

She grunted as she spun the handle to angle the grenade launcher at the beach, gears clanking together as she worked. "I'm Mara."

"Soren," he replied. "I'll load for you."

She jerked her head at the nearby crates filled with poison grenades. "Let's hit our targets."

Soren undid the latch with quick fingers. "Have you only seen revenants?"

"So far. That's not to say something worse isn't on the way."

Soren loaded grenades into the launcher while Mara adjusted the sights to aim at the shore. The release for the first volley was loud, the explosion that followed louder still. Soren didn't have any ear coverings, and the ringing that afflicted him after each launch was something he could only ignore. Right now, the defense of the island and the eradication of revenants was all that mattered.

The warning sirens never changed pitch, only sounding for revenants over the next hour as the wardens eradicated the threat with bullets, poison, and grenades. No return fire ever hit the fort's walls, and no airships or ground forces were ever seen in the sky or on the far shore. The threat this time around was normal in the grand scheme of things, even if the number of revenants blown to bits on the shore was double what they should be.

When the sirens blared the all clear, Soren rocked back on his heels where he crouched by the grenade launcher, eyeing the fully empty crate he'd kicked to the side and the one that was only half full. Mara had worked the grenade launcher with a deft hand, picking and choosing her targets to do the most damage.

Soren leaned toward the open window and peered out at the beach in the distance. The number of body parts strewn across the pockmarked sand was more than he could remember seeing in the past. "It's going to be a lot of bodies to burn."

Mara stood and placed her hands behind her hips, leaning backward to crack her spine. "If only we had that Ashion girl to burn them all for us."

Soren went still, gaze cutting back to Mara. "The one with starfire?"

Mara nodded, ignorant of the way Soren's heart rate sped up. "I was a tithe last year during the attack but old enough to get put on wall duty. Caris used starfire to incinerate all the revenants on the shore. It burned so hot some of the sand turned to glass. We're still finding pieces of it in the ground."

He turned away from the window in favor of completing inventory of their ordnance. "I heard she incinerated the entire beach."

"She casts starfire in a way I've heard people say hasn't been seen in generations outside Eimarille." Mara shrugged, cranking the grenade launcher back into its default position. "But I'm no magician, so who knows what's true in that regard? Still, having starfire to burn the dead would make cleanup go quicker."

Soren only nodded at that, fingers flexing as he sorted the crates and made a note on the logbook of what inventory was used. He'd complete the other column once he returned with the grenades to make the supply whole. He tried not to think about the casual way Mara spoke about starfire, skin prickling with a burn that he ruthlessly suppressed.

Wardens couldn't cast starfire, and Soren would always be a warden.

The aftermath of a revenant incursion on the island came with the interruption of regular tasks. Soren made his way to the underground munitions storage on the opposite side of the fort from the laboratories and then back to the sentry tower he'd stood guard duty at. He made the inventory whole for the next fight before leaving Mara to her watch duty for the rest of the afternoon. He joined other wardens past the walls on the shore to deal with what remained of the revenants.

The poison that had been used in defense of the fort wasn't dangerous to wardens who'd gone through the years of alchemy to gain immunity to the poisons and toxins native to Maricol. Tithes were restricted from the cleanup, none of them having made the full alchemic transition to the rank of warden.

Soren spent the afternoon with other wardens cleaning up their assigned segments of the shoreline, hauling the remains of revenants to the western burn pit for disposal. The smell of rotting bodies finally burning was the only reason he and other wardens put their gas masks on. The filters made the stench bearable as they canvassed the open areas of the island to ensure no bits of revenants remained.

By the time he and the other wardens re-entered the fort, the sun was low on the horizon, and everyone was hungry. They cleaned up at the public sinks near the gate before making their way to the refectory. Tithes had prepared a hearty meal of pan-fried noodles and beef, with a heaping of roasted bitter greens and slices of sourdough bread.

Soren carried his tray to a table in the middle of the large space, joining other wardens already there, all of them more focused on the food than conversation. He cleaned his plates and was nursing the dregs of his chai when the noise in the rectory faded to a murmur. Heads craned around to the door, and Soren looked that way as well, seeing Delani conversing with a knot of older wardens just past the entryway. She clasped a hand to one warden's shoulder before making her way to the nearest table to stand on the bench.

Every warden crammed together at the tables went silent without her needing to ask for their attention. Delani didn't need a voice amplifier to be heard in that quiet.

"A patrol around the Celestine Lake by boat and airship cleared the surrounding area of any enemy movement. Wherever these revenants came from, it was likely from a tributary, and they made their way to the island through the water since no one on watch duty saw movement on the shores," Delani said.

"Could they have been released by submersibles?" someone in the back called out.

"It's a possibility, but none of our depth charges were triggered, and our underwater patrols didn't see any. If they came from the rivers, we'll need to expand our patrols. With winter behind us, the land is more easily traversable now, and the revenants coming out of the war in Ashion will be more of a problem. Reports are coming back from the front line that the numbers of revenants are higher than they were last autumn."

"Both sides are taking losses, and dead soldiers are getting run through Daijal's death-defying machines before they can be burned.

We need to put a stop to that," someone down Soren's table said loudly.

"Any news on the locations of the death-defying machines?" another warden asked.

"We're still hunting for them in Ashion's western provinces, but Daijal is targeting wardens now. Even traveling through the back roads is risky with the troop movement happening."

Wardens still had borders to guard, land to cleanse. Those wardens who'd been recalled from Daijal and Urova had been assigned duties in Ashion to assist that country's army when it came to handling revenants in the battlefield. Eimarille saw it as an alliance even if the wardens did not.

Every war in Maricol's history always involved wardens. They were the ones to ensure the dead were burned, that every genealogy tag taken from a body was sent back to the cities and towns the fallen had once hailed from. Wardens might not have experience with fighting a war, but they certainly had experience with the aftermath.

"Because we anticipate the war escalating over summer, we're reassessing borders in Ashion around the poison fields. I know most of you have been waiting for your assignments, and I promise you'll get them in the next few days."

"What about Rixham and the Wastelands?" a young-sounding warden asked, most likely newly made within the last few months.

"Rixham's guard was doubled last year, and we've had no warnings from them about that border being at issue. The Wastelands remain as they always are, and the wardens on border duty there say they can handle what is being spawned in the red sands by the spores."

Delani stepped down from the bench. They all knew their duty, and Soren wanted to do his. He picked up his tray and returned it to the kitchen before hurrying to catch up with Delani. He wasn't the only one wanting to speak with her, but their conversation needed to be held in private. Delani must have agreed because as soon as she finished with the other wardens, she gestured at Soren. "Walk with me."

The breeze blowing through the air was cool but not cold, and

Soren's field uniform kept him warm enough. The gas lamp lights scattered in intervals down the street hadn't been switched on yet, but the setting sun still provided enough light to see by. Their boots crunched over gravel as Delani headed back to the cluster of administrative buildings rather than the barracks.

"Will you give me a border?" Soren asked after they'd put several buildings behind them on their way back to the governor's office.

"No," Delani said.

"Governor—"

She rounded on him, stepping close, single eye narrowing. "I need wardens here to protect the island and rebuild as much as I need them in the field. You've proven your priorities are not as strictly aligned as they need to be."

Soren's mouth went dry. "I am *loyal*."

"You interfered with a government when that is not our way," Delani said, voice low and hard. "I will not overlook your indiscretions nor your decisions."

"We wouldn't know about the death-defying machines or the *rionetkas* if I hadn't."

Delani stepped back, lips flattening in a hard line. "I'm sure the information would have come to light eventually, but that is beside the point."

"It *is* the point. Governor, I'm an able-bodied warden, and I want to be on the road."

"And I can't disregard the broken one behind you."

Soren lifted his chin, refusing to back down. "We all come from broken roads to be a warden."

Delani was quiet for a few seconds, taking his measure, and she must have still found him wanting, for she shook her head and turned away. "My previous order stands for you. As a warden, you will obey it."

Soren watched her leave, hands clenched into fists, feeling as if the fort was a prison he'd never be free of. Taking a breath, he spun on his feet and made his way back to the barracks. His shift at the telegraph machine had been interrupted by the incursion, but the hour meant the next shift would be taking over.

His room was only large enough to fit a narrow bed and a small dresser, with a weapons rack and a single shelf screwed to the wall. He undid his gun belt with its double holsters and hung it from a peg. The knife strapped to his thigh and the poison short sword secured over one shoulder soon followed.

Soren sat on the bed, the thin mattress sinking beneath his weight. After a moment, he pulled the vow from beneath his shirt and leather vest, staring down at the roaring lion head in profile pressed into the gold. He pressed the tiny button at the top, the face sliding open. Hidden inside was a smear of dried blood, Vanya's vow a promise Soren had carried for years.

He slipped his fingers beneath the top of his vest, sliding them into the inside pocket there and pulling out a folded piece of paper he went nowhere without. When he unfolded it, the ink and seal on the Imperial writ that acted as the Imperial emperor of Solaria's voice was as crisp and bright as when it had first been printed and signed.

Soren might not ever see Vanya again, but the pieces the other man had left behind were ones that Soren could never let go of. Perhaps things would be different if he could, if he'd never known Vanya's affection. But he had, and Soren couldn't pretend they didn't exist the same way he couldn't pretend his heart didn't hurt from Vanya's absence.

Being a warden meant being nameless and stateless, with no stars to guide them down a road that only followed Maricol's borders. Sitting there, holding memories in his hands, all Soren could think about was how much he missed Vanya's touch and how lonely this road was without him.

Five

CALLISTO

Callisto heard the desperate prayers meant for Aaralyn all the way in Solaria.

She paid them no mind until one slipped through, belief meant for the Dawn Star in their plea. She turned her face north, the sun high in the sky over the Southern Plains, her shadow barely a black halo around her feet. The travelers who'd died of thirst in the back roads from drinking out of a bog had already ended their road, guided into the stars by her helping hand.

She left the bodies behind, stepping into the aether and feeling it burn her from the inside out, like an all-consuming fever. The Dawn Star came back to herself in some other land, the prairie grass beneath her feet soaked in blood. She stood on the precipice of a deep trench, one that stretched quite a ways. She could see more dug into the earth behind huge, spiked iron balls meant to deter automatons and vehicles from advancing.

Soldiers hunkered down in the trench she stood over, most of them dead, but there was one who continued to load his rifle with shaky hands, face pale, uniform stained with blood that wasn't all his. He prayed as he reloaded, eyes glassy as he cranked the gears on his rifle to load another round.

"Please, Callisto," he begged around cracked lips, voice carrying an accent found in Ashion frontier towns that bordered Solaria. "Please let me live."

He was hers more than Aaralyn's in that moment. Callisto looked away from the soldier and across the battlefield at the advancing force led by sentinel-class automatons steered not by a human hand but by magic. Those automatons could go where humans couldn't, driven forward by the command of a magician held safe behind the battalion. Callisto watched it approach with dispassionate eyes. Her ears filled with prayers of the dying and the living and the ones who were almost dead, like the young man who clambered up the side of the trench to throw himself against the edge.

He took aim, the last of his squadron to do so, desperate to hold a broken line. Callisto stood witness to the bullets the Ashionen soldier got off before a grenade launched by the sentinel-class automaton landed within the trench. He tried to climb out, to get clear, but the resulting blast flung him past Callisto and onto the bloody battlefield, back ripped to pieces from the explosion.

The Daijalan soldiers in their green uniforms kept advancing, but Callisto ignored them and went to kneel beside the young soldier. He looked at her, through her, with glazed-over eyes, a prayer fading on his lips.

Please.

"I hear you, child," Callisto said.

She drew his soul out of skin and bones, sending the ghost of him into the sky and the stars that shone beyond the brightness of the sun. The aether in her own veins burned in solidarity as he faded to nothing. Callisto curled her fingers against her palm and drew her hand away from the body.

Shouts reached her ears, and Callisto looked over her shoulder at the encroaching enemy line. The lead automaton came inexorably forward, its mechanical gears grinding and clanking together. Callisto straightened, striding down the length of the trench, bullets passing her by as dirt rose around her from another grenade hit.

"She doesn't hear them, you know," a deep voice said from behind her. "She never comes for them."

Callisto rocked to a stop, reaching up with one hand to touch the Lion constellation tattoo wrapped around her throat. The heat of the golden lines always was a comfort amidst the surrounding death. "That is where you are wrong, brother. Aaralyn hears them; she merely chooses who to listen to."

"You would listen to them all. One prayer brought you out of Solaria."

Callisto narrowed her eyes before turning around to face her brother, the Midnight Star dressed in the clothes of a Urovan, thick arms crossed over his broad chest. The sleeves of his shirt were rolled up to his elbows, revealing the golden lines of the Bear constellation tattoo that crawled over the back of his hands and fingers and up his forearms.

Xaxis had always been the most intimidating of their group, but his broad form and bearded visage hid a quiet gentleness few were ever privy to. Urova was a harsh land during the long winter months where the midnight sun never set and the cold was deadly. But his children had made it a home, and they worshipped him as a part of their way of life.

And now that way of life included war.

Explosions nearby that sent dirt and grass high into the air would have deafened anyone but them. Callisto barely noticed it, nor the dirt that fell like rain around them. "I hear my children's prayers no matter where they walk. Aaralyn has her reasons for the ones she answers and the ones she must leave by the wayside."

"She did the same during the Inferno." Xaxis tilted his head to the side, studying her. "I hear you stole a prince."

Callisto shrugged. "I stole nothing not freely given. I hear you delivered a Blade to the princess Innes claimed."

"I'm not here to compare our mistakes."

"I don't consider helping our children a mistake." Callisto jerked her head at the trenches and the dead resting at the bottom of them. "I consider this war Innes crafted the wrong road."

Xaxis followed her gaze, his dark eyes taking in the battlefield. The prayers rising from the earth and metal war machines went unanswered in the face of Innes' desire to find a way back to the stars they had all left behind Ages ago.

"He is tired of never dying."

Callisto snorted at that. "We all died once, and we keep being reborn. Innes is not the only one who yearns to dance amongst the stars like our children when they reach the end of their roads. But we have our own roads, and they are never-ending. We swore we would walk them together, and now he seeks to tear us all apart. You aid him in that."

Xaxis lifted a hand to stroke his fingers over the neatly trimmed beard that shadowed his features. He hadn't yet shaved off the mark of winter, but she knew he would in due time. "He means well."

At that, Callisto made a gesture with her hand, the movement of her fingers an insult of some kind, but she'd forgotten the meaning millennia ago. "He means to dictate progress through his children. Urova is not safe from his desires. You should know that by now."

"Is it so wrong to want a different road?"

"And if his want kills our children? What then?"

"Then perhaps that is progress."

Callisto snorted derisively and looked up at the haze of smoke stretched across the blue sky. "Progress won't change the road we walk. You know that."

Because Maricol was their home and their grave. They'd walked the land and sailed the seas and taught their children how to survive in this world that had saved them so long ago. They'd made a promise through the Ages to keep their feet on the earth and leave the stars alone.

"This war will end in some fashion. I will listen to the prayers that ask for my guidance," Xaxis eventually said.

"When your people pray for deliverance from Daijal's interference, you will know why Aaralyn only listens to some prayers."

Xaxis inclined his head in her direction before the constellation tattoos bled gold and consumed him in starfire, the aether drawing him to some other place. Callisto eyed where her brother once stood before staying to watch the battle through, listening to prayers not meant for her but guiding those with broken roads to the stars anyway in the North Star's absence.

Six

JOELLE

Bellingham was a city surrounded by war, but the sound of it never quite made it through the walls of the House of Kimathi's grand estate. Spring, however, had, and the flowers blooming on the vines and trees lovingly tended throughout the estate lent the air a perfumed scent. The inner courtyard meant for the House's private use was adorned with so many blossoms it rivaled the gardens that once existed in the old Imperial palace grounds.

Vezir Joelle, head of the House of Kimathi, sipped her tea in relative silence as she watched her daughter read through the reports she herself had already reviewed the night before. Karima's dark head was bent over the sheaves of paper, brow furrowed as she studied the latest news from their *vasilyet*'s borders.

"We've lost ground," Karima said when she finished, leaning back in her seat. The low table between them had been cleared of the late-morning meal some time ago, with only the tea tray remaining. The sun shining down on the courtyard had migrated closer to where their table sat beneath the branches of a potted tree.

"Some," Joelle conceded. "The general of our army assures me it is nothing to worry about."

Karima pursed her lips, the motion deepening the lines that bracketed the corners of her mouth. She was dressed in a white-and-gold gown offset by gold and opal jewelry today, her dark hair twisted up in an elaborate style picked through with diamond-encrusted pins. As with Joelle, Karima dressed as if she were royalty, reinforcing the image of their rule. "I find that difficult to believe, Mother."

Joelle set her teacup on the table, the knuckles on that hand throbbing faintly from gripping the delicate handle. She'd taken the salve and potion for the aches in her joints with food, but it hadn't yet carved out the pain she lived with. Her House's healer was worried about her becoming resistant to such relief, and at her age and position, there was only so much medicine she could afford to take. Part of that was the side effects and potency of such medications; the rest of it was not wanting to risk being addled when someone attempted to kill her.

For a time, she'd weathered such potential threats from her daughter. Karima had never been pleased with her right as heir being usurped by Artyom while mourning her daughter, Nicca. She'd ultimately not acted on such desire, and while Karima still grieved for her daughter, she'd seen what such devastating depression could cost her. She'd mourned Artyom strictly during the official mourning period and no longer than that.

Karima was intent on retaking her rightful spot to succeed her mother. To that end, Joelle no longer believed Karima was plotting against her now that Artyom was dead. The ache of losing her son left her with melancholy thoughts at night and when she prayed at the memory wall that held Artyom's name. But Joelle had not survived and come so close to reclaiming her House's rightful place on the Imperial throne by being someone who let emotion control her.

Joelle had plenty of family members to choose an heir from, but the road to the Imperial throne ran through Karima, for Nicca had born Raiah. Artyom's children had as much right to Joelle's title of *vezir* but less so to the Imperial throne at this time. And so Joelle had gone back to her daughter and left Artyom's widow and children by the wayside. These days, Karima accompanied her to every meeting about the war come to their *vasilyet*'s borders.

Karima wasn't the only one present in those moments. Joelle's gaze cut briefly to the Blade who stood in the corner, ever silent and watchful. Daijal's support for their House's endeavors ran through Joelle, kept in check by a pair of Blades who'd set up residence in their household last Twelfth Month. She chafed at the oversight but went along with it because pretending to bow to someone else and toeing the line hopefully meant less intrusion. Besides, Joelle had other ways to pursue her own plans.

For all her supposed power, Eimarille's attention and army were tied up in Ashion despite the support sent to Joelle's *vasilyet*. Joelle knew Eimarille viewed the fight in Solaria as a distraction to Vanya, to keep him focused on his own people and not give in to the begging of Ashion envoys. The Legion guarded the long northern border and skirmished with Daijalan war machines in the northwest amidst thousands of revenants roaming the poison fields and back roads.

Vanya had not yet authorized aerial bombardment of Bellingham, and Joelle doubted he would. She knew he did not want to be viewed like his mother and make the same mistakes that had turned Rixham into a dead city. Killing innocent civilians in an attempt to claw back a *vasilyet* and punish a House wouldn't play well with all the rest of the Houses who had backed him in the Conclave.

In the aftermath of her House being named a traitor by Vanya, Joelle had refused to return to a fold she no longer believed in. The House of Kimathi stood alone as a rallying point for what was coming. If Vanya could not see his rule would end in ruin, then Joelle would wait out his inevitable fall.

"Eimarille is shipping down another death-defying machine to one of the towns on our side of the border. She's emptying the POW camp outside of Istal to provide more bodies for it. The revenants it produces will be deployed within range of the Legion battalions harassing our border," Joelle said.

"And what of our soldiers?" Karima asked.

"Their use of the sentinel-class automatons is what keeps them safe. Trust the generals in charge of war. They know what they are doing."

Especially since the defected Solarian general deployed in the field on their side was a *rionetka* loyal to Joelle and no longer under Eimarille's control. Where that general led, many of the legionnaires under his command had followed. Vanya had yet to push the full might of the Legion against her defected army backed by Daijal weapons and magic. Whenever he did, Eimarille had promised to divide his attention further. The Legion would be handled.

For now, Joelle had to handle her own matters.

The meeting with Karima lasted another hour before she sent her daughter off with political aides for the interview with reporters that would appear in the evening edition of the only broadsheet printing in Bellingham. Propaganda was an important part of keeping power that Joelle never let fall by the wayside. Letting Karima dance those steps at Joelle's direction meant she could control the narrative.

The Blade did not follow either of them when they left the parlor, but Joelle didn't trust the assassin's prying eyes. Neither did she appreciate needing to skulk about her own home, but she'd yet to figure out how to remove the Blades without it getting back to Eimarille.

Her handmaidens escorted her to her bedroom, opting to use the small lift to spare Joelle's knees. She'd taken to napping through the midday hours, needing the rest but also the privacy it allotted her. The Blades never watched her sleep.

When the door closed behind her, her youngest handmaiden opened the closet door and pushed aside the numerous gowns and robes hanging there. The intricately tiled walls hid a narrow door in the corner. The hinges were always oiled and made no sound when the handmaiden used the key Joelle gave her to unlock the door and push it open.

One of her handmaidens was already slipping beneath the covers of Joelle's bed, a wig in place that mirrored Joelle's current hairstyle. The body double was a precaution she'd utilized off and on throughout the years. The rest of her handmaidens ranged themselves around the room to await her return.

"This way, my lady," the handmaiden in the closet said in a low voice.

Joelle took the offered hand and let the other woman guide her into the hidden, narrow spiral staircase built between walls and floors that led underground. The estate boasted several such hidden passages, some meant to exit the estate entirely. This one led to the estate's cellar, a place only the servants ever really accessed except in moments like this. Whether or not the Blades knew of it didn't matter so long as her secret meetings with her own spies were never uncovered.

Joelle stepped out of the narrow stairwell into dimly lit darkness, the cellar only having one other exit that led to the servants' and kitchen areas of the estate. The spies loyal to her House knew how to enter the estate dressed as servants and were always listed on the duty roster under an alias. They went through the physical checks for *rionetkas* that everyone else did and another check by a magician with an affinity for mind magic. So Joelle knew that the young man with a forgettable face was no threat. Even if he was, the starfire she coaxed into existence at the tips of her fingers was enough to make most people hesitate.

She didn't have Vanya's strength, but starfire ran in her bloodline and through her House. Nicca hadn't been able to cast it, but she'd passed it on to Raiah through her blood. Joelle's great-granddaughter was the culmination of all her efforts to reach the Imperial throne in her lifetime, and yet, she'd never properly met the girl. It galled her to know that part of her House was out of reach.

But hopefully not for much longer.

"*Vezir* Joelle," the spy said with a deep bow, keeping his voice low.

"What news have you of the warden?" Joelle asked.

"Soren hasn't left the Warden's Island. The governor still hasn't assigned him a border, and my contact embedded in the construction crew says it's unlikely she will anytime soon."

Joelle frowned. "Why not?"

"Punishment, perhaps. Some of the other wardens know he was the emperor's lover for a time. Not many are pleased about that."

None in the Houses appreciated that relationship either, considering it was Vanya's ill-fated decision to let the warden be privy to the funeral rites of the royal dead that had seen Solaria hit with sanctions.

What no House knew—what she didn't believe Eimarille even knew—was that Soren was most likely the long-thought-dead Ashion prince. Joelle's suspicions had taken root ever since the destruction of the quarry where the first death-defying machine had been hidden. While Soren had not once shown hints of being able to cast starfire, what clues Joelle had gathered pointed to such a likelihood.

While Caris Rourke was beyond her reach, the warden was entirely different. No one knew of his possible bloodline, and if Joelle had him in her grasp, she'd be able to threaten both Vanya and Eimarille. Keeping the warden alive could force both royals' hands to pay Joelle's price as she pitted them against each other—Vanya to save his lover and Eimarille to ensure her brother died so she could secure her claim to the starfire throne.

All of Joelle's plans for blackmail rested on getting control of the warden, but extracting one from their island was near impossible these days and had been even before Eimarille approved the attack on them last year. Even Joelle had been taken aback at that decision when word had reached Bellingham. It had made her rethink how she dealt with the Daijalan queen.

"Construction is still ongoing?" Joelle asked.

The spy nodded. "The crews will stay through at least the end of summer. Things might change depending on how the war goes and if Daijal is successful in annexing Ashion."

"Keep your contact on the island, and stay close yourself. The moment Soren is given a border to guard, I want to know where."

The spy sketched a shallow bow. "Of course, *vezir*."

Joelle snuffed out the sparks of starfire and turned away, heading back the way she'd come through the secret passageway. Her handmaiden ensured the door behind them was securely locked before following her up the stairs and back to her room where nothing was amiss.

"All is well, *vezir?*" the handmaiden who stood guard at the doorway of the closet asked.

"Yes," Joelle replied, thinking about how, someday soon, she would have what her House deserved.

Seven

CARIS

Caris resisted the urge to pinch her nose in frustration and grief as she stared at the tally of the dead and the list of cities and towns that had fallen to Daijal when the front lines had gained ground east. One of the cities had held a production plant, and now it was nothing but rubble, according to the tintype photograph someone had smuggled out with them during the retreat. She picked up the tintype, studying the smudge of shadows on it that had once been a building.

"We can't afford to lose another production line, to say nothing of the people who die for our cause," Caris said into the quiet that had settled over the table after General Clarence Votil finished delivering his report. "Have any of our envoys brought back news of an alliance?"

Meleri shook her head, expression rigidly neutral. "Unfortunately, no. Both E'ridia and Solaria have rebuffed our requests for an alliance or purchase of supplies."

Caris set aside the tintype photograph. "They won't take our aurons?"

"I believe the worry is they aren't sure where the funding would come from."

She could understand why another country would be concerned

about how payment would be enacted. The Ashion banking system had gone through an upheaval at the start of the war, breaking away from the banks in Daijal and reallocating capital amongst them. Bloodlines and companies had helped set an example by not making a run on the banks, but there was only so much cash circulating at the moment.

The bloodlines themselves weren't exactly giving a full-throated defense of Caris' claimed position. She knew that calling herself Rourke without proof would only take her so far. Being able to cast starfire wasn't enough in the long run. The bloodlines of Ashion were split in their support, and the geographical lines weren't easily cut.

Some bloodlines in the eastern province had refused Caris' overtures, aligning themselves with Daijal. Other bloodlines in the western provinces had never taken to Daijal's propaganda and were steadfast in their support of Caris and Ashion. Knowing who was friend and who was foe was a delicate political dance Caris knew she'd made missteps in. Even with Meleri's teachings and backing, it was difficult for Caris to feel like she was a queen.

"Have our envoys keep asking to be heard," Caris said, looking up from the reports and maps scattered across the table. Too many eyes stared back at her as if she held all the answers, and she tried not to flinch at the attention. "Perhaps Solaria and E'ridia will come around in time."

"And if they don't?" Lore asked from her seat to Caris' right.

"I am not Eimarille. I won't interfere with another country's decisions."

Blaine and Honovi weren't sitting in on this meeting, though they were still present in Cosian. The pair had reported to her the sinister machinations Eimarille had employed to try to destabilize their government. *Rionetkas* in high political positions was a chilling threat E'ridia was already facing. News out of Solaria came through a chokehold these days, but Caris was certain the Imperial throne had faced the same enemy.

"We can't rely on others to give us aid. We must continue as if we are alone," Meleri said.

"Which we are," Clarence agreed grimly. "We have no allies, despite every overture we can think of. I don't know what good our diplomats can do if they keep getting the same answer with every request. Daijal keeps pushing the front line closer to us. If we can't keep our production up, if we can't recruit more soldiers, we'll be overrun before the end of summer."

"How is recruiting going? Is there anything I can do?" Caris asked.

Clarence smiled briefly at her, but it seemed strained. "You have done more than enough, Your Royal Majesty."

She'd sat for press interviews and photographs used in recruitment and propaganda posters that were put up in every city and town throughout Ashion. Her face was plastered everywhere, her words a rallying cry for her people, but it all seemed so meaningless in the face of the losses they were sustaining. Caris hated that so many people were willing to die in her name for a freedom that Daijal was trying to steal.

"We may need to rethink our objective. If our timeframe has shrunk, perhaps we shouldn't wait for the fight to come to us," Meleri said.

"We don't have the capacity to bring the fight to Daijal and win," Clarence reluctantly said. He wasn't one to provide false optimism, something Caris appreciated, but it was still disheartening to know the general was doing his best to win this war and it wasn't good enough.

"I'm not talking about Daijal." Meleri looked across the table at Caris. "I'm talking about Amari."

Caris stiffened even as others around the table muttered amongst themselves. She thought of the broadsheet she'd opened the other day with a photograph of her parents splashed across the front page. The news story had reported on their transfer back to Amari for an eventual trial that everyone knew would be a sham.

She'd cried when she'd seen the photograph, Nathaniel barely able to console her. Her parents were alive but prisoners of war. Caris would always wonder if she'd made different choices, if she'd taken a different road, if her parents would be with her right now, seated at this table.

"Amari is a deathtrap. We'd have to push through the front, and our losses would be twice what they are now once Daijal realized our intention. Daijal would throw everything they had at our forces and decimate us. Amari is off the table right now," Clarence said.

"Amari holds the starfire throne. If we can get Caris inside the city, she could claim her birthright, and it would be enough to stop this war."

"You don't know that," Caris said, drawing everyone's attention. "Do you really think Eimarille will bow to me? She doesn't believe we're sisters or that my claim to the Rourke bloodline is valid."

Even with Blaine returned to her and his memories of carrying her out of Amari, Caris knew it still wouldn't be enough for those people who believed Eimarille's truth. Him standing as witness wouldn't change the minds of people who didn't see her as queen.

"My dear, if you put out the North Star's decree, then no one would have the right to question your claim to the throne."

"That's a fairly optimistic view, Mother," Lore said evenly. "We all know Eimarille would undermine Caris' rule. The Inferno happened because the Iverson bloodline sought to eradicate anyone who might have a single claim to royal power who wasn't Eimarille. Bernard knew what he was doing when he gained her as his ward in the aftermath of so much murder. Better every claimant dead than a country split between two queens. That's what Eimarille is trying to do here."

"All the more reason to try for Amari," Meleri persisted.

"You're asking to reset the battlefield. It's not that easy," Clarence argued.

"There won't be a battlefield left to worry about if we're all *dead*. If you're concerned about breaching the city walls, we can enter through the catacombs and bypass their defenses."

Clarence barked out a harsh, disbelieving laugh. "We'd need to fight our way for months through Daijalan forces and war machines to reach the capital. It'd be a suicide push."

"What if we split Eimarille's attention?" Caris asked.

Meleri snapped her teeth together on whatever she was going to say to the general. "Pardon?"

"Eimarille is pitting all her forces against us in Ashion. So, what if we attack somewhere else that isn't the front lines? Get her army to split their focus."

"We have no way to reposition our army and supply lines without them knowing and countering," Clarence said.

Caris shrugged, clutching her hands together on the table. "I wasn't talking about our land forces. What about asking the Tovan Isles for help? We haven't tried sending an envoy to that country yet."

"Because we haven't any ships and no ports to meet them at. Their ambassadors always came to us in our capital," Lore said.

"Surely we sent our own to Port Avi?"

"Not for a decade at least. The Ashion parliament ceded that right to Daijal."

"If we reached out to them through diplomatic channels via another country, it might buy us some time before Eimarille found out," Caris said.

Lore hummed thoughtfully. "As far as distractions would go, an attack on New Haven would certainly catch Eimarille's attention and split the Daijal army's focus."

Clarence stared at them in disbelief. "An attack on Daijal's capital would require far more coordination between countries than we currently have, not to mention the cost and logistics of such an endeavor."

Caris spread her hands. "But it would be a distraction."

"Of a magnitude that we would pay in blood with. I wouldn't even think about moving battalions unless ink was drying on an alliance treaty. Aside from that, we'd have to move our people through Solaria to reach the Gulf of Helia if we were to get land forces on the Tovanians' ship-cities. I am doubtful the Imperial emperor would approve of such staging, not to mention it would tip off Daijal as to what our plan was."

"It's a viable option," Meleri said.

"It's suicide without an alliance."

Caris listened to them argue back and forth for a moment before she raised a hand, catching their attention. "Attacking New Haven should be an option, and so should freeing Amari. If not right now, then later. It's something we should instruct our envoys in Solaria to ask about."

Clarence shook his head. "I would counsel against that."

"Then if we persist on trying to hold an ever-moving line, we need to have a backup plan."

"If you're worried about your extraction from Cosian in the event of a full-frontal attack—"

"I'm not," Caris said sharply. "But my status is the issue I want to discuss. If you would be so kind as to assess who has the highest security classification for this conversation, then please do so."

Clarence narrowed his eyes while Meleri looked slightly alarmed. Caris ignored the duchess' attempts to catch her eye, turning her head to watch as Clarence ordered officers away from the table with a sharp wave of his hand. They filed out, some appearing disgruntled by the order. By the time the door closed, the only ones at the table with her were the Auclairs, Clarence, and Colonel Taiwo Esina, recently back from the front bearing many of the reports scattered on the table between them.

"We are doing everything in our power to keep you safe, Caris," Meleri said.

Caris tried not to hunch her shoulders. "Yes, by keeping me in Cosian."

"It's for your own protection."

"It makes me feel like a prisoner and a sitting target." Caris drew in a deep breath and lifted her chin, meeting Meleri's gaze. "I think it's time I met my brother."

"No." Meleri's refusal was automatic and fierce.

"*Yes.*" When Meleri opened her mouth to argue, Caris cut her off. "This isn't up for discussion. I am going to the Warden's Island. If anything happens to me, Ashion will need someone else to take up the claim to the Rourke bloodline and the starfire throne and fight against Eimarille."

"He is a warden. My understanding is he refuses to be anything else. Trying to convince him otherwise is a wasted effort. It will only make him and the wardens a target, and they have suffered enough."

"Are you worried for the wardens or worried about Alasandair having a right to the starfire throne that supersedes mine?"

Meleri pressed her lips into a thin line before raising her chin. "There is no witness to his claim."

"Blaine says the resemblance to me is uncanny. We take after our birth father that way, while Eimarille looks like Ophelia."

Caris had never quite looked like Portia or Emmitt, but their coloring was close enough no one ever questioned it as she grew up. They'd loved her so much, doted on her without question, that she had never thought differently.

"Appearances are meaningless. He can say he's Prince Alasandair Rourke all he likes, but he has no claim to it, not like you."

"Some say I don't have any claim."

"Caris—"

"You want to put me on the throne by risking the lives of every soldier in our army. You want to lay siege to a city that Daijal has controlled for my entire life. All that risk just to put me on a throne you don't know if I can take. How many have tried to sit on the starfire throne and died for it?"

"None of them were Rourke."

"And if I die, you still need one." Caris leaned forward, pressing her hands flat against the table as she stared Meleri down, Lore and the officers quiet and still in their seats. "Am I to be your queen or your puppet? Would you have me be nothing better than a *rionetka* for your dreams?"

Meleri flinched, the flush of angry determination washing out to a sickly white. "Caris, I never meant—"

"You never meant a lot of things while I was your ward and your cog, and I have forgiven you for that. But if you want me as your queen, then you need to treat me as such. I am the age of majority in Ashion, and I am *tired* of people trying to bend my road to theirs."

Silence settled between them, and Caris pushed her fingertips against the wooden tabletop to keep her hands from shaking. Meleri looked away, gaze momentarily downcast, something like shame in her voice when she finally spoke. "I only want you safe, my queen."

Caris briefly closed her eyes at the honorific before opening them again. "We're at war for our country, not for me. If Ashion is to survive, then we must bring Alasandair on board."

Meleri bowed her head at that and said nothing, but she didn't argue Caris' point again. Letting out a soft breath, Caris looked at Clarence, who gave her a slow nod back.

"If you need an airship, the army will provide you with one," he said.

"You need those airships for the war. Blaine and Honovi have agreed to fly me to the Warden's Island."

"I'll be going with you," Lore said.

Caris managed a smile for the other woman. "I would expect nothing else."

Meleri cleared her throat, drawing Caris' attention. "We'll need to prepare an announcement, then. I'll work on that while you're traveling."

It was a peace offering of sorts, an acknowledgment that Meleri would follow Caris' commands in this moment. "Thank you."

Clarence tapped his finger against the table. "With this sorted, let's bring in the others again and continue our work."

Caris didn't argue that request and settled back in her seat, getting as comfortable as she could for the work ahead.

Eight

NATHANIEL

"Nathaniel."

Nathaniel looked up from stirring jam into his tea, watching Caris enter the formal dining room. The sweetness from the berries went well with the floral notes of the drink, and using the jam helped stretch the household's sugar supplies. Sugar was rationed, and he, like Caris, had donated their additional shares to the nurses, doctors, and healers manning the pair of hospitals within Cosian.

"Is it time to depart?" Nathaniel asked, setting the teaspoon aside.

Caris quirked a smile at him, her dark hair loose and falling to her shoulders. It was short enough that she'd have no trouble tucking it under a leather flight helmet. Her trousers were tailored for a tighter fit, and her blouse was long-sleeved despite the warmth outside, corset belt cinched tight around her thin waist.

"Honovi said the *Celestial Sprite* will launch at noon. Maurus is seeing to our travel trunks and the motor carriages. He said he would retrieve us when they were ready."

"Where's Lore?"

"With the duchess. She left before breakfast but said she'll meet us at the airfield." Caris tilted her head a little, studying him. "What's wrong?"

"I don't know what good will come of me traveling with you to the Warden's Island. You can't speak of any strategy around me. I feel I would only be a threat."

He tried not to sound bitter, for he knew why the precautions were taken by everyone else where he was concerned. But Nathaniel wanted desperately to be of use, to fight, to be something more than the burden it felt like he was.

Caris came to him on quick feet, her boots making no sound on the soft rug spread beneath the dining table. The colors in the rug weren't as vibrant as they'd once been, but it still paired well with the orange and gold wallpaper accents of the room. It made the space feel warm and inviting, cozy for the small Dhemlan family that had lived here over the years.

Caris took the chair beside his at the table, angling it so she faced him rather than the empty room. "I want you with me, for however long I have you."

Nathaniel reached for her hand, fingers tightening around hers. He drew her hand to his mouth, pressing and holding a kiss to her fingers. She stared at him, her gray eyes wide and trusting, and the love in her gaze was something he didn't know if he deserved, not after what he'd done and what he'd become.

They both knew the clockwork metal heart that beat in his chest, powered by alchemy and magic, was the only reason he was alive. His mind couldn't be trusted, and Nathaniel woke up from nightmares every week about the potential treachery he could inflict on those he cared about.

"You have me," Nathaniel promised.

"Then never doubt you belong by my side." She tugged her hand free and pressed it against his chest, over his shirt and waistcoat, all his scars hidden by the clothes he wore. "You've suffered more than any of us, and I won't have anyone blaming you for something that was not your fault."

Nathaniel covered her hand with his, breathing in deeply. He'd lost his family, then his heart and his free will. He had no hope his parents and siblings were alive, not after the seizure of their company and their arrest by debt collectors for the crime of aiding and abetting the Clockwork Brigade. Last he'd heard, they'd been shipped west, and he knew what happened to prisoners of war.

"I can provide nothing to this war. I'm no soldier, and what aid my company once offered was stolen from us."

All the steam trains the Clementine Trading Company once owned and operated had been seized and repurposed for Daijal's needs. He couldn't even be sure any of their employees had escaped the punishment given his family. He hoped they had, for he wouldn't wish that horror on anyone. He knew what it was like to be a dead man walking.

Caris' expression softened, and she shifted on the chair, her knee brushing his. The closeness they indulged in certainly would not have been allowed under the norms of high society. If this war had never happened, Caris' parents would be seated at the table with them, and they wouldn't be so overtly affectionate.

Lore had long since allowed them their privacy, affecting the role of chaperone less and less these days. Caris was of majority age, and while she might be Rourke and Ashion's queen, Nathaniel had fallen for her when she'd been an engineering student with a bright future ahead of her with her bloodline's company, Six Point Mechanics. Her rank as a baroness had never bothered him, but her being queen made him question what he wanted for her own safety and not his own heart—what was left of it.

"Nathaniel," Caris said, never looking away. "You are important to me. I care about you dearly, and my love for you will never be in question."

"Some say it should be."

Her lips twisted sadly, grief flickering across her gray eyes. "Then they are wrong."

Some part of him would always believe the detractors who looked at him askance, who would never trust him with information much less Caris' life. Maurus had become resigned to letting him be in Caris' presence, but he knew the captain of the Royal Guard would put a bullet through his heart if he thought Nathaniel would harm Caris again.

Nathaniel would welcome it if that horror ever came to pass again.

He pulled her hand away from his chest and held it in both of his. Her fingers were bare of rings, and the only one he'd ever given her hung around her neck. Before everything that led up to the riot in Amari last summer and what came after, he'd held fast to the hope of one day offering her an engagement ring and taking her name.

But that was when he thought he'd be the man who could stand whole and devoted beside her, without questioning if his mind was his own or if the next breath he took would be his last.

His desire for intimacy in the bedroom had fallen by the wayside, unwilling to show the scars he now lived with to anyone, even himself. Nathaniel could not look at his reflection in a mirror and refused for a valet to aid him in dressing until his shirt was buttoned up first.

Caris had never seemed to mind that they did nothing more than kiss, enjoying simply being with him, which was a grace Nathaniel hadn't expected. But Caris never initiated anything more than the kisses they shared or the quiet moments when they held each other. She'd confessed, once, that she'd never desired what came with the marriage bed, but she desired him, loved him, even, in her own way, and Nathaniel could not deny her his heart.

"You are the kindest person I know," Nathaniel said, voice a little rough.

She framed his face with her hands, leaning in to kiss him softly on the mouth. "You flatter me."

"I speak nothing but the truth."

She smiled, gaze softening. "So that means you'll not argue about joining me for the journey to the Warden's Island?"

"So long as you keep me ignorant of any information I should not be privy to. I know I'm not the only reason why you want to return there."

"Ksenia made it clear during our last communications that she wants to run further tests on you, but no, you aren't the only reason I'm going."

"Don't tell me secrets that will endanger you," he warned.

She reached up to tug on one of her curls before resting her elbow on the table and slouching a little. "I never wanted to be queen. That's not a secret. I wanted to be an engineer."

"You still are."

"Yes, but now I'm this living banner for Ashion to rally behind, and I hate that people are dying for me. I don't want their deaths to be wasted if something happens to me."

He knew of the assassination attempts directed at him, of the Blades stopped by soldiers and magicians, sometimes at great cost to the Royal Guard. The home they shared was heavily guarded, the streets surrounding their block restricted. Caris' survival was integral to Ashion remaining an independent country. Without her, the push for freedom from Daijal and that country's terrible laws that favored debt bondage would crumble. "The people would fight in your memory."

Her mouth drew down at the corners, something bitter in the twist of her lips. "I won't be a martyr. If Eimarille's Blades ever do reach me, I don't want people to fight for a memory when there is a perfectly acceptable Rourke waiting in the shadows."

Nathaniel shook his head, staring at her beseechingly. "My darling, you shouldn't speak of such things to me."

"I won't treat you as other," she replied fiercely. "I won't treat you as less or be fearful of some *what-if* scenario. People will find out soon enough that Eimarille and I have a brother. It makes no sense to keep you in the dark when that is the whole reason I'm flying to the Warden's Island."

He opened his mouth but couldn't quite find the words. After a moment, he reached for his teacup and took a hefty swallow of the cooling liquid. "Prince Alasandair is alive?"

"The star gods gave us all different roads to walk." She looked away, a pensive expression in her eyes. "I always wondered what it would be like to have a sibling when I was growing up."

Nathaniel set his teacup aside and covered her hand on the table with his. He was fearful of the information she'd revealed somehow being used wrongly by him. If she was certain the news wouldn't be a secret for much longer, Nathaniel was glad to know it so he could be there for her. "I'm certain he must be far kinder than Eimarille."

Caris shrugged one shoulder, gaze cutting back to him. "Alasandair is a warden. He goes by a different name and refuses to claim the Rourke bloodline."

"So you're flying there to try to convince him to join your cause?"

"I can be persuasive."

It was a trait she was becoming more deft at, but Nathaniel hoped she never lost her kindness to the pitfalls of politics. "If he wanted to rule, would you cede him the crown?"

"If I thought he would be better for Ashion than me, I wouldn't hesitate to step aside. I…" She trailed off, pressing her lips together. When she spoke again, her voice came out a little rough, as if she were trying to hold back tears. "I wanted a life with you that wasn't this, but I have you, and I will not regret that. I just hope that if I must take the throne, you will stand with me."

Nathaniel pushed his chair back away from the table and knelt before her, taking both her hands in his again. He looked up at Caris, knowing that the love he felt for her was something that could never be carved out of him the way his heart had been.

"I will walk your road with you until the end. Even if there are days I'm not with you, know that it is not because I refused to be but because I couldn't be. My darling Caris, I promised to love you until my heart breaks, and this life with you is the only one I have ever wanted."

Caris blinked, tears falling from her eyes that she didn't bother to wipe away. "I'll fix your heart first."

He laughed, rising up to kiss her. "You already have. I would be so much less a man without you."

Someone cleared their throat, and Nathaniel broke the kiss, straightening up. Maurus stood in the entryway to the dining room, a politely indifferent expression on his face. "The motor carriages await."

Caris discreetly wiped the tears off her cheeks with the back of her hand. "We're ready."

Nathaniel drew her to her feet and offered his arm, which she gracefully accepted. Maurus led the way out of the estate, and Nathaniel kept Caris tucked close to him, knowing better than to take her love for granted.

Nine

BLAINE

After the weeks spent in Cosian, Blaine was happy to be in the air. Honovi seemed just as pleased to be back on the *Celestial Sprite*, feet planted against the sway of the decking as the airship flew through some choppy air. The airspace around the Eastern Spine always had pockets of turbulence, but Honovi was adept at piloting them through it. Blaine checked the engine readouts one last time before joining Honovi. He rested the metal fingertips of his mechanical prosthetic against the edge of the control panel, eyeing the green glow across the board.

"We should arrive in about an hour," Honovi said as he adjusted a lever, voice coming out a little muffled through the air mask secured to his face. They were at a high enough altitude that everyone had been ordered to don one.

"No signs of Daijalan airships?" Blaine asked.

Caoimhe, from her spot at the radio, snorted. "Our hull colors are clearly marked as an E'ridian airship. If they tried to shoot us down, it would certainly be cause for E'ridia to join the war. I'm doubtful Eimarille wants that."

The airship captain, unlike the *cinn-chinnidh*, understood the threat

164

Daijal presented. She, like most of E'ridia's air force aeronauts, knew they'd be called to the skies eventually. Their defense of Cosian could be seen as an act of self-defense, which was what Blaine knew Honovi would argue if they were brought before the *Comhairle nan Cinnidhean*.

"It would certainly tip things in Ashion's favor," Blaine said.

He wanted Ashion to survive, wanted Caris to take the starfire throne, but neither did he wish to see E'ridia dragged into a war that would surely leave broken clans behind. Blaine knew, with a foreboding sense of certainty, that his homeland might not have a choice in setting their much-vaunted neutrality aside to join the fight. He already had, to an extent, and Honovi refused to let him go it alone.

Honovi pushed away from the control panel, eyes hidden behind brass goggles. "Let's see how Caris and the others are faring. Caoimhe, I'll leave you the controls."

She saluted him and took his spot while Blaine followed Honovi onto the decking. Howling wind whipped around them, stealing through the collar of Blaine's flight jacket to chill his skin for a few seconds before he tugged the zipper up higher. The fur lining kept him warm as he reached for a safety line hooked to the wall just outside the door, clipping it to his belt.

The sound of the engines was louder outside, the shadow cast from the air balloon falling more to the port side as they flew south, with the sun burning its way to the western horizon. The brass goggles Blaine wore didn't block out the sun, but they did keep the wind from stinging his eyes. He and Honovi maneuvered toward the crew cabin and the entrance there that led below decks.

The *Celestial Sprite* wasn't built with comfort in mind, being a war airship and all, but there were a few extra cabins for when passengers came on board. Blaine and Honovi's was in the officer's quarters, despite them being civilians, while the Ashionens had been assigned a tiny cabin and were ordered to remain there for the duration of the flight for their safety. They'd reach their destination before sunset, but no one was taking clear skies for granted in a country at war.

Honovi unclipped his safety line and attached it to the hooks on the side of the crew cabin before entering it. Blaine followed after his husband, the crew cabin slightly warmer than the cold temperatures outside. The cold tended to chill his mechanical prosthesis, making the limb ache at the end of the stump. His flight jackets now had extra insulation on that arm, but the cold would never keep him from performing his duties.

They made their way belowdecks, coming upon the door to the cabin Caris and the other two were at. The Royal Guard had their own bunk across the way, their door open to keep an eye on the hallway. Maurus gave them a polite nod before returning his attention back to the card game his fellow soldiers were playing to pass the time. Blaine knocked on Caris' door, calling out in Ashionen, "It's us."

The lock clicked, and the narrow door swung open. Caris offered him a tired smile. "Not much room, but we'll squish on the bunk and leave you the floor."

Nathaniel and Lore were seated on the bunk bolted to the wall. Like Caris, Lore was dressed in trousers and boots, the fur-lined coat she wore falling to her knees. Her face was bare of the veil she typically wore when traveling, but Blaine had no doubt it was secreted away on her person.

"Just an update to say we'll be landing in an hour or so. You won't have to be down here for too much longer," Honovi said.

"It's fine. I'm just planning what I want to say to Alasandair."

Blaine couldn't stop the way he instinctively looked at Nathaniel. "You shouldn't—"

"Nathaniel already knows. It won't be a secret if what I have planned comes to fruition," Caris said calmly.

Honovi pressed his hand to the small of Blaine's back, urging him inside. Blaine went where directed, knowing this was a conversation they shouldn't have in public. He knew Nathaniel had been added to the passenger manifest because Ksenia, the wardens' master alchemist, wanted to check up on him. He hadn't known Caris had revealed secret information to the other man. "You only mentioned that you wanted to speak to Soren. What is it, exactly, you're planning, and does Meleri know?"

Caris raised her chin. "The duchess knows, but I didn't seek out her permission. Eimarille and I are not the only Rourkes. If something were to happen to me, Ashion needs someone else to rally behind. Alasandair could be that person."

"He doesn't go by Alasandair," Blaine said slowly.

Soren had been insistent that he wasn't the long-thought-dead Ashion prince they seemed to think he was. He'd adamantly denied being a Rourke, despite the clear resemblance he had to Caris. Blaine had been driven near speechless the first time he'd laid eyes on Soren in that meeting room in Glencoe last year. He'd known of Eimarille and Caris surviving the Inferno, had kept Caris' life a secret while he'd lived his own until his road made its way back to hers. Alasandair —*Soren*—had never factored into the fight for the starfire throne and the right to rule Ashion.

He knew Queen Ophelia had three children, but Alasandair's death during the Inferno had been a fact for so long Blaine hadn't wanted to believe what his eyes were telling him. None of them knew anything about Soren except that he was a warden, made through alchemy to be able to survive the poison fields and handle revenants. Wardens were barred from interfering with a country's politics outside delivering border reports.

Caris had grown up a noble, learning her bloodline's business before going to university to become an engineer and how to be a cog and rule under Meleri's guidance. She was still learning the dance of politics but was a far cry better at it now than she'd been even last summer. Blaine couldn't say the same for Soren, if the warden would even believe the truth Caris spoke.

An hour or so later saw them anchored at the Warden's Island and trekking through the fort's heavily guarded gate. Construction was ongoing, but the scars from the attack last summer still dotted the interior. Empty spaces where buildings once stood interrupted the skyline, and rubble, while piled in designated areas, had yet to be removed. More disheartening than the structures was the small number of wardens and tithes they passed.

While Blaine knew that many of the wardens had survived the attack by virtue of being in the poison fields and guarding borders, they'd lost so many tithes that it would set back Maricol's safety by at least a generation.

He couldn't help the way he reached for his left elbow and the metal joint of the mechanical prosthetic. He curled his fingers around the shape of it beneath the sleeve of his flight jacket, a sense of disquiet settling over him as they walked. He hadn't been back to the Warden's Island since his capture, and he thought it wouldn't bother him. Judging by the knots in his stomach, he'd been wrong.

Honovi caught his eye as they walked behind the others and the warden who was their guide. He draped his arm around Blaine's shoulders, pulling him close. "All right?"

He spoke in E'ridian, and Blaine was grateful to hide behind their language. "I will be. It's jarring to be back."

Honovi squeezed his shoulder, and Blaine leaned into the comfort his husband provided. "I won't leave your side this time."

Blaine reached up and touched the chain that held the clarion crystal shard hanging from his throat beneath his marriage torc. Honovi's promise was one Blaine would never take for granted. They'd been separated enough the past few years; he rather hoped their roads would not break apart anytime soon.

The administration building the warden led them to was smaller than the old one he remembered, but that one had been bombed during the attack. Still, it was just as busy inside as he remembered, with wardens surrounded by folios as they worked through border reports. No one looked up at their arrival, busy with their tasks and diligent in completing them. Delani's office was smaller and more cramped than her old one, but she remained a force to be reckoned with, her one good eye studying them as they entered.

"One hopes your time here won't be as exciting as your last visit," Delani said by way of greeting.

Blaine winced, and Honovi's arm tightened briefly around his shoulders before falling away. "We won't be staying very long."

"We'll be staying as long as it takes to convince one of yours to aid us," Caris said evenly. Blaine bit back a sigh at that declaration. Caris' itinerary was known by less than a dozen people, but her absence would be felt after more than a couple of days. Blaine hoped this trip would wrap up quickly, but that depended on how the wardens handled the request.

Delani's gaze slid to Caris, attention sharp in the way of a hunter. "We wardens have never shirked our duties."

"It's not your duty I'm talking about but mine and my desire to share it."

Delani leaned back in her chair, the wood creaking with the motion. "Ah. You're here for Soren. I thought you'd come to ask for more wardens to handle the dead in your eastern province."

"I'm here for Alasandair, yes."

"I have no warden by that name."

Caris frowned but wasn't deterred. "You know him as Soren, then. No matter what name he goes by, I am here for my brother."

"I know who you are here for, but he has stated to me he is not who you believe him to be. As our records were destroyed in the attack, I am unable to verify which country sent him as a tithe. You say he is a Rourke, but Soren insists he is a warden, and you have no witness to prove your declaration unless Blaine speaks for him as well as you."

Delani's formidable attention landed on him, and Blaine stepped forward. "I do not, but surely any warden who could cast starfire would be repudiated based on the Poison Accords."

"Soren claims to not have that power."

"And do you believe him?"

Delani's silence was a clear enough answer, though Blaine didn't press her to speak it. He knew what it would mean if it became known that the wardens had allowed someone who could cast starfire into their ranks. Whatever wardens' governor had signed off on such acceptance would have ruined their vaunted neutrality, and it was that which kept the tithes flowing.

"I believe we're all at a crossroads," Delani finally said as she stood. "But my duty is to the borders of Maricol, not your attempts to secure power. Your birthright doesn't interest me. It is the fallout of this war that does."

"If Soren could help us end this war, wouldn't you want that?" Caris asked.

"It's not about what I want. It's about what everyone else will think of you and him and this history spun from the aether you wish to make a truth. It complicates everything, and my focus must be on the borders, not your crown."

"Will you let Caris speak to him?" Blaine asked.

Delani gestured at the door. "Soren's shift at the telegraph machines ends around sunset. I'll send a runner to let him know you are here, but I won't pull him from his duties. You can wait to have your conversation until tonight. Someone will show you to your rooms."

It was a clear dismissal, one that saw Nathaniel escorting a frustrated Caris out of the office. Lore followed after them, and Blaine would have gone with them if Delani hadn't said, "I'd ask you to stay a moment, Blaine."

Honovi pointedly closed the door and put his back to it, crossing his arms over his chest in a clear indication of his refusal to leave. If Delani had an issue with his presence, she didn't show it. She stepped around her desk and approached the small wet bar tucked between a bookcase and filing cabinet. She pulled the stopper out of a decanter and poured herself a small glass that smelled like *ika*, Urova's favored drink.

"How is your arm?" Delani asked.

Blaine clenched his metal fingers into a fist, the click of gears loud in the room. "I made a new one."

Delani tossed back the *ika* in a quick swallow. "I apologized to your husband last year for the betrayal of one of mine against you. I'll say it again to you. I am sorry for the harm come to you at the hands of a warden."

Raziel hadn't survived her betrayal. Honovi had told him months after his return to Glencoe, when he could bear to think about what had happened on the Warden's Island, that her mind had been stripped of memories by the wardens before she boarded an airship back to E'ridia. She'd been tried and found guilty based on Honovi's testimony and Blaine's medical records. The E'ridian court had made it clear Raziel had acted on her own, that the wardens hadn't condoned her betrayal and knew nothing of it.

Blaine would be lying if he said he didn't have reservations about being alone with a warden these days.

"Just because wardens wear the same field uniform doesn't mean your people share the guilt of a traitor. Raziel made her choice. I'm just lucky I survived it and only lost part of my arm," Blaine said.

"Still, it reflects badly on us wardens, especially because of the origins of *rionetkas*."

"That isn't common knowledge."

"For now. But secrets aren't staying kept these days, and I'm doubtful we'll escape the blame there for long."

It didn't help they no longer had any records to prove they'd thought the warden in question had died in the poison fields of Daijal. Neither did they have records of the tithes who'd come to them for centuries or the border history of the poison fields. So much knowledge had been lost last summer, harming everyone.

Delani stepped in front of her desk and leaned against it, arms crossed over her chest. She studied him for a moment before speaking. "I know you can stand witness for Caris. If it came down to it, could you do the same for Soren?"

Blaine shook his head. "I carried her out of Amari during the Inferno, and my memories speak to that. I never knew where the prince went. A magician skilled in mind magic could easily find if that were a lie."

There were those in Ashion who refused to believe he was a West-ergard, even with his ring. His name had been struck from the nobility genealogies, after all, and he'd not tried to undo it. So far, the people who mattered believed him, but Blaine was aware of how quickly that could change.

"Then that complicates things."

"There aren't any records to suggest one way or the other what Soren is, save the alchemy that lets wardens survive poison that would otherwise kill anyone else. Soren is what you made him to be, and there's no changing that, even if he changes his name," Honovi said.

Delani's bland expression never faltered. In another life, she would have made a formidable political opponent. "And wardens aren't meant to be of royal blood. We have kept to the parameters of the Poison Accords through the Ages. I won't see it break on my watch."

"We're in the Age of Progress. Perhaps it is time for change," Blaine said slowly.

"No." Delani's tone was all steel, refusing to budge. "I will not alter what was agreed to for the sake of saving a government that may crumble before the year is up."

"And if Eimarille takes the entire continent? What then? She's already proven she doesn't care for the duties you wardens uphold. Your livelihood is at stake as much as ours, especially after you pulled wardens out of Daijal."

Delani grimaced. "I'm not willing for countries to think they can control wardens by threatening to murder us all."

"What position do you think you wardens would be in if Eimarille is the only one ruling at the end of this fight?" Honovi asked.

"It would be better if you could control the narrative," Blaine added.

"Nothing good comes of lies, and that is what I would have to work with." Delani shook her head and pushed away from the desk. "I'll speak with Soren after he talks to your queen."

Blaine inclined his head and was escorted out of the office by Honovi. Neither of them spoke until they were outside the building, finding Caris, Nathaniel, and Lore chatting with a familiar warden. Caris gave them a curious look but didn't ask any questions on why they were delayed. Yufei, on the other hand, offered his hand in greeting.

"Glad to see you are well," the warden said, nodding at Blaine's left arm.

"Well enough," Blaine replied. "Are you our guide again?"

"Yes. One hopes you'll have a calm visit."

Blaine cracked a smile. "One hopes."

He sent a silent prayer to the Dusk Star for that, wanting Nilsine to hear it.

SOREN

"The governor wants to speak with you," a tithe said.

Soren looked up from sorting his end-of-day transcriptions into their correct boxes, frowning at the tithe. "Now?"

The tithe nodded, gaze solemn. "She's outside waiting for you."

Soren knew better than to keep Delani waiting. "Run and let her know I'll be out shortly, then head off to dinner if she doesn't need you for anything else."

The tithe darted off at a fast clip between desks, the clack of telegraph machines running loud in the air. Soren put his desk in order for the next warden on shift before taking his leave. He swapped the warmth of the space for the cool, late-spring evening, the sky black in the east and a deep, fading orange in the west. Delani waited for him out front, the tithe nowhere to be found.

"You wanted to speak with me?" Soren asked.

Delani curled her fingers at him as she turned away, heading down the road that led toward the center of the fort. "We have visitors."

"I heard an E'ridian airship landed with a *jarl*."

"Not just a *jarl*."

Her expression was unreadable, but Soren knew whoever was on that airship had to be important, or Delani wouldn't be hunting him down to talk. For one moment, Soren thought it could be Vanya, and it left him *wanting* with such desperation he had to take a deep breath to settle himself. Vanya wouldn't be traveling on an E'ridian airship. What's more, Vanya probably didn't even know where he was, and that made his heart ache. "Who arrived that you needed to personally meet with?"

"The queen of Ashion doesn't want to meet with me. She wants to meet with you."

Delani turned her head to look at him as she spoke, keeping him in view of her good eye. Soren managed to keep the shock off his face through sheer will alone. "Why?"

"You know why."

Soren clenched his teeth together, stopping there in the road. They stood in the shadows between two gas lamp lights, no one else around due to it being the dinner hour. Normally, Soren would be in the refectory taking his evening meal, but the thought of food just then left his stomach churning in protest. "I have nothing to say to the Ashionens."

"Caris claims to be your sister."

Soren looked away, jaw twitching. "I have no family but my fellow wardens."

Delani started walking again, her footfalls quiet on the road. "You were made to be a warden, and the alchemy that runs through you can't be reversed. But I can't trace which country tithed you, and your background could be a problem that harms our standing beneath the Poison Accords. We are not meant to interfere with heads of state, and yet, here you stand."

"I'm no prince."

Delani looked over her shoulder at him. "Perhaps you should rethink that."

Soren caught up to her, matching his stride to Delani's. "You won't give me a border because of my actions in Solaria, and now you won't keep me as a warden based on some stranger's statement?"

"This stranger looks remarkably like you."

"That doesn't make us related."

Delani shrugged. "I was reminded today that Eimarille has no respect for our commitment to keeping Maricol safe. If Ashion falls, we'll have Daijal at the shores of the Celestine Lake and limited support to fight back. There's no guarantee she might not retaliate against us for pulling out of Daijal. I won't see wardens annihilated just so she can more easily conquer another country."

"What does that have to do with me?"

"Listen to what Caris has to say." She didn't outright order him to agree to whatever offer awaited him, but it was heavily implied that he should.

Soren followed Delani to a small building that had been designated for visitors to the island. Men in Ashionen uniforms guarded the entrance. He ignored their stares and followed Delani inside. The gas lamps were all turned to their brightest settings, the light shining warmly all around them. Two people Soren remembered from Glencoe stood in the entryway, both of them dressed in the trousers and shirts of E'ridian aeronauts. The blond had been missing part of his arm last year but seemed to have received a mechanical prosthetic in the time since. The dark-haired man with the intricate metal hair ornaments woven through his long braid gave Soren a friendly enough nod.

"Thank you for agreeing to come," he said in the trade tongue. "I'm Honovi, *jarl* to Clan Storm. We've met before."

"I remember," Soren said warily.

Honovi gestured at the blond man standing beside him. "My husband, Blaine, also of Clan Storm."

"Once of the Westergard bloodline," Blaine said in the same language, just as deft at the pidgin structure as Honovi.

The name didn't mean anything to Soren, and he just stared at them. Delani sighed, hand still on the doorknob and holding it open. "Speak with them and find me after you've thought about what they've said."

Delani nodded goodbye at the E'ridians before leaving Soren to face them alone. Blaine shifted on his feet, angling his body toward the hallway. "Caris flew all this way to speak with you. I hope you'll take the time to hear her out."

"Your queen?" Soren said.

"And your sister."

The pointed statement had Soren rolling his eyes. "I'm a warden. We have no family."

But Delani had given him an order, and as much as Soren wanted to turn around and leave, he trailed after the E'ridians farther into the home. More of the soldiers stood guard outside a receiving room, though the only people who waited for them inside were three Ashionens who weren't dressed like any nobles Soren had met before. The two women and one man all wore practical clothing, and each person had a gas mask clipped to their belt.

Soren's attention settled on the younger woman, her gray eyes the same shade as the ones that stared back at him when he looked in the mirror. Her hair was a darker brown than his, falling to her shoulders in thick waves. She was pretty, not striking, and if she was meant to be queen, she lacked the magnetism Vanya had as emperor, that confidence that came with being a ruler and knowing one's place.

It seemed she was still learning it.

Blaine gestured at the three seated on the sofa and armchair. "May I introduce Mr. Nathaniel Clementine, Lady Lore Auclair, and Her Royal Majesty Queen Caris Rourke."

Wardens didn't bow to any government, and so Soren merely stared at the young woman who claimed to be queen and much more than that where he was concerned. She wore no crown or tiara, no jewelry or other indication of her rank. When Caris stood to greet him, he found her to be shorter than he was, slightly built, but she had faint cuts on her hands from doing work royals typically left for others. She said something in Ashionen, which Soren didn't understand.

"I don't speak your language," he replied in the trade tongue.

Caris blinked at him, and her next words were in the language shared at the edges of every country's borders. "Do you only speak the trade tongue?"

"I know Solarian. My border was in that country."

"You've never been to Ashion?"

"No."

Caris nodded slowly, her gaze never leaving his face. "I'd like to speak to Soren alone."

Lady Lore Auclair said something quick in Ashionen. Soren didn't understand the words, but he understood her tone. Caris shook her head and remained firm in her request. After a moment, the others filed out of the room, closing the door behind them. She retook her seat and gestured at the chair across from her. "Please sit. There are things I want to speak with you about that don't deserve an audience."

Soren thought about leaving, but Delani had wanted him to hear Caris out, so he sat, resting his elbows on his thighs, hands hanging between his knees. The weight of his poison short sword shifted along his back but remained secured. He was dressed for the poison fields, a place he hadn't been to in months, and he would rather be camped outside on the back roads than sitting here.

"Blaine said you were born Alasandair Rourke," Caris said.

"Whatever name you think I had, it was stricken when I came here as a tithe. My name is Soren."

"I know a thing or two about claiming an old name."

"We differ there," Soren said sharply. "I don't want whatever it is you think is mine."

Caris straightened her shoulders, folding her hands together over her knees. She looked tired, a bit strained, but that didn't stop her from speaking her mind. "You must know of the war in Ashion, perpetuated by Daijal and Queen Eimarille Rourke. Our sister is determined to murder me to claim the starfire throne. She will try to murder you as well."

"And you are determined to tie me to a bloodline and a fight that isn't mine. I'm a warden. We remain neutral."

Her mouth twisted slightly, shoulders rising a little toward her ears. "Eimarille keeps sending Blades to try to murder me. My hometown, Cosian, is routinely bombarded by Daijal's war airships. The front line of the war keeps pressing eastward, and soon enough, our defenses will break. No country has accepted our request for aid, and I fear that if Eimarille is successful in killing me, Ashion will truly fall if there isn't another to take up my mantle and stand against her."

"You need an heir," Soren said slowly, thinking of Raiah and everything that Vanya had done and sacrificed to keep his daughter safe.

"Yes."

"You're not married?"

Caris' gaze flicked toward the door behind Soren, and he wondered which of the two—Nathaniel or Lore—she loved. "Not yet."

"You have no husband or wife, no child to carry your bloodline. What makes you think me lying for you will help either one of us?"

"Would it be a lie?" Caris reached up and tucked a stray lock of hair behind her ear, meeting his gaze once again. "Blaine carried me out of Amari when I was a just-born infant under the Dusk Star's guidance. His bloodline guarded the Rourke bloodline for generations, and by doing so, I lived as someone else for the majority of my life."

Soren thought of Callisto and the handful of times she'd guided him down his road. He didn't want to share a past with Caris, but the similarities were difficult to ignore. "I am a warden."

"But you weren't always such."

"We're nameless and stateless once we arrive here as tithes. Whatever past you think to find in me, it doesn't exist. The attack last summer destroyed our records, our history—"

"Which means no one can argue you *aren't* my brother," Caris interrupted.

Soren raised an eyebrow. "I think everyone would see through that lie. You Ashionens live and die by your genealogies like every other country on Maricol. No one would believe I am of your Rourke bloodline."

"They would if you could cast starfire."

Soren resisted the urge to physically recoil from her words. He'd learned much from living within the Imperial court over the years and watching how Vanya comported himself. How one physically reacted was just as telling as the words spoken. "The wardens do not take in those who cast starfire."

Caris slumped a little in her seat before straightening her spine. "You'd still be Rourke, and perhaps that would be enough to put out the North Star's decree if Eimarille's Blades are successful where I am concerned."

"I'm not the answer you were hoping I would be. I'm not your brother."

There was more to family than the blood flowing through one's veins. Soren was twenty-seven years old, and whatever memories he had of his time before becoming a warden, they were meaningless in the face of his duty.

"Could you pretend?" Caris beseeched quietly. "Just until the war is over?"

Soren shook his head. "You're asking me to give up my entire way of life and risk the wardens' standing beneath the Poison Accords."

"Eimarille won't stop with just me or Ashion. She wants to rule the entirety of Maricol. Do you think the wardens will have any freedom beneath her crown? She'd rip up the Poison Accords the moment she's able to. I don't want your people to suffer the way mine have. Maricol needs wardens, but we need you whole and unsubjugated. Daijal already permits debt bondage. Do you think Eimarille won't attempt that with all of you, especially after you pulled out of her country?"

Soren couldn't quite ignore the shiver that slid down his spine at that frank assessment of a possible future. "She wouldn't dare."

Caris managed a half-smile that didn't reach her eyes. "Nathaniel knows what lengths our sister would go to. She made him into a *rionetka* and ordered him to murder me. He very nearly succeeded. My advisors wanted him jailed, but I refused to punish him for something out of his control. You wardens gave him back his mind, but his heart is gone, replaced by clockwork gears. Eimarille doesn't care about the lives she ruins if it gets her what she wants, and what she wants is Maricol. She has the backing of the Midnight Star, so I think she would dare a great deal."

"And what star god backs you?" Soren asked, trying not to think of Callisto and the moments when she'd been so real to him.

"None, at the moment. I've not been blessed by any of them, but I'm not fighting for a star god's favor. I'm fighting for my people." She hesitated before continuing with, "And I'm asking you to fight for them with me."

Soren stared at her, seeing bits of himself in her face and wishing he didn't. Wishing, too, that she was anywhere else but here, asking him to step off the only road he'd ever known. The one that had given him purpose and which had, for a time, given him Vanya.

He stood, walking away from everything she represented—everything he never wanted to be. "I'm not your brother, and I won't be your heir. Find someone else to pretend for you."

He had his hand on the doorknob when Caris spoke again, her voice firm and steady in a way that reminded him of Vanya in that moment. "I tried to deny our bloodline, tried to deny my road, but I ended up walking it anyway. Some roads the star gods deem inevitable."

Soren tightened his grip on the knob but didn't respond, yanking open the door. He left the room, ignoring the people in the hallway and the heavy weight of their stares. Soren headed back into the spring night that had fallen over the island, appetite gone but body filled with a tension he couldn't quite shake.

Eleven

NATHANIEL

Nathaniel stepped into a laboratory brightly lit by gas lamp lights, alchemy potions bubbling away in glass burners, smoke caught by a hooded vent. He couldn't quite ignore the queasy feeling in his stomach about returning to a place he had no good memories of, but the warden who greeted him with a perfunctory smile soothed the rough edges of a panic that had him reaching for Caris' hand.

"Nathaniel," Ksenia said in greeting. The master alchemist was a short, wiry-built warden whose features hinted she was tithed from Urova. Her dark hair was cut short, with a thick white streak running through it at an angle. Like all the other wardens he'd seen since landing, Ksenia was dressed and armed as if she were in the poison fields, the attack last summer lingering even now.

"Good morning, Ksenia," Nathaniel politely returned.

Caris gave his hand a firm squeeze before letting go and moving to the side. She hadn't been in the best of moods after her talk with Soren last night—frustrated and dejected in turns—but she hadn't let that stop her from joining him in the laboratories for his continued care.

Ksenia eyed him critically before jerking her thumb at the metal exam table. "Take your shirt off and get up on the table."

It took him a moment to find his resolve before he reached for his cravat. He slowly undid the strip of silk, setting it down on a nearby stool. He undid the buttons of his waistcoat with fingers that only shook a little, shrugging out of the deep blue and green attire. His white button-down shirt was the last to be removed, and even though he retained his trousers, Nathaniel felt incredibly exposed with his scars on display.

He didn't look down at his chest and torso, didn't want to see the physical mark of someone else's past ownership of him on his skin. The vivisection scars pulled with every breath he took, though the pain wasn't nearly as bad as it had first been. Medicated lotion and pain pills dispensed from an apothecary helped keep the scars from healing too tightly. He still had range of motion, but the rigid scar tissue would always be something he would need to account for in his daily life.

However long that would be.

"Here." Caris startled him as she draped a thin blanket over his shoulders, providing him with some warmth and unintentional protection against prying eyes. Nathaniel clutched at the edges, holding it in place as she came around to face him. She smiled wanly at him before her gaze dropped to his chest. Whatever warmth had been in her eyes was replaced by guilt as she reached out to touch the center of his chest, where the scars crossed through his skin. He couldn't feel her touch, not even the pressure of it. "I'm sorry."

"This was never your fault," he replied in a low voice.

She reached up and cupped his jaw, smoothing her thumb over his cheek. He'd shaved that morning, and his skin felt a little sensitive beneath her touch. "You were hurt because of me, and I will always regret that."

Nathaniel ducked his head to kiss her gently on the mouth, lips closed, grateful that she still saw him in his body when he still had nightmares about it belonging to someone else. "I would beg of you not to."

Caris promised him nothing. Sighing, Nathaniel went and took a seat on the exam table, the metal cold through his trousers and the blanket. Ksenia had her clarion crystal–tipped wand in her right hand, aether bleeding away from it in a soft glow.

"Have you heard different notes?" Ksenia asked.

Her question was directed to Caris, who shook her head. "It's been the same song since last year."

"You're certain? No discordant notes?"

"I would know if the song changed."

Caris' answer was firm, and Ksenia seemed satisfied with it as she turned her formidable attention to Nathaniel. "Lie down."

Nathaniel tightened his grip on the blanket, chest aching inside where his clockwork metal heart beat at a rhythm that never quite matched his emotions. Still, he swung his legs up onto the table and leaned back, letting the blanket fall away to cover the cold metal. The chill still seeped through, and he blinked up at the laboratory ceiling, digging his fingernails into the thin fabric.

Slender fingers curled around his as Caris held his hand, a comfort he had never even dreamed about during those flash moments he sometimes remembered of his nightmare beneath the *Klovod*'s hands.

"I won't leave you," Caris promised.

Nathaniel nodded jerkily as Ksenia stepped closer to the exam table. The master alchemist was more interested in his scars, studying him with the clinical focus of an aetherologist or engineer. She touched the scars with her wand at various points, her magic warmly curling along his skin. It didn't hurt, but he couldn't stop the way his breathing escalated. He didn't like feeling as if he were an experiment.

"Hold still just a bit longer," Ksenia murmured.

Nathaniel took a deep breath and let it out slowly, thinking he could hear the gears in his chest moving. Ksenia's magic remained coiled around his chest, tracing the scars there before the glow disappeared as the magic sank into his skin. He couldn't feel anything after that, though Ksenia's wand never left the spot it touched on his chest.

When she finally lifted her wand, her magic rose out of him, twisting into a pattern in the air that shaped itself into what he thought his clockwork metal heart must look like behind his ribs.

Nathaniel stared at the shape of it before he jerked his gaze away, hating the sight of the thing that kept him alive.

"It's okay," Caris said. "You're okay."

"The bypass of the compulsion spell hasn't shifted," Ksenia said, her words barely easing Nathaniel's anxiety. "Neither has the self-destruct component. Caris confirms the song from the clarion crystals that power it hasn't changed. You're still you, as much as your predicament allows. I'll reinforce the stabilizing spells, but I still see no way to undo it."

Nathaniel swallowed tightly, knowing the chance of him reverting back to his *rionetka* status was still a possibility. "Truly?"

Ksenia sighed. "We lost many of our records in the attack. Aside from that, removing the spells completely would still trigger the self-destruct one and break your heart. It's too much of a risk."

Nathaniel let out a shaky little breath as Caris' grip on his hand tightened. "I rather like being alive."

He managed a ghost of a smile for the woman he loved when he said that, looking up at Caris' face. She smiled back, but there were shadows in her gray eyes he wished he could make disappear. "I rather like you being alive."

It didn't feel like he was some days. He was an abomination, alive through magic and alchemy and beholden to the gears in his chest. It took Caris to remind him otherwise.

Ksenia dragged her wand through the aether, scattering the magic and undoing the spell she'd used to examine his clockwork metal heart. "How has your pain been?"

At that, Nathaniel couldn't hide a grimace as he sat up. "Persistently present."

"Do the pain pills not help?"

Nathaniel swung his legs over the side of the table and gratefully accepted his clothes that Caris fetched for him. "I don't like relying on them. I finished the batch you made me last year, and we requested another one from a resupply station in Cosian, but I still have half of that order left."

They made his head feel cloudy sometimes, making him think he was back under the *Klovod*'s control and causing panic attacks that he hated for anyone to witness. He also didn't want to have to need them to function, even if some days his chest ached from the cold of the metal inside it.

"I'll write you another script and leave you to mind your dosage as you like."

Nathaniel nodded and started to redress himself. When it came time to tie his cravat, Caris gently batted away his hands and did it for him. He held still beneath her ministrations, hands drifting to her hips and resting carefully there. Caris didn't mind his touch and remained beside him once he finished.

"Thank you," Nathaniel said.

Ksenia tucked her wand away in her belt case, eyeing the both of them. "Just keep an ear out for any different notes the clarion crystals sing."

"Always," Caris promised.

Nathaniel tightened his hold on Caris. "We'll head back aboveground if you have no more need for us."

"I'm finished with you. I've heard you might not be finished with us, though," Ksenia said.

"We came for Nathaniel but also for someone else," Caris said slowly.

"I am aware."

"You don't seem particularly surprised," Nathaniel said.

Ksenia shrugged. "I'm a master alchemist and an advisor to the governor. Soren is someone she requested counsel on."

"What do you know of him?" Caris' question came out cautiously, curiously, and Nathaniel couldn't say he himself didn't want to know about the warden she insisted was her brother. Some part of him still disliked knowing that information—disliked knowing anything that someone else could use against him to bring her harm—but he would do his best to bury it if need be.

"Soren is a warden and always will be," Ksenia replied as she turned away from them. "There is no way to unmake him so."

Nathaniel didn't think it was quite the answer Caris was hoping for, but when she would have pressed, he cleared his throat, catching her attention. "Let's go find a meal?"

"Of course," she said.

Yufei waited for them in the hallway, the warden having been tasked with escorting them below. He led them out of the cold and back up into the warm, late-spring sunlight that existed beyond the well-guarded entrance set into the floor. Nathaniel let the chill of the underground laboratories fade away as they stepped outside. He took a deep breath, glad to be out of there, despite the good he knew Ksenia had accomplished. After everything he'd gone through, Nathaniel would never be truly comfortable in a laboratory again.

Caris took his hand in hers and smiled politely at Yufei. "We'd like to go to the refectory."

Yufei shrugged before turning to leave. "You know your way around."

Caris tugged at Nathaniel's hand, and he let her lead him in the opposite direction. He didn't know the fort very well, having spent most of his time there last summer in Ksenia's care below in the laboratories. Caris had a decent sense of direction, though, and she led them to a small scrap of open space between two buildings that could possibly be called a park if one was generous.

The patchwork grass had scattered flowers poking up and a wooden bench situated beneath a flowering tree. Nathaniel took a seat on the bench, tugging Caris down beside him. She leaned against him, resting her head on his shoulder. "I thought you'd prefer to see the sky for a little while longer rather than be cooped up inside."

It was a thoughtful gesture, and Nathaniel turned his head to kiss her forehead. "Thank you."

Caris tucked her legs up on the bench, reaching for his right hand to twine their fingers together. "I'm glad Ksenia cleared you."

Nathaniel stroked his fingers through her hair, a gesture that calmed them both. "I fear the day she won't be able to."

"Don't speak like that."

"You know I only speak the truth."

Caris curled close, resting her ear over his clockwork metal heart. "Just this once, lie to me?"

Nathaniel closed his eyes, tightening his hold on her at the ache in her voice she didn't try to hide. "Is that what you truly want?"

She was quiet for a time, the only sound between them the rustle of the leaves above from the passing breeze. A few petals fell from the flowers blooming overhead, drifting slowly down to the ground. "No."

Caris was pragmatic in a way that he loved. She'd never shied away from a difficult engineering project and seemed to face the war and all its many agonies with the same resolute determination. But he knew how much taking up the crown and claiming a bloodline when she'd lived her life as someone else weighed on her. He knew, too, if her road had been different—if Eimarille's desire for power had been less —they'd be married by now, because there was no life he'd ever live without her.

"I want to grow old with you," Nathaniel confessed. "I want children with you, however we may have them."

"I want that, too."

"I just don't ever want to hurt you."

Caris sighed softly, shifting on the bench so she could rest her head on his shoulder once again. "You never could of your own free will."

Nathaniel swallowed. "Promise me, no matter what, you'll do what you must."

Because the world was bigger than just the two of them as cogs, and as much as he wanted to be selfish and have her to himself, he knew she was learning to put the world first, as any good queen must. He respected her for that—loved her for it, even—because it spoke of the type of person she was in the face of everything.

Caris let go of his hand so she could press her palm over his clockwork metal heart and the scars that held it in place. When she spoke, her voice was steady enough. "I promise."

It was all he could ask for.

Twelve

SOREN

Soren peered over the top of the parapet at the shimmer of moonlight on the Celestine Lake's black waters. The pier in the distance was marked by lit lanterns interspersed along its length. Gas lamps that had been destroyed during the attack last summer had been replaced, as had the pier that acted as the main dock for the Warden's Island. Submersibles had sunk the steamboat used to ferry wardens and tithes across the poisonous waters. The wardens didn't have a functioning dry dock to begin a rebuild, but the Tovan Isles had sent a replacement at the tail end of winter, along with their yearly tithe quota.

The new steamboat was anchored on the opposite shore, manned by a full crew of wardens and automatons. Soren had wanted to board that steamboat every day since its arrival, but he hadn't stepped foot off the Warden's Island since his return, bound by Delani's order to remain. Presently, he'd found no way off the island save one. Caris' offer was a chance for Soren to leave the place that had made him into the man he was to become someone he'd left by the wayside in some other life.

All he had to do was give up everything he was.

"You're not on wall duty this month," Delani said from behind him, drawing Soren out of his thoughts.

"I wanted to clear my head. Am I allowed to do that?"

Delani came to stand next to him, resting her hands against the stone wall. The breeze blowing down the Eastern Spine was cool but not freezing, a hint of summer yet to come. "You aren't a prisoner."

"You haven't let me off the island in months."

"I have my reasons."

"Yes, one in particular won't leave me alone."

Caris had tried to meet with him every day for the past week, politely persistent in a way he'd never known royalty to be. She was doggedly determined to change his mind, believing he was the answer to whatever prayers she'd given up to the star gods. He didn't know how to tell her that he didn't—*couldn't*—want what she was offering but that some part of him wanted to take the way out just to see someplace that wasn't here.

He missed the Southern Plains and the desert.

He missed Vanya.

"You haven't been by to speak with me," Delani said after a long moment where the only sound between them was that of a passing automaton below on the outside of the fort's wall.

"I needed to think."

"About Caris' offer?" Soren pressed his lips together, refusing to look at her. Delani drummed her fingers against the stone. "She thinks you're her brother."

He grimaced. "I am aware."

"I think she's right."

Soren jerked, staring at Delani, but the governor wasn't looking at him. Her head was tipped back, one good eye on the stars that burned clarion crystal bright high above in the clear night sky. "Why?"

"Besides the obvious physical similarities?"

"I'm sure if you looked hard enough, you could find someone else who has the same eyes as she does."

"You're the right age to be the lost prince. You look like her more than you do Eimarille, though I'm sure if the three of you ever stood in the same room, an argument could be made for family."

"I'm not Ashionen. I'm not *Rourke*. I'm a warden."

"Yes, we made you that way. And as Ksenia has seen fit to remind me, we can't unmake you."

He'd spent years and years in and out of the laboratories buried beneath the fort, taking potions and being injected with chemicals, learning to tolerate poisons and toxins bit by bit until they couldn't kill him. He'd trained in weapons and alchemy, learning the science to keep records on the poison fields, all while being taught how to fight against revenants and survive a horde. He had scars from a life lived on the road, guarding his assigned borders, existing in places few others trekked, the rest of society preferring the safety found behind city walls to the wide-open spaces of Maricol.

He was a warden. He didn't know how to be anything else.

And yet.

"You don't need to unmake me," he said quietly.

"I wouldn't even if we had the ability to do so." Delani tipped her head back down, turning to face him full-on so she could see him with her good eye. "You haven't earned a banishment."

Others had, over the centuries. Wardens who'd used their skills to torment the living, dealt with by their brethren accordingly, had lost the right to be a warden when they'd lost their lives at the end of a judgment issued by whoever held the rank of governor.

Only one warden in recent memory had been banished, though for a time, everyone had assumed Olet was dead. But with the knowledge that *rionetkas* were warden-made—that it was one of their own's work destabilizing governments on Eimarille's orders—it meant they could not ignore the fallout. Not forever. And Olet had a kill order out on him now for the crimes he had committed as the *Klovod*.

Wardens were meant to be neutral, to favor no country above another. Even though they'd pulled out of Daijal and Urova, Soren knew he wasn't the only one who regretted the unmanned poison fields. Most citizens weren't responsible for their rulers' decisions, but they suffered from it just the same.

"You want to leave. You want a border again," Delanie said.

Soren licked his dry lips. "I do."

"You guarded Solaria for all the years you've been an active warden. After everything that happened there, I can't send you back."

His heart sank, that sliver of hope he'd been clinging to slipping away. "Then where would you send me?"

He knew before she even spoke, steeling himself for a road away from where his heart lay. "Ashion."

"As a warden or as a prince?" The question came out tight, the words like poison in his mouth.

Delani leaned her weight against the wall, never looking away from his face. "There are no records of where you came from. Whether you were royalty or not, if you becoming a prince could help stop this war, would you do it?"

"Ashion isn't my country."

"Our duty is to all of Maricol's countries."

"Caris wants me to be her heir. To put Ashion first above all others. That's not our way."

"Let it be, for now. If Ashion falls, we'll have Daijal at our shore, and for all our expertise in the poison fields, we are not soldiers. We do not have the capacity to stand against an army."

"And what about after, if they win? If everyone knows or believes I'm this person? How does that reflect on us wardens?"

"Badly," Delani said with an honesty that ached. "The missing records won't help our arguments that we governors and archivists didn't know what you were when you were delivered as a tithe. But you can help set things right."

"By giving up my road."

"We have enough problems with Olet's actions where the *rionetkas* are concerned, and we've lost nearly an entire generation of tithes from the attack last summer. The coming years won't be easy for wardens in the poison fields, and that's if Daijal *doesn't* win the war. If Eimarille succeeds, I fear we face a subjugation far worse than the debt slaves they hold."

Soren stared at Delani for a moment before turning to look back at the shadowed waters of the Celestine Lake and the moonlight reflected there. The quiet of the land around them was broken by the night noises of the fort and the automatons on guard duty. He closed his eyes and remembered what it had been like in that quarry, with its death-defying machine and imprisoned debt slaves, freedom taken from him. He could so easily see his fellow wardens in the same or worse predicament.

He opened his eyes, wondering if this was the road Callisto had wanted him to walk—a broken, empty life where he belonged nowhere, nameless and starless no matter where he stood. "If I go north to pretend to be this prince, would you take me back when this is all over?"

Delani's silence was answer enough, her single eye unblinking as she stared at him. Soren laughed raggedly, dragging a hand through his hair. He would have turned away if she hadn't gripped his shoulder, keeping him close. "We can't unmake you, but to claim you as a warden puts us all at risk."

"That sounds like banishment to me," he bit out. "A warden in all but name."

She smiled a crooked little smile that wasn't meant to comfort. "We must abide by the Poison Accords. Doing so keeps the peace."

"There is no peace in Maricol right now."

"If Ashion wins the war, there will be." Delani let him go, taking a step back. "Do you have any desire to take the starfire throne?"

He recoiled at the question. "*No.*"

She nodded. "Good. Keep that mindset. Wardens aren't meant to rule."

"You would call me anything but a warden."

"I can't fix the mistakes of my predecessors, but I can guard our future. That is what we do as wardens. That is what I am asking you to do. You wanted a border. This is the one I'm giving you."

A future for wardens that had no place for him but where they would still exist, free from the control of any country. Soren didn't know how to be a prince, didn't know how to be anything but a warden, and wardens had been created with one goal in mind: to guard a border, a country, a world against the threat of revenants and the spread of poison fields.

They had a duty, and Delani must have known he would abide by it.

Soren's chest tightened with the desire to scream, but it would change nothing. "I'll see to it."

Delani nodded slowly. "I'll let Caris know. Pack your things for a morning departure."

He walked away from her, and she didn't try to hold him back, his anger and grief a weight on his shoulders that made him want to drag his feet all the way back to the barracks. Soren shut himself away in that small room, staring blankly at the walls of a building he knew he'd never see again after this, not as he had been. Delani wanted him to guard the wardens by becoming someone else, but the only way he'd ever known how to guard anything was as a warden.

"Is this what you wanted from me, Callisto?" Soren asked into the quiet.

It wasn't a prayer, wasn't a cry for help, and maybe if it was, the Dawn Star might have answered. But the star god who had led him to the Warden's Island so very long ago wasn't there to guide him off it when the sun rose. While Caris and Delani would have him act the prince, in the morning, when he boarded the E'ridian airship, he did so as the man he'd always been, wearing the uniform of a people he could no longer claim but who he'd do anything to keep safe.

"I'll be your heir, but I won't be your dead prince," he said on the decking as crew members bustled around them for the launch. "My name is Soren."

Caris held out her hand, chin tilted up, a stubborn look in her gray eyes. "Whatever name you go by, you'll still be my brother."

He didn't know about that, but for the wardens, Soren would try.

Alliances

937 A.O.P.

One

VANYA

A Solarian spy came to Oeiras in Seventh Month, when the summer heat had long since burned away the spring coolness. Vanya wasn't aware of the spy's presence on the Imperial estate until Caelum—who had traveled with him from Calhames back to Oeiras—interrupted Vanya's afternoon of reviewing military updates on the Legion's efforts to fight through another wave of revenants in the House of Kimathi *vasilyet*. The walking dead seemed to outnumber the living these days, which made gaining ground difficult.

"Your Imperial Majesty?" Caelum said from the doorway to the vast office that Vanya felt he lived in more than his bedroom these days.

"Yes?" Vanya replied, not looking up.

"You have a particular guest who wishes an audience."

Vanya paused in his perusal of a rather dense briefing before setting it aside. He looked up and met Caelum's eyes. Someone stood farther back in the antechamber, his *praetoria* legionnaires having not yet let them come forward. Caelum's turn of phrase was one used when a spy had returned to the fold, and Vanya was never one to make them wait.

"The audience is granted," Vanya said as he leaned back in his comfortable chair, the leather warm from how long he'd been sitting there.

Caelum half turned and gestured with his free hand. The person in the antechamber came forward into the office, bowing deeply to Vanya. The pale yellow robe she wore over loose white trousers was neatly embroidered at the edges with green thread. Her blonde hair was tied back in a single thick braid that was twisted around her head and pinned in place like a crown. The gold bangles around her wrists and the few heavy rings she wore indicated a good career as a Solarian merchant but not one well-off enough to earn her name being written in the nobility genealogies.

"Your Imperial Majesty," the spy said.

Caelum closed the door behind them for privacy, though he didn't lock it. The windows that overlooked the private inner courtyard were open, but no one was outside save for discreetly placed *praetoria* legionnaires. None of those guards were within hearing distance.

"Your name?" Vanya asked.

"Bellanca, of no House. I hail from Karnak and was stationed in Ashion for business reasons over the last few weeks. Specifically, Cosian."

Vanya rubbed at his chin, studying her. "My understanding is that Cosian is a restricted city these days. It's Ashion's disputed capital, where their self-claimed queen holds court. It's been bombed several times over since last year."

She dipped her head in a shallow nod. "Yes, I'm well aware of the attacks. I and my company's airship survived the last two attempts. But my company exports durable cloth favored for uniforms, and we were cleared to remain in Cosian. The Ashionen military aides I did business with were desperate to buy."

"And what did you uncover while there?"

Caelum opened the folio he held and pulled out a folded broadsheet, which he set on Vanya's desk. It contained only the front page of an Ashion broadsheet, the language one Vanya was near fluent in. What caught his eye more than the neatly typed words and made his heart skip a beat was the photograph printed large, filling up a good section of the top page. In it, Queen Caris Rourke posed on a porch in a neat blouse, corset belt, and dark trousers, wearing no crown, a slight smile fixed on her face. Standing beside her was a man Vanya would recognize in any clothing, though he much preferred it when he could coax Soren out of them.

He carefully touched his fingers to the imprint of Soren's familiar face on the paper, the warden's expression giving nothing away in the glare of camera lights. The Ashionen suit Soren wore in the photograph lacked the leather he knew the warden preferred. Missing as well were the weapons he knew Soren never went anywhere without, even while walking the halls of the old Imperial palace.

"I know we received news last week of the third Rourke child returning from the dead. While all the broadsheets are referring to him as Prince Alasandair Rourke, there hasn't been a single photograph taken of him until this one shot for the Ashion press two days ago. Bellanca is aware of your warden and decided the news was worth flying back to Solaria for," Caelum said quietly.

"I was in Bellingham when he brought you home some years ago, Your Imperial Majesty," Bellanca added. "That is how I recognized him."

"Thank you for bringing this to my attention," Vanya said, managing to keep his voice steady through a lifetime of practice.

Bellanca glanced at Caelum before bowing and seeing herself out of the office. Caelum went to the side table and poured a glass of the sweet red wine one of the servants had brought in earlier, the carafe damp from condensation. He set the wineglass on the desk and nudged it toward Vanya. "Drink."

Vanya reached for it, taking a sip and thinking about that moment in the train so long ago, when he'd been poisoned with quiet killer and Soren had saved his life in the aftermath of the crash. He crunched a berry between his teeth, swallowing the taste but unable to swallow the hurt and grief that clawed at him as he stared at the Ashion broadsheet.

Caelum sat in front of the desk, adjusting his robes. Gone were the heavier ones of winter, the lighter one today a concession to the heat beyond the office. The mechanical fans that whirred away in the corners above provided enough relief, though that might change the longer summer wore on.

"Did he ever tell you that he was a prince?" Caelum asked.

Vanya had to stop himself from crumpling the broadsheet into a ball and tossing it in the bin. "No. He is a warden."

"Wardens are made from tithes. Before they go to the Warden's Island, they are someone."

I'm a warden, and that's all I'll ever be. Wherever I came from, I can't go back. I can never go home.

Soren's words spoken to him beneath a starry night sky after surviving the revenant incursion at the Imperial palace before Vanya burned it down were seared into his memory. So, too, was the way they'd said goodbye on silken sheets, the heat of the other man's skin bruised into his dreams.

He'd thought he knew all of Soren's secrets after that night. Raiah had survived Artyom's betrayal because of Soren's ability to cast starfire, the strength of which Vanya knew must be on par with his own. That revelation had left him with too many questions—too many moments of second-guessing what they'd been to each other— for Vanya to be rational in the face of that hurt.

It didn't matter that the Dawn Star had interfered in both their lives, changed their roads, to force their paths to cross. Vanya had thought he could have with Soren what he couldn't have with anyone else, but that, too, had been a lie. Knowing that—and now knowing the name Soren must have had before he was tithed—didn't stop the hurt.

"If he is capable of casting starfire as a royal of the Rourke bloodline, then the wardens must have known. They would have broken their own Poison Accords with that admittance," Caelum said.

"The wardens didn't know."

Caelum frowned at him. "How could they have not? Starfire isn't something that is easily ignored by a person who is gifted with it."

Vanya knew that all too well growing up as a young boy with the biting burn of it just beneath his skin. But he also knew what Soren had said—that the wardens didn't know about him because of the Dawn Star—and for all the lies Vanya had been told when they last spoke, he didn't think that had been one.

Callisto had warned him to keep the warden close, after all.

If she had wanted to break his heart, she had succeeded.

"Bring me my *valide*," Vanya said.

Caelum stood and bowed before leaving, closing the door behind him. Once alone, Vanya dragged the broadsheet closer, peering at Soren's face, some part of him wishing the warden stood before him. Despite his anger, he'd worried about Soren, wondered if the warden had been sent north to deal with the tremendous amount of revenants laying claim to the battlefields.

The wardens had yet to send any of their people into Daijal or Urova since the attack, the wardens' governor's order still in effect. For all that they patrolled the poison fields in Ashion, they weren't overtly supporting the war. He knew the ones assigned to the border around the House of Kimathi's *vasilyet* were hard-pressed to give aid to the Legion simply because of the sheer number of revenants. They had the Daijal queen to thank for that, even if Vanya knew Eimarille would never admit to such folly.

Despite the Legion's prowess when it came to their war machines, their sentinel-class automatons needed to be piloted. Placing people in the direct path of the walking dead—where spore contamination was a real risk and its spread through the ranks could be devastating—meant it was slow going. But Vanya would rather a careful push forward than risk scores of legionnaires dying due to spores. Solaria couldn't afford such a loss, not with what was happening up north.

Vanya traced the outlines of Soren's face on the broadsheet, torn between hurt and anger. Closure was out of reach because Soren wasn't there, and Vanya couldn't leave to go where he was. If this was how their roads were to end, he loathed it.

The sound of the doorknob turning had him looking up, watching as Taisiya was escorted inside by Caelum. The Chief Minister well knew when a conversation was meant to be private and so stepped back out into the antechamber. Taisiya sank slowly into a seat before Vanya, attention on the broadsheet rather than him.

"I see you enjoy a life of complications," Taisiya said.

Vanya pushed the broadsheet across his desk so she could reach it. "The purported Ashion queen has announced she found her older brother."

Taisiya reached for it, carefully picking it up and rotating it so she could read the headline. "So your warden is a prince."

"His name isn't in the article."

"His face is, and there are those of the Houses who will recognize it."

Vanya shoved his chair back and stood, walking over to one of the windows to stare out at the courtyard, fingernails biting into his palms. "He claimed to be a warden for the years I knew him. That the wardens didn't know who he was because of the Dawn Star."

"Did *he* know?"

Vanya thought of that night and the anguish in Soren's gray eyes, the promise that he had never used the vow because then he'd have to leave. But Soren had left anyway, pushed away by Vanya's hurt in the wake of so much betrayal. "He never said."

"Can Soren cast starfire?"

He ground his teeth together so hard his jaw clicked. The memory of Artyom holding Raiah and Vanya powerless to save her while Soren gave up all his secrets to do so flashed through his mind. "If I told you no, could you speak that lie as a truth?"

"*Vanya.*" Taisiya's voice came out sharp, like a knife sliding between his ribs. "Did you know when you gave him your vow?"

"*No.*" Vanya spun on his feet, throwing out his arm in a furious gesture. "If I had, do you think I would have offered it?"

"In my experience, one will do anything for love."

"I don't—"

"Look me in the eye and finish that sentence." Her hazel eyes were bright with anger in her narrow face, unblinking in his rapidly fading rage. She held his gaze, and in the end, Vanya was the one to look away first. Taisiya didn't treat it like a victory. "You love him. A warden who is now a prince. Who was, quite possibly, always a prince."

Vanya stared at the painting on the wall depicting the side profile of a roaring lion that represented the House of Sa'Liandel, the animal head surrounded by golden starfire. His House had ruled for centuries and still ruled only because of divine intervention in the face of assassination attempts and treason. He hadn't been strong enough to keep the claim on his own, and the results of the Conclave of Houses would be questioned if it got out that he'd promised a blood vow to a foreign prince, no matter the road Soren had walked as a warden.

"Tell me I do not speak the truth," Taisiya said quietly.

He wanted to, but it would be a lie if he tried. Because—despite *everything*—he did. He loved Soren in a way he hadn't ever learned to love his wife after a year of marriage before Nicca died in childbirth. And it was that love that made him never force Soren to pick a payment for the debt Vanya owed him. Like Soren, Vanya had never wanted to let the other man go.

Except he had.

Vanya looked at Taisiya, and whatever she must have seen in his face made her expression soften. "Oh, my child. The best kind of love will always burn like starfire. I only wish it wouldn't hurt you so."

"It doesn't matter," Vanya rasped. "I can never have him now."

The confession felt dragged out of him, words brittle like summer-dry prairie grass, primed to burn with just one spark. Vanya dragged a hand over his hair, wrenching his gaze away from Taisiya's too-knowing eyes. If Soren truly was the long-thought-dead Ashion prince, then being together was an impossibility. For Vanya couldn't insert himself in some other country's volatile politics for love, because love would not keep his country safe, and Solaria had to come first. His heart—fractured as it was—would always come second.

A cool hand touched his jaw, startling him. He looked down into Taisiya's upturned face, unaware that she had moved to join him by the window. "We must get ahead of this. Once the Houses find out about Soren's past, they will find a way to call for your abdication in the face of the sanctions we're set to receive from the wardens. Solaria may be accused of breaking the Poison Accords, but so have the wardens, and that is something we can't ignore."

The wardens had already suffered enough at Daijal's hands. Vanya didn't want to strike another blow against them, but he knew he had no choice. Not if he wanted to keep the Imperial throne. "I know."

"If you reduce the sanctions by using Soren, the Houses will come around to your rulership."

He flinched at her words, but Vanya knew she was right. "I'll call the wardens' governor tomorrow, after my meeting with the Tovanian ambassador."

What it all came down to was protecting Solaria's borders, and Vanya's heart had no place in those decisions. His heart would break before Solaria could.

It had to.

Two

VANYA

Vanya dressed with care the next morning for the meeting with the Tovanian ambassador and the Solarian diplomatic corps that had traveled west over the ocean to the Tovan Isles. The robes laid out for him were white and gold, the filigree on the crown he wore wrapped around large rubies. The vault where the Imperial jewels were held had been one of the few parts of the old Imperial palace that had survived, solely because they had been located underground. Taisiya seemed pleased with his presentation when he met with her after separate morning meals.

"Your ambassador said they would meet us at the dignitary room," Taisiya said. She wore a shimmering blue-green gown today, with a sheer pale gray robe over it. The ensemble resembled the colors of white-capped waves in the harbor, a quiet nod to the guests who awaited them. Her hair had been tied up, hidden beneath the stiff blue-green headdress she wore, its flat top embroidered with silver thread.

Vanya offered her his arm, and she curled her hand around his elbow, allowing him to escort her down the wide hallway. "I've read the brief Ambassador Grethe delivered yesterday afternoon and spoke with her before dinner. What do you think of the report she delivered?"

"I think the *Uri* has made a wise decision, which we will do our best to reciprocate, but it will bring unwanted attention from the Daijal court."

"We've uncovered many *rionetkas*." It had galled Vanya when he'd received the report on the numbers of Solarian citizens whose lives had been stolen and controlled by the enemy. Learning just how deeply the *rionetkas* had entrenched themselves in the government and Houses had been a quiet sort of horror over the last many months.

The bitterest loss was Amir, former *vezir* of the House of Vikandir. Vanya had considered the man a friend, an ally, and a confidant. Knowing that Amir now lived with a ticking time bomb in his chest, unable to oversee his House anymore, was a devastating blow to the House of Vikandir and the counsel Vanya had sought.

"We don't know if we've found all of them. I fear this alliance will cause Eimarille to attempt further infiltration." Taisiya raised her free hand to briefly touch her chest, over her heart, lingering in the space where vivisection scars would cross if she carried them on her skin. "I would feel safer in a palace and the walls it comes with."

Vanya grimaced, thinking of the timeline stretching out on the rebuild of the palace. "The Imperial estate here in Oeiras will have to do for now."

Taisiya hummed at that but kept her peace. The rest of the walk to the dignitary room was made in silence, only the sound of their footsteps and those of the *praetoria* legionnaires' guarding them echoing in the air. When they turned the last corner, he saw a group of people huddled outside the door to the dignitary room, Caelum amongst them. One of them turned at the sound of their approach before bowing deeply.

"Your Imperial Majesty," Grethe said. "The Tovanian delegation awaits you."

"You've done well as my voice," Vanya said.

Grethe was a decade older than him, tall and lean, with an oval face dominated by a strong nose. Her blonde hair was bleached white from the sun rather than age, and her brown eyes were creased deeply at the corners from laughter. She took the praise with a faint nod of acknowledgment. "I did what I could for Solaria."

"As always."

Last night, she'd handed back the Imperial writ he'd given her before she'd taken the voyage to Port Avi on the Tovan Isles. It had enabled diplomatic talks to finish quicker rather than sending ship-cities and airships across the seas between the two countries. Of the ambassadors he could have sent, Grethe had been the most trustworthy, and his faith in her had proved itself.

"Shall we?" Caelum asked, gesturing at the doors a *praetoria* legionnaire was pushing open.

This time, no press was invited to document the meeting between two nations. Vanya escorted Taisiya inside, seeing the Tovanians were already settled on the floating cabana. Akeheni stood at their arrival, her gaze intent as Vanya and Taisiya approached the saltwater pool. The clothes she wore for today's meeting were far more elaborate than they had been in the past, the collar of her shirt cut in such a way as to show off the vibrant black ink tattooed over her collarbones and up her throat.

The Tovan Isles' *Uri* wore no crowns, as they governed similarly to how the *Comhairle nan Cinnidhean* did in E'ridia. In lieu of clans, Tovanians claimed their ship-cities and the long-held names attributed to those vessels. Akeheni's facial tattoos indicated she was a captain of one such ship-city, as well as an ambassador. The tattoos she revealed now indicated she had been granted a seat on the *Uri*, given the title of chief for one of the six sub-nations that spanned the crews of the ship-cities. It was as good a sign as any the Tovan Isles were serious about the treaty on the table.

"I see congratulations are in order, *Uri'ka* Akeheni," Vanya said, inclining his head out of respect to another ruler.

Akeheni nodded just as regally. "Well met, Emperor. The *Uri* thought it prudent to show our resolve to this alliance. The matriarch of my ship-city's crew nation allowed my mother to cede her seat to me, and I take up her duty with honor to speed things along."

"I've heard from my envoy only good news brings you to our shores."

"Indeed. The *Uri* felt your request was prudent to our shared goals."

"So it seems."

Vanya escorted Taisiya to a low cushioned seat at the edge of the pool. The one reserved for himself was far grander than the others, but he stayed standing for the moment, willing to meet Akeheni on the same level. He turned to face the Tovanian. "To be frank, I was anticipating a much longer wait. What changed?"

He'd sent his envoy across the waves back at the beginning of Sixth Month. It was Seventh Month now, summer heat rising like the Lion constellation in the night sky. It was the Dawn Star's season, though Vanya had yet to direct any prayers toward Solaria's guiding star.

Akeheni pursed her lips, the tattoos around her mouth pulling tight as she crossed her arms over her chest. "We discovered a *rionetka* in one of the lower circles of the *Uri* amidst the talks that were happening regarding the treaty. It was…eye-opening."

Vanya grimaced, well aware of the physical toll taken on the body when one was turned into a *rionetka* and the political fallout that could happen after they were discovered. "Do they still live?"

"Your ambassador counseled us against attempting to undo the magic powering the clockwork metal heart, that it would kill the victim through a self-destruct spell. The *rionetka* could not give the *Uri* an answer on who performed the operation or who they were feeding information to. The ship-city they hailed from had a manifest with a history stretching back to Second Month showing ports of call in Helia, Oeiras, Seaville, and other smaller seaside towns. There is no telling where the operation would have occurred."

"My condolences to the crewmate in question. I well know the travesty of a life caught up in the strings of a *rionetka*."

"We've instituted physical checks, and foreigners are barred from Port Avi without proper clearance. But it prompted the *Uri* to agree to

Solaria's proposed alliance when it comes to patrolling your shores in exchange for the production of munitions built to our specs. I am here to sign that treaty on behalf of the *Uri*."

Vanya raised an eyebrow. "You Tovanians have your own production facilities on your main island. I'm not against the request, but Solaria's Legion is dug in at our northern border and fighting to retake a *vasilyet*. I would be happy to go over the request with my military aides, but your favored weapons are not ours, and reconfiguring a production facility is an undertaking they may counsel against."

"The *rionetka* had access to the supplies their ship-city traded for and bought, which included components for the defensive arsenal. We can't risk using it until it's been subjected to a thorough and extensive review by our engineers and magicians. Rather than trade for hard materials, the *Uri* would rather Solaria produce it for us at a discount. Considering we will be patrolling your shoreline, it will be used in your defense."

"I'll impress upon my military advisors that your request is a fair trade. Daijal won't see it that way once they learn of our treaty."

Akeheni's smile was a sharp thing. "The *Uri* does not care."

Vanya nodded. "Very well, *Uri'ka*. Then let us discuss about how our countries might aid each other."

Both of them got settled as Caelum and Greer facilitated the talks with their Tovanian counterparts. Caelum eventually summoned the handful of military aides who had followed them to Oeiras. At some point, he brought over the telephone that rested on the side table, enabling Vanya to call General Chu Hua, who was back in Calhames.

Taisiya left at the lunch break, off to see to Raiah, while Vanya continued the finalization of the treaty. He didn't need the Senate to vote on it, as Solaria's borders were under Vanya's authority. Getting approval from the Legion, while not required, kept everyone happy.

"We can spare the production facility between Oeiras and Calhames," Chu Hua eventually said, a rumble of approval around her from the other officers she'd summoned for the call echoing through the receiver into Vanya's ear.

"Agreed," Vanya said. A final flurry of chatter across the line finished up with Chu Hua tendering a farewell. Vanya set the receiver back in the pronged cradle and focused on Akeheni. "My advisors are agreeable to the location, as am I. We will set the treaty signing ceremony for tomorrow."

He would need to send word to the Senate about what was being agreed to, and Caelum would need time to round up the press for the ceremony so that news could be distributed via broadsheets in all cities. Overall, the alliance would be worth the anticipated headache he would endure over the next few days, but Vanya didn't believe the Houses would find his decision made in bad faith.

Akeheni stood, pressing a fist over her heart and bowing her head. "May our countries ever have calm waters when we sail together."

"My household has prepared a celebratory meal for us tonight," Vanya said.

"We'll gladly join you."

The meeting broke up, and Vanya exited the dignitary room, swept up in Caelum's political needs. Vanya led the way to his office but found his way blocked by a welcome distraction.

"Papa!" Raiah exclaimed, launching herself at him.

Vanya smiled, gathering her into his arms and holding her close. She was warm, skin sun-kissed from being outside. "Did you convince your governess to give you lessons in the garden today?"

Raiah nodded enthusiastically as he carried her into his office, her braids brushing against his cheek. "I had riding lessons today."

"So it appears."

Vanya carried her to his desk while Caelum handled the files and dealt with the aides that had followed them. He sat in the chair, settling Raiah in his lap. She immediately leaned forward and started going through the items and papers scattered on the desktop, careful not to make a mess but curious as she always was. Vanya spoke with Caelum about the evening schedule, focused on the dinner set to occur in just a couple of hours, when Raiah piped up again.

"Papa, you're missing a photograph."

Vanya waved the others off, not watching them leave the office as he turned his attention back to his daughter. "All the ones of you and your *valide* are here."

The photographs in question were neatly arranged at the corner of his desk in stand-up frames, with others perched on the bookcase behind him. Raiah craned her neck around, blinking her big brown eyes up at him with a frown on her little face. "But you're missing the one with Soren and me. I thought you said you would find it for me?"

Vanya's gaze darted to the tintype photographs, knowing exactly the two she meant. One had been of Soren with Raiah when she was younger, taken of the pair together in the gardens there in Oeiras' Imperial estate before the threat of *rionetkas* was known to them. The other had been of Soren by himself, sitting relaxed in a private room, his gaze focused not on the camera but on Vanya, who had been the one to take the photograph.

He'd taken others of Soren over the years, many of which were scattered across the various Imperial estates, along with some that had always traveled with him. But after Soren had left—after the lies were revealed and the hurt of betrayal had lodged itself in the center of Vanya's chest—he hadn't been able to look at the photographs without wanting to break them at times.

Eventually, he'd taken them down and sent them off to his personal storage, hiding them away, as if he could ever hide the gaping hole that existed in his life these days where Soren once stood. Raiah had been persistent lately in finding them again, but he knew it would be best if she learned to forget about the warden.

Vanya cleared his throat. "I'll ask the servants where they've gone. But I believe it's time for your bath."

She frowned stubbornly at him, but Vanya knew the best way to ward off an argument was to distract her. Handing Raiah off to her governess with a kiss goodbye and a promise to see her before her bedtime staved off another tantrum.

Finally alone in his office, Vanya rubbed at his forehead before reaching for the telephone perched on the side of the desk. He put the receiver to his ear and pressed a button, immediately being connected to the Imperial estate's operator. "Put me through to the wardens' governor."

"Certainly, Your Imperial Majesty," the operator said.

It took time, knowing it was a later hour in the east than it was in Oeiras, but eventually, the wardens' governor joined the call.

"Governor Delani," Vanya said. "We need to discuss the tithes my country owes you."

Three

SOREN

Soren's head ached with the constant chatter of a language he didn't understand. He knew Solarian, and he knew the trade tongue, but he'd never learned Ashionen, and the gap of his understanding was clear in every meeting he attended with Caris over the weeks since flying north. He knew she meant well by wanting to keep him included in the high-level talks with military officers and nobility, but all it did was leave Soren feeling as if he were a bug under an alchemist's microscope.

The room he'd been given in the small estate Caris called home was clean, the closet filled with clothes Soren rarely wore. His preference was still for the field uniform he'd worn for years as a warden, the leather and durable cloth a comfort, even if it made people question his identity as Caris' brother. The broadsheets insisted on referring to him as Prince Alasandair Rourke, according to Caris, much to her chagrin. She still called him Soren, as did everyone in her court, which consisted of exactly one lady-in-waiting in the official records so far and a man who Soren assumed was Caris' betrothed, despite not seeing any rings on either of their fingers.

Nathaniel Clementine was friendly enough, if more than a bit reserved. Lady Lore Auclair knew a bit of Solarian, though her trade tongue was better. Along with her mother and brother, they were the next highest-ranked nobles in the country after Caris, and the three of them had to be more than simply an old bloodline. The meetings they took with the military and others spoke of different roles that no one had yet to inform Soren of. But he'd spent enough time in the Imperial court to know the ebb and flow of political power, and Duchess Meleri Auclair had plenty of it.

Then there were the E'ridians, the *jarl* and his husband, who seemed quite content to remain in Cosian with their single E'ridian war airship despite the fact that country had no alliance with Ashion. Blaine and Honovi were fluent in the trade tongue. Speaking with them was always a relief, a soothing bit of sound after hours spent with the tutor trying their best to teach Soren Ashionen and the manners and habits of a people that had never been his.

The tea and food were different, and some mornings, Soren found himself acutely missing the strong tea or sweet chai he'd always had at Vanya's table and the savory, family-style breakfast spreads favored by Solarians. Ashionen food lacked the spices and chilis he'd grown used to over the years. The food shortage that had hit the eastern provinces meant not everything was available, but Soren didn't really think that mattered. Ashionen food was not as heavily spiced as Solarian, and he had yet to locate any sort of restaurant in the frontier city that served the dishes he missed.

He'd taken to brewing his tea in the kitchen without aid from a cook, making the black tea darker than was preferred by everyone else in the home. It wasn't as strong or as spiced as the kind he'd drunk in Solaria, but it did its job of waking him up before dawn every morning.

The early hours were always quiet in the estate, something Soren appreciated, knowing that it wouldn't be long before his ears were assailed with Ashionen. He was busy sprinkling a spice that smelled similar to one used in chai into his tea when someone cleared their throat behind him. He'd heard their footsteps in the hall before they arrived and so didn't jump at the sound.

"It's early," Blaine said in the trade tongue.

"I'm not leaving," Soren replied with a shrug.

He'd thought about it so many times since arriving in Cosian and stepping off that airship. But Delani had given him a border to guard, and Soren had never in his life walked away from his duty. He wasn't about to start now.

A brief pause before Blaine's footsteps drew closer. "Do you always walk around with your weapons on?"

Out of habit, Soren reached over his right shoulder for the hilt of his poison short sword, the clarion crystal embedded in the pommel cool to the touch. His gloves were tucked into his front pockets while he prepared his tea and the toast in a contraption that Caris had proudly said she and her father had modified together when she was younger. She'd shown him how to drop slices of bread into the two holes while the clarion crystal–powered machine heated the bread to the desired crispness.

His toast was currently resting on a plate, butter melting on both slices, and his tea was almost how he could drink it here. "I've learned it's better to be armed no matter where I am."

Soren tried not to think of everything that had transpired in the Imperial palace before Vanya burned it down to keep Calhames safe. The fight in the star temple would have gone poorly if he'd been without his gear, but even then, he'd still ended up in that coffin in the crypt. Only bowing to his need to survive and casting starfire had enabled him to escape, starting an avalanche of decisions that ended with all his lies laid bare to Vanya, but his princeling and Raiah safe.

"I can't say I disagree with that," Blaine said after a moment.

Soren picked up his teacup and plate, turning to carry them both over to the small prep table the kitchen staff typically ate their meals at. Blaine was already pulling one of the low stools out to sit down, dressed in his sleep clothes, the mechanical prosthetic limb Soren rarely saw him without missing. The stump of his left arm was scarred, skin faintly reddened but healed. Blaine absently massaged his left elbow, wincing as he did so.

"Need a potion?" Soren asked.

Blaine blinked at him before glancing down at his arm. "Ah, no.

Just phantom pains that interrupted my sleep. Potions don't do much for that, and I didn't want to disturb Honovi any more than I already have."

Delani had told Soren how Blaine had come to lose his arm. To know that a warden had sought monetary gain over their brethren during the attack on the Warden's Island had been devastating to learn.

Soren sipped his tea, eyeing Blaine across the prep table. It was early yet, the sun just starting to break on the horizon when he'd stuck his head out the window before coming downstairs. The estate was small, with only a limited number of servants, most of whom didn't live on-site. He expected the kitchen staff to arrive shortly, taking back the prep table.

"Your husband was an ambassador, but he's here as a *jarl*," Soren said.

Blaine nodded, letting go of his left arm to prop his elbows on the table. "He's here because I am here, but he isn't speaking for E'ridia."

"You want to stand witness for Caris. Seems odd E'ridia would be invested in that if they aren't invested in the country."

Blaine's mouth tugged downward at the corner. "Yes, well, the Dusk Star gave me my road, and I must follow it. Honovi is working to convince the *Comhairle nan Cinnidhean* that supporting Ashion in this fight is a worthwhile decision. We'll head back to E'ridia soon enough to continue that argument. Eimarille won't stop her war at the Eastern Spine."

Soren grimaced and couldn't even blame his expression on the tea. "She won't stop until she has the whole of Maricol under her crown."

"I agree, but I'm not in charge, and Ashion needs more support," Blaine said tiredly, reaching up to rub at his eyes with his one remaining hand. "Urova is allied with Daijal, so we can't ask for assistance from that country. Caris' diplomats have petitioned E'ridia and Solaria for aid, but both countries keep refusing. There's been talk of trying to reach the Tovan Isles, but any outreach would run through another country, and I don't think permission would be granted. I fear Ashion as a country won't survive to winter without finding an alliance somewhere, and no one is offering a lifeline."

The tea Soren had taken a sip of went sour on his tongue. He was acutely aware of the vow that hung from his throat. "And if E'ridia won't give it? Will you stay?"

Blaine looked away, expression becoming troubled and resigned. "My road leads to Caris, and it always has."

Soren knew Blaine's history with Caris, how he'd taken her out of Amari when she was just an infant, both of them put on an airship captained by the Dusk Star. Nilsine had left Caris in Cosian and given Blaine to the clans in E'ridia, and the price for Blaine's life was the knowledge he couldn't leave his birth country behind. Soren found they had that in common, if little else. "Your broadsheets talk about me being her heir, but you can't stand witness for me. There are plenty of people who don't believe the story she's trying to sell."

"If you could cast starfire—"

"Even if I could, that proves nothing," Soren interrupted. He still refused to acknowledge that skill, despite the way everyone in Cosian seemed desperate to know if he could command starfire the same way Caris and Eimarille could.

"Doesn't it?"

"Starfire is a rarity, but people argue it shouldn't be a requirement to rule. Look at your clans. Look at the Tovanian ship-cities." Soren picked up a slice of his toast and took a bite, chewing angrily and swallowing before responding. "There are no records of my past or where I come from. Anyone could be Caris' brother. Starfire had nothing to do with it. You all just chose me."

"You told Caris you would be her heir."

"Yes. That doesn't make me Alasandair. The moment you get her on the starfire throne, I'm leaving." Blaine appeared taken aback at that statement, mouth opening to speak, but before he got a word out, the piercing sound of a siren rent the air. Bone-deep instinct yanked Soren to his feet, attention sharpening. "Revenants?"

Blaine winced as he shoved himself to his feet. "Yes, and most likely another aerial attack. The Daijal army has been pairing both together more and more these days. We need to get below."

Soren shook his head. "I'll make my way to the wall."

"Soren—"

But he was already moving, racing out of the home and bypassing the Royal Guards out front who were coordinating with the ones on duty on the street. Captain Maurus Nash was near the gate barking out orders when he caught sight of Soren heading straight for his velocycle.

"What do you think you're doing?" Maurus furiously called out in the trade tongue.

Soren slung himself over the seat of his velocycle, kicking up the stand and starting the engine with a twist of the knob and a wrench on the handlebars. "Heading to the wall."

He'd left his gear on the velocycle since landing in Cosian, still somehow believing he could attend to his duties as a warden even when Delani was insistent he could no longer be one. The warning sirens echoing through the air was a call no warden could ever ignore, and Soren wasn't about to stop now. He grabbed an extra pair of brass goggles from the storage container behind his seat and yanked them on. Then he looked at the closed gate and the soldiers guarding it. "Open the gate."

Maurus' expression twisted. "Your Royal Highness—"

"You want me to be your prince, then you're going to listen to the orders I give. Open the damn gate, or I will do it for you."

The captain swore, hesitating only another second before gesturing sharply at those under his command. A soldier hastily undid the lock on the gate and shoved it open. Soren revved the engine and drove forward, wheels biting into the cobblestones as he headed off the grounds.

Cosian was a city whose streets he'd learned the first week of his arrival inside its walls. Soren knew exactly the path he needed to take to get from the center of the city, through its inner walls, and toward the massive outer ones. The route was one Enmei had suggested when Caris had first introduced him to the other warden.

That had been an awkward meeting between the two, but the other warden had heard him out when he'd requested the best roads to travel if they were called to the walls in an emergency. This definitely counted as an emergency, and Soren was glad for his velocycle as he weaved through streets full of abandoned vehicles as people ran for cover.

He'd not been in Cosian for an attack, though it was impossible to miss the number of soldiers mixed in with civilians. They were the ones racing to their assigned defensive positions, and Soren did his best not to run any of them over. The warning sirens never stopped, and beneath the sound was a repeated warning in Ashionen of the oncoming threat.

Soren pushed his velocycle faster, the vibrations from the engine thrumming through the frame between his legs. He leaned into the curve as he took corners at speeds he normally wouldn't push in a city, but he didn't have a choice. Neither was he the only warden gunning for the outer wall.

Other velocycles turning onto the main boulevard were driven by wardens, more than Soren was used to seeing when on the road. But the war had upended everyone's borders, and the influx of wardens that had once guarded Daijal and Urova now found themselves handling the dead in the wake of a war.

When they all got to the main city gates that led to the trade road, the doors were barred shut. Automatons up on the wall had their Zip guns pointed at the land beyond, while the heavy anti-airship guns were being rotated into position.

Enmei was already at the gate, talking to a soldier whose epaulets and ranking pins showed him to be captain. Enmei didn't look pleased with whatever the captain was telling him, judging by the tight, narrowed-eyed expression on the warden's face.

"—not safe for you to be in the line of fire," the captain argued in the trade tongue.

"Waiting for the bombs to drop inside the city puts us at just as much risk. Your airships are launching to meet the ones coming our way. If we don't deal with the revenants now, we'll be hunting them for days in the basin," Enmei replied.

"General Votil wants the gates kept closed."

"The general doesn't speak for us wardens when it comes to revenants."

Soren braked to a stop, back wheel skidding sideways a little until he planted his feet. He shoved his brass goggles on top of his head to better pin the soldier with a hard look. "Open the gates."

The captain did a double take at his order, blinking rapidly as he stared at Soren. "Your Royal Highness?"

Soren grimaced at the title but didn't protest it. "Our duty is out there, so open the gates."

"You heard him," Enmei said, jerking his thumb at the gates. "Let us through."

The captain swore under his breath before spinning on his feet and shouting out an order. Within moments, the metal gate was pulled upward. Soren looked at Enmei, giving the other warden a tight nod. "Orders?"

"Airships are incoming from the west, but the horde is less than two miles out and moving quick. We think Daijal dropped the revenants sometime before dawn and waited for them to make the trek to the walls. It's been their typical practice as of late."

"What's the defense we take beyond the walls?"

Hordes were typically found in the wild beasts population, though travelers who got lost in the poison fields or near bogs and died were known to cluster together as revenants. Thanks to the death-defying machines, this war produced hordes in terrifying numbers, and a single warden couldn't hope to stand against them.

Enmei strode over to the makeshift armory that had been built, reached down, and flipped open the lid of a crate by his feet. "We keep position by the outside walls, near the trenches. That will ensure we stay under the line of fire from those above. The gates will remain closed after our departure, which means if we need to get clear of the ground, we use a grappling wire."

Wardens were already there, hauling away crates and extra gear that they normally didn't travel with. Enmei handed Soren a grappling crossbow, which he secured to his back over the sheath for his poison short sword with the other warden's help. Then he helped Enmei carry a crate to his velocycle, where they secured it behind the seat. A quick check inside showed the disassembled mechanical pieces of a portable grenade launcher. They were shoulder mounted, meant to be handled by two people.

"How good are you at loading grenades?" Enmei asked.

"I handled them on the island when assigned to the fort's walls," Soren said.

Enmei nodded sharply. "Good. You're with me. I don't care what the governor says. You're still a warden in your blood and training, and we need every last one of us in the poison fields right now."

Other wardens loaded up their own velocycles as they arrived, everyone moving with a grim sort of purpose. Soren was itching to leave by the time the Ashion captain returned to them, a troubled expression on his face. "General Votil has asked that I request you stay within the walls while the wardens do their duty, Your Royal Highness."

Soren kicked up the stand on his velocycle and started the engine. "No."

The Ashionens could want to parade him around all they liked to rally their people, but Soren wasn't about to walk away from his duty as a warden. He followed Enmei through the gates and into the flat land of the Eastern Basin, their tires eating up dirt.

Sparse grass and scattered prickly shrubs stretched across the dry ground on either side of the wide trade road. In the distance, on the horizon, a shadowy smudge that could have been fog was steadily growing larger—Daijalan war airships coming to bomb Cosian. More threatening than that was the moving mass of revenants stalking their way toward the city.

The wardens split up, driving in opposite directions to their assigned positions. The Ashion army had dug trenches into the ground some distance from the outer wall, with heavy artillery positioned by each one. The trenches had been abandoned when the warning sirens started up. The Ashion army couldn't afford to lose its soldiers to revenants and spores and had pulled everyone back inside the walls. If this war was being fought with only the living, the trenches wouldn't have been abandoned, and the wardens wouldn't be out there fighting to keep Cosian safe.

"The wall defense will cut through the horde from a distance. We're to handle those that break through," Enmei said after they reached their position outside the wall.

The poison in the grenades would incapacitate the revenants, keeping them unmoving long enough for the wardens to gather the bodies for dozens of pyres. The chemical concoction had been brewed by the remaining alchemists on the Warden's Island and put into production on an expedited notice for use in the poison fields while the war raged. They were far more potent than what the army could produce. Cleansing the poison fields afterward was going to be the work of a generation once the war was won.

If it was won.

"And the airships?" Soren asked. Before Enmei could speak, a fast-moving shadow passed over them, the wide expanse of it causing him to look up. An Ashion airship flew overhead, gaining altitude, followed by another and then another.

"They'll try to keep Daijal's from bombing the city."

They parked their velocycles on the ground near a trench. Neither of them jumped into the trench itself, instead setting up behind it. The crates were taken off the velocycles and the shoulder-mounted grenade launcher assembled with a speed that spoke of Enmei having done this plenty of times before.

Soren flipped open the lid of the crate that held the poison grenades in padded compartments. He picked one up and loaded it into the rear metal tube of the launcher, listening as the gears clicked into place with sharp sounds. Enmei stayed kneeling, fingers resting against the body of it, near the switch and buttons that would launch the grenade.

In the distance, coming closer, was the horde of revenants.

"Ready on the wall!" someone bellowed above a few minutes later.

"Ready below!" Enmei, Soren, and other wardens ranged down the way shouted back.

Seconds later, the sound of Zip guns going off above filled the air, the heavy *rat-tat-tat* of the rapidly fired bullets loud in Soren's ears. The revenants at the front of the oncoming horde were torn to pieces by the bullets and fell. The ones behind marched over the ruined bodies, some of which still tried to crawl forward, before they, too, fell beneath the onslaught of bullets.

Those on the wall knew not to aim so close to the trenches, which meant when the inevitable happened and revenants lurched forward past that invisible line, Enmei and the other wardens acted. The flare of light and smoke from the grenade launching smelled like hot metal. Soren couldn't follow its trajectory, but he saw when it hit. The explosion of dirt and body parts was obvious, as was the way the revenants within the blast radius all abruptly fell to the ground, the poison from the grenade incapacitating them.

Soren reached for another grenade and loaded it with grim determination, never taking his eyes off the horde of revenants that just kept coming.

Four

SOREN

Soren finally left the wall and returned to the estate Caris called home late in the afternoon. The drive through Cosian this time around went much slower, his way impeded by new damage done from dropped bombs. Damaged gas lamp lights meant the city had to cut off the flow of gas in certain areas while rescue crews dug through the rubble of collapsed buildings, looking for survivors.

Only two airships had managed to break through the Ashion defense, but they'd dropped a dozen bombs between them in the city's outer neighborhoods before being harried off by ground-to-air defenses and eventually shot down. If there were any survivors of those crashes out in the wilds of the Eastern Basin, Soren hoped the bodies burned before they rose as revenants.

His fellow wardens had nearly been overrun at the end, sections of their defense having to pull back and use their grappling crossbows to get hauled out of reach of the walking dead. The poison grenades had gone off closer than any of them would've liked, requiring the need for alchemist intervention starting tomorrow before some of the trenches could be manned again. The outer wall remained intact, which was the only positive.

The damage he passed was difficult to observe, knowing the death count would rise. But it was the Ashion people moving about with grim determination—either directly helping with the search and rescue efforts, pitching in to start clearing debris, or feeding those working—that caught Soren's attention. The resolve he could see and hear in those he passed was proof that Daijal hadn't broken them, but how long they could hold out was anyone's guess.

He braked to a stop at an intersection beyond the second inner wall, staring past the makeshift peacekeeper barrier that had been set up to block civilian traffic from the debris of several collapsed buildings. Bodies were laid out in the street under makeshift funeral shrouds consisting of torn sheets. A star priest moved from one body to the next, providing rites to the dead to see them onward to the stars.

Another velocycle drew up beside his. Enmei's attention was on the dead, a frown tugging at his lips. "The Ashion army needs better air support."

"Isn't there an E'ridian airship in the airfield?" Soren asked, thinking of Blaine and Honovi.

"They were in the air, but one war airship won't win a fight against half a squadron."

Soren looked away from Enmei, returning his attention to the efforts of the living. "How long before Ashionens burn their dead?"

"An aerial attack last autumn destroyed one of the city's crematoriums on the western side. It's only half rebuilt, delayed because of the winter storms. The other one is in the southeast side of the city. The dead will burn tonight, for however long it takes. Mourning will take longer."

It seemed senseless, all these innocent lives lost, simply because Eimarille wanted to rule past the borders she had been given. Soren raised a hand, pressing his fingers over the outline of the vow tucked beneath his shirt, a quiet discomfort eating away at his thoughts.

"Ashion won't win as they are, will they?" he asked quietly.

Enmei twisted his velocycle's handlebars, revving the engine. "No, I don't think so."

The other warden drove off to wherever he stayed in Cosian.

Soren watched the survivors work a little longer before leaving, not wanting anyone to recognize him. He drove back toward the center of the city at a slow speed, mindful of the abandoned vehicles and the people working to put their city back to rights again.

When he finally turned onto the street that held Caris' estate, the Royal Guard let him pass without argument, the number having doubled since the morning. He drove his velocycle up the estate's drive and parked it behind a motor carriage. He removed his brass goggles and shoved them in the travel compartment, along with his gloves. He'd cleaned up as best he could at the facilities assigned to wardens near the main gate, removing any excess poison that might have transferred during the fight.

He needed a bath more than anything, and he couldn't help but think of the bathhouses in Solaria that he'd shared with Vanya. Those didn't exist in Ashion, and he'd have to make do with the small copper tub in the estate's guest washroom. As much as he was looking forward to a hot soak, it would have to wait. When he entered the home, the hallway beyond the foyer rang with loud, arguing voices.

Moments later, a door slammed open, and Caris stalked out of a room down the hallway, heading in the other direction with jerky strides. She disappeared around a corner right as Lore darted out of the room and skidded to a stop in the hallway. "Caris!"

She didn't run after the other woman, though, hands fisted at her side as Blaine stepped out of the room, expression resigned. He said something too low for Soren to hear before touching Lore's shoulder and heading off in the direction Caris had gone in. Lore let out a heavy sigh and turned on her feet, jerking slightly when she caught sight of Soren. With determined steps, she closed the distance between them, a mix of relief and anger on her face.

"You went past the wall when General Votil told you not to," Lore said by way of greeting in stilted trade tongue.

"Your general isn't mine," Soren replied. "I had my duty."

"You aren't a warden anymore." Soren didn't even bother replying to that, merely stepped around her and walked away in the direction Caris and Blaine had gone. "Alasandair!"

Soren grimaced at the use of that name and refused to respond to it. He bypassed the room where Meleri and a handful of people he didn't know were huddled, ignoring the cry of his name the duchess let out.

In the scant few weeks he'd lived in the estate, he knew the one place Caris always went to when she felt out of sorts and needed to clear her head. The door to the small laboratory in the rear garden was shut, but the gas lamp lights were turned on, a soft glow shining through the windows. Soren didn't bother knocking, and instead let himself inside to the furious sound of Caris venting her frustration to Blaine.

Soren couldn't really understand what Caris was saying, but he understood the look of frustration in her gestures, and the grief on her face, even if the tone of her voice was all anger. Caris made a sound not unlike a furious hawk might make. The machinery and chunks of clarion crystals scattered around the worktables vibrated in place, a few tools rolling off the edge to the floor.

Soren watched her take a deep breath, hands clenched into fists, and squeeze her eyes shut. The shaking stopped, everything settling back down. The temperature in the laboratory took a nosedive, the heat Soren had thought had accumulated during the day actually coming from Caris.

"What's wrong?" Soren asked in the trade tongue.

Caris wrenched her eyes open, startled, and stared at him. "You're back."

Blaine twisted around, relief writ clear across his face. "Captain Nash was furious you decided to fight. Caris wanted to join you, but General Votil forbade it."

Soren stared at Caris. "You're not a warden. You can't go past the walls during a revenant attack."

"I could burn them from the top with starfire," Caris shot back waspishly. "I did it on your island."

The shores of the Warden's Island still retained black glass scattered through the sand from her efforts. He'd nearly cut through the sole of a boot from the shards once. "Maybe next time."

Caris smiled thinly, gray eyes hard. "If Meleri has her way, I'll never see the fighting up close."

Blaine sighed tiredly. "You know why we can't have you on the front lines."

Caris raised her hand and spread her fingers. The bright, incandescent glow of starfire crackled into existence against her palm, the shine of it as brilliant as its namesake. "I think I would have better reach than even our best artillery."

"Not if you're dead," Soren retorted.

"I feel as if I'm useless here, treated like a child, when I could be *helping* people."

"You *are* helping people," Blaine said.

Caris' lips twisted bitterly. "Not enough. You know it doesn't matter where I stand. Eimarille wants me dead. She wants Soren dead. It's the only way she can claim the starfire throne. So long as we live, the North Star's decree can be put out, and she will stop at nothing to make sure that doesn't happen."

The vow hung like a noose around Soren's neck, a weight that had never felt as heavy as it did in that moment. He'd thought about it in the weeks since his arrival and he'd learned what Ashion was up against, what it would mean to finally use what was promised, and what would happen if he didn't. But this war was about more than just the starfire throne—it was about the whole of Maricol, even if some countries refused to act. To let Eimarille win would see the subjugation of the wardens, and Delani had tasked him with guarding them.

"If there was a way to get Solaria to ally with you, would you take it?" Soren asked.

Caris curled her fingers over the starfire burning in her hand and snuffed it out before crossing her arms over her chest, giving him an odd look. "Of course, but my diplomats have been unsuccessful in convincing the Imperial emperor or his Senate to change course."

Soren hooked his thumb under his collar, snagging the gold chain of the vow and dragging it free. The medallion spun at the end of the links, glittering in the gas lamp lights that burned in the laboratory. "I saved Vanya's life some years ago. I am owed a debt, and he will pay anything I ask. If you need an alliance, I can get you the Legion."

Caris' eyes went wide, and she didn't immediately speak. Blaine, on the other hand, had no qualms about expressing his shock. *"You're that warden?"*

Soren let the chain go, and the vow thumped heavily against his chest. It took effort to get his answer out, feeling as if the vow itself was strangling him. "Yes."

"What are you talking about?" Caris asked.

Blaine waved his left arm at Soren, gears clicking subtly in his mechanical prosthetic. "When the Imperial emperor was a prince, he was nearly assassinated and thought dead for a few days back in 931. The news made it to E'ridia via telegraph and broadsheets, and then an update came a few editions later, stating he'd survived with the aid of a warden. We never found out the warden's name, though."

"A rival House tried to poison Vanya. At the time, they didn't approve of his marriage. I reached him before the poison could take effect," Soren said.

Caris came around the worktable and approached, only stopping when she stood toe to toe in front of Soren. Her eyes were locked on the vow, gaze unreadable. She didn't try to touch it, which Soren was thankful for. "Would the Imperial emperor truly lend us his Legion?"

Soren wrapped his hand around the medallion, the imprint of the lion cutting into his palm. He tried not to think about the devastation in Vanya's eyes during their last night together. "He will if I ask."

It would forever bar him from Vanya's side, no chance of returning to the man he wanted more than anything. He hadn't lied when he'd told Vanya he would never ask for himself, but Ashion—no, *Maricol*—was worth losing Vanya forever.

It had to be.

"Then you're my newest Solarian diplomat. I assume you know the language?"

Soren smiled tightly. "Better than Ashionen."

"You're lucky we're fluent in trade tongue, or it'd be a headache for all of us." Caris looked over at Blaine, looking more hopeful than she had mere minutes ago. "If Solaria joins the war effort, do you think that would prompt E'ridia to as well?"

Blaine made a face. "The *Comhairle nan Cinnidhean* wouldn't take that as a sign to ally ourselves with your country. It would take more than a given vow to bring the E'ridian air force into play. Honovi is set to fly to Glencoe in a few days. He will argue your case, as always."

"If I can't have your airships, I'll take Solaria's Legion. Let's bring this news to Meleri and Clarence. I anticipate a long evening ahead of us."

Blaine was the first one out of the laboratory while Caris lingered behind. Soren was astute enough at social hints now that he kept his feet planted as well. She met his gaze with a frank steadiness that he returned. "Is there a chance the Imperial emperor would deny your vow, despite your assertations?"

Soren had a feeling Vanya would try, if only fleetingly. The Houses who already distrusted Vanya's decisions wouldn't trust this, but Soren told himself he couldn't think about that. Vanya had offered the vow with no restrictions, and Soren had never thought he'd ever use it, for he'd had no intention of painting Vanya into a corner. But he knew if he brought the vow to Vanya and demanded payment, Vanya would keep his word because if he didn't, the House of Sa'Liandel would lose all the loyalty left to it.

"He won't," Soren said with a sureness he felt down to his bones.

Vanya was, above all else, an honorable man. He would do what was right; of that, Soren had no doubt. It would just break Soren's heart in the process.

Five

SOREN

The wind on an airship was nothing like the sort on the ground. Despite the heat of Seventh Month, the higher altitudes were cold, and Soren was glad for the fur-lined leather flight jacket he'd been given for the journey. It had necessitated leaving his gear in the small cabin assigned to him on the Ashion airship, but it meant he was warm as the airship flew through a cloudless blue sky.

The small glass dome that encompassed the lounge provided a clear view of the surrounding flight deck, the sky beyond, and the balloon above. Certain windows were able to be winched open, but none were at the moment.

The whistling of the passing wind outside was a white noise that helped drown out his thoughts as Oeiras drew ever closer. Their route had taken them south first, away from the fighting to reach Solaria. They'd first touched down in Karnak to bring Caris' diplomatic corps on board, who'd traveled there from Calhames.

They'd been notified the Imperial emperor held court these days in Oeiras while the new Imperial palace was being built. It meant a longer flight, crossing the width of the southern portion of the continent to that eastern city. It was still quicker than if they'd taken a steam train, and Soren couldn't decide which travel option he would have preferred. Either way, Vanya would be waiting for him at the end of the trip, and that knowledge was enough to make Soren's stomach roil uneasily. He couldn't even blame it on the turbulence they'd experienced off and on, though he wished he could.

"You look tired," Lore said in the trade tongue as she sat at his table. Her accent wasn't the best, but it couldn't be helped. Lore's linguistic skills had focused on E'ridian, though she was picking up Solarian out of necessity. They still couldn't have a conversation in that language, but the rest of the diplomatic corps were fluent in it.

"I slept enough," Soren replied.

A crew member approached with a tea set on a silver tray, nimbly serving them the drink. The tables and some viewing benches were bolted to the floor, but the cushioned seats were not. Soren eyed the delicate teacup and the dark tea inside it, wishing for some chai or the spiced red tea he'd come to love over the years. He had to make do with thick cream and honey rather than sugar to make it palatable.

There was a lot of Ashion culture that Soren didn't care for, wasn't comfortable with yet, and didn't know if he ever would be. He'd promised Caris he would be her heir, but he'd give the spot away the moment she claimed the starfire throne and married Nathaniel. They could have as many children as they wanted, and Soren would gladly cede any right to their heritage.

What he wanted couldn't be found in Cosian or Amari or any city in Ashion.

"Lord Dariush, in his capacity as our ambassador, believes your vow will be a miracle," Lore said.

Soren resisted the urge to reach up and touch the shape of the vow beneath his shirt. "I'm not doing this for a miracle."

Lore sipped her tea, watching him with keen hazel eyes. "You seem to think the Imperial emperor will give you anything just because you saved his life. Most rulers wouldn't offer up something like that with no restrictions."

"Vanya didn't know my past."

"Most people don't use a ruler's name with such familiarity."

"I'm a warden. We don't care about titles."

"You're a prince. Perhaps you should remember that before we land."

Soren decided the tea wasn't worth the interrogation. "Perhaps you should let me do the talking when we land. Solarian politics aren't yours."

Even the crash course Lord Dariush had been giving everyone in Solarian politics wasn't enough for Lore and the others to understand the nuances of the Houses and how they orbited the Imperial throne, vying for power.

Soren stood and left the table, heading for the exit. Belowdecks was accessible to the lounge without needing to go out onto the flight deck. Soren chose to spend the last hour of their flight west by himself, in the small cabin, staring at the vow and praying he wasn't making a terrible mistake.

What Soren assumed was the call for landing came through the small speaker bolted above the door sometime later, the words garbled to his ears. Still, he could feel the change of altitude in his ears as the airship descended toward the airfield outside Oeiras. Soren's room didn't have a port window, so he couldn't see the ground, but he felt it when the airship juddered into place in its berth.

He stripped out of his flight jacket and removed his altitude mask from his belt, tossing both on the bed. With practiced ease, he pulled on his pauldron and sheathed poison short sword, his nerves settling a little as he dressed the part of a warden rather than that of a prince. Everyone had protested when he'd refused the trunk of splendid clothes that would be fine for the Ashion nobles but would get them laughed out of the Imperial court. Soren would step foot in Solaria as himself, even if he wasn't sure who that was these days.

A firm knock on his door had him shaking away such thoughts as someone called out in stilted trade tongue, "Your Royal Highness? We're ready to disembark."

Soren picked up his rucksack with the field supplies he never went without and opened the door, finding a military officer waiting for him in the hallway. "I'm ready."

The officer gestured at the rucksack hanging off his shoulder. "The porters can take that for you. We're to be housed in the diplomatic estate, and all the travel trunks will be transported there."

"No, I'll carry it."

Soren slipped into the hallway and headed for the stairwell, taking the steps abovedeck. Heat greeted him, the thick humidity of the coastal *vasilyet* something he remembered from his time spent in Oeiras before.

Lore and the others milled about nearby, clearly waiting for him. Lord Dariush gave him a pleasant enough smile. "The Imperial estate sent an envoy to greet us. I've been told they're led by the Chief Minister."

Caelum had survived the attack on the palace and had never once steered Vanya wrong politically. Soren's interaction with the man over the years had been polite enough, though he doubted that ease would be present today. "Does he know I'm coming?"

"He knows the queen sent a close emissary with a new request and that I am to help facilitate talks. We did not indicate you were on board, but the manifest will. Is there something we should be concerned about?"

"No."

It tasted like a lie on his tongue, but none of the people on the flight deck could tell. Truthfully, Soren didn't know how everyone would react to his appearance in Solaria as a prince rather than a warden, but there was only one way to find out.

He led the delegation off the Ashionen airship, attention on the group of officials in their summer robes waiting for them on the dock. He saw the moment Caelum recognized him, the way the Chief Minister's eyes got fractionally wider once Soren stepped off the gangplank. The older man's blue eyes flicked up and down Soren's body, taking in his attire. But he was ever the politician and saw through the façade Soren was clinging to.

"Prince Alasandair Rourke," Caelum said after a moment, dipping into a shallow bow. "This is a surprise."

"I didn't want it to be," Soren said. "And that's still not a name I go by."

"It's the one used in broadsheets coming out of Ashion."

"I never claimed it."

"Yet you travel with the Ashionen delegation, here on behalf of a supposed queen who claims kinship with you."

"There's a war going on, and I'm here to speak with Vanya about it."

Caelum smiled politely, expression still that neutral mask Soren had seen the other man wear countless times before when dealing with strangers. "His Imperial Majesty has already advised the ambassador with you that Solaria has no intention of allying itself with the war efforts on either side in the countries north of us."

"I still want to speak with Vanya."

"The Ashionen delegation is welcome to the embassy set aside for their country, but His Imperial Majesty is unavailable for the business you seek."

Soren hooked his thumb beneath his collar and snagged the gold chain, dragging the flat medallion from beneath his shirt. The vow glinted in the hot summer sun, the House of Sa'Liandel's crest of a roaring lion in profile stamped clear in gold. "He'll be available for me."

Caelum's gaze locked on the medallion, too good of a politician to lose his neutral mask, but Soren saw the way he went just a shade paler beneath the hot summer sun. "I will make His Imperial Majesty aware of your request. You and your delegation will accompany me to the Imperial estate."

Soren let go of the vow, the medallion thumping against his chest. "Lead the way."

The group of mismatched people started down the pier. Somehow, Lore ended up next to Soren as they walked, keeping pace with him.

"Do you still think the Imperial emperor will accept your vow?"

she asked in a low voice, the trade tongue an outlier in the voices speaking Solarian around them in the airfield.

Soren stared straight ahead, eyes on the high wall surrounding Oeiras, tension starting a slow throb of a headache behind his eyes. "He will."

What he wanted more than that was for Vanya to accept him.

To keep him the way Soren knew Vanya would keep his promise.

Six

VANYA

Vanya was busy reviewing the latest update on the fight to reach Bellingham—he had vetoed yet another request for aerial bombardment of the city—when the door to his office was pushed open without even a knock. He looked up, frowning at the tense expression on Caelum's face. "What is it?"

Caelum bowed deeply. "Forgive me, Your Imperial Majesty. The Solarian diplomatic delegation has arrived."

"My position for Solaria hasn't changed. I don't know why they think it will."

"This time, the ambassador didn't come alone."

Caelum paused for long enough that Vanya set aside his report. "What has you worried? Was one of them a *rionetka*?"

"They all passed the physical checks. No, it's—" Caelum broke off, grimacing, a pained sort of look in his blue eyes. "It's the prince. He came with them."

Vanya froze, breath stuttering in his lungs, a high-pitched ringing tone filling his ears at Caelum's announcement. Lifelong training with controlling his emotions meant he didn't react worse than that, but it was close. Vanya swallowed, the motion like swallowing glass, and it took him a long minute to find his voice. "Why?"

He'd had no communication with Soren since the warden—the *prince*—had left his bed and left his road. That didn't mean Vanya hadn't wanted to know, even in the depths of the hurt left behind, where the other man was and how he was faring. Now he was here, returned, and Vanya knew with a sinking sort of disquiet that he wouldn't like the reason for whatever brought Soren back to him.

Caelum flexed his fingers before folding his hands together in front of him, no judgment seeping into his voice when he spoke. "He carries a vow. One with your House's crest on it. He asked to speak with you."

Vanya flinched with his entire body, glad the blow hadn't hit in the middle of the Imperial court, which he was due to oversee in less than an hour. Vanya closed his eyes and drew in a deep breath, searching for the iron-willed composure that had seen him through the Conclave last year and finding it brittle.

"Is it valid?" Caelum asked into the silence Vanya couldn't bring himself to fill. "The vow? The crest—"

"The vow is rightfully his." Caelum went silent at that statement, and Vanya finally opened his eyes, seeing nothing but concern in his Chief Minister's face. "He asked to speak with me?"

Caelum nodded. "Ambassador Dariush Zayed is with him, though he left the speaking to the prince."

It was strange to hear Soren referred to as that, anger flickering like a spark of starfire in Vanya's chest. He organized the reports on his desk into a pile, covers closed, and took a deep breath before standing, rolling his shoulders to settle his white robe with its gold embroidery. He wasn't yet wearing his crown or other jewels of state, but Caelum seemed to have anticipated that, for a knock on his office door heralded the arrival of an Imperial jeweler.

The woman carried a lacquered jeweler's box and curtsied rather than bowed, inclining her head with reverence. "Your Imperial Majesty."

Caelum directed her to place the box on the credenza before waving her out. He did the duty of taking out the Imperial crown with its gold filigree and deep red rubies and placing it on Vanya's head. "Is there anything else you need?"

"My *valide*. Send her to me," Vanya said.

His circle of trusted aides and family members was tiny these days, but he knew Taisiya would always see reason when he could not. Vanya was pragmatic enough to know that Soren was so much more than a liability to himself and his House and his country.

"I will summon her. The Ashionens are waiting in the dignitary room overlooking the oasis courtyard."

Vanya nodded and led the way to the room in question. It was a grand space made up of marble floors, mosaiced walls, and arched windows that opened into a courtyard that could have been a mirror of the wild jungle spread out beyond Oeiras' walls. Vanya noticed none of the grandeur when he entered after being announced.

All he saw was Soren.

Ten months since the last time they'd breathed the same air, and all Vanya could think was that Soren looked worn and tired, wearing the field uniform of a warden but surrounded by Ashionens. No crown, no trappings of royalty, only the golden vow Vanya had given him years ago as thanks for saving his life.

"I will speak with the prince alone," Vanya said into the tense silence.

Soren flinched, expression one of regret before he hid it all behind the political mask Vanya had taught him to hold when attending the Imperial court. "Here or elsewhere?"

Vanya didn't bother responding, merely headed for the arched doorway that led out to the inner courtyard. He didn't wait to see if Soren would follow, stepping onto the narrow arcade that provided some shade from the sun above. The plants and trees there were different from the desert ones Vanya was used to seeing in Calhames, but the lush greenery in pots and garden plots amidst the tiled courtyard and bubbling pond provided a veneer of privacy. The beauty of the surroundings couldn't soften the emotional blow of Soren's arrival back into his life.

Quiet footsteps behind him finally had Vanya turning around once he'd gone far enough, watching Soren come to a stop an arm's length away, too close and too far all at once. Gray eyes that he'd missed looking into at all hours of the day stared back at him from beneath a thatch of windblown light brown hair. A face he used to wake up to was dappled with shadows from sunlight streaming through the branches of the potted tree they stood under, but the shadows beneath Soren's eyes and within them persisted.

Vanya wanted to hold him close as much as he wanted to push Soren away, torn between all that they'd had together before lies came to light and the betrayal that fed the hurt Vanya still carried. Of all the losses Vanya had experienced, losing Soren had been the worst.

Neither spoke, not for a long few minutes, and when Vanya finally wrangled all his angry, bitter, mournful thoughts into some semblance of words, he found himself with only one question that mattered. "Is this you asking?"

Soren's trembling lips pressed together in a hard line, as if he were holding back whatever was the first thought to come to him. He breathed sharply through his nose before nodding with a decisiveness that appeared a lot like grief. "I always said I would never ask for myself."

Fury burned through Vanya like the molten heat of starfire for a split second. His skin went hot, as if he were too small to contain anything, before he wrangled it into submission. "You also said you were *nameless*, Alasandair Rourke. A *prince* is not nameless."

Soren's hands spasmed ever so slightly before he clenched them into fists. He lifted his chin, gaze never leaving Vanya's. "I haven't claimed that name."

"It is what people call you in every broadsheet and report I read."

"It's not *mine*."

"You are Queen Caris' *heir*. How can you not be Rourke if she claims you as her brother?"

"Because the governor gave me a border to guard, and that border was the wardens themselves. Do you think my people would survive if Eimarille defeats Ashion? She attacked us once already and cares nothing about the dead she uses to further her own gain. I won't see the wardens eradicated because of her ambition. Choosing to follow my governor's order doesn't make me a prince."

The words were said forcibly, passionately, but his tone was a plea Vanya couldn't accept. Only there was a vow Vanya had given when he'd been young and—in ever bitter hindsight—thoughtless. In his attempt to clear a debt owed by himself alone, Vanya had unintentionally damned his entire country.

If Soren had only ever been a warden, the vow would have been insignificant amidst Solaria's politics. Except here he stood before Vanya as a foreign prince, clinging to the only road he'd ever known, one that had led him back to Solaria.

Back to Vanya one last time.

Soren reached up and removed the vow, undoing the clasp with a peculiar hesitancy that spoke of never having done it much, if it all. Vanya wondered if he'd ever taken it off in all the years since it had been gifted, but it didn't matter anymore, not when Soren was finally giving it back. Soren held it out to Vanya, chain clenched in one hand, the medallion swaying from the end of it, glinting in the sunlight.

"This is me finally asking," Soren said hoarsely. "Ashion needs Solaria's Legion."

Vanya choked out a bitter, angry little laugh, staring at the vow before taking it with stiff fingers. The metal felt heavier than he remembered, the weight of what he owed like an insidious anchor. "You lied about everything. Did you ever even care about my country? About *me*?"

Soren's expression twisted, and he swayed forward a little, as if he were going to reach out to Vanya, before he jerked himself back. "Vanya, I—"

"Soren!" Raiah shrieked, shattering the intimate bubble of illusory privacy they'd wrapped themselves in. "*Soren!*"

They both turned toward the entrance to the dignitary room that Raiah tore out of, her skinny little legs pumping beneath her summer gown. Her braids flew behind her as she ran toward Soren with a desperate look on her face and tears in her eyes. For his part, Soren wasn't unaffected, moving away from Vanya so fast there was no chance of stopping him.

Raiah threw herself at Soren, and the warden picked her up as if she weighed nothing. He hugged her close, an arm around her waist and his other hand cradling the back of her skull as Raiah wrapped her arms around his neck, buried her face against his shoulder, and sobbed. "You're back!"

"Hey now, no tears," Soren said raggedly, eyes squeezed shut against his own tears, but Vanya could see the way they dampened his lashes. "I'm right here."

"You were *gone*."

"I know. I *know*, and I am so very sorry for that, but I had to leave." Soren opened his eyes, the color of them like a desert storm when they stared at Vanya. "I had my duty."

It was as much an excuse for Raiah as it was a plea to Vanya. He wanted to discard it, to ignore it, but it would mean pretending that duty meant nothing to him when it was all that he had ever known.

Raiah clutched at Soren harder, her small fingers grappling at his vest around his poison short sword that no one had asked him to give up before being in Vanya's presence. Despite the Ashionens he traveled with, Vanya's people had treated Soren exactly as they always had —someone to be trusted.

After everything, Vanya wasn't sure he could allow such freedom again.

"Raiah, come here," Vanya said, stepping close and reaching for her.

"No!" she shrieked, holding on to Soren tighter. "No! He'll go away again!"

Soren looked as if he'd been punched. "Raiah, I'm not going away right now."

She was young, but she was Vanya's daughter and an Imperial princess and knew enough about how words could mean many things. Her grip on Soren somehow seemed to get tighter. "Right now doesn't include later."

Something that might have been humor at any other moment

flashed across Soren's face before he turned his head to press a kiss against Raiah's. "I know."

Raiah grumbled something too low for Vanya to hear, but which made Soren's lips twitch into a smile. Vanya was about to take her from him when Taisiya stepped into the courtyard and came their way.

"Your absence has been mourned," Taisiya said, her shrewd gaze on Soren.

Soren whispered something to Raiah before bending to set Vanya's daughter on her feet. She still clung to his hand with both of hers, leaning in close, mindful of the weapons he carried. "Taisiya."

"Well met, Soren. Or should it be prince now instead of warden?" Her gaze cut away to the vow Vanya held before he could answer, expression never changing. "I see there are discussions to be had."

"*Valide*," Vanya said warningly.

Taisiya clicked her tongue at him. "The Imperial court awaits. We will discuss this after."

It was the better choice, given who peered curiously through the windows. Vanya didn't care for an audience when the ramifications of the vow he held and the debt he owed was finally acknowledged. "Then let us depart."

Taisiya held out her hand to Raiah. "Come along."

Raiah frantically shook her head. "No! I want to stay with Soren."

"Raiah," Vanya said firmly. "You will go with your *valide*."

Before she could throw a fit, Soren knelt beside her, catching her attention. "Go with Taisiya. I'll be at court as well, and she can show you where I stand."

"You won't be sitting with us?" Raiah asked.

Soren's gaze flicked to Vanya before returning to her. "I must stand with those I came here with."

"But you won't leave?"

"Not right now."

"Promise?"

Soren nodded gravely. "I promise."

Raiah sniffed and let go of his hand so she could wipe the tears from her face. "Okay."

She stepped away from him to go stand with Taisiya, who took her in hand and nodded at Vanya. "We will see you in the Constellation Hall."

Taisiya left with Raiah, his daughter looking back at Soren every step of the way, as if she were afraid he'd disappear. Soren, for his part, never took his eyes from her.

"She missed you," Vanya said roughly.

"I missed her, too," Soren said quietly as he stood.

Vanya refused to look at him, keeping his attention on his daughter. "You were of my household once. I won't have you pretend to be again only for it to hurt her when you must leave."

His name, when Soren spoke it, came out cracked. "Vanya—"

"Go stand with your people, Alasandair. I must tend to mine."

Vanya tucked the vow into his robe's pocket and walked away, refusing to look back how Raiah had despite everything in him crying out to do so.

Seven

VANYA

The Imperial estate in Oeiras was far larger than the ancestral estate the House of Sa'Liandel held in Calhames. Like other Imperial estates across the nation in capital *vasilyet* cities, it acted as a miniature palace for a traveling head of state. It could by no means replace what Vanya had burned down, but it projected the sense of Imperial rule that he needed more so than Calhames could at this time.

The Constellation Hall was a scaled-down version of the throne room that had once existed in the Imperial palace. Like in the Senate, it held a throne, this one carved with the oceanic and jungle motifs of the *vasilyet* it stood in. The embroidered cushions on the seat and back were comfortable enough and had become familiar over the many months he'd sat in it, even if the sea of faces before him changed with every court session.

Vanya held court once a week, allowing petitioners from businesses and guilds, representatives of major and minor Houses, and others to present themselves with social and business requests, looking for Imperial approval. It was rare Vanya issued writs on behalf of the Imperial throne, but it was also a way to take the pulse of his people.

Imperial Empress Zakariya, of the House of Sa'Liandel, had always held court, and that was a habit Vanya had not broken since his mother's death. It was an intimate political and social dance whose usual steps were upended this time by Soren's appearance with the Ashionens. Vanya was certain that news of Soren's return would reach representatives of the press the moment it was polite for anyone to leave, and from there, it would be in the broadsheets before sunset in cities across the country.

Every House would learn that Soren was known now as Prince Alasandair Rourke. That the warden Vanya had led into the royal crypts, who had been the catalyst for the sanctions levied against Solaria by the wardens, was himself a head of state. The repercussions of that would be nothing like what would come when the vow was brought to light and the debt Vanya owed had to be paid.

Vanya had to constantly remind himself not to reach for it, to ignore the weight of it in his pocket. The ghost of his past decision would haunt him soon enough, but for now, he had his subjects to meet. He kept his attention on his people, not the foreigners, hearing what was brought before him and taking everything under advisement, to be reviewed later with his Chief Minister and other advisers. An aide took discreet notes at a small standing writing desk tucked away near the wall but close enough to the throne dais to hear conversation. Taisiya sat in a grand seat beside the dais with Raiah in hand, his daughter on her best behavior.

The Ashionen delegation remained at the back, near the wall with its white-and-gold mosaic depicting the constellations of the six star gods. The Dawn Star's imagery was the most prominent, and Vanya couldn't look at it without remembering the way the golden tattoos had stood out against the dark skin of Callisto's throat. He kept his attention on the crowd, not on the constellations, but that didn't mean he could forget the Dawn Star's words from that morning last year to keep the warden close.

Vanya knew he couldn't, not when Soren had a road that couldn't cross his anymore.

When the presentations were finished, Vanya stood from his throne and stepped off the dais, mingling with the guests in the hall. It was how he always ended court, wanting to put a more personable touch on the proceedings than that of a removed, untouchable ruler. Servants passed by the small groups of people with trays of sweet red wine, the temperature in the room warm from the crowd. The mechanical fans in the corners helped keep the air moving, a soft hum that ran through the drone of conversation.

"I do hope you will take our request under advisement," the representative from the House of Aetos said. Otto wasn't of the main House, having been married into a distant branch of the bloodline. His presence was meant to be an insult despite the request for trade easement he came with. Having the Tovanians patrolling the coastline meant certain harbor restrictions that Seaville was apparently not pleased about on the east coast. It didn't impact trade with E'ridians, but it certainly did with Urovans.

Considering what Vanya knew of that country and its alliance with Daijal, he couldn't quite feel any sympathy for making it difficult for Urovan submersibles to find port.

"The safety of Solaria is important to me. Keeping our borders secure on land and at sea is integral to our sovereignty," Vanya said blandly.

Otto's smile was as sincerely insincere as one could get away with in this crowd. "Of course. The House of Aetos does not disagree with that, but business is important to the economy."

"The economy is worth nothing if our people are dead. The restrictions you protest are for the good of the country, and they will remain."

"Of course, Your Imperial Majesty." A passing servant paused to offer their tray of glasses, the sweet red wine with floating fruit filling each one. Otto reached for two glasses, offering one to Vanya with a sketch of a bow that nearly sloshed the liquid over the rims. "A toast, if you like, to Solaria."

The polite thing to do would be to acknowledge such loyalty to their country. Vanya took the wineglass, fingers slipping from some of the condensation. He raised it in a silent toast to Otto's words before taking a sip. Otto slipped away, replaced by yet another person looking to reinforce their earlier petition with a one-on-one chat.

After the second such conversation, Vanya found the heat in the Constellation Hall increasing despite the fans and the cool drink in his hand. The tips of his fingers started to tingle in a way he thought came from gripping the wineglass too tight until they spasmed. The wineglass slipped out of his grip, his attempt to hold on to it getting lost in the prickling hot awareness that *something wasn't right*. He didn't even feel it when the red wine splashed over his white robes before the wineglass shattered on the marble floor.

Poison, he thought as the noise in the Constellation Hall became curiously muffled. He could still breathe, but he wondered for how much longer.

The weakness spread, and he would've collapsed if someone didn't catch him, guiding him down to the floor. A hand framed his face, tipped his head back, and he found himself staring into beloved gray eyes wide with fear. "Vanya!"

He wanted to speak, wanted to say something more than the hurtful words they'd exchanged already that day, but he found his tongue wouldn't work. Soren looked away from him, talking to someone that Vanya couldn't see, and the numbing weakness was digging into his bones now with a fiery ache in his joints that made him want to flinch, but that seemed to take so much effort.

Soren took his hand that had held the wineglass and wiped it with a small piece of white paper that came away with streaks of orange-red across it. "He's been poisoned."

Vanya would have laughed at that statement because *of course he had*. Cold numbness vied with hot pain as his entire body jerked, heels clattering against the floor. His vision was blurring, and so he couldn't see what was pressed against his lips, but he felt it.

"Drink," Soren told him, still sounding so far away.

It felt like the aftermath of that train wreck so long ago that Vanya didn't question the order. Soren tipped Vanya's head back, and something bitter flowed over his tongue and down his throat. Vanya still had enough control left to swallow the liquid on his own. He closed his eyes, still breathing, still alive, listening desperately as sound slowly returned to him in increments. Eventually, so did the ability to move, hastened by another dose of whatever antidote Soren had given him.

"Otto," Vanya croaked out when he thought his tongue could form the syllables.

"*Praetoria* legionnaires have him in custody. He tried to leave the estate, but they barred him at the gate. It was a contact poison, not one you drank, and you've been out of it for a bit." Cool fingers touched his cheek, shaking ever so slightly, or maybe that was Vanya. "I need you to open your eyes, princeling."

The endearment cut through Vanya like a knife, causing him to suck in air too quickly, and he found himself coughing horrendously as the muscles in his chest spasmed. An arm curled beneath his shoulders, lifting him up so he wasn't completely supine. The new angle made it easier to breathe, and Vanya cracked open his eyes.

The Constellation Hall was empty of the Imperial court but filled with *praetoria* legionnaires. Soren was the one holding him, while Caelum knelt on his other side, appearing as white as Vanya's robes when they weren't stained.

"Raiah?" Vanya asked breathlessly.

"Taisiya is with her. They're both safe," Caelum said.

Vanya grunted, trying to get his fingers to move. One or two twitched, and he grimaced, blinking rapidly. "Can't feel."

"Give it a few more minutes. I gave you a broad antidote to start with, but someone had to bring me my gear so I could mix the correct one," Soren said.

Vanya managed a shallow nod, momentarily closing his eyes. He let Soren continue to hold him up, swallowed another dose of antidote when told to do so, and didn't question the way Soren dealt with Javier when the *praetoria* legionnaire major entered the Constellation Hall. Despite everything that had happened between them, Vanya hadn't removed Soren from his household, and Javier obeyed Soren's orders as if they were Vanya's.

"Was Otto a *rionetka*?" Soren asked.

"No scars and no veil hiding anything. He's alive and acted on his own free will," Javier said.

"Stupidly so, which means he wasn't a Blade. What House does he claim?"

"Aetos," Vanya muttered, clumsily lifting a hand to wipe at the sweat beading on his brow. He didn't know where his crown was but assumed someone had taken custody of it. Vanya opened his eyes, vision marginally better, though a throbbing was starting at his temples, promising a severe headache.

"They supported the House of Kimathi. Whatever orders he'll say he was given, the House of Aetos will deny any association with him. Something tells me there will be no proof of those orders."

"It's tradition for the Houses to deny such power grabs," Caelum said.

"Of course it is." Soren's annoyed disgust was clear for anyone to hear. "Is he of the bloodline, or did he marry in?"

"Married in."

"They'll repudiate him." And oh, despite his absence, Soren's knowledge of the Houses hadn't faded one bit, Vanya discovered. Soren touched two fingers to Vanya's throat, taking his pulse. "All right, princeling. How are you feeling?"

Vanya stared up at Soren's face, vision better than it had been even some minutes ago. The tingling numbness had faded almost everywhere except his fingers, but even he could tell that, too, would pass soon enough. The ache left behind in his muscles from the poison was painful in a way he knew the antidote couldn't fix. The tightness in his chest had nothing to do with surviving an assassination attempt and everything to do with the knowledge of how close he'd come to never having Soren by his side again. "Alive."

"But been better, I'm sure." Soren managed a tight smile, the pressure of his fingers easing but not leaving. Vanya found he didn't mind the lingering touch after so many months of going without. "Your healer is waiting for you in your room."

"What poison was it?"

"Nervbiyan. Otto smeared it on your wineglass using his rings. It's best absorbed through contact and doesn't have a smell, but nothing can mask how it tastes."

Vanya closed his eyes and took a deep breath, glad that it no longer hurt. "I would assume it was done on Joelle's orders."

"Most likely, but you won't find any House admitting to keeping an alliance with hers. Let's get you up."

Moving was far more painful than lying on the floor. It took both Caelum and Soren to get Vanya back on his feet, though his legs didn't quite want to support him. He slumped heavily against Soren, who took his weight without complaint, pulling Vanya's arm across his shoulders to steady him more. When he turned his head to speak, Soren's breath ghosted over Vanya's ear, making him shiver. "Can you walk?"

His mother had always said one must be seen to be believed they were amongst the living after an assassination attempt. "I will not be carried."

"Your stubbornness does you no favors, princeling."

But despite Soren's words, he still helped Vanya walk out of the Constellation Hall on his own two feet, his presence seen by many more *praetoria* legionnaires than had been present before and servants who would no doubt spread the news of his survival.

Soren helped him back to the private wing of the estate, where the Imperial household called home. Taisiya was there to greet them in the main receiving room with Vanya's personal magician skilled in healing magic, but Raiah was nowhere to be found.

"She's being tended to in your bedroom," Taisiya said, correctly reading the concern on his face. "I thought it best she see you more healed than you currently are."

To that, the magician gave a quick little bow. "If you would sit, Your Imperial Majesty. I will tend to you."

Intira was a magician who'd spent most of her life teaching magic at a civilian school in Calhames. She was older than Vanya but younger than Taisiya, with soft features and skin not weathered from the elements. Her healing ability was unparalleled, and ever since Basri, his House's previous magician, had died in the attack on the

Imperial palace, Intira had been the one to care for Vanya and his House when needed.

Her clarion crystal–tipped wand was intricately made from carved wood and polished brass. The aether that flowed out of it was warm, her magic gentle as it settled over his body like a blanket, easing his pain. Vanya breathed in, the ache in his muscles fading, though her magic couldn't take away the cold knot of lingering fear in his gut.

He'd survived yet another assassination attempt, but it could have been so much worse if Soren hadn't been there.

Vanya searched for the warden, finding Soren standing outside the circle of people hovering around him, worried about Vanya the emperor, not the man beneath the crown. Soren caught his gaze, held it, before giving a slow nod of acknowledgment.

And then he left, slipping away, as if he knew he didn't belong in the epicenter of Solaria's government even if he'd long since burrowed his way into Vanya's heart.

Eight

SOREN

The day after Vanya survived yet another attempted assassination, Soren woke with the dawn in his room at the Ashionen embassy at the center of the city. The embassy hadn't been opened in quite some time, as the advance team of diplomatic aides and royal servants had discovered while the rest of them were at the Imperial estate. The room Soren had been given when they finally arrived was far more comfortable than the barracks on the Warden's Island, aired out or otherwise.

Still, the bed had felt empty after having Vanya within reach yesterday, and Soren didn't think anyone would blame him for wanting to return to the Imperial estate. The Royal Guards who had flown with them to Solaria didn't seem keen on him leaving alone, but Soren was adamant about going without an escort.

The lieutenant who blocked his velocycle didn't know a word of Solarian, but Soren could still see her stubbornness. She pointed insistently at the black motor carriage with the Ashionen flag painted on its side, clearly wanting him to be driven in that rather than drive himself.

Soren very deliberately started the engine on his velocycle and pointed at the closed gate. "Open it."

He spoke in the trade tongue, hoping she understood him. Judging by the way she planted her fists on her hips, she probably hadn't.

"What is going on?" Dariush asked brusquely from the porch, speaking in Solarian, which was a relief to Soren.

"I'm leaving for the Imperial estate," Soren said in the same language, not looking away from the lieutenant. "She's in my way. Tell her to move and for the others to open the gate."

"It's early, Your Royal Highness."

"The Solarians will let me in."

The sun might barely be above the horizon, but he knew the Imperial estate would be bustling with people already. Raiah always woke early during the summer months, intent on packing so many activities into the hours of the day, to say nothing of Vanya's schedule. Soren only wanted to get there before Vanya was tied up in government work. He wanted to know that Vanya was all right after everything that had happened. Soren had wanted so badly to stay yesterday, but he knew he hadn't the right to.

Soren turned his head to look at Dariush, seeing the ambassador wasn't dressed for the day yet and had merely thrown on a dressing gown before stepping outside in his house slippers to address what was going on in the forecourt. He squinted against the bright morning sunlight, the day warm already, a precursor for the humid heat that would arrive before noon. After a moment, Dariush said something in Ashionen, his tone firm, which left the lieutenant looking displeased when she snapped something back.

"I presume the Royal Guard will not be able to follow where you go within the Imperial estate?" Dariush finally said to Soren, switching to Solarian.

"There is a reception room they would be confined to. Aside from that, I know this city better than they do. If they try to follow me, I'll lose them in the streets," Soren warned.

"No need to make their jobs more difficult. I've asked them to remain, but please do let us know if you will return tonight or not. The queen made it clear that you are leading the delegation this time, but we want to make sure you are safe while doing so."

"I'll ring you."

With that decided, Soren kicked up the stand and revved the engine, not caring if he woke up anyone sleeping inside the embassy. The lieutenant stepped out of his way, a pinched expression on her face. Soren left them all behind in favor of the Solarian streets.

The coastal city came alive as the sun crept into the sky, salt lingering in the early morning breeze. It was a nice ride, truth be told, but not nice enough to settle his nerves. By the time Soren pulled up in front of the closed gates of the Imperial estate, the tightness in his gut had gotten worse. For all his words to the Ashionens, he wasn't sure if Vanya would want to see him after yesterday.

But the *praetoria* legionnaires standing guard at the gold-painted gates still opened the way for him. Letting out a soft breath, Soren drove into the forecourt and parked his velocycle beneath one of the trees lining the arcade. He'd left the embassy only carrying his weapons and travel antidote kit, the leather bag slung over one shoulder and banging against his hip as he walked. He wasn't sure if Vanya would need it, but Soren wasn't taking any chances.

Caelum met him at the entrance into the estate, the Chief Minister dressed for the day in his robes of office and eyeing Soren with an unreadable expression. "It is early."

Soren gestured vaguely at his kit. "I know your magician saw to Vanya yesterday. I brought my kit in case he needed further attending to."

"His Imperial Majesty is in the bathhouse at the moment, on orders from Intira. He is not expecting you."

"May I see him?"

He had no right to ask, not after he'd finally given up the vow, but Soren asked anyway. Standing there in the shadow of the porch, in a world he had no right to walk through anymore, all Soren could hope was that Caelum would let him pass.

After a moment, Caelum inclined his head and stepped aside, gesturing at the open door. "I assume you know the way?"

Soren had lived in Oeiras for weeks at a time in the past, back when he'd gone to where Vanya was after his duty to the borders was done. "I do."

"Then I'll inform the servants to add another place setting to the morning meal in the private courtyard."

Soren wasn't sure if that was a wise assumption, but he wasn't going to question it. He passed Caelum and entered the Imperial estate, his feet taking him through familiar hallways, past servants who nodded politely at him and *praetoria* legionnaires who never barred his way to the rear of the building, where a stone path led to the private bathhouse.

The domed roof glittered at the base from intricate mosaic work depicting the constellations of the star gods. The pergola above the pathway was draped with sweet-smelling flowering jungle vines. *Praetoria* legionnaires guarded the entranceway, but none left their posts as Soren approached. He entered the bathhouse, the antechamber slightly cooler than it was outside, the place to disrobe empty save for a pair of bath attendants, who glanced at him before going back to their tasks.

Steeling himself, Soren pressed forward, walking through the arched entryway into a circular space that reminded him of the sea lapping at the shore. The tiled floor was done in deep blue, like the bottom of the ocean, while shades grew lighter as the bits of stone and tile and glass crept up the walls in a mosaic of curling waves beneath a soft sky. The inside of the dome above was lined with golden tiles, the pattern acting as the sun. It was beautiful, but not as beautiful as the man lounging in the steaming pool, watching him approach with keen dark eyes.

Petals floated in the water, the scent of bath oils drifting with the steam, the tray they'd come from sitting close by the bath's sole occupant. Vanya had his arms stretched along the edge of the pool, water lapping at his waist and sliding down his chest in tiny droplets. He was naked, certainly a sight to behold, but Soren wasn't sure he had the right to it. He drew to a stop opposite Vanya, toes lined right up to the edge, and waited, never looking away from the other man.

Vanya tilted his head back a little, holding Soren's gaze, eyes dark with a complicated mix of emotions Soren couldn't decipher. "Do I owe you another vow for saving my life again?"

His quiet voice seemed to ring loudly against the bathhouse walls, tone leached of emotion, the banal neutrality he used for political adversaries all that remained. Soren couldn't stop the faint flinch that tugged at him, knowing Vanya would see it. "I never asked for the first one."

"I remember. I thought at the time I was giving it to a nameless warden. Yet it was a foreign prince who asked for what was owed." Vanya blinked slowly, almost lazily, but his gaze was sharp like cut clarion crystal. "My Chief Minister seems to think that is my way out of a debt owed by my House through the vow."

"And would you play your House games with me in such a way?"

"They are all I know."

Soren sighed before unbuckling his pauldron and the strap holding in place the sheath across his back with its poison short sword. "And all I know is how to be a warden."

"You came with the vow and asked as an Ashionen."

"I asked for my people."

Vanya arched an eyebrow. "Both of them?"

Soren dropped his gear to the floor, then unbuckled his gun belt and the stabilizing holster straps secured around his thighs. He pried it all off, bending to set the heavy leather with its dual pistols beside his poison short sword. "Wardens care for all of Maricol's children by guarding the borders everyone lives within."

"You wield starfire. You took the name of a royal bloodline."

Soren yanked off his gloves, tossing them aside before working on the leather waistcoat, never taking his eyes off Vanya. "I took that name at the behest of my governor. No part of the identity the Ashionens gave me can be found in any genealogy. There is no witness to who they think I am."

"You can't be a warden, not as you are."

Soren's fingers stuttered over the buttons of his shirt, nearly ripping one out in the wake of Vanya's words and the bitter truth he spoke. Soren drew in a breath, steadying himself with long practice, and mechanically undid the rest before shrugging off the shirt. "I won't be a prince."

"Then what will you be?"

Soren said nothing to that, silent beneath Vanya's heavy gaze. He pulled off his boots and tossed them aside before stripping out of the rest of his clothes. Then he stepped into the warm water, finding his footing with ease, then waded toward Vanya, who watched him come, still as yet unmoving. Soren closed the distance between them, heartbeat loud in his ears, feeling almost lightheaded when he stepped between Vanya's spread legs. Despite how close they were, it still seemed as if a vast chasm separated them.

Wardens weren't supposed to want, he knew, but Soren had always wanted this, had always wanted Vanya. If his road didn't have Vanya walking beside him, then it wasn't a road he would travel.

Soren crawled onto Vanya's lap, their soft cocks brushing together beneath the warm water as he reached with damp hands to frame Vanya's face. Vanya didn't try to stop him, and Soren searched those eyes for a long moment before curving in close to press their foreheads together, breathing the same air after far too long apart.

"I once said I could never go home again," Soren rasped. "But that's not true. You're my homeland. Not Ashion, not Solaria, not any road that leads me to a border away from you. I don't care about the crown you wear or the one I lost. *You*, Vanya. You are all I have ever wanted."

Warm, firm hands gripped his waist, fingers digging in hard, but he didn't push Soren away. Vanya's voice came out terribly rough, sending a shiver down Soren's spine. "*Soren.*"

He pulled back but didn't go far, mouth hovering over Vanya's, their lips a breath apart as Soren laid bare all that he was. "I love you, princeling. Do with that what you will."

For a moment, Vanya was still beneath him, looking at him with wide, dark eyes. Then he surged upward, one hand skimming up Soren's back to grip his hair as Vanya kissed him with ruinous intent. He tasted like the strong tea Solarians favored, warm and alive beneath Soren's hands as they stole air from each other. Vanya's fingers were tangled tight in Soren's hair, and so when Vanya pulled his head back, breaking the kiss, Soren could only follow where he led.

Warm lips dragged down his throat, teeth scraping against the pulse there. Soren dug his fingers into Vanya's shoulders when the other man sucked a bruise into his skin. "Vanya."

"You walked away, and I should never have let you go," Vanya said harshly.

Soren lifted his hand and touched the side of Vanya's face where it was tucked so close. "I hurt you. I never meant to, but I did."

It hadn't been his intention, knowing how much Vanya needed truth in his life filled with words that didn't mean what they should and a House whittled down by betrayal and tradition. But everything he'd done, every secret he had kept, Soren had done so not out of malice but out of love, and he wanted Vanya to know that.

Vanya's arm curled around his waist, dragging Soren impossibly closer. He sucked in a breath, heat he couldn't blame on the pool settling in his skin and hardening his cock. Vanya pulled Soren's head to the side, and he went, letting Vanya kiss his way up to the hinge of his jaw to nip at his ear.

"Do you know what Callisto told me once?" Vanya said, voice deep and ragged, his cock a growing hardness between them. "That our roads were always meant to cross. You were always meant to be mine, Soren. Even the star gods knew that. I should have believed them."

Soren closed his eyes at that, stomach swooping like he stood on an airship suddenly losing altitude. "Then keep me, princeling, because you always had me."

Vanya groaned, the sound pressed into Soren's skin, before he let go of Soren's hair and blindly reached out for the tray near the ledge. Vials and jars were knocked over with a clatter, but he snagged a sealed one before his hand disappeared beneath the water again. He gripped Soren's thighs, lifting him up out of the water as he stood. Soren wrapped his legs around Vanya's waist, stealing kisses as Vanya walked them across the pool to the stairs, carefully carrying him out of the water. He was taken to one of the wide benches that lined the mosaiced wall, the marble cool beneath his back when Vanya laid him down on it.

Soren curled his hand over the back of Vanya's neck, tugging him down into a heated kiss, Vanya settling between his legs in a way no dream could replicate. Maybe it was the steam from the water drifting through the air that made Soren lightheaded, or maybe it was having everything he'd ever ached for within grasp once more. His skin was primed for touch, practically burning for it, and Vanya was the only person he wouldn't mind becoming ash for.

"You are *mine*," Vanya said fiercely, holding him there as they panted into each other's mouths. "The Ashionens cannot have you, and the wardens do not want you, so you will be mine."

Soren's fingers scrabbled against the ladder of Vanya's ribs, something like a whine crawling out of his throat to leave his lips. "*Yes.*"

It felt like a vow between them, the words a promise that Soren wouldn't break this time. Vanya leaned over him, blocking out the world, leaving only the two of them in that moment. "Then I will have you."

Soren shuddered at the words, managing a jerky nod. Vanya gripped his knee and tugged Soren's leg outward at an angle. He held on to Vanya's shoulders when a slick finger pressed against his hole and slid in deep, no teasing in the touch, just a desperate need that Soren felt in his bones. Soren was so hard already it *hurt*, wanting everything Vanya could give him.

Wanting *Vanya* and able now to have him.

"Do you know," Soren gasped out, looking up into eyes he wanted to see every morning until the end of their road, fingers skating over a beloved face he'd committed to memory so long ago, "I would burn the world for you."

Vanya swore, pressed another finger into Soren, the stretch too much too soon, but he didn't care. Vanya surged forward, kissing him with a ferocity that made their teeth scrape together, the curl of his fingers inside Soren pressing against the spot that made him jerk with pleasure, wanting more, wanting everything.

And Vanya must have felt the same because he pulled his fingers free and shifted forward, pressing the head of his slick cock against Soren's hole, and pushed in and *in*. Soren tipped his head back, mouth open on a silent, strangled gasp of air as Vanya took him, claimed him, the burn of him sliding in some distant ache Soren would always cherish.

Vanya rested their foreheads together, forearms pressed to the bench on either side of Soren's head. Soren hooked the leg not bent near to his chest around Vanya's waist, digging his heel against the small of the other man's back. Vanya shifted on his knees, hips flexing, the motion pushing him impossibly deeper into Soren.

He let out a strangled little sound, and Vanya laughed, low, almost disbelieving, before he levered himself up. Soren groaned when Vanya gripped him by the hips and ground into him, slow and teasingly, because it might have been months since they last took each other apart, but Vanya had always known how to make Soren want no one else.

"I will give Ashion my country's Legion," Vanya said as he pulled out before thrusting back in, all while dragging Soren back down on his cock with that bruising grip of his. The force of it nearly had Soren biting through his tongue. "Because you asked, and I won't break my vow to you."

Soren's hands tried to find purchase above his head on the cold marble, but the edge of the bench was too far away. "Vanya—"

Another brutal thrust, the ache of it making Soren momentarily lose the ability to speak. "And I will *keep* you because you were mine from the first moment I saw you."

The marble was useless, so Soren flailed his arms downward, finding Vanya's to grip the other man's strong forearms and hold on. Another thrust, oil barely slicking the way, and Soren let Vanya take what he wanted, groaning as the pace increased, the sound of their skin slapping together and their harsh breathing echoing in the bathhouse.

"You will be of my House," Vanya bit out, baring his teeth, eyes dark with desire and want and need that Soren knew all too well. Vanya spread Soren's legs wider, forcing Soren's hips up, the next thrust at an angle that made Soren nearly choke on his tongue. He did it again and again, panting hard with the effort. "You won't be nameless because you will carry mine."

Soren came with a shout the *praetoria* legionnaires outside could probably hear through the stone wall, came untouched, Vanya's words like the shock of starfire running through him, lighting him up from the inside out. He shuddered through his orgasm, barely able to breathe as Vanya pounded into him, taking his own pleasure in Soren's body because he could, because he had the right to it and always had.

Vanya finally came with a groan, hips grinding against Soren as he spent himself. His cock throbbed inside Soren, and he weakly clenched around it, shivering at the way Vanya's grip got impossibly tighter. They stayed like that for a moment, breathing heavily, before Vanya slowly pulled out, leaving Soren aching to be filled again. Vanya pushed a finger inside even as he leaned over to kiss Soren, both of them messy and warm and still holding on.

"Our roads were always meant to cross," Vanya murmured against his lips, finger pressing deeper, skating over that too-sensitive spot deep inside. Soren couldn't stop the way his hips jerked, not sure if he wanted more or less, only knowing that he didn't want Vanya to stop touching him. "The Dawn Star guided you to me, and I love you too much to see you walk away once more."

Soren wrapped his arms around Vanya and tugged him down, tucking his face against the curve of Vanya's neck and shoulder. Beyond the walls of the bathhouse was a war and their duties meant for two different countries and the whole of Maricol itself. But here, wrapped up in each other and nothing else, Soren let himself hold on to the only thing that had ever mattered to him.

Vanya never let him go.

Nine

VANYA

Raiah's laughter was something Vanya always cherished, but hearing Soren's voice at his table again was a particular kind of pleasure.

He looked over the decimated serving dishes of the evening meal at where Soren sat beside Raiah, his hand extended to her, with a tiny flicker of starfire curling against his palm. Raiah poked at it the same way she did Vanya's when he pulled the aether through him and cast it in the only form of magic he knew. The starfire didn't burn her, the way it never burned anyone blessed with that power.

"So you're like Papa and me," Raiah said, covering the starfire with her little palm and trying to snuff it out. When she lifted her hand again, the starfire still burned, and she giggled.

Soren's gray eyes flicked up to meet Vanya's across the table, a hesitancy in them that quickly faded. "Yes, but I didn't know for years."

"I always knew I could cast starfire." Raiah stated such news with an imperious tone to her voice as she clambered up to her knees on the cushioned bench.

"Lucky you," Soren said before putting out the starfire.

"Do it again!"

He tugged at one of Raiah's braids. "Some other time. It's getting late."

Taisiya had already excused herself from the table, wanting an evening bath for her old bones, as she'd put it. Vanya had soaked himself that morning on orders from Intira, and the lingering ache from the poison yesterday had disappeared, along with the tension he'd carried since Soren's return to Oeiras. Their reunion that morning had been intense, and not everything that needed to be said had been said, but the important words—those, at least, he'd given voice to. Soren would stay, and that was all Vanya wanted.

"I think it's time for bed," Vanya said before rising to his feet.

Predictably, Raiah protested, begging to stay up. When her pleas fell on deaf ears, she turned to Soren, eyes big and pleading. "If I go to sleep, you might not be here in the morning!"

Vanya saw Soren wince before the warden pasted on a smile that Raiah would never know was full of regret. "I promise I will be here when you wake up."

Despite Soren's words, Raiah sulked for the short walk from the private inner courtyard to her room, demanding Soren carry her and requiring a story be read to her once she was finally in bed. When Vanya offered to do the reading, Raiah shook her head. "I want Soren to read to me."

And Soren, much like Vanya, could deny her nothing. So Vanya sat at the foot of the bed and watched in silence as Soren read to his daughter from a book he remembered from his own childhood. It was still popular with children, and Soren had read it to her before several times back in Calhames, before everything burned.

Eventually, they kissed her good night on the forehead, turned off the gas lamp light in the corner, and left her under the faithful watch of the *praetoria* legionnaires, their numbers doubled after yesterday on Javier's orders. Vanya reached for Soren's hand after the door clicked shut quietly behind them, tugging the other man forward.

"Walk with me," Vanya said.

Soren nodded, never letting go as Vanya led him through the Imperial estate up to the rooftop observation patio. It was situated above the private wing where his household called home these days. The patio was a half-circle in shape, whose tiles still held some of the heat from the day, though it was fading. No overhang impeded a view of the sky, and several chaises were angled toward the edge and the intricate stone railing there.

Oeiras stretched out before them, the coastal city brilliantly illuminated by gas lamps in the warrens of the streets between city walls. The observation patio pointed north, toward the port and harbor that fed into the vast blackness of the sea west of them, distant flickering lights evidence of ships or ship-cities in the waters there. Vanya couldn't hear the sound of the water from where they stood in the heart of Oeiras, nor could he smell the sea salt on the air, but one always knew where the sea was, even inside the city walls.

Calhames was a desert city, born of fire and sometimes drought, but it was the home he knew and loved. Oeiras, with its dangerous jungle on one side and the sea on the other, held its own kind of vibrant beauty. As in both cities, the night sky was a searing darkness overhead, painted with a million pinpricks of stars surrounding the half-moon.

None of it was as beautiful as the man standing beside him.

"Raiah missed you," Vanya said as he leaned his hip against the stone railing.

Soren came to stand next to him, well within arm's reach. The light from gas lamps burning by the stairs they'd come up through didn't reach where they stood, both of them cast in shadow. "You know I missed her as well. I'm sorry she thought I was never coming back."

Vanya's fingers twitched, and he bit back the retort that first came to his tongue, the harshness in the words no longer relevant. "I didn't speak to her about you while you were gone. She wanted me to promise you would return, and I couldn't grant her that wish."

Soren ducked his head before settling his hand on Vanya's hip through the layers of his robe. "I wouldn't have blamed you if you told her I was gone or dead or any such excuse you needed to in order to move on."

"You aren't someone I could ever move on from."

In all the years since Nicca's death, there had only ever been one person in Vanya's bed. He'd bedded no courtesan, man or woman, taken no other lover in any city throughout the years. Soren had captivated him from the moment they met in the wreckage of the train crash years ago, Vanya meant to die and Soren never meant to be his savior. Only here they were, with all their secrets laid bare between them and a world tipping into war.

"Still," Soren said quietly. "Hurting you was the last thing I ever wanted to do."

"You lied to protect yourself and to protect me." At Soren's nod, Vanya let out a rough sound that might have been laughter on some other day. "Your truth wasn't one I wanted to hear last year. I've had time to realize that mistake and regret not listening."

Vanya curled his fingers through a belt loop and pulled Soren with him over to one of the chaises. He sat down, propped up against the high back on one end, and tugged Soren down with him. The warden settled himself between Vanya's legs, his back to Vanya's chest. He'd left his weapons in their room, a concession to Taisiya for the evening meal, and it made it easier to hold him now, like this. Vanya relished the weight of Soren against him as they stretched out on the chaise, tangled together how he liked.

"If our roads were meant to be different, they never would have crossed. Despite everything, my life is richer with you in it," Vanya said.

Soren slid down a little, resting his head back against Vanya's chest. When he spoke, Vanya could feel the thrum of his voice against his ribs. "Returning to you after time spent at a border always felt like coming home."

Vanya tightened his arms around Soren and kissed the top of Soren's head. "I'm glad you were there for us at the Imperial palace."

Raiah wouldn't be alive without Soren's intervention, a fact Taisiya had seen fit to remind him of over the past few months. His darling daughter was his legacy, what he fought for when it came to the Imperial throne. He'd not have either if Soren hadn't been present during the Conclave last year.

"When the memories with Callisto came back to me, I knew I couldn't speak of them. I'd have lost the wardens and you if I did." Soren sighed roughly, voice steady when he spoke again. "I might have lost the wardens anyway, but the thought of losing you was why I never asked. I was selfish."

Vanya hummed softly, looking up at where the Lion constellation burned brightest in the night sky. "We are both selfish for wanting the same thing."

"I still lost you both."

"As you said before," Vanya murmured. "You always had me. My House is yours."

Tension leaked out of Soren, the other man finally relaxing against Vanya. Their voices never became louder than a murmur in the hours that followed. They spoke of the past like it was some distant land despite the immediacy of what lay ahead, born of those choices. Whatever came from their roads merging, Vanya would face it with Soren by his side. He would never regret the pain they'd endured, for it had brought Soren back to him.

Ten

SOREN

The logistics of decamping the Imperial court from Oeiras to Calhames took less time than Soren anticipated. Vanya had apparently been ruling out of Oeiras for quite some time, but the Senate remained ever in Calhames. For all that Vanya had the right and power to issue orders pertaining to war, consulting with his military advisors and notifying the Senate in person seemed prudent, especially with a whisper campaign running through the Houses again after the latest attempted assassination against him.

Hanging above all the political maneuverings was the vow itself that Vanya owed, something that Caelum admitted was giving him migraines and stress ulcers. Vanya's Chief Minister was nothing if not a consummate professional when it came to preparing for the pushback sure to come from Vanya's decision.

"The House of Sa'Liandel pays its debts, whether by gaining power over the House we owe it to or acknowledging what is owed and paying it," Vanya had said the day after their time together spent in the bathhouse.

"You forgot murder," Soren had replied.

Vanya had given him a droll look over their midday meal. "We have to pray to Callisto somehow."

They'd talked about more than politics in the few days they spent together in Oeiras. Soren had stayed in the Imperial estate without apology or explanation to the Ashionen delegation, leaving the others to work their politics without him. For the first time in months, he slept deeply and without dreams while in Vanya's bed. He wouldn't trade it for anything.

Lore, when the Ashionen diplomatic dignitaries met with Vanya about the vow, had expressed her concern about Soren's new position —firmly standing with Vanya and disregarding his rank as heir to Caris. The trade tongue was perhaps not the best language to pursue diplomacy in, but she kept at it, worried for her country and her people, having never quite trusted Soren's position, despite both of them having a singular goal.

"You should fly with us," she said when they met at the gates to the airfield on the day they were to depart. The Imperial procession was long and involved, and Soren would have been with Vanya and Raiah in the midst of it, but Lore had asked for a moment, to which he had agreed.

"We'll end up at the same destination," Soren said.

Lore frowned at him, her gaze impossible to read. "You are Ashionen."

"I never wanted to be. Caris is getting what she wants, what Ashion needs. Let that be enough."

"You are her brother. Will you not support her?"

Weeks of knowing each other in the midst of politics and war didn't make a family. Bloodlines were written down in genealogies, but all that granted was power, which neither he nor Caris had ever truly wanted. But Ashion wanted a queen, and he would not take that from her, not when his road led elsewhere. "I am supporting Maricol."

"Do you even wish to be her heir?"

"I don't want her crown." The words came out flat but firm, a truth Soren would tell anyone who asked. What he wanted, Ashion could not give him, but for the future of Maricol, he'd ensure Caris claimed the starfire throne.

Soren walked away from Lore, not interested in explaining the reason Vanya held his heart. He made his way down the pier toward the pair of Imperial airships. Vanya waited on the pier for him, Raiah in his arms, Taisiya already boarded. When he reached them, Vanya tipped Raiah into his arms, the Imperial princess immediately latching onto Soren.

"She asked that you fly with her," Vanya said, a smile twitching at his lips.

The need for an heir meant Vanya and Raiah always traveled separately, with Taisiya seeing to Raiah's care these days, as the household was still without a majordomo. Soren knew it always made Vanya worry, being separated like this, but he'd traveled the same way as a prince when his mother had been alive. Better their House had a claim on the Imperial throne than to see it fall to another amidst the threat of war.

"Is that what you want?" Soren asked Raiah.

She kicked her legs a little, beaming at him. "Yes! Papa said it was okay."

"Well then. If he agreed, it seems I must."

Raiah cheered, pleased with herself, and Soren smiled at her. He'd missed her while away, and she'd grown so in that time. His absence had been felt deeply by her, from what Vanya had said, and Soren was more than willing to prove he wouldn't be walking away again.

Vanya tweaked one of Raiah's braids. "I shall see you both in Calhames."

Soren held still as Vanya leaned in to first kiss Raiah on the cheek and then him. The gesture, done so publicly, felt like a risk with everything going on, but Vanya had made it clear the other day that trying to hide what they were to each other would be detrimental in the long run. They'd have to come clean with the vow anyway, which Soren knew would be a political nightmare, almost as much as Vanya wanting to marry a warden turned foreign prince.

Soren carried Raiah onto the Imperial airship to his right, trudging up the gangplank while she chattered happily away about what she wanted to do when they got to Calhames. Once on the flight deck, a crew member handed over two fur-lined flight jackets. Soren slung both over his free arm before finding the captain. He conferred briefly with the woman to ensure his velocycle had been put in the cargo hold before heading to the observation lounge located behind the flight cabin. A crew member opened the heavy door for him, and Taisiya, already seated at one of the low sofas, waved them over.

"There you are," she called out.

"Raiah had to say farewell to Vanya," Soren said.

The sofas each came with lap belts, and Soren buckled Raiah in after he set her down and got her jacket on. She leaned forward and made grabby hands at the tea tray situated on the low table, the plates filled with small pressed fruit squares dusted with sugar and the rock sugar sticks she loved so much. Soren handed her one stick and a few of the fruit squares on a small plate, declining when she offered him one.

Praetoria legionnaires settled themselves around the observation deck for the launch, politely ignoring the conversation Taisiya seemed determined to have with him. Thankfully, she waited until they were well in the air and Raiah had her nose pressed to the window on the outskirts of the observation lounge.

"I understand Vanya wishes to bring you into the House," Taisiya said, holding her teacup in both hands. Her robes today were thin for summer weather, but she'd worn a fur-lined cloak as well in anticipation of the chill to come from the flight ahead, and someone had provided her with a thick blanket to drape over her legs.

"He asked," Soren said, meeting Taisiya's gaze.

She raised an eyebrow at him. "And did you accept?"

"Yes."

He'd been part of the household since the moment Vanya had given him the vow all those years ago, but to be of a House came with a wealth of social and political power outsiders rarely gained. Vanya had sworn off marriage after Nicca's death, not wanting to make Raiah a target by bringing another House into the tangle of succession rights. He'd skirt that issue by marrying Soren, but there were a host of other problems that would come from the union.

And Taisiya, as with any good *valide*, knew them all. "The Houses

271

will not care for your ascension."

"Vanya has an heir."

"An heir is not the issue here, and to be quite frank, you haven't the ability to give him one. Many know you as a warden, a people who we owe sanctions to due to the major Houses keeping the old burial traditions alive through the Ages."

"Which you should never have done."

"We prayed how the Dawn Star asked those who ruled to pray."

"You knew it was wrong."

Taisiya shrugged and sipped her tea. "It was wrong only in the risk we and our ancestors took, but it was ours to take. The sanctions are owed, and they will be paid, but the Houses will not take kindly to you gaining even more power over them."

"The wardens aren't the ones who will be marrying Vanya, and the governor says I am no longer a warden."

"A warden cannot be unmade, and you are a foreign prince to the country Vanya owes a vow to. You must see the pitfalls in this endeavor of yours."

"I won't walk away again."

Taisiya's lips quirked upward at the corners, but there was no humor in her eyes. "Good. For all his hurt and anger, Vanya mourned your absence in his life."

Soren found his throat dry and leaned forward to pour himself some tea. The red tea Taisiya favored was far better than the blend he'd had in Ashion. "He knows I never meant to hurt him."

They'd talked about such things late into the night after their reunion, speaking all the words they'd held back over the years, the act like lancing an infected wound. They carried no secrets between each other anymore, only an understanding that everything they'd done—for each other and to each other—had been done out of a sense of duty.

"Most never mean the hurt they give, but that doesn't undo the pain. I am glad you have both come to an accord, despite the delicate and difficult political situation it leaves us in. The House who holds the Imperial throne is never meant to marry for love but for power. Vanya did his duty there, so I suppose he can be granted this."

"Thank you," Soren said wryly.

"Don't thank me yet. You cannot marry Vanya until the war in the north is over and the sanctions are ratified. You will be blamed for both, by virtue of your past."

"I would have died if the Dawn Star had not given me to the wardens."

"You should be thankful it was our guiding star who aided you and not the North Star. If there was ever proof you were meant for Solaria and not Ashion, it would be that, though I anticipate few Houses being pleased about such a truth."

"I want no part of ruling."

"You claim to be the Ashion queen's heir."

"Only because my governor asked me to accept the role. It was the only way to ensure the wardens could be kept safe. Giving it up when the war is over won't be a hardship." Caris had Nathaniel, after all. At some point, if they all survived Eimarille's bid for power, the two would marry and have children and have no need for Soren to owe any claim to the starfire throne.

"What makes you think you'll have no say in ruling if you give up one throne for another?"

"I'm marrying into a House, not marrying to rule. I already told Vanya I would be his consort, but I won't be an emperor."

Taisiya nodded, seemingly pleased with his answer. "We'll find a place for you."

"I'll be with Vanya. That is the only place I need."

Raiah came hurrying back over, sugar stick clenched in one sticky hand while she used her other to tug on his arm. "You're staying?"

Soren smiled over at her, watching the excitement rise in her eyes. "Yes."

She shrieked with glee before burrowing close, hugging him as tight as her skinny arms could. Soren stroked his hand over her braids. When he glanced up, catching Taisiya's eye, the *valide* tipped her head at him in silent acceptance.

This House, this family, was what he'd never prayed for but which Soren would gladly hold on to with everything he had.

Eleven

VANYA

Their arrival in Calhames was met with a fanfare that spawned whispers through the Houses Vanya knew he couldn't ignore. He had no intention of letting things get out of hand, but the Senate and the Houses were not who Vanya had to convince first of the alliance he owed through the vow. It was Imperial General Chu Hua and the rest of his commanding military officers who required persuasion.

The day after they landed in Calhames, Vanya was driven to the Legion's military headquarters in one of the inner rings of the city, between a pair of inner walls that had been built in another Age. The Imperial motorcade bypassed sentinel-class automatons that stood guard at the gate leading into the military grounds. The property held barracks for active-duty legionnaires and the administration buildings geared toward the bureaucracy of war.

In times past, the enemy had been revenants, sometimes thieves on the trade roads, sometimes Houses, and rarely another country since the Age of Separation. Vanya was there today to change the Legion's road, the vow tucked away in his robe's pocket, feeling less like a noose only because Soren accompanied him.

The Ashionen diplomatic delegation had settled into their embassy, their request to join Vanya to plead their case to the commanders of the Legion denied. Their voices would be represented by Soren, despite the wariness directed toward the warden after his clear preference for the Solarian side of politics.

"They won't be pleased with what you owe," Soren murmured as the motor carriage pulled up in front of the main building of the headquarters. Legionnaires stood at attention on the parade grounds, their tan uniforms pristine, red-and-white checkered *effiyehs* unmoving on their heads by the sluggish summer breeze.

"I am their emperor. They will abide," Vanya said.

The motor carriage braked to a stop, and a *praetoria* legionnaire moved quickly to open his door. Vanya climbed out of the motor carriage, crown firmly in place. His white robes tipped in crimson and gold were perhaps a bit too elaborate for a casual meeting, but he had a point to make.

Imperial General Chu Hua saluted him from where she stood at the bottom of the grand steps leading into the building behind her. "Your Imperial Majesty."

Chu Hua had spent her entire military career within the *praetoria* legionnaires, the personal guard of the Imperial throne, but that did not mean her skills at war had been left by the wayside. Of all the officers Vanya had ever known, he'd trusted her the most. Her job, and the job of the *praetoria* legionnaires, was to guard Solaria by guarding the Imperial throne. Their loyalty was to no House, and their decisions were tempered by what was best for the country, not a single person.

"General," Vanya said with a faint smile. "Thank you for making yourself available."

"Always," she replied, gesturing at the military brass standing on either side of her. "We are ever at your service."

"Then let us go inside."

A handful of curious glances were sent Soren's way, but no one protested the warden's inclusion. Chu Hua was well aware of Vanya's favoritism toward Soren, but he knew she wouldn't like what brought them all together today.

Once ensconced in the private meeting room that had no windows and only oil paintings of past battles won hanging on the walls, Vanya looked down the length of the long wooden table at those present. Soren was to his right, with Chu Hua to his left, and a ream of ledgers scattered over maps spread out between everyone.

"You said you wanted to meet about the Legion, Your Imperial Majesty," Chu Hua said.

Vanya nodded, the crown unmoving upon his brow. "I do."

"What concerns do you have for the Legion?"

"None, only a request to prepare for war."

Chu Hua frowned at him, gaze intent. "The Daijal army has not accosted our northern border."

"We both know the fight in the House of Kimathi's *vasilyet* is a proxy one at best. Joelle allowed a death-defying machine to operate within her borders, and we reap the horrors of that decision with revenants that seem never-ending in the northwest corner of our country."

"We are gaining ground."

"Yes, but slowly. I do not wish to move forward with aerial bombardment at this time, but that is something we can reassess later. For now, our focus must be on the war in Ashion."

"It is not our fight."

Vanya steeled himself as he pulled the vow from his pocket, the chain tangled around his fingers. He held it up for the table to see, the gold medallion swinging at the end, before setting it on the table before him. "Soren saved my life when I was a prince. A debt was owed, and my House paid it with a blood vow and a promise to provide whatever he asked for. He has asked for the Legion on behalf of Ashion."

The uproar was instantaneous. More than half of the officers seated at the table rose to their feet in shock and anger, their voices tripping over each other as they protested Vanya's words. Chu Hua was not one of them, sitting stone-faced and quiet amidst the shouting, her gaze flicking between Vanya and Soren. After several minutes of furious unrest, she stood, the motion enough to silence everyone in the room.

"Why now?" Chu Hua asked, looking not at Vanya but at Soren. "Do you wish the starfire throne for yourself and hope to have Solaria aid in you taking it, Prince Alasandair Rourke?"

"No," Soren said into the charged silence. "My governor asked me to claim that name to be Caris' heir and keep Ashion's will to fight alive if she somehow died. But I have not been a prince since the Dawn Star brought me to the Warden's Island and named me as a tithe."

"The broadsheets call you Rourke."

"He is a warden," Vanya said.

"And the wardens have been ever so kind to Solaria as of late."

"The fault of burial falls to every major House, and we will pay it. But what Soren asks for is about more than just Ashion or Solaria. It is about Maricol."

"Eimarille has already struck at the wardens, just as she has struck at Ashion in pursuit of a crown and a throne she doesn't deserve. You know as well as I do that she will not stop at just one country. Borders are meaningless to her. Ashion requests the Legion aid its army in pushing Daijal back and reclaiming their capital," Soren said.

"And in doing so, Solaria will aid in putting a queen on the starfire throne. Your Imperial Majesty, who is to say Caris will be better than Eimarille?" Chu Hua asked.

"No one, but it was not Caris who created the *rionetkas* plaguing our government and others save for Daijal's. It was not Caris who attacked the Warden's Island and decimated the next generation of the only people who can survive the poison fields so the rest of us can live. It was not Caris who started this war," Vanya said.

"Caris is an engineer. She builds things; she doesn't break them. She wants nothing beyond her borders," Soren added.

"She wants the Legion," Chu Hua said flatly.

"She wants an end to the war," Vanya said. "That is something I, as a ruler, can understand."

"The Houses will not like this."

"There will be no Houses left if Eimarille has her way." Vanya reached out and picked up the vow, offering it to Chu Hua. "The

Legion can hold the line with Ashion and push Daijal back. We will have an ally and a debt owed for generations to come. Soren asked, but I am not. I will declare an alliance with Ashion in the Senate later today. I would like my generals to be in accord with me."

Vanya looked around the table, meeting the gaze of each and every officer surrounding him. In the end, it was Chu Hua who took the vow and held it rather than flinging it back in his face how Vanya was certain some of the others would like to do.

"We will face the same threat of revenants in Ashion as we do in the northwest *vasilyet*," Chu Hua warned.

"Yes, but we'll have more wardens to lend aid than we do now. I leave the logistics of war up to you and the other officers, but make no mistake. The Legion will march north to stand against Eimarille. I will not let her take Solaria, and I think we can all agree she will not stop at Ashion's border in her quest for power."

Chu Hua's mouth tightened before she gave a shallow nod. "Of that last point, we are in agreement, Your Imperial Majesty."

"What of Bellingham?" someone down the table asked.

"The Legion will still work to take that city. With the Legion moving north, one hopes the forces there will be split and it will provide us an easier way forward."

Vanya would not bomb that city, not yet. He would not continue his mother's legacy when it came to the ruination of a Solarian city. The progression to that city's walls was slow, but the Legion remained mostly intact because of the commanding officers' caution in the face of an overwhelming number of revenants and deadly poison fields.

Chu Hua looked down at the vow in her hand before meeting his gaze again. "If you order us to war, the Legion will fight."

The production facilities for ammunition and automatons used for war had been running continuously since last summer. They had a glut of supplies, even with giving up one facility to the Tovanians' needs. The logistics of moving a large number of people and weapons across *vasilyets* was something the Legion practiced on a yearly basis as part of their training.

"The debt my House owes will be paid for the sake of Solaria's future," Vanya said.

Chu Hua squared her shoulders before dipping into a deep bow. "By your will, Your Imperial Majesty."

The Houses would not like it, nor would the Senate, but Vanya alone had the power to declare war. If his road had crossed Soren's for anything, he knew it was for this—to keep Solaria a sovereign nation, no matter what Eimarille would prefer.

Twelve

SOREN

Senate sessions were never Soren's favorite things to sit through. The minutiae of politics was dry and cutting, the veiled threats and promises hidden between words and behind smiles enough to give a person a headache. Lore seemed to thrive in it, despite not knowing the language spoken all around them, but she was savvy enough to leave the discussions up to Dariush when their opinion was needed.

The Ashionen delegation had claimed the ambassador table on the Senate floor that day. Soren sat with them when he would have preferred the seat beside Taisiya up on the mezzanine where the Houses watched the proceedings unfold. His concession was to wear the uniform of a warden and not any of the finery the Ashionens had dressed in for their day in the political spotlight.

"Far more cutthroat than Ashion," Lore murmured in the trade tongue, quiet enough that only Soren heard her.

"The Houses play their games, the Senate writes the laws, and the emperor rules over them all," Soren replied.

It was a generalized explanation for the intricate culture—both socially and politically—that ran Solaria's government. Lore made a soft, wordless sound before leaning toward Dariush, who sat on her other side, speaking quietly in rapid Ashionen. Soren tuned them out and focused on the proceedings that provided a cacophony of voices echoing through the Senate chambers. Amidst it all, Vanya was a calm center, flanked by his Legion generals, who, despite their earlier reservations, were aligned with his desires.

"It is not our House that owes the Ashionens. Solaria as a whole should not have to pay for your mistakes," Lady Vesper Aetos, of the House of Aetos, said imperiously from the mezzanine at one point.

"It is your House that attempted to murder me in Oeiras just the other day," Vanya replied in a bored voice, which effectively made Vesper snap her teeth together.

"My House takes offense to your slanderous accusation."

"The proof sits in a jail cell back in Oeiras, one that married into your House as of three years ago. Your noted alliance with the House of Kimathi and now an attempted assassination makes me wonder how much of your House is against Solaria's sovereignty."

The ensuing argument that resulted from Vanya's biting words lasted almost an hour, dragging other Houses into the verbal fray. Soren wisely stayed out of it, and Dariush did the same, even when Lore wondered if they should perhaps engage more than they were.

"No," Soren told her firmly. "The Houses need to be brought to a consensus."

"I thought you said the emperor had the sole power to declare war?" she asked.

"He does, but he'll want the Houses supporting that decision, or they'll try to murder him again. If that happens, the debt he owes dies with him, and Ashion will not get the Legion."

Lore seemed a bit taken aback by that but dutifully stayed quiet and stopped pestering Dariush about politics that weren't hers.

The midday meal was eaten in the Senate chambers, with grilled meat wraps delivered to everyone present, along with sweet red wine that some senators drank more of than was probably polite. The heat of the spices used to flavor the meat made Lore gulp down more water than anyone else at their table. Soren enjoyed the taste of it, having missed the flavors he'd grown to love while at the Warden's Island and in Ashion. The food was eaten, and the arguing continued, every conceivable side pressing their point and hoping for neutrality in the face of the vow, only to be waylaid by Vanya's grim determination to see a debt paid and a war won.

Soren wasn't surprised when the Houses attempted to cast him in a negative light. He didn't defend himself beyond his stated remarks that he'd chosen to become Caris' heir in order to save Maricol because that was the only way the wardens would survive.

"You regret the sanctions owed by your major Houses and the tithes Solaria will have to pay, but tell me," Soren said when pressed. "How will you keep your cities safe when the influx of revenants is clawing at your walls? Will you be the ones to go into the poison fields and fight the walking dead? I did my duty for the wardens and for Maricol. Solaria allying itself with Ashion is how we ensure Maricol survives. We had an Age of Separation for a *reason*."

It was a prudent point that Vanya ran with and which his generals emphasized. The politicking went on well into the evening, long past when the sun had set. In the end, Vanya signed off on the declaration of war with the backing of two-thirds of the Senators, which meant as many Houses were in agreement as well.

It wasn't a unanimous agreement, but it was more than enough for Vanya to count it as a win. When the session finally ended, Vanya made his way to the ambassador table, accepting Dariush's respectful bow with a regal nod. Chu Hua stood at his left and offered a shallow bow as well to the ambassador.

"The broadsheets will announce the declaration of war in the morning. My generals will need to be in contact with your commanders who handle Ashion's war effort," Vanya said.

"I will go with the generals tonight in order to provide the requested information. I can't begin to thank you enough on behalf of my queen for your support, Your Imperial Majesty," Dariush replied.

"I'm not doing it for her."

Soren's name went unspoken, but Dariush's gaze flicked briefly toward him. "Be that as it may, Your Imperial Majesty. Ashion is in your debt."

"I know." Vanya nodded at Soren. "Let us depart."

"You aren't staying?" Lore asked in the trade tongue. "There's still much to discuss."

"I will come by the embassy in the morning," Soren replied.

They didn't need him to facilitate introductions between their military officers when Dariush had that task well in hand. Soren had done his part, risked his heart to see Caris have a chance to win this war. The Ashionens could celebrate their alliance without him.

Soren followed Vanya out of the Senate, both of them ushered into the waiting motor carriage by *praetoria* legionnaires. It was dark out, the gas lamps lit on every street they were driven down. Their return to the House of Sa'Liandel's ancestral estate was done in silence, Vanya having talked enough that his voice had turned rough by the end of the evening.

They passed by the sentinel-class automatons standing guard at the end of the street before pulling into the drive. Vanya tugged Soren out of the motor carriage and led him inside, where a servant met them with a small tray holding two steaming cups of tea to soothe their throats.

"Did my *valide* return?" Vanya asked.

"Hours ago, Your Imperial Majesty," the servant murmured. "Shall I fetch her?"

"Let her rest. We will speak in the morning."

They carried their tea with them to the bedroom Soren had slept in last night, where they'd made better memories to replace the ones from last year. Tonight, though, they were both tired from the long day in the Senate, and so Soren helped Vanya out of his robes out of a desire to sleep more than anything else.

Crawling into bed with Vanya still felt new, a delicate desire that had Soren rolling in close, tucking his head beneath Vanya's chin. He fell asleep to the sound of Vanya breathing, steady and perfect and alive.

Morning came with a packed schedule, one that Soren knew could not be waylaid by lingering in bed, no matter how drugging Vanya's kisses were.

"I need to get to the embassy," Soren said, reluctantly rolling away from Vanya's greedy hands.

"They have the Legion now. They do not need you," Vanya replied.

"Yes, well, I'd like to ring Caris and let her know I'll be staying in Solaria."

Vanya's arm snaked out to wrap around his waist, hauling Soren close again. Warm lips pressed a lingering kiss against the back of his neck, over the knob of his spine there. "You'll give up Ashion?"

Soren skimmed his hand over Vanya's arm, tangling their fingers together over his stomach. "It was never truly mine to give up."

They managed to extract themselves from each other and the bed, servants bustling in once Vanya rang for them to help him get ready for a day of meetings. Soren didn't need any assistance getting dressed. He pulled on his uniform, strapped on his weapons, and stole one more kiss from Vanya before heading for the door.

"I'll see you at dinner," Vanya called after him. "Raiah will expect you for the midday meal."

"I'll return before then."

Soren left, walking through the bustling hallways to the front entrance. A *praetoria* legionnaire had retrieved his velocycle from the garage, probably after being notified by a servant. Soren gave a nod in thanks before slinging his leg over the seat and starting the engine. He retrieved the helmet hanging off one of the handlebars and put it on, the malleable leather over thin metal plates settling around his skull. He fit the brass goggles over his eyes before kicking up the stand with his heel and driving off.

Calhames was a bustling city even that early in the morning in the civic center behind the first inner wall. When Soren made it to the Ashionen embassy, the front gates were unlocked and unguarded. He frowned at the drive beyond the wrought-iron gate, seeing no one outside manning the main entrance. The motor carriages were there, proof that no one had left yet despite the hour. Soren pulled his velocycle up to the gate and set the brakes before kicking down the stand, engine still running. He dismounted and pushed the gate open far enough that he could drive his velocycle through the space.

He parked beside one of the motor carriages and turned off the engine, removing his helmet and brass goggles. Soren left the velocycle behind and walked toward the embassy building. He found it, too, was unlocked, and Soren paused there on the threshold, frowning at the wooden door. Every instinct he had told him something was wrong, but he couldn't flee without knowing what lay beyond the threshold.

Soren reached over his right shoulder and unsheathed the poison short sword, flexing his fingers around the sturdy hilt, thumb resting over the button just beneath the cross guards. He didn't trigger any of the poison held inside the hilt, but it was an option.

He turned the knob with his left hand and pushed the door open on silent hinges, stepping inside. The gas lamps in their sconces were all burning down the hallway, as if no one had bothered to turn them off before heading to bed last night. But more concerning than the light was the body of a Royal Guard soldier lying on the floor of the foyer, the pool of blood spread around them appearing dark and tacky.

Soren had seen plenty of dead bodies over the years, and he knew enough to gauge the time of death for the poor soldier as hours ago rather than minutes. Soren tightened his grip on the hilt of his poison short sword, using his other hand to unholster the pistol on his left hip and thumbing off the safety without looking.

He stepped over the body, listening hard for any noise in the working front of the embassy. No sound came to him beyond the sputtering of the gas lamps he passed. Soren passed two more rooms —a library and receiving room—but only the receiving room held more bodies. Two diplomatic aides who had supported Dariush were sprawled on the floor, both of them victims of gunshot wounds.

He grimaced, heart sinking at the thought of what a political nightmare the murder of the Ashionen diplomatic envoy would be right after Vanya had agreed to join the war. The wise course of action might have been to leave or call the peacekeepers, but the clattering sound of something crashing to the floor in a room farther within the embassy had Soren's head snapping around.

It could be anything—someone dying, someone trying to hide, or a revenant risen from the murdered. Whatever it was, Soren knew he couldn't leave the premises without first checking it out. He left the receiving room and let his pistol lead him down the hallway, clearing every doorway he came to. When he reached the intersection of hallways at the end, he found a trail of bodies, the Royal Guards sprawled on the floor and against the wall, blood smeared everywhere. Beyond them, every door in the hallway was closed except for one.

Soren knew embassies were generally manned by quite a lot of diplomatic officers and aides, and he wondered if all of them were dead. He looked down the hallway and then glanced back the way he'd come. If everyone was dead, he needed to call in more wardens, notify the nearest star temple for transportation of the dead to the crematorium, but everything he knew he had to do got waylaid by the sound of a wavering voice calling out for help.

Lore's voice echoed in his ears, freezing Soren where he stood. Even if he couldn't understand the Ashionen words she spoke, he knew that tone of fearfulness all too well. Steeling himself, Soren crept down the hallway toward the open door, finger resting against the trigger guard of his pistol. He wasn't familiar with the building, though, and a step several breaths later made the wood beneath his feet creak.

The faint rustle of sound he'd heard in the room ahead cut off, and a voice he didn't recognize called out an order in Ashionen that he didn't understand. But the startled, terrified gasp from Lore was proof enough of the threat awaiting him in that room. Fleeing would only leave her to die, and she didn't deserve that. Soren steeled himself and didn't bother hiding his presence. He stepped into the doorway, forcing his expression to remain calm as he took in the scene before him.

The farce of a meeting over tea between Lady Lore and Lady Vesper of the House of Aetos was marred by the body of a diplomatic worker who, thankfully, wasn't Dariush but who hadn't died quickly or easily, judging by the ropy mess of intestines that hung outside their body from a hole carved into their midsection. The gag tied around their mouth had kept whatever screams they'd let loose muffled in their throat. Their hands and legs had been tied to the chair, the rug beneath the furniture stained and damp from blood and other fluids. Soren didn't know if the ambassador lay dead somewhere else in the embassy.

"Lay your weapons down, or her throat will be cut," Vesper said before sipping her tea, as if she fully expected Soren to comply.

Soren's gaze flicked to where Lore sat, pale-faced and stiff-spined, hands fisted over the skirt of her gown. Her head was tipped back, the sharp side of a knife held by a star priest pressed close to her skin. In the star priest's other hand was a clarion crystal–tipped wand, indicating command of the aether.

His slight hesitation had Vesper sighing irritably. "If you use starfire, she will die, Prince Alasandair Rourke."

He rather thought protesting that name and title would fall on deaf ears. "You have to know that murdering the Ashionen diplomatic delegation will not stop the Legion from going north to join the war."

"Perhaps not, but it will be a political land mine for the emperor to traverse. One you will not be present to see. Now, your weapons or her life."

He had no magician hiding him in shadow to sneak up on an unsuspecting target, not like when Artyom had held Raiah in the old Palace. Here, the star priest was one pound of pressure away from slitting Lore's throat, and Soren wouldn't be a warden if he let her die. The risk of setting either the star priest or Vesper on fire had to be weighed against the threat to an innocent life.

Telegraphing every move, Soren moved his finger away from the trigger and thumbed on the safety of his pistol even as he crouched to set his poison short sword on the floor. He set his pistol down as well before moving slowly to unholster the second one hanging off his right hip. He sat that pistol on the floor as well, then unsheathed the dagger on his thigh and dropped it next to his short sword. Only then did he straighten, eyes on Vesper.

The lady who was the voice for the House of Aetos appeared calm and composed, though her outfit wasn't one he'd ever seen her wear before. Gone were the light robes or breezy summer gowns favored by Solarians at the height of summer. In their place, she wore an Ashionen diplomatic uniform, and he wondered if she'd taken it from the premises or already had it before arriving. Either way, Soren knew enough of where her loyalties had lain in the past to see Joelle's interference in what had happened in the embassy.

"You won't kill Lore," Soren said slowly, studying Vesper. "Not here, and not now. The moment you do, you must know *I* will kill *you.*"

Vesper smiled slightly at him, her gaze cold. "She is our assurance that you will comply with what we want."

Soren grimaced, well aware of how true that statement was. "What did Joelle offer you to have you betray your country so thoroughly?"

"There is no betrayal when the House of Sa'Liandel would see us fight for a land that is not ours. I won't help pay a debt that is not mine."

"Vanya is fighting for Maricol, of which Solaria is a part of."

"He's fighting to tear us apart, and I will not see my country ruined because of his House's wants. They've done enough damage, and it stops here."

"By murdering the Ashionen delegation and kidnapping Queen Caris' lady-in-waiting, a member of one of the oldest bloodlines in Ashion? Do you honestly think they won't demand retribution from Vanya for your actions?"

"My House will not be found at fault."

She spoke with such assuredness that Soren wondered if Joelle had been planning such an attack ever since the Ashionen ambassador started begging Solaria for help months ago. He didn't think so grandly of himself as to believe she'd orchestrated all these murders in order to kill him. Vesper and Joelle couldn't have known he would return or that he would return with such a past haunting his road.

No, Soren was certain whoever was meant to walk through the embassy's front doors was meant to die. But if his presence could keep Lore alive, then he would do his best to find his way out of such a difficult situation.

"Joelle aligned herself with Eimarille, and that betrayal will seep into your House as well. You can't call yourself Solarian if you're working with Joelle to tear your country apart."

Vesper set down her teacup with a careful hand, giving away nothing, ever a lady of a House. "You sleeping with the emperor doesn't make you Solarian, not when you're in bed with the Ashionens. I must admit, I hadn't expected your return to our capital, but your arrival certainly presented an opportunity we couldn't ignore."

Soren thought about the promise he'd given Vanya in bed that morning, about the meal he'd been looking forward to sharing, and all the years they'd promised each other if they could just see the war through to the end. All of it slipped away as the seconds were counted off by the clock on the wall, in a place filled with the dead, burying him not unlike he'd once been buried in the royal crypt.

His gaze flicked to Lore, who watched him with wide, watery eyes, a thin trickle of blood sliding down her throat from where the knife had nicked her skin. Her lips trembled, but she didn't beg. She wouldn't have understood the conversation happening around her, but she'd have understood the meaning behind him setting aside his weapons.

"And how do you think to get us out of Calhames and past the active war zone around the House of Kimathi's *vasilyet?*" Soren asked.

Vesper's smile was a slow, cruel thing, eyes shining with a victory that Soren refused to let her enjoy. She reached for a scrap of fabric on the table and lifted it up, the veil shimmering between her fingers. "One lie at a time."

Thirteen

VANYA

Vanya's meeting that morning with some of the senators to discuss proper allocation of the purse to support the needs of the Legion was interrupted by Caelum with an urgency he hadn't seen in quite some time.

"Your Imperial Majesty, I am sorry, but I must speak with you," Caelum said after he'd thrown open the meeting room door and offered a hasty bow.

Concern had Vanya rising from his seat, effectively ending the meeting. "Of course."

He knew better than to ask for details where others could hear. He said nothing as he followed Caelum out into the hall, his Chief Minister making a subtle hand gesture that kept Vanya's teeth locked together.

"Ambassador Zayed is in the Mosaic Room, along with several peacekeepers and a military aide who had driven him back to the Ashion embassy," Caelum said in a low voice.

Ice settled in veins, a spike of worry causing him to miss a step and speak when he should have kept silent. "Soren went to the embassy this morning. Where is he?"

Caelum flinched around his eyes, and bile crept up Vanya's throat.

Caelum kept quiet as they walked through the halls of the Senate at a pace that one could say was hurried but not panicked. When they entered the Mosaic Room, Vanya's attention was reserved for the pale-faced ambassador pacing by the window. The peacekeepers who'd escorted him to the Senate and the military aide snapped to attention, all three of them bowing stiffly to the Imperial degree.

"What is going on?" Vanya demanded the second the door was closed.

Dariush jerked around, still in the same clothes he'd worn to the Senate yesterday for the declaration of war. He looked as if he hadn't slept, dark circles standing out beneath his bloodshot eyes. His hands shook when he dipped into a bow, voice just as unsteady. "Your Imperial Majesty, something horrific has occurred."

Everything inside Vanya spiked like lightning in a desert thunderstorm. "Where is Soren?"

Dariush opened and closed his mouth before rallying himself in a way Vanya could respect if his sanity and heart weren't at risk in that moment. "I joined your military officers at the Legion's headquarters after the Senate session yesterday to facilitate calls between them and our own generals back in Ashion. The calls lasted much of the night, and I acted as translator along with several other military aides. I was invited to sleep there overnight for the scant hours before morning. I accepted and was driven back to the Ashion embassy this morning where..."

His voice trailed off, a distant look coming to his gaze that spoke of reliving a horror Vanya knew he wouldn't like.

"The exterior gates were unlocked and open," Dariush said after giving himself a visible shake. "No guards were on duty. The door was unlocked, and when I entered, there were bodies everywhere."

Vanya sucked in a harsh breath, teeth scraping together. "Bodies?"

Dariush blinked, still clearly in some sort of shock and yet forcing himself to work through it. "Bodies, Your Imperial Majesty. Every single person in the embassy had been murdered by bullets or magic."

Vanya went cold, ears ringing with some noise no one else could hear. He squeezed his eyes shut, wrenching the panic aside as he forced himself to ask the questions that mattered as an emperor and not a man in love. "The people who came with you? The Lady Lore and Sor—the prince. Were they dead as well?"

"No," Dariush said raggedly. "They weren't amongst the dead that we could find, but the prince's weapons were in a room where my counselor had been murdered."

Vanya opened his eyes, staring at the distraught ambassador. Before he could try to speak, one of the peacekeepers with ranking pins depicting him as a captain stepped forward and offered a shallow bow. "We canvassed the area and knocked on the doors of the nearby businesses, Your Imperial Majesty. Someone at a barrister firm in early for work saw a diplomatic aide and a star priest leave with two people who matched the descriptions of Lady Lore and Prince Alasandair Rourke."

Dariush shook his head. "No member of my staff nor anyone who flew here from Ashion would have betrayed us so."

"Can you be sure?" Vanya asked, voice scratchy.

"None were *rionetkas*, if that is your concern."

"Perhaps you didn't look hard enough at those who traveled with you." Vanya raised a hand to forestall Dariush's anticipated protest. "I know a thing or two about betrayal by those held in close regard to me."

Dariush clenched his teeth together, the tendons in his neck standing out before he took a deep breath. "No true Ashionen would sabotage us so. Everyone who has worked under me is aligned with our queen."

Vanya dearly wanted to believe that, but he knew how well someone could play the long game. "Say it was none of yours. That leaves Daijal or Solaria."

He doubted Eimarille was responsible for such an attack. The Daijalan ambassador and diplomatic corps had been expelled from Solaria last year, their embassy empty and barred to anyone but the Solarian government these days. Joelle, on the other hand, he could see her reacting badly to yesterday's war declaration.

He doubted any but the House of Kimathi would have acted so

murderously. Joelle still had her supporters, and while the Conclave might have enshrined his right to rule with Callisto's own blessing, there were ever those who would conspire to see him off the Imperial throne. She would have tapped into such discontent, even from behind Bellingham's walls, and moved swiftly when Vanya was still savoring a desperately argued-for political win.

Vanya looked at Caelum. "I want all trains stopped and airships grounded. Bring me the manifests of those that have already left this morning, their destination, and who owns them."

"You don't believe the lady and the prince are within the capital?" Caelum asked.

Vanya shook his head. "A city-wide search will still occur, but I don't believe we'll find them. What use are hostages if they are here?"

Caelum grimaced. "You will need proof to accuse a House."

"The House in question was already accused."

"Why wouldn't the prince have saved himself with starfire? He is a Rourke, is he not?"

Dariush frowned. "The prince insists he has none."

Vanya knew otherwise, but it wasn't his truth to tell. "He gave up his weapons of his own free will, most likely to save Lady Lore. A warden's first tenant is to protect Maricol's children."

It was so easy to see how Soren would have been manipulated in order to ensure his sister's closest confidant remained alive. Joelle probably hoped such interference would blow back against the declaration of war and drive a rift between the two countries before the alliance was anything more than words. Perhaps she thought Vanya would focus on Soren and not the threat beyond Solaria's borders.

But as much as he loved Soren, he had to love his country more, and Vanya knew the warden would understand, even as it made his heart ache with a grief he could not let himself feel.

"I need to speak with Queen Caris," Vanya said.

"I can facilitate that," Dariush said.

"I'll send the order to the military to close the railway stations and airfields," Caelum said, already gesturing at the military aide to follow him out of the Mosaic Room.

Vanya turned toward the doors. "Come with me, Ambassador."

Dariush fell into step behind him, exactly where someone of high importance but not Imperial royalty would walk. The *praetoria* legionnaires waiting in the hallway fell in around them as Vanya led the way to his working office in the Senate building. He kept his expression bland as he went, aware of the whispers and curious glances thrown his way by the senatorial staff they passed.

The *praetoria* legionnaires cleared his office before allowing him to enter, the spell-detecting device hidden in the gas lamp chandelier above never activating. Vanya sat behind his desk while Dariush stood before it rather than sit, hands clasped together in front of him. Vanya picked up the telephone and put the receiver to his ear, pressing the button that would connect him to the Senate's operator.

"I have a long-distance call to make," Vanya said after the operator greeted him.

"Certainly, Your Imperial Majesty. May I have the number?" she asked.

"The Ashionen ambassador will tell you."

He handed the receiver to Dariush, who hid his surprise at being given access to Vanya's personal telephone line. But he rallied quickly enough, conversing with the operator as she connected him through to whoever handled such things on the Ashionen end. It took several minutes to reach someone who was within the queen's employ and then longer before she could be found and brought on the line for Dariush to explain what was going on.

Eventually, Dariush handed the receiver back to Vanya. "Her Royal Majesty is ready to speak with you."

Vanya took the receiver again, the long-distance call staticky in the silence that stretched between them over a thousand miles. Eventually, Queen Caris Rourke spoke, her voice young-sounding but quietly firm.

"I understand from my ambassador that my brother and Lady Lore Auclair are missing and that my diplomatic corps in Solaria have nearly all been murdered," Caris said evenly in Ashionen.

Vanya let none of the anguish he felt at losing Soren once again seep into his voice as he conversed in the same language. "You have my sincerest apologies for the attack upon your people and territory within Solaria. Rest assured, it is not one I initiated."

"Your people can't have been best pleased about the debt owed to my brother that you are paying with the Legion."

Young, Vanya decided, but quite astute when it came to the fallout of politics. "A common enemy remains even after the dead will be burned. I have no intention of reneging on my promise of aid and an alliance."

"I am relieved to hear that, as we desperately need the support. But that still doesn't tell me who took my people or why."

Vanya quashed the knee-jerk retort that Soren wasn't hers. "I have my suspicions on who but no proof. As to why? Solarians don't see your war as theirs."

Caris made a thoughtful noise that crackled in Vanya's ear over the line. "But you do."

"My country was not spared from the interference of *rionetkas*, and I see Eimarille for the threat she is. She may claim Ashion is hers to rule, but that is not the only country she covets."

"So you risked your people's wrath to support mine."

"I made a vow."

"To my brother. My understanding is he could have asked for anything, and he never did until now."

She didn't need to know Soren's reasoning behind that. Only Vanya knew his lover had kept the vow and never asked for anything before now so as to remain by Vanya's side. "Soren never knew his past."

Caris was quiet for a moment. When she spoke again, her voice was soft and wry. "He dislikes the name Alasandair Rourke."

"He is a warden. It is what he was made to be. Soren can be nothing else, no matter the name your people would give him."

"He is my heir."

"For now," Vanya demurred. "Take solace in the fact he is worth more alive than dead to whomever has him. He and your lady will be a bargaining chip."

"That relieves neither of us of our current dilemma."

"No, but it will not stop me from sending the Legion north nor searching for Soren and Lady Lore. This alliance will not falter." Vanya meant it, the sureness in his voice as hard as steel.

"Thank you. I think my people and my country will survive because of you. I wish others were as open to giving aid."

"I wasn't, at first."

"No, but you were honorable about what you owed. Soren said you would be."

"E'ridia hasn't agreed to an alliance?"

"Not for lack of effort."

"What about the Tovan Isles?"

"Ashion is landlocked. Daijal holds the western coast, and the Ashionen parliament handled diplomatic duties with that country when necessary. My people don't have the proper connections nor permission of passage through foreign territory to open diplomatic channels with that nation."

Vanya looked at Dariush and the intent expression on the ambassador's face as he listened to only one side of the conversation. "Solaria has an alliance with the Tovan Isles. If Ashion needs access to their representatives through Solaria, I will grant such accommodations. Your ambassador can coordinate with mine for an introduction."

Caris made a soft, surprised noise while Dariush did his level best not to give away whatever he was feeling in the face of Vanya's offer.

"Thank you," Caris said again, relief, or perhaps delayed grief, making her voice waver over the line. "Ashion accepts your generosity."

"I look forward to our new alliance."

"As do I."

They didn't chat much longer, the bulk of their conversation finished. After he placed the receiver in the cradle, Vanya looked at Dariush, and the ambassador dipped into a deep bow. "My people thank you, Your Imperial Majesty."

"Who has custody of Soren's weapons?" Vanya asked.

"Ah, I would need to check, but I believe the peacekeepers do. They are the ones investigating the crime scene."

"I want his weapons brought to me."

Vanya knew how much wardens cared for their weapons, had spent many nights watching Soren tend to them before he could coax the other man into bed. A warden's life was only as good as their training and ability to defend themselves in the poison fields. He'd hold on to Soren's poison short sword, his dual pistols, and his dagger until the warden could claim them again.

Because he would.

Dariush inclined his head. "I will retrieve them immediately, Your Imperial Majesty."

He took his leave, closing the door behind him. Left alone in his office, Vanya gave in to the urge to pray, holding his head in his hands while hunched over his desk. "You said our roads were meant to cross. Tell me they still will, Callisto."

But in those few moments where it was just Vanya and his heartbeat before duty came knocking again, the Dawn Star did not answer his prayers.

Fourteen

EIMARILLE

Eimarille looked up from the reports strewn across her desk as the door to her office was pushed open without a knock, the hinges squeaking ever so slightly. Terilyn slipped inside, her clothes meant for an airship and not the Daijal court. Her trousers were neatly tailored, the material thicker for higher altitude. The flower embroidery around the collar and cuffs of her blouse were the only bits of brightness on the fabric. Her plain, fur-lined leather flight jacket was slung over one arm, hair braided tightly around her skull like a crown to fit beneath a helmet.

Eimarille glanced at the clock on the wall and the minutes that had ticked away into hours while she'd been working. "Darling, is it time already?"

"Yes. Maksim's airship departs in an hour."

Eimarille's heart lurched at that, and in the late hour where it was only the two of them, she let her concern show. "I'd send someone else if I could."

Terilyn draped her flight jacket over the back of one of the chairs angled in front of the desk before coming around to where Eimarille sat. She leaned down, and Eimarille tipped her head up to accept the kiss her lover offered.

"You know I go at your command," Terilyn said when they broke apart.

Eimarille tugged on Terilyn's belt, a wordless plea the other woman didn't hesitate to answer. Terilyn climbed onto Eimarille's lap, knees on either side of her, the skirt of Eimarille's gown stretching tight over her legs. She was still in the clothes she'd worn for court that afternoon and the meeting with the military that had come after. She'd not seen Terilyn for most of the day, the Blade's absence something necessary but one which always left Eimarille bereft.

"The emperor will send his Legion north within the next two weeks. You planned for this, and I will see your orders obeyed," Terilyn murmured as she framed Eimarille's face with cool, long-fingered hands.

Eimarille settled her own at Terilyn's waist, mindful of the pistols and knives the other woman carried on her person. "If I could trust anyone else with this task and keep you by my side, I would."

She never slept well when Terilyn was gone, and a part of her always fretted over Terilyn's safety. Rationally, Eimarille knew Terilyn was a well-trained Blade, but that did nothing to ease her fear of losing the one person she'd ever truly loved before her son was born.

And as much as she loved Lisandro—fiercely, devotedly, with every spark of starfire at her command—she loved Terilyn just as much. Terilyn had been Eimarille's port in a storm ever since the Inferno, her home, no matter the city they stood in. Terilyn wanted what Eimarille wanted—the world for themselves and her son—and they'd claim it soon enough.

Terilyn carded her fingers through Eimarille's loose hair before they locked together behind her neck. Eimarille sighed when Terilyn pressed their foreheads together, eyes fluttering shut as they held each other close.

"I will be fine," Terilyn murmured. "It's an airship flight to Matriskav and then another to the northern coast. I've been promised the Urovan navy's fastest submersible to take me under the ice and down the east coast to the forces lying in wait. They'll have your orders within a week for the coordinated attack."

Some things in war—whether an order or a warning—were best delivered in person. Only three people in Daijal outside the military high command knew of the plan created to cripple any alliance Ashion sought to make. Of those three, Eimarille could not leave New Haven for such a long absence, much less an excursion beyond Daijal's borders. That left Terilyn and the *Klovod* to carry out her clandestine orders because a telegram or telephone call wouldn't reach the Urovan forces waiting in the Constellation Sea.

"Make sure the captain is mindful of the Tovanian ship-cities patrolling the coastlines," Eimarille warned, fingers tightening around Terilyn's hips. "I won't have you unable to return to me."

Terilyn moved to press a kiss to the corner of Eimarille's mouth with soft lips. "You worry so. I will be fine."

She wasn't always. She'd come back to Eimarille bruised and cut and burned plenty of times before, never once blaming Eimarille for the aches she endured. She carried scars that should have been on Eimarille's skin from being her Blade and cutting where Eimarille could not. She understood what it cost Terilyn to walk this road beside her, and she would never not be indebted to the other woman. "I worry out of love."

Terilyn hummed softly before pressing another kiss to Eimarille's cheek, skimming her lips over the powder and blush there. Eimarille turned her head, capturing Terilyn's mouth for a long, languid kiss that made her hate the clock ticking away on the wall. Not enough time to divest her lover of the clothes she wore or to lick her way inside the tempting heat between Terilyn's thighs. Her airship waited, as did Eimarille's orders.

"Come back to me," Eimarille murmured when they parted once more.

Terilyn stroked her hands through Eimarille's hair, making a mess of it before she leaned in for one last kiss, fingers ghosting over the edge of Eimarille's jaw. "I'll return well before Seventh Month is over."

The calendar still had days to mark off before Eighth Month arrived, and Eimarille would count down every one like a prayer until Terilyn was back by her side. She sighed as Terilyn slid off her lap, their hands clasped for a lingering moment before Terilyn bent to kiss Eimarille's knuckles. Only then did she finally let go, and Eimarille resisted the urge to drag her back close again.

"Be safe, my darling," Eimarille said.

Terilyn quirked a smile, dark eyes full of a love no one ever saw, before she left, closing the office door behind her with a quiet click. Eimarille pressed her knuckles to her lips, staring blankly at the reports before she gave herself a shake to clear her head. She still had much reading to do for her meeting with the military brass in the morning, but Eimarille knew the next stage of the war was in good hands.

Repurcussions

937 A.O.P.

One

HONOVI

Honovi left the *Comhairle nan Cinnidhean* chambers at the center of the government building with an aching fury he dared not show on his face after the session ended for the day. Despite his effort, he knew his father could read the seething truth in him better than anyone.

"The *Comhairle nan Cinnidhean* hasn't changed its stance since the last time you stood before them. This alliance you seek with Ashion is not viable, and you paint our clan in a bad light by repeatedly bringing it to the table. You must have known the session would have gone this way," Alrickson said with a heavy sigh as they walked through the curved hallways of the capital's governing building, leaving their fellows behind. The gardens situated in the space between the circular buildings were in summer bloom, but Honovi barely spared them a glance.

Honovi clenched his hands into fists and matched his stride with his father's, the hem of his kilt brushing against his knees. "It's my right as *jarl* to request a vote."

"Perhaps, but it is also the *Comhairle nan Cinnidhean*'s right to refrain from bringing it up. I told you that your latest motion would be tabled."

"You could have voted yes to hear it."

"I have before, several times, and always the vote is the same. I couldn't in good conscience proceed when there are other pressing needs to be dealt with. There will be no vote for alliance, now or in the future. You are not Ashion's ambassador, so stop trying to be."

That wasn't an unexpected result of Honovi's continuous lobbying since last year, but it was disheartening, to say the least. "But you agree with me that Eimarille is a threat. That this war she persists in fighting will not end at the Eastern Spine."

"She has made no moves beyond her own borders—"

"What do you think this war with Ashion *is*? And what of the *rionetkas* found in our government?" Honovi all but hissed to keep his voice low as they passed by clerks and political aides. "What of our former Seneschal?"

Alrickson slanted him a look, hair ornaments depicting his rank glinting in his long graying braid with the motion of his head. "There isn't any proof of Daijal interference there."

Honovi snorted his opinion on that and stared straight ahead as they walked to his father's office. "Pretending it's not there doesn't negate the threat, and you know it."

Gregor of Clan Wind, once their country's Seneschal, had been found to be a *rionetka* last year, bearing the vivisection scars on his body of someone else's control. The wardens had been reluctant to advertise their ability to rework the control as they had done with Nathaniel, but they'd eventually sent Ksenia to Glencoe over the winter to handle the operation. They hadn't had Caris to write out the notes the clarion crystals sang or find the dips in his mind, so it had taken much longer.

In the end, Ksenia's efforts had given Gregor back his mind but not his memories or his position. The clans had been forced to vote on an interim Seneschal until the next round of elections arrived to fill it permanently.

It had also made E'ridians wary of giving more aid to the wardens after their initial rush to help in the wake of the attack on the Warden's Island. Rumors were persisting and building that the wardens had a hand in creating the *rionetkas*, despite their sworn duty to protect Maricol under the Poison Accords. Honovi knew the truth would be devastating—that a warden *was* responsible for the horror of *rionetkas*. That the warden in question had been thought dead at the time would not negate the public's opinion on the matter.

Delani, the wardens' governor, had remained silent in the face of such pointed questions, refusing to confirm or deny such a fact. E'ridia would still tithe, as was required by the Poison Accords, but Honovi could see how this might build resentment in the clans. So, too, could he see how the clans' insistence on noninterference would be their undoing if Eimarille had her way.

Honovi held his tongue until they were ensconced in his father's office, the space familiar after years of standing in his father's shadow and learning how to lead a clan as much as how to help govern a nation.

"Father, you know I am right," Honovi said once the door was closed behind them. The whir of the mechanical fan in the corner was white noise, moving the sluggish air, as there wasn't a window for a breeze. Summer was only two weeks away, Seventh Month half over already.

Alrickson went behind his desk and started sorting through the folios left there by a clerk. "I am not in a position to agree with you. You haven't brought us any proof beyond what Blaine insists is the truth."

"The Dusk Star wouldn't have left him with us if we weren't supposed to support his duty."

"His road is not enough to dictate policy."

Honovi bit back the first and second retort that came to his lips. "Will the *Comhairle nan Cinnidhean* wait until Daijal is at our border? Is that our policy now?"

"Ashion's war is not ours."

"Does the attack on the Warden's Island mean nothing, then? Is Solaria's alliance not evidence enough they see Daijal for the threat it is?"

News of that alliance had come out of Calhames nearly two weeks ago. Honovi had left for Glencoe soon after Caris had confirmed it, along with Lore's and Soren's frightening disappearance. The alliance was all the broadsheets were reporting on, even in E'ridia, though Soren's absence had yet to be truly questioned. There'd been no demand sent to either Caris or the Imperial emperor that he knew of, and Honovi knew faith in finding the pair alive was flickering.

But that was information Blaine had sworn him to secrecy about, and Honovi, for all that he was *jarl*, was a husband first these days. He believed in Blaine's road, in his duty to stand as witness for Caris, because in doing so, it would keep Maricol safe and whole, not subjugated by one country determined to assimilate everyone under one crown.

"The Imperial emperor's alliance was dictated by a debt. The Legion is marching north, but it remains to be seen how long the Houses will support such an endeavor," Alrickson said before sitting. He gestured pointedly at the chairs in front of his desk.

Honovi withheld a sigh before obeying the wordless order and claimed a chair. "The Imperial emperor has the Dawn Star's blessing."

"And Queen Eimarille has the support of the Twilight Star. An argument could be made for who is more favored, but it is not one the *Comhairle nan Cinnidhean* will participate in."

Honovi met his father's gaze. "Standing on the sidelines is not the answer."

Alrickson sighed, spreading his hands. "It is not our fight."

"The vote today was wrong."

Honovi knew it in his gut, in his soul, in a way he thought his father might have until he'd voted no. Honovi might be *jarl*, but his father was *ceann-cinnidh*, and it would be years yet until Alrickson ceded the clan seat to him. He knew there were some in Clan Storm who disliked his persistence regarding the dangers of Daijal, but he was resolute in his fear that to ignore what was happening beyond their borders was detrimental to their own sovereignty.

He'd been sounding the alarm since last year, and no one seemed inclined to listen. It didn't matter that he was *jarl* of Clan Storm—he had limited power to make people listen when they'd rather turn the other way.

Unlike his mother and sister, Honovi was no magician. Perhaps he was graced with a little foresight, though he'd forever wish he weren't when the city sirens pierced the walls of the government building just then.

Honovi jerked to his feet, the tone one he'd never heard before outside the yearly tests to ensure the whole system was working. Siren warnings for revenants were a pattern everyone knew, the sound bone-deep and jarring, but this one—this was a nightmare of their own making that had followed the winds back home.

He watched his father stand, all the blood draining out of the older man's face as the siren positioned outside the building blared the inconceivable.

"All airships are to launch in defense of the city. All citizens are to seek immediate shelter."

Alrickson opened his mouth, but before he could say anything, the office door banged open, one of the peacekeepers on duty in the building appearing in the doorway. "*Ceann-cinnidh* Alrickson, *jarl* Honovi, the building is being evacuated. We need to get you to the shelters."

E'ridia had stood for several thousand years, and the clans had not always been so easy with each other. Even after the Age of Separation, when they'd gained sovereignty, learning to govern with so many disparate groups had sometimes degenerated into actual, physical battles. And when aeronauts fought, airships were always involved.

Their country had an old history with aerial bombardments, but the bomb shelters had not been needed in generations. Funds were always allocated in the yearly budget for their continued upkeep and repair over the centuries, but Honovi knew that Glencoe wouldn't have enough to shelter every citizen. They hadn't needed them for war, and the walls kept revenants out.

They would need them now.

The telephone on Alrickson's desk rang, the sound different from the unceasing warning siren. His father snatched up the receiver and pressed it to his ear, nearly knocking the base off the desk in his haste. "*Ceann-cinnidh* Alrickson speaking."

Honovi couldn't hear the person on the other side of the line, and the peacekeeper was gesturing hurriedly at them to move, but his feet remained planted in the office. He stared at his father, watching as that political mask he'd worn for years cracked, a horrifying disbelief filling his gaze. Alrickson swayed on his feet, leaning forward to press his hand to the desk to hold himself steady.

"I understand," he rasped. Seconds later, he placed the receiver in the cradle with a shaking hand. He blinked, focusing on Honovi, eyes terribly wide. "Compass Air Force Base and the Ferric Repair Yard were attacked. Initial reports indicate we've lost nearly half the war airships at the base and almost all those in the yard."

The bitter truth of the situation wasn't a victory for Honovi—it never would be, when it was his country that had been harmed. He looked at his father, the siren still piercing the air as if it were trying to wake the dead as the peacekeeper entreated them to evacuate.

"Daijal was never going to stop at our border," Honovi said.

And E'ridia's insistence for neutrality had crippled their vaunted air force in a preemptive attack no one except for Honovi and Blaine had feared might happen.

Two

TERILYN

Terilyn wedged herself in the corner behind the captain's seat, squinting at the murky, silt-filled water of the swampy wetland that lapped against the front viewport. They'd left the main tract of the river behind yesterday, the Urovan fleet of submersibles pressing ever northwest toward their target. The swamp waters here in this part of Solaria were deep enough to allow for submersibles to travel through the waterways beneath trees whose branches hung low overhead, blocking out the sky and keeping them hidden.

The Urovans hadn't sent an icebreaker ship south—there'd been no need for such a powerful vessel in open waters—but they'd reworked the engineering on the submersibles' prows to cut through overgrowth rather than ice for this endeavor. The water was trending more shallow with every hour they put behind them, and she thought the trees and low-lying plants were starting to thin out.

"Maybe another hour before we hit the shallows, according to the maps," the captain said in Urovan as he pulled on a lever and flicked a toggle with his other hand.

Terilyn pulled her pocket watch free and lifted the lid with her thumbnail to check the time. This far south in Solaria, the sun set faster than it did in Daijal, but they'd reach solid land before sunset truly started, and that was all that mattered. It would be light enough still for the Urovans to execute Eimarille's orders. By Terilyn's calculations, the submersibles tasked with traversing E'ridia's rivers should have already finished their attack. Terilyn would have no way to tell until she reached a city and could pick up a broadsheet.

Eimarille and Terilyn had planned the two-pronged attack during the latter half of this past winter, when it became apparent that Ashion would not stop requesting aid from other countries. They'd picked apart every possible detail with Kote until they had a solid plan in place to head off what support E'ridia and Solaria could provide Ashion.

It meant targeting E'ridia's airfields and repair yards while targeting something else in Solaria altogether. Solaria's Legion was next to impossible to fully cripple, but its forces could be split. One just needed to find the right leverage.

She tucked her pocket watch away and shifted on her feet, arching her back a little to crack it. She'd shed the heavy jacket she'd worn for most of the travel south, the inside of the submersible quickly becoming warmer than was comfortable. It was built to stay insulated in icy-cold seas, not in the middle of a swampy wetland. Someone had popped the hatch after they'd breached the water, and Terilyn tilted her head around the edge of the entryway, hoping to feel a hint of breeze to cool the sweat on her skin.

"How has the artillery fared?" she asked in her native language. Terilyn had gained a faint accent from all her years spent in Daijal, but she'd never lost her proficiency in her mother tongue.

The captain didn't look away from the waterway beyond the large glass panes of the front viewport. "Dry and ready to launch, according to the ordnance officer."

She nodded to herself, watching as the shoreline twisted up ahead, a breeze gently making the branches and vines sway above the submersible. Those on watch hadn't sounded any warnings for revenants, but that didn't mean the dead weren't out there. The water wasn't cleansed the way the lakes and rivers were tended to in the north with filtration machines, the wetlands too vast to easily fix.

Whatever poison was embedded in the Wastelands had encroached in the land out here, spreading spores and poison in this area of Solaria. Frontier towns existed in the wetlands, but no city had ever called it home.

The closest one had ever gotten to the shallows was Rixham.

Eventually, the trees of the swampy wetlands thinned enough to see the horizon through the trees and the convoy that awaited them at the rendezvous point. The distance between Rixham and the wetlands was beyond the capabilities of a submersible to travel without a waterway. They were met instead at the shoreline by trucks that had risked the long trek south from the House of Kimathi's *vasilyet* through dangerous back roads and survived, courtesy of their guide.

The *Klovod* was a man Terilyn knew well after so many years of him orbiting her queen. The former warden had the training and the wherewithal to move the disguised Daijalan troops through Joelle's porous northern border of her *vasilyet* and past the Legion's ever-shifting front lines. He'd been sent to oversee the death-defying machine at Daijal's southern border, bringing with him prisoners of war to turn into revenants, and from there, his orders had sent him deep into Solaria.

Terilyn studied the *Klovod* through the front viewport, the man dressed as the warden he'd long since ceased to be. She shifted on her feet, moving with the motion of the submersible as the captain angled it close to shore. She gave her thanks for a smooth sail after the long days spent together before slipping out of the cramped quarters and through the short, narrow corridor for the ladder leading to the hatch.

She climbed it swiftly, nodding her thanks to the Urovan soldier already outside, who offered his hand to her. She took it, letting him smoothly guide her from submersible to shore. Her feet slid a bit in the muddy banks, but she pitched herself onto dry land for the first time in nearly two weeks, breathing fresh air that didn't leave an aftertaste of metal in the back of her throat.

"Did you encounter any trouble?" Terilyn asked in Daijalan.

"Not when everyone thought we were wardens heading to the

Wastelands for border duty," the *Klovod* said, bite scar on his cheek pulling a bit as he spoke.

These days, most of the wardens were in Ashion, removed from Daijal and Urova, a troubling issue that meant more revenants walking the poison fields of their country than Eimarille preferred. But despite the betrayal Solaria's major Houses had adhered to over the Ages with their royal dead, the wardens hadn't pulled out of that country and continued to back Ashion.

And now Solaria had agreed to an alliance with the false queen.

Eimarille had expected such a problem, planned for it, which was why Terilyn had traveled far. The House of Sa'Liandel had cracks in the loyalties owed to it, even with the Dawn Star's blessing. Some of those cracks had spread for years, and Terilyn was here, behind enemy lines, to ruin a country for her queen.

"The ornithopter is on standby for after. It will take us north, to an abandoned way station between here and Calhames, where an airship is waiting. It'll be a night flight the rest of the way to Daijal," the *Klovod* said.

Terilyn nodded. "Then let's make this transfer quick."

The soldiers who had followed the *Klovod* south had been busy while they waited for the Urovan submersibles to arrive. Trees had been cut down to clear space, metal ramps laid down over soft ground, and the trucks lined up with engines running were ready to receive the long-range grenade launchers Urova had transported for them.

It took time, with the sun sliding ever west in the sky, but Terilyn wasn't willing to rush the unloading. The ordnance that had already leveled E'ridian airfields would now be put to the test against a dead city.

Automatons helped with the unloading of weaponry from the submersibles onto transport trucks, while soldiers worked tirelessly to bolt and weld them into place. The grenade launchers would have received far too much attention to smuggle them through Solaria, especially with the security checks the emperor had initiated. Coordinating this meet-up had taken both time and luck, but when they finally parted ways, they were only a few hours out from the attack on E'ridia when the city walls of Rixham came into view.

Terilyn knew it had been a city holding hundreds of thousands of revenants inside its barricaded walls for going on two decades. It had stood for years as a monument to a mother's grief and a House's folly.

It would fall in the shadow of the emperor's mistakes.

The *Klovod* knew of its defenses from a fellow warden whose duties had always been to guard it. The clockwork cat he'd created for his warden friend years ago had learned the habits, codes, and spells used to keep the barricades around Rixham in place. He'd retrieved such information during the times they'd both leave the poison fields behind in favor of the Warden's Island.

Terilyn wondered if the *Klovod* had meant to betray the wardens for years before the Midnight Star had found him and taught him how to create *rionetkas*. She'd never asked why he harbored such hatred of the people who had made him, but therein, perhaps, was her answer. Tithes were payment and had no rights once given up. All they had was the wardens and the alchemy that would change them or kill them. The wardens could not be surprised some held such bitterness in their hearts.

The sun had touched the horizon when the soldiers and magicians under the *Klovod*'s command got in position on the southeast side of the city. Magicians cast magic from their wands to make everyone appear as part of the topography while soldiers extended the support struts that would stabilize the trucks when the long-distance grenade launchers fired at the high walls in the distance.

The *Klovod* supervised several soldiers as they removed the tarp that kept the ornithopter hidden from view, the blades that helped give it flight rotating idly from the jostling. Satisfied with the preparation efforts going on around her, she made her way to the ornithopter and eyed the two seats inside it.

The soldiers had their own escape avenues, though they were all aware that this could very well be a suicide mission. But they were dedicated to their queen, hand-picked because of their belief in Daijal's right to rule Maricol.

The *Klovod* glanced at her, his face impassive in the dying light. "I had a soldier drop it off here last night. He stayed under cover until we arrived and will be departing with his squad. It's fueled up and ready for us."

"Good," Terilyn said. "Let's see this done."

The wardens had never had any cause to be concerned that the walls around Rixham wouldn't hold. They had spent two decades guarding the walking dead massed inside an abandoned city's streets. Terilyn knew there would be no survivors inside Rixham, only a horde of revenants of a size not seen before in history.

Solaria would bear witness to it now.

The first volley of grenades launched before the light in the west faded, hitting their target dead-on, destroying the thick outer wall of Rixham one explosion at a time. The soldiers knew they'd have a limited amount of time to press the attack before the wardens on duty at the watchtower and the sentinel-class automatons came to defend it.

By then, it was too late.

Terilyn hauled herself up into the passenger seat of the ornithopter, the hair on the back of her neck prickling as a sound rent the air between the booming noise of explosions. It rose like a storm wind, raspy and animalistic, tens of thousands of the walking dead screaming for a release they couldn't comprehend, driven onward by the spores ravaging their desiccated flesh.

For all that she was a Blade, Terilyn was no warden, and the bone-deep fear of revenants almost everyone on Maricol grew up with made her want to *run*.

The volley stopped minutes later, engines thrumming as the soldiers frantically undid the support struts to quickly turn the trucks south. Their evacuation route was in the wetlands, where the Urovan submersibles waited to ferry them out of danger.

The *Klovod* appeared on the other side of the ornithopter so suddenly that Terilyn was half drawing a stiletto from the sheath in her boot before she recognized him. He smirked at her, as if he knew how tightly wound her nerves were. "Your queen will be pleased."

"Just get us in the air," Terilyn said coolly.

The sooner they left the land behind, the better.

The *Klovod* did as ordered, deftly getting the engine up and running, the blades spinning with a speed that vibrated through the framework of the ornithopter. Soon enough, they were in the air, the thrum of the engine making her teeth ache.

Terilyn leaned to the side and craned her head to peer down at the rapidly distancing earth below them. In the last vestiges of the fading sun, she could see a darkness spilling out of the shattered walls surrounding Rixham, spreading ever outward.

Solaria would learn the lesson of burning their dead instead of burying them far too late.

Three

VANYA

In the weeks since Soren's disappearance, Vanya spent most of his days trying to tire himself out so he wouldn't dream about the nightmarish possibilities of his lover's fate.

Taisiya had made it a habit to bully him out of his office on a nightly basis. On one such occasion, Vanya was having an after-dinner drink with Taisiya in the private inner courtyard of the Sa'Liandel estate in Calhames when Caelum interrupted them with a troubled look on his face. "Apologies, Your Imperial Majesty. Governor Delani is insistent that she speak with you."

Vanya frowned and set his glass of brandy down on the table, gesturing Caelum to come closer. "This late?"

"She informs me she tried to reach you at your desk, but when that failed, she called my personal line."

Vanya stood, a knot forming in his stomach, wondering if it was about Soren and, distantly, Lore. He'd had spies scouring Calhames and elsewhere for any hint of where Soren might have been taken, but still no leads had shown up. He hadn't yet dared to initiate communications with Joelle, not wanting to give her any leverage. Vanya had to believe that Soren wasn't dead somewhere, that he would come back to him, as he always did when he left for the poison fields.

Caelum approached, holding out his hand with the televox resting in his palm. Vanya took it and pressed the small device to his ear. "Delani? Did you find Soren?"

"I'm not calling about Soren," Delani said in a tight, raw voice. "I'm calling with a warning for Solaria. Someone attacked Rixham tonight. I got the call from those on duty at the watchtower."

Sound disappeared into a high-pitched ringing in Vanya's ears. He had to lock his knees so as not to stagger backward. *What?*

"Rixham has fallen. You need to warn your people."

Vanya opened his mouth to speak but couldn't find the words. Every sound was stuck in his throat like shards of glass, the horror of something he never thought would pass rising up to ruin him.

Rixham is a dead city. There is nothing living in Rixham.

The mantra was a warning his mother had given voice to in the wake of his older brother's murder decades ago. She'd fought to keep Solaria whole and left the traitorous city still standing but its people dead inside walls that kept them imprisoned. Every House knew what they risked if they targeted what was essentially a grave.

"Why didn't your wardens stop them?" Vanya finally got out.

"They *tried* and died for their efforts, but they got the warning out first. Make no mistake, this problem lies with your House. We wardens could have eradicated the threat if your mother had been willing, but she wasn't."

"You don't know that."

"I was *there*," Delani snarled, fury lacing every bitten-out word. "I warned Zakariya about the risks, even after she pulled back as some of the city burned. She would not heed any of them."

There'd been a warden at the front lines back then when Rixham fell, Vanya vaguely remembered. He'd never known her name, could not place her face these many years later, but to now know it was Delani underscored, perhaps, why she'd seemed to take news of the royal crypts with such anger.

"You changed the maps. You made Rixham a border. You never dealt with the city, proving my mother right—it was too risky to burn it to the ground."

"The spores would carry, and she would not see her people at risk like that, for all that she left them at risk for this very moment. It seems your House haunts everyone's road these days."

Vanya clenched his teeth, mind whirling at the implications of the attack and what it would mean to defend against it. The Legion, he realized with a sinking stomach, would need to be split. Half the forces would now have to be sent south to help protect the cities and towns across Solaria, while the rest kept the country's promise to Ashion.

"I'll summon my war council and reallocate the Legion. I'll make overtures to E'ridia for assistance from their air force and—"

"E'ridia lost a base and a repair yard a couple of hours before Rixham fell," Delani interrupted. "You'll have no support from that quarter."

He closed his eyes, refusing to flinch at that news. "Eimarille planned this well."

For Vanya had no illusions about who was behind the coordinated attacks. He doubted there'd be proof left at Rixham, but Vanya knew what Eimarille stood to gain from crippling E'ridia's air force and diminishing Solaria's Legion. While the attacks hindered Solaria, he would not abandon Ashion, for that was what the Daijal queen hoped for in the wake of such horror.

More than anything, Solaria's alliance with Ashion must stand.

Delani drew in a breath that crackled in his ear. "I will need to send my most experienced wardens south. The ones on duty in the Wastelands are being warned as we speak to take cover and prepare for a long engagement. This is going to be a siege in some areas of your country. Your cleansed lands will be contaminated."

All the fields planted and growing would be worthless if revenants trampled everything and spread spores. His people risked starving, even with the supplies every city was required by law to have in storage for lean years. "What are the numbers?"

"Of revenants in Rixham? Several hundred thousand, easily, even with the passage of time."

Not even the Legion could stand against so many and come away alive and unharmed. An alliance with E'ridia for use of their airships would have been his country's best bet to stem the encroachment of so many revenants, but that was impossible now. The Legion's own war airships didn't have the higher capabilities E'ridia's had, but much of the ones he'd intended to send to Ashion would have to remain in Solaria.

Hordes could cover ground quickly. Revenants never needed sustenance to keep them going. The spores embedded in their bodies kept them walking, kept them searching for a victim to infect, and there were so many in Solaria for them to target.

"I'll call my war council together."

"You do that," Delani replied, judgment thick in her voice before she ended the call.

Vanya pulled the televox away from his ear, staring into the distance, not really seeing anything of the courtyard. Solaria had to come first, he knew that, but some desperate corner of his heart wished he could put more resources toward finding Soren. Only when Taisiya touched his arm and called to him did Vanya orient on the here and now rather than his missing heart.

"What happened?" Taisiya asked, a pleading look in her eyes, as if she already knew the answer and wished for him to lie to her.

Vanya pressed his hand over hers, wishing he could comfort her and knowing he couldn't. "Rixham was attacked and the walls destroyed, freeing the revenant horde."

Four

HONOVI

Dawn's soft light illuminated the Sunrise Valley as the *Celestial Sprite* flew above it, forward and aft gunners on standby to defend against any attack. Honovi stood at the prow beside his father, gloved hands gripping the metal railing as he squinted into the rising sun behind his brass goggles. The breeze of their passage was cool, though Honovi knew the weather would warm up the later it got.

"You and Blaine were right," Alrickson said, his words stolen by the wind. "We should have listened."

Honovi knew the *Comhairle nan Cinnidhean*'s remorse was useless in the wake of the damage that had been wrought, but his anger would help no one. So he kept silent, and his father bowed his head.

The Compass Air Force Base was stationed north of Glencoe, situated not far from the banks of the River Esk. That waterway flowed from the Eastern Spine into the valley floor, streaming north to the wide mouth of the river that poured into the Northern Sea. None of the airships patrolling their borders had seen the danger before it struck. Honovi didn't know how long the Urovan submersibles might have been stalking their waterways, but there was no denying E'ridia had been caught unawares.

Some airships had been able to launch amidst the attack, circling back over the River Esk to hunt the perpetrators. Many Urovan submersibles had managed to escape the aerial bombardment, though some had been destroyed, the remains sunk into the river. But E'ridia's air force had more bombs than depth charges, and that lack had left them reeling in the aftermath.

Enough evidence had been pulled from the river as proof that Urova had been behind the attack. With what everyone knew about their alliance with Daijal, it was easy to see where the true orders had most likely come from, even if no one had any solid proof. The Urovan ambassador, when summoned before the *Comhairle nan Cinnidhean*, had professed ignorance of the attack and offered shallow condolences for E'ridia's dead. The answer had not been anywhere near enough to appease anyone, and the Urovan ambassador and their entire diplomatic corps had been summarily expelled from E'ridia last night. They'd been given less than a day, all while under guard, to close up their embassy in Glencoe and leave the country.

The *Comhairle nan Cinnidhean* was now on its way to see the damage done to the country's premier air force base and largest repair yard, located adjacent to the base. The *cinn-chinnidh* and their *jarls* were flying on separate airships of different makes to ensure if another attack occurred, the core of E'ridia's government wouldn't be completely wiped out.

They hadn't been the only country attacked in such an underhanded way. Blaine had called late last night with the shocking news that the Solarian Legion would now have to split their forces, sending only half as many promised battalions into Ashion for the war efforts because of an attack in Solaria. Apparently, Rixham had fallen, and the Imperial emperor had no choice but to defend Solaria from the internal threat of a massive horde of revenants.

"The Imperial emperor promised Caris the alliance would not break," Blaine had said when Honovi was woken from a brief nap in his father's office to take the call. "But I don't know how much longer he can keep that promise."

Soren and Lore were still missing, with no word on a ransom or any evidence of who had taken them. That, coupled with these two attacks, lent credence to the simmering accusation that Daijal was behind the disruption happening on a global scale. For Honovi could see how each attack was a precision cut into the supports that could have shored Ashion up in the face of war.

The airship juddered against the cables connected to the balloon as they began their descent. In the distance, the horizon was hazy, smoke lingering still from fires that had taken hours to put out through the night. The destruction that eventually came into view was devastating, the sight tearing a wounded noise from Honovi's mouth.

E'ridia had a dozen air force bases scattered throughout the country—within the Sunrise Valley, amidst the coastal hills, and tucked away in the jagged teeth of the Eastern Spine, all of various sizes. Of them all, the Compass Air Force Base was their main training airfield, as well as where many of their war airship squadrons were anchored when not on assignment elsewhere.

Just yesterday, it had been a thriving outpost, the base safely walled off with the airfields stretched around it. Now, as the *Celestial Sprite* and others drew closer, Honovi could see that some portions of the outer wall had been damaged or outright destroyed, putting their defense against revenants in jeopardy, to say nothing of the smoking airfields.

The burned husks of airships smoldered in their anchor berths alongside ruined hangars. Those closest to the river had taken the brunt of the attack, while some areas farther inland had escaped, their anchor berths empty, the airships hopefully having been able to launch. Honovi wouldn't know for sure until they landed and met with the command staff on the ground—whoever had survived.

"Sirs, you'll want to be in the cabin for the final descent," a crew member said from behind them.

Honovi pushed away from the railing, his father following him to the crew cabin situated behind the flight deck. Their shadows stretched away from their feet across the decking as they maneuvered past the crew on duty, the rising sun warm at their backs. Every aeronaut went about their duty with a grim sort of focus, the only sound that of the wind from their passage through the sky and the thrum of the engine in the air. No one seemed inclined to banter right now.

They reached the crew cabin and strapped in for the final descent, the pressure change in Honovi's ears something easily regulated. The air grew a little warmer, too, but Honovi didn't remove his fur-lined flight jacket. He'd opted for trousers over a kilt for today's excursion, as had the rest of those in government. His father had chosen to wear his plaid like all the other *cinn-chinnidh* and their *jarls*. The colors represented Clan Storm, the length of it falling to the ground as a symbol of his rank.

The airships carrying the *Comhairle nan Cinnidhean* descended into the areas of the airfield that had taken the least amount of damage. Ground crews worked diligently to securely anchor each airship and help those on board to disembark. Honovi let Alrickson precede him down the gangplank to the intact pier, both of them nodding at the aeronauts in military uniform who greeted them with salutes.

The pier was long enough, and enough anchor berths had been cleared, that all the airships transporting the *Comhairle nan Cinnidhean* and their heirs were able to land without issue. A select number of reporters from the press had been allowed to travel with them, and Honovi did his best to ignore the pops and flashes of light from those set to document the travesty. It felt disrespectful, almost, but they needed to document the horror for history.

"I wish I could welcome the *Comhairle nan Cinnidhean* under better circumstances," Admiral Kyrre said, his weathered face lined with fatigue and smeared with soot around the outline of where brass goggles had covered his brown eyes. His uniform wasn't much better, but he carried himself with the carriage of a lifelong military man.

"No one ever expected such a tragedy to occur," said Anneli, the new *ceann-cinnidh* of Clan Lightning. Her predecessor, Leena, had survived the attack on the governing body by Gregor last year, but it had taken a toll on her health. She'd elevated her *jarl* to oversee Clan Lightning, and Anneli had taken up the position with a gravity Honovi could appreciate.

Quite a few people glanced in Honovi's direction, but no one said anything. He bit his tongue and let Kyrre lead them toward the outer wall of the base, his voice carrying as he pitched it loud enough to hear.

"We have wardens onsite guarding the damaged sections of the outer wall and engineers working to clear the debris in preparation for a rebuild," Kyrre said.

"How long will that take?" someone called out from behind Honovi.

"Not quick enough to ease anyone's anxiety, but they're working on it."

"And the damage?" Alrickson asked. "How many war airships did we lose?"

Kyrre grimaced, the look he cast over his shoulder grim and tired. "We're still finalizing the count, but more than half that were anchored here."

"And aeronauts?"

"Not everyone has been accounted for yet. I'll take you past some of the damage for you to see."

Honovi swallowed his anger at the thought of the lives lost, knowing it was still far less than the number Ashion had mourned so far. But seeing the damage up close and personal drove home the loss in a way a report over a wire could not.

Everyone was silent when they passed through the city gate into the base, the smell of burning metal and oil still thick in the air. It made Honovi's hand twitch toward the gas mask hanging off his belt, but the admiral hadn't indicated it was necessary. Half a dozen motor carriages waited for them past the wall, though Honovi wondered about their practicality amidst the damage. Still, some of the *cinn-chinnidh* wouldn't be able to trek the breadth of the base on their own, and so he climbed into the motor carriage that Alrickson chose.

Traveling the streets that wound through the base was an exercise in caution as the drivers maneuvered through debris and past damaged buildings. While most of the attack had focused on the airfields, some of the bombs had targeted the infrastructure. Kyrre led them past the outskirts of some of the damaged sections, the bombed-out remnants of buildings being attended to by rescue workers. Bodies lined the street, clothing used in place of funeral shrouds to wrap the dead.

Honovi clenched his hands into fists over his knees as he stared out the window of the motor carriage, taking everything in. Alrickson was silent beside him, head craned toward the damage, expression impossible to read outside the grief in his eyes. They didn't linger, continuing onward. Only one inner wall existed in the base, surrounding the administrative buildings of the air force, and that, at least, was still intact, even if some of the buildings in the outer neighborhood were not.

"The Urovans had new long-range weaponry we weren't prepared for," Kyrre said once everyone had been transported to the forecourt in front of the officer's building. "They aimed from the river and never came on land, but they didn't need to."

"How come no one saw their approach?" Clan Lightning's *jarl* asked. "For the amount of damage done, the attacking force must have been large."

Kyrre, while put on the spot, didn't take the question as an insult to the aeronauts under his command. "No one had any idea that Urova would invade us in such a way. E'ridia hasn't been targeted like this in at least an Age."

E'ridia, Honovi knew, lived by isolationist tendencies in past Ages, but Maricol was too connected these days for that to be a viable answer. It had little to do with the numbers and everything to do with how complacent E'ridia had become as a whole. He cleared his throat, loudly, drawing Kyrre's attention. "Were any Urovans captured?"

"Some, though they're all wounded."

"We'll want to speak with them," Alrickson said.

Kyrre nodded. "That can be arranged after our meeting. Please, follow me."

They were led into the building, down hallways lit by gas lamps, aeronauts in uniform scurrying about with tense expressions on their faces. Kyrre brought them to a utilitarian room with an oval table covered in maps. The windows were closed to keep out the smoke, and the ceiling fans were on their highest settings in anticipation of another hot day. A warden waited for them in the room, along with other officers. The officers all stood and saluted the *Comhairle nan Cinnidhean*, but the warden showed no such deference, remaining seated with a map close at hand.

"I think the most important item on the agenda is our country's aerial capabilities in the wake of this attack. Where do we stand?" Alrickson asked once everyone had taken a seat around the table. There wasn't quite enough room, with some *jarls* and lower-ranked officers forced to sit behind others at the table.

Kyrre's grim expression was answer enough. "We're lucky none of our other bases were targeted, but that isn't saying much. Those ones are smaller and further inland, not located near waterways. Many of the airships down for repair were destroyed, along with a high percentage of the war airship and aeroplane squadrons assigned to the base. Our air force wasn't destroyed, but it was crippled in that we lost airships along with many of the next generation of aeronauts and some of our best fliers."

It was similar to the attack on the Warden's Island, and Honovi couldn't help but glance at the warden, who sat stone-faced on the other side of the table. It was sometimes difficult to know a warden's age, but this one looked to be younger than him.

"What of our forces in other bases?"

"Intact and on alert. Patrols have been stepped up at our borders, but so far, no reports have come back about incursions."

"We summoned the Urovan ambassador last night, but they purported to know nothing about the attack. We as a whole expelled them from the country," Anneli said.

They'd done the same last year to the Daijalan ambassador after the attack on the Warden's Island. Having no avenues of communication open with another country was never advantageous, but after everything that had happened, Honovi couldn't see anyone believing what the Urovans said.

"Trade will be at issue once again," someone down the table warned.

"Trade is the least of our worries," Honovi said before anyone else could argue for or against it. "We all know who is truly behind the attack on our sovereignty, and continuing to ignore that fact sets us up for another attack and the distinct possibility of being invaded. Only next time, if Ashion has fallen, we'll be squeezed on both sides, with Urovan submersibles in our waves and the Daijal army in our land."

"The Eastern Spine would stop them," an officer on the other side of the table protested.

Honovi leaned forward, staring him down, fighting back his fury. "Can you be absolutely certain of that?"

It was telling that no one spoke up.

In the silence, the sound of the warden getting to his feet drew everyone's attention. He settled back on his heels and took in the room with a sweeping glance before speaking. "It is the governor's opinion that the attack on your air force base and the attack on Solaria's city are meant to distract both countries from the war effort in Ashion. We find it suspect that the Imperial emperor agreed to an alliance and sent his Legion to the Ashion queen and then these attacks occurred. While E'ridia has offered no alliance, the preemptive nature of the attacks must be called into question. The governor believes Eimarille is behind what happened yesterday in both countries the same way she was behind the attack on us wardens last year."

Honovi was glad to see the wardens reinforcing the argument he and Blaine had repeatedly brought before the *Comhairle nan Cinnidhean*, but it didn't make him feel any better about the situation at hand. He rose to his feet as well, commanding everyone's attention. "Eimarille has ambitions that will not stop at her border. The *Comhairle nan Cinnidhean* must see that now and must act in the best interest of E'ridia."

"You and your husband have been proponents of war for some time now," Kele, *ceann-cinnidh* of Clan Sky, said evenly.

"We have not," Honovi pushed back. "We have been a proponent of ensuring our sovereignty in the face of an enemy who lies and schemes for power. If our Seneschal being turned into a *rionetka* was not enough to face the threat, then this attack must be, or what excuse will you give to the clans for why we are doing nothing?"

He had to fight not to raise his voice, but he couldn't stop himself from the forcefulness of his words. If the *Comhairle nan Cinnidhean* did nothing, Honovi feared their country wouldn't survive to see a new Age.

Alrickson stood, the sound of his chair scraping across the floor causing Honovi's head to snap around. "The Age of Separation gave us our countries, and the wardens mapped our borders and guarded them for centuries. E'ridia has never sought war beyond our borders, even if we have fought amongst the clans. But E'ridia does not hold with debt bondage, and we cannot ignore this attack inflicted on our people.

"I admit, I have been reluctant to believe my son's persistent belief that Daijal was a threat to us. I thought the strife between Daijal and Ashion had no bearing on us, despite the fact we share a border with one of them. We as a people put our faith in the Eastern Spine and the revenants that hunt amongst its valleys and peaks to hold back the rest of the continent. So much so that we never saw the threat from the sea because Daijal made allies with Urova, and we assumed we would not be targeted. We were wrong. My son and son-in-law were not. The Dusk Star delivered Blaine to us when he was a child, and my clan took him in. His road has led him back to Ashion, and my son follows. I think it is time E'ridia follows as well."

"You wish for us to vote on war?" Aslaung, *ceann-cinnidh* of Clan Mountain, asked.

"I wish for the *Comhairle nan Cinnidhean* to protect E'ridia. If that means allying ourselves with Ashion and Solaria against Daijal and Urova, then so be it. Queen Eimarille might have sought to cripple our air force, but we still have airships to fight with." Alrickson looked down the table on both sides, meeting his contemporaries' gazes. "What say the clans?"

For a moment, the room was silent. In that quiet, Honovi thought his arguments hadn't been enough. That the terrible isolationist ways would win out. Then everyone at the table pounded their fists against it as if they were beating a drum in prayer and he let out a heavy breath, looking to his father. Alrickson nodded decisively before retaking his seat. "Then let us vote."

The military officers and *jarls* had no say in the votes cast by the *Comhairle nan Cinnidhean*. There was no need for a Seneschal to send a declaration of war up to them, not when the laws of E'ridia gave the *Comhairle nan Cinnidhean* the right to declare it on their own. This time, when the war drums would sound, it wouldn't be for a clan-on-clan fight but one that would pitch E'ridia into a fight Ashion was desperately trying to win for them all.

It was the one bright spot in a horrifying aftermath, but it eased something deep within Honovi as E'ridia rallied itself for war. He wanted desperately to relay the news to Blaine but knew the official announcement had to come from the *Comhairle nan Cinnidhean* to Caris.

His father leaned toward him, braid sliding over his shoulder with the motion, the ranking hair adornments there catching the light. "E'ridia has no ambassador for Ashion at this time, but I rather think we'll need one for this fight. I'll put your name forth to take up that mantle again after we contact Queen Caris and notify the Imperial emperor of our intentions. I know asking you to stay in Glencoe would be futile."

Honovi inclined his head. "I will do what my country asks of me."

And if walking that road led him back to Blaine, so much the better.

Five

BLAINE

Dureau popped his head into Blaine's cramped office, appearing tired and haggard. "Caris requested to speak with you."

Blaine straightened from where he'd been hunched over his desk, rubbing absently at his upper arm where the mechanical prosthetic connected. The weight of it was still something he was getting used to, and most days, he could ignore the minor discomfort and the instances of phantom limb pain. It was harder to do when he was tired and stressed, which seemed to be his standard emotional state these days. "Where is she?"

"With Mother in the library. They had a working lunch, which you missed."

Ah, the tightening of his middle wasn't all just stress, but hunger, too, now that he realized the hour. "How is Meleri doing? Any news yet?"

Dureau's lips thinned into a pale line before he retreated from the doorway and back into the hallway. "She's doing her best. We both are."

Both his older sisters were unaccounted for, leaving him the nominal heir to the Auclair bloodline and all it entailed—from a seat in Parliament to Meleri's spymaster rank and the whole of the Clockwork Brigade—if nothing changed. Brielle hadn't been heard from since last year, and Blaine secretly suspected the worst for her and her own family, trapped as they had been when Amari was held under occupation by order of the Daijal court.

Blaine stood, putting the reports he'd been reading back to rights. "Let's not keep them waiting."

Blaine and Dureau made their way to the library on the other side of the borrowed estate. These days, it could double as a military war room, filled as it was with maps, reports and people with security clearance meeting at all hours with Meleri and Caris. Gathering together made it easier for officers to find them, even if it could, theoretically, leave them all a tempting target.

A familiar voice—sounding tinny from coming through a speaker—had Blaine picking up his pace. When Blaine had first been informed yesterday of the attack in his home country, it had taken all his willpower not to drive out to the airfield and hitch a ride on the first E'ridian airship he came upon to fly east. He took solace in the fact that Glencoe hadn't been targeted and that Honovi was *fine*, but he hadn't heard from his husband since their call late last night.

When he entered the library, he found Caris, Meleri, and Enmei huddled around the worktable that had been hauled up from a downstairs room when the Auclair bloodline had first moved in. Sitting in the center of it was a telephone, receiver resting on one of the contraptions the military used to project a call through a speaker for everyone to hear.

"Honovi?" Blaine asked, hoping his ears hadn't heard wrong.

"Blaine," his husband replied, voice echoing through the speaker.

Caris looked up from where she was leaning over the table, body angled toward the telephone, reports spread out between her hands. Her gray eyes were bright, despite the dark circles beneath them. None of them were getting much rest these days. "Honovi is acting as translator with the *Comhairle nan Cinnidhean*. General Votil is on his way to join us. But Blaine, E'ridia is allying itself with Ashion."

Blaine opened his mouth, but nothing came out. He cleared his throat as he stepped up to the table, gaze flicking from Caris to Meleri, then back to the telephone. "Is that true, Honovi?"

He spoke in Ashionen, mindful of the audience, and Honovi kept to the same language. "The attack on our base and repair yard took out a number of airships and aeroplanes, to say nothing of the loss of people. The *Comhairle nan Cinnidhean* took the attack as a declaration of war."

"Eimarille will claim she had nothing to do with it. She'll place the blame on Urova," Meleri pointed out.

"Who are so entirely entwined with her country right now that no one will believe her. Certainly the Imperial emperor does not," Enmei said with a snort.

"E'ridia is prepared to send squadrons west to fight alongside Ashion. A number will be held back to guard our borders, but our admiralty is already working on assignments. We should be able to send the majority of support in a few days, but a small squadron will depart from one of the mountain bases for Cosian today," Honovi explained.

"And will you remain in E'ridia?" Blaine asked.

"No. I will be returning to you, as E'ridia's ambassador to Ashion again."

"I look forward to receiving you in your diplomatic capacity once more," Caris said.

Blaine cleared his throat. "What was the damage we incurred?"

"Deep, but hopefully not insurmountable, given time," Honovi said. He didn't provide numbers, which Blaine could understand, but he still grieved their losses. "The country is incensed and up in arms over the attack."

It had taken a tragedy for E'ridia to commit to war. Blaine knew there would be nothing but heartache on the road to come because of it.

"We'll need to coordinate with the Solarian generals in order to fold your people and their skills into the war effort. General Votil will most likely spearhead that, but is there someone within your admiralty who we should speak to?" Meleri asked.

"I'll get you a name," Honovi promised.

The conversation didn't last much longer, the call having been placed to notify Ashion's queen of E'ridia's intent of an alliance. The nitty-gritty of such a decision would not be left up to her alone, nor anyone else standing at the table or on the other side of the line. Others would need to be brought on board to finalize everything, but for now, the relief that loosened all their shoulders was something Blaine could lean into. Hope was a fragile feeling, but it buoyed all of them in that moment.

When Caris was done speaking, Blaine picked the receiver off the speaker and pressed it to his ear. He switched to E'ridian, not caring if no one else could fully understand. "When will you fly to Cosian?"

"Tomorrow, hopefully. The diplomatic corps is readying an airship for me and the rest of the aides traveling with me," Honovi said.

"Good." Blaine licked his lips, gripping the edge of the table with his right hand. "I miss you. When I heard about the attack, I was so worried you were caught in the crossfire somehow. I don't know what I would have done if you were."

"Not this time. I was lucky. Besides, I did promise you I would try not to get shot again."

"Keep your promise, or I will be highly displeased."

Honovi chuckled. "I will. I'd rather not be relegated to the sofa once we are reunited."

The words were said with so much love in Honovi's tone that Blaine had to close his eyes. "I am sorry it came to this, though."

"It's not your place to apologize."

"It feels like it, some days."

Because of his road and the way it had led him back to Ashion, to Caris, and how Honovi had steadfastly followed despite the disapproval from the ruling body of the country they both belonged to. Blaine considered himself clan, considered himself E'ridian more than anything else these days, but he still had this duty to stand witness.

"The blame lies solely with Eimarille on all fronts. It is not your burden to carry, and it never will be."

Blaine nodded, even though Honovi couldn't see him. "Send your airship's designation to me over the wire number I gave you. I'll be waiting for you in the airfield when you land."

"I will. I love you."

Blaine's lips quirked into a tired smile. "I love you as well."

He finally ended the call, putting the receiver back on the cradle, letting the coil of wire twist itself on top of the maps. He looked across the table at where Caris stood with her arms crossed over her chest, biting her bottom lip.

"I'm glad your people are joining our fight, but I wish the reason that changed their mind had caused your country no harm," she said.

Blaine went around the table to hug her. Caris wrapped her arms around him, tucking her head beneath his chin. She felt too thin beneath her work blouse, stress eating away at all of them. But when she pulled away, the stubborn set to her jaw was not to be discounted.

"As Honovi just reminded me, none of this is your fault. This fight is no longer just about Ashion. We're all fighting for Maricol," Blaine said.

"Yes," Meleri said. "And we have a chance now."

It was most likely the only one they would get.

Six

JOELLE

Joelle sat in her office, holding the telephone to her ear with a shaking hand, the horrified fury she'd felt since learning of Rixham's final fall still eating through her. The line clicked over from an operator, and then Eimarille's calm voice slid through the wire, fueling Joelle's temper.

"I understand you wish to speak with me?" Eimarille asked, voice pleasantly cool in the way a viper might be right before they struck. Only Eimarille already had.

"Do you not understand what you have *done?*" Joelle rasped out.

"I don't believe I know what you are referring to."

Joelle clenched her left hand into a fist, joints aching with the pressure. "Your people brought down Rixham and freed all the revenants there."

"Daijal has made no inroads into Solaria."

The sheer gall of the other woman to deny what had occurred this week left Joelle momentarily speechless. When she found her voice again, it came out strained with incredulity. "You've damned the country I was supposed to rule."

"Did I?" Eimarille asked in a faintly lilting tone. "Were you? Everything was predicated on you using your *vasilyet* as a foil to keep the

Legion occupied. Instead, the Imperial emperor offered his forces to Ashion in an alliance."

"So you thought destroying Rixham's walls and releasing the horde of revenants there a valid response?"

"There will be no evidence showing my supposed involvement in that attack. There are other Houses who do not support the House of Sa'Liandel. Perhaps your country's investigators should start there."

They both knew the words Eimarille spoke were a lie. No House, no matter their stated opposition to the one that had ruled for centuries now, would *ever* target Rixham's walls. They all knew the danger that city presented, like the Wastelands in the south. While Bellingham was one of the most northern cities in Solaria, the revenants would claw at their city walls eventually, and her people would have nowhere to run.

"I never agreed to this."

"You agreed to turn your back on your country for a chance at the Imperial throne. I agreed to aid you in that endeavor, but it is not my fault you've yet to ascend it. You've sacrificed a granddaughter and a son in your desperate ploy to take back something your House hasn't held in centuries. What makes you think it was ever going to be easy? What makes you think the Houses you hope to rule will ever believe you are innocent of all that has occurred? They all sided with Vanya during the Conclave over you."

Eimarille's words made Joelle flinch, glad the other woman couldn't see her reaction. If the Conclave had turned in her favor, if she'd managed to get Raiah into her arms—if, if, *if*. So much of what she'd fought and schemed for had crumbled around her, the situation made worse by Eimarille's orders and not hers. First, the Warden's Island, and now the attacks in Solaria and E'ridia, all of which could be traced back to Joelle in some way, she was certain.

She'd treated this alliance as if it were one with a House, something Joelle could control, when in reality, it wasn't anything but a trap. Eimarille had plans, and they did not include a Solaria ruled by the House of Kimathi, Joelle realized with a dawning sense of shame she would never admit to anyone.

She wondered if the Twilight Star would hear her prayers and would answer them. Considering he'd given his blessing to Eimarille and promised to guide her road, Joelle doubted any of her own would be listened to.

Perhaps she should never have forsaken the Dawn Star after all.

"You think once you kill Caris Rourke, you'll be in the clear," Joelle said slowly as she unclenched her hands, knuckles throbbing. "But your attacks on other countries, while damaging, have done the opposite of what you hoped for. You wanted to isolate Ashion. Instead, you've ensured the countries with the most formidable land army and air force will face you on the battlefield."

"Daijal is prepared to win."

"Killing your sister won't give you the crown nor the right to the starfire throne. Not with your brother still alive."

Joelle knew of the North Star's decree. For all that Innes had shown favor to Eimarille, Aaralyn had given it to no one. It could be inferred that Eimarille would not have it, so long as others of the Rourke bloodline lived. Holding the prince would be leverage against Eimarille in the future, leverage Joelle could use to keep her *vasilyet* and Solaria free.

"News out of Calhames states he is still missing. Caris has no heir."

"Of course," Joelle demurred. "But you can't win so long as one of them still lives."

"And what have you done that makes you so certain I won't win?"

"Ensured someone will always be a challenge to your right to the starfire throne if you are ever able to claim it."

The silence that settled over the call was charged, and when Eimarille finally spoke, her tone was glacial. "You have Alasandair."

"I have a threat to your rule if you seek to ruin Solaria any more than you already have. If you don't wish that to happen, then you will leave me the Imperial throne."

Another fraught silence settled between them. Eventually, Eimarille said, "You will regret defying me."

"I doubt that."

Joelle set the receiver on the cradle, ending the call. She closed her eyes and pressed her fingers over them, wishing she could wipe away some of the decisions she had made in her youth, knowing she could do nothing now but own them. This was her road to walk, and she'd been the one to build it.

Joelle reached for her cane, using it and the desk to lever herself up. She'd taken the call in private, her handmaidens waiting out in the antechamber. The trio on duty stood at her entrance and bowed to her.

"Let's see to our guests, shall we?" Joelle said.

Eimarille could think she had the upper hand, but Joelle was *vezir* of the House of Kimathi. She knew the games the Houses played in her bones. She had spent her entire life owning debts, claiming loyalty, and gaining blackmail material.

None was as important as the prince she'd stolen.

Seven

SOREN

Being a prisoner of war was not a title Soren had ever wanted, much like he'd never wanted to be a prince.

Vesper had left Calhames with them weeks ago, Soren bound by Lore's life to not retaliate as they were herded onto an airship that had flown them northwest. They'd been separated on that flight, both of them drugged, though it hadn't quite stuck for Soren. The alchemy that had turned him into a warden made him immune to many toxins and poisons and some sedatives as well. But waking up early didn't mean anything if Lore wasn't with him.

They'd remained separated during landing and their transportation through Bellingham, driving through streets Soren only vaguely recalled from the time he'd brought Vanya back seemingly from the dead after the train wreck. He wasn't taken to the Imperial estate but to the grand one that had been home to the House of Kimathi for Ages. The basement room he'd been deposited in was windowless, the floor black marble streaked with gold, a circle inlaid with opal carved with precision into the marble so that it touched each wall. A narrow cot, rudimentary toilet, and shallow sink were all the furnishings allowed.

Soren had felt the magic in that cell the moment he'd stepped foot in it, like a heaviness that weighed down the very air. If he'd been a magician, he rather thought it would be impossible to reach the aether for any spells, but he'd been able to summon a curl of starfire that first day, what little good it did him. Lore had not been placed with him, and he didn't know where she was or how she was doing. Breaking out would put her life in jeopardy, and he couldn't risk that.

So Soren stayed in that small, cool cell, given meals twice a day that were never laced with drugs and water that was. He drank it anyway, knowing he needed to keep up his strength, able to shake off its effects quicker than someone who wasn't a warden, even without his field kit.

On the third day, the door had opened, though *vezir* Joelle, of the House of Kimathi, had never stepped foot inside his cell. She'd been flanked by guards and the same magician who had transported them out of Calhames to Bellingham. Soren had stared at her for a moment before getting to his feet, calculating the odds of escape before deciding against it.

"So, you are the warden who has kept my great-granddaughter from me," Joelle had said.

Soren hadn't engaged, knowing well the power of silence. She'd looked at him as if he were some captive animal before letting the door close on him, locking him back inside.

Joelle had not returned since that first meeting, and Soren counted the days that passed by way of meals delivered. He couldn't even be sure the days were correct. Every demand to see Lore he gave the guards who delivered his food was rebuffed, and part of him wondered if she was even alive. Not knowing ate at him, stuck as he was in that cell by his own sense of honor.

At what felt like the two-week mark, perhaps a little more than that, the door to his basement cell opened sometime between his morning and evening meal. The strangeness had Soren rising to his feet, staring at where Joelle stood once again in the gas lamp–lit basement. The guards with her had their pistols drawn, barrels pointed at Soren. The magician with her this time was a young woman whose clarion crystal–tipped wand appeared made of bone and brass, her magic a soft violet as she called on the aether.

"Where is Lady Lore?" Soren demanded.

Joelle curled her hands over the top of her cane, the robes she wore not as elaborate as those meant for government. He wondered about her health, how months of war over secession might have whittled her down. She'd lost her son, her political power, and would have lost her *vasilyet* if she hadn't had Daijal's backing.

Soren knew she'd lose everything else left to her the moment Vanya knew he'd been taken by Joelle.

"Sleeping," Joelle said, a lightness to her tone that put Soren on edge.

"I want to see her."

"Oh, so untrusting for a warden." Joelle smiled, eyes shadows in her face. "My people know to kill her if you so much as summon a flicker of starfire. You will be bound, and you will obey."

As much as Soren didn't want to, he knew he had no choice but to obey if Lore was to live. So he held his hands behind his back when ordered to by the guards, let them place metal shackles around his wrists, and prod him out of the cell with a muzzle pressed to his back, over his spine. Joelle stepped aside so he could exit. Soren found himself looking down at her, the *vezir* so much smaller than he was and yet the cause of so much terror and heartache.

"Good to see you know your place," Joelle murmured.

Soren kept his expression as neutral as he could, refusing to give her the satisfaction of his emotional state. Joelle smirked at him before pointing with her cane, the silent gesture an order the guards immediately followed by shoving Soren forward.

The basement wasn't large, from what he remembered when he'd been dragged down into the dark. What storage it was used for weren't things people needed on a daily basis. The guards led him up a set of stairs into the round room of a star temple. Soren had only seen glimpses of it before when he'd arrived, still sluggish from the drugs in his system and not quite able to fully focus. But the statue of

Callisto at the forefront was something he remembered, the eternal flame burning at her feet a flicker that caught his eye.

He was dragged away from the basement entrance, the metal door nothing as elaborate as the one that had closed up the royal crypts back in Calhames. A pair of handmaidens helped Joelle back up into the star temple, steadying her when the older woman's cane slipped a bit. Soren could only wish she'd lose her balance and fall back down into the basement and break her neck.

Joelle waved off her handmaidens and crossed over to a closed and guarded door on the other side of the star temple. The pistol at his back prodded Soren forward, and he went docilely enough, knowing it wasn't just his life on the line if he disobeyed.

And the life he was trying to protect was presented to him in that side room. Perhaps it had once been used as a place of private prayer, small and windowless as it was. Now, it served as a makeshift alchemist's lab, a metal worktable positioned in the center of the room, Lore laid across it like a dead thing.

They'd stripped her of her gown, leaving her only in her chemise, with a thin blanket drawn up to her breasts. Her arms were on top of the blanket, pale and uncuffed, a catheter resting in the crook of her right elbow. A metal stand was positioned beside the table, holding a large glass vial containing an unknown substance that dripped steadily through the tubing into her vein. That drug was clear, while the one in the vial hanging next to it was a poisonous-looking violet.

Soren tensed, recognizing that shade for the quick-acting poison it was. He eyed that tubing and the poison that was clamped off just before the catheter in Lore's left arm, a minuscule gap ready to be filled and poured into her veins.

A star priestess sat beside Lore, the woman's fingers resting lightly on the clamp that kept the poison at bay. She said nothing, merely stared serenely at all of them. Soren kept his eyes on Lore, watching as her chest rose and fell, eyes closed, lashes dark against the pallor of her cheeks.

"What have you done to her?" Soren demanded.

"Ensured your compliance through her predicament," Joelle said, stepping into the room.

Soren tried to follow her, but a hand fisted itself in his shirt, slamming him up against the side of the doorframe. He gritted his teeth against the pain that lanced down his arm, holding still as the muzzle of the pistol pressed against the side of his throat. He slid his gaze sideways, staring with unblinking eyes at the guard who was having none of it.

Joelle clicked her tongue at him. "You've a temper."

Soren snorted, turning his head with a dismissive motion, doing his best to ignore the guard and the cold metal against his skin. "You tell me how you'd feel if it was someone you knew lying on a table like that."

"I'd let them die if it meant I wouldn't." Joelle lifted her cane and waved the tip of it in his direction. "You, however, have a heart I would gladly replace with a *rionetka*'s if the *Klovod* were still around."

The guard lifted the pistol and dragged Soren upright. Soren fought the urge to forcibly shove him off, knowing what it would cost him if he stepped out of line. He eyed the violet poison in the glass vial, needing to be sure.

"That's bittershade, isn't it?" he asked, thinking of the shrubs with their dangerously poisonous flowers that grew near the peaks of the Eastern Spine. It only bloomed the first few weeks of spring, after the snows melted. The leaves, petals, and pollen were deadly if it touched a person's skin or was ingested or inhaled. Harvesting it took an airship and a warden with skill enough to survive the environment and wandering revenants.

Joelle's lips quirked into a tiny smile. "You know your poisons."

Soren raised an eyebrow as condescendingly as he could. "I'm a warden."

Joelle outright chuckled at that before shifting on her feet to face Lore. "You're a prince."

"To some."

"Eimarille considers you a threat, the same way she considers Caris."

"I don't want the starfire throne."

She seemed surprised at the firmness of his denial. "You lack ambition. Such a stance would see you killed in Solaria."

"You haven't shot me yet."

"I know your worth, both to Eimarille and Vanya."

Soren's heart sank at the mention of Vanya. He'd left their bed with a promise he'd return and had that promise forcibly broken. Coming so close to having the one thing he'd ever wanted—Vanya in his arms again—only to have it snatched away from him was an ache that kept him company in the cell like a nightmare.

"Your honor collars you. All the starfire you possess, and you refuse to use it." Joelle shook her head at that, clear disgust in the gesture.

Soren's gaze flicked to Lore's unconscious form, then back to Joelle. "I put people first, unlike you."

If she thought it an insult, Joelle didn't let it show. "I have done nothing but put people first for the good of Solaria."

"You allied yourself with Eimarille, and look where that's got you." For some reason, that made her flinch ever so slightly around the eyes. Soren took notice, and he wondered what had transpired during the time he'd been a prisoner. "What did she promise you? The Imperial throne?"

"My dealings with Eimarille are of no importance to you."

"I've seen what she's done in Ashion and in the Warden's Island. Do you think she won't do worse to your country?"

At that, Joelle did laugh, a dry, disbelieving sound. "Ah, you don't know."

Soren stiffened. "I've been stuck in a cell. Of course I don't know what has happened outside it."

"Eimarille attacked E'ridia's largest air force base and downed the walls around Rixham in an effort to deprive Ashion of allies. You, Prince Alasandair, are my insurance to deny Eimarille the starfire throne after she kills Caris."

For a moment, the words didn't penetrate. When they did, nausea roiled in his gut so suddenly he had to take a deep breath to settle his stomach. It seemed unfathomable that Eimarille would target Rixham and release the massive horde of revenants trapped behind those city walls, but he didn't think Joelle had any reason to lie.

Joelle stepped closer to him, causing her guards to tense, worried, he supposed, about her safety. But Lore was one pinch away from an excruciatingly painful death, and Soren wouldn't let her die just so that he could save himself.

"Eimarille thinks to split the Legion's forces. She thinks the Houses will cave beneath her grand ambitions. She does not know us and our ways," Joelle said.

"Can you even call yourself Solarian after all you've done?" Soren asked.

Joelle lifted her chin, eyes glittering beneath the gas lamp light, determined to walk a road that would see his own destroyed. "All that I have done, I have done for my country."

"And how many Houses do you think would support you once word got out that your allegiance with Daijal was the cause of the horror crawling out of the south?"

Not even the House of Aetos would stand with her, he was certain. That House would be carved to pieces the same way Joelle's would the moment Soren made it back to Vanya and reported their betrayal. That nebulous future was what he clung to when Joelle had the guards return him to the cell.

After the shackles were removed and the door shut, leaving him in darkness, Soren called forth a flicker of starfire. The brilliant burn flared to life in the palm of one hand, warm and bright, like the eternal flame above.

With nothing else to lose, Soren prayed to the Dawn Star that had guided him down his road since the Inferno, hoping she would hear him.

Eight

BLAINE

The arrival of a small squadron of E'ridian war airships flying toward Cosian in the morning was a sight to see. Unprompted cheers rose up from the ground crew around him in the airfield. Blaine remained on the pier, pressed up against the railing to stay out of the way as the ground crew tasked with anchoring the new arrivals got to work.

He kept an ear out as the engines all changed pitch for the final descent, pleased to note nothing sounded off. Blaine kept his eyes on the *Celestial Sprite* as it finally settled into its anchor berth, aeronauts and ground crew hurrying about to tie the ropes down. Minutes later, the gangplank was cranked out, two ground crew locking it into place on the pier.

Blaine pushed away from the railing when a familiar figure appeared at the top of the gangplank. Honovi cut a dashing figure in his kilt and formal jacket, most likely having discarded his flight clothes during the descent. He was returning as the official ambassador of E'ridia, which necessitated a certain need for formality. His boots were polished, the plaid hanging off his left shoulder and in his kilt carrying Clan Storm colors, and the ranking hair adornments were as Blaine remembered from Amari.

Despite the grim reason that had brought Honovi back to Cosian, his husband managed a smile when he swept Blaine off his feet. Blaine wrapped his arms around Honovi's neck, ignoring the sharp whistles directed their way as he welcomed his husband back with a fierce kiss. Honovi eventually broke the kiss and put Blaine back on his feet but didn't let go.

Blaine rested his hands on Honovi's shoulders, mindful of the grip he kept with his metal fingers. "You made good time."

"More squadrons will arrive within the next few days," Honovi said.

Blaine touched the edge of Honovi's jaw with his right hand for a moment before stepping out of the circle of his arms. "I wish it was under better circumstances."

But he knew, like Honovi, that nothing short of what had happened would've been enough to get the *Comhairle nan Cinnidhean* to join the war effort. The alliance with Ashion still needed to be signed, which Honovi had the authority to do now that he was an ambassador again as well as *jarl*.

"Better the agreement now than never," Honovi murmured.

Blaine could only nod at that before gesturing in the direction of the city walls. "Let's get through the gate, and I'll take you to Caris. She's waiting for us at her family's estate. The officers can make their way to where General Votil is stationed for their orders while we handle the treaty signing."

Honovi wrapped an arm around Blaine's waist, tugging him close as they started walking. "Does the general have a plan of attack already?"

"Yes, but we'll discuss it later." Blaine glanced sideways at him as a ground worker in coveralls jogged around them on the pier. "I don't think you're up to date on Ashion news."

"The front is holding."

"Yes, for now. But I am talking about Caris' parents."

Honovi's grip tightened on his hip. "What happened?"

"Eimarille has ordered a sham trial for them in Amari."

Honovi jerked to a halt midstride, staring at Blaine. "What are the charges?"

"Treason, amongst other ones." Blaine urged him to keep moving. "It was expected."

Honovi grimaced. "They'll be found guilty no matter their barrister's attempt to argue otherwise."

"Yes. For their supposed crimes, they will be sentenced to death."

"How did Caris take the news?"

"Not well. The only person who could calm her down was Nathaniel."

"How is he?"

Blaine thought of the way Nathaniel was so careful to never overhear battle plans or impromptu meetings at the old Dhemlan bloodline estate. How he never failed to cheer Caris up when she came home tired and depressed. Even with the clearance from the wardens, no one trusted him, but Nathaniel was nothing if not understanding of that.

"As well as can be expected, considering his condition."

They chatted a bit more about things that wouldn't get people killed if overheard. Honovi caught Blaine up on their clan, and it was nice to hear how everyone was doing. He missed them, couldn't wait to see everyone once he finally got home. He still had his duty to Caris, and she greeted them from Nathaniel's side when they finally made it inside the city walls and back to the estate.

"Welcome back," Caris said as she pulled away from Nathaniel to throw her arms around Honovi in a tight hug under the watchful eyes of the Royal Guard.

He returned the embrace with a smile, and Blaine couldn't help the fond look he gave them both. Honovi had taken on the role of older brother since his initial introduction to Caris, something Soren had never had an interest in being in the short time the warden had been in Cosian. Honovi never let it interfere with his duties to E'ridia, and Caris never used their relationship to try to extract more than was prudent from him.

Honovi could teach her about ruling in ways that Blaine could not, his outlook different from Meleri, and for that, Blaine was grateful. Caris needed other options, Blaine knew, other ways of viewing the world that weren't bound up in Meleri's ideal of what a queen should be.

"We've tea and a light meal ready for you when you're hungry, but I'm sure you'll want to catch up with Blaine first," Caris said as she pulled back, tucking a lock of dark hair behind one ear. The summer heat had her dressed in a light, short-sleeved blouse and loose, wide trousers that allowed for better airflow. The outfit was one best suited for time spent at home or out and about in the city, not in an engineering lab or for fieldwork. Blaine knew she'd change for the treaty signing ceremony later in the day, but for now, she needn't dress up for them.

"Some time together would be lovely," Honovi agreed.

"We'll be downstairs when you're ready."

The motor carriage transporting Honovi's luggage pulled up behind the one that had driven them. A pair of Royal Guards stepped forward to assist in removing the luggage off the roof and taking everything inside.

Blaine waited for Honovi to finish saying hello to Nathaniel, hovering nearby. Being apart never got any easier, and Blaine relished each time Honovi returned to him. Blaine took him by the hand and led Honovi inside and upstairs to the room they'd claimed as theirs whenever they were in Cosian. It wasn't nearly as big as the one they shared back in Glencoe, but it was private, and Blaine was looking forward to sharing the bed again.

The Royal Guards had stacked Honovi's luggage near the wall, the pile rather more extensive than the last set he'd traveled with. Blaine assumed his duties as ambassador required far more accessories to do his job. Cosian didn't have a proper embassy building, and Blaine knew Meleri was still organizing space in an administrative one that already held the temporary embassy for Solaria.

All of that flew out of Blaine's mind when Honovi shut the door behind the departing soldiers and pushed Blaine up against it. He went easily, lips parting when Honovi's mouth slanted over his. Blaine groaned softly, the sound vibrating between them as he rocked against Honovi, seeking pressure for the sudden ache in his cock. Honovi settled his hands on Blaine's hips, fingers gripping tight as he deepened the kiss.

When they finally broke apart, Honovi turned his head to kiss his way over Blaine's jaw. Blaine reached around his torso to grab his husband's braid with his right hand, mindful of the metal ranking adornments woven and pinned throughout it.

"I missed you," Blaine confessed as he slid a leg between Honovi's and rocked up hard against him, the kilt bunching higher between them. "I slept poorly while you were gone."

Honovi sucked in a sharp breath as he undid Blaine's belt. "We'll sleep tonight. Right now, I want to see if this door will hold you."

Blaine let out a breathless little laugh as Honovi lifted his head, the air heated between them, in the room, summer a heavy weight all around them. Blaine stared into his husband's eyes, thankful he was still there to hold him, to have him like this. Honovi leaned in to steal a kiss, hands already undoing Blaine's belt. He tilted his head back, knocking it against the wooden door, moaning softly when Honovi moved to suck a bruise over the pulse in his throat.

The belt was yanked free and tossed aside, clattering to the floor. Blaine dragged his hands down Honovi's chest, the gears in the metal prosthetic clicking softly. He gripped the fabric of Honovi's kilt and yanked it up even as Honovi undid Blaine's trousers. A warm hand slid beneath his clothes to cup his half-hard cock, and Blaine pushed into the touch, rising onto the balls of his feet, trying to get more pressure.

"Don't tease," Blaine panted, feeling Honovi's teeth against his skin. "It's been weeks."

Honovi groaned, finally pulling away from the heated bruise he'd been sucking into Blaine's throat. He had a wild thought that he'd have to borrow a cravat from Nathaniel to hide it for all the upcoming meetings before Honovi abruptly pulled away. Before Blaine could protest, he was spun around by firm hands and shoved up against the door with a little more force than before.

The wood was cool beneath his right hand when he pressed them against the door for leverage. Honovi yanked his trousers and underwear down his thighs as far as they could go with his legs spread apart. The hem of his shirt fell past his hips, and when Blaine looked down, he could see the front parting around the hard length of his cock. The fabric moved as Honovi yanked it up. A startled noise coming from his husband had Blaine turning his head to look over his shoulder.

A warm finger slid between the crease of his ass, and Blaine shivered as Honovi pressed it inside him in one smooth, easy glide, the way already prepared for him. Honovi looked up to meet his gaze, eyes dark, more pupil than anything else with a lust that had never faded when they found themselves like this.

"Did you think of me when you got yourself ready?" Honovi asked in a gravelly voice.

"I *always* think of you," Blaine retorted, going for tart and ending up breathless when Honovi curled his finger and touched that spot that sent sparks singing through his nerves. His cock twitched in the air, blurting out a glob of stickiness.

"And what if we'd gone straight to the treaty signing table? You'd have sat for hours unfulfilled."

"I'm sure I could have convinced you to take care of me where no one could find us."

Honovi pressed in close, the hard length of his cock sliding between Blaine's thighs, the wet tip of it nudging against his balls. Blaine swallowed thickly, fingers pressing hard against the door. "You'd have had to be quiet. I wouldn't have wanted anyone to walk in and see you like this."

"I can be quiet."

Honovi nipped at his ear, one hand coming around to wrap around Blaine's cock and stroke it with pointed intent. Blaine let out a strangled moan, rocking between the hand on his cock and the finger in his ass, heat pooling in his gut. "Let's see if you can, shall we?"

Blaine hung his head, squeezing his eyes shut as Honovi removed his hands before he felt them again, gripping his hips to yank him backward a little. His fingers scraped down the door as his spine curved, Honovi's thumbs digging into the muscles of his ass to spread him apart. Blaine panted, the sound terribly loud in his ears, as he tried not to tense up in anticipation. But Honovi never made him wait, the blunt head of his cock pressing against his entrance and pushing inside with slow pressure that didn't stop, making room for himself inside Blaine.

Getting filled by his husband's cock made Blaine moan, and he remembered too late he needed to be quiet. Honovi laughed when the sound became strangled as his husband finally slid all the way home, pressed flush against Blaine's ass. Blaine felt the way his cock throbbed inside, the stretch a lovely sort of ache that made his eyes flutter shut.

Honovi's grip gentled somewhat, the brush of fabric from his kilt and Blaine's shirt skimming across his back and upper thighs. Blaine shivered when Honovi pulled out halfway before rocking forward with intent. The force of it had Blaine bracing himself against the door, fingers scratching at the wood, the metal ones gouging deeper than he meant to. He had half a thought to remember to apologize to Caris when Honovi drove all thoughts but those for pleasure out of his mind with his next thrust.

It was so good to be held like this, filled like this, loved like this. Blaine's mouth dropped open on the next thrust, a whine escaping, high and needy, that he choked off lest someone hear it through the door. Honovi's hands wandered away from his hips, sliding around to grip his cock with dry fingers. Blaine jerked forward at the first touch, Honovi following with a thrust that made him pant for more.

"Honovi," he got out, fingers sliding down the door as it creaked on the hinges with the force of them moving against it.

Warm lips brushed against the side of his neck. "Let me take care of you."

Blaine tipped his head back, swallowing around a moan as Honovi angled his next thrust just right, catching that spot inside that lit up everything in his body. Honovi pressed even closer, forcing Blaine fully up against the door, cheek pressed to the cool wood, chest heaving against it as Honovi thrust hard into him. He couldn't spread his legs any more than they already were, trousers tangled around his knees, but it didn't matter, not with the way Honovi was thrusting into him with fierce intent.

While Blaine managed to keep quiet, to bite his tongue against the noises that crawled up his throat, he could do nothing about the sound of the door rattling on its hinges with every forceful thrust of Honovi's cock inside him. The sound was almost like a heartbeat, mingling with the slap of skin coming together, Honovi's ragged breath a match for Blaine's.

Blaine didn't last long, tipping over into orgasm on a particularly hard thrust, spilling into the loose circle of Honovi's fingers. His husband made a pleased sound as he caught the mess, fingers tightening now that his release made the glide easier. Blaine shuddered at the touch, at the way Honovi chased his own release for another minute or two, finally coming with several sharp thrusts that lost their rhythm.

The hinges protested with one final loud creak before Honovi stilled, pressed so close that Blaine could feel the line of his body from shoulders to feet. Only when wetness started to trickle down his inner thighs from where they were joined did Honovi finally pull out.

"Wait here," he murmured.

Blaine pressed his forehead to the door, trying to leach some of the coolness there into his overheated skin. He listened as Honovi ran the faucet in their attached washroom and didn't flinch too much when Honovi returned to clean up the mess they'd both made. Blaine's trousers were salvageable, but he'd need to change his shirt. Honovi, when he finally turned around to meet his husband's gaze, didn't look nearly as ruffled as he felt.

"I don't think they heard you, but they certainly heard us," Honovi said with a faint smirk, glancing aside at the top hinge.

"You were impatient," Blaine replied.

Honovi kissed him softly, tugging at his ruined shirt. "With good reason. But now I am hungry, so let's get you dressed and head downstairs for Caris' tea."

Blaine hummed agreement before easing past his husband to get ready again.

When they made it downstairs, with Blaine in a changed shirt and Honovi looking far too satisfied, Caris didn't say anything, merely raised an eyebrow and smiled softly as she served them some tea.

Nine

CARIS

Caris smoothed her hands over the broadsheet on the table, fingertips lingering over the blurred faces of her parents. The photograph had been taken from a distance, both her parents standing in front of a civic building in Amari, their hands shackled together in front of them. Their clothes, while neat and not of a prison set, hung on their frames in a way she wasn't familiar with. The shadows edging their cheeks were concerning, but she was half a country away from them, in no position to question after their health. She knew anyway that Eimarille wouldn't have been kind to them.

She couldn't even be sure they were alive, despite the article taking up the top front page. Caris was well aware of how manipulative Eimarille was, and planting a story to entice Caris out of Cosian was something she had tried before. Threatening a trial and execution of her parents had surprised no one. Knowing she could not act just yet left Caris aching with regret.

But they had a chance now, she knew, to take back Ashion. She lifted her gaze from the table, glancing down its crowded length in both directions. Officers from the Ashion army, several from the Solarian Legion, and those of the E'ridian air force had gathered in Cosian for a critical alliance meeting. Now that the E'ridian treaty had

357

been signed and their air force committed, Ashion had a chance at surviving—if they could take their capital back.

"A head-on push to Amari will tip our hand well before we make that city's walls," the Imperial General Yiannis Diomandis, of no House, said in heavily accented Ashionen. "Retaking the city is important, but all of Daijal's forces have come to bear in the eastern provinces of your country. Breaking that line will take time, but it won't be quick enough to save who you wish."

Yiannis' face was weathered from years spent beneath the desert sun, his red-and-white checkered *effiyeh* perfectly set on his head, the bulk of the fabric falling to one side. His tan uniform held an assortment of ranking pins, medals, and braid, making him look stiff with the weight of it, but he'd been kind when he greeted Caris with the salute of his people. His expression was still kind but tempered with something like regret as he looked back at her.

"I am aware that Eimarille is prepared to judge my parents guilty well before the ground offensive can get underway, but they would be the first to say that Ashion comes first," Caris said quietly. Which was true, but it didn't lessen her heartache any. Her parents had been cogs in the Clockwork Brigade, a road that had helped lead Caris to this very table. "Ashion *must* come first if we are to keep Daijal from gaining any more ground. I know the plans must change due to the attacks that occurred within your own borders, but the way forward, as General Votil has explained it to me, remains the same. We must retake Amari."

She looked at the maps spread out across the table, battle plans inked into the paper with notes from more than a dozen hands. Caris had gotten better at learning military shorthand and understood the gist of what her generals had planned. Even with the aid of half the Solarian Legion and the squadrons of war airships from E'ridia's air force, pushing Daijal back all the way to Amari would be a huge undertaking.

"To do that, we need a distraction," General Clarence Votil said, glancing at Caris. "Our queen made a suggestion weeks ago that I've had our best strategists working on. With the addition of our allies, it could prove fruitful. We need to split Daijal's focus to break their front lines."

Admiral Eirik nodded in agreement, lifting a hand to stroke his neatly trimmed salt-and-pepper beard. The plaid sections on his shirt tied him to Clan Lightning. "We're all in agreement about the offensive push needed to reach Amari, but it's the distraction we've not decided upon. The Daijal army is entrenched in the provinces, and the revenants are many. What is your plan?"

"New Haven," Caris said. "We need to attack New Haven."

All eyes returned to her, and she lifted her chin beneath their scrutiny. She might not be adept at military strategy, but she knew what a capital city meant to its people. Two could play the game Eimarille had set upon this board when it came down to it.

"The Daijal navy has their port cities and the river mouth sealed off with their ships. We can assume Urova's submersible fleet has some presence in the Gulf of Helia as well," Clarence said.

"The Tovanians can counter that with depth charges and sea mines. They did so around our borders, though not before the Urovans had slipped past the patrols into the wetlands," Yiannis said.

Caris blinked at him. "Your treaty with the Tovanians still stands?"

"It does. We believe the Urovans were already lying in wait within our wetlands to target Rixham before the Tovanian patrols reached the eastern shores of our country. We do not blame them for failing to stop the attack when none of us thought Daijal would ever cross the line as they have."

"If it's a pitched sea battle between Tovanian ship-cities against Daijal's navy and Urova's submersibles, I'll pick the Tovanians. They know the open seas better than anyone." Clarence looked at Caris, using his stick to tap at the small marking on the map that indicated Oeiras on the west of Solaria. "With your approval, Ashion can send another envoy to the Tovan Isles and ask for an alliance."

Caris nodded slowly. "The Imperial emperor agreed to provide an introduction to their ambassador in Oeiras. The sooner we send an envoy south again, the better."

"If we can convince the Tovanians to lend aid with their ship-cities for us to target New Haven, Eimarille will be forced to split her forces and pull some back to her capital. Such an effort will be the crack in their wall we need," Yiannis said.

The officers devolved into a conversation about logistics of pulling off such a feat, something that Caris followed along as best she could before she decided she wasn't needed for this part. Clearing her throat, she stood, causing everyone to stop speaking and rise to their own feet to salute her out of the room after she said her goodbyes.

Maurus waited for her in the hall, the captain of her Royal Guard ever at attention. He and several others escorted her out of the building that had become the command headquarters for the war, the streets surrounding it filled with people in uniform. Those who saw her as she exited the building came to strict attention and saluted. Maurus helped her into the back seat of the motor carriage before climbing behind the steering wheel himself. Their small convoy of vehicles drove away from the civilian-turned-military-occupied buildings in favor of home.

Caris rolled down the window, allowing for a sluggishly warm breeze to blow over her face as they drove. The temperature today was hot, summer in Eighth Month always a ruthless season in the Eastern Basin. She'd grown up with the heat and didn't mind it as much as Meleri or Dureau did. Lore had tolerated it better, and Caris tried not to think too much on what had become of her friend.

Caris stared out the window at the damaged and undamaged streets they passed on the drive back home. Nathaniel was there to greet her when they arrived, opening the door to offer her his hand, as he always did. Whether it was for dancing or a walk or an escort, he thought nothing of being by her side, providing support she desperately needed as she pretended all the while she knew what she was doing.

He lifted his other hand to her face, brushing his knuckles over the arch of her cheekbone. Despite the heat of the day, his shirt was done up to the collar, cravat knotted tight around his throat. "Would you like tea brought to you in your laboratory?"

It was a wonder how he knew what she always needed when sometimes even she didn't know. "Please."

"I'll bring it to you."

Clearing her mind was easier to do when she had something to occupy her hands. Nathaniel saw her to her small laboratory in the rear garden before excusing himself to return to the main house and prepare a tea tray for her. Caris set about opening the windows and turning on all the mechanical fans for better airflow, then tied up her hair and pulled a large folio off the shelf. She set it on her worktable and opened it, peering down at the sketched-out designs for attaching a pistol's barrel to Blaine's mechanical prosthetic.

The sound of the door opening made her hum. "That was quick."

"I suppose twenty-one years *is* quick for me."

The voice didn't belong to Nathaniel. Caris' head jerked up, mouth opening to call for help even as starfire sparked at her fingertips, when the words strangled themselves in her throat.

The woman standing before her wore neat trousers and a white blouse whose short sleeves allowed her to show off the constellation tattoo on her right arm. Caris tracked the lines and starbursts of the Wolf constellation on the North Star's arm, the gold an impossible color in her skin. But then, star gods were the stuff of dreams and prayers, if their history was anything to go by.

Caris shoved away from the worktable and hastily sank down into a curtsy. Her parents had drilled into her a respect for their country's guiding star that had never left her, even if her mother and father had.

"My lady," she croaked out, clenching her hands into fists so they would hopefully stop trembling. She didn't know what had drawn the North Star here, but Caris rather hoped that Aaralyn wouldn't condemn her for the choices she'd made on behalf of Ashion.

"You have grown," Aaralyn said, her voice a rich cadence in Caris' ears.

Caris rose out of her curtsy and dared to lift her head to meet the North Star's gaze. "I haven't a memory of you."

Aaralyn smiled slightly as she stepped closer, the air in the laboratory becoming stifling with her presence. "Not with this face, no."

She reached the worktable, and her features shimmered as if she was pulling on a veil, and Caris' eyes widened at the face revealed to her for a handful of seconds before Aaralyn's natural features returned. "*You* taught me to control my magic?"

For a moment, Aaralyn had stood before Caris as the star priestess who'd taught her in secret when the clarion crystals' songs became too loud for her to resist as a child. Later, it had been that same star priestess who had warned of the dangers of revealing the starfire that burned in her soul. Caris had held those teachings close when she'd left Cosian for Amari several years ago. She'd followed the rules set down for her right up until the riot in Amari, when to keep that secret meant damning her people to die.

"I have been your guiding star since Ophelia prayed for me to save you," Aaralyn said, hazel eyes never blinking.

Caris thought about the beginning of her road that Blaine had told her about and all that came after. She'd wondered but daren't ask her parents, whose road she had overtaken when she was barely hours old. "You gave me away. You bade the Dusk Star to flee with me."

"You have never regretted that."

Caris flinched. "Haven't I, my lady?"

Aaralyn tipped her head to the side, studying Caris with a gravity to her gaze that burned like starfire. Her attention was anything but easy. "You don't, for if you did, you would protest the crown others have given you."

It was a rank in name only, for all the jewels meant for the starfire throne had been destroyed during the Inferno, and the ones Eimarille claimed as hers were Daijal-made. Caris was queen, made that way by everyone's belief, not a crown that had never rested on her head. But it was something Eimarille coveted and which Soren flatly refused the same way he refused his name. Unlike Soren, Caris couldn't bring herself to walk away from what it meant to be of the Rourke bloodline and all it entailed.

"My name isn't even written down in the royal genealogies."

"That was done to protect you. If you'd been in the records, my husband's Blades would have found you."

Caris crossed her arms over her chest, shoulders hunching forward a little. "If you could save me, why couldn't you save Eimarille? Or Soren, who I don't even know is still alive?"

Aaralyn shrugged. "I gave your brother to the Dawn Star and the Eclipse Star to make him a warden."

"And Eimarille?"

Aaralyn stepped closer, resting the fingertips of both hands on the worktable. "I let my husband take her."

"I fail to see how that decision saved her if it brought the world to war."

"Oh, child. It was never about saving one person, or even three, but about ensuring the future of Maricol remains firmly planted *here* and not in the stars."

Caris gave her an odd look. "Maricol is our home. The stars take our ashes when we die. Where else would we go?"

"Where else indeed." Aaralyn smiled slightly, looking both ancient and young but, above all, wholly something else in that moment. "Eimarille's road was always meant to cross yours."

"I'd rather it didn't." But that confrontation was barreling toward Caris like a steam train with no switch light to stop it.

"I've given you a long road to walk, but it must be walked." Aaralyn lifted her hand and reached across the worktable for Caris, fingers brushing across her forehead with a searing touch that had her jerking back, turning her head aside. "Trust your heart, for it will never betray you."

When she looked back, Aaralyn was gone, and Caris wasn't quite certain if it hadn't been a fever dream brought about by the summer heat.

She swallowed, rubbing at her forehead, and tensed when the door opened again. Only this time, it wasn't a star god sweeping in with no apologies, but Nathaniel, who she was always glad to see. Nathaniel frowned at her as he nudged the door shut behind him with his foot. "What's wrong?"

Caris shook her head, wondering if she looked as rattled as she felt. "Nothing. I could use some tea."

"Well then. Let's pour you some."

She drank it plain and hot, needing the bitterness to clear her mind. Nathaniel drank with her, a quiet presence that she leaned against, her shoulder pressed to his arm. If she concentrated, she could hear the sound of his clockwork metal heart and the faint song from the clarion crystals that helped power it. She thought about Aaralyn's words and everything stretching out beyond her on a road that got harder and harder to walk with every dawn she woke up to.

"We're sending a diplomatic envoy to Oeiras to open talks with the Tovan Isles to ally with us and join the war effort. We need their ship-cities to break through the blockade in the Gulf of Helia guarding the way to New Haven," Caris said quietly.

Nathaniel stiffened beside her. "Should you be telling me this?"

She turned her head to look at him, the clarion crystal shard hanging around her neck with the ring he'd given her warm against her skin. "You would never betray me."

"Not of my own free will."

They'd carved it back out of him when it mattered, and he'd never embodied the chains of *rionetka* since. But there was always that fear, she knew, that the *Klovod*'s control could return. "We are not married, but I would have you go to Oeiras on my behalf and plead our country's case."

Nathaniel carefully set his teacup down on the worktable, freeing his hand so he could turn to face her and gently touch her cheek. "I am a living risk to everything you are fighting for, my darling."

She curled her fingers around his wrist, thinking of Aaralyn's words and all the times Nathaniel had held her and shored her up and helped to carry her forward. "If we take no risks, then we won't win."

Caris knew from Vanya that the Tovanians had uncovered *rionetkas* in Port Avi. Whether dead or alive, none would be able to articulate what it was like to be so changed. Nathaniel would encompass all the horrors that Eimarille represented and be a warning as well as a plea.

"Do you not want me here?" Nathaniel asked, voice quiet, almost small.

Caris blinked back the sudden tears that came to her eyes. "I want you with me always."

But there was a war being fought and a throne to be won and a country to ensure it *stayed* a country. None of it a road she had ever wanted to walk, but walk it she must.

And Nathaniel understood that, judging by the slow nod he gave her, a bittersweet smile coming to his lips. "If that is your will, then I will do as my queen commands."

She knew no one would be pleased with her orders, but Caris didn't care. Nathaniel would be her voice, out there in the Gulf of Helia, and if it kept him off the land and out of reach of Eimarille and the *Klovod* and their deadly schemes, so much the better.

"I love you," she said, meaning it with all she was worth.

"And I you."

He kissed her softly, tea a bitter taste on both their tongues. Caris would always want him like this, even if she wanted nothing more in terms of touch. And no matter where Nathaniel went, Caris would know where he stood on a spelled-ink map, could follow and find him anywhere.

His heart would always belong to her, and she vowed never to break it.

Ten

Eimarille watched as the small airship descended into the royal hangar, the ground crew assisting with the anchoring. The royal guard that had escorted her to the airfield outside the city walls of New Haven had closed off one of the main piers and the city gates for her passage. Being at war changed her routine, but New Haven was far from the front lines stretched across the eastern provinces of Ashion.

The broadsheets being sold from street corners that morning all reported on the latest news coming out of Solaria and E'ridia—that the two countries were joining the war effort on behalf of Ashion but with crippled support. The reason for it all walked down the gangplank some ten minutes later, dressed for travel rather than the Daijal court, her long black hair simply braided back and face bare of any of the rouge Eimarille wore. It smeared a little over Terilyn's lips when Eimarille kissed her, but neither woman cared, either about the stains or their audience.

"Welcome home," Eimarille murmured when she finally pulled back. "Excellent work, as always, darling."

Terilyn used her thumb to gently clean up the edge of Eimarille's lip before slipping their hands together. "It was a successful trip, but I am glad to be back by your side."

Eimarille tightened her fingers, tugging Terilyn after her down the pier where her escort waited. "I never had any doubt you would succeed."

It had meant several weeks spent traveling by airship and submersible, but the results were more than Eimarille could have hoped for. Kote had warned that keeping other countries from joining the war was only a delaying tactic, but halving what support could be sent by Solaria and E'ridia bought Daijal more time to dig in and boost the output of their production factories.

The royal guard led the way out of the hangar and into the bright summer sunshine. Eimarille had foregone her crown for the trip to the airfield, but she was ever recognizable to her people. Her arrival had drawn a crowd earlier, and it had only grown during the time spent waiting for Terilyn's airship to anchor in its berth. Eimarille lifted her free hand to wave elegantly at the airfield workers gathered along the piers who cheered at her appearance.

Leaving the airfield amidst the circle of her royal guards took a matter of minutes. The royal motor carriage and its escorting vehicles waited with engines running past the city gates. The driver helped first Eimarille and then Terilyn into the back seat of the motor carriage before getting back behind the steering wheel to drive them back to the palace.

New Haven was a bustling city that would not be home for too much longer. If the war went how Eimarille envisioned it, the palace she'd spent her formative years in here in the west would be nothing but a summer home. Eimarille looked forward to the day when Lisandro would grow up in the city she'd been born in, Amari a capital for the world, not just a single country.

Still, New Haven held some good memories for her. It was where she'd fallen in love with Terilyn, where she'd given birth to her son, where she'd been crowned queen of one country in preparation for all the rest. The palace they eventually entered had long since become hers, nearly all traces of the Iverson bloodline erased from every wing of the vast building. The only remnant of her deceased husband's bloodline greeted them both with outstretched arms.

"You're back!" Lisandro shouted, unable to contain his glee at seeing Terilyn again.

His lessons forgotten, her little prince flung himself at Terilyn with a smile on his face. Eimarille watched with a pleased smile of her own as Terilyn swept Lisandro into her arms, peppering his face with playful kisses. "Hello, *malynshka.*"

The Urovan endearment only made Lisandro smile harder before he wrapped his skinny arms around Terilyn's neck to hug her tight. Eimarille let her son chatter away at Terilyn, the governess knowing his lessons were done for the day without needing to be told. Eimarille followed Terilyn out of the nursery, half listening as Lisandro prattled on about what had happened in her absence. Terilyn kept an interested face for all of it, the adoration in her eyes a kind of love Eimarille had never seen in Wesley's when he'd been alive.

"How about we go for a walk in the gardens?" Terilyn asked, glancing over her shoulder at Eimarille.

"I think that's a splendid idea," she replied.

It was honestly too beautiful of a day to spend most of it inside. Lisandro, free of his lessons, was more than pleased to gallivant down the cobbled pathways that snaked through the grand rear garden. Eimarille had ripped up and replanted them all, undoing all of former Queen Aleesia's hard work in favor of plants and flowers that Terilyn preferred. Which meant summer in the palace gardens smelled how Eimarille thought Urova might, if she ever had the opportunity to visit Matriskav during the same season.

Lisandro eventually returned and wriggled his way between the two of them, shoving his small hands into theirs. It was muscle memory to lift him on the next step and swing him, smiling over at Terilyn as they did so. They walked a short path like that before Lisandro pulled free and skipped ahead once more.

"Joelle has Alasandair in her *vasilyet,*" Eimarille said as they walked after Lisandro.

Terilyn hummed thoughtfully, folding her hands together at the small of her back. "Shall I pay her a visit?"

Eimarille shook her head, thinking about all the nights she'd slept poorly, half her bed cold and empty. "No, you've been gone long enough. But I would carve out her insolence once and for all. I have no use for her House any longer."

"There are Blades who would gladly go south for you to see it done."

"I trust who you think would be best suited for the job at hand. Whatever they require for such an endeavor, they shall have."

"I'll see it done, my love."

"Tomorrow." Eimarille stepped closer so she could wrap her arm around Terilyn's waist, who returned the gesture. "It's been too long since I've been able to hold you in my arms."

She knew peaceful moments like this, with Terilyn by her side and Lisandro dancing on ahead, would be more difficult to come by once she finally convinced Kote to allow her to travel to Amari. Her High General fretted so, but the war would not end in some grand battle as all her officers seemed to think so.

It would end with her.

Stratagem

937 A.O.P.

One

CARIS

"You look tired," Meleri said.

Caris looked up from the speech she had labored over for the past week, the pages of neatly typed-out words the result of long hours at her desk and ink-stained fingers. She'd worked with Honovi and Meleri through many drafts, though she still wasn't happy with the final version—mostly because she doubted herself. But Honovi had assured her the speech was excellent, and Meleri had agreed, even if the duchess hadn't agreed with the schedule Caris was keeping once it was delivered.

"I didn't sleep well. I suppose I should be grateful it is only the press who will see me today," Caris said, rubbing at her eyes.

The speech was to be done over radio, with reporters from dozens of broadsheets to be present in the room with her as she gave it. It would be sent over the wire to every Ashion province, and the reporters would be given copies of it to print in their broadsheets. It was meant to inspire, to give her people faith, but Caris wasn't sure how well her words would work. She'd much prefer using starfire in her country's defense, but everyone had adamantly refused to let her near the front lines.

But staying in Cosian was no longer an option, not with the

building push along those same front lines to force the Daijal army west again. With the addition of the Solarian army and E'ridian airships to the Ashion army's beleaguered forces, the fighting wasn't as desperate, but every mile was still hard-won. Caris would be following behind the main force, taken in secret to small frontier villages and towns, cities when they could, with an airship capable of ferrying her out of harm's way always nearby. There was no point in her being half a country away from Amari once their forces took it back.

If they took it back.

Doubt was an insidious companion that Caris tried not to focus on. But with Nathaniel sent to the Tovan Isles on her behalf, her mornings were lonely before duty took over, and it was a struggle to ignore what she felt were her shortcomings at being queen.

Meleri came into the drawing room, the skirt of her gown rustling with each step. She sat beside Caris on the sofa, folding her thin hands together over her lap. She sat with a straight-backed ease Caris still couldn't achieve despite her years spent as Meleri's ward. Sitting hunched over a worktable meant her shoulders wanted to curve, and Caris always had to remember to straighten them.

"Are you certain you should leave?" Meleri asked carefully.

Her trunks had been packed last night and taken to the airfield to be loaded as cargo in the airship that would fly her west to the town General Votil had cleared for her safety in a province south of Cosian. It wouldn't be a straight flight to Amari, not with the way the fighting fluctuated.

"You know I can't remain here," Caris said. She was a target, and any place she stayed would become threatened. Cosian had seen enough bombings over the last year to reinforce that fact.

"It's not safe beyond the walls."

"It's not safe inside them." Caris set her speech on the low table, shifting on the cushion to better face Meleri. "I know it's not what you want, but this is my duty, and I have to do it."

Meleri studied her with shadowed hazel eyes, the white in her hair having overtaken the pale red color more in the last two years than all the ones before that Caris had known her. "It's not that I don't want you to do your duty. I just want you safe while you try."

Caris looked away, thinking of Lore, who they still had no news of, the same way they had no news of Soren. The calls Caris had taken with Vanya had provided nothing new on the whereabouts of the pair. Caris could only pray they'd find them still alive, but she knew the likelihood of that happening dimmed with every day that passed.

They'd lost weeks already.

"There is so much out there I don't know, that I never even knew I didn't know, but I can't learn it here inside the walls you want to build around me," Caris said quietly, returning her gaze to Meleri, who never looked away. "I never wanted this road, but it is the one I must walk. You need to let me."

Meleri's lips trembled slightly, her stoic determination faltering there in the private moment they shared as queen and duchess, spymaster and former cog. "I know you are Portia's daughter, but you have so much of Ophelia in you as well. She would be proud of you, as I am sure Portia always has been. As am I, my queen."

Queen Ophelia was nothing but a name in history texts to Caris, a past she'd been birthed from but never got to know. That didn't mean she couldn't start now. "When the war is over, will you tell me about her?"

Meleri's lips curved into a bittersweet smile, and she reached to take Caris' hand in hers. "I would be honored to."

Caris nodded, eyes flicking back to the typed-out speech waiting for her. Meleri patted her hand gently before letting go to lever herself to her feet. "Come. You don't want to be late."

Caris reached for the speech, shuffling the papers together before slipping them into her small satchel. Together, they left the room, finding Blaine and Honovi waiting for her at the front door. Blaine would be traveling with her, as would Honovi, who was in charge of captaining the airship assigned to her. While it would be Ashion-made, its crew would be a mix of Ashionen and E'ridian aeronauts.

"All right?" Blaine asked with a familiarity Caris was beginning to miss in all the interactions she'd had of late.

She patted her satchel and smoothed her hand down the soft silk of her day jacket. "Yes. Shall we?"

Blaine nodded and offered up his left arm, his metal prosthetic cool beneath her fingers when she curved her hand over his elbow. Honovi got the door, holding it open for them as they strode out into the warm summer sunlight, the Royal Guard preparing for her departure.

She'd give her speech praising the war effort, hoping to rally her people, and then leave for a city or a town out in the Eastern Basin where Eimarille wouldn't think to look. She'd spend time with bloodlines who knew nothing about her beyond what the press had reported on and hope to forge social connections that would keep Ashion from fracturing further while she waited in the shadows to take the starfire throne.

Caris would be herself and hope it was enough in the end.

Two

NATHANIEL

When Nathaniel passed through the doorway that led into the dignitary room of Oeiras, a piercing alarm went off from hidden spell-detectors. Every single *praetoria* legionnaire within the grand room and outside it in the hall unholstered their pistols with deft speed and aimed the weapons at him.

Chief Minister Caelum raised both his hands in a placating manner, appearing unbothered by the greeting. He spoke in the trade tongue, which was a kindness for Nathaniel and the others with him who weren't quite fluent in Solarian and none of which were fluent in Tovanian. "The Ashionen representatives have been cleared by our magicians and granted leave of the premises by His Imperial Majesty. There is no threat from *rionetkas*, for none stand with us."

Nathaniel froze where he stood just past the doorway, along with the others. As warm as those words made him feel, he didn't breathe until the *praetoria* legionnaires reluctantly holstered their pistols at a wave from the Imperial emperor, though none removed their hands from the grips. Ambassador Dariush Zayed, doing double duty to Solaria and the Tovan Isles as Ashion's envoy, stepped forward and bowed deeply.

"Your Imperial Majesty," Dariush said, offering up the greeting in

Solarian. That phrase, at least, Nathaniel knew, for he'd been taught it on the flight over.

Nathaniel hastily bowed as well, trying not to feel as if the cravat wrapped around his throat was choking him. It'd felt like that for the past week and a half ever since Caris had given the order that he was to be her personal representative to the Tovanians. Predictably, there'd been arguments, all of which she'd ignored, despite the persistent attempts to change her mind. She'd put her foot down as queen and would not be swayed, sending Nathaniel west on an Ashionen airship, carrying a letter written by her own hand that he was meant to deliver to the Tovanian ambassador.

Dariush had already been in Oeiras since Caris had asked him to continue his diplomatic duties in the wake of the murders that had occurred in their embassy in Calhames. Nathaniel had traveled with a hastily gathered group of diplomatic aides to lend support to Dariush's mission in Solaria. He hoped what had occurred in Calhames would not be repeated here in Oeiras.

Imperial emperor Vanya Sa'Liandel, of the House of Sa'Liandel, stared at them with piercing dark eyes, his white robes edged in crimson and gold embroidery gleaming in the sunlight pouring through the high open windows of the strange dignitary room. His golden crown glittered like starfire, drawing the eye.

Vanya nodded gravely to them, his gaze lingering like a heavy thing on Nathaniel, who tried not to shift on his feet. He'd come a long way from being the son of a merchant, but he still didn't feel as if he belonged, either here in this grand Imperial estate or in his own body some days.

"Solaria bids you welcome," Vanya said, opting to speak in the trade tongue. He turned slightly so that he could gesture at the floating cabana behind him, where the Tovanians stood. "May I present *Uri'ka* Akeheni, of the ship-city *Matariki*."

Dariush bowed again, and Nathaniel followed his lead. Dariush kept to the trade tongue when he spoke. "We thank you for your hospitality in facilitating these talks, Your Imperial Majesty. Our queen sends her thanks as well to both you and *Uri'ka* Akeheni."

The Tovanian in question was an imposing figure, standing at the head of her delegation, arms crossed over her chest as she studied them. Caelum ushered them all farther into the room, and when they reached the edge of the pool, Nathaniel was able to make out the tattoos on the ambassador's face. His curiosity was left by the wayside when the emperor addressed him.

"I understand from Queen Caris that you speak for her, Mr. Clementine?" Vanya said.

"Only in so far as I can give voice to the state I have unwillingly found myself in and to sign on my queen's behalf, Your Imperial Majesty," Nathaniel said after a quick glance at Dariush. "The good ambassador is in charge of everything else."

He knew that Dariush had been making headway with the Tovanians ever since Caris had tasked him with initiating alliance talks. Nathaniel knew nothing about the ways of diplomacy, but if it was anything like a business contract, it would be easy to get bogged down in the minutiae of details, and they did not have much time for that.

"What state do you find yourself in?" Akeheni asked.

Nathaniel hesitated a moment before lifting his chin, meeting her gaze without flinching. "I and the rest of my family were arrested before the riot protesting taxes and debt bondage occurred in Amari. While imprisoned, I was—I became—" He swallowed hard, rallying himself after a moment of silence. "The *Klovod* turned me into a *rionetka* and used me to try to murder my queen. The wardens were able to undo the compulsion but not remove it. I still carry magic in my clockwork metal heart, but at least my mind is my own these days."

A soft murmur rose from the group of people on the cabana and those few ranged down the table by the side of the pool. Nathaniel easily read the concern and wariness that appeared on people's faces, but he didn't offer any comfort.

Akeheni frowned at him, her gaze dropping briefly to his chest and the neatly done-up waistcoat and shirt he wore that hid his vivisection scars. "Your queen trusts you?"

She was the only one who did, it seemed like, though Nathaniel didn't give voice to that thought. "Yes."

"A risky choice to make."

"I love her," Nathaniel said quietly. "As she loves me. But we both love our country just as much, and some risks must be taken to win this war. I come here as a warning for the ills that Eimarille will do to anyone but also to show how far we'll go to fight against her."

Akeheni didn't reveal how she felt, but Nathaniel was familiar with the unease people felt when they knew what kind of heart beat in his chest. Still, the Tovanian *Uri'ka* didn't immediately request he be removed from the talks, and Nathaniel was allowed to sit at the table set aside for the Ashionen delegation. The emperor, he noted, did not take a seat, conferring quietly with the Chief Minister for a moment before addressing the room at large.

"My ambassador to the Tovan Isles will remain to ensure Solaria is represented for your talks. We hold an alliance with the Tovanians, and any alliance made will affect our own borders," Vanya said before sweeping out of the room, Caelum following after him.

Dariush cleared his throat from his spot beside Nathaniel before opening up the talks. They didn't have time for flowery courtesy, not with the front lines of the war now grinding west instead of east one incremental mile at a time. He'd left behind the skies filled with airships and the poison fields trampled by the feet of the Legion and Ashion armies, but all of their efforts would be worth nothing if they failed here, at this table.

Nathaniel was a merchant, and in some ways, diplomacy was about selling yourself to the right buyer. But he was not so nearly skilled in that area as Dariush, and so he rarely spoke up in the days that followed, there as Caris' proxy in the event the Tovanians agreed to the desperately needed and wanted alliance.

Five days after their arrival in Oeiras, Nathaniel's breakfast of food not spiced quite as much as it had been the last few times was interrupted by an Ashionen clerk escorting a Tovanian into the embassy's inner courtyard used for all the meals. Dariush paused in ripping a piece of flatbread in half, everyone seated at the low table eyeing the newcomers. Nathaniel had come to learn that, when in another country, diplomats were summoned, never visited.

Dariush proved to be rather adept at unexpected surprises, dropping the bread and hastily swallowing the bite of food he'd taken. Dariush stood and offered a shallow bow in greeting while everyone else remained seated. "Is something amiss?"

"*Uri'ka* Akeheni wishes to speak with Mr. Clementine," the Tovanian said in accented Ashionen.

"We can present ourselves to the *Uri'ka* at the Imperial estate shortly."

The Tovanian shook his head, thick curls swaying with the motion. "Just him."

Nathaniel slowly set down his teacup, the sweet chai turning rancid on his tongue as a spike of panic wound through him. Clearing his throat, he stood beneath Dariush's heavy gaze, offering his own bow to the Tovanian. "I am at the *Uri'ka*'s disposal."

Dariush's fingers snagged the soft cotton of his sleeve, the older man bending his head in a bid for privacy as he switched from the trade tongue to Ashionen. "Do not agree to anything without me present."

Because Nathaniel's words would be binding on behalf of Caris, whereas Dariush's would not. "Of course."

Nathaniel left the inner courtyard, falling into step beside the Tovanian and waved off the clerk. He escorted the Tovanian through the living quarters of the embassy into the ones meant for government work and beyond them to the small forecourt where a motor carriage waited for them. He was surprised to see Akeheni standing beside the open door, an elbow resting on the window frame, the other on the roof of the motor carriage. She smiled at him in greeting, though it did not reach her eyes, the tattoos on her face pulling with the motion.

"Oh," Nathaniel said, startled by her presence. "*Uri'ka*, we would have welcomed you inside."

"Your embassy isn't built with my people in mind. Too unmoving.

I know it is early, but there is someone who wants to meet you back on my ship," Akeheni said.

For one moment, Nathaniel could not move, and it felt as if the *Klovod* had his fingers in his mind again, controlling his limbs and breaking his heart. He knew she was not the enemy, but it still took effort to make his lungs work, and by the time he'd sucked in a strangled breath, Akeheni's expression had settled into something like an apology.

"It is not anyone who would do you harm. They just dislike the land, and our ship is a better place for such conversation we must have," Akeheni said, not unkindly.

Before he'd had his heart carved out, he would've been inclined to trust her. Now, Nathaniel wanted desperately to bring another with him, but the rest of the Ashionen delegation had been denied an invitation. Nathaniel could only join Akeheni in the back seat while the aide got situated behind the steering wheel.

It was a quicker ride to the port than it would've been during midday, the streets not clogged with as many vehicles or people. Those up and about were of the working class, putting in the hours before the searing noon heat would drive everyone inside. The humidity was thick even that early, causing Nathaniel to roll down the window to get air flowing through the motor carriage. The Eastern Basin was hot, but it was a dryer heat than in Oeiras. By the time they made it to the outer wall and through the gate to the river port, Nathaniel's clothes were sticking to his skin from sweat, and he could taste the salt of it on his lips.

Oeiras' port was a bustling mini city of its own, dozens of berths, civilian docks, and commercial loading docks stretching down the shore of the Tirsha River. Anchored at a long pier was a sleek steam-powered ship whose design was far different from the other ships docked in the port. Nathaniel squinted against the sunlight as he got out of the motor carriage, taking it in.

"The frigate is part of our ship-city. It's small enough to traverse the inland waterway when we need to come to shore," Akeheni said.

Its hull was black iron but painted a riot of colors not unlike how the E'ridians painted their airships. No mast was needed for sailing, not like some personal riverboats had, and its pair of chimneys were empty of smoke at the moment. The port and aft sides didn't match in terms of design, with the port side that aligned with the dock having struts protruding outward in a way that indicated they were meant to lock onto something.

"I thought it would be larger," Nathaniel said.

Akeheni chuckled. "It's meant for maneuverability. It connects to our ship-city, which is anchored out at sea while we are here. Come, they are waiting."

Someone up on the high deck called down to them in Tovanian, and Akeheni responded in the same language. Nathaniel didn't know what was being said, but he could follow gestures well enough. The gangplank was winched out, dockworkers securing it to the pier. Akeheni jogged up it with easy steps, Nathaniel following her a little less easily. The river water lapped at the hull of the ship below, and he caught a glimpse of gun holes before he made it to the deck.

Unlike on an airship, no shadows from a balloon offered up shade in the face of the rising sun. Nathaniel lifted a hand to shield his eyes from the glare, gamely following Akeheni across a deck designed for the sea as opposed to the air, no lifelines crossing overhead or hooks needing to be used. He wondered if that changed due to the weather but set that question aside in favor of greeting the person Akeheni led him to meet at the stern.

He was surprised when Akeheni took a knee, fist held over her heart and curly head bowing in respect. When she spoke, she opted for the trade tongue, but her tone held a deep respect that had been offered to no one in the Imperial estate, not even the emperor.

"My guiding star, I have answered your call," Akeheni said.

At first, Nathaniel had thought the golden design on the person's back had been stitched onto a Solarian robe. He froze when he realized that it was no embroidery but the distinct golden lines of a constellation tattoo cutting through tanned brown skin. Part of the golden lines and starbursts that made up the Leviathan tattoo was hidden by the fall of long hair pulled off their neck by sturdy leather ties into a tight queue. When they turned at Akeheni's words, Nathaniel found himself looking into a face he'd seen before in some Star Order prayer books, their visage always an afterthought to his own country's guiding star but still ever present in the religion that all of Maricol's children followed.

Farren quirked a smile at him, their dark eyes pinning him much how he thought a harpoon might pin a leviathan. They were shirtless, their loose linen trousers belted in place around slim hips. They were barefoot, seemingly unbothered by the hot metal deck they stood on. But for all the kindness in their face, Nathaniel could not stop the way his knees went weak, and he staggered in the face of a star god.

"Oh," he said weakly. "Hail to the Eclipse Star."

He hastily locked his knees and bowed, breath a ragged sound in his ears. Despite his unease, his clockwork metal heart still beat at a steady pace, and he kept his gaze on the deck, wondering if the sweat sliding down the back of his neck was from the weather or nerves.

"I don't expect your prayers or your loyalty. You are one of my sister's children," Farren said, their voice lilting a bit with a humor Nathaniel didn't understand.

He rose out of his bow only when Akeheni stood again. He blinked rapidly, looking everywhere but at the star god. "Regardless, I am yours to command."

Farren hummed thoughtfully at that before stepping closer, bringing with them the scent of the sea. The edges of their constellation tattoo curled over their shoulders, the golden points catching the sunlight and glittering on their skin. "Aaralyn would be displeased if I asked that of you."

"I have never had the honor of the North Star's attention."

"Consider yourself lucky. Her favor isn't easy."

Nathaniel thought briefly of the Rourke children and the war spiraling out from their roads and barely contained a wince. "Yes, so I have seen."

Farren studied him for a moment, the shouts of the dockworkers below drifting up to the deck. "Your clockwork metal heart isn't the progress we'd hoped for this Age. I suppose Innes would find it acceptable, but he has always dreamed bigger than I."

Nathaniel gave them a helpless look. "What do you want of me?"

"I wanted to see for myself the future Innes wants to build. It is one I do not approve of."

"Will you help us fix it?"

"Televoxes don't reach across the waves easily, but prayers do. I have been listening and guiding those who must be involved with agreeing to the alliance you seek. My children do not care for the sturdiness of land, but they know what is fought there will eventually spill into the sea."

"The ship-cities are willing to fight," Akeheni said, glancing at him.

Nathaniel, well aware of the intense negotiations that had been ongoing for the past few days, let out a shuddering breath. "Ambassador Zayed will be pleased to hear that."

"Yes, and I will agree to such an effort, if only to stop my brother's madness." Farren tilted their head, gaze unblinking as they studied Nathaniel. "Xaxis might claim the depths under the ice, but the open sea has always been mine and my children's domain. I'll not give it to him or Innes simply for the sake of some long-forgotten dream that should never have been remembered."

Nathaniel had no idea what the Eclipse Star meant by that and so remained silent.

"We have your blessing, then, my guiding star?" Akeheni asked.

Farren inclined their head. "Yes. All the other ship-cities are in agreement as well."

Akeheni looked fiercely pleased about that as she hooked her thumbs over the top of her leather belt. "We shall do you proud."

"And my waves will ever guide you."

Nathaniel let out a careful breath, shoulders loosening a little. "On behalf of my queen and country, I thank you."

"Oh, you'll be coming with my children," Farren said, almost cheerfully, nearly making Nathaniel choke on his breath. "You and all the other soldiers who will storm the shores of Daijal when the blockade is broken."

"But I'm not a soldier," Nathaniel protested weakly.

"You are not, but you must be kept safe long enough to get your queen to Amari." Farren reached out and tapped his chest, their touch seemingly vibrating through his bones down to the metal he carried behind his ribs. "You'll reach the shore again, but for now, let the waves cradle you."

A loud clang startled Nathaniel, and he jerked his head to the side out of instinct to see a pair of deckhands arguing over a crate that had been dropped. When he turned his head around again, he found the space that Farren had occupied empty, but the weight of their touch lingered on him.

"Come," Akeheni said, gesturing for Nathaniel to follow her across the deck once more. "Let us return to the Imperial estate and talk of war."

Three

VANYA

"What is this?" Raiah asked, reaching across Vanya's desk for a pile of reports that needed his attention. The open one was a brief memo updating him on the troop movement of the last company from Ashion's army traveling through Solaria to Oeiras via steam train. They'd arrived at the port two days ago with supplies and war machines, taken by frigate to board the waiting Tovanian ship-city anchored offshore. If things were going as scheduled, the Tovanian navy was even now regrouping in the Gulf of Helia to begin the fight to break the Daijal navy's blockade.

It was Tenth Month, three weeks since Nathaniel had signed the treaty with the Tovan Isles on behalf of Queen Caris. As far as Vanya knew, a battalion was all Ashion could spare to attack Daijal on the west coast. Their movement into Solaria had been done under the guise of assisting the Legion in the south against the revenant horde tearing through the countryside there. That lie would last until the first gun volley was issued by a Tovanian ship-city.

Vanya shifted Raiah on his lap and set the reports aside. "Work."

Raiah pouted at him, tugging on the collar of his robe. "But you promised you would play in the gardens with me."

"After the midday rest, yes, we shall go outside. But I do believe you have lessons this morning."

"I will take her to her teachers," Taisiya said from where she sat on the low sofa in his office, reading a broadsheet. The pair had joined him after their morning meal, Vanya in need of Taisiya's guidance over the mess still making its way across the country from Rixham.

Raiah huffed out a heavy, performative sigh, and Vanya had to work to keep from smiling. He remembered being a child and wanting to be around his older brother and his mother when they'd been away working, and then he'd taken up the learning of it all and realized how exhausting it all was. Raiah was only five, but he hoped to spare her the heavy weight of learning to rule for another year or so.

A knock on his office door had him calling out, "Enter."

He was unsurprised to see Caelum, the Chief Minister his most frequent caller these days. The person who joined him was unfamiliar to Vanya, dressed in neutral-colored robes, her light brown hair twisted up off her neck in a high knot. Her face was plain and unassuming, easily forgettable. She wore no jewelry, carried no sign of rank on her person, but her green-eyed gaze was steady and sharp as she rose out of a deep curtsy.

"Your Imperial Majesty," Caelum said, sounding a little out of breath, as if he'd run across the Oeiras Imperial estate. "Might I introduce a particular guest to you?"

Vanya eyed him sharply, the turn of phrase familiar when it came to the network of spies his Chief Minister handled. "You may."

Taisiya had straightened up at Caelum's query, setting aside the broadsheet. She used her cane to get to her feet, coming around to stand by Vanya's seat at his desk. Raiah, sensing the tension in the room, stopped squirming in his lap.

"Your Imperial Majesty, I have gone by Cinzia for the past several years," the spy said after a nod from Caelum. "I carried out a life of service within the House of Aetos."

Vanya stilled at the mention of that House, eyes narrowing. "Were you within the household?"

Cinzia nodded. "I was adept at ingratiating myself into the major-domo's good graces. After the Conclave, positions opened up after those servants who had doubts about the House of Aetos' loyalty to Solaria left. I remained to be useful and was found acceptable."

Which spoke well of her ability as a spy. "What news do you bring that bade you break your cover to leave that House and Seaville?"

"The House of Aetos' estate is old and has many secret passageways. I managed to gain access to several of them during my time there, one of which led past the family's private quarters. I overheard an evening conversation between Lady Vesper and her *vezir* about aiding *vezir* Joelle by bringing her the foreign prince and lady. They were taken from Calhames to Bellingham alive by Lady Vesper."

Fury coursed through him, hot like starfire, and Vanya had to force himself not to launch out of the chair, mindful of Raiah sitting in his lap. He kept his touch gentle with his daughter, when all he wanted to do was tear down the walls of Bellingham and let the revenants take it once he was assured of Soren's and Lore's safety. Whispers weren't truth, though, but they'd been the spark for any number of House feuds and debts over the centuries. And Vanya had known, deep in his heart, that the most logical place his lover could be was in Joelle's hands.

"How certain are you of what you overheard?" he asked.

"Completely" was Cinzia's firm reply.

"You have no proof," Taisiya murmured in warning. "And Bellingham is not the city you should be focused on."

Vanya offered his *valide* a thin smile. "I am well aware of the land we are losing in the south, but I will not lose *him*."

"Papa?" Raiah asked. "Who?"

Vanya finally stood, holding Raiah in his arms rather than setting her on her feet, and caught Caelum's eye instead of answering Raiah. "I want to speak to General Chu Hua. And send for the head star priest of the main Star Order temple. Tell them to bring me the royal and nobility genealogies."

"Of course. I will get the general on the telephone for you first," Caelum said.

Caelum gestured for Cinzia to follow him out of the office, pulling the door shut behind him. Vanya shifted Raiah in his arms and reached for the reports on his desk, handing them to Taisiya. "These are accountings of the cities and towns under siege from the revenants released from Rixham. The wardens tell me the estimated number is not something they are capable of stopping at this time, not with the ongoing war in the north and not while they are still recovering from the attack on their island and the loss of tithes."

Taisiya took the stack of reports but didn't bother opening any of them. "Taking soldiers and supplies away from either front simply to aid in rescuing Soren will endear you to no one."

Raiah leaned out of Vanya's arms so quickly he almost couldn't right her. "Soren? Where is he?"

"He'll be home soon," Vanya said as he sat her on his desk since she was wriggling all around.

Raiah kicked her feet in open air and stared up at him with wide eyes. "Promise? I miss him. He said he would come back, and he *didn't*."

It felt like taking a knife between the ribs when he remembered the scant time they'd had together in Calhames before Soren was stolen away from him again. "I know, but it's not because he didn't want to. He *did*. And he will return to us."

Vanya would not make a liar out of Soren or himself in giving that promise to his daughter.

Taisiya sighed thickly before setting the reports on the desk, idly flipping through the topmost one. "What do you think the Houses will say or do if you wage war over one man instead of fighting for Solaria?"

"What makes you think I can't do both?"

"Vanya."

He arched an eyebrow at his *valide*, ignoring the frown she offered him. "You think I don't know what is happening here? You think I don't recognize the mess of my mother's choices? She loved Iosiv just as much as she loved Solaria, and she killed for both."

"Don't follow Zakariya's road."

"She had the right of it, in some ways. You must see that." Taisiya's silence was as good as admittance. Vanya nodded before taking her hand in his, running his thumb over her bony knuckles in a comforting way. "I've let Joelle play her games long enough. I am *done* letting the fallout from the Conclave stay my hand."

"You act on whispers."

"We as a House have acted on less. The whisper of a truth will always be stronger than brittle lies to stand on. I haven't set the Legion upon those who took Soren because I didn't know where he'd been taken. I know now."

"Do you?"

"I will order the Legion to work with E'ridia's air force to help break through the defenses around Bellingham. We both know Daijal is behind Joelle's deep reserves there, even if many of the Houses refuse to see it."

"And will you be leading that charge?"

Vanya worked his jaw a bit. "As much as I would like to, no, I will not go to Bellingham."

"Then what will you do?"

"I will head south instead to join the Legion there."

Taisiya jerked her hand free of his, eyes widening. "Outside the walls?"

As much as Vanya wanted to find Soren and bring him home, he had to ensure there was a home left for the warden to come back to. Vanya turned his hand over, calling forth a flicker of starfire, the heat of the aether at its most powerful distillation burning between them. "I am one of the few with strength enough to summon starfire like a firestorm, and we all know the dead must be burned."

That lesson had been reinforced quite adamantly at the end of the Conclave last year. He would not make the same mistake as his ancestors this time.

"Not by you," Taisiya protested.

"I won't be going alone. I will ask those of the Houses who can still wield starfire and are capable of fighting to join me."

"You are our emperor. You should not be anywhere beyond the walls while Solaria fights a war."

"What sort of emperor would I be if I won't fight to save us?"

Taisiya made a tiny throwing-away motion with her hand. "Alive."

Vanya snorted, reaching out to stroke his hand over Raiah's hair, thinking of how happy and relieved they would both be once Soren was returned to them. "I have much to come back to."

"So you will burn the dead at the same time you allow a city to fall?"

"Joelle condemned Bellingham to its fate, not I. And the House of Aetos will pay for their betrayal, both to Solaria and our House."

Taisiya narrowed her eyes, but before she could argue that statement, Caelum let himself back into the office with a faintly harried look on his face. "The operator has the general on the telephone for you."

Vanya reached around Raiah to pull the telephone on the desk closer to him. "I'll take it here."

Caelum nodded and ducked back out. Moments later, the telephone rang, and Vanya picked it up, glad to hear Chu Hua's voice on the other end.

"You wished to speak with me, Your Imperial Majesty?" Chu Hua said over a line that crackled from the distance between them.

"I have it on good authority Joelle kidnapped the Ashion prince and lady with the help of Lady Vesper. The House of Aetos has picked their side, and it is not Solaria's," Vanya said.

"I see."

"Do you?" Vanya couldn't help but turn and meet Taisiya's gaze. "I want E'ridian air support to back up the Legion ranks attempting to break through the defenses around Bellingham. Send extra battalions if you must, but I want Soren brought home."

"You will not be leading the charge?"

"I will be fighting revenants in the south."

The sharp inhalation broke across the line. "Your Imperial Majesty, is that wise?"

"It is necessary."

Unlike Taisiya, Chu Hua didn't argue his intent beyond the initial protest. "I will inform the southern command of your orders and plan for your arrival."

"I hope to not be the only one fighting with starfire, so plan for that as well."

"Of course. Give me an hour."

She was polite enough to let him end the call first, even though he knew he'd given her a headache-worthy task to coordinate his presence in the poison fields against the revenant horde. But she was the best general he had, and he trusted her to protect him and the Imperial throne while he did his best to protect Solaria, his home and his heart.

"Will this be your road, then?" Taisiya asked quietly.

He looked at her, knowing that if he didn't put his all into this fight, they wouldn't have a country at the end of it. If he had to burn down cities to keep the walking dead at bay and bring Soren home, then so be it. "There is no other."

Vanya was, it turned out, ever his mother's son.

Four

JOELLE

Bellingham's warning sirens jerked Joelle out of a deep sleep, hands flailing beneath the thin sheet she slept with during the late-summer heat at the end of Tenth Month. Almost immediately, her door was thrown open by one of her handmaidens, the young woman switching on the gas lamp in the room, bathing them both in burning light.

"What is going on?" Joelle rasped, still struggling to shake off the dregs of sleep.

"I don't know, *vezir*," her handmaiden said gravely.

"Is it revenants?"

As soon as the words left her mouth, a distant explosion echoed through the air, loud enough to hear even through the walls of her House's estate. Joelle flinched with her entire body. "Have our defenses been pushed back so far? How did that happen?"

Her handmaiden's lips pressed into a thin line as she helped Joelle out of bed. "I do not know."

Another handmaiden hurried in, the pair of them helping Joelle into the first set of robes they could get their hands on in the closet. She didn't bother with any jewelry, only her cane, gripping it tightly as she left the bedroom.

Those servants who lived within the estate were awake, though no one had turned on the gas lamp lights throughout the rest of the building. They were all well aware of the directive to stay dark at night whenever possible so as to not mark them a target while the Legion crept ever closer beyond their walls. Joelle's forces had lost ground before the Legion ever since Eimarille had refused to send more soldiers and war machines to the *vasilyet* after their last telephone call.

The captain of the estate's guard found her and Karima in a ground-floor receiving room, her daughter frantic but hiding it better than Joelle thought she would. In the flickering light from a lantern that cast a limited glow, the captain saluted sharply, clutching a televox in one hand. The clarion crystals on the device were dark.

"*Vezir*, the airfield is on fire and the western city gate was damaged. The wall in that section is compromised," Captain Reva said.

Joelle stiffened, forcing back the fear those words brought. "How is the emperor's Legion so close already?"

"It wasn't their forces who attacked—it was our own."

Karima gasped, eyes wide and glittering in the gas lamp light. "How?"

"*Rionetkas*," Joelle hissed out, gripping her cane with both hands to hide how they shook. "How bad is the damage?"

"The gate is gone completely, taken out by an airship's bombing run. The outer wall no longer stands whole," Captain Reva said.

Which meant revenants would be able to gain access to Bellingham, bringing with them poison and spores, tainting the city her House had held since the Age of Separation. "Close off the inner walls. Let no one pass between the gates especially not anyone in the outer ring. Find engineers to deal with the hole in the outer wall *immediately*, and I want magicians searching for *rionetkas*. They can start with the soldiers who so damnably betrayed their duty."

Captain Reva drew in a breath. "Closing the gates will cut off our forces and—"

"My concern is the city and keeping revenants *out*," Joelle said sharply. "Relay my orders to the commanders in the field."

Captain Reva pressed her lips into a thin line and saluted. "Right away, *vezir*."

She left, but Joelle had little hope the defenses she wanted put into place would save her House.

"Mother?" Karima asked quietly, the fear in her voice a brittle thing. "If the airfield is on fire, how are we to leave?"

They'd had a plan, a way to escape if Bellingham was in danger of falling, predicated on Eimarille still being an ally. Now? Fleeing to Daijal was no longer an option, and if their troops had been compromised by *rionetkas*, the streets were just as dangerous. A city's walls were meant to keep threats out, but when the threats were within, escape was far trickier.

"We'll leave for the Imperial estate within the city. Quietly, with only a few guards to escort us," Joelle said.

"How will staying there help us?"

"Because we must assume Eimarille's people are within the city and that they will come *here*. Better to be out of reach while we figure out what to do."

Because the galling, bitter realization that they couldn't stay—not here in their ancestral estate, nor likely Bellingham—sat like poison in her heart. Joelle did not want to run—did not want to give up everything her House had lived for over the Ages—but she'd rather be alive to enact revenge at the end of the day than not.

"What about the Ashionens?"

"We'll take them with us." They'd have to knock out the prince, which was never easy, considering his tolerance to poisons and drugs, and assign a magician to watch over him. Transferring the lady was a bigger problem, considering her still-unconscious state and needing the machine to keep her that way. Joelle glanced at her handmaidens, tipping her head at the closest one. "See to what needs to be done to transfer the prisoners."

Her handmaiden sketched a shallow bow before leaving with

quick strides. Karima watched her go with a frown. "What if Vanya knows?"

Joelle levered herself up to her feet, letting Karima carry the lantern. "If he does, I find his spy network lacking. We've had the warden for weeks now."

"Do you think he'd raze Bellingham to get the warden back?"

Joelle didn't profess to know what Vanya was willing to do or lose or risk to reclaim the warden, but she wasn't going to make it easy for him. She'd lost too much of her House to him since she'd signed the betrothal contract for Nicca years ago. The opportunity to claim the Imperial throne was slipping through her fingers. All her attempts at fostering political support with other Houses and clandestine alliances with Daijal were crumbling in the face of counterattacks she had nothing left to defend against.

More and more, Joelle questioned her decision all those years ago to turn from the Dawn Star and place her loyalty with the Twilight Star.

"It doesn't matter what Vanya will do. What matters is our own efforts to secure our power," Joelle said.

"But we keep *losing*."

"Our House still stands, and we will ensure it stays standing by leaving until it is safe to return."

Karima pressed her lips together in a thin line. "My daughter shouldn't have died for scraps."

Joelle tightened her grip on her cane, silently lamenting that Artyom wasn't with her. He'd been a better heir than Karima ever had. "Obey your *vezir* and do your duty to your House."

Karima bowed her head, knuckles white where she gripped the lantern. She said nothing as she left, taking the light with her. Joelle let out a slow breath, keeping a firm grip on her temper. "Turn on the light."

"Of course," her handmaiden murmured, moving to switch on a small table lamp, providing them with some illumination—enough that Joelle could see the hideous, desiccated face pressed against the glass of the window that looked out upon the rear garden.

She opened her mouth on a warning cry, but nothing came out, voice too tangled by fear to find the words. Her horrified expression must have given enough of a warning, for her handmaiden spun around, and the shriek she let out was cut off by the revenant that crashed through the window, bloated hands reaching for her. The revenant dragged the handmaiden to the floor, mindless in its ferocity to kill the living.

A guard slammed his way into the room, eyes widening in horror as he took in the scene. "*Vezir!*"

He gathered her up in his arms, Joelle dropping her cane so it wasn't in the way. They fled the room for the darkness of the hallways, the sound of shattering glass elsewhere in the estate reaching her ears.

"How did revenants get into the estate?" Joelle asked frantically as she was carried down the hallway.

"We don't know, *vezir*," the guard grunted. "But we must get you *out*."

She curled close to his chest, bones aching from the jostling she endured as he raced through the estate to wherever the rest of the guards were preparing to stand their ground. She didn't see Karima anywhere in the rush to safety, but Joelle breathed out a sigh of relief when she caught sight of her daughter in one of the ground-floor rooms located in the center of the estate, the interior space having no windows.

Joelle tried not to feel as if she were stepping into a grave like the sort that used to rest beneath the old Imperial palace in the royal crypt.

Karima let out a cry of relief at Joelle's arrival. The guard carrying her set Joelle on her feet, and she let Karima grasp her hands and pull her close. "Mother, did you see them?"

"We'll barricade the door," one of the guards said.

Fear spiked through Joelle as she thought of how Artyom must have died in the Imperial palace. "No, we can't stay in here. We need to leave."

"We can't go out *there*," Karima protested, her voice pitched high from fear and disbelief. "They're bombing the city walls, and now we've revenants in our home!"

Joelle flexed her fingers, glancing down at her wrinkled, arthritic hands, which had an ability that hadn't shown up in her daughter or granddaughter. It'd shown up in Raiah, though Joelle bitterly wondered how much was from her bloodline as opposed to Vanya's. "The attack on the walls must be a distraction."

Not by Vanya. He'd never send revenants into a city, not after what he'd survived in Calhames. But Eimarille? The Daijal queen had commissioned death-defying machines and bade the *Klovod* create *rionetkas*. Eimarille had no respect for the living.

Joelle should have remembered that.

The click of a lock sliding into place made Joelle stiffen. She turned on shaky feet, every instinct that had kept her alive through all the games the Houses played crawling through her bones and ringing a warning louder than the sirens going off over the city. She called forth a spark of starfire, something she'd rarely cast except when making a point in the name of her House. She didn't have the strength or depth the House of Sa'Liandel carried in their bloodline, but it was still bright enough to blind if one looked directly at where it burned against her palm.

"Mother?" Karima asked, voice cracking.

The guard who had so thoughtfully carried Joelle through the halls of the estate turned to face them, expression bland, but the coldness in his gaze reminded Joelle of a fanatic. "Queen Eimarille sends her regards."

For all that Joelle could cast starfire, she'd never been trained to use it in defense of her life. It'd been like a parlor trick over the years, proof that her House, for all that it hadn't sat on the Imperial throne for centuries, still could. But it couldn't save her or Karima or the dreams she had for the future of the House of Kimathi.

Starfire had always burned bright, but the bullet that slammed its way into her gut was what snuffed it out.

Through the brutal agony that swallowed up everything, Joelle could just make out the sound of Karima screaming and the cracking sounds of a pistol going off. Everything moved like liquid around her, a blackness clawing at the edges of her vision. A metallic taste flooded her mouth, dribbling out between her lips. Her hold on consciousness, on her body, was a tenuous line that kept fraying there at the end until it broke, cut by a Blade.

Five

SOREN

Even where Soren was hidden below in that small, dark room, he could hear the warning sirens. Pushing himself to his feet, he peered up at the ceiling, seeing nothing in the darkness but more than able to imagine what was going on above.

The House of Kimathi's ancestral estate, and perhaps Bellingham itself, was under attack.

He looked at the door to his prison, the outline limned faintly with light from beyond. He knew where the lock was, knew even with the spells to dampen magic surrounding him that he could melt it off if it wasn't Lore's life keeping him imprisoned. Still, an attack on the city could mean Vanya's forces had finally reached the walls. It could mean rescue was at hand, if Vanya even knew where to look for him.

Soren couldn't count on that. Vesper had been incredibly adept at getting them out of Calhames without anyone noticing, all her lies and the veil she'd worn weaving an illusion of travel for members of the Star Order.

And here he was, trapped once again beneath a Star Temple, in a room that reminded him much of the iron coffin he'd once been welded shut inside. If Bellingham was being attacked, Soren didn't want to be trapped in a corner and killed like a wild beast. But if he tried to leave and was found out, then he risked Lore dying because of him.

Soren crossed the scant space to the door, pressing his ear to the cool metal and listening hard for any sound on the other side. He heard nothing, but that didn't mean no one wasn't out there. A guard had always been present in the basement outside his cell the few times Joelle had deigned to let him out to see Lore in that room above. Lore had never been awake during those visits, always pale and sleeping from drugs, poison a mere hairsbreadth from her veins.

He shifted, pressing his forehead against the metal, and closed his eyes. It'd been hours since his last meal, and he hadn't drunk as much of the drugged water this time, tired and disoriented from being shut away in the dark. Soren couldn't guarantee Lore would still be up there if he got out. He didn't know if Joelle kept Lore elsewhere in between those times he'd been allowed to see her. If he escaped and she wasn't there, she'd die for his efforts before he ever even found her.

Another distant, keening note from the warning sirens filtered down to his ear. Soren frowned, pulling back to stare at the door and weighing his options. Break out and hope to find Lore alive or break out and be responsible for her death. If it was truly the Legion trying to tear down Bellingham's walls, Soren knew he couldn't stay there in the dark and wait to be rescued.

Choice made, he moved his hand and reached for the aether through the thick miasma of spells wrapped around the room. If he'd been a typical magician, wand or no wand, he wouldn't be able to summon anything in the face of the precautions Joelle had set upon him. But starfire was a different beast of power altogether, and Soren clawed it forth from the aether with a determination that left him sweating.

Starfire sparked in his hand, the tiny curl of flame molten bright, forcing him to turn his head aside and blink watering eyes. His vision wasn't used to such brightness, and it hurt, but Soren worked through the pain. He kept his ear pressed to the door, straining to hear anything beyond it as he used starfire to melt the lock clean off the door, his efforts warping the handle as well. He didn't hear anyone move or call out in the basement beyond, making him think the warning sirens had drawn his guards to the surface.

He hoped so.

Soren let the starfire die away except for a spark, the light it gave off enough for him to see the knob. He balanced on one leg, raising his other to use his boot to shove at the door next to the knob. Damaged and warped as it was from the heat in that area, the door opened easily enough on hinges that didn't squeak. He tensed, but none of the spells meant to dampen magic barred his way. Soren let his starfire die and quickly moved to the side of the doorframe, nudging the door open wider with his foot.

When he spared a quick glance around the doorframe, he saw the basement beyond was empty. A lone gas lamp in a sconce burned, but most of the light he could see came from the open entryway above the stairs that led to the star temple.

Soren stepped out of the cell, knowing he had little time to make it to Lore before he was found out. He didn't know what was happening in the estate, but staying put wasn't an option any longer.

He crept toward the stairs, wishing for his pistols or even his poison short sword. But those had been abandoned in Calhames, and all he had was starfire, a type of magic he'd spent most of his life denying.

There in a star temple, in enemy territory, he no longer denied what he'd been born to.

Soren crept up the stairs, starfire curling around the fingers of both hands as he focused on the star temple above. He couldn't hear any voices, but that didn't mean the prayer space would be empty.

The warning sirens hadn't been switched off, and they rang in his ears as he crouched near the top of the entrance. Soren hid the glow of starfire in his fist as he peered over the edge of the underground entrance, getting eyes on the interior of the star temple. He saw no one in the immediate vicinity, nor could he hear any voices over the warning sirens that echoed through the air. The soldiers tasked with guarding him must have been summoned away, and the only reason

Soren could see that happening was an attack on the House of Kimathi's estate.

Which meant he had to move quickly.

Soren hurried the rest of the way up, staying crouched low as he ducked behind the benches, trying to stay hidden. Keeping an ear out for any voices or footsteps, Soren made his way across the star temple to the side room he remembered Lore being held in, hoping she was still there. He paused at the entrance to the narrow hallway leading to it, voices finally reaching his ears.

"We shouldn't be traveling when the Legion is bombing the city," a woman said frantically.

"We do as the *vezir* orders," a man grunted.

"We can't do our duty if all of us are dead!"

"Our orders are to move the prisoners to the Imperial estate for the time being. A motor carriage will be brought around shortly to transport them. Your duty will be to ensure the lady doesn't wake up."

"Do you realize how delicate the state she is in? Keeping her unconscious requires a continuous application of drugs in a precise dosage at exact intervals. Moving her will disrupt the administration of everything."

"You're an alchemist. It's your job to make sure she doesn't wake up."

Soren canted his head a little, wondering if there were more than two people in the hallway and where everyone else might be. If the star temple here was like the one Vanya's House used, then it most likely wasn't fully staffed. The guards might have been momentarily pulled for the defense of the estate, or they were still on duty some-where he couldn't see. Either way, Soren couldn't risk standing around doing nothing, not if Joelle was planning on leaving her estate to hide somewhere else.

Soren flexed his hands, pulling magic from the aether to power his starfire from a spark to a firestorm as he stepped into the entryway to the hall.

The soldier and the star priestess—the same woman who'd sat beside Lore the few times Soren had been allowed to see her—jerked around as the brightness burned away the shadows in the hallway. Soren didn't give them a chance to speak. He cast starfire at them with brutal intent, leaving no inch of them uncovered from the searing, deadly heat.

They died before their bodies even hit the ground, air burned to nothing in their lungs and bodies scorched down to their bones. Soren got rid of the starfire, but he couldn't get rid of the way the hall smelled like a crematorium. Breathing through his mouth, Soren stepped over the pair of charred husks and hurried toward the side room where Lore was kept, hoping no one else was in the room with her. The door wasn't locked, and he twisted the knob, shouldering it open.

The room was empty save for the table Lore lay on, pale and unmoving, still hooked up to that horrible machine, the tubing that held the poison clamped off. Soren didn't breathe a sigh of relief until he'd slid the needles out of her veins, the sedative dripping onto the floor and the poison useless as a shackle to them both. He leaned over Lore, pressing his fingers to the side of her neck to get her pulse— steady but slow. He didn't have his field gear to test what sort of drugs that star priestess who knew alchemy had used on Lore, and neither was he a healer. He'd have to wait until it all flushed out of her body naturally and hope she woke up from it on her own.

Hauling her unconscious form around while he himself had no weapons wouldn't help either of them. Soren chewed on his bottom lip, thinking about his options. While he could burn his way out of the estate, they'd be on the run in a city whose loyalty lay with their *vezir* and not Solaria's emperor.

Swearing softly, Soren dug around in the cupboards of the room. One bay was filled entirely with vials of chemicals the star priestess he'd killed must have been using to keep Lore under. Drawers were filled with prayer candles and matches, while the other set of cupboards held stacks of fabric. He pulled one free, shaking it out, relieved to see it was what he'd been searching for.

The robe was one of the generic ones used by acolytes in the star temple. It lacked the fitted extravagance of a star priest's robe, but that was fine by Soren. It would hide the uniform he wore, identifying him as a warden by sight. Shrugging it on, Soren did up the buttons, grimacing at how wide the sleeves were and how flowing the rest of it was. It would be easy to get it caught on something, and he'd have to be mindful of that. What he really wanted was a pistol or two, a knife, something that he could defend them with that wasn't starfire. For now, he'd have to do without.

He took a couple of vials out of the cupboard and pocketed them, hoping he'd have time later to figure out what had been used on Lore. Soren turned back to the table, easing Lore's limp body into his arms, concerned at how light she was. She looked and felt thinner than she'd been at Calhames, whatever they'd used to keep her unconscious having taken a toll on her body.

"We're getting out of here," Soren grunted, not caring that she couldn't hear him. He couldn't know if the woman he'd killed had spoken the truth—that the Legion had finally broken through Joelle's defense. He wanted to believe it, but in order to get out of Bellingham, he had to assume everyone was the enemy.

The soldier he'd killed had said a motor carriage was being brought around to transport them out of the estate. All Soren needed was a chance to commandeer it and find some way outside the city walls. The poison fields in the *vasilyet* surrounding Bellingham were a risk filled with encroaching front lines of battles and too many revenants, but they risked far more if they stayed.

Soren walked through the star temple as if he belonged, carrying Lore in his arms, head held high, gazing straight ahead. No one had appeared when he'd used starfire earlier, which was concerning in a way. He'd have thought more security would've been present, but perhaps the attack on the city was drawing everyone away.

And then he made it outside, where the motor carriage waited, and found the soldier meant to drive it on the ground with two revenants digging through his guts.

No wonder the star temple had been empty.

Soren immediately hiked Lore over his shoulder to free up one hand, keeping her in place with an arm pressed against the back of her thighs. He raised his right arm, calling forth starfire without any degree of finesse, opting for brute power over anything else as the revenants staggered away from the body toward fresh prey.

The dead caught fire, dried-up husks of bodies nothing more than kindling to Soren's starfire. They went up in flames like a lit pump at a way station. The revenants crumbled in seconds, falling to the flagstone path, nothing but ash. Soren put out the starfire, glad the breeze he'd felt for the first time in weeks was too sluggish to really lift the ash and spread it. He didn't have a gas mask for either himself or Lore, and spores were always a threat.

Grimacing, Soren hurried toward the motor carriage, the rumble of its engine almost too loud in the air between the rise and fall of the warning sirens. The star temple faced the House of Kimathi ancestral estate, and the revenants would've been like beacons as they burned to anyone who would be watching.

Which meant they had to leave.

And fast.

Soren maneuvered Lore into the back seat of the motor carriage, laying her across it and using two of the lap belts to secure her as best he could. He closed the door before turning his attention to the bloody mess of the dead soldier. Soren crouched near the body, the torn uniform useless to him, but the pistol still clutched in the dead soldier's hand was something he could use.

Soren took the pistol, the extra ammunition he found in a belt pouch, and a small serrated knife tucked in the soldier's boot. None of the weapons were the type issued by wardens, but they were better than nothing. He opened the barrel and reloaded it before snapping it back into place, the gears clicking away without issue. Soren tucked the knife into his own boot, clipped the pouch to his own belt beneath the robe he still wore, and straightened up with the pistol in hand.

He returned to the motor carriage and opened the driver's-side door—and had to immediately duck behind it as bullets peppered the air around him and the motor carriage.

Soren cursed, priming the pistol and eyeing the holes in the glass windows of the motor carriage. The angle meant he had the frame of the motor carriage between him and whoever was shooting, but Lore was in the back seat, and he couldn't see if she'd been hit or not.

"I've been told you're quite a thorn in my queen's side," a voice called out in heavily accented Solarian. "It seems we should have murdered you first."

Queen had to mean Eimarille, not Joelle, and Soren spared half a thought to wonder if the *vezir* was even alive anymore. He crouched lower, peering beneath the undercarriage at the three pairs of legs he could see walking toward him down the stone pathway. "Who are you?"

"Believers."

"More like fanatics."

They had to be Blades, which meant the attack on the estate was Eimarille's doing, even if the rest of Bellingham was the Legion's. Soren dropped flat to the ground at the next volley of gunfire, stretching his arm out beneath the motor carriage. He splayed his fingers wide, pushing starfire at the enemy in a ribbon of flame that turned into a wall of heat on the other side of the motor carriage. It forced them to quit shooting and change tactics.

Soren scrambled to his feet, pistol in hand and searching for a target. He kept the wall of starfire burning, knowing it was the best defense he had to keep Lore safe. Movement out of the corner of his eyes had him reacting without thinking, arm swinging around as he aimed and fired in seconds at the man coming around behind him past the edge of starfire.

They wore Solarian robes to blend in, but he doubted they were Solarian. With the way the man moved—speed Soren attributed to an assassin—they could only be Blades. Soren only had so many bullets to spare, and when his first two didn't find their target, he sent the wall of starfire streaking after the Blade. It moved like a snake in prairie grass, a threat the Blade couldn't escape. The starfire swallowed him up whole in a column of flame, his scream a sharp-pitched thing that rang louder than the warning sirens for a brief moment.

Soren turned his attention to the remaining two Blades, not bothering with bullets, instead leaning into his birthright. He didn't have to hide it any longer, and it was the one weapon that could save them, even if it was something a warden should never have. He manipulated the starfire into something that might resemble a wildfire there in the estate. It flared like an explosion before dying down, leaving behind charred plants, scorched stone, and a target for any other soldiers to aim at.

The Blades were nothing but ash in the aftermath, and that was all Soren cared about. His head throbbed from casting starfire, and he couldn't tell if it was because he'd overextended himself after being drugged for so long or if he just didn't have the stamina yet. But he hadn't passed out like he had after that time in the quarry, which meant he could still drive them out of the estate. Getting past the walls was going to be a different problem entirely.

Soren stared down at his hand and the starfire that curled around his fingers like a living thing. In most countries on Maricol, it was a sign of royalty. For Soren, it was nothing but a tool now, and he'd use it however he could to make it back to Vanya.

If he had to burn a city down to escape, then so be it.

Soren breathed out to center himself before letting the starfire fade away. He returned to the motor carriage, where Lore remained unconscious and unharmed from the firefight in the back seat. Getting in the driver's seat, the engine still running, Soren set his pistol beside him on the front bench and undid the brakes.

"I'm coming home, Vanya," Soren murmured as he stepped on the gas pedal and drove forward into a city still under attack, the warning sirens a constant drone in his ears.

Six

EIMARILLE

Eimarille roused from sleep by a gentle hand on her shoulder. She blinked open her eyes, squinting up at Terilyn's face in the early light of dawn seeping past the edges of the curtains in their room. "Darling?"

Terilyn stroked the back of her knuckles over Eimarille's cheeks before slipping her fingers through Eimarille's loose hair to tuck it behind her ear. "I'm sorry to wake you, but Kote called. The operator has him holding for you."

Eimarille sat up, letting the thin, soft blankets they slept in during the summer months slide off her. "I'll take it in my office."

She'd gone to bed with a headache last night, and the taste of the potion she'd drunk to get rid of it lingered on her tongue. Terilyn must have handled whichever servant had knocked on their door before sunrise regarding the call. She still wore her sleep clothes, though she'd thrown a dressing gown over them, the silky fabric belted tight around her thin waist. Terilyn held up the same sort of garment for Eimarille, deftly helping her into it and tying the belt for her.

Eimarille bent her head and pressed a soft kiss to the side of Terilyn's throat. "Bad news?"

410

"I don't know," Terilyn admitted.

A pair of slippers were on the rug beside the bed; Eimarille slid her feet into them. She waved off the servant hovering in the doorway, the woman clearly eyeing the closet and wondering about the time it would take to get Eimarille dressed. While she rarely left the royal wing of the palace without being ready for the Daijal court, some moments necessitated speed over anything else.

The royal guard standing at attention in the hallway outside her private quarters paid her no mind as she and Terilyn left her private suite and hurried toward Eimarille's office. It took some minutes to reach it, but few people were around other than a handful of servants and the posted guards to see them pass. When they reached her office, Terilyn pulled out a key from the pocket of her dressing gown and let them inside. Eimarille switched on the gas lamp lights but left the fans alone. The end of Tenth Month was trending cooler, autumn soon to arrive, and she'd needed the fans less and less lately.

"I requested us some tea. It should be here shortly," Terilyn said as Eimarille went around her wide desk and sat on the leather chair behind it. "The operator is holding on your private line."

"Thank you," Eimarille said and picked up the receiver. She pressed the cold metal to her ears and pushed the button that would bring the operator onto the line. "Put the High General through."

The operator said nothing, but a faint clicking sound filled Eimarille's ear for a moment, and then the line hummed with a solid connection. She could hear voices in the background on Kote's side of the call, but his voice came through the loudest. "Your Royal Majesty, I'm sorry to wake you. I know it's early there in New Haven."

"It's not a hardship. I know you wouldn't be calling if it wasn't important. What news have you from Ashion?"

"It's not Ashion I bring news about." Kote's tone was harsh and grim, making Eimarille sit up straighter, one hand curling into a fist over the cleared-off desk. She never left reports lying around. "It's the Gulf of Helia."

"What?"

"For the last day, the Daijal navy has been the recipient of coordinated attacks from Tovanian ship-cities. The Urovan submersibles that had joined the blockade of the Gulf of Helia haven't been spared either. They've taken hits from depth charges, and we've lost contact with more than a dozen submersibles in critical travel areas, as well as confirmation we've lost two of our flagships."

He gave the report in his usual clipped tone that had no room for emotion. Kote was very good at distilling war updates to the bare-bones information that Eimarille needed to know. That still didn't make it easy to digest the news.

She tightened her grip on the bronze handle of the receiver, half rising out of her seat. "The Tovan Isles have allied with Ashion?"

"All indications point to that."

"How did their representatives even reach the shore to initiate talks? The Tovanians wouldn't have gone to them in Cosian. It's too far from any water."

"We believe they used Solaria as an intermediary. Solaria already had an alliance with the Tovan Isles to patrol their shores, though they were too late getting into position on the east coast to stop our attack on Rixham. Ground troop movement has been in flux for the past several weeks between both countries as the front lines have been pushed back west. Ashion could have moved a battalion through Solaria to reach a western port. Oeiras seems most likely."

Terilyn stood rigid in front of Eimarille's desk, dark eyes narrowed and focused on her. The only thing that got her moving was the rapid knock on the door that heralded the arrival of their early morning tea. Eimarille waited until Terilyn had retrieved the tea tray and shut the door again before speaking again.

"What is their objective?" she asked, watching Terilyn set the tea tray on the desk but refrain from pouring in favor of coming around to stand beside her. Eimarille shifted the receiver against her ear, angling it so they could both hear.

Kote let out a harsh breath that crackled like static. "Breaking the blockade is obvious. But I've had my best strategists and tacticians run the numbers and extrapolate on current movement. We believe the Tovanians are intent on making it to shore for the Ashionens with them to storm New Haven. Which means you need to leave the capital."

Terilyn's arm wrapped around Eimarille's waist, pulling her close. Eimarille leaned against her, finding comfort in her embrace. "We don't know for certain that New Haven is their target."

"No, but it's the most likely one. The majority of our forces are in Ashion, along with every war machine coming off the production line. I will have to pull battalions from the front line and send them back west to fortify the capital, which means we'll have gaps in our forces."

"You're pulling back."

"We're coordinating a calculated defense."

It still sounded like a loss after months and months of victories. "If you do that, it will lessen our ability to keep the Ashion army and their allies from reaching Amari. That's been their target all along."

Because the Ashion capital held the starfire throne, and Caris couldn't be queen without it, the same way Eimarille couldn't.

"And if we lose Daijal's capital, that will be a blow we can't recover from," Kote said. "Regardless, it's not safe for you to remain, not with the Tovanians intent on reaching the shore."

"If I leave this city, there is only one place I will go."

"Your Royal Majesty, I must insist—"

"You can insist all you like, but I will be going nowhere else but Amari during this time. I will not give up the starfire throne to an *imposter*."

The last word nearly stuck in her throat, a knot of fury that she had to force past her teeth. She—who remembered the palace she'd been born into before the Inferno, who had crowned herself, who had carried the Rourke name all this time—*she* was meant to be queen. Eimarille would not willingly give up what she'd been born for: Queen of Maricol.

"Very well," Kote said after a strained silence. "I will meet you in Amari in two days' time to ensure your safety while in that capital. I will notify the royal guard stationed there to expect you in my absence, as I am assured you will be leaving today."

"Terilyn will handle our travel itinerary while I deal with the Daijal court. I can't have it seem that I am fleeing New Haven."

"Which you are, because you must. There is no shame in that."

Eimarille ground her teeth, glad no one but Terilyn was present to see her temper. She wasn't in the mood to wear the neutral political mask she'd cultivated since she was a child. "War is your specialty, High General. Politics is mine."

"Of course." Kote paused before continuing with "Perhaps we have the *Klovod* activate the remaining *rionetkas* in the field and issue a kill order, as we did in Bellingham. Doing so might disrupt more of the fighting and cause the Ashion army to lose some of the ground they've recently gained."

Doing so would also tip their hand in how deeply Eimarille's effort had burrowed into their enemies. But considering the new front they had to fight on, she supposed there was no time like the present for such an attack.

"If you think doing so will be favorable to our war efforts, then do so."

They had little to say after that, and Eimarille ended the call a minute later, dropping the receiver onto the telephone base with a hand that shook ever so slightly from pure, unadulterated rage. Terilyn grasped her fingers and squeezed them tightly, causing Eimarille to jerk her gaze to her lover.

"We'll leave in the late afternoon. A night flight will make you less of a target when we finally cross the central border on the way to Amari. I will see to it the airship is readied for you and Lisandro," Terilyn said softly.

"And yourself, for you will be coming with me."

Terilyn smiled, her dark-eyed gaze softening with a love that had sustained Eimarille since they were both young girls after meeting on that long-ago train ride, each of them on a road guided by a star god. "I will never leave you."

Eimarille closed the scant distance between them to kiss Terilyn fiercely, bringing up her free hand to frame the other woman's face. Terilyn's hands gripped her waist through the thin fabric of the clothes she wore, her touch everything Eimarille would always want. She twisted so her neck wasn't angled so cruelly, allowing her to deepen the kiss to something possessive.

She let her hands fall to Terilyn's thighs, fingers gripping the colorfully patterned dressing gown and dragging it upward. She only let go long enough to undo the thin fabric belt tied around the other woman's waist. Terilyn hummed against her lips, ceding to Eimarille's desire, allowing herself to be turned and pushed down onto the desk, long legs splayed wide. Eimarille dropped gracefully between her legs, hands catching the hem of Terilyn's dressing gown and sliding it up pale, scarred thighs to bunch around her waist.

Eimarille kissed her way up every mark that was revealed, dragging her tongue over the pale, puckered scars that were all her fault. Terilyn never blamed her for those moments where the Blade had fought for her, defended her, killed for her. Eimarille was meant to rule, and Terilyn was meant to see she lived to do so, but she wished it didn't have to hurt her lover so.

"I love you," Eimarille murmured against the soft skin high up on Terilyn's inner thigh. "I love you so much."

Fingers stroked through her hair, trembling in a way they never did when holding a weapon as Eimarille licked over wet heat with a sureness that came from years of doing so. "Show me how much."

Eimarille smiled as she dipped her tongue into Terilyn's slick entrance, feeling as much as hearing the soft moan that escaped her lover's mouth. She slid her left hand higher, slipping two fingers inside Terilyn where her tongue had been. Eimarille rose to her feet, letting the soft fabric of Terilyn's sleeping gown fall around her wrist as she kept her hand where it was. She pressed the heel of her palm against the sensitive clit there, grinding down against it even as she wrapped her lips around one of Terilyn's nipples through thin fabric.

Terilyn arched into her mouth and hand with a gasp, having to brace herself against the desk with one hand. The other was tangled in Eimarille's hair, gripping the long locks as if they were an anchor against the pleasure Eimarille knew how to give her. Eimarille dropped her jaw a little to bite at the tender flesh beneath her teeth, flicking her tongue against the damp fabric molded around the taut nipple. Terilyn jerked beneath her, hand sliding a little against the desk. Her chest heaved, pressing her breast more fully into Eimarille's mouth.

"Don't stop," Terilyn gasped.

Eimarille hummed and lifted her head, kissing her way up warm skin and the line of Terilyn's throat to her mouth. She kissed her deeply, tongue moving at the same languid pace of her fingers as Terilyn ground down against her hand. Her breath came in ragged gasps when Eimarille finally tore her mouth away, staring at Terilyn's flushed face and kiss-swollen lips. She reached up and hooked her fingers around the loose collar of her sleeping gown, dragging it down to reveal one breast to the cool air of the office.

"When I have the world, you'll be right beside me," Eimarille promised before bending her head to bite at that tantalizing nipple, increasing the movement of her fingers, curling them through clenching heat.

Terilyn choked on a cry, hand flying to Eimarille's shoulder as she rose on her tiptoes. Eimarille followed her with hand and mouth, relentless in the pleasure she wanted to give, heat pooling in her own body. She didn't stop until Terilyn came undone around her fingers, clenching down around them as her release spilled around Eimarille's fingers. Her quiet keen in Eimarille's ear ended in a hitched breath as Eimarille kept her hand where it was between her lover's thighs, fingers stilled, releasing the soft skin she'd bruised with her mouth.

She lifted her head, staring at the only person other than her son who had ever held her heart. Terilyn's eyes were closed, dark lashes flickering as she came down from a pleasure high. She was a mess in a way no one else would see, and Eimarille held that gift close, as she always did. Eimarille ghosted her lips over Terilyn's cheek, finally pulling her fingers free, splaying them over Terilyn's thigh.

After a moment, Terilyn cracked her eyes open, the dazed look in them pleasing to Eimarille. Terilyn straightened up, lifting a hand to touch Eimarille's hip. "I could—"

Eimarille shook her head, stealing another quick kiss. "No, darling. Later. My pleasure will keep."

Terilyn sighed softly and allowed Eimarille to put her clothes to rights. By now, the tea had grown cold, but the servants would take care of that, just as Eimarille knew they'd have taken care of preparing a bath for them back in her suite.

Eimarille twined their fingers together and lifted Terilyn's hand to her lips, kissing her scarred knuckles. "When we get to Amari, I want you to execute Caris' parents."

Terilyn smiled softly, leaning forward to press their foreheads together. "Your will is mine."

As it always had been.

Seven

NATHANIEL

Nathaniel peered through the porthole overlooking the starboard side of the ship-city *Matariki*. The pink hues of dawn crept over the horizon, breaking up the vast darkness of the sea and sky that seemed to be as one. The stars were fading, wisps of cloud high up in the sky coming into view with the sun. He leaned his forehead against the cool glass, letting it ease the throb in his head a little. He'd woken up with a headache and an uneasiness in his gut he attributed to lingering seasickness. After several weeks at sea and a handful of pitched naval battles, Nathaniel had thought he'd moved past the illness.

There'd been no activity during the night, no sirens calling crew to their battle stations. The ship-city was a massive piece of engineering that fascinated Nathaniel to no end, rising like an island out of the waters even as it churned through the waves with ease. He'd been amazed at how the frigate he'd boarded in Oeiras had seamlessly attached itself to the ship-city, its engines providing extra power to the whole of *Matariki*.

Its sister frigate on the starboard provided the same sort of support, both smaller ships able to disengage quickly from the main portion of the ship-city. The main deck that sat above the waves was where its heavy artillery and harpoon guns were located, situated in intervals that meant it could cover every side of the ship-city with defensive fire. A cargo hold at the aft had a recessed ramp that, when winched down, led to the water. The space was used to haul leviathans into the belly of the ship-city but also to dispatch *Matariki*'s contingent of submersibles.

When he'd been given a tour of the ship-city, it had felt like a warren of painted iron hallways and countless rooms. Some were used for berths to sleep in, many more were meant for the overall function of the place the crew called home. While *Matariki* could be pressed into battle—as it had been in the past, for the Tovanians had their own history of sea-faring skirmishes between ship-cities—it was meant to be a home first. Port Avi back on the Tovan Isles was where the shipbuilders resided and where their country's laws were decided, but home was found on the open seas.

"How's your stomach faring?"

Nathaniel lifted his head and dragged his gaze away from the endless stretch of water to meet *Uri'ka* Akeheni's eyes. The officer's mess was quieter than the crew's on the other side of the ship-city, but it was still crowded, more so than it typically was, he'd been told. Akeheni had graciously allowed the Ashion officers use of this mess, and people were packed elbows to elbows at the narrow tables bolted to the floor. The officers at the one Nathaniel sat at all handily shifted down the bench to provide their captain room.

"Better than my head, if a little uncomfortable. I haven't needed to use the bucket in my room for at least a week," Nathaniel said in the trade tongue with a faint smile.

A few of the Tovanian officers at the table laughed, the ink on their faces moving with their smiles. Like Akeheni, they sported tattoos on their chins, around their eyes, and across their cheeks and foreheads of delicate designs that depicted rank as much as they depicted their lineages. Nathaniel was still learning what they all meant, but he knew the ones Akeheni sported elevated her to something higher. Akeheni was captain, ambassador, and a ruler of sorts in her own right, and he was continuously deferential to her.

Nathaniel might be Caris' representative out here in open waters, but he had no power or sway over anyone. The treaty had been negotiated and signed, and that alliance granted Akeheni the right to wage war how she saw fit on the waves to bring the troops to shore. So far, that had resulted in dozens of Daijal ships and Urovan submersibles sinking into the ocean's depths before the blockade had pulled back along the Daijalan coast.

It also meant Nathaniel had come to learn what seasickness was like, the opposite of the land sickness Tovanians experienced when away from the motion of their ship-cities. It meant his breakfast was plain, unsalted rice porridge, lacking the bits of dried fish, onion, and fried bread most everyone else had before them. It wasn't what he was used to eating, but at least the ginger tea was soothing, even if it was a bit strong.

Akeheni picked up her spoon and ate a few bites of her steaming porridge before catching his eye. "You should still keep taking your potion."

Nathaniel nodded, biting back a wince at the thought of the terrible-tasting medicine the ship-city's onboard apothecary had given him. But it had quelled his nausea up until this morning, enough that his stomach no longer roiled when the ship-city sometimes did.

Of the many conversations happening around him, Nathaniel only understood the ones happening in Ashionen. Akeheni was kind enough to speak to him and some of the higher-ranked Ashion officers he traveled with in the trade tongue. Nathaniel wasn't ever offended when he was excluded from strategy meetings, left to wander sections of the brightly painted ship-city with an escort. Akeheni might have agreed to take him on, but the vivisection scars on his chest still gave her people pause.

Even though he wasn't privy to battle plans, Nathaniel still knew when maneuvers were underway. It was difficult to miss when the ship-city's sirens suddenly punctured the early morning camaraderie, calling everyone to their stations.

Akeheni stood before anyone else, pushing her bowl into the bin sunk into the wood at the end of the table. Nathaniel hastily followed her actions, along with everyone else, until the bin was filled. Someone flipped the top panel back around and bolted it into place, ensuring that whatever happened in the next few hours, none of the flatware and cutlery would be pitched around the mess, creating a hazard.

Nathaniel lost sight of Akeheni in the initial rush of sailors exiting the mess, but the sailor assigned as his escort for the day appeared by his shoulder in seconds. Matiu flashed him a tight smile before speaking to him in the trade tongue. "Let's get you back to quarters."

Nathaniel nodded jerkily and let Matiu lead the way out of the mess. The small gas lamp above the door with its spinning mirror never stopped flashing; neither did the ones scattered down the corridor Nathaniel found himself in. He kept close to the wall like Matiu, letting Tovanians who clearly had places to be rush past him. The Ashionen officers who'd been out and about were doing the same, all of them knowing this wasn't their ship, wasn't where they could fight, and the best course of action any of them could do as passengers was to stay out of the way and be prepared to evacuate if need be.

Nathaniel, like the other Ashionens, had run through emergency procedures with the Tovanian crew since the moment they boarded. He knew the way back to his berth, the colors painted on the walls changing as Matiu turned down a different direction at a cross-corridor. While some walls held murals, those never went to the floor. The solid colors and integrated stripes helped show which direction on the ship one was in when all you had to navigate by was iron walls.

They were halfway there, if Nathaniel judged the paint correctly, when a searing pain wrenched itself from one side of his chest to the other in the space behind his ribs. He fell to his knees with a strangled cry, one hand going to his chest in a useless gesture. He gripped the fabric of his shirt since he couldn't reach skin, cold creeping through his torso.

"What's wrong?" Matiu asked.

Nathaniel could only mutely shake his head, trying to breathe when his ribs didn't seem to want to expand around the clockwork metal heart that kept him on his road. It took time—long minutes, going by the increasingly frantic escalation of Matiu's prodding, who was surely late to his station in the middle of an emergency—before Nathaniel could uncurl himself from the ball he'd sunk into.

Every muscle in his torso throbbed, bones aching, the weight of his clockwork metal heart heavy in a way he rarely noticed, thanks to the alchemy and magic Ksenia and her wardens had worked into him. But there, in the middle of a Tovanian ship-city, Nathaniel felt as if his heart was an anchor that could drown him.

Something wanted him to kill—that distant thought hovered at the very depths of his mind, cradled in a tangle of magic he knew Caris had helped to unstitch one note at a time from everything that made him a person. Ksenia had tied it all back, barricaded that foreign magic from all that he was with her own skill.

But pushing it aside didn't mean it was gone, and Nathaniel could sense the gap between his own free will and that of the *Klovod*'s desire was as razor-thin as an emergency fence in the poison fields with revenants clawing for a way in.

And the *Klovod* wanted in.

Matiu helped him to his feet, keeping him upright. Nathaniel swayed there for a moment—then *lurched* when a distant, echoing boom from below shook its way through the framework of the ship-city. Matiu shoved him against the wall to brace them both. He grimaced, head tilting as the sirens abruptly changed tone to something Nathaniel couldn't parse.

"What is it?" Nathanial asked.

"Depth charges were deployed, far too close to the hull. Whoever is on duty knows better than to deploy them like that."

Nathaniel knew the ship-city had Tovanian magicians whose magic was tied closely to the sea. Their repertoire included spells that specialized in mapping the area beneath the waves surrounding a ship-city in search of underwater threats or leviathans during hunts.

It was why Tovanian ship-cities were so effective at hunting submersibles. The magicians should have been able to warn the rest of the crew on duty of an incoming attack.

But they wouldn't if any of them were *rionetkas*.

"Akeheni," Nathaniel rasped. "I need to speak with her."

Nathaniel couldn't be sure that request came from him or whatever bits of the *Klovod*'s control was—hopefully—held at bay by warden interference.

Matiu shook his head. "She'll be on the command deck and will have no time for you. I'm to get you back to your berth—"

Nathaniel reached for the Tovanian, gripping his wrist with shaking fingers as crew ran past them. The sirens rang in his ear with a warning that seemed to rise and fall in time with the click of the gears in his clockwork metal heart. "The *Klovod* is trying something. She needs to be warned."

He knew the *Klovod* wasn't a secret amongst the Tovanians. They'd accepted two treaties and a shared alliance based on the knowledge of foreign interference. While no one had solid proof, too many pieces placed Eimarille at the center of a web of machinations that had ruined so many lives. Nathaniel wouldn't let the ship-city sink because of her.

Matiu gripped him by the arm and turned them back the way they'd come. Nathaniel let himself be hauled forward on shaky legs until he could get his feet back under him, the pain in his chest settling into something like a metronome his breath kept time to.

It took time to get to the captain's deck, the location high up top with the best view of the horizon on the ship-city. Nathaniel hadn't been allowed up on his initial tour of the ship-city, but Tai got him through the checkpoints and pushed him through the open doorway being guarded by a crew member outfitted with both a pistol and a heavy blade.

The captain's deck was a space ringed by glass windows that circled the entire room, giving an undisrupted view of the horizon. Nathaniel could see for miles, nothing but waves beyond them and no other ship breaking up the brightening vista. His attention was jerked back to the chaotic scene they'd stepped into, with officers shouting at each other and into radios, people entering and leaving with a clear destination in mind. He couldn't understand anything that anyone was saying, but Matiu didn't hesitate to lead him through the fray.

Sailors manned a section of the command area that looked to be some type of analytical machine. They faced the prow of the ship-city, the lower outside decking in view, along with the heavy guns that were being cranked into position. Nathaniel only got a glimpse of what the sailors were working on before Matiu pushed him toward the area behind them, where officers huddled around a navigation table filled with gridded maps. Amidst the group of Tovanians listening to Akeheni's orders, one person stood out.

A warden.

Matiu said something in Tovanian that had everyone's head jerking around, attention landing on Nathaniel. He contained a flinch, lifting his chin in the face of their judging eyes as he slipped into the trade tongue. "*Uri'ka* Akeheni, I think I know what's happening."

Akeheni half turned to look at him, lips pressed into a grim line. "I can't trust your words."

She didn't need to say why. "I know, but you need to. Just this once."

Caris had sent him here to keep him out of the *Klovod*'s reach, and still he could not escape that repudiated warden's grip. Akeheni knew that; it had been part of the terms of the treaty-signed alliance. But if he was a risk, Nathaniel would be the first to take one of the lifeboats and set himself adrift if it would keep the ship-city on course.

"Ksenia unmade what the *Klovod* did," the warden said, her voice cutting through the chaotic noise around them.

"Unmade doesn't mean gone." Nathaniel tapped a finger against his chest, never looking away from Akeheni's eyes. "I can feel him reaching. I don't think I was the only one out here he found."

"You said you woke with a headache this morning," Akeheni said.

"Yes." He swallowed thickly, well aware of what it meant. "But I am in control of myself."

"We don't know that for sure."

"I know, but in this moment, you must believe me. Please."

Akeheni looked over her shoulder at the warden. "What say you, Binh?"

"Ksenia is our master alchemist, and few in any country can match her skill. Her magic and alchemy would hold, especially this far from the *Klovod*'s reach," Binh replied after a brief pause. "If Nathaniel can sense the *Klovod* in his mind, you should believe him."

"If I was truly a *rionetka* again, I would not be able to *tell* you that I could sense him," Nathaniel said.

He remembered the agonizing horror of being a prisoner in his own body, the way his hands moved without his permission, the words that were spoken that were not his. But everything he did and said here on the ship-city was of his own volition. The *Klovod* might have left fingerprints on his mind and rebuilt his heart, but the control he'd experienced before was no longer there.

Binh frowned thoughtfully. "He is right. My understanding of *rionetka* control is they act like the person they are, and you would not know the difference."

Akeheni didn't let what she thought filter onto her face when she looked back at Nathaniel. "Tell me what you think the *Klovod*'s motive is here?"

"Where are we under attack?" Nathaniel asked.

Akeheni bared her teeth. "Not from without. Our magicians see no Urovan submersibles within range."

"Matiu said the depth charges went off too close to the hull."

"We aren't sinking."

The derisiveness in her tone made Nathaniel want to laugh, but he choked it back. "Your sailors know their duties. *Rionetkas* will take that knowledge and twist it to do harm, and they will have no choice."

"We have precautions against *rionetkas*. Physical checks and spell detectors."

"They aren't infallible. The *Klovod* has ways of infiltrating the governments of our allies."

"We are aware." Akeheni rested a hand on the navigation table, the map beneath her palm crumpling. "If we have *rionetkas* aboard, then they are the ones responsible for releasing the depth charges. Clearing my sailors will take time, which we have precious little of since we are scheduled to meet up with the *Ailani* for an attack on Daijal's ironsides along the coast. We need—"

Akeheni's next words left on a jagged cry as her first mate unexpectedly turned and slammed their knife into her left shoulder. It would have been her heart if Akeheni had been even a shade slower in twisting her body. She jerked back, sliding off the knife as a cry of rage rose from those assembled around her. The noise was disrupted by the crack of a single gunshot from Binh's pistol.

The first mate—the *rionetka*, Nathaniel's numb thoughts supplied —went limp and fell to the floor, a gaping hole on the side of their skull where the bullet had exited. In such tight quarters, it was a miracle the bullet hadn't hit anyone else, though Nathaniel had no clue where it had ended up. All of that musing felt like background noise as he was pushed back by Matiu, Akeheni disappearing beneath a crowd of her people.

Nathaniel couldn't understand anything being said, the Tovanian washing over him in an unceasing wave of sound. He had no weapons, but considering what he'd been and what had occurred just now, Nathaniel made sure to keep his hands in sight and went where Matiu prodded.

He watched as Akeheni was helped by her sailors, saw the worried, sometimes wary glances the crew gave each other. The *rionetka* might have missed the mark in murdering Akeheni, but the seeds of distrust were there in the aftermath.

"You need to clear your ship-city through whatever measures you have for rooting out *rionetkas*," Nathaniel said quietly.

Matiu looked back at him, dark-eyed gaze steady and without judgment. "Can you sense any of them in some way?"

Nathaniel shook his head. "I can sense the *Klovod*'s intent in the back of my mind, but not *rionetkas*. Even when I was under his control, I never knew who the others were."

Caris was the only person he knew of who could differentiate between a *rionetka* and a person who still had their own free will, and that was only because of her ability to hear clarion crystals sing.

Matiu nodded, his grip tightening on Nathaniel's arm. "Let's get you back to your berth."

Nathaniel swallowed and dipped his head in a nod. At least they weren't taking him to the brig.

Eight

NATHANIEL

Binh came for him hours later, when the sun he couldn't see would be high in the sky, and she didn't come alone. Farren smiled at Nathaniel from the corridor where the star god stood behind the warden, dressed like a sailor, their Leviathan tattoo hidden beneath a linen shirt. Binh did not seem to notice, or perhaps she didn't care, who had joined her wanderings. Wardens were nameless and starless, or so all the teachings went.

He wondered how true that would be after this war.

"Akeheni wants to see you. Bring your gear," Binh said.

Nathaniel nodded jerkily. If they wanted him to bring what he'd boarded with, perhaps they weren't going to do him harm. Treaty or no treaty, having a *rionetka* attempt to murder an *Uri'ka* did cast doubt on his situation. He could understand why the Tovanians might not want him on their ship-city any longer. Their reasoning for sending Binh made sense as well. Wardens were best suited to this kind of threat. They handled the walking dead, after all.

Binh waited patiently while Nathaniel hauled out his small travel trunk from beneath the bolted-down bed and stuffed only the necessities into the rucksack stored within. The rest could be tossed overboard for all he cared. Shrugging the straps over his shoulders, Nathaniel followed Binh and Farren out of the room.

They traversed the ship-city to a higher level but not quite as high as the captain's deck. Officer's quarters, Nathaniel realized once they made it to the central area of the ship-city, judging by the paint on the walls. The sailors on guard duty in the corridors they walked down practically bristled with weapons. Farren went seemingly unrecognized, even if Nathaniel was hyperaware of the star god following at his heels. He bit his tongue against the questions he wanted to ask, knowing he had no right to speak them in this place that was, for all intents and purposes, a foreign country.

Binh eventually came to a stop at the end of a corridor, the iron door there guarded by a tall, broad sailor who looked strong enough to lift a Zip gun without assistance. Not that one would fit in the corridor. Binh spoke in rapid-fire Tovanian, and after a moment, the sailor turned to push open the door just enough to speak through the crack. After a moment, he shoved it wider and gestured for them to enter.

Nathaniel stepped into a brightly decorated room, the port windows providing enough illumination that the gas lamp lights were cold. Everything was securely bolted down or locked into place, but the space was decorated more in the way of a home than an office. He could see an open door to a bedroom beyond the receiving suite, a place Akeheni should be but wasn't. Instead, the *Uri'ka* was ensconced on the small sofa, shirt off, her breast band on clear display as the magician finished tracing the red and swollen—but miraculously closed—knife wound with her clarion crystal–tipped wand.

Nathaniel hastily jerked his gaze away, cheeks heating. "Apologies. I didn't realize—"

Akeheni cut him off with a raspy bark of laughter. "We don't stand on manners like that. None of us go in the water clothed when we swim. Skin isn't anything to be ashamed about. If it was, I wouldn't have summoned you."

Nathaniel politely kept his gaze averted. "I am at your disposal."

He heard a rustle of clothing, a murmur of Tovanian he couldn't understand, and then Binh was nudging him toward the chair. Nathaniel slid his rucksack off his shoulders and placed it on the floor before sitting, sparing a swift glance at Akeheni. She'd leaned back on a stash of pillows, grimacing from pain. She waved off whatever the magician said next, pinning Nathaniel with her fierce attention for a moment. Then her gaze slid away, focusing on the star god standing at his back. "My guiding star."

"If you could refrain from getting stabbed while I ferry the Ashionen back to land, that would be wonderful," Farren said lightly, their words causing Nathaniel to jerk in surprise. "Your people need you for the upcoming battle."

Akeheni snorted. "It was not my intention to be stabbed in the first place. How goes hunting the *rionetkas*?"

"Three-quarters of the crew have been checked, and all of the Ashionen soldiers as well. We found two of your people so far who have been turned into *rionetkas*, excluding the one killed in the depth charges hold," Binh answered.

Akeheni's gaze became hooded, the look in her eyes a mix of anger and grief. "Can you wardens save them how you did with Nathaniel?"

"I can't offer that."

"It's your people who created the threat."

"One traitorous warden shouldn't paint the whole as bad," Nathaniel cut in. "And what Ksenia did to me wasn't a fix. Not how you wish it to be."

He could admit that now, so long after the damage was done. No one would give him back the heart he'd been born with, and it was magic and alchemy that let him still walk his road these days, but he knew there was no guarantee it would last. That was a false hope he would give no one.

Akeheni sighed tiredly, closing her eyes for a brief moment before opening them again. "My people believe you brought the threat with you. I need them to focus on the threat in our waters and not a perceived one within the ranks. We'll be hitting the Daijal ships of the line tomorrow, and a sister ship-city has already warned of Urovan submersibles in our area. I need you off my ship-city before then. For your safety as much as my people's."

"Of course."

"Binh will accompany you and escort you through the poison fields in Solaria." At Nathaniel's surprised look, she quirked him a tight smile. "Did you think we'd abandon you in Daijal?"

"Ah, no," he said with as much polite blandness as he could muster.

"The ship-cities not tasked with breaking the blockade and getting Ashionen troops to the shores for the fight at New Haven are patrolling Solaria's coast. I will take you to one, and they will bring you to shore. My sister wishes you back in Ashion to keep your queen from fretting," Farren said.

Akeheni levered herself up off the pillows, leaning forward a little, her wound clearly paining her despite the healing done to it. "Our ship-city wasn't the only one who suffered an attack from *rionetkas*, and the same threat is happening on the continent. The Daijal army has split, sending half its force back to New Haven via steam trains, according to the allied command. Eimarille activated the *rionetkas* because of that threat. You were the only one who did not succumb to the assassination order."

Nathaniel's mouth went desert dry at the implications. He craned his head around, unable to help meeting Farren's gaze, the star god's attention like a heavy weight. "Did any target Caris?"

Farren shrugged with one shoulder. "Aaralyn is not worried."

Akeheni snorted at that, muttering something in Tovanian that made Farren laugh. The Eclipse Star stepped around Nathaniel's armchair to approach her, leaning down to grasp her chin in their hand and bend their head. Farren pressed their nose to hers, foreheads touching, and Akeheni closed her eyes, shoulders slumping.

"The waves will guide you," Farren promised when they straightened.

It felt like a blessing to Nathaniel, a promise, and Akeheni seemed at peace with it. Farren turned to face him, gesturing with one slim hand for him to rise. Nathaniel hastily stood, grabbing his rucksack and slinging it over one shoulder. Farren headed for the door, Binh at their heels, and Nathaniel would have followed, but he hesitated, feet rooted where he stood. He looked back at Akeheni, seeing the *Uri'ka* looking back.

"Thank you," he said. "For your people's support. For the risks you're taking. For all of us."

He meant the words on behalf of himself as much as for Caris because he knew the war would be going differently without this second front the Tovanians were opening up.

"Maricol is meant for all of us, not ruled over by one person. We all owe it to each other to fight," Akeheni said.

Nathaniel turned and bowed deeply to her, giving her respect in the way of an Ashionen. Then he left, following a star god and a warden down to the belly of the ship-city. Sound echoed oddly through layers of iron as they descended. No one questioned their presence, and those sailors they passed sketched absent nods in Farren's direction, as if the star god was just another crew member rather than their nation's guiding star.

Eventually, they ended up in the hold where the submersibles were kept in anchor bays, one already pulled out and ready to launch on the wide ramp that led to the sea. The deep thrum of the engines was loud, the heavy hit of the waves against the iron hull a counterpoint to it. The ship-city's massive propellers churned the sea in the wake stretching behind it.

Sailors had readied the submersible for launch at the top of the ramp, a sleek vessel that didn't look like anything Nathaniel had ever seen before. He desperately wished he could take a look at the engine, but he knew better than to ask. They were under a time crunch, so when Farren gestured for him to climb up to the top of the submersible to the open hatch there, he did so hurriedly.

Binh had gone down first, the space inside almost claustrophobic. If Nathaniel's heart wasn't made of clockwork gears, he rather thought it would be beating faster. Farren followed after him, pausing long enough to haul the hatch closed behind them and twist the wheel to lock and seal it. Then they slid down the ladder with a casual ease that spoke of doing it so many times it was second nature.

"We'll dive after the launch, and it'll be at least a day before we surface. My children packed supplies, and there's a berth you can share in the rear for rest," Farren said as they moved forward toward the pilot's seat in front of the port window there.

"You take the berth. I'll sleep near the controls that launch the torpedoes," Binh said to Nathaniel.

Farren laughed, bright and amused as they flipped some toggles on the controls, one hand settled on a lever. "If you are worried about my brother's children finding us in the deep, they will not."

Binh ignored their words and got settled on the secondary seat behind the pilot's and angled off to the side. Nathaniel stood in the space behind both seats, wrapping both hands around the handle welded into the top of her seat for support. He braced himself as Farren signaled a sailor in the hold through the port window and got an answering gesture back. A grating noise echoed through the hull, and the submersible jerked forward on the skids that led to the ramp. His stomach lurched as the submersible tipped over the edge and down the ramp, the water rushing up to meet them. They hit it with a splash that sent a wave over the port window, blinding them, but only for a moment.

The submersible sank beneath the waves, its engine humming to life as Farren maneuvered the levers in their hands to guide them into the deep.

Nine

Getting out of Bellingham and through the poison fields surrounding the House of Kimathi's *vasilyet* was a nightmare Soren never wanted to experience again. The only reason he and Lore made it out alive was due to starfire. It took a day to sneak out of Bellingham, the city falling after Joelle's death—but to whose forces, he still couldn't say for sure. Nor could he trust anyone in a uniform in a place that still held loyalty to a newly dead House.

Once he got them past the damaged city walls, Soren headed south, burning the expanse of the Southern Plains they traveled through as if he were the beating heart of a grass fire whenever revenants showed up. He had to be careful not to melt the tires off the motor carriage, one hand extended out the window at all times during the drive, starfire ever ready at his fingertips to attack.

He lacked his usual field gear, only having a very limited amount of bullets for the stolen pistol and enough stolen food and water to last just a few days. He had to stop in intervals to try to get Lore to take some water now that she was no longer hooked up to a drip, but she still hadn't woken. It wasn't anything he could fix, there in the back roads, so Soren merely kept driving.

A terrible headache clawed at his concentration over the next two days as he intermittently burned through hordes of revenants before the walking dead could reach them. Even without his maps, Soren remembered some of the back roads through the *vasilyet* and where a handful of way stations should be alongside trade roads. He drove until he found one before the needle on the fuel gauge dipped too low. The way station had been abandoned, the tanks almost empty, but enough was left for him to refuel, even if it wasn't much.

On the fourth day of their escape, with the dark sky beginning to lighten in the east, the motor carriage finally ran out of fuel however many miles south of Bellingham. Soren set the brakes and closed his eyes against the throbbing of his skull. The nausea roiling in his stomach came from overuse of magic he'd never had to wield so desperately before as much as it came from the situation they'd found themselves in.

He let the flicker of starfire at his fingertips die down and opened his eyes, squinting at the flat plains that stretched before them. He saw no shelter, didn't have his maps to figure out where exactly they were in the poison fields, and they hadn't yet reached any squadrons of the Legion he could trust. Soren must have driven past their position, knowing they'd never be able to hold a solid line against the walking dead and Daijal war machines.

The throbbing in his head resonated, getting worse, before Soren realized it wasn't the ache itself but the thrum of an approaching airship's engine. He went still, knowing how badly they stood out against the plains, with no tarp for cover or camouflage. Swearing, Soren undid the lap belt and shoved open the door, getting out.

With nothing to impede his vision, Soren could see the airship coming in from the east, still high enough in the sky that he doubted starfire would make a difference. He still dragged starfire from the aether despite the stabbing pain that erupted behind one eye.

The airship's forward gun turrets never fired as it descended. The closer it came to the ground, the easier it was for Soren to make out the hull's colors and its build, the shape of it looking nothing like an

E'ridian airship. The Legion's crest was painted in gold on the thin metal that shielded the underside of the balloon, glinting in the light of the rising sun. He could make out shadowed figures gathered along the railing, several raising their arms in a greeting he was hesitant to return. A rope ladder was thrown over the side, the length of it unfurling to dangle in the air, and then another.

Soren stayed where he was as the airship skimmed over the ground, the bulk of it blocking out the sun. Its engines were loud in the early morning quiet as it brought its broadside parallel to his position, the gun turrets aiming at the horizon and not his position.

"Hail!" a legionnaire called out before they and others pitched themselves over the railing to climb down the rope ladders.

Soren wanted to believe the legionnaires were on Solaria's side and not Joelle's or Daijal's, but he'd been through too much to take anything at face value. He kept his arm extended, calling forth starfire despite the way it made his head hurt worse. The legionnaire coming his way wore the uniform of a captain, and she raised her own arms in a placating manner, pistol left holstered on her hip.

"Prince Alasandair?" the captain asked.

Soren spread his fingers wider, meeting her gaze through the molten glare of starfire. "Who's asking?"

She drew up sharply, offering him a crisp salute that didn't budge the *effiyeh* on her head one bit. "Captain Elise, at your service. Scouts in the poison fields working with wardens caught sight of your passage and sent word to command. We were dispatched to escort you to Oeiras."

"Not Calhames?"

"The House of Sa'Liandel resides in Oeiras."

None of the legionnaires on the ground made any move to approach him, keeping their hands loose at their sides as their captain handled him as if he were a spooked animal. Soren really couldn't blame her. "What month is it?"

"Tenth Month, in the Fortieth Week of the calendar. It'll be Eleventh Month tomorrow."

Soren wanted to close his eyes but didn't. He'd lost so many weeks as Joelle's prisoner, and he couldn't begin to know what damage Lore had taken in her forced unconsciousness as well. It was fear for her health that finally got Soren to lower his arm and snuff out the starfire, making a fist to hide how his hand shook from weariness. He licked his lips, meeting Elise's gaze. "I have Lady Lore in the motor carriage, and she is in desperate need of care."

"We have a magician on board who is a healer. We'll take care of her and you."

Soren nodded slowly, finally stepping away from the motor carriage and letting the legionnaires swarm forward. Elise gestured for him to join her, knowing better than to reach for him. Soren followed where she led, glancing over his shoulder from time to time to see how Lore was being cared for. He followed Elise to the closest rope ladder, squinting up its length at the railing high above them. Gritting his teeth, Soren reached for a rung as Elise held it still, and he climbed up to the safety of the airship.

He was met on board by more crew and a magician who had her wand out and at the ready, tapping the tip against her thigh. She wore the uniform of a legionnaire and approached him the moment his feet hit the deck.

"Prince Alasandair, if you would follow me belowdecks, I have quarters ready for you," the magician said politely.

"I go by Soren, and I'd rather you tend to Lady Lore first. She's in desperate need of a healing," Soren replied.

The magician dipped her head and gestured at his chest. "Apologies, but I must confirm you aren't a *rionetka*."

Soren didn't mind peeling open his shirt, his vest long since lost to him. He desperately needed clean clothes and a bath, but despite the grime, his skin carried no vivisection scars, to the lieutenant's clear relief. "I was a bargaining chip, and I couldn't be that if I was dead or a *rionetka*."

"Can you tell me what happened? Any injuries I should be aware of?"

It was a lot like reporting back to the magicians on the Warden's Island when he came back from the poison fields over the years, only he kept it very brief, pertinent to their escape. Soren only disclosed what was needed for Lore's health, still not trusting the crew and Legion around him to share the pertinent details that Vanya would need to hear.

The legionnaires hauled Lore over the railing some minutes later in a medical carry, secured over one man's back. The magician took that as her cue and focused her attentions on Lore rather than Soren.

Elise stayed beside him, half her attention on her aeronauts, the rest on him. An aeronaut jogged up to them and passed over a canteen to Elise, who handed it to Soren. "You should know we took Bellingham on the emperor's orders. The House of Kimathi was found dead in their estate. Was it your doing?"

Soren took the canteen and carefully sipped the water, tasting nothing out of the ordinary in it. Then again, if it was poisoned, he'd find out soon enough, but he wanted to believe he was finally safe. "No. There were Blades on the premises. I burned them in order to escape."

"Ah." Elise cleared her throat, gaze flicking up and down his body. "Let's get you settled below."

Soren nodded tiredly, watching the cluster of people handling Lore's transport toward the stairs that would lead belowdecks. He was tired, filthy, and hungry, and he knew everything he'd gone through would catch up to him at some point, but for now, he really just wanted to lie down on a bed and *sleep*.

So that's what he did.

The flight to Oeiras from where they'd picked him up in the poison fields took hours. Soren slept through the flight and only roused when someone knocked on the door to his temporary room and called out that they were anchoring. Soren rolled to his side and sat up on the bunk, hunching carefully so he wouldn't hit his head on the underside of the one above. He knew better than to walk around during a descent and landing, so stayed put until the hard judder of the hull meeting the anchor berth vibrated through the airship for a moment.

Part of Soren didn't believe he'd made it until he stood on the decking, staring at the intact city walls surrounding Oeiras, the breeze bringing with it the familiar scent of the jungle that grew to the west of them.

The pier was crowded below with *praetoria* legionnaires and officials, but Soren didn't see Vanya anywhere. He tried not to be disappointed, even if he couldn't quite stop the worry that settled in his heart.

Elise was the first down the gangplank, with Soren right behind her and the magician following after. The magician oversaw Lore's transport down on a stretcher, the legionnaires carrying her going slow so as to not jostle her. Soren made it to the pier and was a little surprised when the *praetoria* legionnaire lieutenant saluted him in greeting.

"Welcome home," the lieutenant said. "We've orders from the *valide* to take you to the Imperial estate."

Taisiya, not Vanya, which made Soren wonder where the other man was, if he was all right. Questions tumbled through Soren's mind, but he wouldn't get any answers until he got inside Oeiras.

He let the *praetoria* legionnaires hustle them down the pier, clearing the way toward the city gates. The lieutenant bypassed the customs and security line, everyone standing aside to let them pass. Motor carriages with the House of Sa'Liandel crest on the doors waited with their engines running on the street beyond. They were loaded inside with care before being driven away.

Soren slumped in the back seat, head tipped back, tired down to his bones, but he kept his eyes open on the drive to the Imperial estate. The lieutenant didn't speak to him, riding in the front seat with the driver. They passed through several of the inner-city walls before eventually turning down a familiar set of streets.

Soren shoved himself straighter, watching as the Imperial estate came into view behind its high walls and well-guarded gates. A sentinel-class automaton was posted at the gate as well, its Zip gun held at the ready to defend. The motor carriage didn't stop, the gate already open for them, and it went up the drive. The front entrance to the grand estate came into view, but all Soren saw were the two people standing just outside the open door, waiting for him.

Taisiya and Raiah.

He was moving before the motor carriage even braked to a halt, pitching himself out of the back seat with a lack of grace he didn't care about. Raiah's shriek of his name was the best sound he'd heard in weeks, and Soren had to force his chest to expand as he lurched forward to meet her halfway.

"*Soren!*" Raiah cried out.

Taisiya didn't bother trying to hold Raiah back, the little girl racing toward him with tears in her eyes and braids flying behind her. Soren swept her up into his arms and held her as tight as he dared as she sobbed and clutched at him with frantic hands.

"Raiah," Soren managed to get out, her name ragged on his tongue. "Raiah, I'm here."

"You're not allowed to go away *ever again!*" she sobbed. "You have to *stay.*"

Soren watched as Taisiya stepped down from the porch with the aid of her cane and a *praetoria* legionnaire's assistance. Soren kissed the side of Raiah's head, hiking her up higher in his arms as he met Taisiya's gaze. "Vanya?"

"Alive," Taisiya promised. "But not here. The southern front needed him."

Soren tried to steady the heavy pounding of his heart. "Rixham?"

"Yes. He had to split the Legion between the war in Ashion and the threat of the revenant horde. Vanya's capabilities with starfire far exceed everyone else's in the other Houses. He asked for volunteers, but only some heeded the call."

"Did anyone from the House of Aetos go with him?"

Taisiya shook her head. "No. One of our spies uncovered their ties to the House of Kimathi. Because of their betrayal, the House of Aetos has been branded a traitor and is being dealt with."

All Soren felt was relief at her words—relief that Vanya wouldn't be fighting with traitors at his back. "Good."

"How do you fare?"

"Tired, but well enough. They kept Lore sedated with the threat of poison being injected into her veins to keep me compliant. If I had tried anything, they would have killed her."

"But you escaped."

"Yes, because Blades released revenants into the House of Kimathi's estate, and I had a window of time to free Lore amidst the confusion of the attack. Joelle is dead, most likely on Eimarille's orders. I wasn't certain who was attacking Bellingham at the time, which is why I went into the poison fields."

Behind them, the Legion magician was overseeing the transfer of Lore from the motor carriage to the estate. They bowed deeply to Taisiya and Raiah, who still hadn't let go of Soren, keeping her face tucked close to his neck and shoulder. She'd stopped crying, but her sniffles were loud in his ears.

"The lady is in need of deep healing," the magician said.

"Bring her inside. Our House's personal magician will see to her," Taisiya said.

The magician nodded and corralled her charge and their escort inside. Soren watched them go, aware of everything that he needed to do now that he'd made it home. "Caris needs to be told we are alive, but I don't know what's going on in Ashion with the war."

"The front in their eastern provinces has been pushed west since Daijal was forced to split their forces."

Soren dragged his gaze back to Taisiya. "Oh?"

She reached out to pat his arm before turning around. "Come. There is much to discuss. The merchant can help fill you in."

Soren frowned as he matched his pace to hers on the way inside. "Merchant?"

"The one who was a *rionetka* and speaks with his queen's voice."

He nearly missed a step. "Nathaniel? What is he doing here?"

"As I said, we have much to discuss."

Clearly, if Nathaniel was in Oeiras and not Ashion.

Raiah finally lifted her head, wiping at her damp cheeks with the back of her hand. "You need a bath."

Soren barked out a laugh, knowing everyone on the flight to Oeiras and the drive through the city had probably been too polite to mention that. "Yes, I really do."

Taisiya took charge once they were inside the Imperial estate, overseeing Lore being transferred in the care of the House of Sa'Liandel's personal healer. Soren had an irrational urge to keep her in sight, aware the anxiety stemmed from his own time being imprisoned and both their lives hinging on his compliance.

Taisiya brought him into the private royal wing of the Imperial estate, getting them settled in a receiving room that overlooked the private inner courtyard. Servants had set out a spread of light finger foods on the low table, as well as a pitcher of sweet red wine and another of cool water. Soren settled Raiah on the cushion beside him, wrapping his arm around her so she could lean against him.

"Eat slow," Taisiya said. "I had the cooks go light on the spices."

Soren nodded, eyeing the food on offer. He knew he'd lost weight while in Joelle's custody, but he'd eaten what they gave him because that had been his only choice. His appetite had shrunk, and he knew better than to gorge. He started with a plain flatbread and tore off a piece to swipe it through the mild mashed beans mixed with oil in a shallow bowl.

Taisiya poured drinks for them, watering down his wine as a courtesy. Soren didn't decline the drink and ate slowly, easing the hunger gnawing at him. He was tired, and he wanted desperately to speak to Vanya, but he knew he needed to hear what Taisiya had to say first.

"I've summoned the merchant," Taisiya said.

"And what of Vanya?" Soren asked.

"When we are finished here and you are seen to after Lady Lore, we can attempt to contact him. Direct communication is a little difficult when he is fighting."

"Then don't bother. He doesn't need to be distracted. Besides, I'll be going to him."

Taisiya studied Soren across the table with an unblinking gaze. "As a warden?"

Soren never looked away. "He needs my starfire."

Using starfire in defense of Solaria would cement his removal from the wardens. He could not be a warden and keep his people safe from the demands of countries sure to come after the war was over. The Poison Accords had been broken in many ways, and Soren would not break it further. Some part of him would always grieve for that road he'd walked and no longer could, but there was another one ahead of him that led to Vanya.

It would be enough.

"Very well. I'll have an airship prepared to launch tomorrow."

"Taisiya—"

"You need rest," she cut in. "Vanya will hold the line until you arrive."

Soren could only accept the *valide*'s judgment and finished what he could of the food provided. He'd just scooted his plate away from the edge of the table when the door to the receiving room was pushed open and a servant stepped inside, bowing to them.

"Mr. Clementine is here to see you," the servant said.

Taisiya discreetly wiped her fingers on the linen napkin before setting it aside. "He may enter."

Soren watched as Nathaniel stepped inside, a pair of *praetoria* legionnaires at his back. An escort that was little more than guards, not that he didn't blame their caution. Soren hadn't interacted much with Nathaniel back in Cosian—the Ashion commanders had been adamant about keeping the other man in the dark—but he knew enough the merchant shouldn't be here.

The relief in Nathaniel's face was plain for anyone to see as he came out of his bow, speaking in the trade tongue. "*Valide*. Prince Alasandair. I'd heard you and Lady Lore had been rescued."

"Lore is being cared for by the House of Sa'Liandel's healer. Joelle kept her unconscious during our time in Bellingham. I don't know what state she'll be in after she wakes up," Soren cautioned.

"But she's alive." Nathaniel sighed deeply, shoulders loosening. "The Duchess Auclair will be happy to hear that."

"I'm sure they'll want Lore brought back to Ashion. I'll have my secretary handle the logistics of transportation via airship. We can't trust the steam trains at the moment, not with the revenant horde pushing north. Mr. Clementine and Lady Lore will return to Ashion tomorrow if she is cleared to fly," Taisiya said.

"What are you doing here in Oeiras?" Soren asked Nathaniel.

"I was sent here some weeks ago as Caris' proxy to gain an alliance with the Tovan Isles. I sailed with them as a way to keep me out of the *Klovod*'s reach." Nathaniel shook his head, his voice becoming tired. "Even the sea wasn't far enough. *Rionetkas* sneaked on board despite all the precautions to keep them out. The Tovanians put me on a submersible and sent me back here. They kept course to break the blockade in the Gulf of Helia and get our soldiers to shore to lay siege to New Haven."

"What made your people change their mind on that?"

"The need to get Caris to Amari. After Daijal attacked Solaria and E'ridia, there were strategy decisions made I wasn't privy to until I was sent to Oeiras. We're attacking New Haven to force Daijal to pull back their forces on the eastern front."

War was such an ugly thing, and there would be no peace until someone claimed the starfire throne. For all that Solaria was home, Soren could not ignore the ruin ripping Ashion and Daijal apart. The only way to stop it all—in a way that would keep every country separate and intact—was to put Caris on the starfire throne and give her a crown Soren had no desire to ever wear. At some point, he would need to return to Ashion, but he wouldn't do so without seeing Vanya first.

They were interrupted yet again by another knock on the door. This time, it was Intira, the royal healer magician, who came inside, her attention landing unerringly on Soren. "Lady Lore is resting comfortably and should hopefully be roused from her stupor in an hour or so. I'll be better able to assess her then. I understand I have a second patient?"

Soren rubbed his hand up and down Raiah's back and kissed the top of her head before getting to his feet. "Yes."

"Perhaps the exam should take place in the bathhouse," Taisiya said tactfully.

"Please," Soren said, not above begging for time spent in hot water.

Taisiya waved him off. "I'll speak with Mr. Clementine while you are seen to."

Soren left everything in Taisiya's capable hands and followed the healer out of the room.

Ten

SOREN

Taisiya kept her word and had an airship ready to depart south in the morning. His departure wasn't approved by everyone.

"But you *promised* you wouldn't leave!" Raiah wailed during breakfast when Soren broached the subject.

Soren pulled her into his lap to cuddle her, his breakfast forgotten for the moment as he tried to reason with a five-year-old. "Vanya needs me, and so I must go to him. You will be safe here, and we'll return once the threat is handled."

Raiah scowled and pressed her face into his chest. Soren had woken up that morning in Vanya's bed with Raiah curled close to find a brand-new warden's uniform laid out for him on the settee. He'd dressed in the adjacent washroom with quiet regret, for he knew his time wearing the uniform was limited. Then he'd escorted Raiah to the inner courtyard, knowing she wouldn't be happy about his plans. He'd been right.

"No," Raiah growled. "You have to stay."

Soren smoothed his hand over her neatly braided hair and shared a commiserating look with Taisiya. Raiah had cleaved herself to his side since his arrival yesterday, doing her best impression of a barnacle. It tore at him to have to leave her again, but even though the healer would prefer he took some time to rest, Soren knew he was needed.

"Your *valide* will need lots of help while I'm with your papa. Do you think you can help her?" Soren asked, trying a different tact to stave off more tears.

Raiah lifted her head and frowned up at him, eyes a little watery, but she wasn't falling into full-blown sobs yet. "Of course."

She spoke with the same sort of haughtiness Soren had heard from Vanya over the years, and he couldn't help smiling. "Good. I'm glad. Now, let's finish eating, okay? Everything will be all right."

Normally, Soren wouldn't promise such a thing, but Raiah was still so young that he hoped she could be distracted in the coming days from the realities of war and all the machinations of the Houses. She wasn't yet at the age where she officially needed to start learning how to politick. Soren knew Vanya was adamant at giving her a childhood, despite everything that had occurred so far.

They finished breakfast without rushing, Soren eking out just a little more time with Raiah. After the servants had cleared the low table of their dishes, a *praetoria* legionnaire approached, holding a bundle in his arms. He bowed his head and only came closer when Taisiya nodded at him.

"What you requested, *valide*," the man murmured.

He set the bundle on the table and carefully unrolled it. Soren's eyes widened once he caught sight of his poison short sword, his pair of pistols and gun belt, his dagger, as well as a full field kit all wardens carried that consisted of poisons and antidotes. He'd never thought he'd see the weapons he'd been forced to leave back in Calhames weeks and weeks ago again, but here they were.

"We found them amidst the massacre of the Ashion diplomatic envoy after you'd been taken. We have wardens assigned to Oeiras, and I asked them to prepare your weapons when I was informed you were coming home," Taisiya said.

Soren reached for the poison short sword first, the weight of it familiar in his hand. The clarion crystal on its hilt remained whole. When he unsheathed it to carefully check the interior of the hilt where the vials of poison were secured and hidden away amidst tiny, intricate gears, he found them filled to capacity.

He toggled the casing closed and locked it before sheathing the poison short sword again. Then he checked his pistols with motions that had been drilled into him since he was a tithe. Satisfied they were in working order, Soren slid off the bench and stood so he could more easily strap on the gun belt and dagger.

"I don't want you to leave," Raiah said sulkily.

Soren turned back toward her, putting one knee on the bench so he could pick her up and hug her carefully around the wanted weight of his weapons. Raiah kept her arms and legs away from them out of long practice, cuddling close.

"I have to, but I truly promise to return once the fighting is over," Soren murmured.

"When you come back, you have to promise to stay. Papa was sad while you were gone."

Soren held her just a little tighter. "I know. But I apologized to him for making him sad, and I won't again."

"Promise?"

"I promise."

It took everything in Soren to set Raiah back down on the bench to finish her breakfast. He turned to face Taisiya, who reached for him with one wrinkled hand that he took in both of his.

"May your road find its way back to us," Taisiya said. "Our House will be waiting."

Soren managed a smile, gently squeezing her hand before letting go. "Thank you. For everything."

"There is no thanks needed within our House when you are part of it." Soren closed his eyes, stomach swooping at the belief and support and sheer acceptance of her words. When he opened his eyes again, Taisiya's gaze was warm and knowing. "Go to him."

Soren took that as his order and left the inner courtyard, making his way through the Imperial estate. The forecourt was busy with servants and *praetoria* legionnaires tending to their duties. The line of waiting motor carriages wasn't only for Soren. He spotted Nathaniel beside one, the door open and speaking to another person in the back seat. When he stepped closer, he saw Lore's pale face over Nathaniel's shoulder.

She caught sight of him, and the faint smile that came to her lips was full of relief. When she spoke, it was in the trade tongue, and her voice wasn't as smooth as it used to be. "I hear I have you to thank for my rescue."

Nathaniel glanced back before straightening up, offering a hasty bow. "Alasandair."

Soren didn't protest the name and let it be for the moment. "I wish I could have saved us both earlier."

Lore made a jerky motion with her hand, fingers shaking. Soren couldn't be sure it was due to exhaustion or something else. "I'm alive. As any cog would say, that's enough some days."

"Did Intira clear you to travel?"

"Not really, but Caris wants us home, and Lore agreed," Nathaniel said.

"I will rest on the flight over. Nathaniel won't let me do anything else," Lore said.

Nathaniel nodded firmly. "The *valide* was kind enough to send another healer with us to Ashion as a precaution."

"The drugs, while not poison, played merry havoc with my body," Lore said at Soren's questioning look. "I can't walk at the moment, and I am very tired, but I've been told it should pass with rest and exercise. None of which I have the time for. I can still lend aid to the war effort, though, even if it's from a bed. I gave my memories up willingly to a magician last night. My testimony should aid in the report the *valide* intends to submit to the Solarian Senate."

It didn't sound as if the drugs that had kept her unconscious had damaged her mind the way they'd harmed her body. She might not be a military strategist, but she'd led the Clockwork Brigade with her mother. She could parse politics and information brought by their spy network better than most.

"I'm certain Caris will appreciate that, as will Vanya," Soren said.

"What will you do?"

Soren hesitated, unwilling to commit himself to the breadth of possibilities and traps that question offered up. "Vanya requires aid in the south against the revenant horde there. Starfire is the only thing capable of decimating the numbers in the quantities needed. My understanding is he sent out a call to the Houses for those who could cast starfire to join him, but only a few answered."

Soren understood the reason given by the Houses who'd declined—Rixham was the House of Sa'Liandel's failure alone in many ways—but one would think the continuation of their country as a whole would be enough to bring the Houses together.

Apparently not.

"And after?" Lore asked with the persistence of a lady entitled to an answer.

"Eimarille is still a threat," was all Soren said.

The starfire throne was still up for grabs, and Soren knew Maricol wouldn't be as it was if Eimarille claimed it. He'd provide Vanya with support and then see what Caris needed from him. The war wasn't over yet, and he still had his orders from Delani to obey, for as long as he could as a warden.

That seemed to satisfy Lore. She nodded slowly before closing her eyes, clearly ready to rest. Soren murmured his farewells before retreating to the motor carriage that would take him to the airfield and the airship ready to launch the moment he boarded. When next he landed, he'd be reunited with Vanya, and Soren ached with the need to hold the other man in his arms again.

Reckoning

937 A.O.P.

One

VANYA

Eleventh Month dawned with smoke and ash riding the wind, blowing across the summer dry expanse of the grasslands surrounding the frontier town Vanya and the Legion were hunkered down in. Vanya couldn't smell it, not through the filters of his gas mask, but he kept having to wipe a film of ash off his brass goggles.

Avenyah had been evacuated of civilians and now served as the launching point for the Legion's effort to whittle down the Rixham revenant horde clawing its way north. The horde had broken up into countless smaller groups that had spread across the southern half of the continent. The walking dead had essentially laid siege to every frontier village, town, and city south of Calhames. Traveling by road was impossible now, and even steam trains were a risk but one the Legion had to take when getting their soldiers into position.

The wardens had offered their expertise for the fight, with a few dozen attaching themselves to battalions and traveling south with the Legion. Delani couldn't spare the numbers she would have liked, not with so many wardens bogged down by the war in Ashion and trying to get a handle on the numerous walking dead there. The death-defying machines were still active, and with the numbers of dead littering the battlefields, Eimarille had plenty to transmute into revenants.

At the moment, Ashion and its civil war with Daijal was the least of Vanya's worries.

"Someone get those poison bombs in the launchers!" a Legion officer yelled over the hectic sounds of legionnaires shouting at each other along the wall and heavy artillery going off.

Vanya flexed his hands, the flicker of starfire warming the air around his fingers. He, like everyone else in the Legion, wore a uniform in the field in lieu of robes. Vanya's *effiyeh* was checkered gold and red as a mark of the crown he hadn't taken with him out of Oeiras. He turned to look at Javier, the major staring grimly back at him. "Will our position hold here?"

"The revenants are massing near the western gate and the railway station there. I'd rather they didn't break through. The legionnaires can hold the wall here," Javier said.

"Then let's get to the western wall. I need to get up on the observation platform."

Avenyah had no airfield, though it was serviced by railroads. The Legion had barricaded the entrance for defense purposes upon their takeover of the town, but the sheer number of revenants on the other side of the wall was a problem. The Legion couldn't evacuate by steam train if the town was overrun. While the airship anchored above the town's public plaza remained intact, Vanya hated the thought of being evacuated out on it while leaving the rest of his people to die. That wasn't why he'd come south.

Javier nodded. "I have a motor carriage waiting."

Vanya let the major guide him away from the squadrons lining the wall alongside the main gate. The wall surrounding the town wasn't as tall or as thick as the one surrounding a city would be, but it would have been enough against the intermittent incursions of revenants that came up from the Wastelands. With the number of the walking dead presently massed against it and attempting to climb their way into the town, the wall was at risk of being overrun if they didn't burn through the horde.

That duty fell to Vanya, as it had since he'd made it to the fight. This was the third frontier town he'd landed in, hoping to provide a bulwark against the revenants making their way north. Of those in the major Houses who could cast starfire of any degree, only a handful had heeded his call for support. Some minor Houses had sent magicians, and while the Legion was gaining support, Vanya knew many of the Houses hoped he'd die in the poison fields, a victim of his House's many mistakes over the years.

Vanya had no plans to die out here.

Javier drove Vanya to the western side of the town, where sentinel-class automatons ringed the barricaded gate there, Zip guns aimed at the entrance. The automatons were too heavy for the town wall to hold their weight, so legionnaires manned the wall with grenade launchers, sending warden-made poison bombs into the horde.

No one paid Vanya any mind when Javier braked to a halt beside the observation platform, a mechanical contraption that could rise higher than the wall when its four legs were extended. Yadvir waited for them there, the young man giving him a sharp nod in lieu of any formal address. "Your Imperial Majesty."

"Yadvir," Vanya said.

"I'll be joining you on the observation platform for your security."

"I welcome your assistance."

Yadvir had been one of the first to heed his call for aid, joining Vanya when he'd left Oeiras for the battlefield, determined to keep him safe, despite the young man having no inclination for war nor skill with a pistol. Neither was he able to cast starfire, but Yadvir was a magician and had handled himself well during their escape of the old palace last year. His House was a minor one out of Oeiras, but their loyalty was unmatched compared to some of the major Houses.

Those of the Houses who could cast starfire and had heeded the call had been deployed across the south to areas the Legion commanding officers could best put their magic to use. Vanya's position here in this frontier town was where the horde was thickest, drawn to the living on its march north to Calhames.

A legionnaire was already ensconced in the control seat that hung below the circular platform, allowing the pilot to guide it into position. The platform above it provided a circular view of the entire area and space for Vanya to cast starfire.

Vanya, Javier, and Yadvir climbed the ladder to the platform, holding on to the railing as the officer on the ground gave the signal to rise. With a grind of gears, the pilot began their ascent, the platform rising up until it cleared the top of the wall.

The sight that greeted them made Javier swear and Yadvir go pale. Vanya didn't make a sound, gripping the safety railing with both hands as he stared at the oncoming threat. He knew the ground beyond the wall was scorched black from starfire, ash all that remained of half the horde that had greeted his arrival yesterday when his airship made it to Avenyah. But that was difficult to see when the horde had seemingly doubled in size since yesterday. The night had hidden the numbers, despite the near-constant battle the Legion persisted in.

Yadvir gripped his wand tightly, the clarion crystal at the tip encased in sturdy metal wire that didn't impede the glow of the aether that danced around it. "I will guard you as you focus on the horde, Your Imperial Majesty."

"We both will," Javier grunted.

Vanya nodded, gaze sweeping over the mass of walking dead that undulated like waves on the land before them. Burning the dead in such quantities spread out before them took effort and was a risk to the land as well as the people hunkered down behind the walls. He also had to be mindful of the steam train and railroad tracks situated beyond the wall. Too much heat could warp them both, and then the legionnaires would be stuck here until airships could be spared for transport out.

All of that went through Vanya's mind as Javier handed him a spyglass. Vanya pressed it carefully to one of the lenses of his brass goggles, peering through it at the horde of revenants. The Legion was targeting the closest segment of the walking dead with poison bombs and other kinds of explosives. Bullets seemed to do nothing to keep them down, merely tore them to pieces that kept wanting to move.

Fire was the only thing that had ever kept their people safe, and Vanya meant to do his duty to Solaria.

"I'll aim for the rear of the horde and bring the starfire as close as I can," Vanya said before passing back the spyglass. "Have the legionnaires focus their efforts close to the wall to drive them into my starfire."

"Understood," Javier said, already pulling out his televox. They'd traveled with a portable communications tower that was currently set up on the other side of the plaza, giving them a solid line of communication.

Vanya extended his arms in front of him, palms facing outward. He reached for the aether and drew its power through him, starfire erupting into existence around his hands. It burned molten hot, a white-gold flicker of ferocious heat that he sent streaking into the sky like a comet, one volley at a time. The bursts of starfire landed amidst the horde like a match landing in drought-dry kindling.

Starfire ripped through the revenants, fed by the dried-out husks of the walking dead who'd suffered since Rixham had been walled off all those years ago. They went up in flames, and Vanya guided his starfire through the revenant horde with fierce concentration.

Shouts from below resulted in a pause of attack as the legionnaires repositioned their artillery for closer attacks. The revenants tried to escape the starfire by lurching closer to the wall, but they were met by explosions driven by poison bombs that would hopefully incapacitate them.

Vanya flexed his fingers before initiating another volley of starfire, aiming farther to the left than before. He wanted to box the revenants in as much as possible, giving the Legion time to work on eradicating them with warden help. The sky turned hazy with smoke and ash, muting some of the eye-watering brightness of the rising sun that Vanya was staring into.

He squinted through his brass goggles, the rasp of his breathing through the gas mask filters loud in his ears, thrumming through his jawbone. He turned on his feet, concentrating to guide the starfire from a distance.

"A warden is requesting you pull the left flank of your starfire barrier closer to the wall. Revenants are trying to escape in that direction," Javier said.

Vanya nodded and curled his fingers, starfire mimicking the motion as the searing heat of that fiery wall drew ever closer to the frontier town. "Any luck on air support yet?"

"The squadron over Temetry isn't scheduled to leave for our position until midday."

The Legion only had a certain number of military airships at their disposal for use of aerial bombardment on revenants. Some of those squadrons had been shifted out of Ashion once E'ridia joined the fight. More than half of those had been positioned at Solaria's major cities in preparation for defense against the oncoming horde. The rest were meant to fill in the gaps in the vast expanse of open land and poison fields the Legion was fighting within to build a bulwark against the revenant horde. Vanya knew it might not be enough to make a difference.

"We'll make do."

He kept most of his attention on the starfire he controlled, keeping it contained within the revenant horde as it scorched the earth. He fought to keep it from expanding beyond the area, unwilling to risk the threat of a grassfire. Summer might be over, with the Eagle Constellation rising in the sky in honor of the Dusk Star, but that didn't mean the brittle dryness of the desert and hill country would see rainstorms just yet.

Vanya was only distantly aware of the defensive maneuvers happening within the ranks on the wall, most of his attention on burning through revenants without damaging the tracks. Yadvir remained by his side, a constant presence working in tandem with Javier to guard him. Being so high up on the observation platform made him a target, but Vanya wasn't about to hide.

So focused was he on the shifting line of starfire that he missed the initial conversation Javier was having with someone through the televox. He didn't miss when both Javier and Yadvir shouted a warning practically in his ears.

"Get down!" Yadvir cried out, lending action to his words by yanking Vanya to the floor of the observation platform.

Javier instantly dropped as well, bullets peppering the air where they'd been standing and pinging against the body of the observation platform. A roar went up amongst the legionnaires on the ground and wall, a furious sound that was drowned out by an explosion on the ground *inside* the frontier town.

Yadvir snapped his wrist, wand cutting through the air as aether fled the clarion crystal tip. Magic surrounded them in a glittering golden shield while Javier lurched toward the control panel, grabbing for the radio that kept them in contact with the pilot. "Take us down!"

No sooner had he spoken than the gears clicked and metal screeched as the observation platform shuddered, descending toward the ground. Vanya shoved himself up onto one elbow. "Thank you."

Yadvir smiled, more a baring of teeth than anything else. "No thanks needed, Your Imperial Majesty."

"Do we know who was shooting?"

"A legionnaire on the wall. It looks like others took him down."

"We'll check if they're a *rionetka*," Javier said.

If they were a fanatic instead, it still would not change Vanya's course of action. He would continue to remain in the south, moving from town to city and back again, doing all that he could to burn revenants into ash with starfire. It was the least that he owed Solaria.

The observation deck settled on the ground with a judder. Javier kept a hand on Vanya's shoulder, speaking into his televox. After a moment, a pair of *praetoria* legionnaires hustled up to the railing, and Yadvir retracted his shield only after Javier gave the command.

"We've confirmation the attacker was a *rionetka*," the shorter woman reported.

Javier offered Vanya his hand, helping him to his feet. "Their rank?"

"No rank, sir. Enlisted."

Javier met Vanya's gaze. "We should get you under cover."

Vanya shook his head. "I need to get back up there to burn the dead."

He couldn't see the starfire he'd cast, but he could sense it, a weight to his awareness beyond the wall. Leaving the area would mean having to withdraw it from the fight, allowing the revenant horde to claw at the walls. The Legion only had so many poison bombs and bullets to commit to each battle, and starfire was inexhaustible outside his own strength. Their best chance at clearing this portion of the horde was if he stayed put.

Javier didn't argue, much as Vanya knew the major wanted to. Instead, Javier reached for the lever again and shoved it back up, starting the observation platform's ascent all over again. Vanya steadied himself on the ride up, scanning the wall and the sky as he did so. A speck in the northwest caught his eye, too large to be any ash floating across the sky. He watched it for a few seconds, noticing how it grew larger.

"Javier, I thought you said we weren't expecting any airships right now?" Vanya said.

Javier followed his gaze to the horizon. He swore softly before pulling out his televox, presumably to call whichever communications officer was on duty. Yadvir handed Vanya the spyglass, and he put it up against the lens of his brass goggles again. He turned the cylindrical plating a little to sharpen what he was looking at. The airship, while still far away, appeared larger in his eye, big enough that Vanya could see its make was Solarian. When he spied the edges of the Imperial seal painted on its hull, he swore his heart clenched.

"Communications was just notified of its arrival now that the airship is within range. It's come from Oeiras," Javier said.

"My *valide* and daughter?" Vanya asked sharply, fear the first thing to fill his mind.

"No. It carries reinforcements."

Which would be sorely needed, but he couldn't fathom how one airship could hold the number of soldiers they needed. Vanya passed back the spyglass as the airship rapidly closed the distance. The only realistic place for the airship to dock was in the middle of the town on a long anchor line like the other one. Except it didn't head there, choosing instead to hover over the observation deck.

Vanya tilted his head back, watching as the airship descended, the thrum of its engine drowning out everyone's voices. Crew came to the railing, and a rope ladder got tossed over the side. It was long enough the knotted ends thumped against the metal flooring of the observation deck. Javier and Yadvir immediately moved to hold and steady it.

High above, a familiar figure appeared at the railing and deftly flipped over it, grabbing at the rope ladder with sure hands. Vanya drew in a ragged breath, the gas mask filters crackling in his ears as he recognized who they were, forcing his knees to lock, lest he stumble.

"Soren."

It was as if every prayer Vanya had ever uttered to the Dawn Star since Soren had been taken from him was answered in that moment. That fear he'd carried for weeks—of never knowing if he'd see Soren alive again—bled away, replaced by a joy so fierce it made Vanya's heart skip a beat.

Soren climbed down without pause, though he never made it to the last rung. He jumped down to the observation deck before his feet even came level with Vanya's head, finally *there*, within reach, looking thinner than Vanya would have liked but blessedly *alive*. And all Vanya could think about was holding the other man in his arms again after so long apart.

"Vanya," Soren said, gray eyes bright with what Vanya now knew was love after all these years. He wore no gas mask, and Vanya wasted no time in tearing his own off, taking his *effiyeh* with it.

"Soren," Vanya ground out, already reaching for him.

The space between them disappeared as Soren stepped in close, his arms going around Vanya's neck to pull him down into a scorching kiss. It felt like a fever dream to hold him, almost too much after so many weeks of uncertainty—the taste of him, the feel of Soren in his arms—that Vanya couldn't stop the shuddering gasp that escaped him when they finally broke apart.

"You're here," he rasped. "How are you here?"

Gloved fingers gently pressed against his lips, stilling his words. "I wouldn't be anywhere else but here, princeling. I escaped Bellingham with Lore. Taisiya sent her and Nathaniel back to Ashion. You needed me more."

Vanya grabbed his hand, pressing a hard kiss to leather-lined knuckles. The smell of ash in the air was brutally harsh, and he knew he'd have to put the gas mask back on soon, but Vanya stole another kiss first, then another.

"You should know Joelle is dead. Blades killed her in Bellingham," Soren said.

Vanya's lips curled upward. "Good. It means I don't need to tell Raiah I had her mother's House eradicated. Eimarille did it for me."

Joelle had *lost*. The House of Kimathi would be a threat to his House or his daughter no more. The cost to see Joelle dancing amongst the stars was so much, though. Her alliance with Daijal had nearly torn Solaria apart, and even now, what power Vanya held since the Conclave was questionable at best after Rixham's walls fell.

But he was here, and she was not.

"Fight with me?"

Soren's smile was small but filled with a warmth that was for Vanya alone. "Always, princeling."

Two

CARIS

"Lore?" Caris shouted as she slammed her way into the small inn, leaving Blaine and Honovi behind on the street in her rush. The building had once been a bustling business in a midsized plains town south of Amari before the Daijalan army had rolled through and claimed it late last year. "Nathaniel?"

"Upstairs!" came Nathaniel's muffled shout.

Caris ignored the Royal Guard who had entered first for her safety, hurrying toward the stairs with Blaine and Honovi on her heels. She'd cried the other night when she received news of Lore's and Alasandair's survival. Nathaniel's return to the continent was unexpected but not unwelcome. Fontaine had been the ideal place to rendezvous now that it was under Ashion control once more, and she'd been counting the hours to their reunion.

The Ashion army had wrestled back control through vicious fighting over the last few weeks, driving the Daijal army out of Fontaine with the aid of wardens, the Legion, and the E'ridian air force. The push might have been for naught if the Tovan Isles hadn't begun their naval assault to break the blockade in the Gulf of Helia. Reclaiming Fontaine had come at a cost, with the allied command attacking the town in order to keep it. When the Daijal army had

463

abandoned it to shift troops back west to protect New Haven, they'd left destruction in their wake.

Portions of the town had been set aflame during their retreat, the damage contained only through the efforts of the remaining fire brigade and cogs that doubled as magicians who hadn't fled with other refugees. Some areas had been reduced to rubble from E'ridian airship bombing runs, and areas of the outer wall had been utterly destroyed by the Daijal army before they relinquished the town.

That damage meant the civilians who remained, along with the allied soldiers, were at risk of revenant attacks from both within and without. The wardens had organized round-the-clock patrols guarding the broken section of the outer wall with the help of soldiers and magicians. Many areas of Fontaine couldn't be cleared—it would take weeks to root out the walking dead, Ksenia had said—so everyone was restricted to certain areas that could be defended, billeting Ashion soldiers and Solarian legionnaires in abandoned homes and shops. The E'ridians remained on their airships, anchored in the remnants of the airfield or flying patrols.

Caris had made it to Fontaine only after General Votil had reluctantly confirmed that the Daijal army was in retreat and had no plans to try to retake the ruined town. She'd left a small town in the southeast where a bloodline had taken in refugees, the baron in charge there having been skeptical of who she was prior to the visit. He'd changed his opinion, for which Caris was grateful, but she'd left when it became clear that the push to retake Amari would soon begin.

She reached the top of the stairs and darted into the first open door with gas lamp light spilling out of it. Lore smiled wanly from her spot on the bed, wrapped in a thick blanket and looking far too thin and pale for Caris' liking. Nathaniel crouched beside her, holding her hand in a comforting manner, and he turned his head to give Caris a relieved smile.

"She's all right" was the first thing Nathaniel said.

"I can speak for myself," Lore rasped.

"Yes, but you also need to rest."

Caris smiled, lips quivering. She ignored the wetness in her eyes that blurred her vision as she hurried to Lore's side. She bent to embrace the other woman with careful arms.

"Lore," Caris choked out, the rest of what she wanted to say stuck in her throat.

"I'll be all right," Lore promised softly. "Nothing a bit of rest won't cure."

"More than that, if the healer has their way," Nathaniel said.

Caris sniffled a little as she pulled back, shifting so she could kneel beside Nathaniel on the floor so Lore wouldn't have to move her head too much and risk dizziness. She rested her hand on his thigh, the touch outside the bounds of propriety, but she figured she could be forgiven for the breach after everything that had occurred. "If it's rest you need, we can send you to Cosian. Your mother and brother are still back there."

Lore frowned fretfully at her, too-thin fingers clutching at the blanket wrapped around her shoulders. "I should stay. I can help."

"You were hurt. No one will think less of you if you need some time to heal. And I would like to know that you are safe."

"*You* aren't safe out here. Not with *rionetkas* being activated throughout the continent."

"We're aware of the threat and have taken precautions," Blaine said from the doorway as he and Honovi entered the room.

Lore made a face but couldn't hide the exhaustion in her eyes. Still, she argued, because she was forever her mother's daughter and a lady in her own right. "If our army and allies are pushing toward Amari, you'll need what I know from all my years as a cog."

Which was almost her entire life, Caris knew. Dureau had stayed with Meleri in Cosian, and while they had cogs working with the army, none would be more knowledgeable than Lore in her role as Mainspring within the Clockwork Brigade.

"If you're determined to stay, then I won't order you back to Cosian," Caris said after a moment. "Do you think you could join us at the command meeting for a bit?"

Lore nodded. "I'm tired, but I feel as if all I've done is sleep. I need to stay awake. Listening to everyone argue will help with that."

"The command meetings haven't been that bad," Honovi said mildly.

"No, sometimes they're worse, especially when the Imperial generals want their way," Blaine retorted.

"Their way has gained us much ground, even with only half the promised ranks from the emperor."

"Just keep hot tea coming, and I'll stay awake," Lore said.

"Tea won't help you coming off a forced sleep. You'd need stims for that, and I wouldn't recommend those in your current state," Ksenia said from the hallway. Caris glanced over her shoulder and watched as Blaine and Honovi stepped aside so the warden could enter the small room. "Forced sleep is used during medical operations, but keeping someone under for such a long period of time takes alchemist interference, and it isn't without consequences."

"The Imperial healer who saw to her cleared her," Nathaniel said.

Ksenia snorted. "I'll be the judge of Lore's current state."

Lore caught Caris' eye, grimacing slightly. "You should go on ahead to the command meeting. I'll meet you there. I'm sure Ksenia will need to be present as well, and she can escort me."

"I'm not carrying you," Ksenia warned, most of her attention on the field kit she placed on the bed beside Lore. "And you, Nathaniel, are in need of a checkup as well."

Nathaniel sighed before standing and offering his hand to Caris. She took it and stood, stepping closer so he could wrap her up in his arms. Caris closed her eyes and leaned into his embrace, listening to the song from the clarion crystals that powered his clockwork metal heart. The tone and rhythm hadn't changed, still a distant, comforting set of notes at the very edge of her awareness.

"Nathaniel's heart sounds like it always has," Caris said, opening her eyes.

Ksenia shot her an unimpressed look. "You know the protocols we have in place to guard against *rionetkas*. You signed off on them."

"With my full agreement," Nathaniel murmured in Caris' ear.

"I'll stay and bring Lore over once Ksenia has finished examining her. You two should get going," Honovi said, nodding at Caris and Blaine.

Caris reluctantly pulled away. She gave Lore one last hug before leaving with Blaine by her side. The Royal Guard waited for them outside, coming to attention at her arrival. She and Blaine settled into the back seat of a motor carriage whose engine was still running, and their driver pulled into the cobblestone street. Caris stared out the window at the damage done to some of the buildings they passed from bombs dropped by both sides in the fight over the town.

Legion sentinel-class automatons stood guard within and without the outer wall, their massive forms impossible to miss. One was positioned at the building command had chosen to work out of. Its Zip gun was held at a forty-five-degree angle, the legionnaire at the controls in its torso keeping an eye on the near horizon for any threats. The automatons were directed by their pilots, and Caris never ceased to be fascinated by the possibility of the design when used for civilian needs. But her desire to pursue that would have to wait until the war was over.

They were ushered inside the command building by a warden and directed to a room that had originally been several different offices before an engineer tore down the interior walls for more space. Everyone gathered around the table stood at her arrival. Caris nodded gravely at the salutes given to her by her own officers and those from foreign countries.

"I understand there's a plan of attack for Amari being discussed?" Caris said as Blaine pulled out one of the last few empty chairs for her.

"Our forces are in position for the push to break through the Daijalan line, but it's going to take time. High General Kote has reconfigured much of his forces that remain in Ashion around Amari and in the trenches there. Revenants will be a problem as well. Our spies have confirmed a death-defying machine is in use. We've requested more wardens from the governor," Imperial General Chu Hua, of no House, said. Beside her sat General Yiannis Diomandis, a familiar face from Cosian.

"Warden ranks are running thin," General Clarence Votil said from down the table.

"They are still worth an entire squad of legionnaires when it comes to traversing the poison fields and dispatching revenants."

Caris listened as the officers went over the strategy to retake Amari, a battle which would see the Ashion army and Solarian Legion pressing forward with weapons and war machines into the Daijalan defensive line while E'ridian war airships ran bombing runs over the enemy. They would target the capital's outer wall if they could get close enough amidst the staggering number of anti-airship guns in Daijal's use.

Caris wanted to protest that action but held her tongue. Somewhere in Amari were her parents, though she didn't know if they were alive or dead. There'd been no news since the last broadsheet weeks and weeks ago about their transfer to Amari for a trial. If there had been a trial, it hadn't been reported on. She held out hope they were still alive, that they could be saved. If her parents had been executed, Caris knew Eimarille wouldn't pass up announcing such news.

"What it sounds like is the fighting both on the ground and in the air is going to be something no one can pass through until one side wins," Blaine said after an hour of discussion that sometimes segued into arguing. "My goal is to get Caris inside the capital to claim the starfire throne. The E'ridian air force can't be bombing the city when we're inside it."

"And how do you suggest we get you past the fighting? An aerial drop? You'd be lucky if you weren't shot out of the sky," Admiral Eirik said.

"The Clockwork Brigade moved in and out of Amari through the catacombs that exist beneath the capital. There are entrances that open up in the plains well beyond the city walls. If we can access one, we could bring Caris into the city."

"The Duchess Auclair informed me of the catacombs' existence before I left Cosian. She provided a map to traverse the few safe routes, all of which we must assume have been compromised and are in Daijalan control. Too many cogs were turned into *rionetkas*, and too many chains were broken because of it," General Votil said.

Caris leaned forward, an idea unfurling in her mind, one she knew Blaine wouldn't like. "Eimarille activated every *rionetka* in the field recently. All our countries have been dealing with assassination attempts of high-ranking officials, despite our best efforts to check for the hidden threat. Nathaniel never succumbed to the *Klovod's* control this time around, and his order has always been to kill me."

"Caris," Blaine said, sounding pained. "He still can't be trusted."

"By the Tovanians' own report, Nathaniel never succumbed to the orders to destroy the ship-city. He went to find the *Uri'ka* and warn her."

"Our spies presently place the *Klovod* in Amari, along with Eimarille. Can you be certain that by putting Nathaniel in such close proximity, he won't be activated again?" Imperial General Chu Hua asked.

Caris swallowed back the answer her heart wanted to give, knowing it wouldn't be appreciated and only mark her as incredibly naïve. "No, but I trust the work the wardens have done to give him back his mind and free will. Nathaniel carries the vivisection scars of a *rionetka* on his chest. If there are any Daijalans controlling the catacomb tunnels, Nathaniel can pass for what they think him to be, and if his orders were to bring me to Eimarille, who are they to deny him?"

Blaine stiffened beside her. The fact none of the officers at the table immediately denied her idea just proved it could be a way into Amari that wouldn't sacrifice more lives than they were already anticipating losing.

"You would be putting yourself in grave danger, and I don't know if I could condone such an endeavor," General Votil reluctantly said.

"I'm in danger no matter where I stand. I need to get inside Amari, and this is the best way."

"If we could identify one of the outside catacomb entrances and determine whether or not it is within our control or the other side's, we could access it with a small team of fighters," Imperial General Chu Hua finally said, sounding thoughtful.

"If it's on the Daijalan side, we'd need to send people in under cover of night, which would put them more at risk of revenants and an attack once they were spotted," Admiral Eirik pointed out. "If we coordinate a bombing run at that time, we could perhaps carve out a period where it would be safer. I would recommend a warden or two assist in leading your chosen group to the entrance."

"So we do the same thing we did with New Haven and create a distraction by increasing the attack on a different side of the city. Get them to focus elsewhere." The Imperial general looked at Caris. "I assume Nathaniel is accepting of the risk?"

Speaking for him would take away his choice, something Caris hated to do, for she knew how deeply Nathaniel abhorred any action where he could possibly hurt her. "He will be."

Beside her, Blaine held his tongue, but when Caris sneaked a glance his way, she saw him staring back at her, expression impossible to read. After a moment, he inclined his head in her direction. "I will stand witness."

It wasn't agreement, not by a long shot, but she knew Blaine would not hold her back from this course of action if it would see an end to the war. Caris only hoped it wouldn't end with everyone she cared about dancing amongst the stars.

Three

EIMARILLE

The new palace in Amari wasn't home, but it would be when all the fighting was over. It felt a bit like a prison at the moment, reminding Eimarille of her younger years spent in the Daijal court beneath Bernard's control before she extricated herself from his ambition. She'd carved out a space for herself and her son in that country, but returning to Ashion with the intention of staying came with a surprising amount of wistfulness for a childhood lost to her.

Standing on the balcony of her suite, soft robe wrapped around her, Eimarille stared up at the fading stars in the sky, picking out the constellations with long practice before the dawn chased them away. The Eagle constellation was on the rise, the season of the Dusk Star upon them. Where the scent of autumn would linger on the breeze in any other year, presently, it smelled strongly of smoke.

The war was coming to Amari's gates, and as much as Kote wished she'd leave the Ashionen capital, Eimarille had chosen to remain. Much of the population in the city had been trapped inside its walls since last year when she'd hobbled the Ashionen parliament and sought to break the Clockwork Brigade. People weren't starving—supplies were never withheld—but the loyalty of those who called the

471

capital home had always been in doubt. She'd sought to limit the damage they could do, but she wondered if it had been enough.

"Such bitter thoughts for a fine morning."

Eimarille tightened her grip around the railing, staying where she was as Innes stepped onto the balcony from the bedroom, where Terilyn still slept. "The Ashion army and its allies are half a day's fight from the city. There is nothing *fine* about that, my lord."

The enemy had been carving trenches of their own to meet the ones around Amari, and it wouldn't be long until the fighting escalated.

The Twilight Star came to stand beside her, gazing at the dark gardens of the palace, the layout different from the one she'd run through in the old palace before it burned. She wondered what Innes saw, if he never noticed the changes in the world he'd walked for Ages.

"I promised you a crown, and you have it," Innes said with a gentleness that almost made Eimarille flinch.

"And the starfire throne?"

"My wife is, perhaps, unforgiving in that aspect. I chose you, and she chose another."

Eimarille turned her head to stare at Innes. "But you saved me from the Inferno so that I could return and claim what was rightfully mine."

"And Aaralyn took offense to my decision to do so. Hence this war."

Past the palace walls, in a public park for all to see and ever burning, was the starfire throne. It sat in the remnants of the old palace's throne room, a visual statement of the country's defiance, something Eimarille had tried for years to—if not snuff out—at least gain the loyalty of her people.

"If I went there now and put out the North Star's decree? What then?"

"Is that doubt I hear in your voice, child?" Innes finally deigned to look at her, his eyes eerily bright in the dark, as if starfire was eating him up from the inside. "You know what I think of doubt."

"This is my road, the one you gave me. I have walked it proudly."

But she hadn't yet gone to the starfire throne and attempted to sit in it, to put out the starfire that had burned to ash those who had tried. The North Star was not her guiding star, and she could not be certain her bloodline—written as it was in the royal genealogy—would be enough to put out the decree. Knowing Caris and Alasandair were out there, fighting against her, was enough to make her doubt, and she hated them for that.

"You must do what is right for Maricol. I have guided you here, but like all my children, you must decide to take your next step," Innes said.

Eimarille firmed her jaw, refusing to look away from his strange and otherworldly stare. "I will be queen, as is my right, and my son will rule after me."

Innes smiled, lifting a gloved hand to settle it on her shoulder in a manner she'd found comforting as a child, but which left her feeling chilled now. "Then do not let them win."

Kote hadn't wanted her to come to Amari, cognizant of the threat that came from the front line being pushed west. Despite her attacks on E'ridia and Solaria, those two countries had still allied themselves with Ashion. Their specific strengths on the land and in the air had been overwhelming the Daijalan army. Now, with battalions sent west to hold New Haven against an invasion, her forces here were weaker.

They were prepared for a siege and bombing runs. The safe rooms below the palace had all been set up before she even landed in Amari, and Lisandro would play in a suite of rooms there today as he had yesterday. The palace in the civic center of the capital would be a target her enemies would be unable to resist, but Eimarille refused to flee like she'd been forced to as a child.

Whatever Innes saw in her face, in her eyes, made him nod. Then he let her go and retreated back into the bedroom. Eimarille knew if she followed him, he would not be there, so she stayed where she was for a while longer, only moving when Terilyn pressed up against her, familiar arms winding around her waist. A pointed chin rested on her shoulder, quiet breathing a soft sound in her ear. Neither spoke as they watched the sunrise, pink spreading through the gray as golden rays broke the horizon.

"Bring me the Dhemlans," Eimarille said softly.

"Of course," Terilyn replied. She pressed a kiss against Eimarille's neck, her lips cool and dry, before slipping away to see to the request.

Eimarille stayed there for a little longer before finally heading inside, where it was warmer, and servants had prepared a bath for her. She washed and was dressed afterward in a deep blue gown with a high neck and long sleeves, the incorporated cape falling gently around her shoulders and upper arms to the floor. She requested and was brought her crown, which she placed on her head with sure hands, the gold and diamonds glittering in the gas lamp light.

She held court in the morning in a throne room that was more subdued than the one she'd left behind in New Haven. The courtiers were nervous, hiding their fear behind silk fans and strained smiles. Eimarille remained serene in the face of their skittishness, projecting a quiet strength that did little to calm everyone. Only when she saw Terilyn quietly enter the throne room did Eimarille call for everyone's attention.

Eimarille watched from the gilded throne as Terilyn led the shackled Dhemlans into the throne room, her Blade dressed in unre-markable trousers and day jacket, her hair secured in a knot with plain pins. Terilyn had dressed for the task at hand, and when she pushed the baron and his wife to their knees before her, Eimarille rather thought the pair knew what that task was.

Baron Emmitt Dhemlan and Baroness Portia Dhemlan were thinner than they had been when Eimarille last saw them in Istal. Their drab clothes hung badly on their frames, cheeks hollowed out from stress and poor rations. Criminals weren't entitled to comfort, and they'd had little of it since their capture last year. Despite their predicament, they still raised their chins to her with defiance in their tired eyes.

"You were tried by a jury of your peers and found guilty," Eimarille said, not needing to project her voice to fill the throne room. The courtiers surrounding them were all deathly silent.

"A farce of a trial. Everyone knows it was a lie," Portia said tremulously.

The broadsheets had extensively covered the trial for the handful of days it'd been ongoing in the courtroom. It hadn't been enough to lure their daughter to Amari, but now it didn't matter. "You were still found guilty, and it's past time for your sentencing."

Before she'd even finished speaking, Terilyn was already slitting their throats. Emmitt died first, Terilyn's dagger flashing in her hand as she drew it across his throat with a sureness that spilled blood all down his front and over the marble floor. Portia let out a strangled cry full of grief before her voice was taken from her, along with her life. She struggled, because the dying always did, but Terilyn's dagger kissed her throat as it had her husband's.

Eimarille watched them bleed out at the foot of her throne, the pool of blood steadily growing around where they lay. It didn't take long before they stopped moving, eyes going distant and sightless. Terilyn spent that time cleaning her dagger. "What would you like done with them?"

Eimarille stood and stepped down from the dais, careful to steer clear of the blood, as the courtiers bowed or curtsied to her on shaking legs. "Deliver the bodies to the death-defying machine. I'll want them ready to greet their daughter when she arrives."

There was no doubt Caris would find her way inside Amari. When she did, Eimarille would show her the cost of defiance.

Four

SOREN

Soren stared through the spyglass at the scorched earth surrounding yet another southern frontier town, seeing nothing but ash where revenants once stood. It hadn't been his doing this time, but Vanya's. Soren had been well east of this location yesterday, burning his way through revenants intent on harassing the coastal towns that dotted the hill country on that side of the continent. He'd taken an airship on a night flight to Vanya, knowing he could no longer stay in Solaria but reluctant to leave all the same.

"Do you doubt my ability to handle revenants with starfire?" Vanya asked from beside him on the town wall, voice dry.

Soren pulled the spyglass away from his eye and adjusted it down to its smaller size before handing it back to the legionnaire who'd offered it to him. "I doubt your ability to be subtle, but I see nothing in the ashes I need to fix."

Vanya chuckled, the sound tired. He looked it, too, with dark circles under his expressive eyes, lines pressed into his face from the constant use of brass goggles and a gas mask.

Soren reached out to touch his thumb to one such lingering indentation, the shadow there turning out to be a faint bruise. "I should have let them take Seaville."

"Most of the citizens there do not deserve that, and the House of Aetos is being seen to."

Neither he nor Vanya had set foot in Seaville, but *praetoria* legionnaires had. The House of Aetos had been arrested for treason for their alliance with the House of Kimathi and, through them, Daijal, as well as the murder of a foreign diplomatic corps and the kidnapping of a foreign prince and noble lady. The charges were ones even the Senate couldn't argue against, not with Soren's own testimony along with Lady Lore Auclair's—their memories attested to by star priest magicians well-versed in mind magic—underpinning it all.

Considering Soren's dual standing as a prince and a warden, the Senate had only been able to stand aside and allow the *praetoria* legionnaires to arrest and detain the House of Aetos for their betrayal to the Imperial throne and, by extension, Solaria. It wasn't even about the House of Sa'Liandel, but the future of their country, and for that reason, the House of Aetos had found no support amongst the major or minor Houses.

They hadn't gone quietly, from what Soren knew.

The *vezir* and Vesper, along with everyone down to the cadet branches of the House of Aetos, were imprisoned in Calhames. Vanya had spared no one listed in the nobility genealogies, and every member of that House would pay for the choice to pit themselves against Solaria.

"Will you execute them?" Soren asked.

Vanya caught his hand and turned to press a kiss to Soren's knuckles. "Eventually. They'll have a trial, because I'll not have anyone say I did it out of spite over you."

He had, Soren knew. *Everyone* knew. But politically speaking, the accusations wouldn't stem from targeting Soren but Prince Alasandair of Ashion. The distinction would save the House of Sa'Liandel from further recriminations—publicly, at least.

"Delani is sending more wardens. She wants me to head north."

"I know."

Vanya didn't appear happy about that, but he hadn't protested the order when it'd been received. Soren had been working to shore up the Legion as they fought to push back the Rixham horde for the past two weeks. He'd have preferred to stay in Solaria, but the allied forces in Ashion were closing in on Amari, and he was needed for that final fight. Delani needed him to be a warden just a little while longer before he could lay down that mantle, as much as it would ache to do so.

Vanya reached up and lifted free of his uniform the medallion he'd given to Soren all those years ago and recently accepted back. Now, he pressed it once more into Soren's hand, the vow warm from resting against skin, the chain dangling in the air between them.

"I want those in Ashion to know you belong to me, that you will carry my name when this is all over. That to insult you is to insult me," Vanya said in a low voice.

Soren could be forgiven for snagging Vanya by the collar of his uniform and yanking him into a fierce kiss. "There was never any doubt where I was concerned."

He would go to Ashion, fight to put Caris on the starfire throne, and walk away from everything Rourke. He would give up the life of a warden to keep them safe, doing his duty to the bitter end. His road had only ever led to Vanya, and Soren would not change course, not now, not for anyone.

Soren hung the vow around his neck, the weight of it settling him. He hadn't realized how much he'd missed it until he wore it once more. He touched it with careful fingers, having memorized the feel of the lion's face years ago, the same way he'd memorized the look in Vanya's eyes that he now knew was love.

"I'll see you to your airship, and I will see you when you return to me."

"Yes," Soren promised, because home would always be Vanya and the life they could make together, and his road would ever lead him there.

Five

BLAINE

Three weeks after Lore's and Nathaniel's return, Blaine was wishing for solid decking underfoot while trudging through a garrison trench in ankle-deep mud. A passing autumn storm that did nothing but turn the plains between Amari and Fontaine into a swamp had created what felt like small bogs in the trenches. The muck was terrible for his mechanical prosthetic, and he kept it covered as best he could with sleeve and glove, but he swore he could feel grit in the gears.

The rain had driven the haze from the sky, though Blaine hadn't removed his gas mask since they landed less than an hour ago. The front lines of the fight were miles and miles from the allied command's location, buried where it was in a bunker accessible only via trench and fiercely guarded by soldiers, automatons, wardens, and magicians.

Blaine's fur-lined leather flight jacket was a little too warm for the ground, but it was durable, so he kept it on. He spared a glance over his shoulder at where Caris walked behind him, with Nathaniel and Royal Guards in plain military uniforms taking up the rear of their line. All of them wore gas masks and hard helmets like him, the lot of them just as filthy from the knees on down. Their escort—a grim-faced sergeant who'd hurried them off their airship transport upon landing—never slowed his pace.

A shadow swept over the trench, and Blaine looked up through his brass goggles, squinting through weak sunlight at the pair of airships passing overhead, escorted by aeroplanes. The bit of sky he could see was limited, but he could see they were of E'ridian make, and they flew at the height favored for a precision bombing run.

The E'ridian air force had enacted a limited bombing run of the enemy trenches dug in around Amari during the storm yesterday. Aeroplane squadrons were running long patrols and radioing back updates on troop movements as they worked to keep the sky over their location clear. Keeping command hidden was done out of necessity, but the risk of being overrun was always there, whether by the Daijal army or the revenants that made it through their defenses to claw against the field fencing.

Blaine hadn't agreed to let Caris leave Fontaine until they were ready to make a run for the catacomb entrance. Unfortunately, all of the ones that led to accessible tunnels mapped out by the Clockwork Brigade years ago were behind enemy lines. It had taken fierce fighting over the last week to get control of even one entrance. Traveling to its location would have to be done at night to keep everyone safe, but there was still a chance of failure.

No one liked the odds, but Caris was determined to go. Despite the danger of it all, Blaine knew she had to get inside Amari. Better to try underground than via airship since half the anti-airship guns were still active around the city. Bombing runs had managed to take out the rest, but they'd lost airships in the effort. Presently, Blaine was focusing on the things within his control to ensure Caris survived. That meant coordinating with command now that they were on the battlefield and preparing to go beyond the field fencing and into the trenches.

The sergeant finally brought them to a cement frame wrapped around a metal door. Two soldiers guarded it, both coming to attention when they spied the embroidered badge over Caris' left breast that depicted the Rourke bloodline's crest. It was a subtle notation of rank, the only thing Blaine would allow her to wear to distinguish who she was on the battlefield. She wore a veil beneath her gas mask as an extra precaution. He still fretted that it wasn't enough to stop a *rionetka* or sniper from finding her.

The sergeant pushed open the door, entering the bunker. Blaine and the others followed him into a narrow corridor lit by intermittent gas lamp lights. A tingle washed through him as he passed through the cement frame, magic curling against his skin. He glanced to the side, seeing the spell etched into the gray cement. He didn't know the underlying spell but assumed it was for security.

The muddied cement floor they walked on sloped downward to the command bunker, hidden as deep underground as excavators were capable of digging. Everything above and outside it was muffled, the quiet almost strange. Blaine pressed his thumb against the sigil ring he wore, the one his father had given him so long ago in the city he was returning to once more. As much as Blaine wanted to be on the airship where Honovi was, he had his duty as a Westergard to stay by Caris' side.

The room they were led to was fairly large, but the ceiling was low. Telegraph machines clattered and hummed away in one corner, their wires fed through a small hole in the cement to run through the dirt all the way to the communications tower located above some distance away from their underground position. The command table, filled with all manner of maps and reports of the battlefield, had the commanding officers of three nations huddled around it, but Blaine's gaze settled unerringly on the warden.

Blaine rocked to a halt, speaking the name he knew the other man preferred over all others. "Soren?"

"I hear you're going past enemy lines," Soren said in greeting in the trade tongue.

"Soren!" Caris moved past Blaine, hurrying over to where her brother stood. She didn't hug him when she reached him, though Blaine knew she wanted to. She was tactile like that with people she was familiar with. She did reach out and lay her hand on his arm in greeting. "I'm so glad to see you safe."

Soren cracked a smile but didn't pull away. "How is Lady Lore?"

"She's helping sort intelligence in Fontaine, a town south of here. She's doing better, though, and can walk again for very short distances."

"I'm glad to hear it. You can remove your gas mask if you like. The air in here is clean." Gray eyes the same shade as Caris' flicked to Blaine. "I came north after helping get some of the revenant horde under control with Vanya."

"Is that something we need to worry about?" Blaine asked as he reached up to unclip his gas mask, breathing in warm, stale air through his nose rather than a filter.

"Perhaps not until winter, if you're lucky. You've enough of the walking dead to deal with amidst the trenches."

"The prince arrived a couple of hours ago on an airship that kept pace with a steam train. He came with several Legion companies for reinforcements. Imperial General Chu Hua has assigned those legionnaires to the front, many of whom are already aiding the push to distract the Daijalans from our true target," General Votil said.

"I'll be going with you into Amari," Soren said, looking at Caris. "You've a mad plan, and you'll need a warden to get you to your destination."

Blaine bit back a wince, heart rate picking up at the thought of both Rourkes out in the battlefield and risking death on a desperate chance. It made him want to pray, but he didn't know to whom—the star god of his birth country or the one who guided the country that had taken him in. He doubted he'd be granted compassion from either.

"When do we leave?" he asked.

"Tonight," General Votil said. "Your escort is being briefed in another bunker, and you're to join them shortly."

Blaine glanced at Nathaniel, who appeared pale-faced but determined. Across the bunker, Caris stared back at him, her hand still on Soren's arm, the pair of them the entire reason three countries had come together as allies to ensure they *remained* separate countries. "Then I suppose we should hear what the plan is."

The plan in question—strategy they couldn't wholly rely on once they fled the safety of the rear trenches for the bloody front—found them hours later hunkered down near a cross-section trench that would lead them toward the bitter, bloody front.

The core group consisted of Blaine, the Rourke siblings, and Nathaniel, along with wardens, magicians, and fighters from two countries. The lot of them would join up with yet more soldiers and legionnaires on the battlefield north of them, some of whom would follow them into the catacombs. Once inside Amari, Blaine's group would head for the civic center of Amari while the others went to sabotage the Daijalans posted at the city's outer wall.

All of their plans to retake the city hinged on the catacomb tunnels being accessible, intact, and not overrun with traps. It was a lot to ask for, but every last person going with them had volunteered.

Blaine watched Soren confer with another warden at the front. Despite the sun having gone down and the stars coming out, Blaine could see him fairly well with the help of night lenses fitted over his brass goggles. Everyone had been issued a set, the spelled devices capable of allowing their wearer to see with a limited degree in the dark.

Half the wardens with them carried long-range weaponry in the form of shoulder-mounted grenade launchers capable of firing off their specialized poison grenades. The toxic explosives could incapacitate revenants, but the poisons were also deadly to the living. Two birds, one bomb, as Ksenia had happily explained last year when the wardens began producing their poison weapons again once the underground laboratories on the Warden's Island were fully manned and running after the attack.

The wardens knew what to look for in the dark when it came to revenants. They'd be leading the infiltration group forward behind the battalions that had broken up the front line and claimed the area where the catacomb entrance was. Airships on both sides were initiating bombing runs, the night flights coming with their own risks, while those on the ground had to hope they wouldn't get caught in an explosion from a dropped bomb.

Blaine followed Soren and the other warden through the cross-section, boots pulling free of the mud with a wet squelch. Soren, he knew, could fend for himself. From here on out, Blaine would put himself between Caris and every threat that would keep her from the starfire throne. The weight of his marriage torc around his throat was a reminder of who he had to return home to.

They trekked through the dark, at the bottom of muddy trenches, passing through cross-sections that connected the garrison trenches with the communication trenches in the vast land outside Amari. Their route would keep them out of the front trenches but not the battle. The catacomb entrance was in open land, no trenches close to it, and the allied forces hadn't had the time to dig new ones to claim it. The only route to it was over open land.

Eventually, they reached the end of a trench, the ladder leading out manned by a soldier and a magician. Amidst the sound of distant explosions, their group climbed out of the trench. Several vehicles waited above with their engines running hot, the heavy-duty trucks and velocycles military issued rather than scavenged. They were built with thicker metal panels and sturdier tires for back roads, most coming with attached Zip guns.

Soren climbed onto a velocycle, eschewing the protection of a truck cab. Blaine waited until Caris made it up out of the trench to join her in a truck near the middle of the convoy, and everyone else hurriedly claimed their spots.

Caris reached for Blaine's hand once they were buckled in; he couldn't feel her touch or grip, seeing as how she'd grabbed his left one. He carefully closed his gloved metal fingers around hers, trying to offer what comfort he could.

"Stay with me, no matter what," Blaine said quietly.

Caris' smile was a flash of teeth, there and gone again, through the oddly lit night around them. "I will."

It was a risk to travel in the vehicles, even with magicians to hide their passage, but the risk was greater without them. The convoy drove away from the main section of the trenches. Explosions and gunfire echoed in the air and cut through the dark sky in distant, radiant bursts. No one spoke in the truck, and Blaine stayed hunkered down in the back with Caris.

Sometime later, the radio crackled to life in the truck, and Soren's voice came out in stilted Ashionen before repeating the warning in accentless Solarian. "Revenants sighted."

Other voices radioed in—wardens acknowledging the warning and rattling off their movements. Velocycles sped past their truck a few seconds later, heading toward the threat Blaine still couldn't see. Both sides of the conflict were fighting against each other but also against the walking dead, and that made for poor positioning all around.

"Starfire could clear the way," Caris muttered.

"You know you can't use it yet," Blaine said.

They'd agreed that Caris and Soren would refrain from casting starfire in the field unless it was an absolute last resort needed to survive. The moment starfire was seen, it would paint a target on their backs, and it wouldn't be long before the Daijalan army shifted course to try to take them out. The restriction removed one of their best weapons from the battlefield, but not using it would hopefully get them closer to their goal in the interim.

But first, they had to survive.

The soldier manning the Zip gun in the truck ahead of them abruptly swung the gun around to the right and started shooting. The soldier positioned in the passenger seat of their own truck followed suit, the sound loud enough to make Blaine's teeth rattle in his skull.

Something heavy slammed against the side of their truck, nearly tipping them over, and the soldier stopped shooting. Glass shattered, and Blaine covered his face with his arm to protect it. The driver jerked the steering wheel to the left to try to escape the massive revenant wild beast that had reached the convoy, undeterred by the countless bullets that had cut into its dead body. Seen through the night lenses, the decaying wild beast looked like a ragged nightmare as its huge horned head swung back around toward the truck, intent on ramming them again.

Caris shrieked, driven up against the door as the truck's engine revved loudly. Blaine found his pistol with his right hand, snapped the safety off, and aimed at the dead through the shattered window, finger tight on the trigger.

Six

SOREN

Soren turned his velocycle in a sharp arc, then swore under his breath as he maneuvered it through torn-up earth, heading to where a trio of revenant wild beasts was harassing the trucks.

"I didn't think death-defying machines were large enough for those things," a fellow warden shouted as she came up beside him.

Soren grimaced. "They aren't."

Or they weren't. Who knew what nastiness Eimarille had come up with since the last time he'd seen one of those horrible machines in person?

Soren shoved that thought aside, needing to focus on the threat at hand. Someone had given an order to the gunners not to shoot as the wardens drove into the line of fire toward the revenants. He aimed himself at the revenant wild beast that had attacked the truck he knew Caris was in. Tossing a grenade at it would put the convoy and Caris at risk, but if the blast came from within, it would be less of a threat.

"Let's get it away from the trucks and feed it a treat," Soren yelled over the sound of velocycle engines. "I'll get in close."

The wardens near him shouted their agreement, falling into a formation that would make it easy for them to weave quickly around the revenants. It was training they'd all gone through as tithes, four of them acting as bait for the hulking corpse doing its best to hunt through metal for the living flesh within.

Mindless but spore-driven, the revenant wild beasts were more difficult to corral and put down than if they'd been human-shaped. Doing such work at night while close to the ongoing battle made it even worse. That didn't stop Soren from driving forward to cut a U-turn near the revenant wild beast, tearing his poison short sword from its sheath on his back to score the blade over the putrid rotting flesh hanging from the revenant's rib cage.

Dead as it was, it couldn't feel pain, but the attack caused its attention to turn from those in the truck to the prey Soren was pretending to be. He revved his velocycle's engine, driving away from the revenant and enticing it to follow. A fellow warden cut between them to circle around and use their axe to harry the revenant farther away from the convoy.

Soren twisted the handlebars of his velocycle, back wheel skidding out and around as he abruptly changed direction. His teeth clacked together from the abrupt motion, but his hand unerringly found a poison grenade on his bandolier and yanked it free. He waited as the other warden drove the revenant toward him, herding it away from the convoy, shadow and light playing merry havoc with his vision through the night lenses. That massive mouth opened, jaw hanging from ragged tendon and stringy flesh. He pulled the pin on the grenade and tossed it into its gaping maw. "Get clear!"

He took his own advice, driving away from the revenant wild beast. Seconds later, it exploded with a muffled, wet sound that sent torn-up pieces of the rotting body flying into the air. Soren didn't see where any of it landed, thankfully out of range of the mess. Two more explosions rent the air as wardens handled the other revenant wild beasts in the same way.

Soren drove back to the truck where Caris and Blaine sat, pulling up alongside it to gesture at the driver. "Keep moving!"

The truck lurched forward, tires spinning for a moment before gaining traction. The rest of the convoy followed as the wardens took up guard positions again, everyone on edge. Another warden took up the lead, guiding everyone forward over pitted land strewn with jagged metal and spirals of barbed wire lining trenches still in use.

Soren knew the last few weeks had seen utterly brutal fighting around Amari and that the entrenched Daijal army hadn't given up ground easily. A truck halfway down the line weaved around a cluster of slagged metal that once used to be an automaton and rolled over a hidden mine, the explosion star-bright in the night. He swore, glancing back at the fiery outline of the truck, the soldiers inside it more than likely dead. The explosion would have marked their location, and they had to get clear.

Soren drove to the head of the convoy and signaled for the warden there to halt before signaling the same to the truck behind her. The convoy rumbled to a stop, engines still running, but the soldier cut it when Soren ordered him to.

"We're still not close to the entrance," warned Halyna, one of the wardens' master cartographers.

"And we don't want the enemy to know where we're heading. We'll need to travel the rest of the way by foot through the garrison and dugout trenches," Soren said.

She didn't protest, even if a few of the soldiers did as Soren drove down the line, verbally giving out the order for the march. The wardens remained on their velocycles, the two-wheeled vehicles capable of maneuvering in the field the way a four-wheeled vehicle couldn't.

"We'll move in groups," a legionnaire captain said.

Soren looked at Halyna, unable to see her eyes through their brass goggles and the night shadowing them. "Do you have the route?"

"Yes, but it's within the ranks of our battalions, which means it's within striking distance of Daijal's army."

"We'll all be within striking distance of Daijal if we don't get inside the city." Soren pointed at the legionnaire captain. "Get everyone down into the trench."

They weren't clear of the battle, and while no bombs had dropped in their immediate area, Soren knew that could change in an instant. The legionnaires gathered everyone into smaller groups, with wardens assigning themselves as guides. Soren made his way to where Caris, Blaine, and Nathaniel crouched near a truck with several soldiers. He went to a knee beside her and signaled for Halyna to join them.

"What direction do we need to take now?" Soren asked.

"A little more northeast. Scouts reported earlier the area we need to head to is clear of mines," Halyna said.

"Brilliant. So we only need to worry about bullets and bombs," Blaine muttered.

"The armies are making themselves a target so we don't become one. The least we can do for them is move quickly," Soren said.

"How long will it take?" Caris asked.

"As long as it needs to."

In the dark, her mouth firmed into a hard line. "Then let's get moving."

Soren offered her his hand, the first time he could ever recall reaching out to her, and she took it without hesitation. Caris rose up and followed him with a determination that spoke of the kind of queen she'd be if they could only get her on the starfire throne.

Fighting at night was terrible for everyone. The area between the frontlines and where command sat had felt like a pockmarked grave when passing through it. Now, as they entered the edges of an active battlefield, Soren couldn't help but think the poison fields and revenants were easier to deal with than the sheer chaos occurring around Amari.

The Ashion army captain traveling with them communicated via televox with the rear forces they approached. Their arrival had been expected, and a squad of soldiers were aboveground at the entrance to the rear garrison trench, keeping watch and ready to cover them. Group by group, they climbed down the ladder into the trench, the soldiers below barely acknowledging them.

Soren's boots hit mud, but it didn't impede him much from following Halyna. She led them with unerring steps through the trench, moving around barricaded anti-airship guns and other heavy artillery fire bay positions. Spiderlike automatons scuttled along the edges of the trench, the Zip guns welded to their boxy forms firing intermittently at targets they couldn't see.

Something whistled through the air, and he reached behind him for Caris' arm, throwing them flat to the muddy ground. "Get down!"

Blaine threw himself over Caris seconds before the bomb hit somewhere behind them and exploded. Soren didn't see the explosion, but he heard it, his ears ringing from the terrible sound. The ground rumbled with the hit, but nothing tore through the air near them. The screams coming from well behind them told him where it had most likely landed.

Soren shoved himself out of the muck, wiped mud off his face, and thumped Blaine on the shoulder. "Keep moving."

Between the two of them, they got Caris back on her feet, with everyone in their group marching after Halyna once again. He didn't know if the bomb had taken out any of the soldiers that had come with them, but it wasn't something Soren could stop and deal with at the moment. They maneuvered around soldiers on duty, some wounded, some not, some clearly dead but not yet dealt with.

Eventually, they reached the end of the garrison trench, the earth sloping up to the ground above, where an automaton stood guard amidst the pieces of others that had been destroyed by enemy fire. Halyna clambered up the ladder only far enough to get eyes on the ground and orient their position.

"How is it looking?" Soren called up.

"The front-line trenches are taking a beating, but the garrison trenches are holding. We're in the dugout line and far enough back we shouldn't be targeted by snipers on the city wall. They have airships to contend with at the moment," Halyna said.

"And the catacomb entrance?"

Halyna ducked back down and pulled out a map from her belt pouch. Soren waited patiently while she studied the trench lines carefully inked into the grid drawn around Amari. "Quarter of a mile away, according to the map. I'll check our route."

She hauled herself back up, pulling a spyglass from the other side of her belt and extending it to full length. The metal was painted black, with no gloss, and hopefully, no one would catch sight of the tiny glass lens she peered through. Soren waited tensely at the bottom of the ladder and didn't move until Halyna pulled the spyglass away from her face. "I see the landmark. Let's go."

Soren's heart rate didn't ease at all during the time they left the dugout trench for open ground beneath a night sky full of stars and distant aerial explosions. They ran, crouched low to the ground, other groups following after them. He kept Caris between himself and Blaine, with Blaine insisting on taking the position that would get him shot first if snipers looked their way. The prairie was flat enough they'd stand out, but he hoped the ongoing fighting would continue to be enough of a distraction.

Eventually, they made it to an outcropping of rock half-embedded in the ground. The stone looked as if it had been cut from a quarry and abandoned. Soren wondered how many times it had been passed over by wardens or other travelers. It was near Amari, yes, but nowhere close to a trade road, and travelers rarely left the safety of the roads.

They huddled behind the rock, the stone blocking Amari from view. Blaine kneeled and used his hands to brush aside dirt, fingers digging for something. When he found it, he let out a pleased grunt before pulling a key from a pocket, the chain it was attached to glinting in Soren's night lenses. He watched as Blaine pried open a tiny metal flap and inserted the key into a depressed hole that was the lock. He turned it, and Soren had to strain his hearing to catch the sound of grinding gears as mechanisms moved below the earth.

"Ready?" Blaine asked.

Halyna had her wand out while Soren held his pistol steady. The rest of the Royal Guards kept their own pistols out and ready to fire. Blaine twisted the key one more degree, and a handle rose from the metal plating, locking into place. Blaine gripped it and braced himself, pulling open the hatch that was only wide enough for one person at a time to pass through. It lay flat against the ground, revealing a dark hole hidden behind the rocks.

Nothing exploded; no one jumped out to attack. All Soren saw was an inky blackness that was their only way inside the capital city. He holstered his pistol and took the handheld gas light that Caris gave him. He stepped closer to the catacomb entrance, clicking the device on to shine a light down into that black hole. The light was too weak to reach far, but Soren saw a ladder and what he thought might be the ground below. He switched it off and handed the device back to Caris. "I'll go first."

No one protested, all of them aware that if revenants waited for them out of sight, Soren had the best chance at surviving their attack. Steeling himself, he twisted around and angled his body over the ladder. It creaked from his weight but held fast, and he climbed down into the eerie, quiet dark of the catacombs.

His feet eventually hit the floor, and he cast a bit of starfire to light the immediate area. The space was empty, dust drifting thickly through the air. Tilting his head back, he called out an all clear. One by one, the others climbed their way down to join him, the space nearly suffocating with so many bodies pressed between the narrow walls.

"Which way?" Caris asked, her voice hushed.

"Whatever way we take, you and I will need to keep everyone safe," Soren said, flicking sparks of starfire away from his fingers in a pointed gesture.

Caris nodded determinedly. "You lead. I'll follow."

Soren could only do as she asked.

Seven

CARIS

Caris was glad she wasn't claustrophobic, but after spending hours in the catacomb tunnel, she could feel the tight space getting to her. Walking beside Soren behind a pair of Royal Guards and Halyna, with Blaine and Nathaniel at her back, only soothed her anxiety a little. All of them except the wardens were in borrowed Daijalan uniforms, having changed clothes once below.

Starfire cast from both herself and Soren danced far ahead of them in a line of fireballs down the tunnel, pushing back the dark. In the time they'd been marching underground, they hadn't come across any threat, but she knew how quickly that could change. In such tight quarters, with no cover to hide behind, fighting could quickly become a bloody bottleneck.

Halyna had tasked herself with the duty of casting shields if they were attacked. The time she'd buy them would hopefully be enough for Soren and Caris to burn whomever or whatever tried to approach them from farther up ahead. Caris' stomach clenched at the thought of killing people again, but not defending herself and those with her would result in their annihilation and the ruin of Maricol.

All of those worries pulled at the edges of her thoughts, making it nearly impossible for her curiosity to get the best of her regarding the makeup of the tunnel. The metal paneling and seams were different than anything she'd come across before, and if the situation wasn't so fraught, she'd love to study the design of it all. It made her wonder about the history of Maricol and the Ages that had come before. Some long-forgotten ancestor must have built the catacombs, but the reason was lost to them now.

She knew the Clockwork Brigade had a secret way to smuggle debt slaves out of Amari, but she hadn't known about the catacombs. She wondered if Meleri would have ever told her. Caris thrust those bitter thoughts aside, knowing they didn't help her here. Right now, as tired as she was, her focus had to be on the tunnel they were traversing.

"How much farther?" Nathaniel asked.

"We'll be approaching the outer wall soon," Halyna said.

"How do you know for sure?"

"Just because we can't see the ground doesn't mean we can't deduce distance."

Wherever they were, it was deep enough that the sound of fighting from above was impossible to hear. The tunnel had dipped deep into the ground after they'd left the access point behind. Caris assumed the air would be cold and stale, but her gas mask made it impossible to tell. She could feel the chill of the depth they were at through her borrowed uniform. Walking kept her warm, but only marginally.

"Doing all right?" Soren asked in a low voice, wiggling his fingers and letting starfire spark at the tips to clarify his question.

Caris nodded jerkily. "Just a little tired."

Keeping up a constant burn of starfire made sweat bead on her brow above her brass goggles, but Caris wasn't about to snuff it out. No gas light sconces existed down here in the catacomb tunnel, which meant starfire and the handful of handheld gas lights were all the illumination they had.

Which was enough to bring into clarity movement up ahead.

Soren grabbed her by the arm, rocking them both to a stop. Halyna had halted, causing the Royal Guards to stop as well. Caris stood on tiptoe to peer over their shoulders at the figures far down the tunnel, at the edge of light from starfire. The raspy moans of things not living echoed strangely against the metal walls.

Revenants.

Halyna cast her magic, drawing on the aether to create a pale white shield of energy that spread like a spiderweb between them and the oncoming threat. Soren shouldered his way to the front, and Caris hesitated a moment before doing the same. Her awareness of the starfire became more focused, and she looked to Soren for what to do next.

"Keep walking. Caris and I will keep the starfire contained. I don't want to burn up oxygen. The rest of you, stay back and hold your fire," Soren said.

Halyna started forward without argument, arm held out in front of her, clarion crystal–tipped wand gripped firmly in hand. The spark of aether at the tip grew brighter as they closed the distance between themselves and the revenants.

Soren glanced at her. "Push your starfire to engulf them. Burn them hot and quick, but try to keep it away from the tunnel walls."

Caris nodded. "I'll follow your lead."

The revenants came ever closer, all of them with the too-fresh look to them that spoke of dying sometime recently and being run through a death-defying machine to aid the Daijalan war effort. Whoever they'd been—whether soldiers or citizens or debt slaves— none of them deserved to be used in such a way. The dead were meant to be burned, ashes sent to dance amongst the stars. They would not find the sky so deep underground.

Between Soren and herself, they managed to incinerate the revenants that packed the catacomb tunnel. Despite their best effort to keep the starfire burning in midair, the heat of it still scorched the surrounding tunnel.

Starfire decimated the revenants until nothing remained but ash that kicked up in puffs during their passage. Caris cast her starfire farther down the tunnel again, following Soren's lead. Halyna kept her shield up, the soft glow of it a marker of their position, but they'd rather safety over anything else at the moment.

"Eimarille might have had her people flood the catacombs with revenants. Not every route was accessible even before the riot last year. Causing cave-ins in some of them could hinder the stability of the buildings above them. She'd want the city intact," Blaine said quietly from behind her.

"She'd blame any destruction on the Clockwork Brigade and the Ashionens rebelling," Nathaniel replied.

"Amari survived the Inferno. It will survive this," Caris said.

Once they got inside the capital, she hoped their path would take them past the prison where her parents were supposedly being kept, according to the broadsheets. Caris was willing to take the bait Eimarille had made them out to be if it meant she'd get her parents back.

But first, they had to make it through the catacombs and whatever other horrors Eimarille had left for them to survive.

Eight

HONOVI

"Get us higher, and bring us around on the port side!" Caoimhe yelled.

The *Celestial Sprite* juddered hard as Honovi wrenched the levers to provide the engine with more power by emptying the ballast. Their ascent was rough, but they cleared the airspace where the anti-airship munitions were exploding, the sound like never-ending thunder in the weak light of dawn.

Honovi steered them around, seeing only sky all around them through the surrounding windows of the flight cabin. Scattered between their position and the horizon were airships from both sides of the war, all of them jockeying for control of the skies. Aeroplanes flew fast between airships, dodging bullets from Zip guns and artillery sent up from below as they attacked with their own guns.

"Sun is coming up," their navigator said.

Caoimhe studied the gauges rather than the maps long since tossed aside during the night. "Get us in formation with the others. I want the sun behind us."

With the allied forces having pushed in from the east, it meant they had the upper hand in the early morning during sunrise, while sunset aided the Daijal army. Flying with the sun behind them meant the enemy didn't have good line of sight for attacks. That didn't mean it would stop them from fighting.

"Falling into staggered formation," Honovi said as he kept half his attention on the gauges and the other half on the controls.

Most of the airships deployed in the skies over Amari were E'ridian. The Ashion army had lost many of theirs through attrition since last year, and the Legion's expertise lent itself more to land-based war machines than those that flew. Even with Eimarille's attack on Compass Air Force Base and the Ferric Repair Yard back in E'ridia, their air force was still something to be reckoned with.

The radio crackled to life, and Caoimhe snatched it up. Honovi kept his attention on steering them into position with the sun behind them. Other E'ridian airships joined them high above the reach of anti-airship artillery as aeroplanes flew around them, tangling with Daijalan aeroplanes in dog fights over the prairie.

The aerial battlefield had moved away from the trenches, spreading out around the plains surrounding Amari. Regrouping would help focus their efforts on a bombing run of the city walls, something Honovi knew the Daijalans were preparing to defend against, as they had before. But E'ridia had sent more airships to support the retaking of Amari, and Daijal had lost plenty in the past two weeks of heavy battle. Their war machines on the ground could be mass-produced, but airships took time to build. With Daijal trying to defend two fronts, Ashion and its allies had a better chance to break through now than they had before.

"All gunners, be ready for a line fight. Bombardiers, pick your targets," Caoimhe said sometime later on a local announcement through the radio, her voice echoing through the airship.

Honovi maneuvered the levers and toggles to pilot the *Celestial Sprite* forward. A glance to either side out the flight deck windows showed other airships flying with him in formation. Enough distance between them meant squadrons of aeroplanes could pass through and meet the enemy aeroplanes head-on.

E'ridian airships still had the higher altitude, and they used that to their advantage when many began to descend in sharp dives, picking out their targets of enemy airships. Artillery from the *Celestial Sprite*'s fore gunners ripped through the air in bright lines of passage, arcing toward the balloon of the airship in their sights. Honovi took in Caoimhe's yelled orders and kept them in the current dive as aeroplanes buzzed past them, picking out their own targets. They came in at an angle, Honovi reading gauges and controls as he kept them dancing in the air with the other airship, just barely out of reach of their runners due to the angle of their guns and altitude.

The *Celestial Sprite*'s gunners had no problem targeting the enemy airship. The streaks of their bullets led the way in the dive as he piloted the airship closer. The distance between the two airships was negligible when bullets were involved, and his airship's gunners didn't waste time with targeting the balloon. Their attacks went straight for the engine, ripping across the hull on the way to that vulnerable spot.

An aeroplane flew between them, above the line of fire, and took out an enemy aeroplane off their port side. The explosion filled the sky with smoke, making it difficult to see any oncoming threat. Honovi piloted them lower, flattening out the dive as he banked hard to starboard. His feet skidded against the decking even as he braced himself against the swing of the airship against the wires that connected it to the balloon. Honovi dug his heels in and wrenched himself back into position.

"Pull up! Pull up!" Caoimhe yelled.

Honovi obeyed without argument, yanking at the levers and switching toggles to get the *Celestial Sprite* to ascend as quickly as possible. They weren't quite fast enough as the airship they'd been targeting exploded, the force of the blast rocking their hull harder than expected. He flew them through black smoke with steady hands, squinting into the distance at their next target—another airship and, if they were lucky, the outer city wall eventually.

They still had bombs to drop, and Honovi had every intention of breaking down the gate to provide his husband and the others with reinforcements inside the capital.

Nine

NATHANIEL

They came out in sunlight, in an alleyway behind a building whose windows were all closed and dark. Nathaniel squinted against how bright it was, glad to be out of the catacomb tunnel and its tight space. The number of revenants Caris and Soren had burned through had been concerning, and he tried not to think about the dust and ash coating his trousers, telling himself none of it was spores.

Their small group had survived the revenants below, and Soren made sure the grate that doubled as a hatch was secured and locked. Revenants couldn't really climb, but no one wanted to take the chance of leaving an access point open to that threat.

"Does anyone know where we are?" Caris asked.

"Between the second and third inner city walls. Southeastern quadrant, so we won't have to cross the Serpentine River," Blaine said, looking at the map.

"We'll just have to cross every Daijalan soldier on duty between here and the civic center. At least the uniforms will help," Maurus said.

"We just need to make sure no one on our side of the fight shoots at us," Soren said mildly.

Nathaniel watched as Blaine unclipped a televox from his belt, flicking it open with his thumb. "I'll ring Honovi and get an assessment of the walls if he answers."

They could all hear the distant sound of explosions, which meant the fighting from last night hadn't stopped. What advance their side of the battle had made was impossible to know from their current position.

Waiting for the *jarl* to answer the call was a tense few moments. Blaine's shoulders never lost the tightness to them, even when it was obvious someone had answered the call. "Good to hear your voice. My group is in. What of the skies?"

The call was brief, lasting only seconds, which made sense if Honovi was captaining an airship in the midst of battle. Blaine's expression of grim determination didn't change, but at least Nathaniel didn't see any grief in his eyes.

"Any news?" Caris asked worriedly.

Blaine nodded. "He couldn't say much, but he did say most of the anti-aircraft guns have been destroyed."

"They probably took portions of the outer wall with them. We'll have to expect revenants in the streets in the outer neighborhoods," Soren said.

"Honestly, I wouldn't put it past Eimarille to release them in every neighborhood."

Amari had restricted travel since last year while under occupation. The silence from people they'd left behind after the riot—most notably Meleri's oldest daughter, Brielle, and her family—came with a waning hope they'd find anyone alive. Considering the accusations and executions Eimarille had indulged in for weeks while visiting the nobility in Ashion some months back, Nathaniel knew the odds weren't good.

"Let's get moving," Maurus said, holding his long rifle up against his chest. "We have a ways to go before we reach the inner wall."

The wardens were placed in the center of the formation Maurus ordered everyone into. It put everyone wearing a Daijalan military uniform on the outside of the group, giving the impression those in the center were prisoners being escorted somewhere, though

Nathaniel didn't know how anyone would miss the weapons on the wardens. Maurus had Nathaniel marching up front with him, as they would rely on the vivisection scars Nathaniel carried to hopefully get them past any checkpoints. If they were operating under orders of the *Klovod* and Eimarille through a supposed *rionetka*, then hopefully no one would question their passage.

"Don't remove your gear or your veil," Blaine told Caris.

She nodded. "I won't."

They left the alleyway at a quick march that Nathaniel struggled to match the first few steps, but he soon fell into the rhythm of it. No vehicles were on the main street, with many of the shop and apartment windows they passed boarded up. He couldn't tell if they'd been abandoned or if it was in defense of the fighting going on. The capital was eerily empty where they were, with most of the soldiers likely assigned to the trenches outside the city or on the outer wall. That didn't mean no one was patrolling the streets.

They turned a corner, coming upon a barricade of stone and barbed wire cutting across the street at the other end of the block. Iron caltrops designed large enough to stop a tank were scattered up and down the street. Their group wasn't immediately fired upon, and Nathaniel wondered if it was due to the uniforms or because they were so blatantly walking where the enemy typically wouldn't.

"Hold your position for identification," someone called out through a bullhorn, the crackle of feedback loud in the air.

"I'll do the talking, but be ready to act as a *rionetka* if needed," Maurus muttered.

Nathaniel nodded and watched warily as two soldiers extracted themselves from behind the barricade and jogged toward their position. They wore helmets and brass goggles, but their gas masks were hooked to their belts rather than being worn. Their rifles were held across their chests, ready to bring up and shoot at a moment's notice.

"What is your squad doing here? All soldiers not on barricade duty were told to report to the trenches," the woman said, the chevron patch on her shoulder identifying her as a sergeant.

"We were sent back from the front by our captain," Maurus

replied. "These wardens defected, and we're escorting them to their debrief."

The sergeant didn't seem convinced. "Prisoners that have some worth are to be remanded into custody at the jail. Debriefing is not part of the process right off the battlefield."

"The *Klovod* is expecting these wardens," Nathaniel said, taking a risk to join the conversation. At the sergeant's sharp look, Nathaniel slowly raised his hands toward his throat, undoing the buttons of his uniform jacket and the shirt beneath, pulling back the clothes to reveal the vivisection scars on his chest. "I have my orders, and the soldiers with me are helping me to complete them."

"*Rionetka*. No better than the walking dead." The sergeant spat on the cobblestones between them. "All right, then. We'll escort you past the barricade."

"The squadrons at the wall couldn't spare a vehicle from the fight. Do you have one available?"

"There's a truck you can use."

She offered it up reluctantly, but requests from a *rionetka* were as good as one sent by their high command, it seemed. Nathaniel's predicament got them past the barricade and into a troop transport truck that would cut their traveling time in half. He sat up front with Maurus while the rest took seats on the benches beneath the cloth canopy on the truck bed behind the cab.

They were barely around the corner of the block when the narrow window between the cab and the truck bed was pulled down. Nathaniel glanced over his shoulder at Caris as she leaned forward, clearly not buckled in. "We need to head for the jail."

"That isn't where the starfire throne is," Maurus said, staring straight ahead.

"No, but it's where the broadsheets said my parents were being kept."

"You don't know that for certain," Blaine said from deeper in the truck, his voice a little muffled. "Those stories are weeks old by now."

"The jail, Maurus. Please don't force me to make it an order."

The desperate urgency in her voice made Nathaniel briefly close his eyes. "I could maybe talk our way inside?"

"We don't know if that will work again," Maurus argued.

"It's worth trying." Nathaniel opened his eyes and craned his head around, feeling the vivisection scars pull with the motion as he twisted in his seat. He reached for Caris' hand where it was curled over the window edge, resting his on top of hers. "It has to be."

"It will be a trap," Blaine warned.

"Everything inside this city is a trap," Caris said.

They'd spring every last one if it meant they got her on the starfire throne, but Nathaniel knew she'd hate the cost of it—that she already did.

Nathaniel gave her hand a firm squeeze before facing forward again. "Head for the jail. I'll play my part."

Eimarille had turned him into a *rionetka* with the intent of using him against Caris and Ashion. Now, he'd use that same status to undermine her the same way she'd done to every country in Maricol.

Ten

BLAINE

"This is a terrible idea," Blaine muttered as the truck braked to a halt in the walled-off forecourt of the city jail. They'd passed three more barricades before reaching the innermost wall of Amari, where Nathaniel's status as a *rionetka* had barely been enough to get them through the checkpoints.

"I'm not sure pressing forward as we are was a better one," Caris said, her voice coming out with a crackle through the gas mask. She didn't sound like herself or even look it in the gear she wore, which Blaine was thankful for. How long their disguises would last was anyone's guess at this rate, though.

He fiddled with the glove covering the mechanical prosthetic, making sure it fit beneath the sleeve of his uniform. His jacket was a size larger to help accommodate the bulk of his left forearm, and Blaine was keenly aware that his face and predicament had been known by Daijalan debt collectors. It wasn't too far-fetched to think he was still on a kill-or-capture list somewhere.

They climbed out of the truck, those dressed as soldiers gathering around the wardens. Everyone still had on their brass goggles and gas masks, which Blaine was glad to see wasn't considered out of the ordinary amongst the soldiers who peeled away from the gate to come meet them.

"Why aren't you at your duty stations? Who sent you this way?" the captain barked.

Maurus didn't seem bothered by the other man's animosity. "We've orders from the *Klovod* through a *rionetka* to bring him these wardens."

Blaine watched how the captain's head turned to peruse the unbuttoned front of Nathaniel's uniform and the scarred skin it revealed. "I wasn't informed of such orders."

"Are you informed of every order that comes into the field?" Maurus retorted, able to push back because his stolen uniform carried the same rank as the other officer's. "I've been following mine."

The captain's gas mask and brass goggles made it impossible to read the man's expression. "The *Klovod* isn't here. He's with the high command at the palace."

"Then you can provide us clearance through the barricades so we can keep obeying our orders. These wardens have insight on the Ashionens' next possible field maneuvers. High command and the *Klovod* will want to hear it."

The captain didn't speak for a moment, his hesitance worrisome. "I need to call this in. You lot can wait inside while I do so."

Blaine wasn't sure being trapped inside the jail's administrative building was a wise decision, but Maurus didn't argue for any of them to remain outside. Considering the way other nearby soldiers had their hands resting on their holstered pistols, Blaine wasn't willing to make a scene.

They followed the Daijalan captain up the steps and through the entrance of the jail. It hadn't been converted inside in any way toward the war effort if one ignored how peacekeepers were absent and every available desk was taken over by a Daijalan soldier. They passed cells in a holding area filled with people who looked to be civilians, all of whom were alive, if more than a little bruised and battered.

"Prisoners of war?" Blaine asked.

"Arrested cogs and other dissidents," the Daijalan captain replied curtly. "They're being processed. The wardens won't be held in this area."

"Where will they be held?"

"A proper cell."

"That wasn't what we were promised," Halyna said, speaking up so Soren wouldn't have to reveal himself.

"I won't have traitors running free in here. You will wait in a cell."

Well, that was one way to get inside the jail proper.

They followed the Daijalan captain through a steel door that separated the administrative side of the building from the jail itself. The space that was revealed cut through the length of the building all the way to the rear. The ceiling was three stories above them, revealing three floors of jail cells that looked out into the main area.

Blaine glanced around, taking in what he could see. While almost every cell was full, the jail was eerily quiet of voices, the only sound coming from the footfalls of patrolling guards. He wasn't sure if that was due to magic or fear, but the answer soon presented itself.

They arrived at a cell on the first floor, the ones on either side of it empty, creating an ocean of space that seemed odd. It held two prisoners who huddled on the floor, backs to them. Blaine couldn't say what gave him a feeling of unease when looking at them, but he knew something wasn't right. The wardens realized what was wrong almost immediately, having spent a lifetime training and guarding against the dead.

"You're keeping revenants in here?" Halyna demanded angrily.

The Daijalan captain inserted a key into the lock of one of the empty cells. "You wardens should feel right at home beside them."

He pulled open the cell door, metal hinges creaking, clearly expecting the wardens to walk inside. And perhaps they would have done so to keep up appearances if Caris hadn't broken cover, speaking up for the first time while surrounded by enemies. Her voice came out cracked and horrified through the filter of her gas mask as she lurched toward that cell housing revenants. "Mother?"

If she'd kept quiet, perhaps the veil she wore would have kept her hidden, but there was no muffling grief in a place like this.

Blaine grabbed Caris by the arm, heart pounding as he yanked her back while the Daijalan soldiers all around them reacted to her outcry by aiming every pistol at them. A voice came from above, cold and familiar from a chase through this very city's streets last year. Blaine glanced up, meeting the gaze of a woman who wanted them all dead on behalf of her queen.

"Welcome back, usurper," Terilyn said from the mezzanine.

Eleven

SOREN

Soren cast starfire with the intent to defend, which ultimately meant killing the Daijal soldiers nearest them with a searing burst of heat, sending those on the mezzanine scattering. The starfire was enough to make the soldiers fall back and look for cover.

"We need to leave!" he snapped. They shouldn't have detoured to begin with, though some part of him could understand Caris' need to reunite with the people she loved. But the revenants in that cell with dried-out husks for faces were no longer her parents.

"No!" Caris shrieked, fighting Blaine's grip. "*No!*"

Her brass goggles were fogged up from tears that had nowhere to go. She kept fighting Blaine, who clearly didn't want to hurt her. Nathaniel solved the problem of her panic by hoisting her over his shoulder and ignoring the way she pounded his back with her fists.

"They're gone," Nathaniel told her, voice breaking. "I'm sorry, my love, but they're gone, and we can't lose you, too."

The sound of pistols going off made Soren instinctively duck. He gestured sharply with one arm, causing starfire to rise higher in the air around them to act as cover. He did his best to keep it away from the prisoners in the cells, but if the heat melted the locks off, well, so be it. And if it burned the Daijalan soldiers who couldn't escape quickly enough, so much the better.

Soren opened up a route between walls of starfire back the way they'd come since it was the only way out. Maurus led the Royal Guard in a charge for the door, pistols out and ready to shoot. Blaine stayed beside Nathaniel, who refused to put Caris down, while Halyna took up the rear with Soren.

"Our cover is blown. We aren't getting past the barricades between here and the palace," Blaine called out.

"That was a given," Soren grunted.

"So what do we do?"

With the allied forces still locked in pitched battles in the trenches and the outer wall only partially broken through, they couldn't rely on the cavalry to arrive. They'd have to fight their own way through the handful of miles between the jail and the palace, and they didn't have the bullets to survive that.

"We evacuate who we can and burn everything down between us and the palace. The city survived the Inferno once before. I'm sure it'll survive another."

Blaine made a strangled, horrified sound that Soren ignored. Maurus had reached the door leading back to the administrative side of the jail but hadn't opened it yet. The Ashionen ordered everyone to stand aside out of shooting range before pointing at Soren.

"Ready?" Maurus barked out.

It didn't take a genius to know what he was asking for, and Soren nodded. He drew the starfire closer, shifting some of it into a rope of burning flame that he shoved through the doorway once Maurus yanked open the door.

The screams from the other side mixed with the crack of pistols going off, but the bullets melted in starfire before finding any targets. The soldiers on the other side didn't have time to escape the searing heat and died for their efforts. Soren shoved the wall of starfire forward, keeping it ahead of them as they all scrambled through the doorway. He let the starfire behind them in the jail die down once they all made it into the hallway.

Nathaniel set Caris back on her feet, though he kept her hand in his as they raced through the abandoned work area, kicking up ash along the way. The entrance was ahead, all the desks between their position and the door hastily abandoned. The only people left in the work area were the ones locked up in the holding cell for processing.

"Let us out!" one of them yelled.

Soren ignored their cries for freedom, all his attention focused on the forecourt he could see out the front windows. "Everyone get down!"

They dove for the floor as the thunderous sound of bullets tore through windows and walls. Soren slammed his back against a desk and unholstered his pistol. He looked over at where Halyna was crouched, one of the Royal Guards having handed back to her the shoulder-mounted-grenade launcher.

"I can buy us a few moments for you to get us a way out," Halyna said.

Soren nodded, pulling starfire from the aether. "Do it."

The suppressive fire from the Daijalan soldiers outside never stopped, forcing them all to stay hunkered down. Vibrations through the floor made Soren grimace, the sensation a warning that a sentinel-class automaton was moving into position. They wouldn't survive the strafing fire of a Zip gun.

Halyna finished loading her grenade launcher and hefted it onto her shoulder, the long-distance weapon primed to shoot. She'd only have one chance to take her shot, and she took it with a calmness all wardens were trained to carry when in the poison fields. The flare of the launch sizzled out the rear of the wide barrel as the chemical grenade streaked through a broken window, exploding amongst the soldiers outside. Soren didn't know what poison or toxin had been inside the grenade, but the screams from everyone in range of the explosion outside told him it was probably one of the more painful types.

Soren looked back at Halyna, mouth open, but the words on the tip of his tongue never made it out whole. They turned into a shout of warning that came too late as Terilyn appeared out of the lingering smoke behind the other warden and slit her throat.

"Hold fire! Hold fire!" a voice yelled from outside. Abruptly, the guns went quiet.

The Blade dropped Halyna's body and threw herself behind a desk for cover, escaping the burst of starfire Soren sent her way. He snuffed it out with a curse. He couldn't simply burn everything around him, not when he didn't know where everyone on his side of the fight was taking cover. He'd have to get in close with Terilyn in order to kill her, all while the enemy kept them boxed in.

"The Blade killed Halyna," Soren called out, scrambling after her. He stayed low, not trusting the absence of bullets. Maurus swore, and Soren hoped someone was with Caris to keep her safe. His focus had to be Terilyn.

Soren lunged for the desk Terilyn had taken cover behind, unsurprised to find she wasn't there. The brass goggles he wore impeded his sight, so he shoved them on top of his head and unclipped his gas mask. Revealing his face meant revealing his identity, but that wouldn't matter if he was dead.

He unsheathed his poison short sword, pressing his thumb to the tiny button beneath the crosshairs. It released a thin stream of poison from the vials in the hilt and internal tubing to trickle down the blade to coat it. The paralyzing chemical agent was meant to bring down revenants, but it would do fine against a Blade. Soren slid out from behind the desk and cut diagonally across the floor for the desk opposite him where Blaine was crouched.

"I expect they're holding fire because Terilyn is inside with us," Soren said in a low voice. "Try to get Caris to use her starfire and clear the front. I'll handle the Blade."

Blaine craned his head around, looking over his shoulder. Soren followed his gaze to where Caris and Nathaniel were crouched behind another desk. Caris huddled in Nathaniel's arms, small in a way Soren knew they couldn't afford her to be.

"She's in shock," Blaine said.

"We don't have time for her to grieve. Get her up and get her fighting before reinforcements come."

"Terilyn might be a good bargaining chip."

"I'm through with bargains."

Soren shoved himself back the way he'd come, focused on hunting Terilyn in the confines of the room they were in, with no way out. Not the best odds, but Soren would make them work in his favor —somehow.

All his people were behind him, and odds were that Terilyn would try to murder them. With that in mind, Soren cast starfire on the area in the rear, not caring where it landed. Wood and paper went up in flames, electric sparks fizzing out as wires popped and burst before melting.

A shadow streaked out from behind a desk, coalescing into a figure that lunged for the entrance back into the jail. Soren sent starfire arcing toward Terilyn but missed, the heat of it hitting the wooden floor and eating a hole right through it. He let it all die down, sparing the others the heat of the magic, before throwing himself toward that same door. He let starfire lead him through it, using it to melt the bullets Terilyn aimed his way.

Before he could orient himself to her position, Terilyn lunged toward him, quick and lethal, stiletto extended. Soren brought his poison short sword around to parry, starfire flickering around them both while nearby prisoners screamed. Their blades clashed together, and Terilyn twisted close again. Soren drove his other elbow toward her face, but she dodged, went low, her other hand snapping out, fisted for a hit, only it was a lie.

Something sharp pierced his thigh through the weave of his trousers. Soren grunted, locking his knee as whatever Terilyn had injected him with made that area go numb. Terilyn tossed the small syringe aside, her hand flicking to another weapon strapped to her body. Soren shifted his weight and spun, snapping his other leg out and catching her in the chest, sending her reeling back. She wasn't a revenant and so managed to duck the sweeping cut of his poison short sword where her head used to be.

"Poison?" Soren asked incredulously. "You know I spent my entire life becoming immune to most of them."

"The *Klovod* made this one especially for wardens," Terilyn snapped.

"Terrible craftmanship. The alchemist masters back on the island would be so disappointed."

Even as he spoke, he could feel a weakness spreading down his leg, up to his hip, but Soren could still move. Whatever the *Klovod* had created, perhaps it could incapacitate a warden in time. But the alchemy running through Soren's veins would hopefully counter it long enough for him to finish this fight.

He planted his feet firmer on the floor, concentrating more on the starfire curling through the air than his sense of balance. Fighting was muscle memory, something he could handle because pushing through the pain or worse while alone in the poison fields was something he'd trained for as a tithe.

He hadn't trained at all to wield starfire, but reaching for the aether and manipulating the raw magic into something ferocious was almost instinctive these days. After the past couple of weeks wielding it in defense of Solaria, the power of it came easily to him.

Soren no longer had to hide behind the mantle of a warden, the only road he thought he'd ever walk now lost to him. He'd do his duty to the wardens and leave it all behind, because his home was in the south, in Solaria, by Vanya's side, and he would not die here in a country that had never been his at the hands of a Blade who belonged to Eimarille.

Soren wrapped Terilyn in starfire, twisting molten white-hot flame around her body like ivy, forcing her to halt mid-lunge, her dark eyes wide in her face. The starfire hadn't touched her yet, but he could see the way her skin sizzled from the heat of it, the panic in her dark eyes something not even her own training as a Blade could push aside.

"I suppose it's too much to hope you'll betray Eimarille and get us through the checkpoints between here and the palace without me having to burn everything to the ground?" Soren asked.

Terilyn's mouth firmed, her grip on the stiletto never wavering even as starfire melted the blade of her weapon. "My loyalty is to my queen."

"I thought as much."

He didn't try to change her mind—fanatics weren't worth the effort. Terilyn's scream of agony was cut short before it could get high-pitched, starfire covering her in a pillar of fire.

In the end, there wasn't even ash left of her.

Soren turned to leave and stumbled, his left leg nearly giving out. He staggered upright, scowling down at the spot where she'd got him with the needle. He pried a travel-sized antidote kit from his belt pouch and took out a small vial. The broad antidote would hopefully help counter whatever poison had been in the needle. Downing it in one swallow, he slid the empty vial back into the kit and tucked it away into his belt pouch.

"Will you let us out?" The question came from a man whose face was half bruises. He shared a cell with two other prisoners, all of whom were looking at Soren.

"I don't have a key for your cells, nor do I know where it is kept," Soren said.

"The supervisor room overlooks the cell block. The controls there can override the individual locks and open the cell doors."

Soren glanced at the entrance. "I can't stay to help you."

"We just need a chance to flee. Please, don't leave us here to die like this."

Soren's gaze tracked down the rows of cells to the one he knew the revenants to be in. He couldn't open all the cell doors, release the prisoners and have them walking into reach of revenants. He made his way toward that cell in question, ignoring the numbness in areas of his left leg. He could still walk, and that meant he could still fight.

Soren stopped in front of the cell, staring at the dead who had once been Caris' parents. The revenants were on their feet, fingers with ragged flesh hanging off the digits wrapped around the metal posts. He couldn't see what they must have looked like in the bones protruding through desiccated flesh on their faces, eyes sunken and dried-out holes. He stayed out of reach, knowing how quickly revenants could move, driven by spores, always looking for the living to propagate.

There was no saving them now.

Soren raised a hand, starfire sparking at his fingertips, and set the dead alight.

They made no sound as they burned, bodies crumbling beneath the excessive heat until nothing was left of them but the memories their daughter would carry. Caris could grieve them at a memory wall. Soren let the starfire die, scorch marks all that was left of the people who had raised Caris.

This was his duty, and Soren hoped she would understand.

He left the cell block and located the control room, a window overlooking the floor of the cell block. The analytical engine was powered on, and Soren flicked toggles, pressed buttons, and raised small levers until he heard the gears of every cell door opening inside the cell block at the same time.

He didn't wait to watch the prisoners walk free. Soren headed back to the administrative side of the building on shaky legs, carefully entering the workroom he'd left everyone else in, staying low to remain behind cover.

The front wall had been blasted through in one section, but no damage existed inside. The scorch marks were familiar, as was the melted, twisted metal of the window frames. Starfire had taken it out, which meant Blaine had convinced Caris to finally join the fight. Soren discovered, when he crept closer to the front of the building, that she hadn't fought for long.

The forecourt of the jail was littered with melted vehicles, half-burned bodies, scorch marks, and a sentinel-class automaton that was little more than slag. Soren found Blaine, Caris, and the Royal Guard facing off against a man dressed as a warden who hadn't arrived with them, one who held Nathaniel in front of him like a living shield. Nathaniel didn't move, didn't fight, standing rigid in the man's grip while the clarion crystal tip of a wand pressed firmly against the underside of his jaw. Even from where he stood, Soren could see the way Nathaniel shivered, as if he was fighting against invisible chains, but they were all in his mind.

Soren didn't have to guess who this man was. "Olet."

The former warden's gaze jerked toward Soren, mouth twisting in annoyance. "That is not my name any longer."

"The *Klovod*, then. It doesn't change your betrayal any less."

"The wardens betrayed all of us who came to them as tithes."

"Let Nathaniel go," Caris pleaded, trying to take a step forward but held back by Blaine's grip on her arm. "*Please.*"

"I think you've had my *rionetka* long enough."

"He isn't yours."

The *Klovod* smiled condescendingly, but his attention remained on Soren. "Where is the Blade?"

"Dead, just like Petra," Soren said.

Soren spoke the name of the warden who had guarded the border around Rixham for years and who he knew had been assigned to it once more when the wall had fallen around that city. He remembered Tock, Petra's strange clockwork cat, and what Ksenia had said about that automaton. How it had been gifted to Petra by a fellow warden out of care, perhaps out of love, but that love had died in the poison fields.

The *Klovod* shrugged one shoulder. "If you hope I have sentiment for my past life, you are sorely mistaken. But the girl's sentiment will be enough to let me walk away freely."

"Will it?" Soren asked, starfire curling around his fingers.

Caris shot him a frantic look, wrenching herself around Blaine. "Soren, don't!"

The *Klovod* took a step back, Nathaniel following in lockstep. "I think my *rionetka* dying would wound her better than any bullet. Eimarille will see to it."

Soren had killed Artyom when the man had held Raiah hostage during the Conclave, but he had been within touching distance then. He wasn't now, and Caris looked about ready to fight him and not the *Klovod* if he tried anything that might harm Nathaniel.

He weighed the cost of effort to get Nathaniel back right now against the fight he knew they were heading into with their push toward the palace. He wasn't sure if Caris could set fire to the city, and if she couldn't, then that responsibility would fall on him. If that was the case, then he needed to conserve his strength until his body fought off the poison.

The *Klovod* took advantage of his hesitation and Caris' refusal to allow harm to come to Nathaniel. He snapped his wand toward them, magic cascading out of the clarion crystal, the sheer force behind the spell like a bomb that sent them all flying.

Soren crashed into the wall behind him, the weakened wood breaking. He fell to the damaged floor of the jail, entire body aching, head reeling. He coughed through the dust his landing sent into the air. Training got him back to his feet, shaky though his balance was, the poison the *Klovod* had created a bit more insidious than he was expecting. But he was still breathing, sight was still functioning, and his thoughts were clear enough that Soren focused on the others rather than himself.

"Caris!" Blaine cried out.

Soren stumbled out of the jail, finding the forecourt empty of the *Klovod* and Nathaniel. The Royal Guard was scattered from the hit, some of the soldiers picking themselves up while a few appeared to be unconscious. Blaine was on his feet, crouched beside Caris' limp form. Soren hurried over to them.

"She's alive, just dazed," Blaine told him when Soren knelt on her other side.

Caris' eyelids fluttered before finally opening, gaze not quite focused. Soren ran his fingers over her skull and discovered a patch of bloody hair near the crown of it. Caris flinched away from his touch, curling in on herself.

"Concussion, maybe," Soren said.

"Nathaniel?" Caris rasped.

"The *Klovod* took him."

Soren curled his hand beneath her head and assisted Blaine in helping her up. Caris sat hunched between them, breathing heavily through her gas mask. Her brass goggles were askew, and Soren hesitated a moment before he removed them, along with her gas mask. The veil she wore beneath them showcased a face that wasn't hers. Caris fumbled at the metal clasp around her throat, managing to undo it and tear the veil off. The blonde hair and green eyes disappeared, revealing a face that Soren could admit shared features with his own.

Her gray eyes met his own, watery with tears, but her jaw was set in a stubborn way. "We're going after Nathaniel."

"Caris," Blaine said tightly. "We need to get you to the palace. You need to put out the North Star's decree and end this war."

"Claiming the starfire throne won't end the war. Bringing two countries together won't be fixed in a day. But my parents are *dead*, and I won't lose Nathaniel how I've lost them."

Her voice cracked when she spoke, gaze flickering over Soren's shoulder at the jail behind them. "The *Klovod* mentioned Eimarille. Odds are he might return to her with Nathaniel to lure you in."

"We don't know that for certain," Blaine said.

"She'll be in the palace," Caris muttered. She patted at the belt of her borrowed uniform until she found the travel pouch connected there. She withdrew from it a wad of paper that unfolded into a map of Amari. "But we need to know where Nathaniel is."

Soren watched as she spread the map between her legs, hunching over it. She unhooked a thin gold necklace, a tangle of pendants, a ring, and a shard of clarion crystal hanging from the chain. Caris clenched it in one hand, letting it hang over the map. Only when the clarion crystal jerked at the end and pulled on the chain of its own accord did Soren realize what he was looking at. "Who gave you a spelled map?"

"Your people did."

"They put a clarion crystal shard in Nathaniel's chest in case he became a *rionetka* again so we could find him," Blaine said.

The crystal pointed at a spot several streets from their location. The *Klovod* hadn't made it far with Nathaniel, but reaching them would be a problem if they didn't take extreme measures. The number of security checkpoints between them and the palace would impede their progress, but Soren was prepared to burn the city down if need be.

"Can you call your husband? Get him to bomb the area north of the palace?" Soren asked.

"He's an aeronaut, not a military officer. The airship might have different orders," Blaine warned, though he still took out his televox.

Maurus jogged over to them, gas mask and brass goggles still in place. "We have a truck ready for transport. It's out on the street and missed being damaged."

Soren offered Caris his hand. "Let's go."

She took it, the gold chain pressed between their palms, reminding him of the vow Vanya had given him. Caris clutched the map to her chest as Soren helped her toward the street while Blaine pleaded with his husband for aerial support.

"Did you burn them?" Caris asked in a low voice, staring straight ahead. "My parents? Did you burn them?"

"To ash," Soren said quietly.

Her lips trembled when he glanced at her, eyes wide and wet as tears trickled down her cheeks. "Thank you."

Her voice came out small and grieved, full of a pain Soren would never know because tithes never had parents growing up. "The dead are my duty. The living must be yours."

The future of a country rested on her thin shoulders, and Soren didn't envy her the road everyone on their side wanted her to walk.

Twelve

EIMARILLE

When the bombs dropped north of the palace, they shook the earth and walls of the vast structure. Eimarille wavered on her feet as if it were an earthquake, gripping the war table with tight fingers before finding her balance again. Kote glanced up at the ceiling where the gas lamp chandeliers swayed from the shaking, a grimace tugging at his mouth. "The bombing runs are getting closer."

Eimarille rested one hand on the long dining room table that had been repurposed for command use. Kote had taken over one wing of the palace for use by the Daijalan commanding officers overseeing the war effort. The officers in the trenches around Amari and those trying to keep New Haven from succumbing to the siege kept relaying updates back to Kote and his high command, searching for guidance.

"What is the likelihood of our airships being able to initiate a counterattack?" Eimarille asked.

"Low. We've lost too many over the last few weeks trying to hold back E'ridia's push west. Any airships in reserve would have to be called away from New Haven."

Which was impossible, given the travel time, to be effective. They were needed to support Daijal's capital against the siege. Eimarille had exchanged one unsafe capital for another, but while her son was

522

hidden away in the safe room beneath the palace, she could not join him. If ever Eimarille was to claim what was rightfully hers for Lisandro's sake, then she could not hide.

A communications officer hurried through the door at the far end of the room, making a beeline for where Eimarille stood with Kote. The young man handed over a piece of paper to the high general, the message written out in blocky script. "Sir, a message from the *Klovod*."

Eimarille extended her hand to Kote. "Let me see."

He passed it over after sparing the message a brief glance. Eimarille read it, lips pursing. "He has Nathaniel Clementine with him."

"Which means the usurper is past the walls," Kote said.

Eimarille's hand drifted toward the televox clipped to her belt beneath her day jacket. Terilyn had yet to ring her, and her lack of communication was worrisome. When they'd received the call from soldiers in the city of the supposed wardens being transported under guard by a *rionetka*, there on the *Klovod*'s orders, Terilyn had left to coordinate the ambush at the Amari jail. "The *Klovod* doesn't mention Terilyn."

"Have faith in your Blade's work. I am certain she is—"

The echoing *boom* of an explosion rattled the room's window and sent everyone stumbling. Kote braced her even as he barked out orders to the soldiers around them. Eimarille's ears rang, her thoughts going immediately to her son.

"They're hitting the palace. We need to get you to the safe room," Kote said in a low voice.

"No." Eimarille carefully shrugged out of his grip, standing up straighter. "That hit was a mistake. They won't risk a heavy run without knowing where their precious traitor is, and they won't turn the starfire throne into rubble."

She knew that in her bones, confident she was right. The Ashionens and their allies had refrained from bombing Amari directly until now. Many of its citizens were loyal to the other side, and she'd kept the capital closed over the last year to use them as a deterrent. As harsh as the fighting was in the trenches, the city had so far been spared heavy bombing runs.

Kote inclined his head at her statement. "We must stay vigilant. They've already broken through the outer wall, despite our best efforts."

"The inner walls will hold. They won't want the city to succumb to revenants more than it already has."

She'd made a calculated choice to flood the catacombs with revenants. Causing cave-ins risked the buildings above, but the dead could remain down there as a threat indefinitely. Eimarille had believed the Duchess Auclair would reveal the existence of the catacombs to the Ashion army and their allies. So Eimarille had ensured the way through the tunnels would remain perilous, even if one could cast starfire. However the traitors had gotten inside Amari, Eimarille would ensure they didn't leave the capital alive.

"I will see Lisandro, and then I will need an escort to the starfire throne," Eimarille said.

Kote looked as if he wanted to argue but held his tongue in the face of Eimarille's order. "Of course, Your Royal Majesty."

Eimarille left the command room surrounded by the royal guard, who whisked her to the safe rooms beneath the palace. The gas lamp–lit hallway leading to them bristled with soldiers, all of them willing to lay down their lives to ensure her son's safety. They saluted her arrival and had the heavy iron door at the far end open for her by the time she reached it.

Eimarille took the stairs down on light feet, the space below brightly lit. Soldiers were posted inside as well, standing up against the wall and not interfering with the servants, nursemaids, and governess in charge of keeping Lisandro distracted from everything happening above.

"Mama!" Lisandro cried out, abandoning his lessons in favor of running toward her in a way unbecoming of a little prince, but she hadn't the heart to chastise him.

Eimarille knelt, gathering him in her arms and hugging him close. His small arms wrapped around her neck, and she breathed him in. Eimarille stood, carrying Lisandro with her over to the nearest armchair. She sank into it, barely aware of the servants curtsying and leaving deeper into the suite of rooms, the soldiers trailing after them.

For a moment, it was just herself and her son in the city she'd been born in thirty-one years ago. She'd wanted to make Amari home for him, and she would, once the war was over. Eimarille smoothed back Lisandro's blond hair and kissed the top of his head. "My darling little prince."

"Mama, will you stay?" Lisandro asked. "It sounds loud upstairs."

Eimarille hated that he was scared, but she braved a smile for him, wishing desperately that Terilyn was there with her to help soothe him. "I promise to make it quiet for you. Until then, you must stay down here and be my brave boy. Can you do that for me?"

"Of course!"

Eimarille hugged him tight, squeezing her eyes against the sudden hint of wetness that dampened her lashes. But her voice was steady and calm when she said her goodbyes. "I will always love you. I promised you the world, and I will give it to you."

He was too young, even at five years of age, to understand the lengths she had gone and would go to secure his future. She'd bided her time as a hostage ward in Daijal growing up, bowed to the pressure to marry a man she'd never loved in exchange for a chance to eradicate the Iverson bloodline and take their throne. Lisandro would carry on *her* bloodline, ever a Rourke, and she'd pave his road as best she could. Which meant leaving him behind in the safety of that suite of rooms and returning to the fight above, where Kote met her, grim-faced and determined, in the hall.

"What is it?" Eimarille asked.

"Amari is burning."

Eimarille froze, some long-since-buried fear coming alive once more to grip at her. For a moment, she could smell smoke, could feel the ash that choked the air coating her skin. But it was all just a memory of that long-ago, frantic night when Innes had orchestrated her escape from the old palace and taken her west under the watchful, covetous eye of Daijal's ambassador at the time.

Innes, who had been silent in the face of her prayers the past few days.

"Show me."

Kote led her down the hallway and then another, taking her to a room that overlooked the forecourt of the palace. The tall windows let in weak afternoon sunlight, the balcony doors locked tight. Eimarille undid the lock and stepped outside, ignoring Kote's protest. The air was on the chillier side, the breeze carrying with it the scent of gunpowder. Airships dotted the sky above the city, plumes of smoke rising in their wake throughout the city from bomb drops.

Eimarille breathed in the smell of smoke, the glow of fire eating through buildings in the city's civic center, creeping ever closer. "Tell the *Klovod* to meet us at the starfire throne."

"I'll ready your escort," Kote said.

It was time she faced the North Star's decree. Eimarille had carried the Rourke bloodline since the day she was born, her name written in the royal genealogies. Aaralyn might favor another's road, but Eimarille's was still just as valid. She was Rourke, and she would put out that ever-burning starfire to take the throne.

It was what Innes had promised her, after all.

It was everything that was owed to her.

Thirteen

INNES

The starfire throne burned with his wife's love, an inferno of determination that had seen them, once, leave a distant hell behind to escape into the stars. Aaralyn had yearned for freedom the same way he had. Innes had thought to instill that yearning in their children, thought of all the ones to carry his belief of progress forward into a new Age, it would be Eimarille.

"You're grieving."

Innes didn't look away from the starfire throne, staring into its burning depths as the sounds of war echoed in his ears and in his memories, distant and half-forgotten as they were. "I wanted more than this for them. For us. You won't let us have it."

"Why can't you see that we are home?"

The ache in Aaralyn's voice finally had him turning around, facing her as he so rarely had since he'd claimed Daijal for himself. She wore well-worn trousers and a fitted short-sleeve blouse, a corset belt tight around her waist. The glittering lines of the constellation tattoo on her right arm burned like his own, a mark of this world that would never leave them.

Just as he knew he could never leave her, despite everything.

"Let Eimarille have the throne. Let her and our children have the world. Let the future be the stars once more. Let us be *free*," he said.

Aaralyn stepped close, resting her hands on his shoulders, and he couldn't push her away. She stared up at him, beautiful and forever young, eternal in this world and in the aether. He searched her eyes and found no recrimination for all that he'd done, all that he'd wanted, only a forgiveness that made him want to scream.

"Our children have always had this world. And you have always had me. Leave this road behind, husband. Come walk with me once more." She raised a hand to cup his face, her touch as warm as the starfire at his back. "I have missed you. So have the others. Have you not missed us?"

He'd kept his distance, interacting with his fellow star gods only rarely over the last few centuries. Perhaps the isolation had driven him mad, but he would never know. The one constant—in his dreams and in his waking wanderings—had always been his guiding star.

Had always been his wife, even when she was not beside him.

"I won't stop trying to reach the stars," he said, pressing her hand to his face.

"If it happens, let it happen in some other Age, but it cannot happen this way. There is no peace in war, no salvation in conquering. You *know* that."

Innes closed his eyes, turning his face into her touch. "Have I become that which we fled from?"

It was a horror he hadn't ever contemplated in the years of guiding his children down a road he thought was the only way to the stars. Had he been so blind?

Aaralyn's fingertips pressed into his skin. "I will not let you become our nightmare. Why else do you think I have done what was needed?"

Defiance and secrets and rallying their brethren to bring all the countries of Maricol to bear against his choices. Always holding out her hand to him every time their roads crossed.

And they had always crossed.

"I cannot stop this. There are roads yet for our children to walk."

"Then let us guide them. Together, how we always have."

She drew him into a kiss and drew him away from mistakes made out of love and the desire for something more, letting Maricol teeter on the precipice of change.

Behind them, as they bled into the aether, the starfire throne burned.

Fourteen

CARIS

"Take cover!"

Caris tumbled to the ground behind a building's corner, dragged there by Blaine as gunfire erupted from the heavily guarded boulevard leading to the palace. Hands grabbed at her, hauling her farther back amidst the group of fighters that had grown since they'd left the jail behind. In the intersection they'd been attempting to enter, a bomb exploded. Starfire called forth by Soren erupted between them and the threat, melting whatever shrapnel might have tried to find a home in their bodies.

"All right?" Honovi asked, staring down at her through his brass goggles, voice coming out a crackle through his gas mask's filter.

He, like the other E'ridians with them on the ground, had jumped from their airships when several had dived low on a bombing run, following Blaine's marker he'd shot off. Not all of the aeronauts had made it to the ground—their parachutes made them easy targets in the sky—but Honovi had, and Caris was grateful for his presence.

"I'm fine," Caris got out as he helped her back to her feet.

She wiped at her throat with the back of her hand, smearing the sweat there. Like the others in that first group to infiltrate Amari via the catacombs, Caris had discarded her Daijalan uniform jacket. They no longer needed to wear it, not after what had occurred in the jail, nor did they want to risk any friendly fire. Pretending to be something they weren't would no longer aid them. Besides, Eimarille knew they were coming, their arrival impossible to miss as buildings went up in flame ahead of them.

Some of it was her doing. Most of it was Soren's. He'd taken it upon himself to cleanse the city the same way he might cleanse the poison fields. Except no alchemy was in use here, only starfire, the aether never in fear of running out. Even now, Soren stood near the intersection, hands moving as he wielded starfire with a sureness Caris wished she could emulate.

The raging fire that had eaten through a block of buildings on the other side crossed the street under Soren's control, starfire cascading over cobblestones. An Ashionen magician had their wand pointed at the fire that remained burning on the buildings, using magic to create wind that drove the smoke upward rather than into the street they huddled in.

"We need to break through their defenses," Blaine said as he planted himself next to Caris. "Soren said he can burn them out."

Caris flinched behind her brass goggles and gas mask, grateful that both hid her dismay. "Can he ensure the fire won't spread? We aren't here to cause another Inferno."

"He says he is able to."

Caris wanted to call up starfire but knew she needed to conserve her strength. She didn't have Soren's training that enabled him to press forward no matter what, for the poison fields were never kind to a lone warden who let their guard down. Caris had spent her entire life growing up loved and cared for, never needing to fight until she became a cog and then queen, and she'd repaid that love by letting her parents die.

She wrenched that knot of grief aside, trying not to cry. Soren had seen that her mother and father had become ash, and that was better than the horror of the revenants they'd been turned into.

"Then let him. What of the airships?"

Honovi tipped his head back for a brief moment, staring at the sky.

"Caoimhe said she and the other airships would keep bombing the streets around the palace to keep the Daijalans at the barricades from reaching our position."

Caris hated that they'd resorted to bombing runs, knowing far too many citizens would die from the attack. Not everyone who called Amari home was beholden to Daijal, but she knew enough about public sentiment these days that their side would take much of the blame in the near future. Perhaps the history books would look upon their choices with a better eye, but Caris could see no positives in war.

Maurus pushed his way through a knot of royal guards, giving Caris a sharp nod. "We're moving forward behind Soren's wall of starfire."

Caris let herself be put in the center of a group of soldiers, Blaine ever by her side as everyone readied themselves for a march. She couldn't see Soren up ahead, but she saw his efforts clear enough when it was deemed safe enough for her to turn the corner.

Starfire extended from one side of the street to the other, a white-gold wall of heat that warmed the air to an uncomfortable degree. It was stifling but not deadly, and it was a defensive wall that no bullet or bomb could get through. Fighting starfire with guns was a useless gesture. One had to fight starfire with starfire to win.

Caris shouldn't have been surprised Eimarille knew that.

The wall of starfire abruptly flared higher than Caris had seen Soren command it to burn, spinning like a vortex. Caris froze, watching in horror at the way it jerked and twisted in the air, arcing back toward their position in the street, bringing with it a searing heat that would burn the air in their lungs before it even burned their skin if given half the chance. She knew it wasn't Soren's doing, and Caris desperately threw up one hand toward the threat, reaching for control of the starfire.

"*No!*" she shouted.

She sank her awareness into heat, into the aether, broadening it in a way she hadn't experienced before. Like years before, in a moment she only half remembered, instinct drove her power, enabling Caris to sink the very essence of herself into the roaring starfire threatening to consume them and rip it free of the person wielding it.

Threads like sun flares seen through an astronomer's great telescope burst into the sky, filling her vision with a brightness that should have hurt but didn't. Caris gasped, arms held overhead, hands clenched into fists, watching as the vortex of starfire ripped itself apart between the forceful will of three people.

Blaine's hand on her shoulder was an anchor Caris leaned into as she gasped for breath. She stared through the shimmering heat of diminishing starfire at the end of the boulevard and the park that resided there over the grave of the old palace.

In the center of that intersection, surrounded by a large group of soldiers and backed by automatons, all of whose weapons were pointed in their direction, stood Eimarille. The crown she wore glittered brilliantly gold from the afternoon sunlight and the fierce glow of starfire that she summoned back to her. Beside her, gripped tight in the *Klovod*'s hold, stood Nathaniel. Caris couldn't help the soft, pained noise that escaped her lips.

"Steady," Blaine said in a low voice.

Maurus and others put themselves between Caris and Eimarille, their own rifles and pistols at the ready. Burning brightly between both sides was a thin wall of starfire controlled by Soren. Caris squared her shoulders and pushed her way to the front, ignoring everyone's protest. Blaine remained by her side, Honovi a comforting presence at her back. When she made it to Soren's position, Caris placed herself to his left, shoulder to shoulder, and raised her chin.

"You've been telling lies to the people of Ashion," Eimarille said, her voice pitched loud enough for them to hear, even over the distant sounds of explosions. "You are no queen, and traitors to the crown will be executed."

Caris stared at Eimarille through the shimmer of starfire, aware of their people fanning out around them, behind them, preparing to fight. They were outnumbered, outgunned, but they hadn't fought this hard, come this far after so many months, to give in now.

She reached up and removed her brass goggles, then her gas mask, clipping both to her belt. She no longer wore the veil, that woven thread magic tucked away in a pocket. Here, now, she would stand as herself. "The North Star declared my right to the Rourke bloodline."

The starfire gathered in Eimarille's upturned palm twisted and grew, becoming a burning sphere. "You are not written in the royal genealogies. The Midnight Star ensured *my* name remained. Give up your road. Both of you."

"No," Soren said. "I have no desire for your throne or your crown, but I won't let you keep it. Not after what you did to the wardens."

If there had ever been love between Eimarille and Soren when they were young children, it had withered like dry prairie grass amidst a drought-filled summer heat. Caris wondered what their lives might have been like if they'd all grown up together. She'd never know, and Eimarille would never care.

"Very well. Then your roads end here."

Starfire exploded from Eimarille's hand, streaking into the sky like launched grenades, coming their way. Soren couldn't get his defensive wall of starfire high enough in time to block all of it, which left it to Caris to counter the assault that broke through. She raised her hands to the sky, threading her awareness through the starfire, trying to break Eimarille's control of the aether. The starfire jerked to a halt midair, burning like a dozen stars come down to earth. Caris grimaced, arms shaking with the effort to hold it back.

Guns went off, the sound coming from above them—someone must have made it to an unburned roof—and down the street, Eimarille made a wide cutting motion with her arm. The starfire ripped itself away of Caris' tenuous defense, streaking to the side toward the buildings on either side of the street. Starfire hit with an explosion of heat that nearly knocked Caris to her knees. It would have if Blaine hadn't grabbed at her to keep her upright.

Soren threw his right arm outward to the side, fingers spread wide before slowly curling toward his palm as he fought to make a fist. Caris watched as the starfire in the building there began to decrease as Soren put it out. She could sense what he was doing and tried to emulate it on the starfire burning to the left of them.

The starfire went out, leaving blackened, smoking buildings behind. Whoever had been on the roof was no longer shooting, most likely dead. Caris glanced over worriedly at Soren when he wavered on his feet. The wall of starfire moved with him, Eimarille clearly fighting him for control.

"I will ask one last time for your surrender," Eimarille called out, not sounding fazed at all from the effort she was putting into the fight. "Do so, and I will give you the merchant you are so very fond of."

Caris' heart lurched painfully, one hand coming up reflexively to press over the ring hidden beneath her shirt. She looked at Nathaniel through the shimmering heat of Soren's starfire, aching to have him by her side. "You have never granted mercy."

"Mercy? When you've turned half of Ashion against me? This is *my* country."

"A queen is meant to rule, not inflict cruelties on their people. But that's all you've ever done inside and outside our borders."

"You know nothing about ruling."

"I never wanted to, but I do now because I had no other choice."

Eimarille didn't seem impressed with her statement. Perhaps she saw it as bluster; Caris doubted she saw it as a threat. Eimarille raised her arm and rotated her wrist, the gesture causing the automatons to aim their Zip guns and fire. Soren's starfire wall went opaque, so white Caris nearly felt scorched by it. The dull roar of the Zip guns echoed in the air, but no bullets made it through.

The Zip guns went silent a minute later. Then the starfire Soren controlled was ripped apart in the center, sending their entire side scattering out of range of the bullets that streamed through that opening. Blaine hauled Caris away while Honovi handled Soren, both dragged to opposite sides of the street.

"We need to double back and find another way into the park," Blaine said.

Caris shook her head, blinking sweat out of her eyes. "Eimarille will have soldiers at every entrance and down every street. It's not worth it to try."

"Caris—"

"I can't run, Blaine. I won't."

He shoved his brass goggles off his eyes, leaning in close while their side exchanged fire with the Daijalans. His eyes searched hers before he bowed his head. "If I were Ashionen, I would be proud to call you my queen."

She managed a smile somehow, knowing it was as close to a vow of service Blaine would ever give her. He was E'ridian in every way that mattered, but the Westergard bloodline had long been struck from the royal genealogies, and her name had never known its pages. Yet here they both were, determined to fulfill their duties to Ashion.

"I don't have a throne yet."

Blaine helped her to her feet, the pair of them hemmed in by Royal Guards and other soldiers for protection, no one ready to back down. "Then let's get you one."

Fifteen

CARIS

Caris faced Soren's wavering starfire, straining to see Eimarille through it as a strange calm settled over her. Around her, the soldiers that had marched with her through the trenches and the catacombs and those that had arrived later in the streets shouted orders at each other as they readied to fight.

Honovi helped Soren to his feet, the warden looking pale-faced and bruised-eyed. Soren hadn't been as steady since the jail, but there wasn't time to ask how he was doing. Honovi raised his arm, pulling the trigger on a pistol that let loose a marker into the sky, purple smoke exploding over their position.

"What—" Caris gasped out.

"It'll summon a bombing run around us. Caoimhe and the others know to look for it. Come on," Blaine said.

The wall of starfire peeled apart in sections, holes opening. Ashion soldiers scrambled for cover in shattered doorways of buildings along the street and behind Legion-made bulletproof shields. Blaine tried to drag her off the street, but Caris dug in her heels. "No. You can't all keep fighting and dying for me."

She tore free of his grip and raised her hands, palms facing outward, and summoned starfire. It poured out of her, curling to fill in the gaps of Soren's defensive wall. Gunfire erupted on the other side, but no bullets made their way through.

"You need to burn the street where they stand before Eimarille does the same to us," Soren said.

Caris shot him an anguished look. "Nathaniel is back there."

Soren's gaze was implacable, no judgment in his eyes, only a ruthless sort of determination Caris knew she'd never be able to match. "You have to, or we all die."

The choice was taken from her by Eimarille. She could sense the other woman's power sliding along her own, the starfire writhing like a dying beast. Soren swore, his words drowned out by the roar of fire as it suddenly expanded.

Caris frantically tried to keep the starfire at bay, dimly aware of Soren trying to assist. But Eimarille's skill at manipulating the aether proved far better than theirs, and she broke through their attempt to hold her back. The force of the push sent them all flying. Caris crashed into Blaine, who took the brunt of their landing. Her head bounced off his shoulder, heat washing over them and everyone else as they rolled over the street. She lashed out blindly, pushing back against the starfire that threatened to consume them.

She rolled off Blaine, getting shakily to her feet, watching through blurred vision as the starfire twisted and arched over the street, kept at bay by her strength of will. Screams filled the air as a handful of soldiers went up in pillars of starfire before Soren's heavy presence against her awareness blocked any such further attacks from Eimarille. So Eimarille shifted her target—instead of people, every single rifle their side carried burst into flame. Again, Caris felt Soren trying to ward Eimarille off, and when the flames were snuffed out, she rather thought Eimarille had done it, not Soren.

"Tell everyone to get back," Caris said, staring down the street at Eimarille, watching the other woman approach with measured strides, trailed by the *Klovod* and Nathaniel.

"Caris—" Blaine protested.

"Do it! Soren and I can't fight her if we're worried about keeping all of you alive. You need to find cover."

"My road is your road until I see you on the starfire throne."

She didn't have time to argue with him. Blaine refused to move, and so did Maurus once her order was relayed. The rest of the Royal Guard stayed, too, as did the others. No one left, even when she wished they would. She didn't want any more people to die for her in the fight to see their country freed of Daijal rule.

Honovi seemed to have the same idea as Blaine, refusing to leave Soren's side as the warden met her in the middle of the street. Sweat beaded on his brow, and tremors made his fingers twitch, but Soren didn't look in any danger of collapsing.

"I'll take out their guns and the automatons as they did ours and then focus on the *Klovod*. The governor wants him alive, if possible," Soren said.

"The rest of us will engage with her soldiers," Maurus said from behind them. "Wardens and magicians up front. Let's keep the enemy away from our queen."

Caris met Soren's eyes, and he stared back at her with a steely determination in them that helped steady her. "Try to get Nathaniel free—"

She broke off as a shadow passed over them all. She jerked her head around, watching in horror as, with a casual flick of her wrist, Eimarille sent a fast-moving, snaking vortex of starfire toward the airship preparing for a bombing run.

Caris raised her arm toward the sky and desperately tried to redirect the starfire, but she was too late. The airship exploded like a bomb a few streets over, the concussive force of it rattling through the air.

"There will be more attempts," Honovi said grimly.

Soren raised his hands, palm up, fingers spread wide. Starfire flickered to life against his palms, bright like tiny stars. "Good."

Bursts of starfire erupted from his hands into the sky like fireworks, guided by his will, to arc over the street toward the Daijalan force that backed Eimarille. He targeted the automatons first, and Caris made sure Soren would hit them by lashing out at Eimarille.

Caris wielded starfire like a cudgel, forcing Eimarille to defend herself and not the soldiers behind her. The other woman rocked to a halt, arms raised and hands braced against the starfire that sought to surround her. With a twist of power Caris felt in her gut, Eimarille wrenched the starfire from her control, letting it wrap around her arms like a fiery banner.

"You will die here," Eimarille said, even as the automatons behind her exploded from Soren's attack.

Caris swallowed against a desert-dry throat. "No, I won't."

"I was promised a crown. I will not let you take it from me."

It took everything Caris had to hold off Eimarille's next attack, feeling as if all the moisture was sucked out of her body with the starfire the other woman called forth. She staggered, but Blaine kept her upright, never leaving her side. She was only dimly aware of Soren moving away, working to keep Daijalan bullets at bay as he sought to remove their rifles and pistols from the fight. Caris had to trust he and the others could handle the soldiers while she drew Eimarille's attention and ire.

Eimarille's control was better than hers, but their strength in calling forth starfire was about equal. Caris kept it at bay from herself and Blaine and did her best to keep Eimarille's attacks from reaching the others.

With guns out of play and automatons melted to scrap, soldiers resorted to close and deadly fighting, with the wardens and their poison grenades taking the lead. A circle of starfire kept them all at bay, trapped on the outside while Caris faced the woman who would have been her older sister in some other life, down some other road.

"Eimarille, please! You rule Daijal. Can't that be enough?" Caris asked desperately as starfire twisted between them like stormy waves of searing heat.

"I am Rourke. Ashion is mine by right of blood," Eimarille spat back.

"You can't reason with her, so don't try," Blaine said from behind Caris, guarding her back with Honovi.

"Did you hope to rule with your Blade?" Soren called out from where he was fighting with the *Klovod*, their poison short swords clashing against each other in a furious duel.

Eimarille went deathly still at his words, fingers curled like claws around flickers of starfire. "What have you done?"

"I killed her."

If grief had a sound, Caris thought it would have resembled the terrible, wordless scream that escaped Eimarille's throat just then. Eimarille rounded on Soren, thrusting one arm toward him and releasing an inferno of starfire that consumed the area he and the *Klovod* fought in.

"Soren!" Caris shouted.

Eimarille turned again to face her, white-faced with grief and rage, gray-blue eyes glimmering with tears that reflected the light of starfire surrounding her. "If I must live without my love, then so will you."

The threat had Caris running before she even knew she was moving. "Nathaniel!"

She was ready to push back against starfire, to keep him from burning to ash, but it wasn't his body she needed to protect—it was his clockwork metal heart.

Eimarille yanked free a clarion crystal rod from where it hung from her belt. Caris recognized the song of it only because she was close enough now to hear it, the notes the same as the one that sang inside Nathaniel's chest, ever a comfort to her. When Eimarille dropped the clarion crystal onto the ground and slammed her boot heel down on it, that precious song broke.

Nathaniel staggered forward, like a puppet with its strings cut, both hands going to his chest. His mouth worked, but nothing came out. The world went quiet, and Caris didn't know she was screaming until sound rushed back to her like a cresting wave hitting the shore.

"Nathaniel!"

Caris fell to her knees beside him, heedless of Eimarille at her back, of anything but the man she gathered into her arms. He was seizing, fingers clawing at his chest, eyes full of a terrified horror as he stared up at her.

"Caris," he gasped out, struggling to breathe.

She could hear the discordant notes of shattered clarion crystal emanating from his clockwork metal heart, the self-destruct spell having been activated by Eimarille's actions. The threads of Ksenia's magic that had held back the *Klovod*'s control were still present but rapidly fading as the mechanics and alchemy and magic that had kept Nathaniel alive since being turned into a *rionetka* broke apart.

"You'll be okay," Caris gasped out, lifting one shaking hand to push his hair away from his eyes as she clutched him close. "The wardens can save you, I know they can."

"No, they can't," Eimarille said, heat growing at Caris' back from a summoning of starfire. "And no one will—"

Eimarille broke off with a wet gurgle, the silence that followed her unfinished words enough to momentarily wrench Caris' attention away from Nathaniel. She glanced over her shoulder, watching as Soren slid his poison short sword free of Eimarille's chest. He'd stabbed her in the back and didn't bother to catch their sister's body as it fell to the ground.

Soren stared at Caris through fading starfire, something like pity in his gray eyes. "She was right. There's no alchemy in the world that can save him."

Caris choked on an ugly, cracked sound before the world blurred from her tears. She turned her head around, staring down into Nathaniel's rapidly paling face as the fight amongst the soldiers around them raged on beyond the ring of defensive starfire Soren held up, the screams of denial from the Daijalans ringing through the air. All of it seemed so distant in that moment as she held Nathaniel close, her tears falling onto his face to mingle with his.

"Please don't leave me," Caris begged.

Nathaniel's shaking hand curled over her wrist, fingers resting against her pulse, his grip barely even there. "My darling, I love you, and I would have lived for you, but there is no living with a broken heart like mine."

"I love you," she said, voice cracking around the sob that tore through her, fingers pressed to his throat, searching for a pulse that was fading away like the last bits of magic giving him unnatural life. Nathaniel had promised her, once before, that he would love her until his heart broke, and he kept that promise to the end of his road, there in her arms. "I will walk this road for the both of us."

"You will make a grand queen. I so wish… I could have seen it."

Nathaniel's mouth curled into a smile that had only ever been for her, the fractured song in his broken clockwork metal heart fading into nothing, its silence ringing in her ears as he slipped away into a peace she could not follow.

Caris stroked his cheek, staring into eyes that saw no more, and choked on her breath, on her tears, on the grief that welled up in her like a bitter funeral dirge. When she opened her mouth, nothing came out but a scream that matched Eimarille's in its wretchedness of knowing one would have to live a life alone.

"Caris," Blaine said from far away. "You have to let him go."

"No," she cried into Nathaniel's hair, clutching at him, at everything she'd hoped to keep after the war and would now no longer have. "*No!*"

Strong hands gripped her wrists, and she fought them, not wanting to let Nathaniel go, but they pulled her away from him anyway. She keened, some animalistic sound of loss that carried no words. Blaine's face, when she finally recognized who held her, was full of grief and sorrow.

"Honovi will watch over him, but we have to get you to the starfire throne."

She hated Blaine in that moment for asking her to leave behind the only man she'd ever loved. For reminding her of the fighting still happening in the capital and outside it, of the war that had been fought in her name and Eimarille's, and all the death that lay in the wake of her road—a road that was much lonelier than it had ever been before. But if she turned away now, it would be a betrayal to everything and everyone she'd lost, to all the newly empty spaces in her own broken heart.

So Caris let Blaine pull her to her feet, let him carry her forward while she carried her burdens and grief. She leaned against him, staring blankly at the pool of blood spreading away from Eimarille's body, too tired and heart-sore for hate to take root.

"Why?" Caris asked, voice raw from screaming, throat burning from overuse.

"I don't think we'll ever know," Blaine said quietly.

Soren held out his hand to her, his poison short sword still dripping with their sister's heart's blood. The *Klovod* lay sprawled on the ground some distance away; alive or dead, she couldn't tell. "Come. You have a duty."

She didn't want it. She never had. But Caris still took his steady hand with hers that shook. Soren gave it a careful squeeze before leading her out of the circle of starfire he'd been holding up. Caris looked back at where Nathaniel lay at Honovi's feet as Soren burned their way forward, until Blaine urged her to turn away. "Your road leads ahead, not behind."

Caris was barely cognizant of their run to the public park that held the starfire throne, their soldiers pushing Eimarille's back. It burned there in the remnants of the old palace's throne room, a beacon that had set the course of war before Caris had even known she was Rourke. But she knew who she was now—grief-stricken and broken-hearted, but a Rourke, forever and always.

When she finally stood before the starfire throne, that seat of power that had torn her life apart since her birth, whether she'd known it or not, Caris wanted to look away. She'd lived her entire life in the shadow of the shattered legacy it provided, walking a road that was always going to return to it. "I don't want it."

"I know," Blaine replied, quiet and sad. "I'm sorry."

Caris let go of her brother and her witness, walking forward on a road she'd only ever walk alone from here on out. She approached the starfire throne with stumbling steps, the heat of that ever-burning decree drying her tears. She came to a stop in front of it, holding out a hand so that her fingers trembled a hairsbreadth from a star god's eternal power.

Caris pressed her lips together and stepped into starfire, pushing the searing heat aside, making space to sit on the throne. Starfire flared bright and hot and golden all around her, blocking out the world for a moment. Then it sputtered and died out, leaving behind the throne and Caris and a kingdom that was now hers alone to rule. She stared at Soren and Blaine, at the remnants of their soldiers approaching, at the desperately wounded Daijalans beyond, all of them bearing witness to her right by blood.

Then Caris bent over her knees, held her head in her hands, and cried.

Homecoming

937 A.O.P.

One

BLAINE

"Lord Westergard."

Blaine withheld a sigh at the title, which had been reinserted into the nobility genealogies at Meleri's insistence. He hadn't been a lord in a very long time and much preferred being known as a *jarl*'s husband. Still, he turned to greet the man who'd called out to him, pasting on a polite smile.

Melvin Khaur, of the Khaur bloodline, and his husband, Ezra, strode down the hallway in the Ashion parliament toward him. The Marshal of the Clockwork Brigade wore trousers and a day jacket tailored in the Daijalan style. Blaine didn't mind the bright colors and heavy embroidery, though he knew it made the pair stand out, which was likely the point.

"Mr. Khaur," Blaine said politely.

"Please, Melvin is fine. I'm glad we caught you."

Blaine glanced at the thick folio tucked under the other man's arm, near bursting at the seams with its contents. "I was actually just leaving. I'm not overseeing the council today, but I had some documents to drop off for the queen. I believe Dureau has the gavel this session."

Creating the Council of Reconstruction and Reunification had been one of the first things Caris had done as queen, days after the ink had dried on the treaty of surrender the ranking Daijalan general had signed. Eimarille's heir was five years old, and High General Kote Akina had died in defense of Lisandro during the siege of the palace. No one had been certain at the time who had the authority to sign for Daijal, but an officer out of New Haven had been found once that city surrendered to Ashion forces, backed by Tovanian ship-cities at the shoreline.

Eimarille's death had gone a long way toward breaking Daijal's spirit, too many of the nobility and citizens tired of feeding their sons and daughters to war and the death-defying machines. Surrender had come more quickly than many had anticipated.

Winding down from war took time, though. Just because it was deemed over didn't mean the fighting had stopped. Pockets of Daijalan resistance still cropped up, and Blaine knew further dissent was in their future once Caris formally rescinded Daijal's right to debt slaves and dissolved that country in its entirety. Blaine was glad the Khaur bloodline had survived the nobility purge Eimarille had enacted, but he did hope Melvin didn't stop looking for a knife in the back. The nobles who had immersed themselves in the now disbanded Daijalan court weren't pleased with the demotion of their political power and would look for someone to blame.

"How is Lady Lore faring?" Ezra asked.

"Still more than capable of politicking with the best of them."

Lore needed a cane to get around on her good days and a wheel-chair on her bad ones. Her body still hadn't fully recovered from her forced coma while a prisoner of the House of Kimathi. Physical therapy helped, as did medicinal potions concocted by Ksenia, but recovery was slow going. Still, she would recover, and while her body needed assistance sometimes, her mind was as clear and sharp as ever.

As a lady-in-waiting and close confidant to Caris, the duty of taking over their bloodline's parliament seat had fallen to Dureau while Lore acted in their queen's stead when necessary. Lady Brielle and her family had died during the occupation of Amari by Daijal forces. Blaine knew Meleri, Lore, and Dureau mourned the loss deeply.

"I'll pass on your well-wishes," Blaine said, politely finding an excuse to leave.

Melvin, ever keen on such subtle cues, inclined his head out of respect. "Please do."

They parted ways, with Blaine heading toward the entrance to parliament, finally able to extract himself from the building's illustrious halls. The day was overcast and gray, with a sharp wind that smelled of rain that had yet to fall. His kilt twisted around his legs, the heavy plaid wool keeping him warm as he hurried down the wide steps leading to the Ashion parliament.

A motor carriage waited on the street, engine still running. A familiar figure got out from the back seat and held the door open for him. Blaine paused only long enough to brush a kiss over Honovi's cheek before sliding into the back seat.

"I thought you'd be longer," Honovi said as he climbed in beside Blaine.

"I tried not to get waylaid." He didn't mind playing messenger between the palace and parliament, not when it was Caris' personal instructions that needed to be delivered. Despite having control of the capital, they were all still wary of important information getting lost or mishandled. "The Marshal finally made it to Amari."

Honovi reached for Blaine's metal hand, curling his gloved fingers around the metal digits. "What's the latest news out of Daijal?"

"I didn't ask. The Marshal can provide it to Dureau, and he can report to Caris."

Ashion wasn't his country, and Blaine didn't want anyone thinking he was responsible for its reconstruction. He and Honovi had plans to stay through winter to ensure Caris didn't buckle under the weight of ruling as she got her feet under her, as well as to make sure Ashion kept its promises to E'ridia for the aid his country had given.

After that, they would return to E'ridia, where Honovi would focus on his role as *jarl* in preparation for taking over his father's position on the *Comhairle nan Cinridhean* next year. Honovi would be *ceann-cinnidh* for Clan Storm, and Blaine was looking forward to maybe teaching again.

He and Honovi spoke little on the short drive to the heavily guarded palace, passing bombed-out buildings and patched-over cobblestone streets. War hadn't been kind to the capital, and the scars it had left behind would take months, if not years, to erase. Priority was given to the outer walls, large sections of which had been destroyed from bombing runs by the E'ridian air force. Even with engineers returned to the city, it was a race against time to get the sections rebuilt before winter arrived.

The third week of Thirteenth Month was cold as autumn gave in to the oncoming winter, but it wasn't yet cold enough to freeze the dead. Revenants roamed the continent, more than there had ever been, even after the civil war between Daijal and Ashion. The fall of Rixham had contributed to the hordes, and the trade roads were more dangerous now than ever before.

With the number of wardens less than they had been and many of the tithes killed during Eimarille's attack on the Warden's Island last year, hunting down revenants and cleansing the poison fields would be the work of generations of wardens yet to come. Already, cities and towns were begging the wardens' governor for assistance, but there were only so many of her people that Delani could safely send out.

Wardens still patrolled around the capital and trekked far into the poison fields no one fought in any longer, hunting down revenants. They had a long, hideous task ahead of them, with fewer wardens to take up the much-needed duty. Despite the need for wardens, there was one who could no longer guard a border, and no amount of cajoling could convince him to take up his birthright.

Blaine and Honovi found themselves stepping into yet another spat between Soren and Meleri when they arrived back at the palace. The two paused in the doorway to the private office Caris had claimed. It was really more a large receiving room, but it gave her room to pace when she got antsy, and it had a nice view of the rear gardens.

"We keep having the same argument, and my answer is never going to change," Soren snapped in the trade tongue, arms crossed over his chest as he glared at Meleri. "I won't take the Rourke name. It was struck from the royal genealogies once already. Leave it lost."

Meleri frowned, her wan face bearing more wrinkles than Blaine remembered. "You are still Caris' heir—"

"Not anymore. She's promised to name Lisandro heir."

Meleri turned her head to stare at where Caris was still dutifully signing her name over every piece of paper Lore put before her. "I thought we were going to discuss that?"

"There's no discussion to be had," Caris replied tiredly. "We can't banish Lisandro without making him an enemy down the road. Neither can we allow him to be adopted by a different bloodline for fear of them grooming him to hate us."

"He may very well hate us anyway once he is old enough to understand the truth."

Caris passed a signed paper back to Lore and sighed down at the next, which was placed in front of her. "What would you have me do, Meleri? I won't kill him."

Blaine saw the way Meleri flinched at the flatly given statement. He would never regret a child's life, but he could admit that things would be easier politically if Lisandro had not survived the palace siege.

They'd found Eimarille's son in the safe rooms built beneath the palace, cradled in the arms of his nursemaid, who had nowhere to run. Escaping through the catacombs was impossible, and unlike his mother, who had been spirited away during the Inferno, there had been no one left to see him to safety.

Lisandro would grow up a political prisoner of his mother's name and ambitions. Giving him another name would not stop him from being a Rourke. Caris was living proof of that. Having Caris adopt him rather than another bloodline was the only way forward for two fractured countries.

In the end, Eimarille got what she wanted after all, whether anyone liked it or not. Lisandro would be Caris' heir, and somehow, she and the others would have to learn to love the boy. He would be king one day, and Blaine could only hope the boy wouldn't take after his mother in all the ways that mattered.

"I would never lay the parent's guilt at the feet of a child," Meleri said.

Caris lifted her gaze from the paper, bruises beneath her eyes from too little sleep. "Good. Because the Infernal War was Eimarille's design and hers alone. She turned the living into revenants, tore people's hearts out and replaced them with clockwork metal ones, and sabotaged every government on Maricol. That is a legacy Lisandro will have to face, but I won't let anyone blame him for it."

Blaine winced at the faint catch he heard in Caris' voice when she spoke of clockwork metal hearts. He knew, like everyone else in that room, how deeply she still grieved for Nathaniel. The *Klovod* who'd caused so much horror had survived Soren's rage during the battle and was being held in the makeshift jail, guarded round the clock by wardens who were also magicians. He would have a trial, eventually, and be found guilty no doubt, then executed for his crimes. It still wouldn't be enough punishment for what he'd done.

"Start him learning from you now. My father did so with me," Honovi said.

"Vanya plans to do the same with Raiah," Soren offered.

Blaine crossed the room to stand by Caris' desk, eyeing the official documents she was signing. "A pity you can't use a press to run these through and stamp your name."

Caris smiled up at him. "Your mechanical prosthetic would come in handy right now."

"Alas, I can't forge your signature." Lore laid the last document in front of her to sign, and once her signature was inked on it, Caris shoved her chair back and stood. The sound her spine made as she stretched made Blaine wince. "That sounds terrible."

"It feels terrible."

He couldn't be sure she wasn't talking about the rank she now held, but Blaine wasn't going to ask. "They're right, you know. Showing Lisandro how to govern from a young age will allow you to mold him into the kind of king you would like him to be."

"He hates me," Caris said quietly. "I don't blame him."

She had denied any and all mind magic to be used on the boy to meddle with his memories or emotions. Blaine had been fiercely pleased with her defense of Lisandro in that way, even if, perhaps, it might have made caring for him easier.

"In ten years, Lisandro will have lived his life with you in it, which will be longer than he'll have lived it with Eimarille. I know what it's like to reach that kind of milestone." Blaine glanced back at where Honovi stood, his husband staring back with only affection in his eyes. "I had a family and a clan that loved me after I lost my parents and bloodline. You can be that for Lisandro, and you will be enough. Love him, no matter how much it hurts."

Caris tipped her head back and blinked rapidly. Blaine politely didn't watch her try to hold back her tears. When she had her emotions back under control, she held out her hands to him, and Blaine took them in his own flesh and metal ones.

"I will miss you when you return to E'ridia," Caris said, voice surprisingly steady. She was learning already how to hide herself, and it made Blaine ache, but he couldn't take her grief or her pain away.

"We won't stay gone forever."

"Besides, we have a few more months before we depart. Our borders are not closed to your country," Honovi said.

Caris let go of Blaine's hands. "Thank you. We're just about to have the midday meal. I hope you two will join us?"

Blaine nodded. "Of course."

It was nice, for once, to share a meal with friends without wondering when the next attack would come. If the laughter was muted and the smiles hard to hold, well, no one ever said living after war was easy.

Two

CARIS

Caris watched as the Urovan ambassador bowed his way out of the throne room, a headache blooming at her temples. She wished she could blame the weight of the crown she wore, but she'd woken up with the pain.

"It will be a very long time before anyone trusts Urova again, even with the peace treaty in place," General Clarence Votil said once the doors were shut.

"The new Isar has formally apologized for his country's involvement in the Infernal War."

"Apologies are meaningless in the face of their crimes. Isar Dávgon should have validated the information his ambassador and military officers were giving him."

"They were all *rionetkas*, and he was killed by one when Eimarille ordered them all to assassinate their targets."

Clarence shrugged expansively. "Every other country initiated physical checks for *rionetkas*. My understanding is Urova never did. The new Isar apologizes now because Maricol is united against Urova, and the wardens refused to patrol their poison fields until they surrendered. The alliance his predecessor had formed with Eimarille is meaningless these days, and he knows it."

Caris agreed with that, but she also knew alienating an entire country they shared a border with was not the best way to keep Ashion safe. "They've been sanctioned, the same way Solaria and Daijal have been."

The tithes those countries owed as payment for sanctions would go far to fill the warden ranks again, but it would be years before any were ready for the poison fields. The tithes Daijal sent would be the last that country ever paid under the Poison Accords, as it would cease to be a country and folded back into Ashion in the near future.

She resisted the urge to pick at the gold leaf that covered the intricately carved armrests of her throne. It wasn't the one that had burned with starfire, merely an exact replica that Eimarille had ordered be created. Caris wondered if they had the budget to replace it. Perhaps next year. Enough aurons were being channeled into her formal coronation next month, even with her putting her foot down about the costs. She'd wanted a simple ceremony, but Meleri was turning it into a grand occasion to enforce the truth of Caris' claim to the throne.

"Is that the last submission for the court today?" she asked.

"Yes, my queen," Lore said from where she sat beside the throne dais in her wheelchair, a diary spread open on her lap. "You do have a meeting in parliament this afternoon with the Council of Reconstruction."

She needed to remember to take something for her headache before that meeting, or time with the council would make it worse. "Of course. If you'll excuse me."

She stood from the throne and left, keeping her head steady beneath the crown. Weeks since the peace treaty was signed, and she still hadn't become used to it—the crown, her rank, this road. She bit the inside of her cheek, blinking back a sudden onset of tears. Grief came and went, the process nowhere near linear.

The Royal Guard followed her into the private wing of the palace, to the suites that were home now, even if they held none of the warmth and memories of the Dhemlan estate back in Cosian. She bypassed her own rooms in favor of the nursery, the design of the space something she hadn't allowed anyone to change. Eimarille had decorated it for Lisandro's comfort, and Caris would not take that from him.

The Royal Guard stayed outside while Caris entered the nursery in time to see Lisandro throw himself onto the floor, pounding his fists against it as he shrieked. "No! I don't want to do lessons! I want my mama!"

She flinched but smoothed away the guilt before nodding her dismissal of the nursemaid and governess. Both women curtsied to her before exiting the room. Caris approached Lisandro and sank to her knees beside him. She gently placed her hand on his back, a touch he allowed.

"I'm sorry I'm not your mother, but I'm here now," Caris said.

"Don't want you," Lisandro hiccupped.

Caris smiled sadly down at her nephew, whom she would raise as a son, and rubbed his back. "I know. I wish I could give you what you want. For now, would you like a hug?"

Lisandro turned his face to the side, cheeks blotchy and wet from crying. He sniffled loudly, staring with his blue eyes so unlike Eimarille's. It made it easier to look at him and see less of her, despite the features and hair she knew came from Eimarille. Caris didn't let herself look away or think about how her sister had looked when she'd destroyed Caris' whole world.

"Okay," he finally said after a long moment.

Caris opened her arms to him and let Lisandro crawl into her lap. She held the boy close, the awkwardness of their first hug having faded over the weeks since she'd taken him into her care. He blamed her for his mother not being there for him anymore, unaware and too young to understand that Caris was the reason Eimarille was dead.

I don't know how to tell you what she did and what I had to do. I don't know if you will ever forgive me.

The thought was a running circle of anxiety she hadn't yet figured out the answer to. What she knew for certain was that she couldn't lie to him, not how her own parents and Meleri had about her past. But the truth hurt, it always would, and she wanted to spare him that pain for as long as she could until he was old enough to hopefully understand.

"How about a treat, hm? And then maybe a walk in the garden?" Caris asked.

Lisandro nodded his head against her chest, his tears probably staining her gown, but she didn't care. She guided him to his feet and got to hers, offering her hand for him to take if he so wanted. She would never force affection or help onto him and had adamantly ordered the same for all who cared for Lisandro. She'd let him keep his boundaries as his road guided him through this transition.

Lisandro sniffed loudly and scrubbed at his nose with his sleeve. He eyed her hand for a long moment before reaching for it, his small fingers curling against her palm. Caris smiled gently at him, putting as much warmth into it as she could before leading him out of the nursery.

They ate cinnamon cakes brought up by a servant with a pot of flowering tea favored by Daijalans. It seemed to soothe Lisandro, and by the time they made it to the gardens at the rear of the palace, the redness from his fit had finally left his cheeks.

Caris let him wander ahead, exploring as young children liked to do. None of the plants were blooming, and many of the trees were bare, but there was still beauty to be found amongst the garden paths. She'd spent many a day out there, walking to clear her mind, and sharing that bit of peace with Lisandro was the least she could do.

Soren found them in one of the far groves with a pond that had giant, brightly colored goldfish swimming in its waters. Lisandro didn't notice his arrival, too busy poking at the fish that came to the surface and seeing if they would eat the lilies floating in the water.

Soren took a seat on the bench beside Caris, stretching out his legs. He still wore the uniform and carried the weapons of a warden, despite no longer being officially counted amongst their ranks. He'd never caved to Meleri's or others' demands in that regard. Soren had always known who and what he was, refusing to alter his road for a country he insisted was not his.

Caris knew eventually Soren would give up being a warden, if only to preserve them. When the time came for him to walk away forever, he wouldn't be staying in Ashion, and she would never begrudge him the life he so keenly wanted in Solaria.

"How is Lisandro faring?" Soren asked.

"He misses his mother the same way I do mine," Caris said. She picked at the skirt of her gown, keeping her attention on Lisandro, for she knew if she looked at Soren, she would cry. "Thank you, again, for doing what I couldn't, for sending their ashes to dance amongst the stars."

"You needn't thank me for doing my duty."

Her parents' names had gone up on the official memory wall reserved for those in the royal genealogies at the main star temple in Amari, alongside Nathaniel's. So many names were being etched into memory walls in towns and cities across the country. Many of the remembered dead had been burned in mass pyres, while still many more walked the poison fields as revenants.

Caris folded her hands together over her lap. "I'm thinking of having a private memory wall built in the garden out here for Lisandro and I."

"You want to put Eimarille's name on it?"

"I want Lisandro to have a private place to reflect without others judging him for loving the woman who was his mother."

"And you?"

"I'll put the names of my parents on it and Nathaniel's."

It would hurt to always be reminded of Eimarille and what she'd done, but Caris wouldn't blame the woman who could have been her sister in front of Lisandro—not while he was young and incapable of understanding. There would be time for explanations when he grew older.

Caris lifted a hand to touch her necklace with careful fingers. The gold chain held the sigil ring Nathaniel had given her as his promise to love her always and a shard of clarion crystal that would never find its other half on a map again.

They'd held a private funeral service for Nathaniel two days after he died, just herself, Blaine, Honovi, Soren, Lore, and Meleri present in the star temple. She'd cried and cried during it, aching from the loss of no longer having him by her side to walk her road together.

"Nathaniel and I, we were a war story. It was never going to end with anything but this grief. I know that now," Caris said thickly.

"Don't mourn forever. Find some joy in what's left. The war is over now, and we need to stop and look at what was left behind," Soren said.

"I miss him. I think I always will." She tipped her head back, staring at the sky. "I haven't learned to give up the things he left me."

Nathaniel had been her first and only love, and the thought of cracking open her heart again for another left her wanting to weep. Perhaps, one day, she'd learn to love again, but it wouldn't be anytime soon. Until then, Caris would carry the pieces of Nathaniel's memory with her and build a world for the both of them around the space he'd left behind.

"One day, you will, and he'll always shine down on you from the stars."

It was bitter comfort, there in a garden surrounded by the only ones left of the Rourke bloodline, the three of them barely family. But Caris had always been good at building things, and she thought, catching Lisandro's eye when the boy looked back at her, smiling gently at him, that perhaps they could build it together.

Three

SOREN

The first month of winter and last month of the year saw the official coronation of Caris and her designation of Lisandro as her heir, permanently removing Soren from the line of succession. It meant his last border duty as a warden that Delani had given him was finished. The Warden's Island would not take him in as a warden, his ability to cast starfire and his no longer hidden ties to the Rourke bloodline proof he could never be neutral by their laws. Delani had made that clear in the few telephone calls they'd had in the weeks following Daijal's surrender. It was a repudiation, but it hurt less than Soren ever thought it could.

"Does Caris know you're leaving?"

Soren craned his head around and watched Blaine approach him on the mezzanine overlooking the grand ballroom below. The dance floor was crowded beneath the massive crystal chandeliers, the nobility dressed in their finest, military officers from Ashion, Solaria, and E'ridia in pristinely pressed uniforms, diplomats from those same countries, and a scattering of wardens who all looked drably out of place.

He had been told the Ashion fashion styles for high society were all scandalously out-of-date, but no one was going to be seen spending heaps of aurons on new suits and gowns for Caris' coronation when the country was still in the grips of post-war deprivation.

Blaine had opted for a kilt and a formal evening coat styled so that it fell to his waist, one sleeve shorter than the other to accommodate his metal prosthetic. His gold marriage torc was on display around his throat, hair braided back and adorned with metal hair ornaments, and knee-high black boots shined to perfection. There would be no mistaking him for anything other than E'ridian tonight, and Soren rather thought that was the point.

"What makes you think I'm leaving?" Soren asked.

Blaine leaned against the railing beside him, gaze on the dancers below. "Meleri told me the palace staff had orders to prepare your velocycle for transport."

"The duchess is probably happy about that."

"I think she'd rather you remain as heir over Lisandro, but we all know Ashion was never going to be your home."

Which was true. His home—his road—had only ever led him to Solaria, to one man. "I leave at sunset. I won't hold up the Legion's airship any longer than that. They have other stops to make along the way back to Calhames."

Blaine nodded. "Caris will want to say goodbye to you."

Soren picked out Caris in the crowd, her red ball gown and golden crown easy to spot in a sea of people. "This is all for her. Let her enjoy it."

"She's here because it's her duty, not because this was what she wanted for her life." Blaine sighed, drumming the fingers of his metal hand against the railing. "I think she'd accept it better if she still had Nathaniel."

But she didn't, and Soren couldn't be for her what Nathaniel had been in terms of support. "She'll have the Auclairs and the favor of the North Star. Caris couldn't have put out the decree if that weren't the case."

"One hopes." Blaine nodded at the ballroom spread out below them. "Don't leave until I can extract Caris from the clutches of her admirers and sycophants."

He and Caris had discussed much over the weeks since the Infernal War ended, but Soren supposed a proper goodbye would be best. "I'll be in the grand foyer."

They parted ways, with Soren leaving the glitter and glitz of Ashion high society behind him, a world far removed from the poison fields he'd grown up in. He made his way through the palace, the grand hallways still in the midst of renovation to showcase Ashion art and history, not Daijal's. Caris hadn't wanted to wait for everything to be completed before having her coronation. Better to start the new year off with no question of who ruled as she tried to integrate Daijal back into Ashion. It would be a lifetime task, he knew, but he rather thought she'd succeed.

The grand foyer attached to the main entrance of the palace was brightly lit, with Royal Guards stationed at the door. Soren chose to wait inside where it was warm, enjoying the quiet that came without being hemmed in by a crowd.

"Soren," Caris called out from down the long hallway sometime later, hurrying toward him in a way undignified of royalty. She was alone save for the trio of Royal Guards who always seemed to follow her around for her protection, one of whom was Maurus.

"Caris."

She came to a breathless stop in front of him, the skirt of her ball gown brushing against the toes of his boots. She looked every inch the queen her people wanted her to be, the remnants of the girl who'd grown up in Cosian wanting to be an engineer impossible to see now. "Blaine said you are leaving tonight."

Soren shrugged. "This was never meant to be my home."

"I hope Solaria will be it for you."

Caris smiled sweetly at him before leaning forward to embrace him. Soren wrapped his arms around her, holding her tight, and closed his eyes. Some part of him wondered what their lives could have been like—him and Caris and Eimarille—if the Inferno had never happened, if their roads were never meant to fork. But there was no use wondering about a road lost to them.

When Caris finally pulled away, her eyes were clear and dry, a steadiness to her gaze he was glad to see. "You'll call and write? I know you don't see yourself as Rourke, but I'd like to still know you as my brother."

"I'll call, and I'll write," Soren promised. He knew of her now, knew there was no point in pretending their ties did not exist. "Take care of yourself, little sister."

Caris beamed at him, still so young to bear the burdens of a country on her shoulders, but he knew she wouldn't buckle. They were more alike in that way than anyone would know.

Soren leaned forward and kissed her forehead before walking out of the palace into the cold twilight of winter. His breath puffed out in soft clouds of white as he took the steps down to the drive, where his velocycle waited. The Royal Guards on duty snapped off crisp salutes, which Soren didn't return. He buttoned up his jacket, swung his leg over the seat, and started the engine with a twist of the key in the ignition.

Pulling away, Soren didn't look back and drove out of the palace grounds, letting the single lamp headlight lead the way through Amari. He passed through heavily guarded checkpoints at every inner wall gate, always getting clearance to pass. The outer wall had finally been rebuilt in every broken section, and while there was a hard curfew at sunset where the gates remained closed, he was allowed through the one leading to the airfield.

"Hangar Three," the guard on duty said, pointing him toward the long main pier. "Ground crew is gone for the night."

"I'll manage," Soren said.

He walked his velocycle down the pier toward the only hangar that was lit. The iron doors used by the ground crew were closed against any possible revenant threat, but they opened at his knock. The legionnaire guarding that door bowed deeply at his arrival.

"We'll handle your velocycle," the legionnaire politely said.

Soren was glad to converse in Solarian again, the language far less grating to his ears than Ashionen had been over the past months. "Thank you."

He left his velocycle in capable hands and made his way to the gangplank that led to a Solarian airship. The crew got him settled, and Soren watched the launch through a port window in his tiny room, Amari growing smaller and smaller as the airship ascended. Pockets of darkness indicating bombed-out ruins were still scattered across Amari, but he knew by this time next year, they'd all be filled in with gas lamp light.

Soren wouldn't be around to see that progress, but Caris would tell him all about it one day.

Four

VANYA

Vanya's repurposed office in the Senate building lacked a fireplace, but the winter chill wasn't so bad he needed one. His winter robes were designed to keep him warm, and the aide who attended him ensured his tea was never cold. Vanya looked at the clock on the wall, noting the time. Taisiya was due with Raiah shortly so that they might have their midday meal together at one of the newly redone restaurants that made his daughter's favorite spiced lentil soup. He was looking forward to leaving the stacks of folios on his desk for later review.

The months following the end of the Infernal War had not been easy for Solaria or his House. Vanya had kept the Imperial throne only by his actions in the south and Callisto's lingering blessing. His depth of starfire was not matched by anyone, and he'd given favor to the Houses, both major and minor, that had sent those who could cast starfire to defend against revenants.

His favor couldn't overshadow the eradication of the House of Kimathi by Daijalan hands or the House of Aetos by his own. Blades had murdered Joelle, and Vesper had been given the choice of a firing squad or poison after being found guilty of colluding with a traitor and a foreign country. Their actions had damned their

Houses to death, but Vanya felt no guilt over their court-ordered deaths, not if it meant Solaria remained whole and free of foreign subjugation.

Two cities now stood without a major House to rule their *vasilyet*. Vanya was working with the House of Vikandir and the House of Balaskas to determine which minor House would be best to be uplifted into a position of generational power. He wasn't going to carve up those *vasilyets* as his mother had done with Rixham. And unlike with Rixham, the Senate and the Houses hadn't protested removing the Houses. The shadow of the Infernal War crossed borders, and no country had gone untouched by Eimarille's machinations.

Part of the Legion was still lending aid to Ashion in the north, providing military support to help fill in the gaps of that army's heavily depleted ranks. Queen Caris had been grateful for his alliance still, even knowing he hadn't done it for her. She was young to the throne but knew what she wanted for her country, and it was nothing like what Eimarille had envisioned. Vanya had no doubt Caris would keep to the treaties their diplomats were drawing up.

He scrawled his signature across another military order and set it aside before reaching for the next. He flipped it open and paused halfway through reading the first paragraph when someone knocked on his office door. "Enter."

His Chief Minister opened the door, an unreadable look on his face. "A warden is here to see you, Your Imperial Majesty."

Vanya stilled, fingers tightening around his pen. He'd had an open line of communication with the wardens' governor to coordinate the payment of tithes Solaria owed for the sanctions incurred, as well as the continued defense against the revenant horde still crawling up from the south. He'd sent Delani's last warden off with the latest border report a week ago and didn't expect them back until the new year.

But there was one warden he'd been aching to see for months already, having to console himself with the sound of a well-loved voice in his ears over a telephone instead. "Who?"

Caelum pushed the door open wider, moved aside, and bowed his head. "Yours."

Soren stepped inside the office, wearing the uniform of a warden, poison short sword strapped to his back and pistols holstered to his belt. He appeared healthy and whole, and the smile that bloomed on his face wasn't hesitant at all.

"Hello, princeling," Soren said.

Vanya didn't know he was moving until he was halfway across the office. Soren met him there in the middle as Caelum discreetly left and closed the door behind him. Vanya drew Soren into his arms and kissed him as if he were starving for air, the ache of months from not holding the warden washing away. Holding Soren again was like rising up from a dream, everything he'd ever wanted finally returned to him.

"You came back," Vanya rasped once he finally broke the kiss.

Soren smiled. "Of course."

Vanya cradled Soren's face in his hands, stroking his thumb over the arch of his cheekbone, looking into those gray eyes he knew he'd see every morning from here on out. "I am glad you kept your vow."

"You promised me your name and a place in your House. I've nowhere else to go but back to you, and I came home gladly."

Vanya kissed him again, the words he wanted to say stuck in his throat. Soren kissed him back just as fiercely, his fingers digging into Vanya's shoulders. Vanya turned them around and walked Soren backward until they reached the desk. Soren wrenched his head aside and let out a breathless laugh as Vanya kissed down his throat, catching himself with one arm on the desktop and nearly toppling over a pile of folios.

"Caelum told me on the walk over that Taisiya and Raiah will be here shortly," Soren said.

Vanya bit lightly over the pulse fluttering in Soren's neck. "I am aware of that."

If it were anyone else, Vanya would make them wait until he'd had his fill of the man he loved. Vanya reluctantly stepped back but didn't get far by virtue of one of Soren's legs curling around his own, keeping him close. Soren raised his gloved hand and brushed his knuckles over Vanya's cheek.

"Caris is queen, and I'm no longer welcome back at the Warden's Island. Delani released me from my duties as a warden. I've no more borders to guard."

He didn't sound angry or sad, not how Vanya thought he might. If anything, Soren seemed relieved. Vanya reached up to cup Soren's face with one hand. "Guard my heart. That's all I'll ever ask of you as my consort."

Soren gripped his robe and pulled Vanya in for a kiss that was gentle but no less intense than the others they'd shared. "I love you."

"And I you, until the end of our roads." Vanya pressed their foreheads together, reaching up to grip Soren's wrist, listening to him breathe. "Welcome home, my beloved."

Whatever Soren might have said was interrupted by the door to Vanya's office banging open and Raiah shrieking her excitement. "Soren!"

Soren hastily dropped his leg so Vanya could step out of the way as his daughter launched herself at the warden. Soren laughed, getting his hands beneath her arms so he could lift her up. Raiah wrapped her arms around his neck and continued to shout his name, clearly excited he'd returned.

"She missed you," Taisiya said with a welcoming smile as she entered the office.

"I missed her, too. All of you," Soren said.

"Well, you're just in time for the start of the weeklong new year celebration."

"There's going to be fireworks *every night!*" Raiah said, leaning back a little so she could look Soren in the face. "You'll watch them with us, won't you?"

Soren laughed, the sound soothing Vanya in a way little else outside his daughter could. "Of course. I'm not going anywhere now."

"I'll have the servants find you a set of robes to wear when we get back to the estate," Taisiya said.

Vanya thought Soren would protest that, but at Vanya's raised eyebrow, Soren merely shrugged. "I can't wear a warden's uniform anymore, and I've always liked your robes."

The idea of Soren dressed in Solarian garb, no longer easily standing out from the crowd as a warden or other, pleased him.

"If you wear our robes, will you wear a crown like Papa?" Raiah asked.

"Yes," Vanya said before Soren could answer in the negative. "He will."

It was Soren's turn to arch an eyebrow, staring at Vanya. "Will I, now?"

Vanya stepped close, wrapping his arms around Soren and his daughter, holding on to the entirety of his world and refusing to let go. "You'll be my consort. You already said yes, and a consort wears a crown."

"And if I don't want it?"

"For me, you will."

For a moment, Vanya thought Soren would deny him this want—this partnership, this marriage he would see written into the royal genealogies held by the Star Order in Solaria. Soren had declined the name and the throne and the crown of Ashion, refusing even to remain as Caris' heir. Vanya should have known the answer would be different for him.

"I'll wear it for you, the same way I wear your vow," Soren finally promised.

"Mine will be prettier," Raiah said, pouting only a little.

Soren threw back his head and laughed, the sound mingling with Taisiya's. Vanya smiled at his daughter and took her into his arms. "Of course it will be. Only the prettiest of crowns for my princess."

Soren stepped back, but Vanya didn't let him get far. He took Soren's hand in his, giving it a squeeze, and led them all out of the office. They walked through the Senate building, and Vanya didn't hide the way he held on to Soren, how the other man walked beside him as his equal, and let everyone draw their own conclusions.

They ate the midday meal together as a family and ended it with a handheld flaky berry pie, of which Raiah ate two. The sugar rush when they returned to the estate afterward was predictable.

That night, they took to the rooftop of his House's ancestral estate, all of them wearing warm robes against the cold breeze, the dark sky clear of clouds overhead. The moon was a crescent against deep black, the Viper Constellation ascending above it, the season of the Twilight Star beginning.

The first explosion of color against the starry night sky made Raiah gasp and clap gleefully where she stood by the railing next to Taisiya's seat. The estate's gas lamp lights had all been muted to better enjoy the fireworks, but Vanya could still make out Soren's face in the glow. He looked beautiful in a set of white-and-crimson robes Taisiya had insisted she'd had lying around just in case. They matched Vanya's in style, the golden vow hanging from his throat.

Vanya couldn't help but reach for it, fingers wrapping around the cool metal, the edges of the roaring lion pressing against his palm. Soren turned his head, a soft smile quirking at the corner of his mouth.

"Do you regret it?" Soren asked, tapping his finger against the back of Vanya's hand that held the vow.

"No," Vanya said, simple and easy, a truth he didn't have to think about. "Regretting it would mean I regret you, and there is no road I walk where that would be true."

Vanya tugged on the chain, drawing Soren into a kiss as fireworks burst overhead, the sound of his people celebrating in the streets beyond the security of the estate ringing through the air. Raiah's happy laughter overrode it all, his daughter safe and alive. Vanya knew he'd get to raise her with Soren, raise her into an empress that would make the House of Sa'Liandel proud, one who would be capable of holding the Imperial throne long after his and Soren's ashes danced in the stars.

"Papa, look!" Raiah cried out.

He broke the kiss and let the vow go but held Soren close because he could now. He smiled at where Raiah stood, pointing at the sky, feeling Soren lean in close, his head resting against Vanya's shoulder, a warm and coveted dream made real.

"I see it," Vanya said, looking out across Calhames and the fireworks exploding above, the stars eternally burning beyond, his road solid underfoot with Soren beside him. "It's beautiful."

Five

AARALYN

Aaralyn walked down the beach toward Helia on the last day of the year, leaving no footprints in her wake. The sun was setting across the Gulf of Helia in the west, a hundred shades of red and gold like starfire burning across the sky. Her shadow stretched long over the sand at this hour, and high tide sent the waves far up the shore, seafoam lapping at the edges of her boots as she walked. The wind was bitterly cold, but she didn't feel it. She had never felt the cold since the aether replaced her blood with molten starfire Ages ago.

The red-orange glow from the setting sun flared brighter for a moment, then faded as another person came to walk beside her. Aaralyn tilted her head in Callisto's direction but never slowed her stride. "Sister."

"Sister," Callisto drawled, the Dawn Star fisting her Solarian robes in both hands to lift them out of reach of the tide.

Three more steps and another flare of starfire brought Nilsine to them, wearing the fur-lined leather flight jacket of an E'ridian aeronaut. The Dusk Star tossed her braid with its metal hair adornments over one shoulder and matched her stride to the other two. "I hope this won't take long."

"As long as it needs to," Aaralyn said easily.

The tide receded then rushed up the shore again, bringing with it a flash of starfire and Farren, barefoot and shirtless but wearing colorful trousers. The Eclipse Star kicked their foot through the receding wave, sending droplets of water arcing into the sky, glittering like clarion crystal. "Next time, we gather on one of my ship-cities."

"No," Callisto said immediately.

Farren threw back their head and laughed, striding over wet sand, never minding the waves that washed up to tangle sea foam around their ankles. "You are missing out, sister."

"I like my feet planted firmly on the earth, thank you."

"We all do, but the sea is just another kind of land if you think about it."

Another flare of starfire, and Xaxis appeared, the Midnight Star wrapped up in a heavy winter coat and the *ushan* favored by his children. "Next time, I would rather we not wage a war."

"As would I," Aaralyn said.

A last flare of starfire on the shore up ahead burned bright against the encroaching dark. Innes appeared from within its fiery depths, the Twilight Star ever prideful beneath their attention. "It was needed."

Callisto planted her feet on the sand, along with the others. "Was it truly? We agreed when we first came here and were changed that we would each claim a country to guide. No one of us held the right to the entire continent and Maricol's seas."

"We also decreed we would not reach for the stars," Farren said, almost tartly.

Innes turned his head to stare at the setting sun, the features of his face bathed in its fading light. "Our children will reach for them one day, as we did."

His voice carried an ache in it for the memory of a home Aaralyn only ever saw in her deepest dreams anymore. She crossed the distance between them and took Innes' hand in hers, tangling their fingers together. When he would not look at her, she touched his chin with her other hand, turning his head so that he had to face her as the rest of their siblings gathered around them.

"Maricol saved us even as it remade us. We have a duty to those who came after us to show them this world is home," Aaralyn said.

"We spent thousands of years culling the seeds of progress, but they were always going to grow. Progress cannot be stopped."

Nilsine crossed her arms over her chest and turned to face the sunset. "Perhaps we should cultivate a new Age, hm?"

Callisto snorted and faced west as well. "What do you think this war was all about?"

Innes turned his face into Aaralyn's touch, his breath warm against the skin of her palm. She so missed having him close, the last few centuries an ache she'd had to endure alone. "Husband, we tried it your way. Let us go back to how we were before, where we walked this road together and guided our children as one."

"Would you still have me? After all I've done?" Innes asked.

"Yes." Daijal would become a footnote in the long history of the Ages they all sought to build in the centuries and millennia that stretched out ahead of them. Ashion would be whole once more, as it had been at the beginning and would be until the end.

"I would appreciate not being drawn into your spats next time," Nilsine said.

"It brought your children out of isolation," Xaxis rumbled.

Nilsine waved off his words. "I was working on that."

Aaralyn let them squabble in the ways they had long, long ago, when they'd served beneath her in the space between stars. It was familiar, this bond with them, this love they all shared for each other and the children they guided.

Innes stepped out of reach but didn't go far, didn't disappear as he had over the past few centuries. "A new beginning?"

Aaralyn looked west, the six of them watching the last remnants of sunlight fade away as the sun slipped beneath the horizon. The sky was a blanket of deep blue turning black as night encroached from the east, bringing with it a million and more stars to light the road ahead.

"A new Age," Aaralyn said.

Prelude

61 A.O.R.

One

CARIS

Caris marked the first-year anniversary of the Infernal War as a day of national remembrance, shared by representatives from every country still in existence. The memory walls across Ashion overflowed with names, the pews in star temples packed with those left behind. Caris did her duty as queen, a pillar of strength for the mourners to look to. After the sermon, after she laid a wreath at the feet of the North Star's statue carved into the memory wall in Amari, Caris was whisked away back to the palace for a state dinner.

"At least rationing is over and done with," Lore said as she adjusted the drape of Caris' gown. "I'm looking forward to dessert."

"Will there be cake?" Lisandro asked from where he stood beside the throne to Caris' right. At six years old, he was a reserved boy these days, the war and loss of his mother having changed him as it had everyone.

"You'll have some in the nursery," Caris promised.

Lisandro fiddled with the lapels of his formal suit jacket, the golden circlet he wore as heir glittering brightly in the gas lamp light. "Berry cake, please, Aunt Caris."

"I have it on good authority the cooks have made one special just for you."

He smiled at her, with none of the anger he used to carry, time easing his pain and grief. Children were resilient, but he remembered his mother, and Caris had no desire to force him to see her as a replacement. She was learning to love him as if he was hers, learning, too, what it meant to be a parent regardless of names and titles.

"There, I think that's done it." Lore stepped back, discreetly smoothing down the skirt of her own gown, the rich emerald green of it suiting her.

Caris studied the exquisitely designed ball gown she wore, with its lace appliques and clarion crystal beads, the jewelry that caught the light, and the necklace that held Nathaniel's ring and clarion crystal shard. The crown on her head was newly requisitioned, lighter than the one she'd been coronated in, and filled with so many diamonds it had made her blanch when she first saw it.

"Thank you," Caris said, adjusting the white satin sash that crossed one shoulder. "Hopefully, this won't take too long."

"Not more than an hour, Your Royal Majesty," the palace's head historian promised before returning his attention to the photographer and their assistant overseeing the last tweaks to the cameras.

Caris shared a pained look with Lore, who bit her lip and ducked her head to hide her laughter. Caris was glad to see Lore had healed enough over the past year to find humor again and stand on her own two feet without need of a cane or a wheelchair these days.

"Only an hour," Caris muttered under her breath.

She'd counted days like that since the end of the Infernal War, getting through the aftermath through sheer will alone at times. This was no different, even if Lisandro was better at being still than he had been when he was five.

Eventually, the photographer indicated he was ready, and Caris sat up straighter on her throne, holding out her hand to Lisandro. Her nephew placed his hand in hers, and she settled them on the gilded armrest of the throne, both of them staring into the lens of the camera. This portrait sitting was to aid in documenting Lisandro as her heir, their first official royal portrait together as Rourkes.

Caris straightened her shoulders and raised her chin, crown

settled firmly on her head. She stared at the camera, fixed a smile on her face, and held it, wishing for all the world in that moment that Nathaniel was seated beside her, his hand in hers. But he wasn't there, and Caris smiled for the camera in the throne room, the flash of the bulb nearly blinding her—

—and months later, she smiled when she welcomed the wardens' governor to parliament—

—she smiled when she signed a treaty with the Tovan Isles in New Haven some years after the war—

—and she smiled when Lisandro stopped mourning his mother and came to her—

—she smiled at every opening of the Ashion parliament that she presided over and—

—when Blaine and Honovi adopted an orphaned boy into their clan and brought him on an airship one year to meet her and—

—she smiled when she shook the Imperial emperor's hand some years after the end of the Infernal War, her brother in blood only but never name by his side as consort, finally happy, and—

—she smiled when Lisandro earned his commission from the Ashion officer's school, a proud young man who hugged her fiercely, an embrace splashed across the broadsheets to further dispel the rumor they were at odds with each other—

—and she smiled when he fell in love and married Captain Hyacinth Votil's daughter and—

—Caris never stopped smiling through the years that came after the Infernal War and the start of the Age of Rebirth decreed by the star gods. The portraits of her life could be found in tintype photographs and oil paintings in homes across the continent, moments captured in perpetuity of a girl grown to womanhood and wedded to her country rather than the man she never stopped loving, whose memory hung from her throat and never left her, the song of it heard in her dreams.

And one day, decades after she was crowned, Caris settled herself on that bench in the palace garden beneath a flowering tree, in a hidden grove that held a pond and a private memory wall that carried only a handful of names. At the age of eighty-two, her bones ached from years lived, but the spring day was warm after a cold winter, and she soaked up the sun like her granddaughter's favorite cat.

Her vision wasn't the best these days, the glasses perched on her nose ever present. Still, she could make out the names on the memory wall well enough, tracing the letters carved into marble.

"I wish you could have seen it," Caris said into the quiet of the garden, speaking to ghosts. "You would have loved it, I think. This world we made."

"You did well. Never doubt that."

Caris jerked, startled, but a warm hand pressing down on her shoulder kept her on the bench. She looked up and up, staring into the ageless face of the North Star. Aaralyn looked younger than her granddaughter, radiant in the way all the star gods were. "My lady."

Aaralyn gently patted Caris' shoulder before folding her hands together in front of her. She was dressed as a noblewoman, the capped sleeves of her gown showing off the golden constellation tattoo that covered her right arm. "Queen Mother."

Caris bowed her head, empty of a crown these days. Lisandro ruled in her place and had for quite some time, her nephew whom she loved as a son presiding over the reunified country that was Ashion with a gravity Caris had been the one to impart to him. Lisandro made a fine king, respected and even-handed when it came to ruling, and she was ever proud of the man he'd become. "Are you satisfied?"

"Quite. It was a long time coming, but Ashion was always meant to be whole again. That is your legacy. Your people will cherish it, as they have cherished you."

Aaralyn's shadow on the ground disappeared. Caris raised her head, ready to call out to the North Star, to offer a prayer, but the words stuck in her throat as she saw who walked down the garden path toward her.

An impossible ghost from her past approached, the faded memory of him sharpening in her mind just then. It hurt to breathe, tears coming to her eyes as he stopped in front of her and bowed. As he straightened, he offered her his hand, smiling all the while.

"My darling Caris," Nathaniel said. "Will you walk with me?"

"Oh, Nathaniel," Caris breathed, the sun overhead filling the sky and washing everything out, but it didn't matter, for all she saw were the stars in his warm brown eyes.

At the end of her road, Caris reached for Nathaniel's hand.

Do you want more Soren and Vanya?
Visit https://bit.ly/TQSF-bonus for a bonus short story.

To stay updated on all Hailey Turner book news, join my newsletter.

If you like urban fantasy and mythology, check out Hailey Turner's Soulbound series, starting with *A Ferry of Bones & Gold*.

Glossary

Short descriptions of words, acronyms, and phrases used in the story that weren't readily explained in text. Included as well are character names.

A.O.C.: Age of Constellations. A past Age on Maricol that occurred after A.O.S. and before A.O.P.

A.O.P.: Age of Progress. A past Age that ended after the Infernal War.

A.O.R.: Age of Rebirth. The current Age that follows A.O.P.

A.O.S.: Age of Starfall. The first Age on Maricol that encompassed landing and initial colonization of Maricol. This Age held the Dying Times and the Great Separation.

Aaralyn: Star god. Also known as the North Star, patron goddess of life. Apex star god of the Star Order. Her constellation is the Wolf, and her tattoo is located on her right arm.

Aeronaut: One who captains or crews on an airship.

Aether: The fifth element that powers magic and clarion crystals, located in an otherworldly plane.

Aetos, Vesper: Solarian. Listed in the nobility genealogies. Heir to the House of Aetos.

Age: Denotations of historical and current eras.

Airfield: A landing field located outside major cities and large towns for the anchorage of airships.

Airship: A lighter-than-air craft powered by steam engines and commercial flight balloons.

Akina, Kote: Daijalan. High General of the Daijal army.

Alida: Solarian. Former majordomo to Vanya's household. Deceased.

Alrickson: E'ridian. Listed in the royal genealogies. Current *ceann-cinnidh* of Clan Storm.

Amari: City. Capital of Ashion.

Ashion: Country. Debt bondage is outlawed within its borders. Its capital city is Amari. The country's patron guiding star is Aaralyn, the North Star. The country's affirmed constellation is the Wolf.

Ashionen: Denoting ties to or nationality of Ashion. Language descriptor.

Auclair, Brielle: Ashionen. Listed in the nobility genealogies. Named Whisper in the Clockwork Brigade. Oldest child of Meleri.

Auclair, Dureau: Ashionen. Listed in the nobility genealogies. Named Locke in the Clockwork Brigade. Youngest child of Meleri.

Auclair, Lore: Ashionen. Listed in the nobility genealogies. Named Mainspring in the Clockwork Brigade. Middle child of Meleri.

Auclair, Meleri: Ashionen. Listed in the nobility genealogies. Spymaster. Named Fulcrum in the Clockwork Brigade. Head of the Auclair bloodline.

Auron: Currency. Used in every country on Maricol.

Automaton: A clockwork machine that varies in size, shape, and use. Generally powered by steam engines but can also be powered by clarion crystals and the aether.

Avenyah: Town. Located in Solaria.

Balaskas, Cybele: Solarian. Listed in the nobility genealogies. *Vezir* to the House of Balaskas. Head of her House.

Bellingham: City. Located in Solaria.

Blade: Secretive Daijalan Star Order sect of assassins.

Blaine: E'ridian. Listed in the nobility genealogies. Clan Storm.

Married to Honovi. Last surviving member of the Westergard bloodline.

Bloodline: Those of noble and royal families who can trace their lineage back thousands of years through genealogies to prove genetics not damaged by poison.

Broadsheets: Daily printed publication containing news.

Caelum: Solarian. Chief Minister to the Imperial throne.

Calhames: City. Capital of Solaria.

Callisto: Star god. Also known as the Dawn Star, patron goddess of death. Her constellation is the Lion, and her tattoo is located on her neck and throat.

Caoimhe: E'ridian. Clan Sky. Air force aeronaut captain.

Catacombs: Ancient tunnels and passageways built beneath Amari with lost technology.

Ceann-Cinnidh: (pl. *cinn-chinnidh*) Ruling rank in E'ridia. Position in the *Comhairle nan Cinnidhean*.

Chu Hua: Solarian. Imperial General of the Legion.

Civil War: The first war between bloodlines that ultimately cleaved Ashion into two countries, forming Daijal in the west and leaving Ashion in the east.

Clans: Distinctive groups within E'ridia. Currently number six in total.

Clarion crystal: Crystal mined from the earth that can transmute the aether into magic or energy, depending on the cut.

Clementine, Nathaniel: Ashionen. Merchant and heir to the Clementine Trading Company. Cog in the Clockwork Brigade.

Clockwork Brigade: Underground rebellion originating in Ashion that exists to free debt slaves in Daijal and smuggle them to freedom in other countries, as well as work against the Daijal court.

Cog: A rebel belonging to the Clockwork Brigade.

Collector's Guild: A powerful association formed in Daijal that helps companies and individuals find and retrieve escaped debt slaves.

Comhairle nan Cinnidhean: Ruling body of E'ridia.

Conclave of Houses: Solarian political tradition wherein the

Houses gather to issue a public judgment on the ruling House and loyalties are bartered for support.

Constellation: Stars in the sky that represent a star god in a celestial map.

Cosian: City. Located in Ashion.

Daijal: Country. Debt bondage is sanctioned within its borders and an integral part of its economy. Its capital city is New Haven. The country's patron guiding star is Innes, the Twilight Star. The country's affirmed constellation is the Viper.

Daijalan: Denoting ties to or nationality of Daijal. Language descriptor.

Dávgon: Urovan. Listed in the royal genealogies. Ruler of Urova.

Death-defying machine: Machine that can turn the dead into revenants on a mass scale.

Debt bondage: Legalized slavery that results from citizens in Daijal putting up their lives as collateral on bank loans and being forced to pay it off with work when they cannot afford monetary payment. Bank loans with life collateral come with astronomically high interest rates, ensuring the people who are collected for bondage never escape it. The debt can be applied to families and rolled into generations.

Debt collector: A bounty hunter working for the Collector's Guild who hunts down and retrieves escaped debt slaves.

Debt slave: Someone who has sold themselves as collateral to a bank to pay off a loan. Their status is denoted by bank numbers tattooed onto their necks.

Delani: Warden. Current wardens' governor.

Dhemlan, Emmitt: Ashionen. Listed in the nobility genealogies. Engineer and owner of the Six Point Mechanics Company. Caris' adoptive father.

Dhemlan, Portia: Ashionen. Listed in the nobility genealogies. Engineer and owner of the Six Point Mechanics Company. Caris' adoptive mother.

Dying Times, the: A period of time during A.O.S. when the planet's ancient colonists struggled to adapt to Maricol's poison and deal with the threat of revenants.

E'ridia: Country. Debt bondage is outlawed within its borders. Its capital city is Glencoe. The country's patron guiding star is Nilsine, the Dusk Star. The country's affirmed constellation is the Eagle.

E'ridian: Denoting ties to or nationality of E'ridia. Language descriptor.

Emperor/Empress: Ruler of Solaria who has claim to the Imperial throne.

Farren: Star god. Also known as the Eclipse Star, dual patron god and goddess of the sea. Their constellation is the Leviathan, and their tattoo is located on their back.

Foxborough: City. Located in Ashion.

Garnier, Sabine: Daijalan. Listed in the nobility genealogies. Magician. Cog in the Clockwork Brigade. Deceased.

Genealogies: Identification records that track families from the earliest Age on Maricol. Created in the past to weed out genetic mutations caused by poison. Currently used as class markers.

Glencoe: City. Capital of E'ridia.

Great Separation, the: A period of time during A.O.S. when the people of Maricol split into different countries under the guidance of the star gods.

Haighmoor: City. Located in Ashion.

Helia: City. Located in Daijal.

Honovi: E'ridian. Listed in the royal genealogies. Clan Storm. Aeronaut captain, *jarl* to a *ceann-cinnidh*, and ambassador for his country.

Houses: Noble bloodlines in Solaria.

Imperial throne: Seat of power in Solaria.

Inferno: A coup by Daijal against Ashion, perpetuated by a star god, that resulted in the Rourke bloodline and all cadet branches being annihilated.

Innes: Star god. Also known as the Twilight Star, patron god of fire. His constellation is the Viper, and his tattoo is located on both shoulders and his pectorals.

Isar: Ruler of Urova.

Istal: City. Located in Daijal.

Iverson, Aleesia: Daijalan. Listed in the royal genealogies. Queen of Daijal. Deceased.

Iverson, Bernard: Daijalan. Listed in the royal genealogies. King of Daijal. Deceased.

Iverson, Wesley: Daijalan. Listed in the royal genealogies. Prince of Daijal. Deceased.

Jarl: Title of an heir to a *ceann-cinnidh* in E'ridia.

Karnak: City. Located in Solaria.

Khaur, Ezra: Daijalan. Listed in the nobility genealogies. Cog in the Clockwork Brigade.

Khaur, Melvin: Daijalan. Listed in the nobility genealogies. Magician. Named Marshal in the Clockwork Brigade, providing him with an officer-level position to guide cogs.

Kimathi, Artyom: Solarian. Listed in the nobility genealogies. Son of Joelle and Heir to the House of Kimathi. Deceased.

Kimathi, Joelle: Solarian. Listed in the nobility genealogies. *Vezir* to the House of Kimathi. Head of her House.

Kimathi, Karima: Solarian. Listed in the nobility genealogies. Daughter of Joelle and mother to Nicca.

Kimathi, Nicca: Solarian. Listed in the nobility genealogies. Granddaughter to Joelle Kimathi. Wife to Vanya Sa'Liandel. Deceased.

Klovod, **the:** Urovan word for *puppet master.* Ex-warden who is a magician and the creator of *rionetkas.*

Ksenia: Warden. Current master alchemist of the wardens.

Legion: Standing army of Solaria.

Legionnaire: Soldier in the Legion.

Magic: The transmuted form of aether.

Magician: A person gifted with the ability to control the aether and transmute it into magic and control it with a wand.

Maksim: Urovan. Listed in the nobility genealogies. Urovan ambassador to Daijal.

Maricol: World. Named from a linguistic shift of the word *miracle.* The planet refugees from a galactic war drifted to after their generation ships were thrown off course. Its high levels of alkaline, alkaloids, spores, poisons, and toxins require continuous alchemist intervention for people to survive.

Matriskav: City. Capital of Urova.

Mind magic: A type of magic some magicians are skilled with that can interfere with a person's thoughts and memories. Can also be used to control people.

Molina, Javier: Solarian. Major and magician in the Legion and in charge of the *praetoria* legionnaire.

Month: Part of the Fourteen Month calendar Maricol runs on.

Motor carriage: Four-wheel ground vehicle.

New Haven: City. Capital of Daijal.

Nilsine: Star god. Also known as the Dusk Star, patron goddess of wind. Her constellation is the Eagle, and her tattoo is located on her right thigh.

Northern Plains: Geographical area spanning much of Ashion and part of Daijal.

Oeiras: City. Located in Solaria.

Ornithopter: Flight machine with spinning blades powered by a steam engine.

Poison Accords: Binding agreement between all countries to tithe citizens to the wardens to ensure continued cleansing of the poison fields inside their borders and removal of revenants.

Port Avi: City. Capital of the Tovan Isles.

***Praetoria* legionnaire:** A soldier in a specialized unit who guards the Imperial throne and the House that controls it.

Provence: An administrative district in Ashion and Daijal. Generally overseen by a noble bloodline.

Raziel: Warden.

Revenant: (pl. revenants) Dead infected by spores that rise to walk again.

Rionetka: (pl. *rionetkas*) Urovan word for *puppet*. People controlled through mechanical means, the aether, and mind magic.

Rixham: City. Located in Solaria. Permanently walled off and inhabited by revenants.

Rourke, Alasandair: (*see* Soren) Ashionen. Listed in the royal genealogies. Deceased prince of Ashion.

Rourke, Caris: Ashionen. Listed in the royal genealogies. Magician. Engineer and heir to the Six Point Mechanics Company. Heir to the Ashion throne through blood.

Rourke, Eimarille: Ashionen and Daijalan. Listed in the royal genealogies. Queen of Daijal. Heir to the Ashion throne through blood.

Rourke, Lisandro: Ashionen and Daijalan. Listed in the royal genealogies. Prince and son of Eimarille and Wesley.

Rourke, Ophelia: Ashionen. Listed in the royal genealogies. Deceased queen of Ashion.

Sa'Liandel, Raiah: Solarian. Listed in the royal genealogies. Daughter of Vanya and Nicca. Heir to the Imperial throne and member of the House of Sa'Liandel.

Sa'Liandel, Taisiya: Solarian. Listed in the royal genealogies. *Valide* of Solaria and member of the House of Sa'Liandel.

Sa'Liandel, Taye: Solarian. Listed in the royal genealogies. Emperor Consort of Solaria and member of the House of Sa'Liandel. Deceased.

Sa'Liandel, Vanya: Solarian. Listed in the royal genealogies. Prince then Emperor of Solaria. Member of the House of Sa'Liandel.

Sa'Liandel, Zakariya: Solarian. Listed in the royal genealogies. Empress of Solaria and member of the House of Sa'Liandel. Deceased.

Seaville: City. Located in Solaria.

Sextant: Double reflecting mirrored instrument used for navigation.

Ship-city: Mechanized Tovanian ships that traverse Maricol's oceans and seas.

Solaria: Country. Debt bondage is outlawed within its borders. Its capital city is Calhames. The country's patron guiding star is Callisto, the Dawn Star. The country's affirmed constellation is the Lion.

Solarian: Denoting ties to or nationality of Solaria. Language descriptor.

Soren: Warden who guards a Solarian border and secretly capable of casting starfire. Formerly known as Prince Alasandair Rourke, Queen Ophelia's only son and middle child.

Spores: The reproductive unit of a plant and fungus that reanimates the dead to ensure future continuous propagation.

Star god: One of six immortals who are the guiding stars for the citizens and countries of Maricol. Each star god was a refugee during the Age of Comets. Upon landing on Maricol thousands of years ago, they were poisoned by the planet and the aether to such a degree that they cannot die and became revered as gods.

Star Order: Continent-wide religion that worships the six star gods.

Starfire: The most powerful application of transmuting aether into magic and an extremely rare ability. Considered a mark of royalty or someone with connection to a royal bloodline.

Submersible: Underwater vehicle.

Telegraph: Point-to-point text messaging machine.

Televox: Handheld communication device. A newer invention.

Terilyn: Urovan. Blade.

Tithe: Citizen of any country given as payment under the Poison Accords to the wardens. Tithes are trained at the Warden's Island and turned into wardens through alchemy. Not all tithes survive the process.

Tovan Isles: Country. Debt bondage is outlawed within its borders. Its capital city is Port Avi. The country's patron guiding star is Farren, the Eclipse Star. The country's affirmed constellation is the Leviathan.

Tovanian: Denoting ties to or nationality of the Tovan Isles. Language descriptor.

Trade tongue: Language drawn from all others on Maricol into a pidgin form spoken for trade.

Uri: Confederation of ship-cities that are loosely grouped into six sub-crew nations. The six appointed chiefs are the ruling body of the Tovan Isles.

Uri'ka: Title for a chief that is part of the *Uri*, the ruling body of the Tovan Isles.

Urova: Country. Debt bondage is outlawed within its borders. Its capital city is Matriskav. The country's patron guiding star is Xaxis, the Midnight Star. The country's affirmed constellation is the Bear.

Urovan: Denoting ties to or nationality of Urova. Language descriptor.

Valide: Title belonging to the matriarch of the ruling House that holds the Imperial throne in Solaria.

Vasilyet: An administrative district in Solaria governed by a major House and overseen by a *vezir*.

Veil: A woven device created with thread magic that can alter a person's facial appearance.

Velocycle: Shortened from velocity cycle. Two-wheel ground vehicle.

Veran: Town. Located in Ashion.

Vezir: Governing official of a *vasilyet*. Typically head of a major House.

Wand: A device used by magicians to focus the aether into magic, usually with the help of clarion crystal.

Warden: A person who is tithed from a country by order of the Poison Accords into the ranks of wardens. They become stateless and neutral. Alchemy is used to make them immune to most poisons and toxins found in the poison fields. Their sole job is to patrol the borders between countries and the ones between the living and dead, as well as map the poison fields for later alchemy intervention to cleanse the land.

Warden's Island, the: Island located in the middle of the Celestine Lake, where wardens are trained and report back to. Considered a neutral administrative city under the Poison Accords.

Wastelands: Desert. Located in Solaria and rife with revenants and spores.

Xaxis: Star god. Also known as the Midnight Star, patron god of earth. His constellation is the Bear, and his tattoo is located on his hands and forearms.

Zip gun: A rapid-fire, multibarrel firearm.

Author's Notes

This book, and the series as a whole, was a labor of love some days, but I'm so glad I made it to the end. Thank you for coming along this journey with me as I dipped my fingers into an epic fantasy romance that was inspired by a single Taylor Swift song. Shout-out to the number of times I listened to *exile* on repeat. I could karaoke it in my sleep at this point.

All my thanks to the usual cohort of friends who are always there for me when life gets crazy: Lily Morton, May Archer, Lucy Lennox, and Aimee Nicole Walker.

I would be thrilled and grateful if you would consider reviewing *The Queen's Starfire Throne*. I appreciate all honest reviews, positive or negative. Reviews definitely help my books get seen, so thank you!

Connect with Hailey

Keep up with book news by joining Hailey Turner's newsletter and get several free short stories.

Join the reader group on Facebook: Hailey's Hellions

Follow Hailey on Instagram.

Follow Hailey's author page on Facebook.

Follow Hailey on Facebook.

Follow Hailey on Goodreads.

Follow Hailey on Pinterest.

Follow Hailey on BookBub.

Visit Hailey's website for more information on her books and merch.

Other Works By Hailey Turner

M/M SCIENCE FICTION MILITARY ROMANCE

Captain Jamie Callahan, son of a wealthy senator and socialite mother, is a survivor.

Staff Sergeant Kyle Brannigan, a Special Forces operative, is a man with secrets.

Alpha Team, the Metahuman Defense Force's top-ranked field team, is where the two collide and their lives will never be the same.

<u>Metahuman Files</u>

In the Wreckage

In the Ruins

In the Shadows

In The Blood

In The Requiem

In the Solace

<u>A Metahuman Files: Classified Novella</u>

Out of the Ashes

New Horizons

Fire In The Heart

M/M URBAN FANTASY

Patrick Collins is a broken mage running from his past.

Jonothon de Vere is a god pack alpha werewolf searching for a home.

In a world where magic is real, myths and legends exist, and gods walk the earth, Patrick and Jono are thrown together by the Fates themselves to fight against an enemy that threatens to consume the world. For if the gods fall and demons from every hell rise up, humanity won't stand a chance.

<u>Soulbound</u>

A Ferry of Bones & Gold

All Souls Near & Nigh

A Crown of Iron & Silver

A Vigil in the Mourning

On the Wings of War

An Echo in the Sorrow

A Veiled & Hallowed Eve

<u>Soulbound Universe Standalones</u>

Resurrection Reprise

Secondhand Skin

LGBTQ+ EPIC STEAMPUNK-INSPIRED FANTASY

Welcome to Maricol, where the land will kill you, kinship turns the gears of war, and burning the dead lest they come back to life is the only way to survive.

<u>Infernal War Saga</u>

The Prince's Poisoned Vow

The Emperor's Bone Palace

The Queen's Starfire Throne

<u>Infernal War Saga Novella</u>

An Emporium of Hearts

CONTEMPORARY GAY ROMANCE

Short stories previously published in the Heart2Heart Charity Anthologies.

<u>From the Heart: A Short Story Collection</u>

AUDIOBOOKS

All of Hailey Turner's audiobooks are available on your favourite listening platform.

Thanks for reading!